THE OXFORD BOOK OF
IRISH SHORT STORIES

William Trevor was born in Mitchelstown, County Cork in 1928 and spent his childhood in provincial Ireland. He attended a number of Irish schools and later Trinity College, Dublin. He was awarded an honorary CBE in 1977 for his services to Literature, and was made a Companion of Literature in 1994. He is also a member of the Irish Academy of Letters. He was awarded the David Cohen British Literature Prize by the Arts Council of England in 1999 and the Bob Hughes Lifetime Achievement Award in Irish Literature in 2008. William Trevor's latest short story collection is *Cheating at Canasta* (2007) and his most recent novel *Love and Summer* (2009). His other books include, *The Ballroom of Romance and Other Stories* (1972), *Angels at the Ritz and Other Stories* (1975), *Fools of Fortune* (1983, the Whitbread Novel Award), *Felicia's Journey* (1994, Whitbread Book of the Year and the *Sunday Express* Book of the Year), and *The Hill Bachelors* (2000, PEN/Macmillan Silver Pen Award for Short Stories and the 2001 *Irish Times* Irish Literature Prize for Fiction).

THE
OXFORD BOOK OF
IRISH
SHORT STORIES

Edited by
WILLIAM TREVOR

OXFORD
UNIVERSITY PRESS

OXFORD
UNIVERSITY PRESS

Great Clarendon Street, Oxford OX2 6DP

Oxford University Press is a department of the University of Oxford.
It furthers the University's objective of excellence in research, scholarship,
and education by publishing worldwide in

Oxford New York

Auckland Cape Town Dar es Salaam Hong Kong Karachi
Kuala Lumpur Madrid Melbourne Mexico City Nairobi
New Delhi Shanghai Taipei Toronto

With offices in

Argentina Austria Brazil Chile Czech Republic France Greece
Guatemala Hungary Italy Japan Poland Portugal Singapore
South Korea Switzerland Thailand Turkey Ukraine Vietnam

Oxford is a registered trade mark of Oxford University Press
in the UK and in certain other countries

Published in the United States
by Oxford University Press Inc., New York

British Library Cataloguing in Publication Data

Data available

Library of Congress Cataloging in Publication Data

Data available

Printed in Great Britain
on acid free paper by
Clays Ltd, St Ives plc

ISBN 978-0-19-958314-0

CONTENTS

vi *Contents*

viii *Contents*

INTRODUCTION

The modern short story may be defined as the distillation of an essence. It may be laid down that it has to have a point, that it must be going somewhere, that it dare not be vague. But art has its own way of defying both definitions and rules, and neither offer much help when examining, more particularly, the short stories of Ireland. In putting this anthology together, I was driven back, again and again, to a consideration of the part that storytelling has played, and continues to play, in Irish life. An Irish flair in this direction has long been recognized as a national characteristic. Stories of one kind or another have a way of pressing themselves into Irish conversation, both as entertainment and as a form of communication. For centuries they have been offered to strangers, almost as hospitality is: tall stories, simple stories, stories of extraordinary deeds, of mysteries and wonders, of gentleness, love, cruelty, and violence. And side by side with speculation about their source, the question has always been: why are they so delighted in, why do they so naturally form part of Irish vernacular?

Not long ago I had a little business with a police sergeant in County Mayo. I called at his remote roadside house at midday one Sunday only to be told by his housekeeper that he was not yet back from Mass and 'wherever else he may have called'. If I drove back along the road, taking it easy so as not to be too soon for him, I would meet him this side of the crossroads.

I drove slowly and before I arrived at the crossroads there he was, ambling towards me on his bicycle. He dismounted when I stopped. I passed on a message from a mutual acquaintance, and then he pointed at the distant hills and told me a story about a pedlar who years ago had sought refuge there after his elopement with 'a captain's wife' from Galway. Inspiration, loosened by the pints of porter that had followed the sergeant's devotions, gathered an unhurried momentum; the telling took twenty minutes.

The reason for our encounter shrank in importance; the story that had by chance come out of it mattered more. In detail it would have been different from the last time the sergeant told it, the circumstances being different, and parrot-like repetition being too tediously mundane. In the same way, the more familiar account of the farmer who was sold a locket at a fair after assurances that the likeness it contained strongly resembled himself, has hundreds of versions, depending on the storyteller. A different reason for the purchase may be given, and the continuing narrative varies from whim to whim. In one, the farmer's wife observes her husband's surreptitious glances at some object he takes from an inner pocket. She roots for it while he is asleep and is infuriated to discover it is a portrait of a fancy woman. 'And a gnarled, filthy old creature at that!' she sneers to the priest with whom she eventually shares the confidence. Examining the miniature for himself, the priest decides the woman isn't in her right mind: what he's looking at is a florid, hamlike countenance of a man. It is vaguely familiar: it could even be a crude attempt at a likeness of himself, only it doesn't pass muster because it lacks both style and dignity. Then he remembers: this must be his predecessor in the parish, a man legendary for the way his mean-spirited soul leapt out at you from his ugly little eyes.

In some versions of this tale the action proceeds into further complications; in others, extra characters are introduced, with twists and highlights, and a particular storyteller's trade-mark. Only the fact that people everywhere must once have experienced mirrored glass for the first time remains constant.

It is not unlikely that this story and the police sergeant's had their origins elsewhere, the Irish contribution to their survival being the immediacy of the spoken word and the transformations necessary to capture a local imagination. J. M. Synge, on the Aran Islands at the turn of the century, records an 'illiterate peasant':

'Have you any gold on you?' said the man.

'I have not,' said O'Conor.

'Then you'll pay me the flesh off your body,' said the man.

They went into a house, and a knife was brought, and a clean white cloth was put on the table, and O'Conor was put on the cloth.

Then the little man was going to strike the lancet into him, when says lady O'Conor—

'Have you bargained for five pounds of flesh?'

'For five pounds of flesh,' said the man.

'Have you bargained for any drop of his blood?' said lady O'Conor.

'For no blood,' said the man.

'Cut out the flesh,' said lady O'Conor, 'but if you spill one last drop of his blood I'll put that through you.' And she put a pistol to his head.

What in England, centuries ago, had been the makings of sophisticated theatre remained a word-of-mouth tale on the harsh Atlantic seaboard, and for good measure Synge was next entertained with the plot of Cymbeline. At about the same time the Irish Folklore Commission began its long trawl of rural districts, recording folktales they rarely had to search far to find. Sean O'Sullivan, who translated many from the Irish, later recalled: 'The old man or woman in these districts who had no folktales to tell was the exception. It is generally conceded that the parish of Carna, in West Galway, had more unrecorded in 1935 than did all the rest of Western Europe. The Commission's workers, as well as other individual collectors, were fortunate in finding the art of storytelling in full vigour in many districts, with outstanding narrators in possession of large repertoires.'

But in spite of such enthusiasm, the *seanchaí*—the old hearthside storyteller—was on the way out. The wandering tale-bearer who begged his way from parish to parish was a far less familiar figure than he had been, and even before the folklore commission had properly begun its task that bustling midwife of the Irish Literary Renaissance, Lady Gregory, was complaining that the great legends of the past were no longer being disseminated. She herself gathered them together from the confusion and contradictions of tattered manuscripts. Adopting a pleasant, fireside voice, she promised 'plain and simple words, in the same way my old nurse used to be telling me stories from the Irish long ago, and I a child at Roxborough'. So the lost epic myths—featuring Cuchulain, and Deirdre, and Queen Maeve and Ailell, and Findabair of the Fair Eyebrows, and the Brown Bull of Cuailgne, and Cruachan of the Enchantments—were returned to the people, as a golden age was revived to furnish the Celtic Twilight.

It happened one time before Maeve and Ailell rose up from their royal bed in Cruachan, they began to talk with one another. 'It is what I am thinking,' said Ailell, 'it is a true saying, "Good is the wife of a good man." ' 'A true saying, indeed,' said Maeve, 'but why do you bring it to mind at this time?' 'I bring it to mind now because you are better to-day than the day I married you.' 'I was good before I ever had to do with you,' said Maeve. 'How well we never heard of that and never knew it until now,' said Ailell, 'but only that you stopped at home like any other woman, while the enemies at your boundaries were slaughtering and destroying and driving all before them, and you not able to hinder them.'

'That is not the way it was at all,' said Maeve, 'but of the six daughters of my father Eochaid, King of Ireland, I was the best and the one that was thought most of. As to dividing gifts and giving counsel, I was the best of them, and as to battle feats and arms and fighting, I was the best of them. It was I had fifteen hundred soldiers, sons of exiles, and fifteen hundred sons of chief men. And I had these,' she said, 'for my own household; and long with that my father gave me one of the provinces of Ireland, the province of Cruachan; so that Maeve of Cruachan was the name that was given to me.'
(From 'Cuchulain of Muirthemne' by Lady Gregory)

Breathing life into the dust of ancient writings has been continuing in Ireland ever since, but even without that assistance, and despite the passing of the *seanchaí*, the native habit of storytelling has managed to survive pretty well in everyday life. Many years ago when I was living in Portlaoise (then Maryborough) a young carpenter from Limerick walked into the town's only fish-and-chip shop in search of lodgings. He was warmly welcomed; there was indeed a vacant room. But some weeks later the shop's proprietors—normally a robust couple—appeared to be unwell. Their pale faces and the disturbed look in their eyes were said to be due to lack of sleep. And then the story came out: at night, distressful moaning emanated from the carpenter's bedroom, with knockings, and voices that were not its occupant's. Every morning the lodger's sheets were wringing wet with sweat. In the end he was asked to leave, but so notorious had the events become in the town that he found it impossible to find alternative accommodation and was obliged to give up his employment and to move on. The rooms above the fish-and-chip shop became quiet again, but just in case anything had been left behind a priest carried out the ceremony of exorcism.

Forty years later, seeming to be a stranger in a public house of the neighbourhood, I was told the story of the haunted carpenter. Its essentials were intact and as I remembered them: the young man red-haired, the fish-and-chip shop couple as stolidly matter-of-fact as the fare they served. Yet the truth of reality had been transformed into the truth of fiction, and a fresh emphasis was working its way through the embroidery to communicate the wonder there had been. Written down, in comparison, the tale of the carpenter who trudges from town to town is as ordinary as the lodgings he haunted. Similarly, the tale of the pedlar and the captain's wife falls flat on paper, that of the vain farmer loses the greater part of its intricate comedy, and Synge's transcriptions lack the drama that the skill of the storyteller would naturally have supplied. Sean O'Sullivan observes: '. . . an English translation of tales told by such expert storytellers as, for example, Éamonn a Búrc, Peig Sayers, Muiris (Sheáin) Connor, and Jimmy Cheallaigh— to name but a few—gives but a pale shadow of the original Irish narration. The voices, with their many modulations, are silent on the printed page; the audience is absent; only the pattern of narrative and the procession of motifs remain.'

The desire to introduce listeners to people they don't know— which is somewhere near the heart of all storytelling, anecdotal or otherwise—isn't something that disappears simply because passing time brings changes. It remains a strong desire in Ireland, and it continues to be satisfied. Readers of the *Irish Times* in the days of its most renowned columnist, Myles na gCopaleen, will be familiar with the establishing of an off-stage character at the Drimnagh bus stop.

'The brother can't look at an egg . . . Can't stand the sight of an egg at all. Rashers, ham, fish, anything you like to mention—he'll eat them all and ask for more. But he can't go the egg. Thanks all the same but no eggs. The egg is barred.'

The brother's subsequent adventures are lovingly recounted. The setting is 'the digs', the landlady's health or foibles a source of the action. 'The rheumatism was at her for a long time. The brother ordered her to bed, but bedamn but she'd fight it on her feet . . . On New Year's Day she got an attack that was something fierce, all classes of stabbing pains down the back. Couldn't move a hand to help herself. Couldn't walk, sit or stand.'

Myles na gCopaleen wrote as Flann O'Brien, an identity that disguises one of Ireland's most inventive, and perceptive, novelists. But it required little perception to pinpoint the Irish passion for peopling bus stops or any other mundane setting with colourful characters, and for retailing, with innate ease, episodes of interest. 'Wait till you've heard this.' And when you've heard it: 'Isn't that the quare one?' Nor is it enough, for example, for a Corkman or a Wexfordman simply to question the famed wit and rattling conversation of the Dubliner. In order to promote his denial that they truly exist he would more naturally choose to illustrate it by recalling the two elderly drinkers in the corner of a Dublin snug whose evening is lightened by a single exchange. 'They say the

Chinaman eats the bamboo,' remarks one, and having dwelt on that observation while the pair's glasses are several times refilled, his companion eventually contributes: 'Is that so?'

It is against this background of a pervasive, deeply rooted oral tradition that the modern short story in Ireland must inevitably be considered. 'A young art,' Elizabeth Bowen rightly observed, 'a child of this century.' Joyce in Ireland and Chekhov in Russia turned the antique inside out: the larger-than-life figures enacting highly charged drama in a mystic past were sent packing. With revolutionary abruptness, the stories that now pressed for attention appeared to be about nothing at all. Added to which, they often dealt in underdogs—what Frank O'Connor called 'small men'— and increasingly as the century wore on, in hard-done-by women. The novel had seized upon the heroics that for so long had distinguished the fiction of the myths, the sagas, and the parables. The modern short story grew out of what remained, but it was a growth so fruitful that its emergence as a literary form could not be denied. Its newness was not dissimilar to the newness of the Impressionists and the post-Impressionists. Its intensity left behind an echo, a distinctive imprint on the mind. It withheld as much information as it released. It told as little as it dared, but often it glimpsed into a world as large and as complicated as anything either the legend or the novel could provide. Portraiture thrived within its subtleties.

What was happening internationally suited Ireland particularly well, and the Irish contribution to this very different kind of story was destined to be as generous as that same contribution has been to the older form. It is occasionally argued that the Irish genius for the short story is related to the fact that when the novel reared its head Ireland wasn't ready for it. This is certainly true. In England, for instance, the great Victorian novel had been fed by the architecture of a rich, stratified society in which complacency and hypocrisy, accompanied by the ill-treatment of the unfortunate and the poor, provided both fictional material and grounds for protest. Wealth had purchased leisure and a veneer of sophistication for the up-and-coming middle classes; stability at home was the jewel in the imperial crown. In Ireland there was disaffection, repressed religion, the confusion of two languages, and the spectre of famine. The civilized bookishness of writing novels, and reading them, was as alien in an uneasy, still largely peasant society as timeless afternoons of village cricket still are in the busy, aspiring Ireland of the late twentieth century. While in England readers waited impatiently for another episode of *The Old Curiosity Shop* or *David Copperfield*, in Ireland the cleverness of a story, or the manner of its telling, still persisted as a talking point. The roots of the antique tale continued to grow, and with hindsight they did so to the advantage of the modern art. In the stories of George Moore, and certainly in those of Somerville and Ross, there are cunningly preserved traces of the old tradition. Seumas O'Kelly's classic, 'The Weaver's Grave', is an example of the antique form in the process of drifting into modernism. But far more important for the new generation of writers was the heritage of an audience for whom fiction of brief duration—irrespective of how it was offered—was the established thing. The receptive nature of this audience—a willingness to believe rather than find instant virtues in scepticism—allowed the modern story to thrive, as the old-fashioned tale had. Stories, far more than novels, cast spells, and spells have been nurtured in Ireland for as long as imperial greed has been attempting to hammer its people into a subject class. The Irish short story has come to appeal to audiences far beyond its home one, but the confidence born of instinct and familiarity has encouraged the art of the spell to continue. The understanding of a mode of communication is not easily abandoned. The Irish delight in stories, of whatever kind, because their telling and their reception are by now instinctive.

To this day, the novel has not flourished in the same way. Novels are widely and eagerly read—the Irish are among the world's most voracious readers—but certain short stories are as highly regarded as anything in the longer form. English fiction writers tend to state that their short stories are leavings from their novels. In Ireland I have heard it put the other way around.

This anthology seeks to place in proximity stories that have little in common beyond the fact that all of them have been influenced by a culture that made much of the fiction it could best absorb. Some derive their strength from their brevity, others require a considerable spread in order to arrive most tellingly at their point. Moore's 'Albert Nobbs' would have lost its impact if he'd written it within the confines of Wilde's 'The Sphinx without a Secret', and although anthologists by necessity are often obliged to avoid longer stories, length is such a vital element in the form that it seems wrong not to display how it is put to use. It is misleading to assign the lengthy story to the realm of the novella because it appears vaguely to belong there. In fact it doesn't: a novella is a short novel, with all the novel's paraphernalia and tendency to ramble; a long short story is what it says it is.

I have omitted Shaw and O'Casey because they conveyed their ideas more skilfully in another medium; and Samuel Beckett, together with several contemporary novelists, for the same reason. But a handful of stories, though coming from writers not usually associated with the form, are of a quality that demands their inclusion, and I have not resisted that. Once upon a time the bane of Irish writing was the stage Irishman; now it is what Francis Stuart calls 'the soft centre'. Both are insidiously destructive and because of their presence several skilfully contrived stories, from different periods, are not here.

I have preferred Gerald Griffin to John Banim and, as with Moore and Le Fanu, O'Kelly and Joyce, I have given William Carleton the space his writing demands. The flavour of the oral tradition is captured as well as it can be in Seumas MacManus's retelling of a Donegal fairy story and in the folk-tales gathered by Sean O'Sullivan; otherwise its influence must be gleaned by reading between the lines. Liam O'Flaherty, Frank O'Connor, and Sean O'Faolain are each represented twice, to emphasize their place as the three most influential Irish writers in the genre since Joyce and Elizabeth Bowen established Ireland at the forefront of the modern short story.

Delving for roots in the past has concerned me more than speculating about the future. There is a distinct group of Irish writers who were born in the 1920s and 1930s, and this collection might sensibly end with them. But it seems perverse not to offer a taste at least of the succeeding generation, now confidently moving from promise to achievement. Bernard Mac Laverty and Desmond Hogan represent it here, and the stories of Clare Boylan, Ita Daly, Aidan C. Mathews, Sebastian Barry, Neil Jordan, Helen Lucy Burke, Rita Kelly, Lucille Redmond, Ronan Sheenan, and many others, may be read in their own collections.

WILLIAM TREVOR

Irish Short Stories

The Hour of Death

Edited and translated from the Irish, as are the five subsequent folk-tales, by Sean O'Sullivan

The old people used to say that in the olden times everybody knew the exact time when he would die.

There was a man who knew that he would die in autumn. He planted his crops the previous spring, but instead of building a fine firm fence around them, all he did was to plant a makeshift hedge of a few rushes and ferns to guard the crops. It so happened that God (praise and glory to Him!) sent an angel down on earth to find out how the people were getting on. The angel came to this man and asked him what he was doing. The man told him.

'And why haven't you a better fence than that makeshift to protect your crops?' asked the angel.

'It will do me,' said the man, 'until I have the crop stored. Let those who succeed me look after their own fences. I'll die this autumn.'

The angel returned and told the Almighty what had happened. And from that day on, people lost foreknowledge of the hour of death.

Fionn in Search of his Youth

One fine day, Fionn mac Cumhaill and fourteen of his men were hunting on the top of Muisire Mountain. They had spent the whole day since sunrise there but met no game.

Late in the evening, Fionn spoke, ' 'Tis as well for us to face for home, men. We're catching nothing, and it will be late when we, hungry and thirsty, reach home.'

'Upon my soul. We're hungry and thirsty as it is,' said Conán.

They turned on their heels and went down the mountainside, but if they did, they weren't far down when a dark black fog fell on them. They lost their way and didn't know whether to go east or west. Finally they had to sit down where they were.

'I'm afraid, men, that we're astray for the evening,' said Fionn. 'I never yet liked a fog of this kind.

After they had sat for a while talking and arguing, whatever look Diarmaid gave around, he saw a beautiful nice lime-white house behind them.

'Come along, men, to this house over there,' said he. 'Maybe we'll get something to eat and drink there.'

They all agreed and made their way to the house. When they entered, there was nobody before them but a wizened old man who was lying in a bent position at the edge of the hearth and a sheep which was tied along by the wall. They sat down. The old man raised his head and welcomed Fionn and his men heartily.

'By my soul,' said Diarmaid to himself. ' 'Tisn't very likely that our thirst or hunger will be eased in this hovel.'

After awhile, the old man called loudly to a young woman who was below in a room telling her to come up and get food ready for Fionn and his men. Then there walked up the floor from below, a fine strapping handsome young woman, and it didn't take her long to get food and drink ready for them. She pulled a long ample table out into the middle of the floor, spread a tablecloth on it, and laid out the dinner for the Fianna. She seated Fionn at the head of the table and set every man's meal in front of him. No sooner had each of them put the first bite of food into his mouth than the sheep which was tied along the wall stretched and broke the hard hempen tying that was holding her and rushed towards the table. She upset it by lifting one end of it and not a scrap of food was left that wasn't thrown to the floor in front of the Fianna.

'The devil take you,' cried Conán. 'Look at the mess you have made of our dinner, and we badly in need of it.'

'Get up, Conán, and tie the sheep,' said Fionn.

Conán, looking very angry at the loss of his dinner, got up against his will and walked to the sheep. He caught her by the top of the head and tried to drag her toward the wall. But if he broke his heart in the attempt, he couldn't tie her up. He stood there looking at her.

'By heavens,' said he. 'As great a warrior and hero as I am, here's this sheep today, and I can't tie her. Maybe someone else can?'

'Get up, Diarmaid, and tie the sheep,' said Fionn.

Diarmaid stood up and tried, but if he did, he failed to tie her. Each of the fourteen men made an attempt, but it was no use.

'My shame on ye,' said the old man. 'To say that as great as your valour has ever been, ye can't tie an animal as small as a sheep to the side of the wall with a bit of rope.'

He got up from the edge of the hearth and hobbled down the floor. As he went, six pintsful of ashes fell from the backside of his trousers, because he had been so long lying on the hearth. He took hold of the sheep by the scruff of the head, pulled her easily in to the wall, and tied her up. When the Fianna saw him tie the sheep, they were seized with fear and trembling, seeing that he could do it after themselves had failed, brave and all though they were. The old man returned to his place by the fire.

'Come up here and get some food ready for Fionn and his men,' he called to the young woman.

She came up from the room again, and whatever knack or magic she had, she wasn't long preparing new food to set before them.

'Start eating now, men; ye'll have no more trouble,' said the old man. 'This dinner will quench your thirst and hunger.'

When they had eaten and were feeling happy with their stomachs full, they drew their chairs back from the table. Whatever peering around Fionn had—he was always restless—he looked toward the room and saw the young woman sitting on a chair there. He got a great desire to talk to her for a while. He went down to the room to her.

'Fionn mac Cumhaill,' said she; 'you had me once and you won't have me again.'

He had to turn on his heel and go back to his chair. Diarmaid then went down to her, but he got the same answer; so did each of the rest of the Fianna. Oisín was the last to try, but she said the same thing to him. She took him by the hand and led him up the floor till she stood in front of the Fianna.

'Fionn mac Cumhaill,' said she; 'ye were ever famous for strength and agility and prowess, and still each of you failed to tie the sheep. This sheep is not of the usual kind. She is Strength. And that old man over there is Death. As strong as the sheep was, the old man was able to overcome her. Death will overcome ye in the same way, strong and all as ye are. I myself am a planet sent by God, and it is God who has placed this hovel here for ye. I am Youth. Each of you had me once but never will again. And now, I will give each of you whatever gift he asks me for.'

Fionn was the first to speak, and he asked that he might lose the smell of clay, which he had had ever since he sinned with a woman who was dead.

Diarmaid said that what he wanted was a love spot on his body, so that every young woman who saw it would fall in love with him.

Oscar asked for a thong which would never break for his flail.

Conán asked for the power of killing hundreds in battle, while he himself would be invulnerable.

On hearing this, Diarmaid spoke.

'Alas!' said he. 'If Conán is given the power of killing hundreds, for heaven's sake, don't let him know how to use it. He's a very strong, but a very vicious, man, and if he loses his temper, he won't leave one of the Fianna alive.'

And that left Conán as he was ever afterward. He never knew how to use this power that he had, except once at the Battle of Ventry, when he looked at the enemy through his fingers and slew every one of them.

Each of the Fianna in turn asked for what he wanted. I don't know what some of them asked for, but Oisín asked for the grace of God. They say that he went to the Land of Youth and remained there until Saint Patrick came to Ireland, so that he would get the proper faith and knowledge of God and extreme unction when he died. He got them too, for when he returned to Ireland, Saint Patrick himself baptized him and anointed him before he died.

Cromwell and the Friar

There was a gentleman named O'Donnell living in Ireland long ago. He was very friendly with a certain friar.

'Things will change very much in Ireland before long,' said the friar to O'Donnell one day. 'The English will invade Ireland, and they will have a leader named Cromwell, who will evict every Irish gentleman from his lands and settle his own followers on them. The best thing for you to do now,' said the friar, 'is to cross over to England. Go around England, and ask every Englishman you meet to sign in your book a promise that he will never take your lands from you. Keep on going like that until you make off to Cromwell, and ask him to sign the promise too. He's a shoemaker at present.'

Very well. O'Donnell started out and never stopped until he reached England. He let on to be a fool and went around, asking everyone he met on the streets to sign the promise that they would never take his lands or house from him. He finally made off to Cromwell's house, and he went in to get a patch sewn on the side of one of his shoes. He asked Cromwell would he do the job, and Cromwell said he would. O'Donnell took off the shoe, and Cromwell patched it for him. O'Donnell handed him a guinea.

'A thousand thanks,' said Cromwell. 'That's good payment.'

'Now,' said O'Donnell, 'I hope that you will sign this book, promising never to take my house and lands from me.'

'Of course, I'll sign it,' said Cromwell. 'Why shouldn't I?'

He took the book and signed his name to the promise. When that was done, O'Donnell returned to Ireland. A few years after that, a great change took place in England. Cromwell rose very high and took the power from the king. Then he came to Ireland. He started to evict people from their lands, gentlemen and everybody—they were all the same. He killed some of them and finally came to O'Donnell's house. He knocked at the door.

'Get out of here quickly. Long enough you've been here,' said Cromwell.

O'Donnell went out to him.

'I hope you won't evict me until we have dinner together,' said he.

'What kind of dinner have you?' asked Cromwell.

'Roast duck,' said O'Donnell.

'That's fine,' said Cromwell. 'I like roast duck.'

He went in, and the two of them started to eat. When the meal was over, O'Donnell produced his book.

'Do you recognize that writing?' asked O'Donnell.

'I do,' said Cromwell. ' 'Tis my own. But how did you get it? And how did you know that I would rise so high?'

O'Donnell couldn't get out of it; he had to tell him.

'A holy friar that was here told me that a great change was to come over Ireland and that a shoemaker named Cromwell would come to put me out of my land.'

'You must send for the holy friar to come to me now,' said Cromwell. 'And, if he doesn't, I'll cut off his head.'

O'Donnell went off to the friar and brought him back to Cromwell.

'Where did you get this knowledge?' asked Cromwell.

'I got it from heaven,' replied the friar.

'Well, you must tell me now how long I will live?' said Cromwell.

'You will live as long as you wish,' said the holy friar.

'Then I'll live for ever,' said Cromwell.

'And how long will I live?' asked an English gentleman who was with Cromwell. 'Will I have a long life?'

'If you're alive after passing the door of the next forge ye meet, you'll live a long time,' said the friar.

'I'll live for ever so,' said the gentleman.

Very well. Cromwell didn't evict O'Donnell. He left him as he was and went his way with the English gentleman and his troop of soldiers. When they were passing the door of a forge, Cromwell stopped.

'Here's a forge,' said he. 'That's luck, for there's a shoe loose on one of the horses.'

He jumped off the horse and went in. The smith was inside.

'Hurry up and put a shoe on this horse for me,' said Cromwell.

The poor smith was shaking with terror, as he ran about from corner to corner of the forge, looking for a good piece of iron. He was afraid to choose any piece, fearing it would be bad, and he was terrified of Cromwell and his soldiers. Cromwell himself went searching too, and he spied the barrel of an old gun stuck over one of the rafters.

'This is good iron,' said he.

He pulled it down and threw it on the hearth. He was a smith's son himself and he knew a good deal about forges and smithcraft. He used to blow the bellows for his father when he was a boy. He took hold of the bellows and started to blow the fire for a while. The English gentleman was standing outside the door of the forge with his two elbows leaning on the fence. A shot went off from the barrel of the gun and went clean through his body, killing him. No sooner did the gun go off than Cromwell ran out, jumped on the back of his horse, and spurred it as hard as he could on the road toward Dublin.

On the way whom should he see, walking on the road ahead of him but the holy friar. The friar ran in fear to hide behind the parapet of a bridge.

'Come out of there, you devil!' shouted Cromwell. 'If I have to go down for you, I'll cut the head off you.'

The friar came up to him.

'It wasn't you who saw me,' said he to Cromwell, 'but the man behind you on the horse.'

'What man is behind me?' asked Cromwell.

'There's a man sitting on the horse behind you,' said the friar.

Cromwell turned to look, and there was the devil sitting behind him. He dug the spurs into his horse immediately and faced for Dublin. From there he crossed to England and never returned to Ireland. After spending a while in England, Cromwell became restless. The King of Spain died and was succeeded by his young son, who had no great sense or judgement for ruling the country. Cromwell thought of a great plan. He wrote to the young king and invited him to England to marry his daughter. When the young Spanish king received the invitation, he sent for his advisers and told them about it.

'That's only a trick of Cromwell's,' they said. 'He only wants to get a foothold in this country and take it for himself. Write back to him and tell him you would be pleased with the match in a year's time. In the meantime, strengthen your army, and when it is strong enough, write and tell him that you won't marry the devil's daughter.'

Very well! When the year was up, the Spanish king wrote to

Cromwell to say that he wouldn't marry the devil's daughter. Cromwell was shaving himself when the letter arrived. He had one cheek shaved, and he opened the letter before shaving the other to see what the news was. When he found out what the letter said, all he did was catch hold of the razor and cut his throat. He fell down dead.

About the time that Cromwell killed himself there was a ship going into Liverpool. The captain saw, coming toward him in the sky, a fiery chariot drawn by mastiffs which cried out: 'Clear the way for Oliver Cromwell!'

At the same moment, in Cois Fharaige, in County Galway, a little girl was having an argument with her mother.

'May the devil stick in your throat,' cried the mother.

The girl began to choke immediately. The priest was sent for, and he began to pray, calling on the devil to leave her throat. He called a second time, and the devil appeared.

'Where were you the first time I called?' asked the priest.

'I was where Cromwell was dying,' said the devil.

'Where were you the second time I called?'

'I was coming here as fast as I could.'

The priest banished him into the air in a shower of fire.

The Girl and the Sailor

Long ago a lot of women and girls used to go to Catherciveen to sell buttermilk. There would often be ten or twelve churns of the milk at the Cross and great demand for it.

I heard that one day the women and girls were at the Cross as usual selling the milk. Among them was a girl from Rinnard, who had a churn in a donkey cart. She was standing in the cart with a measure in her hand to sell to anybody who came to her. Below at the pier, a ship was tied up while her cargo was being unloaded. Two of the crew walked up toward the Cross where the women were, and one of them turned to the girl from Rinnard and asked her what price the buttermilk was.

'A penny a quart,' said she.

'All right,' said the sailor. 'Give me a quart of it. I'm thirsty.'

She handed him the quart of milk, and he gave her a penny. He put the saucepan to his mouth and drank the milk while the other sailor looked on. When he had finished, he handed the saucepan back to her. He was standing near the cart in which she was, and he wiped his mouth with a corner of her apron. The two sailors then went off down the street. What did the girl do but jump off the cart and away with her down the street after the man who had wiped his mouth with her apron. She left the ass and the cart and the churn behind her. Some relatives of hers who were on the street tried to stop her and get her to return to the cart, but if they did, she paid no heed to them. Whenever the sailors went into a public house, she followed them and stood near the sailor who had touched her apron. It was idle for her relatives to separate them.

Later on in the day, a relative of hers heard what had happened. He went along the street and into a public house where the three of them were standing at the counter. The girl had her back to him when he entered. He went up behind her, took out his knife, and cut the string of her apron. It fell on the floor. No sooner did it fall than the girl went off out the door of her own accord and went back to her cart and churn.

The man who had cut the strings picked up the apron, took it into the kitchen, and shoved it into the centre of the fire. He stood there until it was burned.

All that were at the fair couldn't separate her from the sailor until the apron was taken off her. May God guard us all!

The Four-leafed Shamrock and the Cock

There was a great fair being held in Dingle one day long ago. 'Tis a good many years ago, I think. All of the people were gathered there as usual. Whoever else was there, there was a showman there, and the trick that he had was a cock walking down the street ahead of him, drawing a big, heavy beam tied to his leg. At least, all the people thought that it was a beam, and everyone was running after him, and as he went from street to street, the crowd was getting bigger all the time. Each new person who saw the cock and the beam joined in the procession.

Then there came up the street a small old man carrying a load of rushes on his back. He wondered what all the people were looking at. All that he could see was a wisp of straw being dragged along by a cock. He thought that everybody had gone mad, and he asked them why they were following the cock like that.

Some of them answered him, 'Don't you see the great wonder?' they said. 'That great beam of wood being dragged after him by that cock, and he's able to pull it through every street he travels and it tied to his leg?'

'All that he's pulling is a wisp of straw,' replied the old man.

The showman overheard him saying this. Over to him he went, and he asked him how much he wanted for the load of rushes he had on his back. The old man named some figure—to tell the truth, I can't say how much—but whatever it was, the showman gave it to him. He would have given him twice as much. As soon as the showman took the load of rushes off the old man's back, the old man followed after the crowd, but all that he could see was the cock pulling a heavy beam tied to his leg. He followed him all over Dingle.

What happened was that the old man had a four-leafed shamrock, unknown to himself, tied up in the load of rushes. That's what made what he saw different from what the people saw, and that's why the showman paid him three times the value for the rushes. He told the people, and they gave up the chase.

I heard that story among the people, and it could be true, because the four-leafed shamrock has that power.

The Cow that ate the Piper

There were three spalpeens coming home to Kerry from Limerick one time after working there. On their way, they met a piper on the road.

'I'll go along with ye,' said the piper.

'All right,' they said.

The night was very cold, freezing hard, and they were going to perish. They saw a dead man on the road with a new pair of shoes on his feet.

'By heavens!' said the piper. 'I haven't a stitch of shoes on me. Give me that spade to see can I cut off his legs.'

'Twas the only way he could take off the shoes. They were held on by the frost. So he took hold of the spade and cut off the two feet at the ankles. He took them along with him. They got lodgings at a house where three cows were tied in the kitchen.

'Keep away from that grey cow,' said the servant girl, 'or she'll eat your coats. Keep out from her.'

They all went to sleep. The three spalpeens and the piper stretched down near the fire. The piper heated the shoes and the dead man's feet at the fire and got the shoes off. He put on the shoes and threw the feet near the grey cow's head. Early next morning, he left the house wearing his new pair of shoes. When the servant girl got up, she looked at the door. It was bolted, and the three spalpeens were asleep near the fire.

'My God!' she cried. 'There were four of ye last night, and now there are only three. Where did the other man go?'

'We don't know,' they said. 'How would we know where he went?'

She went to the grey cow's head and found the two feet.

'Oh my!' she cried. 'He was eaten by her.'

She called the man of the house.

'The grey cow has eaten one of the men,' said she.

'What's that you're saying?' said the farmer.

'I'm telling the truth,' said she. 'There's only his feet left. The rest of him is eaten.'

The farmer got up. 'There were four of ye there last night, men,' said he.

'There were,' said one of the spalpeens, 'and our comrade has been eaten by the cow.'

'Don't cause any trouble about it,' said the farmer. 'Here's five pounds for ye. Eat your breakfast and be off. Don't say a word.'

They left when they had the breakfast eaten. And they met the piper some distance from the house, and he dancing on the road. Such a thing could happen!

Conal and Donal and Taig

Translated and retold by Seumas MacManus

Once there were three brothers named Conal, Donal and Taig, and they fell out regarding which of them owned a field of land. One of them had as good a claim to it as the other, and the claims of all of them were so equal that none of the judges, whomsoever they went before, could decide in favour of one more than the other.

At length they went to one judge who was very wise indeed and had a great name, and every one of them stated his case to him.

He sat on the bench, and heard Conal's case and Donal's case and Taig's case all through, with very great patience. When the three of them had finished, he said he would take a day and a night to think it all over, and on the day after, when they were all called into court again, the Judge said that he had weighed the evidence on all sides, with all the deliberation it was possible to give it, and he decided that one of them hadn't the shadow of a shade of a claim more than the others, so that he found himself facing the greatest puzzle he had ever faced in his life.

'But,' says he, 'no puzzle puzzles me long. I'll very soon decide which of you will get the field. You seem to me to be three pretty lazy-looking fellows, and I'll give the field to whichever of the three of you is the laziest.'

'Well, at that rate,' says Conal, 'it's me gets the field, for I'm the laziest man of the lot.'

'How lazy are you?' says the Judge.

'Well,' said Conal, 'if I were lying in the middle of the road, and there was a regiment of troopers come galloping down it, I'd sooner let them ride over me than take the bother of getting up and going to the one side.'

'Well, well,' says the Judge, says he, 'you are a lazy man surely, and I doubt if Donal or Taig can be as lazy as that.'

'Oh, faith,' says Donal, 'I'm just every bit as lazy.'

'Are you?' says the Judge. 'How lazy are you?'

'Well,' said Donal, 'if I was sitting right close to a big fire, and you piled on it all the turf in a townland and all the wood in a barony, sooner than have to move I'd sit there till the boiling marrow would run out of my bones.'

'Well,' says the Judge, 'you're a pretty lazy man, Donal, and I doubt if Taig is as lazy as either of you.'

'Indeed, then,' says Taig, 'I'm every bit as lazy.'

'How can that be?' says the Judge.

'Well,' says Taig, 'if I was lying on the broad of my back in the middle of the floor and looking up at the rafters, and if soot drops were falling as thick as hailstones from the rafters into my open eyes, I would let them drop there for the length of the lee-long day sooner than take the bother of closing the eyes.'

'Well,' says the Judge, 'that's very wonderful entirely, and,' says he, 'I'm in as great a quandary as before, for I see you are the three laziest men that ever were known since the world began, and which of you is the laziest it certainly beats me to say. But I'll tell you what I'll do,' says the Judge, 'I'll give the field to the oldest man of you.'

'Then,' says Conal, 'it's me gets the field.'

'How is that?' says the Judge; 'how old are you?'

'Well, I'm that old,' says Conal, 'that when I was twenty-one years of age I got a shipload of awls and never lost nor broke one of them, and I wore out the last of them yesterday mending my shoes.'

'Well, well,' says the Judge, says he, 'you're surely an old man, and I doubt very much that Donal and Taig can catch up to you.'

'Can't I?' says Donal; 'take care of that.'

'Why,' said the Judge, 'how old are you?'

'When I was twenty-one years of age,' says Donal, 'I got a shipload of needles, and yesterday I wore out the last of them mending my clothes.'

'Well, well, well,' says the Judge, says he, 'you're two very, very old men, to be sure, and I'm afraid poor Taig is out of his chance anyhow.'

'Take care of that,' says Taig.

'Why,' said the Judge, 'how old are you, Taig?'

Says Taig, 'When I was twenty-one years of age I got a shipload of razors, and yesterday I had the last of them worn to a stump shaving myself.'

'Well,' says the Judge, says he, 'I've often heard tell of old men,' he says, 'but anything as old as what you three are never was known since Methusalem's cat died. The like of your ages,' he says, 'I never heard tell of, and which of you is the oldest, that surely beats me to decide, and I'm in a quandary again. But I'll tell you what I'll do,' says the Judge, says he, 'I'll give the field to whichever of you minds the longest.'

'Well, if that's it,' says Conal, 'it's me gets the field, for I mind the time when if a man tramped on a cat he usen't to give it a kick to console it.'

'Well, well, well,' says the Judge, 'that must be a long mind entirely; and I'm afraid, Conal, you have the field.'

'Not so quick,' says Donal, says he, 'for I mind the time when a woman wouldn't speak an ill word of her best friend.'

'Well, well, well,' says the Judge, 'your memory, Donal, must certainly be a very wonderful one, if you can mind that time. Taig,' says the Judge, says he, 'I'm afraid your memory can't compare with Conal's and Donal's.'

'Can't it,' says Taig, says he. 'Take care of that, for I mind the time when you wouldn't find nine liars in a crowd of ten men.'

'Oh, oh, oh!' says the Judge, says he, 'that memory of yours, Taig, must be a wonderful one.' Says he: 'Such memories as you three men have were never known before, and which of you has the greatest memory it beats me to say. But I'll tell you what I'll do now,' says he; 'I'll give the field to whichever of you has the keenest sight.'

'Then,' says Conal, says he, 'it's me gets the field; because,' says he, 'if there was a fly perched on the top of yon mountain, ten miles away, I could tell you every time he blinked.'

'You have wonderful sight, Conal,' says the Judge, says he, 'and I'm afraid you've got the field.'

'Take care,' says Donal, says he, 'but I've got as good. For I could tell you whether it was a mote in his eye that made him blink or not.'

'Ah, ha, ha!' says the Judge, says he, 'this is wonderful sight surely. Taig,' says he, 'I pity you, for you have no chance for the field now.'

'Have I not?' says Taig. 'I could tell you from here whether that fly was in good health or not by counting his heart beats.'

'Well, well, well,' says the Judge, says he, 'I'm in as great a quandary as ever. You are three of the most wonderful men that ever I met, and no mistake. But I'll tell you what I'll do,' says he; 'I'll give the field to the supplest man of you.'

'Thank you,' says Conal. 'Then the field is mine.'

'Why so?' says the Judge.

'Because,' says Conal, says he, 'if you filled that field with hares, and put a dog in the middle of them, and then tied one of my legs up my back, I would not let one of the hares get out.'

'Then, Conal,' says the Judge, says he, 'I think the field is yours.'

'By the leave of your judgeship, not yet,' says Donal.

'Why, Donal,' says the Judge, says he, 'surely you are not as supple as that?'

'Am I not?' says Donal. 'Do you see that old castle over there without door, or window, or roof in it, and the wind blowing in and out through it like an iron gate?'

'I do,' says the Judge. 'What about that?'

'Well,' says Donal, says he, 'if on the stormiest day of the year you had that castle filled with feathers, I would not let a feather be lost, or go ten yards from the castle until I had caught and put it in again.'

'Well, surely,' says the Judge, says he, 'you are a supple man, Donal, and no mistake. Taig,' says he, 'there's no chance for you now.'

'Don't be too sure,' says Taig, says he.

'Why,' says the Judge, 'you couldn't surely do anything to equal these things, Taig?'

Says Taig, says he: 'I can shoe the swiftest race-horse in the land when he is galloping at his topmost speed, by driving a nail every time he lifts his foot.'

'Well, well, well,' says the Judge, says he, 'surely you are the three most wonderful men that ever I did meet. The likes of you never was known before, and I suppose the likes of you will never be on the earth again. There is only one other trial,' says he, 'and if this doesn't decide, I'll have to give it up. I'll give the field,' says he, 'to the cleverest man amongst you.'

'Then,' says Conal, says he, 'you may as well give it to me at once.'

'Why? Are you that clever, Conal?' says the Judge, says he.

'I am that clever,' says Conal, 'I am that clever, that I would make a skin-fit suit of clothes for a man without any more measurement than to tell me the colour of his hair.'

'Then, boys,' says the Judge, says he, 'I think the case is decided.'

'Not so quick, my friend,' says Donal, 'not so quick.'

'Why, Donal,' says the Judge, says he, 'you are surely not cleverer than that?'

'Am I not?' says Donal.

'Why,' says the Judge, says he, 'what can you do, Donal?'

'Why,' says Donal, says he, 'I would make a skin-fit suit for a man and give me no more measurement than let me hear him cough.'

'Well, well, well,' says the Judge, says he, 'the cleverness of you two boys beats all I ever heard of. Taig,' says he, 'poor Taig, whatever chance either of these two may have for the field, I'm very, very sorry for you, for you have no chance.'

'Don't be so very sure of that,' says Taig, says he.

'Why,' says the Judge, says he, 'surely Taig, you can't be as clever as either of them. How clever are you, Taig?'

'Well,' says Taig, says he, 'if I was a judge, and too stupid to decide a case that came up before me, I'd be that clever that I'd look wise and give some decision.'

'Taig,' says the Judge, says he, 'I've gone into this case and deliberated upon it, and by all the laws of right and justice, I find and decide that you get the field.'

OLIVER GOLDSMITH · 1730–1774

Adventures of a Strolling Player

I am fond of amusement, in whatever company it is to be found; and wit, though dressed in rags, is ever pleasing to me. I went some days ago to take a walk in St James's Park, about the hour in which company leave it to go to dinner. There were but few in the walks, and those who stayed, seemed by their looks rather more willing to forget that they had an appetite than gain one. I sat down on one of the benches, at the other end of which was seated a man in very shabby clothes.

We continued to groan, to hem, and to cough, as usual upon such occasions; and, at last, ventured upon conversation. 'I beg pardon, sir,' cried I, 'but I think I have seen you before; your face is familiar to me.' 'Yes, sir,' replied he, 'I have a good familiar face, as my friends tell me. I am as well known in every town in England as the dromedary, or live crocodile. You must understand, sir, that I have been these sixteen years Merry Andrew to a puppet-show; last Bartholomew Fair my master and I quarrelled, beat each other, and parted; he to sell his puppets to the pincushion-makers in Rosemary Lane, and I to starve in St James's Park.'

'I am sorry, sir, that a person of your appearance should labour under any difficulties.' 'O, sir,' returned he, 'my appearance is very much at your service; but though I cannot boast of eating much, yet there are few that are merrier: if I had twenty thousand a year, I should be very merry; and, thank the fates, though not worth a groat, I am very merry still. If I have threepence in my pocket, I never refuse to be my three halfpence; and if I have no money, I never scorn to be treated by any that are kind enough to pay my reckoning. What think you, sir, of a steak and a tankard? You shall treat me now, and I will treat you again when I find you in the Park in love with eating, and without money to pay for a dinner.'

As I never refuse a small expense for the sake of a merry companion, we instantly adjourned to a neighbouring alehouse, and in a few moments had a frothing tankard and a smoking steak spread on the table before us. It is impossible to express how much the sight of such good cheer improved my companion's vivacity. 'I like this dinner, sir,' says he, 'for three reasons: first, because I am naturally fond of beef; secondly, because I am hungry; and, thirdly and lastly, because I get it for nothing: no meat eats so sweet as that for which we do not pay.'

He therefore now fell to, and his appetite seemed to correspond with his inclination. After dinner was over, he observed that the steak was tough; 'and yet, sir,' returns he, 'bad as it was, it seemed a rump-steak to me. Oh, the delights of poverty and a good appetite! We beggars are the very foundlings of Nature; the rich she treats like an arrant stepmother; they are pleased with nothing: cut a steak from what part you will, and it is unsupportably tough; dress it up with pickles—even pickles cannot procure them an appetite. But the whole creation is filled with good things for the beggar; Calvert's butt out-tastes champagne, and Sedgeley's home-brewed excels tokay. Joy, joy, my blood! though our tastes lie nowhere, we have fortunes wherever we go. If an inundation sweeps away half the grounds of Cornwall, I am content; I have no lands there; if the stocks sink, that gives me no uneasiness; I am no Jew.' The fellow's vivacity, joined to his poverty, I own, raised my curiosity to know something of his life and circumstances; and I entreated that he would indulge my desire. 'That I will, sir,' said he, 'and welcome; only let us drink to prevent our sleeping; let us have another tankard while we are awake; let us have another tankard; for, ah, how charming a tankard looks when full!

'You must know, then, that I am very well descended; my ancestors have made some noise in the world; for my mother cried oysters, and my father beat a drum: I am told we have even had some trumpeters in our family. Many a nobleman cannot show so respectful a genealogy: but that is neither here nor there. As I was their only child, my father designed to breed me up to his own employment, which was that of a drummer to a puppet-show. Thus the whole employment of my younger years was that of interpreter to Punch and King Solomon in all his glory. But, though my father was very fond of instructing me in beating all the marches and points of war, I made no very great progress, because I naturally had no ear for music; so, at the age of fifteen, I went and listed for a soldier. As I had ever hated beating a drum, so I soon found that I disliked carrying a musket also; neither the one trade nor the other was to my taste, for I was by nature fond of being a gentleman: besides, I was obliged to obey my captain; he has his will, I have mine, and you have yours: now I very reasonably concluded, that it was much more comfortable for a man to obey his own will than another's.

'The life of a soldier soon therefore gave me the spleen. I asked leave to quit the service; but, as I was tall and strong, my captain thanked me for my kind intention, and said, because he had a regard for me, we should not part. I wrote to my father a very dismal penitent letter, and desired that he would raise money to pay for my discharge; but the good man was as fond of drinking as I was (Sir, my service to you),—and those who are fond of drinking never pay for other people's discharges: in short, he never answered my letter. What could be done? If I have not money, said I to myself, to pay for my discharge, I must find an equivalent some other way; and that must be by running away. I deserted, and that answered my purpose every bit as well as if I had bought my discharge.

'Well, I was now fairly rid of my military employment; I sold my soldier's clothes, bought worse, and, in order not to be overtaken, took the most unfrequented roads possible. One evening as I was entering a village, I perceived a man, whom I afterwards found to be the curate of the parish, thrown from his horse in a miry road, and almost smothered in the mud. He desired my assistance; I gave it, and drew him out with some difficulty. He thanked me for my trouble, and was going off; but I followed him home, for I loved always to have a man thank me at his own door. The curate asked an hundred questions; as, whose son I was; from whence I came; and whether I would be faithful? I answered him greatly to his satisfaction, and gave myself one of the best characters in the world for sobriety (Sir, I have the honour of drinking your health), discretion, and fidelity. To make a long story short, he wanted a servant, and hired me. With him I lived but two months; we did not much like each other; I was fond of eating, and he gave me but little to eat; I loved a pretty girl, and the old woman, my fellow servant, was ill-natured and ugly. As they endeavoured to starve me between them, I made a pious resolution to prevent their committing murder; I stole the eggs as soon as they were laid; I emptied every unfinished bottle that I could lay my hands on;

whatever eatable came in my way was sure to disappear: in short, they found I would not do; so I was discharged one morning, and paid three shillings and sixpence for two months' wages.

'While my money was getting ready, I employed myself in making preparations for my departure; two hens were hatching in an out-house; I went and habitually took the eggs; and, not to separate the parents from the children, I lodged hens and all in my knapsack. After this piece of frugality, I returned to receive my money, and, with my knapsack on my back, and a staff in my hand, I bid adieu, with tears in my eyes, to my old benefactor. I had not gone far from the house when I heard behind me the cry of "Stop thief!" but this only increased my dispatch; it would have been foolish to stop, as I knew the voice could not be levelled at me. But hold, I think I passed those two months at the curate's without drinking. Come, the times are dry, and may this be my poison if ever I spent two more pious, stupid months in all my life.

'Well, after travelling some days, whom should I light upon but a company of strolling players. The moment I saw them at a distance my heart warmed to them; I had a sort of natural love for everything of the vagabond order: they were employed in settling their baggage, which had been overturned in a narrow way; I offered my assistance, which they accepted; and we soon became so well acquainted that they took me as a servant. This was a paradise to me; they sung, danced, drank, ate, and travelled, all at the same time. By the blood of the Mirabels, I thought I had never lived till then; I grew as merry as a grig, and laughed at every word that was spoken. They liked me as much as I liked them; I was a very good figure, as you see; and, though I was poor, I was not modest.

'I love a straggling life above all things in the world; sometimes good, sometimes bad; to be warm today, and cold tomorrow; to eat when one can get it, and drink when (the tankard is out) it stands before me. We arrived that evening at Tenterden, and took a large room at the Greyhound, where we resolved to exhibit *Romeo and Juliet*, with the funeral procession, the grave, and the garden scene. Romeo was to be performed by a gentleman from the Theatre Royal in Drury Lane; Juliet by a lady who had never appeared on any stage before; and I was to snuff the candles: all excellent in our way. We had figures enough, but the difficulty was to dress them. The same coat that served Romeo, turned with the blue lining outwards, served for his friend Mercutio: a large piece of crape sufficed at once for Juliet's petticoat and pall: a pestle and mortar, from a neighbouring apothecary's, answered all the purposes of a bell; and our landlord's own family, wrapped in white sheets, served to fill up the procession. In short, there were but three figures among us that might be said to be dressed with any propriety: I mean the nurse, the starved apothecary, and myself. Our performance gave universal satisfaction: the whole audience were enchanted with our powers, and Tenterden is a town of taste.

'There is one rule by which a strolling player may be ever secure of success; that is, in our theatrical way of expressing it, to make a great deal of the character. To speak and act as in common life, is not playing, nor is it what people come to see: natural speaking, like sweet wine, runs glibly over the palate, and scarce leaves any taste behind it; but being high in a part resembles vinegar, which grates upon the taste, and one feels it while he is drinking. To please in town or country, the way is, to cry, wring, cringe into attitudes, mark the emphasis, slap the pockets, and labour like one in the falling sickness: that is the way to work for applause; that is the way to gain it.

'As we received much reputation for our skill on this first exhibition, it was but natural for me to ascribe part of the success to myself: I snuffed the candles, and let me tell you, that without a candle-snuffer the piece would lose half its embellishments. In this manner we continued a fortnight, and drew tolerable houses; but the evening before our intended departure, we gave out our very best piece, in which all our strength was to be exerted. We had great expectations from this, and even doubled our prices, when behold one of the principal actors fell ill of a violent fever. This was a stroke like thunder to our little company: they were resolved to go, in a body, to scold the man for falling sick at so inconvenient a time, and that too of a disorder that threatened to be expensive; I seized the moment, and offered to act the part myself in his stead. The case was desperate; they accepted my offer; and I accordingly sat down, with the part in my hand and a tankard before me (Sir, your health), and studied the character, which was to be rehearsed the next day, and played soon after.

'I found my memory excessively helped by drinking; I learned my part with astonishing rapidity, and bid adieu to snuffing candles ever after. I found that Nature had designed me for more noble employments, and I was resolved to take her when in the humour. We got together in order to rehearse; and I informed my companions, masters now no longer, of the surprising change I felt within me. "Let the sick man," said I, "be under no uneasiness to get well again; I'll fill his place to universal satisfaction: he may even die if he thinks proper; I'll engage that he shall never be missed." I rehearsed before them, strutted, ranted, and received applause. They soon gave out that a new actor of eminence was to appear, and immediately all the genteel places were bespoke. Before I ascended the stage, however, I concluded within myself, that, as I brought money to the house, I ought to have my share in the profits. "Gentlemen," said I, addressing our company, "I don't pretend to direct you; far be it from me to treat you with so much ingratitude: you have published my name in the bills with the utmost good nature; and, as affairs stand, cannot act without me; so, gentlemen, to show you my gratitude, I expect to be paid for my acting as much as any of you, otherwise I declare off; I'll brandish my snuffers, and clip . candles as usual." This was a very disagreeable proposal, but they found that it was impossible to refuse it; it was irresistible, it was adamant: they consented, and I went on in King Bajazet; my frowning brows bound with a stocking stuffed into a turban, while on my captiv'd arms I brandished a jack-chain. Nature seemed to have fitted me for the part; I was tall, and had a loud voice; my very entrance excited universal applause; I looked round on the audience with a smile, and made a most low and gracious bow, for that is the rule among us. As it was a very passionate part, I invigorated my spirits with three full glasses (the tankard is almost out) of brandy. By Allah! it is almost inconceivable how I went through it; Tamerlane was but a fool to me; though he was sometimes loud enough too, yet I was still louder than he: but then, besides I had attitudes in abundance: in general I kept my arms folded up thus upon the pit of my stomach; it is the way at Drury Lane, and has always a fine effect. The tankard would sink to the bottom before I could get through the whole of my merits: in short, I came off like a prodigy; and such was my success, that I could ravish the laurels even from a sirloin of beef. The principal gentlemen and ladies of the town came to me, after the play was over, to compliment me upon my success: one praised my voice, another my person. "Upon my word," says the squire's lady, "he will make one of the finest actors in Europe; I say it, and I think I am something of a judge."—Praise in the beginning is agreeable enough, and we receive it as a favour; but when it comes in great quantities, we regard it only as a debt, which nothing but our merit could extort: instead of thanking them, I internally applauded myself. We were desired to give our piece a second time; we obeyed, and I was applauded even more than before.

'At last we left the town, in order to be at a horse-race at some distance from thence. I shall never think of Tenterden without fears of gratitude and respect. The ladies and gentlemen there, take my word for it, are very good judges of plays and actors. Come, let us drink their healths, if you please, sir. We quitted the town, I say; and there was a wide difference between my coming in and going out: I entered the town a candle-snuffer, and I quitted it an hero!— Such is the world; little today, and great tomorrow. I could say a great deal more upon that subject; something truly sublime, upon the ups and downs of fortune; but it would give us both the spleen, and so I shall pass it over.

'The races were ended before we arrived at the next town, which was no small disappointment to our company; however, we were resolved to take all we could get. I played capital characters there too, and came off with my usual brilliancy. I sincerely believe I should have been the first actor of Europe, had my growing merit been properly cultivated; but there came an unkindly frost, which nipped me in the bud, and levelled me once more down to the common standard of humanity. I played Sir Harry Wildair; all the country ladies were charmed: if I but drew out my snuff-box, the whole house was in a roar of rapture; when I exercised my cudgel, I thought they would have fallen into convulsions.

'There was here a lady who had received an education of nine months in London; and this gave her pretensions to taste, which rendered her the indisputable mistress of the ceremonies wherever she came. She was informed of my merits; everybody praised me; yet she refused at first going to see me perform: she could not conceive, she said, anything but stuff from a stroller; talked something in praise of Garrick, and amazed the ladies with her skill in enunciations, tones, and cadences: she was at last, however, prevailed upon to go; and it was privately intimated to me what a judge was to be present at my next exhibition: however, no way intimidated, I came on in Sir Harry, one hand stuck in my breeches, and the other in my bosom, as usual at Drury Lane; but, instead of looking at me, I perceived the whole audience had their eyes turned upon the lady who had been nine months in London; from her they expected the decision which was to secure the general's truncheon in my hand, or sink me down into a theatrical letter-carrier. I opened my snuff-box, took snuff; the lady was solemn, and so were the rest; I broke my cudgel on Alderman Smuggler's back: still gloomy, melancholy all: the lady groaned and shrugged her shoulders; I attempted, by laughing myself, to excite at least a smile; but the devil a cheek could I perceive wrinkled into sympathy: I found it would not do; all my good humour now became forced; my laughter was converted into hysteric grinning; and, while I pretended spirits, my eye showed the agony of my heart: in short, the lady came with an intention to be displeased, and displeased she was; my frame expired; I am here, and—the tankard is no more!'

The Limerick Gloves

I

It was Sunday morning, and a fine day in autumn; the bells of Hereford cathedral rang, and all the world smartly dressed were flocking to church.

'Mrs Hill! Mrs Hill!—Phœbe! Phœbe! There's the cathedral bell, I say, and neither of you ready for church, and I a verger,' cried Mr Hill, the tanner, as he stood at the bottom of his own staircase. 'I'm ready, papa,' replied Phœbe; and down she came, looking so clean, so fresh, and so gay, that her stern father's brows unbent, and he could only say to her, as she was drawing on a new pair of gloves, 'Child, you ought to have had those gloves on before this time of day.'

'Before this time of day!' cried Mrs Hill, who was now coming down stairs completely equipped, 'before this time of day! she should know better, I say, than to put on those gloves at all: more especially when going to the cathedral.'

'The gloves are very good gloves, as far as I see,' replied Mr Hill. 'But no matter now. It is more fitting that we should be in proper time in our pew, to set an example, as becomes us, than to stand here talking of gloves and nonsense.'

He offered his wife and daughter each an arm, and set out for the cathedral; but Phœbe was too busy in drawing on her new gloves, and her mother was too angry at the sight of them, to accept of Mr Hill's courtesy: 'What I say is always nonsense, I know, Mr Hill,' resumed the matron: 'but I can see as far into a millstone as other folks. Was it not I that first gave you a hint of what became of the great dog, that we lost out of our tan-yard last winter? And was it not I who first took notice to you, Mr Hill, verger as you are, of the hole under the foundation of the cathedral? Was it not, I ask you, Mr Hill?'

'But, my dear Mrs Hill, what has all this to do with Phœbe's gloves?'

'Are you blind, Mr Hill? Don't you see that they are Limerick gloves?'

'What of that?' said Mr Hill; still preserving his composure, as it was his custom to do as long as he could, when he saw his wife was ruffled.

'What of that, Mr Hill! why don't you know that Limerick is in Ireland, Mr Hill?'

'With all my heart, my dear.'

'Yes, and with all your heart, I suppose, Mr Hill, you would see our cathedral blown up, some fair day or other, and your own daughter married to the person that did it; and you a verger, Mr Hill.'

'God forbid!' cried Mr Hill; and he stopped short and settled his wig. Presently recovering himself, he added, 'But, Mrs Hill, the cathedral is not yet blown up; and our Phœbe is not yet married.'

'No: but what of that, Mr Hill? Forewarned is forearmed, as I told you before your dog was gone; but you would not believe me, and you see how it turned out in that case; and so it will in this case, you'll see, Mr Hill.'

'But you puzzle and frighten me out of my wits, Mrs Hill,' said the verger, again settling his wig. '*In that case and in this case!* I can't understand a syllable of what you've been saying to me this half hour. In plain English, what is there the matter about Phœbe's gloves?'

'In plain English, then, Mr Hill, since you can understand nothing else, please to ask your daughter Phœbe who gave her those gloves. Phœbe, who gave you those gloves?'

'I wish they were burnt,' said the husband, whose patience could endure no longer. 'Who gave you those cursed gloves, Phœbe?'

'Papa,' answered Phœbe, in a low voice, 'they were a present from Mr Brian O'Neill.'

'The Irish glover,' cried Mr Hill, with a look of terror.

'Yes,' resumed the mother; 'very true, Mr Hill, I assure you. Now, you see, I had my reasons.'

'Take off the gloves directly: I order you, Phœbe,' said her father, in his most peremptory tone. 'I took a mortal dislike to that Mr Brian O'Neill the first time I ever saw him. He's an Irishman, and that's enough, and too much for me. Off with the gloves, Phœbe! When I order a thing, it must be done.'

Phœbe seemed to find some difficulty in getting off the gloves, and gently urged that she could not well go into the cathedral without them. This objection was immediately removed, by her mother's pulling from her pocket a pair of mittens, which had once been brown, and once been whole, but which were now rent in sundry places; and which, having been long stretched by one who was twice the size of Phœbe, now hung in huge wrinkles upon her well-upturned arms.

'But, papa,' said Phœbe, 'why should we take a dislike to him because he is an Irishman? Cannot an Irishman be a good man?'

The verger made no answer to this question, but a few seconds after it was put to him, observed that the cathedral bell had just done ringing; and, as they were now got to the church door, Mrs Hill, with a significant look at Phœbe, remarked that it was no proper time to talk or think of good men, or bad men, or Irishmen, or any men, especially for a verger's daughter.

We pass over in silence the many conjectures that were made by several of the congregation, concerning the reason why Miss Phœbe Hill should appear in such a shameful shabby pair of gloves on a Sunday. After service was ended, the verger went, with great mystery, to examine the hole under the foundation of the cathedral; and Mrs Hill repaired, with the grocer's and the stationer's ladies, to take a walk in the Close; where she boasted to all her female acquaintance, whom she called her friends, of her maternal discretion in prevailing upon Mr Hill to forbid her daughter Phœbe to wear the Limerick gloves.

In the mean time, Phœbe walked pensively homewards; endeavouring to discover why her father should take a mortal dislike to a man, at first sight, merely because he was an Irishman; and why her mother had talked so much of the great dog, which had been lost last year out of the tan-yard; and of the hole under the foundation of the cathedral! What has all this to do with my Limerick gloves? thought she. The more she thought, the less connection she could perceive between these things: for as she had not taken a dislike to Mr Brian O'Neill at first sight, because he was an Irishman, she could not think it quite reasonable to suspect him of making away with her father's dog; nor yet of a design to blow up Hereford cathedral. As she was pondering upon these matters, she came within sight of the ruins of a poor man's house, which a few months before this time had been burnt down. She recollected that her first acquaintance with her lover began at the time of this fire; and she thought that the courage and humanity he showed, in exerting himself to save this unfortunate woman and her children, justified her notion of the possibility that an Irishman might be a good man.

The name of the poor woman, whose house had been burnt down, was Smith: she was a widow, and she now lived at the extremity of a narrow lane in a wretched habitation. Why Phœbe thought of her with more concern than usual at this instant we need not examine, but she did; and, reproaching herself for having neglected it for some weeks past, she resolved to go directly to see the widow Smith, and to give her a crown which she had long had in her pocket, with which she had intended to have bought play tickets.

It happened that the first person she saw in the poor widow's kitchen was the identical Mr O'Neill. 'I did not expect to see any body here but you, Mrs Smith,' said Phœbe, blushing.

'So much the greater the pleasure of the meeting; to me, I mean, Miss Hill,' said O'Neill, rising, and putting down a little boy, with whom he had been playing. Phœbe went on talking to the poor woman; and, after slipping the crown into her hand, said she would call again. O'Neill, surprised at the change in her manner, followed her when she left the house, and said, 'It would be a great misfortune to me to have done any thing to offend Miss Hill; especially if I could not conceive how or what it was, which is my case at this present speaking.' And, as the spruce glover spoke, he fixed his eyes upon Phœbe's ragged gloves. She drew them up in vain; and then said, with her natural simplicity and gentleness, 'You have not done any thing to offend me, Mr O'Neill; but you are some way or other displeasing to my father and mother, and they have forbid me to wear the Limerick gloves.'

'And sure Miss Hill would not be after changing her opinion of her humble servant for no reason in life, but because her father and mother, who have taken a prejudice against him, are a little contrary.'

'No,' replied Phœbe; 'I should not change my opinion without any reason; but I have not yet had time to fix my opinion of you, Mr O'Neill.'

'To let you know a piece of my mind, then, my dear Miss Hill,' resumed he, 'the more contrary they are, the more pride and joy it would give me to win and wear you, in spite of 'em all; and if without a farthing in your pocket, so much the more I should rejoice in the opportunity of proving to your dear self, and all else whom it may consarn, that Brian O'Neill is no fortune-hunter, and scorns them that are so narrow-minded as to think that no other kind of cattle but them there fortune-hunters can come out of all Ireland. So, my dear Phœbe, now we understand one another, I hope you will not be paining my eyes any longer with the sight of these odious brown bags, which are not fit to be worn by any Christian arms, to say nothing of Miss Hill's, which are the handsomest, without any compliment, that ever I saw; and, to my mind, would become a pair of Limerick gloves beyond any thing: and I expect she'll show her generosity and proper spirit by putting them on immediately.'

'You expect, sir!' repeated Miss Hill, with a look of more indignation than her gentle countenance had ever before been seen to assume. 'Expect!' If he had said hope, thought she, it would have been another thing: but expect! what right has he to expect?

Now Miss Hill, unfortunately, was not sufficiently acquainted with the Irish idiom, to know, that to expect, in Ireland, is the same thing as to hope in England; and, when her Irish admirer said I expect, he meant only in plain English, I hope. But thus it is that a poor Irishman, often, for want of understanding the niceties of the English language, says the rudest when he means to say the civillest things imaginable.

Miss Hill's feelings were so much hurt by this unlucky 'I expect', that the whole of his speech, which had before made some favourable impression upon her, now lost its effect; and she replied with proper spirit, as she thought, 'You expect a great deal too much, Mr O'Neill; and more than ever I gave you reason to do. It would be neither pleasure nor pride to me to be won and worn, as you were pleased to say, in spite of them all; and to be thrown, without a farthing in my pocket, upon the protection of one who expects so much at first setting out.—So I assure you, sir, whatever you may expect, I shall not put on the Limerick gloves.'

Mr O'Neill was not without his share of pride and proper spirit; nay, he had, it must be confessed, in common with some others of his countrymen, an improper share of pride and spirit. Fired by the lady's coldness, he poured forth a volley of reproaches; and ended by wishing, as he said, a good morning, for ever and ever, to one who could change her opinion, point blank, like the weathercock. 'I am, miss, your most obedient; and I expect you'll never think no more of poor Brian O'Neill, and the Limerick gloves.'

If he had not been in too great a passion to observe any thing, poor Brian O'Neill would have found out that Phœbe was not a weathercock: but he left her abruptly, and hurried away, imagining all the while that it was Phœbe, and not himself, who was in a rage. Thus, to the horseman, who is galloping at full speed, the hedges, trees, and houses, seem rapidly to recede; whilst, in reality, they never move from their places. It is he that flies from them, and not they from him.

On Monday morning Miss Jenny Brown, the perfumer's daughter, came to pay Phœbe a morning visit, with face of busy joy.

'So, my dear!' said she: 'fine doings in Hereford! but what makes you look so downcast? To be sure you are invited, as well as the rest of us.'

'Invited where?' cried Mrs Hill, who was present, and who could never endure to hear of an invitation in which she was not included. 'Invited where, pray, Miss Jenny?'

'La! have not you heard? Why, we all took it for granted that you and Miss Phœbe would have been the first and foremost to have been asked to Mr O'Neill's ball.'

'Ball!' cried Mrs Hill; and luckily saved Phœbe, who was in some agitation, the trouble of speaking. 'Why, this is a mighty sudden thing: I never heard a tittle of it before.'

'Well, this is really extraordinary! And, Phœbe, have you not received a pair of Limerick gloves?'

'Yes, I have,' said Phœbe, 'but what then? What have my Limerick gloves to do with the ball?'

'A great deal,' replied Jenny. 'Don't you know, that a pair of Limerick gloves is, as one may say, a ticket to this ball? for every lady that has been asked has had a pair sent to her along with the card; and I believe as many as twenty, besides myself, have been asked this morning.'

Jenny then produced her new pair of Limerick gloves; and as she tried them on, and showed how well they fitted, she counted up the names of the ladies who, to her knowledge, were to be at this ball. When she had finished the catalogue, she expatiated upon the grand preparations which it was said the widow O'Neill, Mr O'Neill's mother, was making for the supper; and concluded by condoling with Mrs Hill for her misfortune in not having been invited. Jenny took her leave, to get her dress in readiness: 'for,' added she, 'Mr O'Neill has engaged me to open the ball, in case Phœbe does not go: but I suppose she will cheer up and go, as she had a pair of Limerick gloves as well as the rest of us.'

There was a silence for some minutes after Jenny's departure, which was broken by Phœbe, who told her mother that, early in the morning, a note had been brought to her, which she had returned unopened; because she knew, from the hand-writing of the direction, that it came from Mr O'Neill.

We must observe that Phœbe had already told her mother of her meeting with this gentleman at the poor widow's, and of all that had passed between them afterwards. This openness, on her part, had softened the heart of Mrs Hill; who was really inclined to be good-natured, provided people would allow that she had more penetration than any one else in Hereford. She was moreover a good deal piqued and alarmed by the idea that the perfumer's daughter might rival and outshine her own. Whilst she had thought herself sure of Mr O'Neill's attachment to Phœbe, she had looked higher; especially as she was persuaded, by the perfumer's lady, to think that an Irishman could not be a bad match: but now she began to suspect that the perfumer's lady had changed her opinion of Irishmen, since she did not object to her own Jenny's leading up the ball at Mr O'Neill's.

All these thoughts passed rapidly in the mother's mind; and, with her fear of losing an admirer for her Phœbe, the value of that admirer suddenly rose in her estimation. Thus, at an auction, if a lot is going to be knocked down to a lady, who is the only person that has bid for it, even she feels discontented, and despises that which nobody covets; but if, as the hammer is falling, many voices answer to the question, Who bids more? then her anxiety to secure the prize suddenly rises; and, rather than be outbid, she will give far beyond its value.

'Why, child,' said Mrs Hill, 'since you have a pair of Limerick gloves; and since certainly that note was an invitation to us to this ball; and since it is much more fitting that you should open the ball than Jenny Brown; and since, after all, it was very handsome and genteel of the young man to say he would take you without a farthing in your pocket, which shows that those were misinformed who talked of him as an Irish adventurer; and since we are not certain 'twas he made away with the dog, although he said its barking was a great nuisance; there is no great reason to suppose he was the person who made the hole under the foundation of the cathedral, or that he could have such a wicked thought as to blow it up; and since he must be in a very good way of business to be able to afford giving away four or five guineas' worth of Limerick gloves, and balls and suppers; and since, after all, it is no fault of his to be an Irishman; I give it as my vote and opinion, my dear, that you put on your Limerick gloves and go to this ball; and I'll go and speak to your father, and bring him round to our opinion; and then I'll pay the morning visit I owe to the widow O'Neill, and make up your quarrel with Brian. Love quarrels are easy to make up, you know; and then we shall have things all upon velvet again; and Jenny Brown need not come with her hypocritical condoling face to us any more.'

After running this speech glibly off, Mrs Hill, without waiting to hear a syllable from poor Phœbe, trotted off in search of her consort. It was not, however, quite so easy a task as his wife expected to bring Mr Hill round to her opinion. He was slow in declaring himself of any opinion; but, when once he had said a thing, there was but little chance of altering his notions. On this occasion, Mr Hill was doubly bound to his prejudice against our unlucky Irishman; for he had mentioned with great solemnity at the club which he frequented, the grand affair of the hole under the foundation of the cathedral; and his suspicions that there was a design to blow it up. Several of the club had laughed at this idea; others, who supposed that Mr O'Neill was a Roman Catholic, and who had a confused notion that a Roman Catholic *must* be a very wicked, dangerous being, thought that there might be a great deal in the verger's suggestions; and observed that a very watchful eye ought to be kept upon this Irish glover, who had come to settle at Hereford nobody knew why, and who seemed to have money at command nobody knew how.

The news of this ball sounded to Mr Hill's prejudiced imagination like the news of a conspiracy. Ay! ay! thought he; the Irishman is cunning enough! But we shall be too many for him: he wants to throw all the good sober folks of Hereford off their guard, by feasting, and dancing, and carousing, I take it; and so to perpetrate his evil designs when it is least suspected; but we shall be prepared for him, fools as he takes us plain Englishmen to be, I warrant.

In consequence of these most shrewd cogitations, our verger silenced his wife with a peremptory nod, when she came to persuade him to let Phœbe put on the Limerick gloves, and go to the ball. 'To this ball she shall not go; and I charge her not to put on those Limerick gloves, as she values my blessing,' said Mr Hill. 'Please to tell her so, Mrs Hill, and trust to my judgement and discretion in all things, Mrs Hill. Strange work may be in Hereford yet: but I'll say no more; I must go and consult with knowing men, who are of my opinion.'

He sallied forth, and Mrs Hill was left in a state which only those who are troubled with the disease of excessive curiosity can rightly comprehend or compassionate. She hied her back to Phœbe, to whom she announced her father's answer; and then went gossiping to all her female acquaintance in Hereford, to tell them all that she knew, and all that she did not know; and to endeavour to find out a secret where there was none to be found.

There are trials of temper in all conditions: and no lady, in high or low life, could endure them with a better grace than Phœbe. Whilst Mr and Mrs Hill were busied abroad, there came to see Phœbe one of the widow Smith's children. With artless expressions of gratitude to Phœbe, this little girl mixed the praises of O'Neill, who, she said, had been the constant friend of her mother, and had given her money every week since the fire happened. 'Mammy loves him dearly, for being so good-natured,' continued the child: 'and he has been good to other people as well as to us.'

'To whom?' said Phœbe.

'To a poor man who has lodged for these few days past next door to us,' replied the child; 'I don't know his name rightly, but he is an Irishman; and he goes out a-haymaking in the daytime, along with a number of others. He knew Mr O'Neill in his own country, and he told mammy a great deal about his goodness.'

As the child finished these words, Phœbe took out of a drawer some clothes, which she had made for the poor woman's children, and gave them to the little girl. It happened that the Limerick gloves had been thrown into this drawer; and Phœbe's favourable sentiments of the giver of those gloves were revived by what she had just heard, and by the confession Mrs Hill had made, that she had no reasons, and but vague suspicions, for thinking ill of him. She laid the gloves perfectly smooth, and strewed over them, whilst the little girl went on talking of Mr O'Neill, the leaves of a rose which she had worn on Sunday.

Mr Hill was all this time in deep conference with those prudent men of Hereford, who were of his own opinion, about the perilous hole under the cathedral. The ominous circumstance of this ball was also considered, the great expense at which the Irish glover lived, and his giving away gloves; which was a sure sign he was not under any necessity to sell them; and consequently a proof that, though he pretended to be a glover, he was something wrong in disguise. Upon putting all these things together, it was resolved, by these over-wise politicians, that the best thing that could be done for Hereford, and the only possible means of preventing the immediate destruction of its cathedral, would be to take Mr O'Neill into custody. Upon recollection, however, it was perceived that there was no legal ground on which he could be attacked. At length, after consulting an attorney, they devised what they thought an admirable mode of proceeding.

Our Irish hero had not that punctuality which English tradesmen usually observe in the payment of bills: he had, the preceding year, run up a long bill with a grocer in Hereford; and, as he had not at Christmas cash in hand to pay it, he had given a note, payable six months after date. The grocer, at Mr Hill's request, made over the note to him; and it was determined that the money should be demanded, as it was now due, and that, if it was not paid directly, O'Neill should be that night arrested. How Mr Hill made the discovery of this debt to the grocer agree with his former notion that the Irish glover had always money at command, we cannot well conceive; but anger and prejudice will swallow down the grossest contradictions without difficulty.

When Mr Hill's clerk went to demand payment of the note, O'Neill's head was full of the ball which he was to give that evening. He was much surprised at the unexpected appearance of the note: he had not ready money by him to pay it; and, after swearing a good deal at the clerk, and complaining of this ungenerous and ungentleman-like behaviour in the grocer and the tanner, he told the clerk to be gone, and not to be bothering him at such an unseasonable time; that he could not have the money then, and did not deserve to have it at all.

This language and conduct were rather new to the English clerk's mercantile ears: we cannot wonder that it should seem to him, as he said to his master, more the language of a madman than a man of business. This want of punctuality in money transactions, and this mode of treating contracts as matters of favour and affection, might not have damned the fame of our hero in his own country, where such conduct is, alas! too common; but he was now in a kingdom where the manners and customs are so directly opposite, that he could meet with no allowance for his national faults. It would be well for his countrymen if they were made, even by a few mortifications, somewhat sensible of this important difference in the habits of Irish and English traders, before they come to settle in England.

But, to proceed with our story. On the night of Mr O'Neill's grand ball, as he was seeing his fair partner, the perfumer's daughter, safe home, he felt himself tapped on the shoulder by no friendly hand. When he was told that he was the king's prisoner, he vociferated with sundry strange oaths, which we forbear to repeat, 'No, I am not the king's prisoner! I am the prisoner of that shabby rascally tanner, Jonathan Hill. None but he would arrest a gentleman, in this way, for a trifle not worth mentioning.'

Miss Jenny Brown screamed when she found herself under the protection of a man who was arrested; and, what between her screams and his oaths, there was such a disturbance that a mob gathered.

Among this mob there was a party of Irish haymakers, who, after returning late from a hard day's work, had been drinking in a neighbouring ale-house. With one accord they took part with their countryman, and would have rescued him from the civil officers with all the pleasure in life, if he had not fortunately possessed just sufficient sense and command of himself, to restrain their party spirit, and to forbid them, as they valued his life and reputation, to interfere, by word or deed, in his defence.

He then dispatched one of the haymakers home to his mother, to inform her of what had happened; and to request that she would get somebody to be bail for him as soon as possible, as the officers said they could not let him out of their sight till he was bailed by substantial people, or till the debt was discharged.

The widow O'Neill was just putting out the candles in the ball-room when this news of her son's arrest was brought to her. We pass over Hibernian exclamations: she consoled her pride by reflecting that it would certainly be the most easy thing imaginable to procure bail for Mr O'Neill in Hereford, where he had so many friends who had just been dancing at his house, but to dance at his house she found was one thing, and to be bail for him quite another. Each guest sent excuses; and the widow O'Neill was astonished at what never fails to astonish every body when it happens to themselves. 'Rather than let my son be detained in this manner for a paltry debt,' cried she, 'I'd sell all I have within half an hour to a pawnbroker.' It was well no pawnbroker heard this declaration: she was too warm to consider economy. She sent for a pawnbroker, who lived in the same street, and, after pledging goods to treble the amount of the debt, she obtained ready money for her son's release.

O'Neill, after being in custody for about an hour and a half, was set at liberty upon the payment of his debt. As he passed by the cathedral in his way home, he heard the clock strike; and he called to a man, who was walking backwards and forwards in the churchyard, to ask whether it was two or three that the clock struck. 'Three,' answered the man; 'and, as yet, all is safe.'

O'Neill, whose head was full of other things, did not stop to inquire the meaning of these last words. He little suspected that this man was a watchman, whom the over-vigilant verger had stationed there to guard the Hereford cathedral from his attacks. O'Neill little guessed that he had been arrested merely to keep him from blowing up the cathedral this night. The arrest had an excellent effect upon his mind, for he was a young man of good sense: it made him resolve to retrench his expenses in time, to live more like a glover and less like a gentleman; and to aim more at establishing credit, and less at gaining popularity. He found, from experience, that good friends will not pay bad debts.

II

On Thursday morning, our verger rose in unusually good spirits, congratulating himself upon the eminent service he had done to the city of Hereford, by his sagacity in discovering the foreign plot to blow up the cathedral, and by his dexterity in having the enemy held in custody, at the very hour when the dreadful deed was to have been perpetrated. Mr Hill's knowing friends farther agreed it would be necessary to have a guard that should sit up every night in the churchyard; and that as soon as they could, by constantly watching the enemy's motions, procure any information which the attorney should deem sufficient grounds for a legal proceeding, they should lay the whole business before the mayor.

After arranging all this most judiciously and mysteriously with friends who were exactly of his own opinion, Mr Hill laid aside his dignity of verger; and assuming his other character of a tanner proceeded to his tan-yard. What was his surprise and consternation, when he beheld his great rick of oak bark levelled to the ground; the pieces of bark were scattered far and wide, some over the close, some over the fields, and some were seen swimming upon the water! No tongue, no pen, no muse can describe the feelings of our tanner at this spectacle! feelings which became the more violent from the absolute silence which he imposed on himself upon this occasion. He instantly decided in his own mind, that this injury was perpetrated by O'Neill, in revenge for his arrest; and went privately to the attorney to inquire what was to be done, on his part, to secure legal vengeance.

The attorney unluckily, or at least as Mr Hill thought, unluckily, had been sent for, half an hour before, by a gentleman at some distance from Hereford, to draw up a will; so that our tanner was obliged to postpone his legal operations.

We forbear to recount his return, and how many times he walked up and down the close to view his scattered bark, and to estimate the damage that had been done to him. At length that hour came which usually suspends all passions by the more imperious power of appetite—the hour of dinner; an hour of which it was never needful to remind Mr Hill by watch, clock, or dial; for he was blessed with a punctual appetite, and powerful as punctual: so powerful, indeed, that it often excited the spleen of his more genteel, or less hungry wife—'Bless my stars, Mr Hill,' she would oftentimes say, 'I am really downright ashamed to see you eat so much; and when company is to dine with us, I do wish you would take a snack by way of a damper before dinner, that you may not look so prodigious famishing and ungenteel.'

Upon this hint, Mr Hill commenced a practice, to which he ever afterwards religiously adhered, of going, whether there was to be company or no company, into the kitchen regularly every day, half an hour before dinner, to take a slice from the roast or the boiled before it went up to table. As he was this day, according to his custom, in the kitchen, taking his snack by way of a damper, he heard the housemaid and the cook talking about some wonderful fortune-teller, whom the housemaid had been consulting. This fortune-teller was no less a personage than the successor to

Bampfylde Moore Carew, king of the gipsies, whose life and adventures are probably in many, too many, of our readers' hands. Bampfylde, the second king of the gipsies, assumed this title, in hopes of becoming as famous, or as infamous, as his predecessor: he was now holding his court in a wood near the town of Hereford, and numbers of servantmaids and 'prentices went to consult him— nay, it was whispered that he was resorted to, secretly, by some whose education might have taught them better sense.

Numberless were the instances which our verger heard in his kitchen of the supernatural skill of this cunning man; and whilst Mr Hill ate his snack with his wonted gravity, he revolved great designs in his secret soul. Mrs Hill was surprised, several times during dinner, to see her consort put down his knife and fork, and meditate. 'Gracious me, Mr Hill, what can have happened to you this day? What can you be thinking of, Mr Hill, that can make you forget what you have upon your plate?'

'Mrs Hill,' replied the thoughtful verger, 'our grandmother Eve had too much curiosity; and we all know it did not lead to good. What I am thinking of will be known to you in due time, but not now, Mrs Hill; therefore, pray, no questions, or teasing, or pumping. What I think, I think; what I say, I say; what I know, I know; and that is enough for you to know at present: only this, Phœbe, you did very well not to put on the Limerick gloves, child. What I know, I know. Things will turn out just as I said from the first. What I say, I say; and what I think, I think; and this is enough for you to know at present.'

Having finished dinner with this solemn speech, Mr Hill settled himself in his arm-chair, to take his after-dinner nap: and he dreamed of blowing up cathedrals, and of oak bark floating upon the waters; and the cathedral was, he thought, blown up by a man dressed in a pair of woman's Limerick gloves, and the oak bark turned into mutton steaks, after which his great dog Jowler was swimming; when, all on a sudden, as he was going to beat Jowler for eating the bark transformed into mutton steaks, Jowler became Bampfylde the second, king of the gipsies; and putting a horsewhip with a silver handle into Hill's hand, commanded him three times, in a voice as loud as the town crier's, to have O'Neill whipped through the market-place of Hereford: but, just as he was going to the window to see this whipping, his wig fell off, and he awoke.

It was difficult, even for Mr Hill's sagacity, to make a sense of this dream: but he had the wise art of always finding in his dreams something that confirmed his waking determinations. Before he went to sleep, he had half resolved to consult the king of the gipsies, in the absence of the attorney; and his dream made him now wholly determined upon this prudent step. From Bampfylde the second, thought he, I shall learn for certain who made the hole under the cathedral, who pulled down my rick of bark, and who made away with my dog Jowler; and then I shall swear examinations against O'Neill without waiting for attorneys. I will follow my own way in this business: I have always found my own way best.

So, when the dusk of the evening increased, our wise man set out towards the wood to consult the cunning man. Bampfylde the second, king of the gipsies, resided in a sort of hut made of the branches of trees: the verger stooped, but did not stoop low enough, as he entered this temporary palace; and, whilst his body was almost bent double, his peruke was caught upon a twig. From this awkward situation he was relieved by the consort of the king; and he now beheld, by the light of some embers, the person of his gipsy majesty, to whose sublime appearance this dim light was so favourable that it struck a secret awe into our wise man's soul; and, forgetting Hereford cathedral, and oak bark, and Limerick gloves, he stood for some seconds speechless. During this time, the queen very dexterously disencumbered his pocket of all superfluous articles. When he recovered his recollection, he put with great solemnity the following queries to the king of the gipsies, and received the following answers:

'Do you know a dangerous Irishman, of the name of O'Neill, who has come, for purposes best known to himself, to settle at Hereford?'

'Yes, we know him well.'

'Indeed! And what do you know of him?'

'That he is a dangerous Irishman.'

'Right! And it was he, was it not, that pulled down, or caused to be pulled down, my rick of oak bark?'

'It was.'

'And who was it that made away with my dog Jowler, that used to guard the tan-yard?'

'It was the person that you suspect.'

'And was it the person whom I suspect that made the hole under the foundation of our cathedral?'

'The same, and no other.'

'And for what purpose did he make that hole?'

'For a purpose that must not be named,' replied the king of the gipsies; nodding his head in a mysterious manner.

'But it may be named to me,' cried the verger, 'for I have found it out, and I am one of the vergers; and is it not fit that a plot to blow up the Hereford cathedral should be known *to* me, and *through* me?'

> 'Now, take my word,
> Wise men of Hereford,
> None in safety may be,
> Till the *bad man* doth flee.'

These oracular verses, pronounced by Bampfylde with all the enthusiasm of one who was inspired, had the desired effect upon our wise man; and he left the presence of the king of the gipsies with a prodigiously high opinion of his majesty's judgement and of his own, fully resolved to impart, the next morning, to the mayor of Hereford, his important discoveries.

Now it happened that, during the time Mr Hill was putting the foregoing queries to Bampfylde the second, there came to the door or entrance of the audience chamber, an Irish haymaker, who wanted to consult the cunning man about a little leathern purse which he had lost, whilst he was making hay, in a field near Hereford. This haymaker was the same person who, as we have related, spoke so advantageously of our hero, O'Neill, to the widow Smith. As this man, whose name was Paddy M'Cormack, stood at the entrance of the gipsies' hut, his attention was caught by the name of O'Neill; and he lost not a word of all that passed. He had reason to be somewhat surprised at hearing Bampfylde assert it was O'Neill who had pulled down the rick of bark. 'By the holy poker,' said he to himself, 'the old fellow now is out there. I know more o' that matter than he does—no offence to his majesty: he knows no more of my purse, I'll engage now, than he does of this man's rick of bark and his dog: so I'll keep my tester in my pocket, and not be giving it to this king o' the gipsies, as they call him; who, as near as I can guess, is no better than a cheat. But there is one secret which I can be telling this conjuror himself; he shall not find it such an easy matter to do all what he thinks; he shall not be after ruining an innocent countryman of my own, whilst Paddy M'Cormack has a tongue and brains.'

Now Paddy M'Cormack had the best reason possible for

knowing that Mr O'Neill did not pull down Mr Hill's rick of bark; it was M'Cormack himself, who, in the heat of his resentment for the insulting arrest of his countryman in the streets of Hereford, had instigated his fellow haymakers to this mischief; he headed them, and thought he was doing a clever, spirited action.

There is a strange mixture of virtue and vice in the minds of the lower class of Irish; or rather a strange confusion in their ideas of right and wrong, from want of proper education. As soon as poor Paddy found out that his spirited action of pulling down the rick of bark was likely to be the ruin of his countryman, he resolved to make all the amends in his power for his folly: he went to collect his fellow haymakers and persuaded them to assist him this night in rebuilding what they had pulled down.

They went to this work when every body except themselves, as they thought, was asleep in Hereford. They had just completed the stack, and were all going away except Paddy, who was seated at the very top, finishing the pile, when they heard a loud voice cry out, 'Here they are, Watch! Watch!'

Immediately, all the haymakers, who could, ran off as fast as possible. It was the watch who had been sitting up at the cathedral who gave the alarm. Paddy was taken from the top of the rick, and lodged in the watchhouse till morning. 'Since I'm to be rewarded this way for doing a good action, sorrow take me,' said he, 'if they catch me doing another the longest day ever I live.'

Happy they who have in their neighbourhood such a magistrate as Mr Marshal! He was a man who, to an exact knowledge of the duties of his office, joined the power of discovering truth from the midst of contradictory evidence; and the happy art of soothing, or laughing, the angry passions into good-humour. It was a common saying in Hereford—that no one ever came out of Justice Marshal's house as angry as he went into it.

Mr Marshal had scarcely breakfasted when he was informed that Mr Hill, the verger, wanted to speak to him on business of the utmost importance. Mr Hill, the verger, was ushered in; and, with gloomy solemnity, took a seat opposite to Mr Marshal.

'Sad doings in Hereford, Mr Marshal! Sad doings, sir.'

'Sad doings? Why, I was told we had merry doings in Hereford. A ball the night before last, as I heard.'

'So much the worse, Mr Marshal; so much the worse; as those think with reason that see as far into things as I do.'

'So much the better, Mr Hill,' said Mr Marshal, laughing; 'so much the better; as those think with reason that see no farther into things than I do.'

'But, sir,' said the verger, still more solemnly, 'this is no laughing matter, nor time for laughing; begging your pardon. Why, sir, the night of that there diabolical ball, our Hereford cathedral, sir, would have been blown up—blown up from the foundation, if it had not been for me, sir!'

'Indeed, Mr Verger! And pray how, and by whom, was the cathedral to be blown up? and what was there diabolical in this ball?'

Here Mr Hill let Mr Marshal into the whole history of his early dislike to O'Neill, and his shrewd suspicions of him the first moment he saw him in Hereford; related in the most prolix manner all that the reader knows already, and concluded by saying that, as he was now certain of his facts, he was come to swear examinations against this villainous Irishman, who, he hoped, would be speedily brought to justice, as he deserved.

'To justice he shall be brought, as he deserves,' said Mr Marshal; 'but, before I write, and before you swear, will you have the goodness to inform me how you have made yourself as certain, as you evidently are, of what you call your facts?'

'Sir, that is a secret,' replied our wise man, 'which I shall trust to you alone'; and he whispered into Mr Marshal's ear that his information came from Bampfylde the second, king of the gipsies.

Mr Marshal instantly burst into laughter; then composing himself said, 'My good sir, I am really glad that you have proceeded no farther in this business; and that no one in Hereford, beside myself, knows that you were on the point of swearing examinations against a man on the evidence of Bampfylde the second, king of the gipsies. My dear sir, it would be a standing joke against you to the end of your days. A grave man, like Mr Hill; and a verger too! Why, you would be the laughing-stock of Hereford!'

Now Mr Marshal well knew the character of the man to whom he was talking, who, above all things on earth, dreaded to be laughed at. Mr Hill coloured all over his face, and, pushing back his wig by way of settling it, showed that he blushed not only all over his face but all over his head.

'Why, Mr Marshal, sir,' said he, 'as to my being laughed at, it is what I did not look for, being as there are some men in Hereford to whom I have mentioned that hole in the cathedral, who have thought it no laughing matter, and who have been precisely of my own opinion thereupon.'

'But did you tell these gentlemen that you had been consulting the king of the gipsies?'

'No, sir, no: I can't say that I did.'

'Then I advise you, keep your own counsel, as I will.'

Mr Hill, whose imagination wavered between the hole in the cathedral and his rick of bark on one side, and between his rick of bark and his dog Jowler on the other, now began to talk of the dog, and now of the rick of bark; and when he had exhausted all he had to say upon these subjects, Mr Marshal gently pulled him towards the window, and putting a spy-glass into his hand, bid him look towards his own tan-yard, and tell him what he saw. To his great surprise, Mr Hill saw his rick of bark rebuilt. 'Why, it was not there last night,' exclaimed he, rubbing his eyes. 'Why, some conjuror must have done this.'

'No,' replied Mr Marshal, 'no conjuror did it: but your friend Bampfylde the second, king of the gipsies, was the cause of its being rebuilt; and here is the man who actually pulled it down, and who actually rebuilt it.'

As he said these words, Mr Marshal opened the door of an adjoining room, and beckoned to the Irish haymaker, who had been taken into custody about an hour before this time. The watch who took Paddy had called at Mr Hill's house to tell him what had happened, but Mr Hill was not then at home.

It was with much surprise that the verger heard the simple truth from this poor fellow; but no sooner was he convinced that O'Neill was innocent as to this affair, than he returned to his other ground of suspicion, the loss of his dog.

The Irish haymaker now stepped forward, and, with a peculiar twist of the hips and shoulders, which those only who have seen it can picture to themselves, said, 'Plase your honour's honour, I have a little word to say too about the dog.'

'Say it then,' said Mr Marshal.

'Plase your honour, if I might expect to be forgiven, and let off for pulling down the jontleman's stack, I might be able to tell him what I know about the dog.'

'If you can tell me any thing about my dog,' said the tanner, 'I will freely forgive you for pulling down the rick: especially as you have built it up again. Speak the truth now: did not O'Neill make away with the dog?'

'Not at all at all, plase your honour,' replied the haymaker: 'and the truth of the matter is, I know nothing of the dog, good or bad; but I know something of his collar, if your name, plase your honour, is Hill, as I take it to be?'

'My name is Hill: proceed,' said the tanner, with great eagerness. 'You know something about the collar of my dog Jowler?'

'Plase your honour, this much I know any way, that it is now or was the night before last, at the pawnbroker's there, below in town; for, plase your honour, I was sent late at night (that night that Mr O'Neill, long life to him! was arrested) to the pawnbroker's for a Jew, by Mrs O'Neill, poor creature! she was in great trouble that same time.'

'Very likely,' interrupted Mr Hill: 'but go on to the collar; what of the collar?'

'She sent me,—I'll tell you the story, plase your honour, *out of the face*—she sent me to the pawnbroker's for the Jew; and, it being so late at night, the shop was shut, and it was with all the trouble in life that I got into the house any way: and, when I got in, there was none but a slip of a boy up; and he set down the light that he had in his hand, and ran up the stairs to waken his master: and, whilst he was gone, I just made bold to look round at what sort of a place I was in, and at the old clothes and rags and scraps; there was a sort of a frieze trusty.'

'A trusty!' said Mr Hill; 'what is that pray?'

'A big coat, sure, plase your honour: there was a frieze big coat lying in a corner, which I had my eye upon, to trate myself to; I having, as I then thought, money in my little purse enough for it. Well, I won't trouble your honour's honour with telling of you now how I lost my purse in the field, as I found after; but about the big coat, as I was saying, I just lifted it off the ground, to see would it fit me; and, as I swung it round, something, plase your honour, hit me a great knock on the shins: it was in the pocket of the coat, whatever it was, I knew; so I looks into the pocket, to see what it was, plase your honour, and out I pulls a hammer and a dog-collar; it was a wonder, both together, they did not break my shins entirely: but it's no matter for my shins now: so, before the boy came down, I just out of idleness spelt out to myself the name that was upon the collar: there were two names, plase your honour; and out of the first there were so many letters hammered out I could make nothing of it, at all at all; but the other name was plain enough to read any way, and it was Hill, plase your honour's honour, as sure as life: Hill, now.'

This story was related in tones and gestures which were so new and strange to English ears and eyes, that even the solemnity of our verger gave way to laughter—Mr Marshal sent a summons for the pawnbroker, that he might learn from him how he came by the dog-collar. The pawnbroker, when he found from Mr Marshal that he could by no other means save himself from being committed to prison, confessed that the collar had been sold to him by Bampfylde the second, king of the gipsies.

A warrant was immediately despatched for his majesty: and Mr Hill was a good deal alarmed, by the fear of its being known in Hereford that he was on the point of swearing examinations against an innocent man, upon the evidence of a dog-stealer and a gipsy.

Bampfylde the second made no sublime appearance, when he was brought before Mr Marshal; nor could all his astrology avail upon this occasion: the evidence of the pawnbroker was so positive, as to the fact of his having sold to him the dog-collar, that there was no resource left for Bampfylde but an appeal to Mr Hill's mercy. He fell on his knees, and confessed that it was he who stole the dog; which used to bark at him at night so furiously that he could not commit certain petty depredations, by which, as much as by telling fortunes, he made his livelihood.

'And so,' said Mr Marshal, with a sternness of manner which till now he had never shown, 'to screen yourself, you accused an innocent man; and by your vile arts would have driven him from Hereford, and have set two families for ever at variance, to conceal that you had stolen a dog.'

The king of the gipsies was, without farther ceremony, committed to the house of correction. We should not omit to mention, that, on searching his hut, the Irish haymaker's purse was found, which some of his majesty's train had emptied. The whole set of gipsies decamped, upon the news of the apprehension of their monarch.

Mr Hill stood in profound silence, leaning upon his walking-stick, whilst the committal was making out for Bampfylde the second. The fear of ridicule was struggling with the natural positiveness of his temper: he was dreadfully afraid that the story of his being taken in by the king of the gipsies would get abroad; and, at the same time, he was unwilling to give up his prejudice against the Irish glover.

'But, Mr Marshal,' cried he, after a long silence, 'the hole under the foundation of the cathedral has never been accounted for: that is, was, and ever will be, an ugly mystery to me; and I never can have a good opinion of this Irishman, till it is cleared up; nor can I think the cathedral in safety.'

'What,' said Mr Marshal, with an arch smile, 'I suppose the verses of the oracle still work upon your imagination, Mr Hill. They are excellent in their kind. I must have them by heart that, when I am asked the reason why Mr Hill has taken an aversion to an Irish glover, I may be able to repeat them:

"Now, take my word,
Wise men of Hereford,
None in safety may be,
Till the bad man doth flee" '

'You'll oblige me, sir,' said the verger, 'if you would never repeat those verses, sir; nor mention, in any company, the affair of the king of the gipsies.'

'I will oblige you,' replied Mr Marshal, 'if you will oblige me. Will you tell me honestly whether now that you find this Mr O'Neill is neither a dog-killer nor a puller down of bark ricks, you feel that you could forgive him for being an Irishman, if the mystery, as you call it, of the hole under the cathedral was cleared up?'

'But that is not cleared up, I say, sir,' cried Mr Hill, striking his walking-stick forcibly upon the ground, with both his hands. 'As to the matter of his being an Irishman, I have nothing to say to it: I am not saying any thing about that, for I know we all are born where it pleases God; and an Irishman may be as good as another. I know that much, Mr Marshal; and I am not one of those illiberal-minded ignorant people that cannot abide a man that was not born in England. Ireland is now in his majesty's dominions, I know very well, Mr Marshal; and I have no manner of doubt, as I said before, that an Irishman born may be as good, almost, as an Englishman born.'

'I am glad,' said Mr Marshal, 'to hear you speak, almost, as reasonably as an Englishman born and every man ought to speak; and I am convinced that you have too much English hospitality to persecute an inoffensive stranger, who comes amongst us trusting to our justice and good nature.'

'I would not persecute a stranger, God forbid!' replied the verger, 'if he was, as you say, inoffensive.'

'And if he was not only inoffensive, but ready to do every service in his power to those who are in want of his assistance, we should not return evil for good, should we?'

'That would be uncharitable, to be sure; and moreover a scandal,' said the verger.

'Then,' said Mr Marshal, 'will you walk with me as far as the widow Smith's, the poor woman whose house was burnt last winter! This haymaker, who lodged near her, can show us the way to her present abode.'

During his examination of Paddy M'Cormack, who would tell his whole history, as he called it, *out of the face*, Mr Marshal heard several instances of the humanity and goodness of O'Neill, which Paddy related to excuse himself for that warmth of attachment to his cause, that had been manifested so injudiciously by pulling down the rick of bark in revenge for the arrest. Amongst other things, Paddy mentioned his countryman's goodness to the widow Smith: Mr Marshal was determined, therefore, to see whether he had, in this instance, spoken the truth; and he took Mr Hill with him, in hopes of being able to show him the favourable side of O'Neill's character.

Things turned out just as Mr Marshal expected. The poor widow and her family, in the most simple and affecting manner, described the distress from which they had been relieved by the good gentleman and lady, the lady was Phœbe Hill; and the praises that were bestowed upon Phœbe were delightful to her father's ear, whose angry passions had now all subsided.

The benevolent Mr Marshal seized the moment when he saw Mr Hill's heart was touched, and exclaimed, 'I must be acquainted with this Mr O'Neill. I am sure we people of Hereford ought to show some hospitality to a stranger, who has so much humanity. Mr Hill, will you dine with him tomorrow at my house!'

Mr Hill was just going to accept of this invitation, when the recollection of all he had said to his club about the hole under the cathedral came across him; and, drawing Mr Marshal aside, he whispered, 'But sir, sir, that affair of the hole under the cathedral has not been cleared up yet.'

At this instant, the widow Smith exclaimed, 'Oh! here comes my little Mary' (one of her children, who came running in): 'this is the little girl, sir, to whom the lady has been so good. Make your curtsy, child. Where have you been all this while?'

'Mammy,' said the child, 'I've been showing the lady my rat.'

'Lord bless her! Gentlemen, the child has been wanting me this many a day to go to see this tame rat of hers; but I could never get time, never: and I wondered too at the child's liking such a creature. Tell the gentlemen, dear, about your rat. All I know is, that, let her have but never such a tiny bit of bread, for breakfast or supper, she saves a little of that little for this rat of hers: she and her brothers have found it out somewhere by the cathedral.'

'It comes out of a hole under the wall of the cathedral,' said one of the elder boys; 'and we have diverted ourselves watching it, and sometimes we have put victuals for it, so it has grown, in a manner, tame like.'

Mr Hill and Mr Marshal looked at one another during this speech; and the dread of ridicule again seized on Mr Hill, when he apprehended that, after all he had said, the mountain might, at last, bring forth—a rat. Mr Marshal, who instantly saw what passed in the verger's mind, relieved him from this fear, by refraining even from a smile on this occasion. He only said to the child, in a grave manner, 'I am afraid, my dear, we shall be obliged to spoil your diversion. Mr Verger, here, cannot suffer rat-holes in the cathedral; but, to make you amends for the loss of your favourite, I will give you a very pretty little dog, if you have a mind.'

The child was well pleased with this promise; and, at Mr Marshal's desire, she then went along with him and Mr Hill to the cathedral, and they placed themselves at a little distance from that hole which had created so much disturbance. The child soon brought the dreadful enemy to light; and Mr Hill, with a faint laugh, said, 'I'm glad it's no worse: but there were many in our club who were of my opinion; and, if they had not suspected O'Neill too, I am sure I should never have given you so much trouble, sir, as I have done this morning. But, I hope, as the club know nothing about the vagabond, that king of the gipsies, you will not let any one know any thing about the prophecy, and all that? I am sure, I am very sorry to have given you so much trouble, Mr Marshal.'

Mr Marshal assured him that he did not regret the time which he had spent in endeavouring to clear up all these mysteries and suspicions; and Mr Hill gladly accepted his invitation to meet O'Neill at his house the next day. No sooner had Mr Marshal brought one of the parties to reason and good-humour, than he went to prepare the other for a reconciliation. O'Neill and his mother were both people of warm but forgiving tempers: the arrest was fresh in their minds; but when Mr Marshal represented to them the whole affair, and the verger's prejudices, in a humorous light, they joined in the good-natured laugh, and O'Neill declared that, for his part, he was ready to forgive and to forget every thing, if he could but see Miss Phœbe in the Limerick gloves.

Phœbe appeared the next day, at Mr Marshal's, in the Limerick gloves; and no perfume ever was so delightful to her lover as the smell of the rose leaves, in which they had been kept.

Mr Marshal had the benevolent pleasure of reconciling the two families. The tanner and the glover of Hereford became, from bitter enemies, useful friends to each other; and they were convinced, by experience, that nothing could be more for their mutual advantage than to live in union.

WILLIAM CARLETON · 1794–1869

The Death of a Devotee

I will long remember the 14th of January, in the year 18——. On that day I had dined with the priest of our parish, who was, at the period spoken of, an old man, in an infirm state of health. Indeed, he considered this warning in its proper light, and held himself prepared for that great tribunal, before which, sooner or later, we must all appear. Father Moyle was a proof that we ought to carry our charity into every variety of human condition; and that it is possible for a man, under the most difficult circumstances, to raise himself above their disadvantages. He had been educated, and resided for some time, abroad, where he encountered many vicissitudes, strongly and painfully contrasted. These trials, imposed on him, when his heart, as he himself expressed it, had been strongly beset, he did not endure to the end. More he never intimated; but, from the emotion he usually betrayed, whenever he alluded to this mysterious topic, I thought it was evident that some secret grief—perhaps the remembrance of some bitter fall, lay coiled round his heart. He was a venerable looking man, much bent with his years—being then 76; his face had been good, and was still interesting, from the expression of habitual sorrow which settled upon it; his hair was as white as snow. Altogether his case was a peculiar one. He certainly appeared to have been gifted with a good understanding, joined to much simplicity of character. That he entertained Scriptural views of religion, there is no doubt; and it would seem as if he had been coerced into them by the chastening hand of affliction, or goaded into truth by the inward lashings of remorse. He had tried to build his peace and his security upon sand—had addressed himself to the miserable fragments of guilty mortality;—but the connection of every thing human with so corrupt and diseased a thing as his own heart, rose up in painful reality before him, and he felt that this unholy affinity—this community of sin and frailty between himself and his mediators, only rendered an application to human intercession or dead works, unprofitable. He was, however, a man, even in his old age, of many weaknesses, and capable of being much influenced, in consequence of his easiness of disposition, by the force of erroneous opinions long wrought into his duties and habits. Whether the abstraction produced by that seriousness which is inseparable from remembered guilt or sorrow, might not have rendered him less capable of going out of himself, and entering into the spiritual circumstances of others, I cannot determine; certain it is that he was engrossed altogether by himself—that his views of truth, though correct, were not urged upon others so strongly as they might have been, and that he discharged the duties of his sacred calling, like a man who felt that the greatness of his own danger prevented him from assisting others. There is some allowance, however, to be made for his years, and the natural decay which time and affliction bring upon the mind as well as the constitution; but another and juster motive may appear by and bye.

On the 14th of January, 18——, as I have said, I dined with him and his curate. After dinner, we amused ourselves by discussing several common topics of conversation, and sometimes by dipping into the classics, until it was after nine o'clock. A little before that time the wind, accompanied by heavy rain, began to blow with unusual force. 'You are storm-staid,' said he to me, 'for this night; so I will go to bed, and leave Father John and you to settle that passage between you; it has become a severe night, but you are under a friendly roof, and your family know that you are safe.' He then retired to his chamber, which was a small closet off the room where we sat, and Father John and I, after remaining up until past eleven o'clock, withdrew to our respective apartments for the night. In the course of an hour, however, or upwards, we were awakened by the violence of the storm, which had increased with great fury.

The priest's house was situated in a hollow, somewhat resembling an old excavation, scooped out of the south side of a hill. It had probably been a limestone quarry, the banks of which, in order to prevent waste, had been levelled in. A young grove intermingled with some fine old elms, grew on the hill immediately above the house, and a good garden was laid out on the slope before the door. As a residence, it was tastefully situated, and commanded two or three graceful sweeps of a sunlit river, on whose bank stood a picturesque ruin. A well wooded demesne, a cultivated country, and a range of abrupt mountains, through a cleft in which a road trailed up, whose white track was visible in the darkness of the mountain soil, closed the prospect. Indeed, from the remarkable site of the house, one would be apt to suppose that it was well sheltered from wind and storm; the reverse, however, was the fact; for, whenever the wind came from the north-west, it divided itself, as it were, behind the hill, which was long and ridgy, and rushed round with great violence until it met again in the cavity in which the priest's house was built, where the confluence of the opposing tides formed a whirlwind far more destructive than the direct blast. Between one and two o'clock the strength of the storm, though startling, had nothing in it to excite particular alarm. Every moment, however, it became more violent: abrupt and rapid gusts, that poured down from each side of the hill, swept round the house, straining its rafters and collar beams until they cracked. It soon became terrible;—lights were got, and, although there was scarcely a crevice in the house, through which a breath of air on an ordinary night could come, yet, so great was the strength of the wind, that arrowy blasts shot in every direction through the rooms, with such force as to extinguish the lights when brought within their range. Still it increased, and the thunder-groans of the tempest were tremendous. The night hitherto had not been very dark; indeed, no windy night is so; but we now perceived the darkness to increase most rapidly, until it was utter and palpable. The straining of the house and rafters were excessive—every light body was carried about like chaff—many of the trees were crashed to pieces, and huge branches reft from their parent trunks, were borne away like straws, wherever the fury of the elements carried them.

Some time before this, Father Moyle made his appearance—he was pale and trembling, and seemed apprehensive of much danger—for he said it was his opinion that the house could not stand much longer under this strong grappling of the tempest.

'I fear,' said he, 'that either the roof or the walls will be blown in, and, in that case, there would certainly be danger;—John,' he continued, addressing the curate, 'get me my stole and some holy water; in that storm we may hear the voice of an angry God, and our duty now is supplication and prayer.'

When he got the holy water and stole, he put on the latter, and began to read certain prayers in the Latin tongue, set apart for allaying storms;—while uttering these, he frequently cut the sign of the cross in the air, threw holy water first against the point from which he conceived the wind blew, then in every direction, and finally on every person, animal, and fixture in the house. We, in the mean time, could only lend our inward assent to the prayers he repeated. When near the conclusion of the ceremony, he paused, then leaned over the table for a few minutes, with his hands on his face;—he seemed as if recollecting himself, for he instantly knelt down, and prayed aloud in much agitation. One of the prayers he selected on this occasion is called the 'Litany of Jesus', and it is almost impossible to conceive the woe begone, the utter lowliness of spirit, with which he repeated the words subjoined to the various epithets which are given to our Redeemer. 'Lamb of God, that takest away the sins of the world, have mercy upon us,' proceeded from his lips, as if he felt in this awful hour, when the wrath of God was heard, as it were, in the terrors of the storm, that the serene and merciful character of the Lamb without stain, was indeed touchingly beautiful, and full of hope to the sinner.

The night was now pitchy dark, though, for a few minutes before this, fearful lulls were noticed, which excited fresh alarm. We could now look out through the windows, and the dark confused air, in connection with the aspect of the sky, was really appalling;—at the verge of the horizon the heavens were of a lurid copper colour, appearing as if they glowed with a fiery hotness: this was motionless, whilst the massive clouds, from which the lightning shot in every direction, sped rapidly in dark irregular piles, seemingly to one point of the sky. The moon became visible by glimpses, and flew through the heavens in the direction from which the tempest came, with the speed of the wind.

Hurricanes are of rare occurrence in Ireland, or when they do visit us, it is always found that they are local. I do not now remember over what extent of country this one may have swept, but I know it put forth such dreadful power, that it seemed as if the very elements went forth to battle. During all this time Father Moyle sat, for he was weak and agitated, and I thought evinced symptoms of terror; in this, however, I was mistaken, for it was a far different sensation from fear of the storm which affected him.

'I think, Sir,' said I, 'it cannot last long now; and, as the house has not already sustained any damage, I trust it will weather it out.'

'Such a hurricane as this,' he replied, 'I have never known in these kingdoms;—but I once remember such a storm; and would to heaven that I could wipe out the recollections attending it from my memory: however,' he continued, in much distress as if to himself, 'it may not be—it may not be—they *will* be remembered.'

The mind is, indeed, a mystery, and it is strange how emotions may be awakened by many circumstances apparently unconnected with them. That night appeared to be to him a dreadful memento, and, as far as I could judge from subsequent circumstances, the thunder of the tempest could not stifle the still small voice of conscience.

The goodness of God has ordained that all violent convulsions of nature shall be but of short duration. The storm gradually subsided;—the servants ventured out to examine the state of the house and offices, and we, after their return, went again to bed.

It seemed, however, that this night was destined to be one of toil to the clergymen. We were scarcely down, when a violent knocking at the door indicated some sudden claim upon their spiritual aid. This was the case;—a frail house in the neighbourhood had fallen in, and crushed one of the inmates almost to death; he was, they said, quite speechless, and they feared that if great haste were not made, he would depart ere the priest's arrival. The curate accordingly dressed himself, and accompanied the messengers to the scene of death. In the mean time Father Moyle had gone to rest; but the others were scarcely gone half an hour, when a second knocking gave intimation of another sick call.

'Open the door,' said a voice—'for the sake of the Blessed Mother, will you open the door fast?'

'What's the matther?' said one of the servants, who was still up.

'Death's the matther,' said the man, entering quite out of breath. 'John Lynch is dyin'—and may the Holy Mother of God have mercy upon me, but you could hear him skreechin', clear an' clane, above the wind and tundher an' all: Oh! Mike, Mike, his voice is still ringin' in my ears, so sharp, wild, an' unnatural, bekase you see it has the sound of death in it. "The priest!—the priest!" he shouts—"the priest—bring me Father Moyle—bring me Father Moyle—no man but *him* will do me;"—then forgettin' *that* for a minute, he goes on—"pray for me—pray for me—will none of yees pray for my guilty sowl?—Ye careless pack, won't yees offer up one prayer for me;—but, bring me the priest first—yees needn't pray till *he* comes—it would be no use—bring me the priest, for the sake of the Livin' Mother!" May I never commit another sin, but his voice would chill the marrow in your bones, or make your teeth cranch, it's so wild an' unnatural.'

'He must wait till mornin',' said the servant, 'for Father John's gone out on another sick call, and Father Moyle's past attendin' any, as you know yourself, for the last three years; any how, he wouldn't be able to venthure out such an unmerciful night as this.'

'Must wait, is it?' said the man, 'who can stop death will you tell us?—why, man, the dead rattle was in his throath when I left him; so say no more, but waken up Father Moyle in a jiffey, or he'll never overtake him livin'.'

This the servant peremptorily refused to do, whilst the other as peremptorily insisted on his compliance; at length, after much bickering, which was near ending in blows, the servant brought him into the priest's bed-room.

'Here,' said he, 'spake to him yourself; for me, I would see you up to the neck in Loughmacall, before I'd axe him to go out sich a terrible night entirely as this is; it's as much, man, as his life's worth.'

'Father Moyle,' said the man, going over to him, 'are you asleep, your reverence? humbly axin' pardon for disturbin' you at this hour of the night.'

'What's the matter?' said the priest.

'Death, your reverence,' said the man: 'John, poor fellow, is departin';—I left the dead rattle in his throath;—so, time's short, Sir.'

'God help him, for I am totally incapable of going to him,' said the priest, 'I'm too weak, my friend, and worn, to venture out on any night, much less so dreadful a one as this.'

'I'm sorry to hear it, your reverence,' replied the messenger, 'but, for all that, you must strive to come, whether or not.'

'I hope he won't die,' said Father Moyle, 'till morning, or till Father John returns.'

'Can the man wait for nothin'?' said the other, 'will death wait for any man?—will God wait, that's more greater again nor death?'

'Well,' said the priest, 'we must commit him to the mercy of his Redeemer; for, if *my* presence were to save him, I am unable to go, from bodily weakness.'

'Rise up, Sir,' said the countryman, in a commanding tone:—'without you I'll not go—once for all I say it; so you must come, whether you are sick or not, if I should carry you on my back—an' well able I am to do that same. Sure I'd put the hair of my head or the hands on my body undher your feet to sarve you; but a day's pace or quietness I'd never see, if he died without you; so you *must* come, yer reverence.'

'Don't be *musting* his reverence, you had better,' said the servant who was present, 'for fraid I'd make it worse for you, nabour.'

'Won't I?' shouted the man, in an angry voice; 'I tell you his bitter curse—the curse of God, of his holy Mother, an' of all the saints, is upon me, if I come back widout Father Moyle, for he'll have no priest but *him*.'

'My friend,' said the priest, 'I tell you once for all it is impossible—I am unable.'

'By that holy book on your chair,' said the man, in a state bordering on despair and phrenzy, 'if you don't get up an' come off along wid me, I'll drag you head foremost out of that bed you're lyin' on; if *he's* to be damned, that's no reason that *I* should be so too, wid so many bitter curses upon my head, if I'd not bring you, an' me undhertuck it—promised before God an' his blessed Mother, not to come back widout you.'

'Who *is* the sick person?' inquired the priest.

' 'Tis my brother, John Lynch, that has *ett* my bit an' sup, an' slep undher the one roof for many a long night wid me an' mine.'

The only reply to this was a cry from Father Moyle, such as I have seldom heard from human lips. The servant was dreadfully alarmed, and instantly called upon me, saying that he believed Father Moyle was dying. As I slept in a closet, divided from that of the priest, only by a thin partition, of course I was apprised of what had taken place, and, in a few minutes, was dressed and in the room. Never did I perceive so awful and mysterious an appearance as he presented when I entered: his arms were lifted up convulsively, as if in supplication or astonishment—his face was death-like, but somewhat distorted out of its natural lineaments—his brows were uplifted wildly like those of a man in affright, and the pupils of his eyes were almost turned inwards, as if the fearful vision which he contemplated was actually in his own brain. He was speechless, and I, as well as the servant, feared that death was upon him.

'What, Sir, is the matter with you?' I inquired: but he made no reply.

'This, you ruffian,' said I to the countryman, 'is your work, and most certainly, if he is dying, you will answer for it.'

I then shook him a little, and he drew his breath heavily. 'My dear Sir,' said I, 'will you tell me what's the matter?'

He recovered somewhat;—'Will I tell you?' said he, repeating my words more fully. He looked at me, however, vacantly, and did not appear to be collected. I then repeated the question, and he started as if he had been pierced with an arrow. 'Alas!' said he, 'you know not what you ask!'

The state of the dying man now rushed upon him. 'Help me up,' said he quickly, 'help me up—and oh! let not one moment be lost, for this man's case is terrible.'

'You cannot venture out,' said I, 'such a night—the wind is still tempestuous, and the rain is falling in torrents.'

'Get my horse,' said he to the servant, not heeding me; 'saddle my horse instantly,' and in a moment he was up, and in the act of dressing himself. 'Not even the certainty of my own death as the consequence,' he continued, 'would prevent me—yes,' said he, 'I *am* able—see how strong I am!' and he extended his trembling arms to their full length, whilst the drops of agony hung about his temples.

His conduct during that night was altogether mysterious, and I had not sufficient decision or energy to guide him—I was absorbed in astonishment.

'Are *you* ready?' said he to me, 'for you must accompany us.'

'I will in a moment,' said I; 'but the consequence I fear will be fatal to yourself.'

'No,' said he, taking my hand, 'I know that your apprehension for me proceeds from kindness and affection: I will not feel the tempest—not *that* tempest;' and, as he pronounced the word *that*, he pointed outwards, then touched his breast significantly, intimating that the storm was within; and, as he did it, he shrunk and shivered, as if he was endeavouring to throw back some oppressive thought that clung to him. At length tears came to his relief, and they fell from his eyes copiously.

'It is altogether a mystery,' thought I, 'and resembles nothing I have ever seen or heard.'

He then, with our assistance, wrapped two or three great coats about him, and tied a large cotton kerchief over his hat and under his chin, and the horse being now ready, we set out, the stranger and I accompanying him.

As we went along, the appearance of the sky was awfully

tempestuous: broad streaks of angry red, such as we had noticed before, appeared here and there in the firmament: others of different shades, ribbed like the sea sand, were also visible; these stormy sweeps were motionless, and not only were deeply tinged with the hue of fire, but seemed to burn like a red furnace. Beneath these were the cloud drifts passing furiously above us—all ebon black, except those about the moon, that had their edges rimmed with pale silver, which only stood out against the dark mass it surrounded in more ghastly relief. The desolation of the country, as we passed along, was calculated to heighten the natural appearance of the heavens. Voices of men and women were heard screaming on the blast, as they struggled along the roofs of their houses, placing beams, boards, stones, and even mud, upon the remaining thatch, to prevent it from being altogether carried away; lights, too, were seen flitting in lanthorns, or such substitutes as they could invent for them, to enable them to take a more accurate survey of the ravages of the storm. On arriving at the bridge below the priest's house, I could perceive that the rapid flood, on whose dusky surface the struggling moonbeams played with snatches of dead light, that glinted darkly and uncertainly on its troubled eddies, nearly filled the span of the arch, and the road itself was strewed with branches of trees, and with thatch that had been carried away from the adjoining houses. Below the bridge was a *holme*, over which the waters swept with a tumultuous roar that might be heard at the distance of miles, if the night were calm; and to the right rose the gloomy outline of Slieuguillen, fixed in awful stillness amidst the confusion which prevailed in the dark air beneath and around it.

At length we came to a cluster of houses, mostly built of mud, about a mile or better from the priest's, where our guide caught the bridle, and led the horse to the door of the house in which the dying man lay. His name, as we have said, was Lynch. For a considerable time he had been abroad, and lived in the capacity of a servant with Father Moyle, who held an ecclesiastical appointment in France, for upwards of fourteen years. Lynch had been a devotee, or voteen, and, for some time previous to his death, was remarkable for the exemplary regularity with which he attended his church duties. He fasted, prayed, and mortified himself with the most rigorous severity, and was known as 'Lynch, the voteen', in consequence of his austere practices. His personal disposition, however, was never amiable, and what he mistook for holiness,

instead of smoothing down the asperities of his natural temper, or
diffusing about him that serenity which is inseparable from true
religion, only rendered him more dark, peevish, and repulsive. He
had returned to Ireland with Father Moyle, and lived in the same
parish ever since; but it was only within the last few years of his life
that he became a voteen. Before that period, he was a reckless and
hardened man, silent, fierce, and malignant; and, though not
without an ordinary share of intelligence, totally illiterate.

Father Moyle had been anxious to ascertain the state of his
religious feelings, before entering into conversation with him;
accordingly, when the man came out to the door on our arrival, the
priest desired him to be silent, and not to let any person within
apprise the sick man of our presence. We accordingly entered
without noise, and stood for some minutes to hear the expressions
and ravings uttered by this singular man. His principal cry was 'the
priest', alternated with a querulous and impatient entreaty to be
prayed for by those about him—for he himself did not attempt to
utter a single prayer.

'Biddy,' he exclaimed, 'is the priest never to come?—is he never
to come?—and must I face God without him? Oh, merciful Mother
of God, what am I to do, if I die without bein' anointed or
absolved?'

'Whisht, John, a hagur,' said the woman, who was his wife; 'sure
you needn't feel so much afeard—you weren't that bad a man, any
how. Didn't you attend your duties, an' sure there wasn't a man in
the parish said more prayers, or fasted as much; besides, avourneen
machree, sure you have the Coard of blessed St Francis, an' what's
before every thing else, the blessed an' holy Scapular of the Mother
of God herself upon your body—sure you needn't be so much
afeard; God will be merciful to you for *their* sakes—besides, is your
prayers an' fastins to go for nothing?'

'I know all that,' said he, 'lave my sight, an' don't be tellin' me
what I know—lave my sight;' and he darted a fierce look at her,
whilst his eyes kindled with living fire, like those of a serpent. This
painful comparison was really suggested to me at the moment; for
it required an effort of close attention to disentangle the sharp, dry
sounds of his voice from the husky death-rattle emitted from the
lower part of his throat, resembling in some degree the noise of the
rattle-snake when irritated.

'Why am I afeard, then?' said he, 'will you tell me that—now that death has got into me?—yet it's thrue what you say, though I can't feel it; but if Father Moyle would come, *he* could comfort me. Merciful Virgin, I can't die;—is he comin'?—is he comin'? Oh, that *one* day of my life had never passed—it lies black and heavy on my heart, for all I confessed it! Will yees pray for me?—do ye hear?— but ye don't, nor ye don't care what becomes of my sowl, ye pack— oh, pray for me! Biddy, will you lay down that jug, I'm not dry? Down on your knees—pray—throw yourselves on the ground— your sowls are not stained like mine;—a dhrink, a dhrink, a dhrink!—I'm burnin', sowl an' body, I'm burnin';—ye must take me out of this bed, and put me in some cool place, for oh, I'm burnin'!'

'John, dear, keep yourself asy,' said his wife, 'sure the priest will be here in less than no time, avourneen; it's the sickness that disturbs you.'

'No, it's not the sickness—I would give the world wide that it was only *that*. Is Father Moyle comin'?—but I suppose none of ye went for him yet; ye want to have me die like a dog;—sprinkle the holy wather on me, an' hould up this scapular till I kiss it in honour of the blessed Virgin. Is there no priest?—is there no sign of Father Moyle yet?—*he* knows *all*. But, merciful Virgin, wouldn't I be now a happy man, if I had never seen either him or France! An' he's not comin'?—oh! oh'

As he uttered the latter part of the sentence, Father Moyle, who stood beside me, grasped my arm tightly, as if to support himself, and gave a groan that echoed back that of the dying man with fearful truth. The man's voice was every moment getting more husky, and even when he didn't speak, the tough rattle rose and fell with his breath, in a manner that intimated the near approach of dissolution.

On entering, we found two or three half-lit turf slumbering on the hearth, which gave the house a cold and desolate look, and a chair placed at the bed, which was protected at the foot and sides by straw mats made to perform the office of curtains. On the dresser was a glimmering rush candle, stuck in the cleft of a wooden candle-stick, by the light of which I could perceive a bottle of whiskey, and an egg-cup beside it by way of a glass. Above the bed, between the thatch and rafters, were two or three branches of withered palm, now covered with soot and dust; in a little blind window beyond the bed, stood an earthen jug, containing holy water, in which was a small branch of heath, as a *Spargess* with which they sprinkled it, from time to time, not only upon the sick man, but over the whole bed, the four corners of the house, the door, windows, and chimney, lest the evil one, or any of his spirits, should lurk within, for the purpose of seizing upon the parted soul. A wooden crucifix was also placed at the foot of the bed, inside the mat, from which it was expected that the dying sinner was to be able to draw comfort. Along with the large scapular which invested him, he had bound round his body many folds of hard whip-cord, knotted in several places, to render the wearing of it more efficacious and penitential: this was called the order of St Francis, and every one knows that the Scapular is the order of the Blessed Virgin. Around his neck, there was also a small four-cornered bit of black cloth, like a flat pin-cushion, which contained several written charms against sudden death, and the dangers of fire and water; it also enclosed a leaf from the missal, containing what was called a 'golden prayer', said to prevent any person having it about him in the hour of death from being damned, and finally, a blessed candle, in the light of which it was his expectation to die. In a bit of broken tea cup beside him lay a little black paste, made of the ashes of the candles used at Mass, mixed up with holy water to the consistence of paste, and with this he formed, or rather caused to be formed, every quarter of an hour, the sign of the cross upon his breast. With respect to his personal appearance, he had been a man of great muscular power, with large bones, broad shoulders, and black bushy eye-brows, that met sternly across his forehead. Indeed, as he lay stretched before me, I was much struck with the herculean fragment of him which remorse and sickness had left behind. When the candle was brought near him, I could see his appearance more distinctly, and truly it was wild and repulsive. His face was ghastly and so much emaciated, that the bones and sinews had only a thin membrane of yellow skin over them; his black hair was matted, and shot up through the holes of his tattered night-cap, and down about his neck and jaws, in hard pointed locks, that stirred when he moved, as if they were instinct with separate life. His nose was thin and worn away—his gaunt cheeks deeply indented on each side, and his eyes had that sharp and gleaming look, which sometimes characterizes the agonies of death. But his voice! O! his voice! Its intonations were hot and fiery—they breathed of torture. No wonder that it rang so powerfully in the ears of the messenger, for never in my life did such sounds fall upon my ear. There was something in them so sharp, pervading, and deadly, or as the man forcibly expressed it, so unnatural, that they seemed like nothing pertaining to humanity. I cannot define the sensation which I felt, but I shuddered with a species of cold terror to which my nature had never been subjected before. Desperate was the grappling—the clinging, where nothing was to be clung to, of a soul which every moment was losing the last consolations of immortal hope—receding as they were amidst the withering anticipations of a futurity for which it was not prepared, but from the tremendous grasp of which it had no refuge. The tones of that voice were rife with utter despair, and his hollow shriekings seemed to be echoed back to mortal ears from the confines of eternal misery in another life. His spirit was parched up, and struggled with appalling strength between the black retrospect of unpardoned crime, and the terrible reality of present and future misery. It was, indeed, a scene never to be forgotten. On our first entering the house, he was lying on his back; but after the expiration of a few minutes, he turned nearly, but not altogether, on his side, and I had an opportunity of surveying him more closely. His face, as I said, was pale; it now seemed cadaverous; but, notwithstanding this, I could perceive shades of pain that scorched both soul and body flitting rapidly and darkly over his countenance; convulsive moisture hung in froth about his temples, and a dark ring, formed by its oozey wreck, was visible about his mouth and the root of his hair; his eyes were fierce and bloodshot; but in addition to this, his black brows painfully knit, and the deadly paleness of the face, shifting into expressions of varied misery, were indeed such only as could be found in a mortal divided on the gulf of eternity, between the inward scourgings of despair and the searching agonies of disease.

> 'In that dread moment, how the frantic soul
> Raved round the walls of her clay tenement,
> Ran to each avenue, and shrieked for help;—
> But shrieked in vain!'

There was only a rush-light in the hand of the man who stood over him, and its faint rays seemed to throw all their light upon his haggard and collapsed features, giving them, if possible, a more ghastly expression than they really had.

The priest now went forward to the bed-side. 'John!' said he.

'Ha,' exclaimed the other, 'that's his voice!' and he actually sat up in the bed, whilst a gleam of gloomy delight played over his haggard features, like the light of an angry sun sinking amid the clouds of an evening storm. 'Ha, ha!' he shrieked with singular exultation, 'you're come, thank God;—now you *must* save me; now you must keep your *promise*—it mustn't rest upon my head, for you *said* it.'

'You had better all retire,' said Father Moyle to us, 'until I strive to compose this man's mind.'

We accordingly withdrew into the next house, which being what the peasantry call 'under the roof' with the other, was only divided from that in which the sick man lay, by a gable of mud. He could not have been less than two hours with him, during which period I occasionally went out to observe if the ceremonies usual on such occasions were performed. I could hear their voices in loud and earnest conversation, particularly that of the dying man, whose sharp tones, even at that distance, I felt to be loaded with anguish and pain. At length, Father Moyle, alarmed by a sudden paroxysm which seized Lynch, summoned us in.

It appeared that the spiritual hopes of the sick man could not be directed to the right source, and Father Moyle felt his own state as a sinner too strongly, to lull him into a false security. The fact was, that the hour of conversion appeared to have gone by, for he was not able to change his views of salvation from the opinions that had long determined him to wrong objects. He could not give up, even at the remonstrances of a priest, his scapulars, his cords, his absolutions, and extreme unctions. He knew his Redeemer, if he knew him at all, only as constituting *one* among a crowd of intercessors, and he wanted absolution from the hand of a brother sinner, as his final remedy. It may be asked how a man like him, who had hitherto placed so much confidence in these dead rites, could maintain better hopes in the hour of death? To this I reply, that the man's heart had never undergone a Christian change; he cried peace where there was no peace: but now he was in the throes of death, and conscience came out to vindicate its own rights. The countenance of a just God shone sternly over his bed of death—the delusions of self-deception melted away—and he stood before God in all the naked deformity of his corrupt nature. But his case was also a peculiar one; for it was quite evident, from certain of his expressions, that remorse for some great crime, stung him to the soul.

'Heaven and earth, is there no mercy?' he exclaimed, 'what brought you to me, if you couldn't give me comfort?—you had no business here; I thought you would take more pains with me—for you know *you're* bound to do it—you *know* that;' and he glared angrily at the priest.

The latter, however, seemed to have been kindled into the pure glow of that Gospel truth which he attempted in vain to place within the dying man's grasp. The scene was touching. He raised himself over him with calm solemnity, that derived much of its venerable beauty from the contrast presented between Christian hope and the raving distraction of a sinner writhing under the conviction of unpardoned guilt, whose death-bed was surrounded by nothing but darkness and misery. It was truly affecting, indeed, to contemplate the reverend form of the priest standing over the bed of death, his snowy locks giving to his careworn features an expression of solemn grace, such as became the messenger of mercy. I think he is yet in my eye, as the dim light fell upon his meek countenance, raising his eyes and his arms to heaven, in attestation at once of the truth of his message, and of the trembling anxiety with which he delivered it. Long, and earnest, and heart-rending was the struggle between guilt and mercy—between the long-cherished, the delusive hopes of the perishing sinner, and the simple command to surrender up the idols of the heart—to believe on the Lord Jesus Christ, and live. The only reply to all this was a continual cry for absolution.

'Absolve me—for the sake of the Blessed Mother, absolve me, I say!' shrieked Lynch, as he stretched out his fleshless arms, with the most intense supplication, to the priest. 'Let me get absolution, an' die.'

'I too am a sinner,' replied the priest; 'think not to draw consolation from *me*. I cannot, nor will I, mock the awful power of God by the unmeaning form of a rite, particularly when the heart is dead to a living faith.'

'Anoint me, then,' said the other—'anoint me; surely you won't let me die like a heretic or a dog, without the benefit of *that*, at laste?'

'I am myself,' replied the priest, 'on the brink of the grave, and I cannot trifle either with your salvation or my own. I could not meet my Redeemer, if I turned away your heart from *Him*, in this awful hour. Tell me that you renounce every thing, except HIM ALONE, and I will then speak peace to your soul.'

'Sure I do believe on my Redeemer,' replied the man—'didn't I always believe on him? I only want absolution.'

'Hear me, you deluded man,' said the priest: 'as I shall stand before the throne of judgment, and as God liveth, there is none but God who can give you absolution.'

A murmur of surprise and disapprobation at this strange doctrine burst from all present: the priest looked round, but he was firm.

'Heaven and earth, cannot *you* do it?' asked the other, distractedly.

'No!' replied the priest, solemnly; 'to forgive sins is the province of God *alone*, as well as to give grace for repentance and faith.'

'God of heaven!' cried the other, in a kind of impotent fury, 'why didn't you tell me this before?'

The priest gasped for breath, and only answered with a groan that shook his whole frame.

'Is there no hope?' asked Lynch.

'Repent,' said the priest—'repent from the bottom of your heart, and believe that Christ died for you, and rest assured, that if your sins were ten thousand times greater than they are, they can be made whiter than snow. Can you, therefore, believe that Christ died for *you*?'

'I can, I can,' said the other: 'didn't I always believe it?'

A gleam of delight passed over the priest's features, and he turned up his eyes gratefully to heaven. He proceeded—'Can you believe that nothing else but repentance and that faith which I have described, are able to save you?'

'I can, I can,' said the man; 'will you absolve me *now*?'

'Do you renounce all trust in this, and in this?' said Father Moyle, taking up the Cord of St Francis and the Scapular, both of which the other had pressed to his bosom. The man clutched them more closely, and was silent. 'Answer me,' said Father Moyle, 'ere it be too late.'

'Here,' said the man, 'I can give up the Coard of St Francis; but—but—is it to give up the Ordher of the Mother of God? No, no, I couldn't give up *that*; I darn't make *her* my enemy.'

'Do you feel that a form of absolution, or the application of extreme unction, from me, *cannot* pardon your sins?'

'Sure I know they *can*,' replied the other.

The priest clasped his hands despairingly, and looked up to heaven for strength to sustain him under his heavy trial; and the tears streamed down his cheeks. Like a faithful champion, however, he was determined not to surrender the soul of this miserable man without another struggle. He knelt again, and prayed aloud in a strain of the most fervent and exalted piety, whilst his glowing words, which he requested the other to repeat after him, though couched in beautiful simplicity (he had been the most eloquent man of his day), breathed forth the holy energy of intense faith. With tears, with supplications, and with deep groanings, did he direct the hopeless man to the fountain of love, pardon, and repentance. With sincere affection and tenderness did he endeavour to lead him to God; strongly did he struggle, and urge, and entreat, pleading only in the name of one mediator between God and man. He prayed, however, alone; the heart of the dying man was not in the prayer— the aspirations of his spirit rose not to the throne of grace: on the contrary, he manifested symptoms of impatience and irritability; he hugged and kissed his cords and his scapular, like a man given over to some strong delusion; and, from time to time, dipped his thumb into the holy water, or black paste, and then formed the sign of the cross upon his forehead, lips, and breast.

When the prayer was over, the priest spoke to him again with redoubled earnestness, and with still streaming eyes, pressed, entreated, and commanded him to cast away all but Christ, who, he told him, would not give his glory to another. Vain was every exertion to accomplish *this*—fruitless every struggle. His hopes, his habits, his opinions, his experience, had all been twined round his idols, and these idols were grown into his innermost heart; how could he cast them out now, without tearing up the heart in which they were rooted? To witness such a death-bed—to contemplate him striving to hope against hope—was worth a thousand homilies. But, in fact, he had *no* hope; and it was this pervading conviction— so strongly at variance with his creed and opinions—this fatal error of mistaken trust, and the inward torture of actual despair, that constituted his misery.

When the prayer was over, he commanded them to raise and support him in a sitting posture. He now breathed short, trembled, or rather shivered unusually, every two or three minutes, and cried at intervals for absolution and the unction. I remarked, that as he sat, thus supported, in the miserable bed, his eyes, which were fixed keenly on the priest, shone with yellow but intense glare, whether in supplication or anger I could not say; but, wherever the latter moved, the sick man's eyes followed him with a riveted gaze which he seemed incapable of changing. Such a look was really enough to make a man's flesh creep.

'Will you not absolve me?' he inquired.

'I cannot absolve myself,' said the priest; 'none can absolve you but God, to whom I implore you, John, to raise your head in sincere repentance.'

'Do you *remember* then?' said Lynch.

'I do, I do,' replied the other; 'but *this* hour is not *that*—the hand of God is fastened on us; death and judgment are both present.'

Lynch again shivered terribly.

'You will not?' he shouted out hollowly and hoarsely, whilst his eyes darted at him, and the dead-creak was quite loud over his words: 'then,' said he, 'may my eternal misery rest upon your head, where it ought to rest!' and he fell back faintly in the bed.

Father Moyle staggered, but I caught and supported him.

'Father of all mercies,' he exclaimed, 'support me under this great trial!' and, as he uttered the words, he wiped the big drops of anguish off his face. He was not, however, to be daunted. Again he grappled with him, wrestled, fought, disputed every inch, under the banner of the Cross, but with no success—the man would give up nothing: he did not refuse to go to Christ, but he brought the enemies of his God along with him.

Matters now took a most singular and unexpected turn. Those who were present had, for some time before this last scene, considered the conduct of the priest unjustifiable, for they knew not his views, nor the responsibility of his duties; they now attacked him in the language of anger and exasperation, and he endeavoured meekly and calmly, to give them a correct view of that which, *as a minister of Christ*, he ought to do. But this was doctrine which they understood not. That a priest should be incapable of forgiving sins, they considered rank heresy, and they told him so. Like the poor creature on the bed, they expected that he *could* save him if he would, and they were determined to compel him to do so. Their language became high, and their visages fierce—so much so, that I myself began to feel apprehensions as to the result of this strange business: at all events, I saw clearly that they *would* effect their object.

'Father Moyle,' said the man who had come for him, brother to Lynch, 'it's no use in spakin' any more about it: this door is now bolted,'—he bolted it as he spoke,—'and out of this house you will not go, if you don't give that dyin' man the rites of the church. One word for all, I've said it.'

The priest, who knew their determined character and prejudices on this subject, saw the difficulties of his situation; but he trembled at the thought of making this awful compromise between conscience and humanity. They were knit to their purpose.

'Come,' said the brother, 'bring up the little table to the bed: it's a folly to talk—I'll not see my brother die in this state, and a priest in the house with him. Bring the table quick,' said he to the woman, in a voice of passion—'what are you about?—and put the candle on it.'

'My friend,' said the priest, and he trembled excessively, 'I'm an infirm old man, and very incapable of bearing any kind of a severe shock; do not, therefore, for the sake of God, compel me to do what my conscience condemns. I have endeavoured to lead him to Christ, as a sinner, like myself, wanting mercy and pardon; but I cannot administer a dead service which would only involve myself in deep guilt, without benefiting him.'

'That's all fine,' replied the other; 'but walk up, your Reverence: not a word now—it *must* be done;' and he forcibly led the trembling old man up to the table.

'Let the priest alone, Larry,' said the woman, alarmed at seeing him under his grasp.

'Keep off of me,' said he, 'or I'll knock you down. Come, Sir, we'll all go in to the little room; and now fall to your duty.'

The timid old man turned his eyes to heaven and fell against the corner of the bed, senseless and convulsive. The woman gave a scream of terror, and ran to his assistance, and I aided her in raising him. The sick man, who did not speak during this scene, watched the proceedings with the eye of a lynx; but the death-rattle became louder and more harsh, in proportion as his interest in what was going forward increased.

We placed Father Moyle on a chair, and were endeavouring to recover him, when a loud knocking was heard at the door, and immediately after, the curate's voice, desiring to be admitted. It appeared that the servant told him, on his returning from the sick call, that he feared something must have happened to Father Moyle—an alarm which the severity of the night, his illness, and his long absence, sufficiently justified. The curate felt the same apprehension, and, on hearing whither he had gone, followed him.

'In the name of heaven,' said he, on seeing the situation of Father Moyle, 'what does this mean?'

'Never you heed that,' said Lynch's brother, 'it won't signify— give this man the rites of the church, while he has life and sense in him, and *we'll* take care of Father Moyle. Come,' said he, 'we'll bring him, chair and all, into the next house, an' in a short time he'll be well enough.'

This the curate refused to do, until he saw that Father Moyle, who now opened his eyes and drew his breath, was likely to recover. In the mean time, he was removed to the other house, whither we all accompanied him, leaving the curate and the dying man together. When the last rites of the church were administered, we returned, and, reader, he who clung to his idols, his scapulars, and his unctions, lay before us, calm and composed, apparently prepared to meet that Redeemer on whom he refused to ground his sole hopes of salvation! The wooden crucifix was either in his hands or next his heart, according as the caprice of the moment dictated.

'Denis,' said he to his brother, 'I have one commandment to lay on you before I die—will you do it?'

'You know, John,' replied the other, 'if 'tis what I'm able to do, I'll do it, God willin'; any thing, John avourneen, that could give you ase or pace where you're goin'.'

'Well,' said the other, ' 'tis this—I lay it upon you to make three stations to Loughderg, for myself—*three*, remember, *in my name*: an' you don't know but may be 'tis yer garden angel I'd be for this, when my soul's relased out of Purgathory. Will you promise, before God, to fulfil this?'

'I promise before God that I will,' said the brother, 'if I'm spared: or, if I don't live to do it myself, that I'll lay it upon some one else to finish it.'

'Well, God be praised!' said the sick man: 'if you will light this bit of blessed candle, that I may have the light of it shinin' upon me, I will now die happy.'

This was complied with; and in less than twenty minutes after these words, he expired.

When Father Moyle saw that the miserable man was gone, a dark shade of intense misery settled upon his countenance; he had been standing over him whilst in the throes of dissolution, and truly he appeared to feel pang for pang; but when the last convulsion quivered away into the stillness of utter death, he dropped down on the chair as if seized with another fit; the upper part of his face was cold, but his throat and lips were so dry and parched, that he gasped for breath. It was not without a strong trial of Christian fortitude that he was able to contemplate the death and life of the unrepentant being who had gone to judgment, and between whom and himself there had been evidently a mysterious community of knowledge which it is out of our power to reveal. His natural feelings were strong and acute, but the consolations of religion, notwithstanding his sufferings, calmed and supported him under them. When he had regained a little strength, and was sufficiently composed, we prepared to go.

Ere we left the house, I went over and took a last glimpse of the corpse. It was an unpleasant object to view: his black, bushy brows, bent into a scowl by the last agonies, contrasted disagreeably with his pallid face, and gave his countenance an expression of 'grim repose', exactly in keeping with his character, and the delusive security in which he died.

GERALD GRIFFIN · 1803–1840

The Brown Man

> All sorts of cattle he did eat,
> Some say he eat up trees,
> And that the forest sure he would,
> Devour up by degrees.
> For houses and churches, were to him geese and turkeys,
> He ate all and left none behind,
> But some stones, dear Jack, which he could not crack,
> Which on the hills you'll find.
>
> *Dragon of Wantley*

The common Irish expression of 'the seven devils' does not, it would appear, owe its origin to the supernatural influences ascribed to that numeral, from its frequent association with the greatest and most solemn occasions of theological history. If one were disposed to be fancifully metaphysical upon the subject, it might not be amiss to compare credulity to a sort of mental prism, by which the great volume of the light of speculative superstition is refracted in a manner precisely similar to that of the material, every day sun, the great refractor thus showing only *blue* devils to the dwellers in the good city of London, *orange* and *green* devils to the inhabitants of the sister (or rather step-daughter), island, and so forward until the seven component hues are made out, through the other nations of the earth. But what has this to do with the story? In order to answer that question, the story must be told.

In a lonely cabin, in a lonely glen, on the shores of a lonely lough, in one of the most lonesome districts of west Munster, lived a lone woman named Guare. She had a beautiful girl, a daughter named Nora. Their cabin was the only one within three miles round them every way. As to their mode of living, it was simple enough, for all they had was one little garden of white cabbage, and they had eaten that down to a few heads between them, a sorry prospect in a place where even a handful of *prishoc* weed was not to be had without sowing it.

It was a very fine morning in those parts, for it was only snowing and hailing, when Nora and her mother were sitting at the door of their little cottage, and laying out plans for the next day's dinner. On a sudden, a strange horseman rode up to the door. He was strange in more ways than one. He was dressed in brown, his hair was brown, his eyes were brown, his boots were brown, he rode a brown horse, and he was followed by a brown dog.

'I'm come to marry you, Nora Guare,' said the Brown Man.

'Ax my mother fusht, if you plaise, sir,' said Nora, dropping him a curtsy.

'You'll not refuse, ma'am;' said the Brown Man to the old mother, 'I have money enough, and I'll make your daughter a lady, with servants at her call, and all manner of fine things about her.' And so saying, he flung a purse of gold into the widow's lap.

'Why then the heavens speed you and her together, take her away with you, and make much of her,' said the old mother, quite bewildered with all the money.

'Agh, agh,' said the Brown Man, as he placed her on his horse behind him without more ado. 'Are you all ready now?'

'I am!' said the bride. The horse snorted, and the dog barked, and almost before the word was out of her mouth, they were all whisked away out of sight. After travelling a day and a night, faster than the wind itself, the Brown Man pulled up his horse in the middle of the Mangerton mountain, in one of the most lonesome places that eye ever looked on.

'Here is my estate,' said the Brown Man.

'A'then, is it this wild bog you call an estate?' said the bride.

'Come in, wife; this is my palace,' said the bridegroom.

'What! a clay-hovel, worse than my mother's!'

They dismounted, and the horse and the dog disappeared in an instant, with a horrible noise, which the girl did not know whether to call snorting, barking, or laughing.

'Are you hungry?' said the Brown Man. 'If so, there is your dinner.'

'A handful of raw white-eyes,* and a grain of salt!'

'And when you are sleepy, here is your bed,' he continued, pointing to a little straw in a corner, at sight of which Nora's limbs shivered and trembled again. It may be easily supposed that she did

* A kind of potato.

not make a very hearty dinner that evening, nor did her husband neither.

In the dead of the night, when the clock of Mucruss Abbey had just tolled one, a low neighing at the door, and a soft barking at the window were heard. Nora feigned sleep. The Brown Man passed his hand over her eyes and face. She snored. 'I'm coming,' said he, and he arose gently from her side. In half an hour after she felt him by her side again. He was cold as ice.

The next night the same summons came. The Brown Man rose. His wife feigned sleep. He returned, cold. The morning came.

The next night came. The bell tolled at Mucruss, and was heard across the lakes. The Brown Man rose again, and passed a light before the eyes of the feigning sleeper. None slumber so sound as they who *will* not wake. Her heart trembled, but her frame was quiet and firm. A voice at the door summoned the husband.

'You are very long coming. The earth is tossed up, and I am hungry. Hurry! Hurry! Hurry! if you would not lose all.'

'I'm coming!' said the Brown Man. Nora rose and followed instantly. She beheld him at a distance winding through a lane of frost-nipt sallow trees. He often paused and looked back, and once or twice retraced his steps to within a few yards of the tree, behind which she had shrunk. The moon-light, cutting the shadow close and dark about her, afforded the best concealment. He again proceeded, and she followed. In a few minutes they reached the old Abbey of Mucruss. With a sickening heart she saw him enter the church-yard. The wind rushed through the huge yew-tree and startled her. She mustered courage enough, however, to reach the gate of the church-yard and look in. The Brown Man, the horse, and the dog, were there seated by an open grave, eating something; and glancing their brown, fiery eyes about in every direction. The moon-light shone full on them and her. Looking down towards her shadow on the earth, she started with horror to observe it move, although she was herself perfectly still. It waved its black arms, and motioned her back. What the feasters said, she understood not, but she seemed still fixed in the spot. She looked once more on her shadow; it raised one hand, and pointed the way to the lane; then slowly rising from the ground, and confronting her, it walked rapidly off in that direction. She followed as quickly as might be.

She was scarcely in her straw, when the door creaked behind, and her husband entered. He lay down by her side, and started.

'Uf! Uf!' said she, pretending to be just awakened, 'how cold you are, my love!'

'Cold, inagh? Indeed you're not very warm yourself, my dear, I'm thinking.'

'Little admiration I shouldn't be warm, and you laving me alone this way at night, till my blood is snow broth, no less.'

'Umph!' said the Brown Man, as he passed his arm round her waist. 'Ha! your heart is beating fast?'

'Little admiration it should. I am not well, indeed. Them praties and salt don't agree with me at all.'

'Umph!' said the Brown Man.

The next morning as they were sitting at the breakfast-table together, Nora plucked up a heart, and asked leave to go to see her mother. The Brown Man, who ate nothing, looked at her in a way that made her think he knew all. She felt her spirit die away within her.

'If you only want to see your mother,' said he, 'there is no occasion for your going home. I will bring her to you here. I didn't marry you to be keeping you gadding.'

The Brown Man then went out and whistled for his dog and his horse. They both came; and in a very few minutes they pulled up at the old widow's cabin-door.

The poor woman was very glad to see her son-in-law, though she did not know what could bring him so soon.

'Your daughter sends her love to you, mother,' says the Brown Man, the villain, 'and she'd be obliged to you for a *loand* of a *shoot* of your best clothes, as she's going to give a grand party, and the dress-maker has disappointed her.'

'To be sure and welcome,' said the mother; and making up a bundle of clothes, she put them into his hands.

'Whogh! whogh!' said the horse as they drove off, 'that was well done. Are we to have a mail of her?'

'Easy, ma-coppuleen, and you'll get your 'nough before night,' said the Brown Man, 'and you likewise, my little dog.'

'Boh!' cried the dog, 'I'm in no hurry—I hunted down a doe this morning that was fed with milk from the horns of the moon.'

Often in the course of that day did Nora Guare go to the door, and cast her eye over the weary flat before it, to discern, if possible, the distant figures of her bridegroom and mother. The dusk of the second evening found her alone in the desolate cot. She listened to every sound. At length the door opened, and an old woman, dressed in a new *jock*, and leaning on a staff, entered the hut. 'O mother, are you come?' said Nora, and was about to rush into her arms, when the old woman stopped her.

'Whisht! whisht! my child!—I only stepped in before the man to know how you like him? Speak softly, in dread he'd hear you—he's turning the horse loose, in the swamp, abroad, over.'

'O mother, mother! such a story!'

'Whisht! easy again—how does he use you?'

'Sarrow worse. That straw my bed, and them white-eyes—and bad ones they are—all my diet. And 'tisn't that same, only—'

'Whisht! easy, agin! He'll hear you, may be—Well?'

'I'd be easy enough only for his own doings. Listen, mother. The fusht night, I came about twelve o'clock—'

'Easy, speak easy, eroo!'

'He got up at the call of the horse and the dog, and staid out a good hour. He ate nothing next day. The second night, and the second day, it was the same story. The third—'

'Husht! husht! Well, the third night?'

'The third night I said I'd watch him. Mother, don't hold my hand so hard . . . He got up, and I got up after him . . . Oh, don't laugh, mother, for 'tis frightful . . . I followed him to Mucruss church-yard . . . Mother, mother, you hurt my hand . . . I looked in at the gate—there was great moonlight there, and I could see every thing as plain as day.'

'Well, darling—husht! softly! What did you see?'

'My husband by the grave, and the horse, . . . Turn your head aside, mother, for your breath is very hot . . . and the dog and they eating.—Ah, you are not my mother!' shrieked the miserable girl, as the Brown Man flung off his disguise, and stood before her, grinning worse than a blacksmith's face through a horse-collar. He just looked at her one moment, and then darted his longer fingers into her bosom, from which the red blood spouted in so many streams. She was very soon out of all pain, and a merry supper the horse, the dog, and the Brown Man had that night, by all accounts.

SHERIDAN LE FANU · 1814–1873

Green Tea

PROLOGUE
MARTIN HESSELIUS, THE
GERMAN PHYSICIAN

Though carefully educated in medicine and surgery, I have never practised either. The study of each continues, nevertheless, to interest me profoundly. Neither idleness nor caprice caused my secession from the honourable calling which I had just entered. The cause was a very trifling scratch inflicted by a dissecting knife. This trifle cost me the loss of two fingers, amputated promptly, and the more painful loss of my health, for I have never been quite well since, and have seldom been twelve months together in the same place.

In my wanderings I became acquainted with Dr Martin Hesselius, a wanderer like myself, like me a physician, and like me an enthusiast in his profession. Unlike me in this, that his wanderings were voluntary, and he a man, if not of fortune, as we estimate fortune in England, at least in what our forefathers used to term 'easy circumstances'. He was an old man when I first saw him; nearly five-and-thirty years my senior.

In Dr Martin Hesselius I found my master. His knowledge was immense, his grasp of a case was an intuition. He was the very man to inspire a young enthusiast like me with awe and delight. My admiration has stood the test of time and survived the separation of death. I am sure it was well-founded.

For nearly twenty years I acted as his medical secretary. His immense collection of papers he has left in my care, to be arranged, indexed and bound. His treatment of some of these cases is curious. He writes in two distinct characters. He describes what he saw and heard as an intelligent layman might; and when in this style of narrative he had seen the patient either through his own hall-door to the light of day, or through the gates of darkness to the caverns of the dead, he returns upon the narrative, and in the terms of his art, and with all the force and originality of genius, proceeds to the work of analysis, diagnosis, and illustration.

Here and there a case strikes me as of a kind to amuse or horrify a lay reader with an interest quite different from the peculiar one which it may possess for an expert. With slight modifications, chiefly of language, and of course a change of names, I copy the following. The narrator is Dr Martin Hesselius. I find it among the voluminous notes of cases which he made during a tour in England about sixty-four years ago.

It is related in a series of letters to his friend Professor Van Loo of Leyden. The professor was not a physician, but a chemist, and a man who read history and metaphysics and medicine, and had, in his day, written a play.

The narrative is therefore, if somewhat less valuable as a medical record, necessarily written in a manner more likely to interest an unlearned reader.

These letters, from a memorandum attached, appear to have been returned, on the death of the professor in 1819, to Dr Hesselius. They are written, some in English, some in French, but the greater part in German. I am a faithful, though I am conscious by no means a graceful translator, and although here and there I omit some passages, and shorten others, and disguise names, I have interpolated nothing.

I

DR HESSELIUS RELATES HOW HE MET THE REV. MR JENNINGS

The Rev. Mr Jennings is tall and thin. He is middle-aged, and dresses with a natty, old-fashioned high-church precision. He is naturally a little stately, but not at all stiff. His features, without being handsome, are well formed, and their expression extremely kind, but also shy.

I met him one evening at Lady Mary Heyduke's. The modesty and benevolence of his countenance are extremely prepossessing.

We were but a small party, and he joined agreeably enough in the conversation. He seems to enjoy listening very much more than contributing to the talk; but what he says is always to the purpose and well said. He is a great favourite of Lady Mary's, who, it seems, consults him upon many things, and thinks him the most happy and blessed person on earth. Little knows she about him.

The Rev. Mr Jennings is a bachelor, and has, they say, sixty thousand pounds in the funds. He is a charitable man. He is most anxious to be actively employed in his sacred profession, and yet, though always tolerably well elsewhere, when he goes down to his vicarage in Warwickshire, to engage in the actual duties of his sacred calling, his health soon fails him, and in a very strange way. So says Lady Mary.

There is no doubt that Mr Jennings' health does break down in generally a sudden and mysterious way, sometimes in the very act of officiating in his old and pretty church at Kenlis. It may be his heart, it may be his brain. But so it has happened, three or four times or oftener, that after proceeding a certain way in the service, he has on a sudden stopped short; and after a silence, apparently quite unable to resume, he has fallen into solitary, inaudible prayer, his hands and his eyes uplifted, and then pale as death, and in the agitation of a strange shame and horror, descended trembling, and got into the vestry-room, leaving his congregation, without explanation, to themselves. This occurred when his curate was absent. When he goes down to Kenlis now, he always takes care to provide a clergyman to share his duty, and to supply his place on the instant should he become thus suddenly incapacitated.

When Mr Jennings breaks down quite, and beats a retreat from the vicarage, and returns to London—where, in a dark street off Piccadilly, he inhabits a very narrow house—Lady Mary says that he is always perfectly well. I have my own opinion about that. There are degrees, of course. We shall see.

Mr Jennings is a perfectly gentlemanlike man. People, however, remark something odd. There is an impression a little ambiguous. One thing which certainly contributes to it, people I think don't remember or, perhaps, distinctly remark. But I did, almost immediately. Mr Jennings has a way of looking sidelong upon the carpet, as if his eye followed the movements of something there. This, of course, is not always. It occurs only now and then. But often enough to give a certain oddity, as I have said, to his manner, and in this glance travelling along the floor there is something both shy and anxious.

A medical philosopher, as you are good enough to call me,

elaborating theories by the aid of cases sought out by himself, and by him watched and scrutinized with more time at command, and consequently infinitely more minuteness than the ordinary practitioner can afford, falls insensibly into habits of observation, which accompany him everywhere, and are exercised, as some people would say, impertinently, upon every subject that presents itself with the least likelihood of rewarding inquiry.

There was a promise of this kind in the slight, timid, kindly, but reserved gentleman, whom I met for the first time at this agreeable little evening gathering. I observed, of course, more than I here set down; but I reserve all that borders on the technical for a strictly scientific paper.

I may remark that when I here speak of medical science, I do so, as I hope some day to see it more generally understood, in a much more comprehensive sense than its generally material treatment would warrant. I believe the entire natural world is but the ultimate expression of that spiritual world from which, and in which alone, it has its life. I believe that the essential man is a spirit, that the spirit is an organized substance, but as different in point of material from what we ordinarily understand by matter, as light or electricity is; that the material body is, in the most literal sense, a vesture, and death consequently no interruption of the living man's existence, but simply his extrication from the natural body—a process which commences at the moment of what we term death, and the completion of which, at furthest a few days later, is the resurrection 'in power'.

The person who weighs the consequences of these positions will probably see their practical bearing upon medical science. This is, however, by no means the proper place for displaying the proofs and discussing the consequences of this too generally unrecognized state of facts.

In pursuance of my habit, I was covertly observing Mr Jennings with all my caution—I think he perceived it—and I saw plainly that he was as cautiously observing me. Lady Mary happening to address me by my name, as Dr Hesselius, I saw that he glanced at me more sharply, and then became thoughtful for a few minutes.

After this, as I conversed with a gentleman at the other end of the room, I saw him look at me more steadily, and with an interest which I thought I understood. I then saw him take an opportunity of chatting with Lady Mary, and was, as one always is, perfectly aware of being the subject of a distant inquiry and answer.

This tall clergyman approached me by-and-by; and in a little time we had got into conversation. When two people who like reading, and know books and places, having travelled, wish to discourse, it is very strange if they can't find topics. It was not accident that brought him near me, and led him into conversation. He knew German, and had read my *Essays on Metaphysical Medicine*, which suggest more than they actually say.

This courteous man, gentle, shy, plainly a man of thought and reading, who, moving and talking among us, was not altogether of us, and whom I already suspected of leading a life whose transactions and alarms were carefully concealed, with an impenetrable reserve from, not only the world, but his best beloved friends—was cautiously weighing in his own mind the idea of taking a certain step with regard to me.

I penetrated his thoughts without his being aware of it, and was careful to say nothing which could betray to his sensitive vigilance my suspicions respecting his position, or my surmises about his plans respecting myself.

We chatted upon different subjects for a time, but at last he said:

'I was very much interested by some papers of yours, Dr Hesselius, upon what you term Metaphysical Medicine—I read them in German, ten or twelve years ago—have they been translated?'

'No, I'm sure they have not—I should have heard. They would have asked my leave, I think.'

'I asked the publishers here, a few months ago, to get the book for me in the original German; but they tell me it is out of print.'

'So it is, and has been for some years; but it flatters me as an author to find that you have not forgotten my little book, although,' I added laughing, 'ten or twelve years is a considerable time to have managed without it; but I suppose you have been turning the subject over again in your mind, or something has happened lately to revive your interest in it.'

At this remark, accompanied by a glance of inquiry, a sudden embarrassment disturbed Mr Jennings, analogous to that which makes a young lady blush and look foolish. He dropped his eyes, and folded his hands together uneasily, and looked oddly, and you would have said guiltily, for a moment.

I helped him out of his awkwardness in the best way, by appearing not to observe it; and going straight on, I said: 'Those revivals of interest in a subject happen to me often; one book suggests another, and often sends me back on a wild goose-chase over an interval of twenty years. But if you still care to possess a copy, I shall be only too happy to provide you; I have still got two or three by me—and if you allow me to present one I shall be very much honoured.'

'You are very good indeed,' he said, quite at his ease again, in a moment: 'I almost despaired—I don't know how to thank you.'

'Pray don't say a word; the thing is really so little worth that I am only ashamed of having offered it, and if you thank me any more I shall throw it into the fire in a fit of modesty.'

Mr Jennings laughed. He inquired where I was staying in London, and after a little more conversation on a variety of subjects he took his departure.

II

THE DOCTOR QUESTIONS LADY MARY, AND SHE ANSWERS

'I like your vicar so much, Lady Mary,' said I, as soon as he was gone. 'He has read, travelled, and thought, and having also suffered, he ought to be an accomplished companion.'

'So he is, and, better still, he is a really good man,' said she. 'His advice is invaluable about my schools, and all my little undertakings at Dawlbridge, and he's so painstaking, he takes so much trouble— you have no idea—wherever he thinks he can be of use: he's so good-natured and so sensible.'

'It is pleasant to hear so good an account of his neighbourly virtues. I can only testify to his being an agreeable and gentle companion, and in addition to what you have told me, I think I can tell you two or three things about him,' said I.

'Really!'

'Yes, to begin with, he's unmarried.'

'Yes, that's right—go on.'

'He has been writing, that is he *was*; but for two or three years, perhaps, he has not gone on with his work; and the book was upon some rather abstract subject—perhaps theology.'

'Well, he was writing a book, as you say; I'm not quite sure what it was about, but only that it was nothing that I cared for; very likely you are right, and he certainly did stop—yes.'

'And although he only drank a little coffee here to-night, he likes tea, at least did like it, extravagantly.'

'Yes, that's *quite* true.'

'He drank green tea a good deal, didn't he?' I pursued.

'Well, that's very odd! Green tea was a subject on which we used almost to quarrel.'

'But he has quite given that up,' said I.

'So he has.'

'And, now, one more fact. His mother or his father, did you know them?'

'Yes, both; his father is only ten years dead, and their place is near Dawlbridge. We knew them very well,' she answered.

'Well, either his mother or his father—I should rather think his father, saw a ghost,' said I.

'Well, you really are a conjurer, Dr Hesselius.'

'Conjurer or no, haven't I said right?' I answered merrily.

'You certainly have, and it *was* his father: he was a silent, whimsical man, and he used to bore my father about his dreams, and at last he told him a story about a ghost he had seen and talked with; and a very odd story it was. I remember it particularly, because I was so afraid of him. This story was long before he died— when I was quite a child—and his ways were so silent and moping, and he used to drop in sometimes, in the dusk, when I was alone in the drawing-room, and I used to fancy there were ghosts about him.'

I smiled and nodded.

'And now, having established my character as a conjurer, I think I must say good-night,' said I.

'But how *did* you find out?'

'By the planets, of course, as the gipsies do,' I answered, and so, gaily, we said good-night.

Next morning I sent the little book he had been inquiring after, and a note, to Mr Jennings, and on returning late that evening, I found that he had called at my lodgings and left his card. He asked whether I was at home, and asked at what hour he would be most likely to find me.

Does he intend opening his case, and consulting me 'professionally', as they say? I hope so. I have already conceived a theory about him. It is supported by Lady Mary's answers to my parting questions. I should like much to ascertain from his own lips. But what can I do consistently with good breeding to invite a confession? Nothing. I rather think he meditates one. At all events, my dear Van L, I shan't make myself difficult of access; I mean to return his visit to-morrow. It will be only civil, in return for his politeness, to ask to see him. Perhaps something may come of it. Whether much, little, or nothing, my dear Van L, you shall hear.

III
DR HESSELIUS PICKS UP SOMETHING IN LATIN BOOKS

Well, I have called at Blank Street.

On inquiring at the door, the servant told me that Mr Jennings was engaged very particularly with a gentleman, a clergyman from Kenlis, his parish in the country. Intending to reserve my privilege, and to call again, I merely intimated that I should try another time, and had turned to go, when the servant begged my pardon, and asked me, looking at me a little more attentively than well-bred persons of his order usually do, whether I was Dr Hesselius; and, on learning that I was, he said, 'Perhaps then, sir, you would allow me to mention it to Mr Jennings, for I am sure he wishes to see you.'

The servant returned in a moment, with a message from Mr Jennings asking me to go into his study, which was in effect his back drawing-room, promising to be with me in a very few minutes.

This was really a study—almost a library. The room was lofty, with two tall slender windows, and rich dark curtains. It was much larger than I had expected, and stored with books on every side, from the floor to the ceiling. The upper carpet—for to my tread it felt that there were two or three—was a Turkey carpet. My steps fell noiselessly. The book-cases standing out, placed the windows, particularly narrow ones, in deep recesses. The effect of the room was, although extremely comfortable, and even luxurious, decidedly gloomy and, aided by the silence, almost oppressive. Perhaps, however, I ought to have allowed something for association. My mind had connected peculiar ideas with Mr Jennings. I stepped into this perfectly silent room, of a very silent house, with a peculiar foreboding; and its darkness and solemn clothing of books—for except where two narrow looking-glasses were set in the wall they were everywhere—helped this sombre feeling.

While awaiting Mr Jennings' arrival, I amused myself by looking into some of the books with which his shelves were laden. Not among these, but immediately under them, with their backs upward, on the floor, I lighted upon a complete set of Swedenborg's *Arcana Cœlestia*, in the original Latin, a very fine folio set, bound in the natty livery which theology affects, pure vellum namely, gold letters, and carmine edges. There were paper markers in several of these volumes; I raised and placed them, one after the other, upon the table, and opening where these papers were placed, I read in the solemn Latin phraseology a series of sentences indicated by a pencilled line at the margin. Of these I copy here a few, translating them into English:

'When man's interior sight is opened, which is that of his spirit, then there appear the things of another life, which cannot possibly be made visible to the bodily sight . . .'

'By the internal sight it has been granted me to see the things that are in the other life, more clearly than I see those that are in the world. From these considerations it is evident that external vision exists from interior vision, and this from a vision still more interior, and so on . . .'

'There are with every man at least two evil spirits . . .'

'With wicked genii there is also a fluent speech, but harsh and grating. There is also among them a speech which is not fluent, wherein the dissent of the thoughts is perceived as something secretly creeping along within it . . .'

'The evil spirits associated with man are, indeed, from the hells, but when with man they are not then in hell, but are taken out thence. The place where they then are is in the midst between heaven and hell, and is called the world of spirits—when the evil spirits who are with man, are in that world, they are not in any infernal torment, but in every thought and affection of the man, and so, in all that the man himself enjoys. But when they are remitted into their hell, they return to their former state . . .'

'If evil spirits could perceive that they were associated with man, and yet that they were spirits separate from him, and if they could flow into the things of his body, they would attempt by a thousand means to destroy him; for they hate man with a deadly hatred . . .'

'Knowing, therefore, that I was a man in the body, they were continually striving to destroy me, not as to the body only, but especially as to the soul; for to destroy any man or spirit is the very delight of the life of all who are in hell; but I have been continually protected by the Lord. Hence it appears how dangerous it is for man to be in a living consort with spirits, unless he be in the good of faith . . .'

'Nothing is more carefully guarded from the knowledge of associate spirits than their being thus conjoint with a man, for if they knew it they would speak to him, with the intention to destroy him . . .'

'The delight of hell is to do evil to man, and to hasten his eternal ruin . . .'

A long note, written with a very sharp and fine pencil, in Mr Jennings' neat hand, at the foot of the page, caught my eye. Expecting his criticism upon the text, I read a word or two, and stopped; for it was something quite different, and began with these words, *Deus misereatur mei*— 'May God compassionate me.' Thus warned of its private nature, I averted my eyes, and shut the book, replacing all the volumes as I had found them, except one which interested me, and in which, as men studious and solitary in their habits will do, I grew so absorbed as to take no cognizance of the outer world, nor to remember where I was.

I was reading some pages which refer to 'representatives' and 'correspondents', in the technical language of Swedenborg, and had arrived at a passage, the substance of which is that evil spirits, when seen by other eyes than those of their infernal associates, present themselves, by 'correspondence', in the shape of the beast (*fera*) which represents their particular lust and life, in aspect direful and atrocious. This is a long passage, and particularizes a number of those bestial forms.

IV

FOUR EYES WERE READING THE PASSAGE

I was running the head of my pencil-case along the line as I read it, and something caused me to raise my eyes.

Directly before me was one of the mirrors I have mentioned, in which I saw reflected the tall shape of my friend Mr Jennings, leaning over my shoulder, and reading the page at which I was busy, and with a face so dark and wild that I should hardly have known him.

I turned and rose. He stood erect also, and with an effort laughed a little, saying:

'I came in and asked you how you did, but without succeeding in awaking you from your book; so I could not restrain my curiosity, and very impertinently, I'm afraid, peeped over your shoulder. This is not your first time of looking into those pages. You have looked into Swedenborg, no doubt, long ago?'

'Oh dear, yes! I owe Swedenborg a great deal; you will discover traces of him in the little book on *Metaphysical Medicine*, which you were so good as to remember.'

Although my friend affected a gaiety of manner, there was a slight flush in his face, and I could perceive that he was inwardly much perturbed.

'I'm scarcely yet qualified, I know so little of Swedenborg. I've only had them a fortnight,' he answered, 'and I think they are rather likely to make a solitary man nervous—that is, judging from the very little I have read—I don't say that they have made me so,' he laughed; 'and I'm so very much obliged for the book. I hope you got my note?'

I made all proper acknowledgements and modest disclaimers.

'I never read a book that I go with, so entirely, as that of yours,' he continued. 'I saw at once there is more in it than is quite unfolded. Do you know Dr Harley?' he asked, rather abruptly.

[In passing, the editor remarks that the physician here named was one of the most eminent who had ever practised in England.]

I did, having had letters to him, and had experienced from him great courtesy and considerable assistance during my visit to England.

'I think that man one of the very greatest fools I ever met in my life,' said Mr Jennings.

This was the first time I had ever heard him say a sharp thing of anybody, and such a term applied to so high a name a little startled me.

'Really! and in what way?' I asked.

'In his profession,' he answered.

I smiled.

'I mean this,' he said: 'he seems to me, one half, blind—I mean one half of all he looks at is dark—preternaturally bright and vivid all the rest; and the worst of it is, it seems *wilful*. I can't get him—I mean he won't—I've had some experience of him as a physician, but I look on him as, in that sense, no better than a paralytic mind, an intellect half dead. I'll tell you—I know I shall some time—all about it,' he said, with a little agitation. 'You stay some months longer in England. If I should be out of town during your stay for a little time, would you allow me to trouble you with a letter?'

'I should be only too happy,' I assured him.

'Very good of you. I am so utterly dissatisfied with Harley.'

'A little leaning to the materialistic school,' I said.

'A *mere* materialist,' he corrected me; 'you can't think how that sort of thing worries one who knows better. You won't tell anyone—any of my friends you know—that I am hippish; now, for instance, no one knows—not even Lady Mary—that I have seen Dr Harley, or any other doctor. So pray don't mention it; and, if I should have any threatening of an attack, you'll kindly let me write, or, should I be in town, have a little talk with you.'

I was full of conjecture, and unconsciously I found I had fixed my eyes gravely on him, for he lowered his for a moment, and he said:

'I see you think I might as well tell you now, or else you are forming a conjecture; but you may as well give it up. If you were guessing all the rest of your life, you will never hit on it.'

He shook his head smiling, and over that wintry sunshine a black cloud suddenly came down, and he drew his breath in through his teeth, as men do in pain.

'Sorry, of course, to learn that you apprehend occasion to consult any of us; but command me when and how you like, and I need not assure you that your confidence is sacred.'

He then talked of quite other things, and in a comparatively cheerful way, and after a little time I took my leave.

V

DR HESSELIUS IS SUMMONED TO RICHMOND

We parted cheerfully, but he was not cheerful, nor was I. There are certain expressions of that powerful organ of spirit—the human face—which, although I have seen them often, and possess a doctor's nerve, yet disturb me profoundly. One look of Mr Jennings haunted me. It had seized my imagination with so dismal a power that I changed my plans for the evening, and went to the opera, feeling that I wanted a change of ideas.

I heard nothing of or from him for two or three days, when a note in his hand reached me. It was cheerful, and full of hope. He said that he had been for some little time so much better—quite well, in fact—that he was going to make a little experiment, and run down for a month or so to his parish, to try whether a little work might not quite set him up. There was in it a fervent religious expression of gratitude for his restoration, as he now almost hoped he might call it.

A day or two later I saw Lady Mary, who repeated what his note had announced, and told me that he was actually in Warwickshire, having resumed his clerical duties at Kenlis; and she added, 'I begin to think that he is really perfectly well, and that there never was anything the matter, more than nerves and fancy; we are all nervous, but I fancy there is nothing like a little hard work for that kind of weakness, and he has made up his mind to try it. I should not be surprised if he did not come back for a year.'

Notwithstanding all this confidence, only two days later I had this note, dated from his house off Piccadilly:

'DEAR SIR—I have returned disappointed. If I should feel at all able to see you, I shall write to ask you kindly to call. At present I am too low and, in fact, simply unable to say all I wish to say. Pray don't mention my name to my friends. I can see no one. Bye-and-by, please God, you shall hear from me. I mean to take a run into Shropshire, where some of my people are. God bless you! May we, on my return, meet more happily than I can now write.'

About a week after this I saw Lady Mary at her own house, the last person, she said, left in town, and just on the wing for Brighton, for the London season was quite over. She told me that she had heard from Mr Jennings' niece, Martha, in Shropshire. There was nothing to be gathered from her letter, more than that he was low and nervous. In those words, of which healthy people think so lightly, what a world of suffering is sometimes hidden!

Nearly five weeks had passed without any further news of Mr Jennings. At the end of that time I received a note from him. He wrote:

'I have been in the country, and have had change of air, change of scene, change of faces, change of everything and in everything—but *myself*. I have made up my mind, so far as the most irresolute creature on earth can do it, to tell my case fully to you. If your engagements will permit, pray come to me today, tomorrow, or the next day; but, pray defer as little as possible. You know not how much I need help. I have a quiet house at Richmond, where I now am. Perhaps you can manage to come to dinner, or to luncheon, or even to tea. You shall have no trouble in finding me out. The servant at Blank Street, who takes this note, will have a carriage at your door at any hour you please; and I am always to be found. You will say that I ought not to be alone. I have tried everything. Come and see.'

I called up the servant, and decided on going out the same evening, which accordingly I did.

He would have been much better in a lodging-house, or hotel, I thought, as I drove up through a short double row of sombre elms to a very old-fashioned brick house, darkened by the foliage of these trees, which overtopped and nearly surrounded it. It was a perverse choice, for nothing could be imagined more triste and silent. The house, I found, belonged to him. He had stayed for a day or two in town, and, finding it for some cause insupportable, had come out here, probably because, being furnished and his own, he was relieved of the thought and delay of selection, by coming here.

The sun had already set, and the red reflected light of the western sky illuminated the scene with the peculiar effect with which we are all familiar. The hall seemed very dark, but, getting to the back drawing-room, whose windows command the west, I was again in the same dusky light.

I sat down, looking out upon the richly-wooded landscape that glowed in the grand and melancholy light which was every moment fading. The corners of the room were already dark; all was growing dim, and the gloom was insensibly toning my mind, already prepared for what was sinister. I was waiting alone for his arrival, which soon took place. The door communicating with the front room opened, and the tall figure of Mr Jennings, faintly seen in the ruddy twilight, came, with quiet stealthy steps, into the room.

We shook hands, and, taking a chair to the window, where there was still light enough to enable us to see each other's faces, he sat down beside me, and, placing his hand upon my arm, with scarcely a word of preface began his narrative.

VI
HOW MR JENNINGS MET HIS COMPANION

The faint glow of the west, the pomp of the then lonely woods of Richmond, were before us, behind and about us the darkening room, and on the stony face of the sufferer—for the character of his face, though still gentle and sweet, was changed—rested that dim, odd glow which seems to descend and produce, where it touches, lights, sudden though faint, which are lost, almost without gradation, in darkness. The silence, too, was utter; not a distant wheel, or bark, or whistle from without; and within the depressing stillness of an invalid bachelor's house.

I guessed well the nature, though not even vaguely the particulars of the revelations I was about to receive, from that fixed face of suffering that, so oddly flushed, stood out, like a portrait of Schalken's, before its background of darkness.

'It began,' he said, 'on the 15th of October, three years and eleven weeks ago, and two days—I keep very accurate count, for every day is torment. If I leave anywhere a chasm in my narrative tell me.

'About four years ago I began a work which had cost me very much thought and reading. It was upon the religious metaphysics of the ancients.'

'I know,' said I; 'the actual religion of educated and thinking paganism, quite apart from symbolic worship? A wide and very interesting field.'

'Yes; but not good for the mind—the Christian mind, I mean. Paganism is all bound together in essential unity, and, with evil sympathy, their religion involves their art, and both their manners, and the subject is a degrading fascination and the Nemesis sure. God forgive me!

'I wrote a great deal; I wrote late at night. I was always thinking on the subject, walking about, wherever I was, everywhere. It thoroughly infected me. You are to remember that all the material ideas connected with it were more or less of the beautiful, the subject itself delightfully interesting, and I, then, without a care.'

He sighed heavily.

'I believe that every one who sets about writing in earnest does his work, as a friend of mine phrased it, *on* something—tea, or coffee, or tobacco. I suppose there is a material waste that must be hourly supplied in such occupations, or that we should grow too abstracted, and the mind, as it were, pass out of the body, unless it were reminded often of the connection by actual sensation. At all events I felt the want, and I supplied it. Tea was my companion—at first the ordinary black tea, made in the usual way, not too strong: but I drank a good deal, and increased its strength as I went on. I never experienced an uncomfortable symptom from it. I began to take a little green tea. I found the effect pleasanter, it cleared and intensified the power of thought so. I had come to take it frequently, but not stronger than one might take it for pleasure. I wrote a great deal out here, it was so quiet, and in this room. I used to sit up very late, and it became a habit with me to sip my tea—green tea—every now and then as my work proceeded. I had a little kettle on my table, that swung over a lamp, and made two or three times between eleven o'clock and two or three in the morning, my hours of going to bed. I used to go into town every day. I was not a monk, and, although I spent an hour or two in a library hunting up authorities and looking out lights upon my theme, I was in no morbid state as far as I can judge. I met my friends pretty much as usual and enjoyed their society, and, on the whole, existence had never been, I think, so pleasant before.

'I had met with a man who had some odd books, German editions in medieval Latin, and I was only too happy to be permitted access to them. This obliging person's books were in the City, a very out-of-the-way part of it. I had rather out-stayed my intended hour, and, on coming out, seeing no cab near, I was tempted to get into the omnibus which used to drive past this house. It was darker than this by the time the 'bus had reached an old house you may have remarked, with four poplars at each side of the door, and there the last passenger but myself got out. We drove along rather faster. It was twilight now. I leaned back in my corner next the door, ruminating pleasantly.

'The interior of the omnibus was nearly dark. I had observed in the corner opposite to me at the other side, and at the end next the horses, two small circular reflections, as it seemed to me of a reddish light. They were about two inches apart, and about the size of those small brass buttons that yachting men used to put upon their jackets. I began to speculate, as listless men will, upon this trifle, as it seemed. From what centre did that faint but deep red light come, and from what—glass beads, buttons, toy decorations

—was it reflected? We were lumbering along gently, having nearly a mile still to go. I had not solved the puzzle, and it became in another minute more odd, for these two luminous points, with a sudden jerk, descended nearer the floor, keeping still their relative distance and horizontal position, and then, as suddenly, they rose to the level of the seat on which I was sitting, and I saw them no more.

'My curiosity was now really excited, and, before I had time to think, I saw again these two dull lamps, again together near the floor; again they disappeared, and again in their old corner I saw them.

'So, keeping my eyes upon them, I edged quietly up my own side, towards the end at which I still saw these tiny discs of red.

'There was very little light in the 'bus. It was nearly dark. I leaned forward to aid my endeavour to discover what these little circles really were. They shifted their position a little as I did so. I began now to perceive an outline of something black, and I soon saw, with tolerable distinctness, the outline of a small black monkey, pushing its face forward in mimicry to meet mine; those were its eyes, and I now dimly saw its teeth grinning at me.

'I drew back, not knowing whether it might not meditate a spring. I fancied that one of the passengers had forgot his ugly pet, and wishing to ascertain something of its temper, though not caring to trust my fingers to it, I poked my umbrella softly towards it. It remained immovable—up to it—*through* it. For through it, and back and forward it passed, without the slightest resistance.

'I can't, in the least, convey to you the kind of horror that I felt. When I had ascertained that the thing was an illusion, as I then supposed, there came a misgiving about myself and a terror that fascinated me in impotence to remove my gaze from the eyes of the brute for some moments. As I looked it made a little skip back, quite into the corner, and I, in a panic, found myself at the door, having put my head out, drawing deep breaths of the outer air, and staring at the lights and trees we were passing, too glad to reassure myself of reality.

'I stopped the 'bus, and got out. I perceived the man look oddly at me as I paid him. I daresay there was something unusual in my looks and manner, for I had never felt so strangely before.

VII
THE JOURNEY: FIRST STAGE

'When the omnibus drove on, and I was alone upon the road, I looked carefully round to ascertain whether the monkey had followed me. To my indescribable relief I saw it nowhere. I can't describe easily what a shock I had received, and my sense of genuine gratitude on finding myself, as I supposed, quite rid of it.

'I had got out a little before we reached this house, two or three hundred steps. A brick wall runs along the footpath, and inside the wall is a hedge of yew, or some dark evergreen of that kind, and within that again the row of fine trees which you may have remarked as you came.

'This brick wall is about as high as my shoulder, and happening to raise my eyes I saw the monkey, with that stooping gait, on all fours, walking or creeping, close beside me on top of the wall. I stopped, looking at it with a feeling of loathing and horror. As I stopped so did it. It sat up on the wall with its long hands on its knees looking at me. There was not light enough to see it much more than in outline, nor was it dark enough to bring the peculiar light of its eyes into strong relief. I still saw, however, that red foggy light plainly enough. It did not show its teeth, nor exhibit any sign of irritation, but seemed jaded and sulky, and was observing me steadily.

'I drew back into the middle of the road. It was an unconscious recoil, and there I stood, still looking at it. It did not move.

'With an instinctive determination to try something—anything, I turned about and walked briskly towards town, with askance look, all the time watching the movements of the beast. It crept swiftly along the wall, at exactly my pace.

'Where the wall ends, near the turn of the road, it came down, and with a wiry spring or two brought itself close to my feet, and continued to keep up with me as I quickened my pace. It was at my left side, so close to my leg that I felt every moment as if I should tread upon it.

'The road was quite deserted and silent, and it was darker every moment. I stopped dismayed and bewildered, turning, as I did so, the other way—I mean towards this house, away from which I had been walking. When I stood still the monkey drew back to a distance of, I suppose, about five or six yards, and remained stationary, watching me.

'I had been more agitated than I have said. I had read, of course, as everyone has, something about "spectral illusions", as you physicians term the phenomena of such cases. I considered my situation, and looked my misfortune in the face.

'These affections, I had read, are sometimes transitory and sometimes obstinate. I had read of cases in which the appearance, at first harmless, had, step by step, degenerated into something direful and insupportable, and ended by wearing its victim out. Still, as I stood there, but for my bestial companion quite alone, I tried to comfort myself by repeating again and again the assurance, "the thing is purely disease, a well-known physical affection, as distinctly as small-pox or neuralgia. Doctors are all agreed on that, philosophy demonstrates it. I must not be a fool. I've been sitting up too late, and I daresay my digestion is quite wrong, and, with God's help, I shall be all right, and this is but a symptom of nervous dyspepsia." Did I believe all this? Not one word of it, no more than any other miserable being ever did who is once seized and riveted in this satanic captivity. Against my convictions, I might say my knowledge, I was simply bullying myself into a false courage.

'I now walked homeward. I had only a few hundred yards to go. I had forced myself into a sort of resignation, but I had not got over the sickening shock and the flurry of the first certainty of my misfortune.

'I made up my mind to pass the night at home. The brute moved close beside me, and I fancied there was the sort of anxious drawing toward the house, which one sees in tired horses or dogs, sometimes, as they come toward home.

'I was afraid to go into town, I was afraid of anyone's seeing and recognizing me. I was conscious of any irrepressible agitation in my manner. Also, I was afraid of any violent change in my habits, such as going to a place of amusement, or walking from home in order to fatigue myself. At the hall door it waited till I mounted the steps, and when the door was opened entered with me.

'I drank no tea that night. I got cigars and some brandy and water. My idea was that I should act upon my material system, and by living for a while in sensation apart from thought, send myself forcibly, as it were, into a new groove. I came up here to this drawing-room. I sat just here. The monkey then got upon a small table that then stood *there*. It looked dazed and languid. An irrepressible uneasiness as to its movements kept my eyes always upon it. Its eyes were half closed, but I could see them glow. It was looking steadily at me. In all situations, at all hours, it is awake and looking at me. That never changes.

'I shall not continue in detail my narrative of this particular night. I shall describe, rather, the phenomena of the first year, which never varied essentially. I shall describe the monkey as it appeared in daylight. In the dark, as you shall presently hear, there are peculiarities. It is a small monkey, perfectly black. It had only one peculiarity—a character of malignity—unfathomable malignity. During the first year it looked sullen and sick. But this character of intense malice and vigilance was always underlying that surly languor. During all that time it acted as if on a plan of giving me as little trouble as was consistent with watching me. Its eyes were never off me. I have never lost sight of it, except in my sleep, light or dark, day or night, since it came here, excepting when it withdraws for some weeks at a time, unaccountably.

'In total dark it is visible as in daylight. I do not mean merely its eyes. It is *all* visible distinctly in a halo that resembles a glow of red embers, and which accompanies it in all its movements.

'When it leaves me for a time it is always at night, in the dark, and in the same way. It grows at first uneasy, and then furious, and then advances towards me, grinning and shaking, its paws clenched, and, at the same time, there comes the appearance of fire in the grate. I never have any fire. I can't sleep in the room where there is any—and it draws nearer and nearer to the chimney, quivering, it seems, with rage, and when its fury rises to the highest pitch it springs into the grate, and up the chimney, and I see it no more.

'When first this happened I thought I was released. I was now a new man. A day passed—a night—and no return, and a blessed week—a week—another week. I was always on my knees, Dr Hesselius, always, thanking God and praying. A whole month passed of liberty; but, on a sudden, it was with me again.

VIII
THE SECOND STAGE

'It was with me, and the malice which before was torpid under a sullen exterior was now active. It was perfectly unchanged in every other respect. This new energy was apparent in its activity and its looks, and soon in other ways.

'For a time, you will understand, the change was shown only in an increased vivacity, and an air of menace, as if it was always brooding over some atrocious plan. Its eyes, as before, were never off me.'

'Is it here now?' I asked.

'No,' he replied, 'it has been absent exactly a fortnight and a day—fifteen days. It has sometimes been away so long as nearly two months, once for three. Its absence always exceeds a fortnight, although it may be but by a single day. Fifteen days having past since I saw it last, it may return now at any moment.'

'Is its return,' I asked, 'accompanied by any peculiar manifestation?'

'Nothing—no,' he said. 'It is simply with me again. On lifting my eyes from a book, or turning my head, I see it, as usual, looking at me, and then it remains, as before, for its appointed time. I have never told so much and so minutely before to anyone.'

I perceived that he was agitated, and looking like death, and he repeatedly applied his handkerchief to his forehead; I suggested that he might be tired, and told him that I would call, with pleasure, in the morning, but he said:

'No, if you don't mind hearing it all now. I have got so far, and I should prefer making one effort of it. When I spoke to Dr Harley, I had nothing like so much to tell. You are a philosophic physician. You give spirit its proper rank. If this thing is real—'

He paused, looking at me with agitated inquiry.

'We can discuss it by-and-by, and very fully. I will give you all I think,' I answered, after an interval.

'Well—very well. If it is anything real, I say, it is prevailing, little by little, and drawing me more interiorly into hell. Optic nerves, he talked of. Ah! well—there are other nerves of communication. May God Almighty help me! You shall hear.

'Its power of action, I tell you, had increased. Its malice became, in a way, aggressive. About two years ago, some questions that were pending between me and the bishop having been settled, I went down to my parish in Warwickshire, anxious to find occupation in my profession. I was not prepared for what happened, although I have since thought I might have apprehended something like it. The reason of my saying so is this—'

He was beginning to speak with a great deal more effort and reluctance, and sighed often, and seemed at times nearly overcome. But at this time his manner was not agitated. It was more like that of a sinking patient, who has given himself up.

'Yes, but I will first tell you about Kenlis, my parish.

'It was with me when I left this place for Dawlbridge. It was my silent travelling companion, and it remained with me at the vicarage. When I entered on the discharge of my duties, another change took place. The thing exhibited an atrocious determination to thwart me. It was with me in the church—in the reading-desk—in the pulpit—within the communion rails. At last it reached this extremity, that while I was reading to the congregation it would spring upon the open book and squat there, so that I was unable to see the page. This happened more than once.

'I left Dawlbridge for a time. I placed myself in Dr Harley's hands. I did everything he told me. He gave my case a great deal of thought. It interested him, I think. He seemed successful. For nearly three months I was perfectly free from a return. I began to think I was safe. With his full assent I returned to Dawlbridge.

'I travelled in a chaise. I was in good spirits. I was more—I was happy and grateful. I was returning, as I thought, delivered from a dreadful hallucination, to the scene of duties which I longed to enter upon. It was a beautiful sunny evening, everything looked serene and cheerful, and I was delighted. I remember looking out of the window to see the spire of my church at Kenlis among the trees, at the point where one has the earliest view of it. It is exactly where the little stream that bounds the parish passes under the road by a culvert; and where it emerges at the road-side a stone with an old inscription is placed. As we passed this point I drew my head in and sat down, and in the corner of the chaise was the monkey.

'For a moment I felt faint, and then quite wild with despair and horror. I called to the driver, and got out, and sat down at the road-side, and prayed to God silently for mercy. A despairing resignation supervened. My companion was with me as I re-entered the vicarage. The same persecution followed. After a short struggle I submitted, and soon I left the place.

'I told you,' he said, 'that the beast has before this become in certain ways aggressive. I will explain a little. It seemed to be actuated by intense and increasing fury whenever I said my prayers, or even meditated prayer. It amounted at last to a dreadful interruption. You will ask, how could a silent immaterial phantom effect that? It was thus, whenever I meditated praying; it was always before me, and nearer and nearer.

'It used to spring on a table, on the back of a chair, on the chimney-piece, and slowly to swing itself from side to side, looking at me all the time. There is in its motion an indefinable power to dissipate thought, and to contract one's attention to that monotony, till the ideas shrink, as it were, to a point, and at last to nothing—and unless I had started up, and shook off the catalepsy, I have felt as if my mind were on the point of losing itself. There are other ways,' he sighed heavily; 'thus, for instance, while I pray with my eyes closed, it comes closer and closer, and I see it. I know it is not to be accounted for physically, but I do actually see it, though my lids are closed, and so it rocks my mind, as it were, and overpowers me, and I am obliged to rise from my knees. If you had ever yourself known this, you would be acquainted with desperation.'

IX
THE THIRD STAGE

'I see, Dr Hesselius, that you don't lose one word of my statement. I need not ask you to listen specially to what I am now going to tell you. They talk of the optic nerves, and of spectral illusions, as if the organ of sight was the only point assailable by the influences that have fastened upon me—I know better. For two years in my direful case that limitation prevailed. But as food is taken in softly at the lips, and then brought under the teeth, as the tip of the little finger caught in a mill crank will draw in the hand, and the arm, and the whole body, so the miserable mortal who has been once caught firmly by the end of the finest fibre of his nerve is drawn in and in, by the enormous machinery of hell, until he is as I am. Yes, Doctor, as *I* am, for while I talk to you, and implore relief, I feel that my prayer is for the impossible, and my pleading with the inexorable.'

I endeavoured to calm his visibly increasing agitation, and told him that he must not despair.

While we talked the night had overtaken us. The filmy moonlight was wide over the scene which the window commanded, and I said:

'Perhaps you would prefer having candles. This light, you know, is odd. I should wish you, as much as possible, under your usual conditions, while I make my diagnosis, shall I call it—otherwise I don't care.'

'All lights are the same to me,' he said. 'Except when I read or write, I care not if night were perpetual. I am going to tell you what happened about a year ago. The thing began to speak to me.'

'Speak! How do you mean—speak as a man does, do you mean?'

'Yes; speak in words and consecutive sentences, with perfect coherence and articulation; but there is a peculiarity. It is not like the tone of a human voice. It is not by my ears it reaches me—it comes like a singing through my head.

'This faculty, the power of speaking to me, will be my undoing. It won't let me pray, it interrupts me with dreadful blasphemies. I dare not go on, I could not. Oh! Doctor, can the skill, and thought, and prayers of man avail me nothing!'

'You must promise me, my dear sir, not to trouble yourself with unnecessarily exciting thoughts; confine yourself strictly to the narrative of *facts*; and recollect, above all, that even if the thing that infests you be, as you seem to suppose, a reality with an actual independent life and will, yet it can have no power to hurt you, unless it be given from above: its access to your senses depends mainly upon your physical condition—this is, under God, your comfort and reliance: we are all alike environed. It is only that in your case, the "*paries*", the veil of the flesh, the screen, is a little out of repair, and sights and sounds are transmitted. We must enter on a new course, sir—be encouraged. I'll give to-night to the careful consideration of the whole case.'

'You are very good, sir; you think it worth trying, you don't give me quite up; but, sir, you don't know, it is gaining such an influence over me: it orders me about, it is such a tyrant, and I'm growing so helpless. May God deliver me!'

'It orders you about—of course you mean by speech?'

'Yes, yes; it is always urging me to crimes, to injure others, or myself. You see, Doctor, the situation is urgent, it is indeed. When I was in Shropshire, a few weeks ago' (Mr Jennings was speaking rapidly and trembling now, holding my arm with one hand, and looking in my face), 'I went out one day with a party of friends for a walk: my persecutor, I tell you, was with me at the time. I lagged behind the rest: the country near the Dee, you know, is beautiful. Our path happened to lie near a coal mine, and at the verge of the wood is a perpendicular shaft, they say, a hundred and fifty feet deep. My niece had remained behind with me—she knows, of course, nothing of the nature of my sufferings. She knew, however, that I had been ill, and was low, and she remained to prevent my being quite alone. As we loitered slowly on together, the brute that accompanied me was urging me to throw myself down the shaft. I tell you now—oh, sir, think of it!—the one consideration that saved me from that hideous death was the fear lest the shock of witnessing the occurrence should be too much for the poor girl. I asked her to go on and take her walk with her friends, saying that I could go no further. She made excuses, and the more I urged her the firmer she became. She looked doubtful and frightened. I suppose there was something in my looks or manner that alarmed her; but she would not go, and that literally saved me. You had no idea, sir, that a living man could be made so abject a slave of Satan,' he said, with a ghastly groan and a shudder.

There was a pause here, and I said, 'You *were* preserved nevertheless. It was the act of God. You are in His hands and in the power of no other being: be therefore confident for the future.'

X
HOME

I made him have candles lighted, and saw the room looking cheery and inhabited before I left him. I told him that he must regard his illness strictly as one dependent on physical, though *subtle* physical causes. I told him that he had evidence of God's care and love in the deliverance which he had just described, and that I had perceived with pain that he seemed to regard its peculiar features as indicating that he had been delivered over to spiritual reprobation. Than such a conclusion nothing could be, I insisted, less warranted; and not only so, but more contrary to facts, as disclosed in his mysterious deliverance from that murderous influence during his Shropshire excursion. First, his niece had been retained by his side without his intending to keep her near him; and, secondly, there had been infused into his mind an irresistible repugnance to execute the dreadful suggestion in her presence.

As I reasoned this point with him, Mr Jennings wept. He seemed comforted. One promise I exacted, which was that should the monkey at any time return, I should be sent for immediately; and, repeating my assurance that I would give neither time nor thought to any other subject until I had thoroughly investigated his case, and that to-morrow he should hear the result, I took my leave.

Before getting into the carriage I told the servant that his master was far from well, and that he should make a point of frequently looking into his room.

My own arrangements I made with a view to being quite secure from interruption.

I merely called at my lodgings, and with a travelling-desk and carpet-bag set off in a hackney carriage for an inn, about two miles out of town, called 'The Horns', a very quiet and comfortable house with good thick walls. And there I resolved, without the possibility of intrusion or distraction, to devote some hours of the night, in my comfortable sitting-room, to Mr Jennings' case, and so much of the morning as it might require.

[There occurs here a careful note of Dr Hesselius' opinion upon the case, and of the habits, dietary, and medicines which he prescribed. It is curious—some persons would say mystical. But, on the whole, I doubt whether it would sufficiently interest a reader of the kind I am likely to meet with, to warrant its being here reprinted. The whole letter was plainly written at the inn where he had hid himself for the occasion. The next letter is dated from his town lodgings.]

I left town for the inn where I slept last night at half-past nine, and did not arrive at my room in town until one o'clock this afternoon. I found a letter in Mr Jennings' hand upon my table. It had not come by post, and, on inquiry, I learned that Mr Jennings' servant had brought it, and, on learning that I was not to return until to-day and that no one could tell him my address, he seemed very uncomfortable, and said that his orders from his master were that he was not to return without an answer.

I opened the letter and read:

'DEAR DR HESSELIUS.—It is here. You had not been an hour gone when it returned. It is speaking. It knows all that has happened. It knows everything—it knows you, and is frantic and atrocious. It reviles. I send you this. It knows every word I have written—I write. This I promised, and I therefore write, but I fear very confused, very incoherently. I am so interrupted, disturbed.

Ever yours, sincerely yours,
ROBERT LYNDER JENNINGS.'

'When did this come?' I asked.

'About eleven last night: the man was here again, and has been here three times to-day. The last time is about an hour since.'

Thus answered, and with the notes I had made upon his case in my pocket, I was in a few minutes driving towards Richmond to see Mr Jennings.

I by no means, as you perceive, despaired of Mr Jennings' case. He had himself remembered and applied, though quite in a mistaken way, the principle which I lay down in my *Metaphysical Medicine*, and which governs all such cases. I was about to apply it in earnest. I was profoundly interested, and very anxious to see and examine him while the 'enemy' was actually present.

I drove up to the sombre house, and ran up the steps and knocked. The door, in a little time, was opened by a tall woman in black silk. She looked ill, and as if she had been crying. She curtseyed, and heard my question, but she did not answer. She turned her face away, extending her hand towards two men who were coming downstairs; and thus having, as it were, tacitly made me over to them, she passed through a side-door hastily and shut it.

The man who was nearest the hall, I at once accosted, but being now close to him I was shocked to see that both his hands were covered with blood.

I drew back a little, and the man, passing downstairs, merely said in a low tone, 'Here's the servant, sir.'

The servant had stopped on the stairs, confounded and dumb at seeing me. He was rubbing his hands in a handkerchief, and it was steeped in blood.

'Jones, what is it? what has happened?' I asked, while a sickening suspicion overpowered me.

The man asked me to come up to the lobby. I was beside him in a moment, and, frowning and pallid, with contracted eyes, he told me the horror which I already half guessed.

His master had made away with himself.

I went upstairs with him to the room—what I saw there I won't tell you. He had cut his throat with his razor. It was a frightful gash. The two men had laid him on the bed, and composed his limbs. It had happened, as the immense pool of blood on the floor declared, at some distance between the bed and the window. There was carpet round his bed, and a carpet under his dressing-table, but none of the rest of the floor, for the man said he did not like a carpet in his bedroom. In this sombre and now terrible room, one of the great elms that darkened the house was slowly moving the shadow of one of its great boughs upon this dreadful floor.

I beckoned to the servant, and we went downstairs together. I turned off the hall into an old-fashioned panelled room, and there standing, I heard all the servant had to tell. It was not a great deal.

'I concluded, sir, from your words, and looks, sir, as you left last night, that you thought my master seriously ill. I thought it might be that you were afraid of a fit, or something. So I attended very close to your directions. He sat up late, till past three o'clock. He was not writing or reading. He was talking a great deal to himself, but that was nothing unusual. At about that hour I assisted him to undress, and left him in his slippers and dressing-gown. I went back softly in about half-an-hour. He was in his bed, quite undressed, and a pair of candles lighted on the table beside his bed. He was leaning on his elbow, and looking out at the other side of the bed when I came in. I asked him if he wanted anything, and he said "No".

'I don't know whether it was what you said to me, sir, or something a little unusual about him, but I was uneasy, uncommon uneasy about him last night.

'In another half hour, or it might be a little more, I went up again. I did not hear him talking as before. I opened the door a little. The candles were both out, which was not usual. I had a bedroom candle, and I let the light in, a little bit, looking softly round. I saw him sitting in that chair beside the dressing-table with his clothes on again. He turned round and looked at me. I thought it strange he should get up and dress, and put out the candles to sit in the dark, that way. But I only asked him again if I could do anything for him. He said, "No", rather sharp, I thought. I asked if I might light the candles, and he said, "Do as you like, Jones." So I lighted them, and I lingered about the room, and he said, "Tell me truth, Jones; why did you come again—you did not hear anyone cursing?" "No, sir," I said, wondering what he could mean.

' "No," said he, after me, "of course, no"; and I said to him, "Wouldn't it be well, sir, you went to bed? It's just five o'clock"; and he said nothing but, "Very likely; good-night, Jones." So I went, sir, but in less than an hour I came again. The door was fast, and he heard me, and called as I thought from the bed to know what I wanted, and he desired me not to disturb him again. I lay down and slept for a little. It must have been between six and seven when I went up again. The door was still fast, and he made no answer, so I did not like to disturb him, and thinking he was asleep I left him till nine. It was his custom to ring when he wished me to come, and I had no particular hour for calling him. I tapped very gently, and getting no answer I stayed away a good while, supposing he was getting some rest then. It was not till eleven o'clock I grew really uncomfortable about him—for at the latest he was never, that I could remember, later than half-past ten. I got no answer. I knocked and called, and still no answer. So not being able to force the door, I called Thomas from the stables, and together we forced it, and found him in the shocking way you saw.'

Jones had no more to tell. Poor Mr Jennings was very gentle and very kind. All his people were fond of him. I could see that the servant was very much moved.

So, dejected and agitated, I passed from that terrible house, and its dark canopy of elms, and I hope I shall never see it more. While I write to you I feel like a man who has but half waked from a frightful and monotonous dream. My memory rejects the picture with incredulity and horror. Yet I know it is true. It is the story of the process of a poison, a poison which excites the reciprocal action of spirit and nerve, and paralyses the tissue that separates those cognate functions of the senses, the external and the interior. Thus we find strange bed-fellows, and the mortal and immortal prematurely make acquaintance.

CONCLUSION
A WORD FOR THOSE WHO SUFFER

My dear Van L—, you have suffered from an affection similar to that which I have just described. You twice complained of a return of it.

Who, under God, cured you? Your humble servant, Martin Hesselius. Let me rather adopt the more emphasized piety of a certain good old French surgeon of three hundred years ago: 'I treated, and God cured you.'

Come, my friend, you are not to be hippish. Let me tell you a fact.

I have met with, and treated, as my book shows, fifty-seven cases of this kind of vision, which I term indifferently 'sublimated', 'precocious', and 'interior'.

There is another class of affections which are truly termed— though commonly confounded with those which I describe— spectral illusions. These latter I look upon as being no less simply curable than a cold in the head or a trifling dyspepsia.

It is those which rank in the first category that test our promptitude of thought. Fifty-seven such cases have I encountered, neither more nor less. And in how many of these have I failed? In no one single instance.

There is no one affliction of mortality more easily and certainly reducible, with a little patience and a rational confidence in the physician. With these simple conditions I look upon the cure as absolutely certain.

You are to remember that I had not even commenced to treat Mr Jennings' case. I have not any doubt that I should have cured him perfectly in eighteen months, or possibly it might have extended to two years. Some cases are very rapidly curable, others extremely tedious. Every intelligent physician who will give thought and diligence to the task will effect a cure.

You know my tract on *The Cardinal Functions of the Brain.* I there, by the evidence of innumerable facts, prove, as I think, the high probability of a circulation, arterial and venous in its mechanism, through the nerves. Of this system, thus considered, the brain is the heart. The fluid, which is propagated hence through one class of nerves, returns in an altered state through another, and the nature of that fluid is spiritual, though not immaterial, any more than, as I before remarked, light or electricity are so.

By various abuses, among which the habitual use of such agents as green tea is one, this fluid may be affected as to its quality, but it is more frequently disturbed as to equilibrium. This fluid being that which we have in common with spirits, a congestion found upon the masses of brain or nerve, connected with the interior sense, forms a surface unduly exposed, on which embodied spirits may operate: communication is thus more or less effectually established. Between this brain circulation and the heart circulation there is an intimate sympathy. The seat, or rather the instrument of exterior vision, is the eye. The seat of interior vision is the nervous tissue and brain, immediately about and above the eyebrow. You remember how effectually I dissipated your pictures by the simple application of iced eau-de-cologne. Few cases, however, can be treated exactly alike with anything like rapid success. Cold acts powerfully as a repellant of the nervous fluid. Long enough continued it will even produce that permanent insensibility which we call numbness, and a little longer, muscular as well as sensational paralysis.

I have not, I repeat, the slightest doubt that I should have first dimmed and ultimately sealed that inner eye which Mr Jennings had inadvertently opened. The same senses are opened in delirium tremens, and entirely shut up again when the over-action of the cerebral heart, and the prodigious nervous congestions that attend it, are terminated by a decided change in the state of the body. It is by acting steadily upon the body, by a simple process, that this result is produced—and inevitably produced—I have never yet failed.

Poor Mr Jennings made away with himself. But that catastrophe was the result of a totally different malady, which, as it were, projected itself upon that disease which was established. His case was in the distinctive manner a complication, and the complaint under which he really succumbed was hereditary suicidal mania. Poor Mr Jennings I cannot call a patient of mine, for I had not even begun to treat his case, and he had not yet given me, I am convinced, his full and unreserved confidence. If the patient do not array himself on the side of the disease, his cure is certain.

Albert Nobbs

I

When we went up to Dublin in the 'sixties, Alec, we always put up at Morrison's Hotel, a big family hotel at the corner of Dawson Street, one that was well patronised by the gentry from all over Ireland, my father paying his bill every six months when he was able, which wasn't very often, for what with racing stables and elections following one after the other, Moore Hall wasn't what you'd call overflowing with money. Now that I come to think of it, I can see Morrison's as clearly almost as I do Moore Hall: the front door opening into a short passage, with some half-dozen steps leading up into the house, the glass doors of the coffee-room showing through the dimness, and in front of the visitor a big staircase running up to the second landing. I remember long passages on the second landing, and half-way down these passages was the well. I don't know if it's right to speak of the well of a staircase, but I used to think of it as a well. It was always being drummed into me that I mustn't climb on to the banisters, a thing I wished to do, but was afraid to get astride of them, lest I should lose my head and fall all the way down to the ground floor. There was nothing to stop me from reaching it, if I lost my balance, except a few gas lamps. I think that both the long passages led to minor stairs, but I never followed either lest I should miss my way. A very big building was Morrison's Hotel, with passages running hither and thither, and little flights of stairs in all kinds of odd corners by which the visitors climbed to their apartments, and it needed all my attention to remember the way to our rooms on the second floor. We were always on the second floor in a big sitting-room overlooking College Green, and I remember the pair of windows, their lace curains and their rep curtains, better than the passages, and better than the windows I can remember myself looking through the pane, interested in the coal carts going by, the bell hitched on to the horse's collar jangling all the way down the street, the coalman himself sitting with his legs hanging over the shafts, driving from the wrong side and looking up at the windows to see if he could spy out an order. Fine horses were in these coal carts, stepping out as well as those in our own carriage.

I'm telling you these things for the pleasure of looking back and nothing else. I can see the sitting-room and myself as plainly as I can see the mountains beyond, in some ways plainer, and the waiter that used to attend on us, I can see him, though not as plainly as I see you, Alec; but I'm more knowledgeable of him, if you understand me rightly, and to this day I can recall the frights he gave me when he came behind me, awaking me from my dream of a coalman's life—what he said is forgotten, but his squeaky voice remains in my ears. He seemed to be always laughing at me, showing long, yellow teeth, and I used to be afraid to open the sitting-room door, for I'd be sure to find him waiting on the landing, his napkin thrown over his right shoulder. I think I was afraid he'd pick me up and kiss me. As the whole of my story is about him, perhaps I'd better describe him more fully, and to do that I will tell you that he was a tall, scraggy fellow, with big hips sticking out, and a long, thin throat. It was his throat that frightened me as much as anything about him, unless it was his nose, which was a great high one, or his melancholy eyes, which were pale blue and very small, deep in the head. He was old, but how old I cannot say, for everybody except children seems old to children. He was the ugliest thing I'd seen out of a fairy-book, and I'd beg not to be left alone in the sitting-room; and I'm sure I often asked my father and mother to take another set of rooms, which they never did, for they liked Albert Nobbs. And the guests liked him, and the proprietress liked him, as well she might, for he was the most dependable servant in the hotel: no running round to public-houses and coming back with the smell of whisky and tobacco upon him; no rank pipe in his pocket; and of all, no playing the fool with the maid-servants. Nobody had ever been heard to say he had seen Albert out with one of them—a queer, hobgoblin sort of fellow that they mightn't have cared to be seen with, but all the same it seemed to them funny that he should never propose to walk out with one of them. I've heard the hall-porter say it was hard to understand a man living without taking pleasure in something outside of his work. Holidays he never asked for, and when Mrs Baker pressed him to go to the salt water for a week, he'd try to rake up an excuse for not going away, asking if it wasn't true that the Blakes, the Joyces, and the Ruttledges were coming up to town, saying that he didn't like to be away, so used were they to him and he to them. A strange life his was, and mysterious, though every hour of it was before them, saving the hours he was asleep, which weren't many, for he was no great sleeper. From the time he got up in the morning till he went to bed at night he was before their eyes, running up and down the staircase, his napkin over his arm, taking orders with cheerfulness, as if an order were as good as a half-crown tip to him, always good-humoured, and making amends for his lack of interest in other people by his willingness to oblige. No one had ever heard him object to doing anything he was asked to do, or even put forward an excuse for not being able to do it. In fact, his willingness to oblige was so notorious in the hotel that Mrs Baker (the proprietress of Morrison's Hotel at the time) could hardly believe she was listening to him when he began to stumble from one excuse to another for not sharing his bed with Hubert Page, and this after she had told him that his bed was Page's only chance of getting a stretch that night. All the other waiters were married men and went home to their wives. You see, Alec, it was Punchestown week, and beds are as scarce in Dublin that week as diamonds are on the slopes of Croagh Patrick.

But you haven't told me yet who Page was, Alec interjected, and I thought reprovingly. I'm just coming to him, I answered. Hubert Page was a house-painter, well known and well liked by Mrs Baker. He came over every season, and was always welcome at Morrison's Hotel, and so pleasant were his manners that one forgot the smell of his paint. It is hardly saying too much to say that when Hubert Page had finished his job everybody in the hotel, men and women alike, missed the pleasant sight of this young man going to and fro in his suit of hollands, the long coat buttoned loosely to his figure with large bone buttons, going to and fro about his work, up and down the passages, with a sort of lolling, idle gait that attracted and pleased the eye—a young man that would seem preferable to most men if a man had to choose a bed-fellow, yet seemingly the very one that Albert Nobbs couldn't abide lying down with, a dislike that Mrs Baker could understand so little that she stood staring at her confused and embarrassed waiter, who was still seeking excuses for his dislike to share his bed with Hubert Page. I suppose you fully understand, she said, that Page is leaving for Belfast by the morning train, and has come over here to ask us for a bed, there not being one at the hotel in which he is working? Albert answered that he understood well enough, but was thinking—He began again to fumble with words. Now, what are you trying to say? Mrs Baker asked, and rather sharply. My bed is full of lumps, Albert answered. Your mattress full of lumps! the proprietress rapped out; why, your mattress was repicked and buttoned six months ago, and came back as good as any mattress in the hotel. What kind of story are you telling me? So it was, ma'am, so it was, Albert mumbled, and it was some time before he got out his next excuse: he was a very light sleeper and had never slept with anybody before and was sure he wouldn't close his eyes; not that that would matter much, but his sleeplessness might keep Mr Page awake. Mr Page would get a better stretch on one of the sofas in the coffee-room than in my bed, I'm thinking, Mrs Baker. A better stretch on the sofa in the coffee-room? Mrs Baker repeated angrily. I don't understand you, not a little bit; and she stood staring at the two men, so dissimilar. But, ma'am, I wouldn't be putting Mr Nobbs to the inconvenience of my company, the house-painter began. The night is a fine one; I'll keep myself warm with a sharp walk, and the train starts early. You'll do nothing of the kind, Page, she answered; and seeing that Mrs Baker was now very angry Albert thought it time to give in, and without more ado he began to assure them both that he'd be glad of Mr Page's company in his bed. I should think so indeed! interjected Mrs Baker. But I'm a light sleeper, he added. We've heard that before, Albert! Of course, if Mr Page is pleased to share my bed, Albert continued, I shall be very glad. If Mr Nobbs doesn't like my company I should—Don't say another word, Albert whispered, you'll only set her against me. Come upstairs at once; it'll be all right. Come along.

Good-night, ma'am, and I hope—No inconvenience whatever, Page, Mrs Baker answered. This way, Mr Page, Albert cried; and as soon as they were in the room he said: I hope you aren't going to cut up rough at anything I've said; it isn't at all as Mrs Baker put it. I'm glad enough of your company, but you see, as I've never slept with anybody in my life, it may be that I shall be tossing about all night, keeping you awake. Well, if it's to be like that, Page answered, I might as well have a doze on the chair until it's time to go, and not trouble you at all. You won't be giving me any trouble; what I'm afraid of is—but enough has been said; we have to lie down together, whether we like it or whether we don't, for if Mrs Baker heard that we hadn't been in the same bed together all the fault would lie with me. I'd be sent out of the hotel in double-quick time. But how can she know? Page cried. It's been settled one way, so let us make no more fuss about it.

Albert began to undo his white neck-tie, saying he would try to lie quiet, and Page started pulling off his clothes, thinking he'd be well pleased to be out of the job of lying down with Albert. But he was so dog-tired that he couldn't think any more about whom he was to sleep with, only of the long days of twelve and thirteen hours he had been doing, with a walk to and from his work; only sleep mattered to him, and Albert saw him tumble into bed in the long shirt that he wore under his clothes, and lay himself down next to the wall. It would be better for him to lie on the outside, Albert said to himself, but he didn't like to say anything lest Page might get out of his bed in a fit of ill-humour; but Page, as I've said, was too tired to trouble himself which side of the bed he was to doss on. A moment after he was asleep, and Albert stood listening, his loosened tie dangling, till the heavy breathing from the bed told him that Page was sound asleep. To make full sure he approached the bed stealthily, and overlooking Page, said: Poor fellow, I'm glad he's in my bed, for he'll get a good sleep there and he wants it; and considering that things had fallen out better than he hoped for, he began to undress.

He must have fallen asleep at once, and soundly, for he awoke out of nothingness. Flea! he muttered, and a strong one, too. It must have come from the house-painter alongside of me; a flea will leave anyone to come to me. And turning round in bed he remembered the look of dismay that had appeared on the housemaids' faces yesterday on his telling them that no man would ever love their hides as much as a flea loved his, which was so true that he couldn't understand how it was that the same flea had taken so long to find him. Fleas must be as partial to him, he said, as they are to me. There it is again, trying to make up for lost time! and out went Albert's leg. I'm afraid I've awakened him, he said, but Hubert only turned over in the bed to sleep more soundly. It's a mercy indeed that he is so tired, Albert said, for if he wasn't very tired that last jump I gave would have awakened him. A moment after Albert was nipped again by another flea, or by the same one, he couldn't tell;

he thought it must be a second one, so vigorous was the bite, and he was hard put to it to keep his nails off the spots. I shall only make them worse if I scratch, he said, and he strove to lie quiet. But the torment was too great. I've got to get up, he muttered, and raising himself up quietly, he listened. The striking of a match won't awaken him out of that sleep! and remembering where he had put the match-box, his hand was on it at once. The match flared up; he lighted the candle, and stood a while overlooking his bed-fellow. I'm safe, he said, and set himself to the task of catching the flea. There he is on the tail of my shirt, hardly able to move with all the blood he's taken from me. Now for the soap; and as he was about to dab it upon the blood-filled insect the painter awoke with a great yawn, and turning round, he said: Lord amassy! what is the meaning of this? Why, you're a woman!

If Albert had had the presence of mind to drop her shirt over her shoulders and to answer: You're dreaming, my man, Page might have turned over and fallen asleep and in the morning forgotten all about it, or thought he had been dreaming. But Albert hadn't a word in her chops. At last she began to blub. You won't tell on me, and ruin a poor man, will you, Mr Page? That is all I ask you, and on my knees I beg it. Get up from your knees, my good woman, said Hubert. My good woman! Albert repeated, for she had been about so long as a man that she only remembered occasionally that she was a woman. My good woman, Hubert repeated, get up from your knees and tell me how long you have been playing this part. Ever since I was a girl, Albert answered. You won't tell upon me, will you, Mr Page, and prevent a poor woman from getting her living? Not likely, I've no thought of telling on you, but I'd like to hear how it all came about. How I went out as a youth to get my living? Yes; tell me the story, Hubert answered, for though I was very sleepy just now, the sleep has left my eyes and I'd like to hear it. But before you begin, tell me what you were doing with your shirt off. A flea, Albert answered. I suffer terribly from fleas, and you must have brought some in with you, Mr Page. I shall be covered in blotches in the morning. I'm sorry for that, Hubert said; but tell me how long ago it was that you became a man. Before you came to Dublin, of course? Oh, yes, long before. It is very cold, she said, and shuddering, dropped her shirt over her shoulders and pulled on her trousers.

II

It was in London, soon after the death of my old nurse, she began. You know I'm not Irish, Mr Page. My parents may have been, for all I know. The only one who knew who they were was my old nurse, and she never told me. Never told you! interjected Hubert. No, she never told me, though I often asked her, saying no good could come of holding it back from me. She might have told me before she died, but she died suddenly. Died suddenly, Hubert repeated, without telling you who you were! You'd better begin at the beginning.

I don't know how I'm to do that, for the story seems to me to be without a beginning; anyway I don't know the beginning. I was a bastard, and no one but my old nurse, who brought me up, knew who I was; she said she'd tell me some day, and she hinted more than once that my people were grand folk, and I know she had a big allowance from them for my education. Whoever they were, a hundred a year was paid to her for my keep and education, and all went well with us so long as my parents lived, but when they died the allowance was no longer paid, and my nurse and myself had to go out to work. It was all very sudden: one day the Reverend Mother (I got my education at a convent school) told me that Mrs Nobbs, my old nurse, had sent for me, and the first news I had on coming home was that my parents were dead and that we'd have to get our own living henceforth. There was no time for picking and choosing. We hadn't what would keep us until the end of the month in the house, so out we had to go in search of work; and the first job that came our way was looking after chambers in the Temple. We had three gentlemen to look after, so there was eighteen shillings a week between my old nurse and myself; the omnibus fares had to come out of these wages, and to save sixpence a day we went to live in Temple Lane. My old nurse didn't mind the lane; she had been a working woman all her life; but with me it was different, and the change was so great from the convent that I often thought I would sooner die than continue to live amid rough people. There was nothing wrong with them; they were honest enough; but they were poor, and when you are very poor you live like the animals, indecently, and life without decency is hardly bearable, so I thought. I've been through a great deal since in different hotels, and have become used to hard work, but even now I can't think of

Temple Lane without goose-flesh; and when Mrs Nobbs' brother
lost his berth (he'd been a bandmaster, a bugler, or something to do
with music in the country), my old nurse was obliged to give him
sixpence a day, and the drop from eighteen shillings to fourteen and
sixpence is a big one. My old nurse worried about the food, but it
was the rough men I worried about; the bandsman wouldn't leave
me alone, and many's the time I've waited until the staircase was
clear, afraid that if I met him or another that I'd be caught hold of
and held and pulled about. I was different then from what I am
now, and might have been tempted if one of them had been less
rough than the rest, and if I hadn't known I was a bastard; it was
that, I think, that kept me straight more than anything else, for I
had just begun to feel what a great misfortune it is for a poor girl to
find herself in the family way; no greater misfortune can befall
anyone in this world, but it would have been worse in my case, for I
should have known that I was only bringing another bastard into
the world.

I escaped being seduced in the lane, and in the chambers the
barristers had their own mistresses; pleasant and considerate men
they all were—pleasant to work for; and it wasn't until four o'clock
came and our work was over for the day that my heart sank, for
after four o'clock till we went to bed at night there was nothing for
us to do but to listen to the screams of drunken women; I don't
know which was the worser, the laughter or the curses.

One of the barristers we worked for was Mr Congreve; he had
chambers in Temple Gardens overlooking the river, and it was a
pleasure to us to keep his pretty things clean, never breaking one of
them; it was a pleasure for my old nurse as well as myself, myself
more than for her, for though I wasn't very sure of myself at the
time, looking back now I can see that I must have loved Mr
Congreve very dearly; and it couldn't be else, for I had come out of
a convent of nuns where I had been given a good education, where
all was good, quiet, refined and gentle, and Mr Congreve seemed in
many ways to remind me of the convent, for he never missed
Church; as rare for him to miss a service as for parson. There was
plenty of books in his chambers and he'd lend them to me, and talk
to me over his newspaper when I took in his breakfast, and ask
about the convent and what the nuns were like, and I'd stand in
front of him, my eyes fixed on him, not feeling the time going by. I
can see him now as plainly as if he were before me—very thin and

elegant, with long white hands, and beautifully dressed. Even in the old clothes that he wore of a morning there wasn't much fault to find; he wore old clothes more elegantly than any man in the Temple wore his new clothes. I used to know all his suits, as well I might, for it was my job to look after them, to brush them; and I used to spend a great deal more time than was needed taking out spots with benzine, arranging his neck-ties—he had fifty or sixty, all kinds—and seven or eight greatcoats. A real toff—my word he was that, but not one of those haughty ones too proud to give one a nod. He always smiled and nodded if we met under the clock, he on his way to the library and I returning to Temple Lane. I used to look round after him saying: He's got on the striped trousers and the embroidered waistcoat. Mr Congreve was a compensation for Temple Lane; he had promised to take me into his private service, and I was counting the days when I should leave Temple Lane, when one day I said to myself: Why, here's a letter from a woman. You see, Mr Congreve wasn't like the other young men in the Temple; I never found a hairpin in his bed, and if I had I shouldn't have thought as much of him as I did. Nice is in France, I said, and thought no more about the matter until another letter arrived from Nice. Now what can she be writing to him about? I asked, and thought no more about it until the third letter arrived. Yesterday is already more than half forgotten, but the morning I took in that last letter is always before me. And it was a few mornings afterwards that a box of flowers came for him. A parcel for you, sir, I said. He roused himself up in bed. For me? he cried, putting out his hand, and the moment he saw the writing, he said: Put the flowers in water. He knows all about it, I said to myself, and so overcome was I as I picked them up out of the box that a sudden faintness came over me, and my old nurse said: What is the matter with thee? She never guessed, and I couldn't have told her if I had wished to, for at the time it was no more than a feeling that so far as I was concerned all was over. Of course I never thought that Mr Congreve would look at me, and I don't know that I wanted him to, but I didn't want another woman about the place, and I seemed to know from that moment what was going to happen. She isn't far away now, in the train maybe, I said, as I went about my work, and these rooms will be mine no longer. Of course they never were mine, but you know what I mean.

A week later he said to me: There's a lady coming to luncheon here, and I remember the piercing that the words caused me; I can feel them here still; and Albert put her hand to her heart. Well, I had to serve the luncheon, working round the table and they not minding me at all, but sitting looking at each other lost in a sense of delight; the luncheon was forgotten. They don't want me waiting about, I thought. I knew all this, and said to myself in the kitchen: It's disgraceful, it's wicked, to lead a man into sin—for all my anger went out against the woman, and not against Mr Congreve; in my eyes he seemed to be nothing more than a victim of a designing woman; that is how I looked at it at the time, being but a youngster only just come from a convent school.

I don't think that anyone suffered more than I did in those days. It all seems very silly now when I look back upon it, but it was very real then. It does seem silly to tell that I used to lie awake all night thinking to myself that Mr Congreve was an elegant gentleman and I but a poor serving girl that he'd never look twice at, thinking of her only as somebody to go to the cellar for coal or to the kitchen to fetch his breakfast. I don't think I ever hoped he'd fall in love with me. It wasn't as bad as that. It was the hopelessness of it that set the tears streaming down my cheeks over my pillow, and I used to stuff the sheet into my mouth to keep back the sobs lest my old nurse should hear me; it wouldn't do to keep her awake, for she was very ill at that time; and soon afterwards she died, and then I was left alone, without a friend in the world. The only people I knew were the charwomen that lived in Temple Lane, and the bugler, who began to bully me, saying that I must continue to give him the same money he had had from my old nurse. He caught me on the stairs once and twisted my arm until I thought he'd broken it. The month after my old nurse's death till I went to earn my living as a waiter was the hardest time of all, and Mr Congreve's kindness seemed to hurt me more than anything. If only he'd spared me his kind words, and not spoken about the extra money he was going to give me for my attendance on this lady, I shouldn't have felt so much that they had lain side by side in the bed that I was making. She brought a dressing-gown to the chambers and some slippers, and then more luggage came along; and I think she must have guessed I was in love with Mr Congreve, for I heard them quarrelling—my name was mentioned; and I said: I can't put up with it any longer; whatever the next life may be like, it can't be worse than this one for me at least; and as I went to and fro between Temple Lane and the chambers in Temple Gardens I began to think how I might make away with myself. I don't know if you know London, Hubert? Yes, he said; I'm a Londoner, but I come here to work every year. Then if you know the Temple, you know that the windows of Temple Gardens overlook the river. I used to stand at those windows watching the big brown river flowing through its bridges, thinking all the while of the sea into which it went, and that I must plunge into the river and be carried away down to the sea, or be picked up before I got there. I could only think about making an end to my trouble and of the Frenchwoman. Her suspicions that I cared for him made her harder on me than she need have been; she was always coming the missis over me. Her airs and graces stiffened my back more than anything else, and I'm sure if I hadn't met Bessie Lawrence I should have done away with myself. She was the woman who used to look after the chambers under Mr Congreve's. We stopped talking outside the gateway by King's Bench Walk—if you know the Temple, you know where I mean. Bessie kept talking, but I wasn't listening, only catching a word here and there, not waking up from the dream how to make away with myself till I heard the words: If I had a figure like yours. As no one had ever spoken about my figure before, I said: Now what has my figure got to do with it? You haven't been listening to me, she said, and I answered that I had only missed the last few words. Just missed the last few words, she said testily; you didn't hear me telling you that there is a big dinner at the Freemason's Tavern tonight, and they're short of waiters. But what has that got to do with my figure? I asked. That shows, she rapped out, that you haven't been listening to me. Didn't I say that if it wasn't for my hips and bosom I'd very soon be into a suit of evening clothes and getting ten shillings for the job. But what has that got to do with my figure? I repeated. Your figure is just the one for a waiter's. Oh, I'd never thought of that, says I, and we said no more. But the words: Your figure is just the one for a waiter's, kept on in my head till my eyes caught sight of a bundle of old clothes that Mr Congreve had given me to sell. A suit of evening clothes was in it. You see, Mr Congreve and myself were about the same height and build. The trousers will want a bit of shortening, I said to myself, and I set to work; and at six o'clock I was in them and down at the Freemason's Tavern answering questions, saying that I had been accustomed to waiting at table. All the waiting I had done was bringing in Mr Congreve's dinner from the kitchen to the sitting-room: a roast chicken or a chop, and in my fancy it seemed to me that the waiting at the Freemason's Tavern would be much the same. The head waiter looked me over a bit doubtfully and asked if I had had experience with public dinners. I thought he was going to turn me down, but they were short-handed, so I was taken on, and it was a mess that I made of it, getting in everybody's way; but my awkwardness was taken in good part and I received ten shillings, which was good money for the sort of work I did that night. But what stood to me was not so much the ten shillings that I earned as the bit I had learned. It was only a bit, not much bigger than a threepenny bit; but I had worked round a table at a big dinner, and feeling certain that I could learn what I didn't know, I asked for another job. I suppose the head waiter could see that there was the making of a waiter in me, for on coming out of the Freemason's Tavern he stopped me to ask if I was going back to private service as soon as I could get a place. The food I'd had and the excitement of the dinner, the guests, the lights, the talk, stood to me, and things seemed clearer than they had ever seemed before. My feet were of the same mind, for they wouldn't walk towards the Temple, and I answered the head waiter that I'd be glad of another job. Well, said he, you don't know much about the work, but you're an honest lad, I think, so I'll see what I can do for you; and at the moment a thought struck him. Just take this letter, said he, to the Holborn Restaurant. There's a dinner there and I've had word that they're short of a waiter or two. Be off as fast as you can. And away I went as fast as my legs could carry me, and they took me there in good time, in front, by a few seconds, of two other fellows who were after the job. I got it. Another job came along, and another and another. Each of them jobs was worth ten shillings to me, to say nothing of the learning of the trade; and having, as I've said, the making of a waiter in me, it didn't take more than about three months for me to be as quick and as smart and as watchful as the best of them, and without them qualities no one will succeed in waiting. I have worked round the tables in the biggest places in London and all over England in all big towns, in Manchester, in Liverpool, and Birmingham; I am well known at the old Hen and Chickens, at the Queen's, and the Plough and Harrow in Birmingham. It was seven years ago that I came here, and here it would seem that I've come to be looked on as a fixture, for the Bakers are good people to work for and I didn't like to leave them when, three years ago, a good place was offered to me, so kind were they to me in my illness. I suppose one never remains always in the same place, but I may as well be here as elsewhere.

Seven years working in Morrison's Hotel, Page said, and on the second floor? Yes, the second floor is the best in the hotel; the money is better than in the coffee-room, and that is why the Bakers have put me here, Albert replied. I wouldn't care to leave them; they've often said they don't know what they'd do without me. Seven years, Hubert repeated, the same work up the stairs and down the stairs, banging into the kitchen and out again. There's more variety in the work than you think for, Hubert, Albert answered. Every family is different, and so you're always learning. Seven years, Page repeated, neither man nor woman, just a perhaper. He spoke these words more to himself than to Nobbs, but feeling he had expressed himself incautiously he raised his eyes and read on Albert's face that the words had gone home, and that this outcast from both sexes felt her loneliness perhaps more keenly than before. As Hubert was thinking what words he might use to conciliate Albert with her lot, Albert repeated the words: Neither man nor woman; yet nobody ever suspected, she muttered, and never would have suspected me till the day of my death if it hadn't been for that flea that you brought in with you. But what harm did the flea do? I'm bitten all over, said Albert, scratching her thighs. Never mind the bites, said Hubert; we wouldn't have had this talk if it hadn't been for the flea, and I shouldn't have heard your story.

Tears trembled on Albert's eyelids; she tried to keep them back, but they overflowed the lids and were soon running quickly down her cheeks. You've heard my story, she said. I thought nobody would ever hear it, and I thought I should never cry again; and Hubert watched the gaunt woman shaking with sobs under a coarse nightshirt. It's all much sadder than I thought it was, and if I'd known how sad it was I shouldn't have been able to live through it. But I've jostled along somehow, she added, always merry and bright, with never anyone to speak to, not really to speak to, only to ask for plates and dishes, for knives and forks and such like, tablecloths and napkins, cursing betimes the life you've been through; for the feeling cannot help coming over us, perhaps over the biggest as over the smallest, that all our trouble is for nothing and can end in nothing. It might have been better if I had taken the plunge. But why am I thinking these things? It's you that has set me thinking, Hubert. I'm sorry if—Oh, it's no use being sorry, and I'm a great silly to cry like this. I thought that regrets had passed away with the petticoats. But you've awakened the woman in me. You've brought it all up again. But I mustn't let on like this; it's very foolish of an old perhapser like me, neither man nor woman! But I can't help it. She began to sob again, and in the midst of her grief the word loneliness was uttered, and when the paroxysm was over, Hubert said: Lonely, yes, I suppose it is lonely; and he put his hand out towards Albert. You're very good, Mr Page, and I'm sure you'll keep my secret, though indeed I don't care very much whether you do or not. Now, don't let on like that again, Hubert said. Let us have a little chat and try to understand each other. I'm sure it's lonely for you to live without man or without woman, thinking like a man and feeling like a woman. You seem to know all about it, Hubert. I hadn't thought of it like that before myself, but when you speak the words I feel you have spoken the truth. I suppose I was wrong to put off my petticoats and step into those trousers. I won't go so far as to say that, Hubert answered, and the words were so unexpected that Albert forgot her grief for a moment and said: Why do you say that, Hubert? Well, because I was thinking, he replied, that you might marry. But I was never a success as a girl. Men didn't look at me then, so I'm sure they wouldn't now I'm a middle-aged woman. Marriage! whom should I marry? No, there's no marriage for me in the world; I must go on being a man. But you won't tell on me? You've promised, Hubert. Of course I won't tell, but I don't see why you shouldn't marry. What do you mean, Hubert? You aren't putting a joke upon me, are you? If you are it's very unkind. A joke upon you? no, Hubert answered. I didn't mean that you should marry a man, but you might marry a girl. Marry a girl? Albert repeated, her eyes wide open and staring. A girl? Well, anyway, that's what I've done, Hubert replied. But you're a young man and a very handsome young man too. Any girl would like to have you, and I dare say they were all after you before you met the right girl. I'm not a young man, I'm a woman, Hubert replied. Now I know for certain, cried Albert, you're putting a joke upon me. A woman! Yes, a woman; you can feel for yourself if you won't believe me. Put your hand under my shirt; you'll find nothing there. Albert moved away instinctively, her modesty having been shocked. You see I offered myself like that feeling you couldn't take my word for it. It isn't a thing there can be any doubt about. Oh, I believe you, Albert replied. And now that that matter is settled, Hubert began, perhaps you'd like to hear my story; and without waiting for an answer she related the story of her unhappy marriage: her husband, a house-painter, had changed towards her altogether after the birth of her second child, leaving her without money for food and selling up the home twice. At last I decided to have another cut at it, Hubert went on, and catching sight of my husband's working clothes one day I said to myself: He's often made me put these on and go out and help him with his job; why shouldn't I put them on for myself and go away for good? I didn't like leaving the children, but I couldn't remain with him. But the marriage? Albert asked. It was lonely going home to an empty room; I was as lonely as you, and one day, meeting a girl as lonely as myself, I said: Come along, and we arranged to live together, each paying our share. She had her work and I had mine, and between us we made a fair living; and this I can say with truth, that we haven't known an unhappy hour since we married. People began to talk, so we had to. I'd like you to see our home. I always return to my home after a job is finished with a light heart and leave it with a heavy one. But I don't understand, Albert said. What don't you understand? Hubert asked. Whatever Albert's thoughts were, they faded from her, and her eyelids dropped over her eyes. You're falling asleep, Hubert said, and I'm doing the same. It must be three o'clock in the morning and I've to catch the five o'clock train. I can't think now of what I was going to ask you, Albert muttered, but you'll tell me in the morning; and turning over, she made a place for Hubert.

III

What has become of him? Albert said, rousing herself, and then, remembering that Hubert's intention was to catch the early train, she began to remember. His train, she said, started from Amiens Street at—I must have slept heavily for him—for her not to have awakened me, or she must have stolen away very quietly. But, lord amassy, what time is it? And seeing she had overslept herself a full hour, she began to dress herself, muttering all the while: Such a thing never happened to me before. And the hotel as full as it can hold. Why didn't they send for me? The missis had a thought of my bed-fellow, mayhap, and let me sleep it out. I told her I shouldn't close an eye till she left me. But I mustn't fall into the habit of sheing him. Lord, if the missis knew everything! But I've overslept myself a full hour, and if nobody has been up before somebody soon will be. The greater haste the less speed. All the same, despite the difficulty of finding her clothes, Albert was at work on her landing some twenty minutes after, running up and down the stairs, preparing for the different breakfasts in the half-dozen sitting-rooms given to her charge, driving everybody before her, saying: We're late today, and the house full of visitors. How is it that 54 isn't turned out? Has 35 rung his bell? Lord, Albert, said a housemaid, I wouldn't worry my fat because I was down late; once in a way don't hurt. And sitting up half the night talking to Mr Page, said another maid, and then rounding on us. Half the night talking, Albert repeated. My bed-fellow! Where is Mr Page? I didn't hear him go away; he may have missed his train for aught I know. But do you be getting on with your work, and let me be getting on with mine. You're very cross this morning, Albert, the maid-servant muttered, and retired to chatter with two other maids who were looking over the banisters at the time.

Well, Mr Nobbs, the head porter began, when Albert came running downstairs to see some visitors off, and to receive her tips—well, Mr Nobbs, how did you find your bed-fellow? Oh, he was all right, but I'm not used to bed-fellows, and he brought a flea with him, and it kept me awake; and when I did fall asleep, I slept so heavily that I was an hour late. I hope he caught his train. But what is all this pother about bed-fellows? Albert asked herself, as she returned to her landing. Page hasn't said anything, no, she's said nothing, for we are both in the same boat, and to tell on me would be to tell on herself. I'd never have believed if—Albert's modesty prevented her from finishing the sentence. She's a woman right enough. But the cheek of it, to marry an innocent girl! Did she let the girl into the secret, or leave her to find it out when—The girl might have called in the police! This was a question one might ponder on, and by luncheon time Albert was inclined to believe that Hubert told his wife before—She couldn't have had the cheek to wed her, Albert said, without warning her that things might not turn out as she fancied. Mayhap, Albert continued, she didn't tell her before they wedded and mayhap she did, and being one of them like myself that isn't always hankering after a man she was glad to live with Hubert for companionship. Albert tried to remember the exact words that Hubert had used. It seemed to her that Hubert had said that she lived with a girl first and wedded her to put a stop to people's scandal. Of course they could hardly live together except as man and wife. She remembered Hubert saying that she always returned home with a light heart and never left it without a heavy one. So it would seem that this marriage was as successful as any and a great deal more than most.

At that moment 35 rang his bell. Albert hurried to answer it, and it was not till late in the evening, between nine and ten o'clock, when the guests were away at the theatres and concerts and nobody was about but two maids, that Albert, with her napkin over her shoulder, dozed and meditated on the advice that Hubert had given her. She should marry, Hubert had said; Hubert had married. Of course it wasn't a real marriage, it couldn't be that, but a very happy one it would seem. But the girl must have understood that she was not marrying a man. Did Hubert tell her before wedding her or after, and what were the words? She would have liked to know the words. For after all I've worked hard, she said, and her thoughts melted away into meditation of what her life had been for the last five-and-twenty years, a mere drifting, it seemed to her, from one hotel to another, without friends; meeting, it is true, sometimes men and women who seemed willing to be friendly. But her secret forced her to live apart from men as well as women; the clothes she wore smothered the woman in her; she no longer thought and felt as she used to when she wore petticoats, and she didn't think and feel like a man though she wore trousers. What was she? Nothing, neither man nor woman, so small wonder she was lonely. But Hubert had put off her sex, so she said . . . Albert turned over in her mind the possibility that a joke had been put upon her, and fell to thinking what Hubert's home might be like, and was vexed with herself for not having asked if she had a clock and vases on the chimney-piece. One of the maids called from the end of the passage, and when Albert received 54's order and executed it, she returned to her seat in the passage, her napkin over her shoulder, and resumed her reverie. It seemed to her that Hubert once said that her wife was a milliner; Hubert may not have spoken the word milliner; but if she hadn't, it was strange that the word should keep on coming up in her mind. There was no reason why the wife shouldn't be a milliner, and if that were so it was as likely as not that they owned a house in some quiet, insignificant street, letting the dining-room, back room and kitchen to a widow or to a pair of widows. The drawing-room was the workroom and showroom; Page and his wife slept in the room above. On second thoughts it seemed to Albert that if the business were millinery it might be that Mrs Page would prefer the ground floor for her showroom. A third and fourth distribution of the 'premises' presented itself to Albert's imagination. On thinking the matter over again it seemed to her that Hubert did not speak of a millinery business but of a seamstress, and if that were so, a small dressmaker's business in a quiet street would be in keeping with all Hubert had said about the home. Albert was not sure, however, that if she found a girl willing to share her life with her, it would be a seamstress's business she would be on the look-out for. She thought that a sweetmeat shop, newspapers and tobacco, would be her choice.

Why shouldn't she make a fresh start? Hubert had no difficulties. She had said—Albert could recall the very words—I didn't mean you should marry a man, but a girl. Albert had saved, oh! how she had tried to save, for she didn't wish to end her days in the workhouse. She had saved upwards of five hundred pounds, which was enough to purchase a little business, and her heart dilated as she thought of her two successful investments in house property. In six months' time she hoped to have six hundred pounds, and if it took her two years to find a partner and a business, she would have at least seventy or eighty pounds more, which would be a great help, for it would be a mistake to put one's money into a falling business. If she found a partner, she'd have to do like Hubert; for marriage would put a stop to all tittle-tattle; she'd be able to keep her place at Morrison's Hotel, or perhaps leave Morrison's and rely on jobs; and with her connection it would be a case of picking and choosing the best: ten and sixpence a night, nothing under. She dreamed of a round. Belfast, Liverpool, Manchester, Bradford, rose up in her imagination, and after a month's absence, a couple of months maybe, she would return home, her heart anticipating a welcome—a real welcome, for though she would continue to be a man to the world, she would be a woman to the dear one at home. With a real partner, one whose heart was in the business, they might make as much as two hundred pounds a year—four pounds a week! And with four pounds a week their home would be as pretty and happy as any in the city of Dublin. Two rooms and a kitchen were what she foresaw. The furniture began to creep into her imagination little by little. A large sofa by the fireplace covered with a chintz! But chintz dirtied quickly in the city; a dark velvet sofa might be more suitable. It would cost a great deal of money, five or six pounds; and at that rate fifty pounds wouldn't go very far, for they must have a fine double-bed mattress; and if they were going to do things in that style, the home would cost them eighty pounds. With luck these eighty pounds could be earned within the next two years at Morrison's Hotel.

Albert ran over in her mind the tips she had received. The people in 34 were leaving tomorrow; they were always good for half a sovereign, and she decided then and there that tomorrow's half-sovereign must be put aside as a beginning of a sum of money for the purchase of a clock to stand on a marble chimney-piece or a mahogany chiffonier. A few days after she got a sovereign from a departing guest, and it revealed a pair of pretty candlesticks and a round mirror. Her tips were no longer mere white and yellow metal stamped with the effigy of a dead king or a living queen, but symbols of the future that awaited her. An unexpected crown set her pondering on the colour of the curtains in their sitting-room, and Albert became suddenly conscious that a change had come into her life: the show was the same—carrying plates and dishes upstairs and downstairs, and taking orders for drinks and cigars; but behind the show a new life was springing up—a life strangely personal and associated with the life without only in this much, that the life without was now a vassal state paying tribute to the life within. She wasn't as good a servant as heretofore. She knew it. Certain absences of mind, that was all; and the servants as they went by with their dusters began to wonder whatever Albert could be dreaming of.

It was about this time that the furnishing of the parlour at the back of the shop was completed, likewise that of the bedroom above the shop, and Albert had just entered on another dream—a dream of a shop with two counters, one at which cigars, tobacco, pipes and matches were sold, and at the other all kinds of sweetmeats, a shop with a door leading to her wife's parlour. A changing figure the wife was in Albert's imagination, turning from fair to dark, from plump to slender, but capturing her imagination equally in all her changes; sometimes she was accompanied by a child of three or four, a boy, the son of a dead man, for in one of her dreams Albert married a widow. In another and more frequent dream she married a woman who had transgressed the moral code and been deserted before the birth of her child. In this case it would be supposed that Albert had done the right thing, for after leading the girl astray he had made an honest woman of her. Albert would be the father in everybody's eyes except the mother's, and she hoped that the child's mother would outgrow all the memory of the accidental seed sown, as the saying runs, in a foolish five minutes. A child would be a pleasure to them both, and a girl in the family way appealed to her more than a widow; a girl that some soldier, the boot-boy, or the hotel porter, had gotten into trouble; and Albert kept her eyes and ears open, hoping to rescue from her precarious situation one of those unhappy girls that were always cropping up in Morrison's Hotel. Several had had to leave the hotel last year, but not one this year. But some revivalist meetings were going to be held in Dublin. Many of our girls attend them, and an unlucky girl will be in luck's way if we should run across one another. Her thoughts passed into a dream of the babe that would come into the world some three or four months after their marriage, her little soft hands and expressive eyes claiming their protection, asking for it. What matter whether she calls me father or mother? They are but mere words that the lips speak, but love is in the heart and only love matters.

Now whatever can Albert be brooding? an idle housemaid asked herself as she went by. Brooding a love-story? Not likely. A marriage with some girl outside? He isn't over-partial to any of us. That Albert was brooding something, that there was something on his mind, became the talk of the hotel, and soon after it came to be noticed that Albert was eager to avail himself of every excuse to absent himself from duty in the hotel. He had been seen in the smaller streets looking up at the houses. He had saved a good deal of money, and some of his savings were invested in house property, so it was possible that his presence in these streets might be explained by the supposition that he was investing new sums of money in house property, or, and it was the second suggestion that stimulated the imagination, that Albert was going to be married and was looking out for a house for his wife. He had been seen talking with Annie Watts; but she was not in the family way after all, and despite her wistful eyes and gentle voice she was not chosen. Her heart is not in her work, Albert said; she thinks only of when she can get out, and that isn't the sort for a shop, whereas Dorothy Keyes is a glutton for work; but Albert couldn't abide the tall, angular woman, built like a boy, with a neck like a swan's. Besides her unattractive appearance, her manner was abrupt. But Alice's small, neat figure and quick intelligence marked her out for the job. Alas! Alice was hot-tempered. We should quarrel, Albert said, and picking up her napkin, which had slipped from her knee to the floor, she considered the maids on the floor above. A certain stateliness of figure and also of gait put the thought into her mind that Mary O'Brien would make an attractive shopwoman. But her second thoughts were that Mary O'Brien was a Papist, and the experience of Irish Protestants shows that Papists and Protestants don't mix.

She had just begun to consider the next housemaid, when a voice interrupted her musing. That lazy girl, Annie Watts, on the look-out for an excuse to chatter the time away instead of being about her work, were the words that crossed Albert's mind as she raised her eyes, and so unwelcoming were they that Annie in her nervousness began to hesitate and stammer, unable for the moment to find a subject, plunging at last, and rather awkwardly, into the news of the arrival of the new kitchen-maid, Helen Dawes, but never dreaming that the news could have any interest for Albert. To her surprise, Albert's eyes lighted up. Do you know her? Annie asked. Know her? Albert answered. No, I don't know her, but—At that moment a bell rang. Oh, bother, Annie said, and while she moved away idling along the banisters, Albert hurried down the passage to enquire what No. 47 wanted, and to learn that he needed writing-paper and envelopes. He couldn't write with the pens the hotel furnished; would Albert be so kind as to ask the page-boy to fetch some J's? With pleasure, Albert said; with pleasure. Would you like to have the writing-paper and envelopes before the boy returns with the pens, sir? The visitor answered that the writing-paper and envelopes would be of no use to him till he had gotten the pens. With pleasure, sir; with pleaure; and whilst waiting for the page to return she passed through the swing doors and searched for a new face among the different young women passing to and fro between the white-aproned and white-capped chefs, bringing the dishes to the great zinc counter that divided the kitchen-maids and the scullions from the waiters. She must be here, she said, and returned again to the kitchen in the hope of meeting the newcomer, Helen Dawes, who, when she was found, proved to be very unlike the Helen Dawes of Albert's imagination. A thick-set, almost swarthy girl of three-and-twenty, rather under than above the medium height, with white, even teeth, but unfortunately protruding, giving her the appearance of a rabbit. Her eyes seemed to be dark brown, but on looking into them Albert discovered them to be grey-green, round eyes that dilated and flashed wonderfully while she talked. Her face lighted up; and there was a vindictiveness in her voice that appeared and disappeared; Albert suspected her, and was at once frightened and attracted. Vindictiveness in her voice! How could such a thing have come into my mind? she said a few days after. A more kindly girl it would be difficult to find. How could I have been so stupid? She is one of those, Albert continued, that will be a success in everything she undertakes; and dreams began soon after that the sweetstuff and tobacco shop could hardly fail to prosper under her direction. Nobody could befool Helen, and when I am away at work I shall feel certain that everything will be all right at home. It's a pity that she isn't in the family way, for it would be pleasant to have a little one running about the shop asking for lemon drops and to hear him calling us father and mother. At that moment a strange thought flitted across Albert's mind—after all, it wouldn't matter much to her if Helen were to get into the family way later; of course, there would be the expense of the lying-in. Her second thoughts were that women live happily enough till a man comes between them, and that it would be safer for her to forgo a child and choose an older woman. All the same, she could not keep herself from asking Helen to walk out with her, and the next time they met the words slipped out of her mouth: I shall be off duty at three today, and if you are not engaged—I am off duty at three, Helen answered. Are you engaged? Albert asked. Helen hesitated, it being the truth that she had been and was still walking out with one of the scullions, and was not sure how he would look upon her going out with another, even though that one was such a harmless fellow as Albert Nobbs. Harmless in himself, she thought, and with a very good smell of money rising out of his pockets, very different from Joe, who seldom had a train fare upon him. But she hankered after Joe, and wouldn't give Albert a promise until she had asked him. Wants to walk out with you? Why, he has never been known to walk out with man, woman or child before. Well, that's a good one! I'd like to know what he's after, but I'm not jealous; you can go with him, there's no harm in Albert. I'm on duty: just go for a turn with him. Poke him up and see what he's after, and take him into a sweetshop and bring back a box of chocolates. Do you like chocolates? Helen asked, and her eyes flashing, she stood looking at Joe, who, thinking that her temper was rising, and wishing to quell it, asked hurriedly where she was going to meet him. At the corner, she answered. He is there already. Then be off, he said, and his tone grated. You wouldn't like me to keep him waiting? Helen said. Oh, dear no, not for Joe, not for Joseph, if he knows it, the scullion replied, lilting the song.

Helen turned away hoping that none of the maids would peach upon her, and Albert's heart rejoiced at seeing her on the other side of the street waiting for the tram to go by before she crossed it. Were you afraid I wasn't coming? she asked, and Albert, not being ready with words, answered shyly: Not very. A stupid answer this seemed to be to Helen, and it was in the hope of shuffling out of a tiresome silence that Albert asked her if she liked chocolates. Something under the tooth will help the time away, was the answer she got; and they went in search of a sweetmeat shop, Albert thinking that a shilling or one and sixpence would see her through it. But in a moment Helen's eyes were all over the shop, and spying out some large pictured boxes, she asked Albert if she might have one, and it being their first day out, Albert answered: Yes; but could not keep back the words: I'm afraid they'd cost a lot. For these words Albert got a contemptuous look, and Helen shook her shoulders so disdainfully that Albert pressed a second box on Helen—one to pass the time with, another to take home. To such a show of goodwill Helen felt she must respond, and her tongue rattled on pleasantly as she walked, crunching the chocolates, two between each lamp-post, Albert stinting herself to one, which she sucked slowly, hardly enjoying it at all, so worried was she by the loss of three and sixpence. As if Helen guessed the cause of Albert's disquiet, she called on her suitor to admire the damsel on the box, but Albert could not disengage her thoughts sufficiently from Helen's expensive tastes. If every walk were to cost three and sixpence there wouldn't be a lot left for the home in six months' time. And she fell to calculating how much it would cost her if they were to walk out once a week. Three fours are twelve and four sixpences are two shillings, fourteen shillings a month, twice that is twenty-eight; twenty-eight shillings a month, that is if Helen wanted two boxes a week. At this rate she'd be spending sixteen pounds sixteen shillings a year. Lord amassy! But perhaps Helen wouldn't want two boxes of chocolates every time they went out together—If she didn't, she'd want other things, and catching sight of a jeweller's shop, Albert called Helen's attention to a cyclist that had only just managed to escape a tram car by a sudden wriggle. But Albert was always unlucky. Helen had been wishing this long while for a bicycle, and if she did not ask Albert to buy her one it was because another jeweller's came into view. She stopped to gaze, and for a moment Albert's heart seemed to stand still, but Helen continued her chocolates, secure in her belief that the time had not yet come for substantial presents.

At Sackville Street bridge she would have liked to turn back, having little taste for the meaner parts of the city, but Albert wished to show her the north side, and she began to wonder what he could find to interest him in these streets, and why he should stand in admiration before all the small newspaper and tobacco shops, till she remembered suddenly that he had invested his savings in house property. Could these be his houses? All his own? and, moved by this consideration, she gave a more attentive ear to Albert's account of the daily takings of these shops, calculating that he was a richer man that anybody believed him to be, but a mean one. The idea of his thinking twice about a box of chocolates! I'll show him! and coming upon a big draper's shop in Sackville Street she asked him for a pair of six-button gloves. She needed a parasol and some shoes and stockings, and a silk kerchief would not be amiss, and at the end of the third month of their courtship it seemed to her that the time had come for her to speak of bangles, saying that for three pounds she could have a pretty one—one that would be a real pleasure to wear; it would always remind her of him. Albert coughed up with humility, and Helen felt that she had 'got him', as she put it to herself, and afterwards to Joe Mackins. So he parted easily, Joe remarked, and pushing Helen aside he began to whip up the *rémoulade*, that had begun to show signs of turning, saying he'd have the chef after him. But I say, old girl, since he's coughing up so easily you might bring me something back; and a briarwood pipe and a pound or two of tobacco seemed the least she might obtain for him. And Helen answered that to get these she would have to ask Albert for money. And why shouldn't you? Joe returned. Ask him for a thin 'un, and mayhap he'll give you a thick 'un. It's the first quid that's hard to get; every time after it's like shelling peas. Do you think he's that far gone on me? Helen asked. Well, don't you? Why should he give you these things if he wasn't? Joe answered. Joe asked her of what she was thinking, and she replied that it was hard to say: she had walked out with many a man before but never with one like Albert Nobbs. In what way is he different? Joe asked. Helen was perplexed in her telling of Albert Nobbs' slackness. You mean that he doesn't pull you about, Joe rapped out; and she answered that there was something of that in it. All the same, she continued, that isn't the whole of it. I've been out before with men that didn't pull me about, but he seems to have something on his mind, and half the time he's thinking. Well, what does it matter, Joe asked, so long as there is coin in the pocket and so long as you have a hand to pull it out? Helen didn't like this description of Albert Nobbs' courtship, and the words rose to her lips to tell Joseph that she didn't want to go out any more with Albert, that she was tired of her job, but the words were quelled on her lips by a remark from Joe. Next time you go out with him work him up a bit and see what he is made of; just see if there's a sting in him or if he is no better than a capon. A capon! and what is a capon? she asked. A capon is a cut fowl. He may be like one. You think that, do you? she answered, and resolved to get the truth of the matter next time they went out together. It did seem odd that Albert should be willing to buy presents and not want to kiss her. In fact, it was more than odd. It might be as Joe had said. I might as well go out with my mother. Now what did it all mean? Was it a blind? Some other girl that he—Not being able to concoct a sufficiently reasonable story, Helen relinquished the attempt, without, however, regaining control of her temper, which had begun to rise, and which continued to boil up in her and overflow until her swarthy face was almost ugly. I'm beginning to feel ugly towards him, she said to herself. He is either in love with me or he's—And trying to discover his purpose, she descended the staircase, saying to herself: Now Albert must know that I'm partial to Joe Mackins. It can't be that he doesn't suspect. Well, I'm damned.

IV

But Helen's perplexity on leaving the hotel was no greater than Albert's as she stood waiting by the kerb. She knew that Helen carried on with Joe Mackins, and she also knew that Joe Mackins had nothing to offer Helen but himself. She even suspected that some of the money she had given to Helen had gone to purchase pipes and tobacco for Joe: a certain shrewdness is not inconsistent with innocence, and it didn't trouble her much that Helen was perhaps having her fling with Joe Mackins. She didn't want Helen to fall into evil ways, but it was better for her to have her fling before than after her marriage. On the other hand, a woman that had been bedded might be disatisfied to settle down with another woman, though the home offered her was better than any she could get from a man. She might hanker for children, which was only natural, and Albert felt that she would like a child as well as another. A child might be arranged for if Helen wanted one, but it would never do to have the father hanging about the shop: he would have to be got rid of as soon as Helen was in the family way. But could he be got rid of? Not very easily if Joe Mackins was the father; she foresaw trouble and would prefer another father, almost any other. But why trouble herself about the father of Helen's child before she knew whether Helen would send Joe packing? which she'd have to do clearly if they were to wed—she and Helen. Their wedding was what she had to look to, whether she could confide her sex to Helen tonight or wait. Why not tonight as well as tomorrow night? she asked herself. But how would she tell it to Helen? Blurt it out—I've something to tell you, Helen, I'm not a man, but a woman like youself. No, that wouldn't do. How did Hubert tell her wife she was a woman? If she had only asked she'd have been spared all this trouble. After hearing Hubert's story she should have said: I've something to ask you; but sleep was so heavy on their eyelids that they couldn't think any more and both of them were falling asleep, which wasn't to be wondered at, for they had been talking for hours. It was on her mind to ask how her wife found out. Did Hubert tell her or did the wife—Albert's modesty prevented her from pursuing the subject; and she turned on herself, saying that she could not leave Helen to find out she was a woman; of that she was certain, and of that only. She'd have to tell Helen that. But should the confession come before they were married, or should she reserve it for the wedding night in the bridal chamber on the edge of the bed afterwards? If it were not for Helen's violent temper—I in my nightshirt, she in her nightgown. On the other hand, she might quieten down after an outburst and begin to see that it might be very much to her advantage to accept the situation, especially if a hope were held out to her of a child by Joe Mackins in two years' time; she'd have to agree to wait till then, and in two years Joe would probably be after another girl. But if she were to cut up rough and do me an injury! Helen might call the neighbours in, or the policemen, who'd take them both to the station. She'd have to return to Liverpool or to Manchester. She didn't know what the penalty would be for marrying one of her own sex. And her thoughts wandered on to the morning boat.

One of the advantages of Dublin is that one can get out of it as easily as any other city. Steamers were always leaving, morning and evening; she didn't know how many, but a great many. On the other hand, if she took the straight course and confided her sex to Helen before the marriage, Helen might promise not to tell; but she might break her promise; life in Morrison's Hotel would be unendurable, and she'd have to endure it. What a hue and cry! But one way was as bad as the other. If she had only asked Hubert Page! but she hadn't a thought at the time of going to do likewise. What's one man's meat is another man's poison, and she began to regret Hubert's confession to her. If it hadn't been for that flea she wouldn't be in this mess; and she was deep in it! Three months' company isn't a day, and everybody in Morrison's Hotel asking whether she or Joe Mackins would be the winner, urging her to make haste else Joe would come with a rush at the finish. A lot of racing talk that she didn't understand—or only half. If she could get out of this mess somehow—But it was too late. She must go through with it. But how? A different sort of girl altogether was needed, but she liked Helen. Her way of standing on a doorstep, her legs a little apart, jawing a tradesman, and she'd stand up to Mrs Baker and to the chef himself. She liked the way Helen's eyes lighted up when a thought came into her mind; her cheery laugh warmed Albert's heart as nothing else did. Before she met Helen she often feared her heart was growing cold. She might try the world over and not find one that would run the shop she had in mind as well as Helen. But the shop wouldn't wait; the owners of the shop would withdraw their offer if it was not accepted before next Monday. And today is Friday, Albert said to herself. This evening or never. Tomorrow Helen'll be on duty all day; on Sunday she'll contrive some excuse to get out to meet Joe Mackins. After all, why not this evening? for what must be had better be faced bravely; and while the tram rattled down the long street, Rathmines Avenue, past the small houses atop of high steps, pretty boxes with ornamental trees in the garden, some with lawns, with here and there a more substantial house set in the middle of three or four fields at least, Albert meditated, plan after plan rising up in her mind; and when the car turned to the right and then to the left and proceeded at a steady pace up the long incline, Rathgar Avenue, Albert's courage was again at ebb. All the subterfuges she had woven—the long discussion in which she would maintain that marriage should not be considered as a sexual adventure, but a community of interests—seemed to have lost all significance; the points that had seemed so convincing in Rathmines Avenue were forgotten in Rathgar Avenue, and at Terenure she came to the conclusion that there was no use trying to think the story out beforehand; she would have to adapt her ideas to the chances that would arise as they talked under the trees in the dusk in a comfortable hollow, where they could lie at length out of hearing of the other lads and lasses whom they would find along the banks, resting after the labour of the day in dim contentment, vaguely conscious of each other, satisfied with a vague remark, a kick or a push.

It was the hope that the river's bank would tempt him into confidence that had suggested to Helen that they might spend the evening by the Dodder. Albert had welcomed the suggestion, feeling sure that if there was a place in the world that would make the telling of her secret easy it was the banks of the Dodder; and she was certain she would be able to speak it in the hollow under the ilex-trees. But speech died from her lips, and the silence around them seemed sinister and foreboding. She seemed to dread the river flowing over its muddy bottom, without ripple or eddy; and she started when Helen asked her of what she was thinking. Albert answered: Of you, dear; and how pleasant it is to be sitting with you. On these words the silence fell again, and Albert tried to speak, but her tongue was too thick in her mouth; she felt like choking, and the silence was not broken for some seconds, each seeming a minute. At last a lad's voice was heard: I'll see if you have any lace on your drawers; and the lass answered: You shan't. There's a pair that's enjoying themselves, Helen said, and she looked upon the remark as fortunate, and hoped it would give Albert the courage to pursue his courtship. Albert, too, looked upon the remark as fortunate, and she tried to ask if there was lace on all women's drawers; and meditated a reply that would lead her into a confession of her sex. But the words: It's so long since I've worn any, died on her lips; and instead of speaking these words she spoke of the Dodder, saying: What a pity it isn't nearer Morrison's. Where would you have it? Helen replied—flowing down Sackville Street into the Liffey? We should be lying there as thick as herrings, without room to move, or we should be unable to speak to each other without being overheard. I dare say you are right, Albert answered, and she was so frightened that she added: But we have to be back at eleven o'clock, and it takes an hour to get there. We can go back now if you like, Helen rapped out. Albert apologised, and hoping that something would happen to help her out of her difficulty, she began to represent Morrison's Hotel as being on the whole advantageous to servants. But Helen did not respond. She seems to be getting angrier and angrier, Albert said to herself, and she asked, almost in despair, if the Dodder was pretty all the way down to the sea. And remembering a walk with Joe, Helen answered: There are woods as far as Dartry—the Dartry Dye Works, don't you know them? But I don't think there are any pretty spots. You know Ring's End, don't you? Albert said she had been there once; and Helen spoke of a large three-masted vessel that she had seen some Sundays ago by the quays. You were there with Joe Mackins, weren't you? Well, what if I was? Only this, Albert answered, that I don't think it is usual for a girl to keep company with two chaps, and I thought—Now, what did you think? Helen said. That you didn't care for me well enough—For what? she asked. You know we've been going out for three months, and it doesn't seem natural to keep talking always, never wanting to put your arm round a girl's waist. I suppose Joe isn't like me, then? Albert asked; and Helen laughed, a scornful little laugh. But, Albert went on, isn't the time for kissing when one is wedded? This is the first time you've said anything about marriage, Helen rapped out. But I thought there had always been an understanding between us, said Albert, and it's only now I can tell you what I have to offer. The words were well chosen. Tell me about it, Helen said, her eyes and voice revealing her cupidity to Albert, who continued all the same to unfold her plans, losing herself in details that bored Helen, whose thoughts returned to the dilemma she was in—to refuse Albert's offer or to break with Joe; and that she should be obliged to do either one or the other was a disappointment to her. All you say about the shop is right enough, but it isn't a very great compliment to a girl. What, to ask her to marry? Albert interjected. Well, no, not if you haven't kissed her first. Don't speak so loud, Albert whispered; I'm sure that couple heard what you said, for they went away laughing. I don't care whether they laughed or cried, Helen answered. You don't want to kiss me, do you? and I don't want to marry a man who isn't in love with me. But I do want to kiss you, and Albert bent down and kissed Helen on both cheeks. Now you can't say I haven't kissed you, can you? You don't call that kissing, do you? Helen asked. But how do you wish me to kiss you, Helen? Well, you are an innocent! she said, and she kissed Albert vindictively. Helen, leave go of me; I'm not used to such kisses. Because you're not in love, Helen replied. In love? Albert repeated. I loved my old nurse very much, but I never wished to kiss her like that. At this Helen exploded with laughter. So you put me in the same class with your old nurse! Well, after that! Come, she said, taking pity upon Albert for a moment, are you or are you not in love with me? I love you deeply, Helen, Albert said. Love? she repeated: the men who have walked out with me were in love with me—In love, Albert repeated after her. I'm sure I love you. I like men to be in love with me, she answered. But that's like an animal, Helen. Whatever put all that muck in your head? I'm going home, she replied, and rose to her feet and started out on the path leading across the darkening fields. You're not angry with me, Helen? Angry? No, I'm not angry with you; you're a fool of a man, that's all. But if you think me a fool of a man, why did you come out this evening to sit under those trees? And why have we been keeping company for the last three months, Albert continued, going out together every week? You didn't always think me a fool of a man, did you? Yes, I did, she answered; and Albert asked Helen for a reason for choosing her company. Oh, you bother me asking reasons for everything, Helen said. But why did you make me love you? Albert asked. Well, if I did, what of it? and as for walking out with you, you won't have to complain of that any more. You don't mean, Helen, that we are never going to walk out again? Yes, I do, she said sullenly. You mean that for the future you'll be walking out with Joe Mackins, Albert lamented. That's my business, she answered. By this time they were by the stile at the end of the field, and in the next field there was a hedge to get through and a wood, and the little path they followed was full of such vivid remembrances that Albert could not believe that she was treading it with Helen for the last time, and besought Helen to take back the words that she would never walk out with her again.

The tram was nearly empty and they sat at the far end, close together, Albert beseeching Helen not to cast her off. If I've been stupid today, Albert pleaded, it's because I'm tired of the work in the hotel; I shall be different when we get to Lisdoonvarna: we both want a change of air; there's nothing like the salt water and the cliffs of Clare to put new spirits into a man. You will be different and I'll be different; everything will be different. Don't say no, Helen; don't say no. I've looked forward to this week in Lisdoonvarna, and Albert urged the expense of the lodgings she had already engaged. We shall have to pay for the lodgings; and there's the new suit of clothes that has just come back from the tailor's; I've looked forward to wearing it, walking with you in the strand, the waves crashing up into cliffs, with green fields among them, I've been told! We shall see the ships passing and wonder whither they are going. I've bought three neckties and some new shirts, and what good will these be to me if you'll not come to Lisdoonvarna with me? The lodgings will have to be paid for, a great deal of money, for I said in my letter we shall want two bedrooms. But there need only be one bedroom; but perhaps I shouldn't have spoken like that. Oh, don't talk to me about Lisdoonvarna, Helen answered. I'm not going to Lisdoonvarna with you. But what is to become of the hat I have ordered for you? Albert asked; the hat with the big feather in it; and I've bought stockings and shoes for you. Tell me, what shall I do with these, and with the gloves? Oh, the waste of money and the heart-breaking! What shall I do with the hat? Albert repeated. Helen didn't answer at once. Presently she said: You can leave the hat with me. And the stockings? Albert asked. Yes, you can leave the stockings. And the shoes? Yes, you can leave the shoes too. Yet you won't go to Lisdoonvarna with me? No, she said, I'll not go to Lisdoonvarna with you. But you'll take the presents? It was to please you I said I would take them, because I thought it would be some satisfaction to you to know that they wouldn't be wasted. Not wasted? Albert repeated. You'll wear them when you go out with Joe Mackins. Oh, well, keep your presents. And then the dispute took a different turn, and was continued until they stepped out of the tram at the top of Dawson Street. Albert continued to plead all the way down Dawson Street, and when they were within twenty yards of the hotel, and she saw Helen passing away from her for ever into the arms of Joe Mackins, she begged Helen not to leave her. We cannot part like this, she cried; let us walk up and down the street from Nassau Street to Clare Street, so that we may talk things over and do nothing foolish. You see, Albert began, I had set my heart on driving on an outside car to the Broadstone with you, and catching a train, and the train going into lovely country, arriving at a place we had never seen, with cliffs, and the sunset behind the cliffs. You've told all that before, Helen said, and, she rapped out, I'm not going to Lisdoonvarna with you. And if that is all you had to say to me we might have gone into the hotel. But there's much more, Helen. I haven't told you about the shop yet. Yes, you have told me all there is to tell about the shop; you've been talking about that shop for the last three months. But, Helen, it was only yesterday that I got a letter saying that they had had another offer for the shop, and that they could give me only till Monday morning to close with them; if the lease isn't signed by then we've lost the shop. But do you think, Helen asked, that the shop will be a success? Many shops promise well in the beginning and fade away till they don't get a customer a day. Our shop won't be like that, I know it won't; and Albert began an appraisement of the shop's situation and the custom it commanded in the neighbourhood and the possibility of developing that custom. We shall be able to make a great success of that shop, and people will be coming to see us, and they will be having tea with us in the parlour, and they'll envy us, saying that never have two people had such luck as we have had. And our wedding will be—Will be what? Helen asked. Will be a great wonder. A great wonder indeed, she replied, but I'm not going to wed you, Albert Nobbs, and now I see it's beginning to rain. I can't remain out any longer. You're thinking of your hat; I'll buy another. We may as well say good-bye, she answered, and Albert saw her going towards the doorway. She'll see Joe Mackins before she goes to her bed, and lie dreaming of him; and I shall lie awake in my bed, my thoughts flying to and fro the livelong night, zigzagging up and down like bats. And then remembering that if she went into the hotel she might meet Helen and Joe Mackins, she rushed on with a hope in her mind that after a long walk round Dublin she might sleep.

At the corner of Clare Street she met two women strolling after a fare—ten shillings or a sovereign, which? she asked herself—and terrified by the shipwreck of all her hopes, she wished she were one of them. For they at least are women, whereas I am but a perhapser—In the midst of her grief a wish to speak to them took hold of her. But if I speak to them they'll expect me to—All the same her steps quickened, and as she passed the two street-walkers she looked round, and one woman, wishing to attract her attention, said: It was almost a love dream. Almost a love dream? Albert repeated. What are you two women talking about? and the woman next to Albert said: My friend here was telling me of a dream she had last night. A dream, and what was her dream about? Albert asked. Kitty was telling me that she was better than a love dream; now do you think she is, sir? I'll ask Kitty herself, Albert replied, and Kitty answered him: A shade. Only a shade, Albert returned, and as they crossed the street a gallant attached himself to Kitty's companion. Albert and Kitty were left together, and Albert asked her companion to tell her name. My name is Kitty MacCan, the girl replied. It's odd we've never met before, Albert replied, hardly knowing what she was saying. We're not often this way, was the answer. And where do you walk usually—of an evening? Albert asked. In Grafton Street or down by College Green; sometimes we cross the river. To walk in Sackville Street, Albert interjected; and she tried to lead the woman into a story of her life. But you're not one of them, she said, that think that we should wash clothes in a nunnery for nothing? I'm a waiter in Morrison's Hotel. As soon as the name of Morrison's Hotel passed Albert's lips she began to regret having spoken about herself. But what did it matter now? and the woman didn't seem to have taken heed of the name of the hotel. Is the money good in your hotel? Kitty asked; I've heard that you get as much as half-a-crown for carrying up a cup of tea; and her story dribbled out in remarks, a simple story that Albert tried to listen to, but her attention wandered, and Kitty, who was not unintelligent, began to guess Albert to be in the middle of some great grief. It doesn't matter about me, Albert answered her, and Kitty being a kind girl said to herself: If I can get him to come home with me I'll help him out of his sorrow, if only for a little while. So she continued to try to interest him in herself till they came to Fitzwilliam Place; and it was not till then that Kitty remembered she had only three and sixpence left out of the last money she had received, and that her rent would be due on the morrow. She daren't return home without a gentleman; her landlady would be at her; and the best time of the night was going by talking to a man who seemed like one who would bid her a curt good-night at the door of his hotel. Where did he say his hotel was? she asked herself; and then, aloud, she said: You're a waiter, aren't you? I've forgotten which hotel you said. Albert didn't answer, and, troubled by her companion's silence, Kitty continued: I'm afraid I'm taking you out of your way. No, you aren't; all ways are the same to me. Well, they aren't to me, she replied. I must get some money to-night. I'll give you some money, Albert said. But won't you come home with me? the girl asked. Albert hesitated, tempted by her company. But if they were to go home together her sex would be discovered. But what did it matter if it were discovered? Albert asked herself, and the temptation came again to go home with this woman, to lie in her arms and tell the story that had been locked up so many years. They could both have a good cry together, and what matter would it be to the woman as long as she got the money she desired. She didn't want a man; it was money she was after, money that meant bread and board to her. She seems a kind, nice girl, Albert said, and she was about to risk the adventure when a man came by whom Kitty knew. Excuse me, he said, and Albert saw them walk away together. I'm sorry, said the woman, returning, but I've just met an old friend; another evening, perhaps. Albert would have liked to put her hand in her pocket and pay the woman with some silver for her company, but she was already half-way back to her friend, who stood waiting for her by the lamp-post. The street-walkers have friends, and when they meet them their troubles are over for the night; but my chances have gone by me; and, checking herself in the midst of the irrelevant question, whether it were better to be casual, as they were, or to have a husband that you could not get rid of, she plunged into her own grief, and walked sobbing through street after street, taking no heed of where she was going.

Why, lord, Mr Nobbs, whatever has kept you out until this hour? the hall-porter muttered. I'm sorry, she answered, and while stumbling up the stairs she remembered that even a guest was not received very amiably by the hall-porter after two; and for a servant to come in at that time! Her thoughts broke off and she lay too tired to think any more of the hall-porter, of herself, of anything. If she got an hour's sleep it was the most she got that night, and when the time came for her to go to her work she rose indifferently. But her work saved her from thinking, and it was not until the middle of the afternoon, when the luncheon-tables had been cleared, that the desire to see and to speak to Helen could not be put aside; but Helen's face wore an ugly, forbidding look, and Albert returned to the second floor without speaking to her. It was not long after that 34 rang his bell, and Albert hoped to get an order that would send her to the kitchen. Are you going to pass me by without speaking again, Helen? We talked enough last night, Helen retorted; there's nothing more to say, and Joe, in such disorder of dress as behooves a scullion, giggled as he went past, carrying a huge pile of plates. I loved my old nurse, but I never thought of kissing her like that, he said, turning on his heel and so suddenly that some of the plates fell with a great clatter. The ill luck that had befallen him seemed well deserved, and Albert returned upstairs and sat in the passages waiting for the sitting-rooms to ring their bells; and the housemaids, as they came about the head of the stairs with their dusters, wondered how it was that they could not get any intelligible conversation out of the love-stricken waiter. Albert's lovelorn appearance checked their mirth, pity entered their hearts, and they kept back the words: I loved my old nurse, etc. After all, he loves the girl, one said to the other, and a moment after they were joined by another housemaid, who, after listening for a while, went away, saying: There's no torment like the love torment; and the three housemaids, Mary, Alice, and Dorothy, offered Albert their sympathy, trying to lead her into little talks with a view to withdrawing her from the contemplation of her own grief, for women are always moved by a love story. Before long their temper turned against Helen, and they often went by asking themselves why she should have kept company with Albert all these months if she didn't mean to wed him. No wonder the poor man was disappointed. He is destroyed with his grief, said one; look at him, without any more colour in his face than is in my duster. Another said: He doesn't swallow a bit of food. And the third said: I poured out a glass of wine for him that was left over, but he put it away. Isn't love awful? But what can he see in her? another asked, a stumpy, swarthy woman, a little blackthorn bush and as full of prickles; and the three women fell to thinking that Albert would have done better to have chosen one of them. The shop entered into the discussion soon after, and everybody was of opinion that Helen would live to regret her cruelty. The word cruelty did not satisfy; treachery was mentioned, and somebody said that Helen's face was full of treachery. Albert will never recover himself as long as she's here, another remarked. He'll just waste away unless Miss Right comes along. He put all his eggs into one basket, a man said; you see he'd never been known to walk out with a girl before. And what age do you think he is? I put him down at forty-five, and when love takes a man at that age it takes him badly. This is no calf love, the man said, looking into the women's faces, and you'll never be able to mend matters, any of you; and they all declared they didn't wish to, and dispersed in different directions, flicking their dusters and asking themselves if Albert would ever look at another woman.

It was felt generally that he would not have the courage to try again, which was indeed the case, for when it was suggested to Albert that a faint heart never wins a fair lady she answered that her spirit was broken. I shall boil my pot and carry my can, but the spring is broken in me; and it was these words that were remembered and pondered, whereas the joke—I loved my old nurse, etc.—raised no laugh; and the sympathy that Albert felt to be gathering about her cheered her on her way. She was no longer friendless; almost any one of the women in the hotel would have married Albert out of pity for her. But there was no heart in Albert for another adventure; nor any thought in her for anything but her work. She rose every morning and went forth to her work, and was sorry when her work was done, for she had come to dread every interval, knowing that as soon as she sat down to rest the old torment would begin again. Once more she would begin to think that she had nothing more to look forward to; that her life would be but a round of work; a sort of treadmill. She would never see Lisdoonvarna, and the shop with two counters, one at which tobacco, cigarettes and matches were sold, and at the other counter all kinds of sweetstuffs. Like Lisdoonvarna, it had passed away, it had only existed in her mind—a thought, a dream. Yet it had possessed her completely; and the parlour behind the shop that she had furnished and refurnished, hanging a round mirror above the mantelpiece, papering the walls with a pretty colourful paper that she had seen in Wicklow Street and had asked the man to put aside for her. She had hung curtains about the windows in her imagination, and had set two armchairs on either side of the hearth, one in green and one in red velvet, for herself and Helen. The parlour too had passed away like Lisdoonvarna, like the shop, a thought, a dream, no more. There had never been anything in her life but a few dreams, and henceforth there would be not even dreams. It was strange that some people came into the world lucky, and others, for no reason, unlucky; she had been unlucky from her birth; she was a bastard; her parents were grand people whose name she did not know, who paid her nurse a hundred a year to keep her, and who died without making any provision for her. She and her old nurse had to go and live in Temple Lane, and to go out charing every morning; Mr Congreve had a French mistress, and if it hadn't been for Bessie Lawrence she might have thrown herself in the Thames; she was very near to it last night, and if she had drowned herself all this worry and torment would have been over. She was more resolute in those days than she was now, and would have faced the river, but she shrank from this Dublin river, perhaps because it was not her own river. If one wishes to drown oneself it had better be in one's own country. But why is it a mistake? For a perhapser like herself, all countries were the same; go or stay, it didn't matter. Yes, it did; she stayed in Dublin in the hope that Hubert Page would return to the hotel. Only to Hubert could she confide the misfortune that had befallen her, and she'd like to tell somebody. The three might set up together. A happy family they might make. Two women in men's clothes and one in petticoats. If Hubert were willing. Hubert's wife might not be willing. But she might be dead and Hubert on the look-out for another helpmate. He had never been away so long before; he might return any day. And from the moment that she foresaw herself as Hubert's future wife her life began to expand itself more eagerly than ever in watching for tips, collecting half-crowns, crowns, and half-sovereigns. She must at least replace the money that she had spent giving presents to Helen, and as the months went by and the years, she remembered, with increasing bitterness, that she had wasted nearly twenty pounds on Helen, a cruel, heartless girl that had come into her life for three months and had left her for Joe Mackins. She took to counting her money in her room at night. The half-crowns were folded up in brown-paper packets, the half-sovereigns in blue, the rare sovereigns were in pink paper, and all these little packets were hidden away in different corners; some were put in the chimney, some under the carpet. She often thought that these hoards would be safer in the Post Office Bank, but she who has nothing else likes to have her money with her, and a sense of almost happiness awoke in her when she discovered herself to be again as rich as she was before she met Helen. Richer by twenty-five pounds twelve and sixpence, she said, and her eyes roved over the garret floor in search of a plank that might be lifted. One behind the bed was chosen, and henceforth Albert slept securely over her hoard, or lay awake thinking of Hubert, who might return, and to whom she might confide the story of her misadventure; but as Hubert did not return her wish to see him faded, and she began to think that it might be just as well if he stayed away, for, who knows? a wandering fellow like him might easily run out of his money and return to Morrison's Hotel to borrow from her, and she wasn't going to give her money to be spent for the benefit of another woman. The other woman was Hubert's wife. If Hubert came back he might threaten to publish her secret if she didn't give him money to keep it. An ugly thought, of which she was ashamed and which she tried to keep out of her mind. But as time went on a dread of Hubert took possession of her. After all, Hubert knew her secret, and somehow it didn't occur to her that in betraying her secret Hubert would be betraying his own. Albert didn't think as clearly as she used to; and one day she answered Mrs Baker in a manner that Mrs Baker did not like. Whilst speaking to Albert the thought crossed Mrs Baker's mind that it was a long while since they had seen the painter. I cannot think, she said, what has become of Hubert Page; we've not had news of him for a long time; have you heard from him, Albert? Why should you think, ma'am, that I hear from him? I only asked, Mrs Baker replied, and she heard Albert mumbling something about a wandering fellow, and the tone in which the words were spoken was disrespectful, and Mrs Baker began to consider Albert; and though a better servant now than he had ever been in some respects, he had developed a fault which she didn't like, a way of hanging round the visitor as he was preparing to leave the hotel that almost amounted to persecution. Worse than that, a rumour had reached her that Albert's service was measured according to the tip he expected to receive. She didn't believe it, but if it were true she would not hesitate to have him out of the hotel in spite of the many years he had spent with them. Another thing: Albert was liked, but not by everybody. The little red-headed boy on the second floor told me, Mrs Baker said (her thoughts returning to last Sunday, when she had taken the child out to Bray), that he was afraid of Albert, and he confided to me that Albert had tried to pick him up and kiss him. Why can't he leave the child alone? Can't he see the child doesn't like him?

But the Bakers were kind-hearted proprietors, and could not keep sentiment out of their business, and Albert remained at Morrison's Hotel till she died.

An easy death I hope it was, your honour, for if any poor creature deserved an easy one it was Albert herself. You think so, Alec, meaning that the disappointed man suffers less at parting with this world than the happy one? Maybe you're right. That is as it may be, your honour, he answered, and I told him that Albert awoke one morning hardly able to breathe, and returned to bed and lay there almost speechless till the maid-servant came to make the bed. She ran off again to fetch a cup of tea, and after sipping it Albert said she felt much better. But she never roused completely, and the maid-servant who came up in the evening with a bowl of soup did not press her to try to eat it, for it was plain that Albert could not eat or drink, and it was almost plain that she was dying, but the maid-servant did not like to alarm the hotel and contented herself with saying: He'd better see the doctor tomorrow. She was up betimes in the morning, and on going to Albert's room she found the waiter asleep, breathing heavily. An hour later Albert was dead, and everybody was asking how a man who was in good health on Tuesday could be a corpse on Thursday morning, as if such a thing had never happened before. However often it had happened, it did not seem natural, and it was whispered that Albert might have made away with himself. Some spoke of apoplexy, but apoplexy in a long, thin man is not usual; and when the doctor came down his report that Albert was a woman put all thought of the cause of death out of everybody's mind. Never before or since was Morrison's Hotel agog as it was that morning, everybody asking the other why Albert had chosen to pass herself off as a man, and how she had succeeded in doing this year after year without any one of them suspecting her. She would be getting better wages as a man than as a woman, somebody said, but nobody cared to discuss the wages question; all knew that a man is better paid than a woman. But what Albert would have done with Helen if Helen hadn't gone off with Joe Mackins stirred everybody's imagination. What would have happened on the wedding night? Nothing, of course; but how would she have let on? The men giggled over their glasses, and the women pondered over their cups of tea; the men asked the women and the women asked the men, and the interest in the subject had not quite died down when Hubert Page returned to Morrison's Hotel, in the spring of the year, with her paint pots and brushes. How is Albert Nobbs? was one of her first enquiries, and it fired the train. Albert Nobbs! Don't you know? How should I know? Hubert Page replied. I've only just come back to Dublin. What is there to know? Don't you ever read the papers? Read the papers? Hubert repeated. Then you haven't heard that Albert Nobbs is dead? No, I haven't heard of it. I'm sorry for him, but after all, men die; there's something wonderful in that, is there? No; but if you had read the papers you'd have learnt that Albert Nobbs wasn't a man at all. Albert Nobbs was a woman. Albert Nobbs a woman! Hubert replied, putting as much surprise as she could into her voice. So you never heard? And the story began to fall out from different sides, everybody striving to communicate bits to her, until at last she said: If you all speak together, I shall never understand it. Albert Nobbs a woman! A woman as much as you're a man, was the answer, and the story of her courtship of Helen, and Helen's preference for Joe Mackins, and Albert's grief at Helen's treatment of her trickled into a long relation. The biggest deception in the whole world, a scullion cried from his saucepans. Whatever would she have done with Helen if they had married? But the question had been asked so often that it fell flat. So Helen went away with Joe Mackins? Hubert said. Yes; and they don't seem to get on over well together. Serve her right for her unkindness, cried a kitchen-maid. But after all, you wouldn't want her to marry a woman? a scullion answered. Of course not; of course not. The story was taken up by another voice, and the hundreds of pounds that Albert had left behind in many securities were multiplied; nearly a hundred in ready money rolled up in paper, half-crowns, half-sovereigns and sovereigns in his bedroom; his bedroom—her bedroom, I mean; but we are so used to thinking of her as a him that we find it difficult to say her; we're always catching each other up. But what I'm thinking of, said a waiter, is the waste of all that money. A great scoop it was for the Government, eight hundred pounds. The pair were to have bought a shop and lived together, Mr Page, Annie Watts rapped out, and when the discussion was carried from the kitchen upstairs to the second floor: True for you, said Dorothy, now you mention it, I remember; it's you that should be knowing better than anybody else, Mr Page, what Albert's sex was like. Didn't you sleep with her? I fell asleep the moment my head was on the pillow, Page answered, for if you remember rightly I was that tired Mrs Baker hadn't the heart to turn me out of the hotel. I'd been working ten, twelve, fourteen hours a day, and when he took me up to his room I tore off my clothes and fell asleep and went away in the morning before he was awake. Isn't it wonderful? A woman, Hubert continued, and a minx in the bargain, and an artful minx if ever there was one in the world, and there have been a good many. And now, ladies, I must be about my work. I wonder what Annie Watts was thinking of when she stood looking into my eyes; does she suspect me? Hubert asked herself as she sat on her derrick. And what a piece of bad luck that I shouldn't have found Albert alive when I returned to Dublin.

You see, Alec, this is how it was. Polly, that was Hubert's wife, died six months before Albert; and Hubert had been thinking ever since of going into partnership with Albert. In fact Hubert had been thinking about a shop, like Albert, saying to herself almost every day after the death of her wife: Albert and I might set up together. But it was not until she lay in bed that she fell to thinking the matter out, saying to herself: One of us would have had to give up our job to attend to it. The shop was Albert's idea more than mine, so perhaps she'd have given up waiting, which would not have suited me, for I'm tired of going up these ladders. My head isn't altogether as steady as it used to be; swinging about on a derrick isn't suited to women. So perhaps it's as well that things have fallen out as they have. Hubert turned herself over, but sleep was far from her, and she lay a long time thinking of everything and of nothing in particular, as we all do in our beds, with this thought often uppermost: I wonder what is going to be the end of my life. What new chance do the years hold for me?

And of what would Hubert be thinking, being a married woman? Of what else should she be thinking but of her husband, who might now be a different man from the one she left behind? Fifteen years, she said, makes a great difference in all of us, and perhaps it was the words, fifteen years, that put the children she had left behind her back into her thought. I wouldn't be saying that she hadn't been thinking of them, off and on, in the years gone by, but the thought of them was never such a piercing thought as it was that night.

She'd have liked to have jumped out of her bed and run away to them; and perhaps she would have done if she only knew where they were. But she didn't, so she had to keep to her bed; and she lay for an hour or more thinking of them as little children, and wondering what they were like now, Lily was five when she left home. She's a young woman now. Agnes was only two. She is now seventeen, still a girl, Hubert said to herself; but Lily's looking round, thinking of young men, and the other won't be delaying much longer, for young women are much more wide-awake than they used to be in the old days. The rest of my life belongs to them. Their father could have looked after them till now; but now they are thinking of young men he won't be able to cope with them, and maybe he's wanting me too. Bill is forty, and at forty we begin to think of them as we knew them long ago. He must have often thought of me, perhaps oftener than I thought of him; and she was surprised to find that she had forgotten all Bill's ill-usage, and remembered only the good time she had had with him. The rest of my life belongs to him, she said, and to the girls. But how am I to get back to him? how, indeed? . . . Bill may be dead; the children too. But that isn't likely. I must get news of them somehow. The house is there; and lying in the darkness she recalled the pictures on the wall, the chairs that she had sat in, the coverlets on the beds, everything. Bill isn't a wanderer, she said; I'll find him in the same house if he isn't dead. And the children? Did they know anything about her? Had Bill spoken ill of her to them? She didn't think he would do that. But did they want to see her? Well, she could never find that out except by going to see. But how was she going to return home? Pack up her things and go dressed as a man to the house and, meeting Bill on the threshold, say: Don't you know me, Bill? and are you glad to see your mother back, children? No; that wouldn't do. She must return home as a woman, and none of them must know the life she had been living. But what story would she tell him? It would be difficult to tell the story of fifteen years, for fifteen years is a long time, and sooner or later they'd find out she was lying, for they would keep asking her questions.

Be sure, said Alec, 'tis an easy story to tell. Well, Alec, what story should she tell them? In these parts, Alec said, a woman who left her husband and returned to him after fifteen years would say she was taken away by the fairies whilst wandering in a wood. Do you think she'd be believed? Why shouldn't she, your honour?

A woman that marries another woman, and lives happily with her, isn't a natural woman; there must be something of the fairy in her. But I could see it all happening as you told it, the maid-servants and the serving-men going their own roads, and the only fault I've to find with the story is that you left out some of the best parts. I'd have liked to know what the husband said when she went back to him, and they separated all the years. If he liked her better than he did before, or less. And there is a fine story in the way the mother would be vexed by the two daughters and the husbands, and they at her all the time with questions, and she hard set to find answers for them. But mayhap the best bit of all is when Albert began to think that it wouldn't do to have Joe Mackins hanging round, making their home his own, eating and drinking of the best, and when there was a quarrel he'd have a fine threat over them, as good as the Murrigan herself when she makes off of a night to the fair, whirling herself over the people's heads, stirring them up agin each other, making cakes of their skulls. I'm bet, fairly bet, crowed down by the Ballinrobe cock. And now, your honour, you heard the Angelus ringing, and my dinner is on the hob, and I'll be telling you what I think of the story when I come back; but I'm thinking already 'tis the finest that ever came out of Ballinrobe, I am so.

The Sphinx without a Secret

An etching

One afternoon I was sitting outside the Café de la Paix, watching the splendour and shabbiness of Parisian life, and wondering over my vermouth at the strange panorama of pride and poverty that was passing before me, when I heard some one call my name. I turned round, and saw Lord Murchison. We had not met since we had been at college together, nearly ten years before, so I was delighted to come across him again, and we shook hands warmly. At Oxford we had been great friends. I had liked him immensely, he was so handsome, so high-spirited, and so honourable. We used to say of him that he would be the best of fellows, if he did not always speak the truth, but I think we really admired him all the more for his frankness. I found him a good deal changed. He looked anxious and puzzled, and seemed to be in doubt about something. I felt it could not be modern scepticism, for Murchison was the stoutest of Tories, and believed in the Pentateuch as firmly as he believed in the House of Peers; so I concluded that it was a woman, and asked him if he was married yet.

'I don't understand women well enough,' he answered.

'My dear Gerald,' I said, 'women are meant to be loved, not to be understood.'

'I cannot love where I cannot trust,' he replied.

'I believe you have a mystery in your life, Gerald,' I exclaimed; 'tell me about it.'

'Let us go for a drive,' he answered, 'it is too crowded here. No, not a yellow carriage, any other colour—there, that dark-green one will do;' and in a few moments we were trotting down the boulevard in the direction of the Madeleine.

'Where shall we go to?' I said.

'Oh, anywhere you like!' he answered—'to the restaurant in the

Bois; we will dine there, and you shall tell me all about yourself.'

'I want to hear about you first,' I said. 'Tell me your mystery.'

He took from his pocket a little silver-clasped morocco case, and handed it to me. I opened it. Inside there was the photograph of a woman. She was tall and slight, and strangely picturesque with her large vague eyes and loosened hair. She looked like a *clairvoyante*, and was wrapped in rich furs.

'What do you think of that face?' he said; 'is it truthful?'

I examined it carefully. It seemed to me the face of some one who had a secret, but whether that secret was good or evil I could not say. Its beauty was a beauty moulded out of many mysteries—the beauty, in fact, which is psychological, not plastic—and the faint smile that just played across the lips was far too subtle to be really sweet.

'Well,' he cried impatiently, 'what do you say?'

'She is the Giocanda in sables,' I answered. 'Let me know all about her.'

'Not now,' he said; 'after dinner;' and began to talk of other things.

When the waiter brought us our coffee and cigarettes I reminded Gerald of his promise. He rose from his seat, walked two or three times up and down the room, and, sinking into an armchair, told me the following story:—

'One evening,' he said, 'I was walking down Bond Street about five o'clock. There was a terrific crush of carriages, and the traffic was almost stopped. Close to the pavement was standing a little yellow brougham, which, for some reason or other, attracted my attention. As I passed by there looked out from it the face I showed you this afternoon. It fascinated me immediately. All that night I kept thinking of it, and all the next day. I wandered up and down that wretched Row, peering into every carriage, and waiting for the yellow brougham; but I could not find *ma belle inconnue*, and at last I began to think she was merely a dream. About a week afterwards I was dining with Madame de Rastail. Dinner was for eight o'clock; but at half-past eight we were still waiting in the drawing-room. Finally the servant threw open the door, and announced Lady Alroy. It was the woman I had been looking for. She came in very slowly, looking like a moonbeam in grey lace, and, to my intense delight, I was asked to take her in to dinner. After we had sat down I remarked quite innocently, "I think I caught sight of you in Bond Street some time ago, Lady Alroy." She grew very pale, and said to me in a low voice, "Pray do not talk so loud; you may be overheard." I felt miserable at having made such a bad beginning, and plunged recklessly into the subject of the French plays. She spoke very little, always in the same low musical voice, and seemed as if she was afraid of some one listening. I fell passionately, stupidly in love, and the indefinable atmosphere of mystery that surrounded her excited my most ardent curiosity. When she was going away, which she did very soon after dinner, I asked her if I might call and see her. She hesitated for a moment, glanced round to see if any one was near us, and then said, "Yes; tomorrow at a quarter to five." I begged Madame de Rastail to tell me about her; but all that I could learn was that she was a widow with a beautiful house in Park Lane, and as some scientific bore began a dissertation on widows, as exemplifying the survival of the matrimonially fittest, I left and went home.

'The next day I arrived at Park Lane punctual to the moment, but was told by the butler that Lady Alroy had just gone out. I went down to the club quite unhappy and very much puzzled, and after long consideration wrote her a letter, asking if I might be allowed to try my chance some other afternoon. I had no answer for several days, but at last I got a little note saying she would be at home on Sunday at four, and with this extraordinary postscript: "Please do not write to me here again; I will explain when I see you." On Sunday she received me, and was perfectly charming; but when I was going away she begged of me if I ever had occasion to write to her again, to address my letter to "Mrs Knox, care of Whittaker's Library, Green Street." "There are reasons," she said, "why I cannot receive letters in my own house."

'All through the season I saw a great deal of her, and the atmosphere of mystery never left her. Sometimes I thought that she was in the power of some man, but she looked so unapproachable that I could not believe it. It was really very difficult for me to come to any conclusion, for she was like one of those strange crystals that one sees in museums, which are at one moment clear, and at another clouded. At last I determined to ask her to be my wife: I was sick and tired of the incessant secrecy that she imposed on all my visits, and on the few letters I sent her. I wrote to her at the library to ask her if she could see me the following Monday at six. She answered yes, and I was in the seventh heaven of delight. I was infatuated with her: in spite of the mystery, I thought then—in consequence of it, I see now. No; it was the woman herself I loved. The mystery troubled me, maddened me. Why did chance put me in its track?'

'You discovered it, then?' I cried.

'I fear so,' he answered. 'You can judge for yourself.

'When Monday came round I went to lunch with my uncle, and about four o'clock found myself in the Marylebone Road. My uncle, you know, lives in Regent's Park. I wanted to get to Piccadilly, and took a short cut through a lot of shabby little streets. Suddenly I saw in front of me Lady Alroy, deeply veiled and walking very fast. On coming to the last house in the street, she went up the steps, took out a latch-key, and let herself in. "Here is the mystery," I said to myself; and I hurried on and examined the house. It seemed a sort of place for letting lodgings. On the doorstep lay her handkerchief, which she had dropped. I picked it up and put it in my pocket. Then I began to consider what I should do. I came to the conclusion that I had no right to spy on her, and I drove down to the club. At six I called to see her. She was lying on a sofa, in a tea-gown of silver tissue looped up by some strange moonstones that she always wore. She was looking quite lovely. "I am so glad to see you," she said; "I have not been out all day." I stared at her in amazement, and pulling the handkerchief out of my pocket, handed it to her. "You dropped this in Cumnor Street this afternoon, Lady Alroy," I said very calmly. She looked at me in terror, but made no attempt to take the handkerchief. "What were you doing there?" I asked. "What right have you to question me?" she answered. "The right of a man who loves you," I replied; "I came here to ask you to be my wife." She hid her face in her hands, and burst into floods of tears. "You must tell me," I continued. She stood up, and, looking me straight in the face, said, "Lord Murchison, there is nothing to tell you."—"You went to meet some one," I cried; "this is your mystery." She grew dreadfully white, and said, "I went to meet no one."—"Can't you tell the truth?" I exclaimed. "I have told it," she replied. I was mad, frantic; I don't know what I said, but I said terrible things to her. Finally I rushed out of the house. She wrote me a letter the next day; I sent it back unopened, and started for Norway with Alan Colville. After a month I came back, and the first thing I saw in the *Morning Post* was the death of Lady Alroy. She had caught a chill at the Opera, and had died in five days of congestion of the lungs. I shut myself up and saw no one. I had loved her so much, I had loved her so madly. Good God! how I had loved that woman!'

'You went to the street, to the house in it?' I said.

'Yes,' he answered.

'One day I went to Cumnor Street. I could not help it; I was tortured with doubt. I knocked at the door, and a respectable-looking woman opened it to me. I asked her if she had any rooms to let. "Well, sir," she replied, "the drawing-rooms are supposed to be let; but I have not seen the lady for three months, and as rent is owing on them, you can have them."—"Is this the lady?" I said, showing the photograph. "That's her, sure enough," she exclaimed; "and when is she coming back, sir?"—"The lady is dead," I replied. "Oh, sir, I hope not!" said the woman; "she was my best lodger. She paid me three guineas a week merely to sit in my drawing-rooms now and then."—"She met some one here?" I said; but the woman assured me that it was not so, that she always came alone, and saw no one. "What on earth did she do here?" I cried. "She simply sat in the drawing-room, sir, reading books, and sometimes had tea," the woman answered. I did not know what to say, so I gave her a sovereign and went away. Now, what do you think it all meant? You don't believe the woman was telling the truth?'

'I do.'

'Then why did Lady Alroy go there?'

'My dear Gerald,' I answered, 'Lady Alroy was simply a woman with a mania for mystery. She took these rooms for the pleasure of going there with her veil down, and imagining she was a heroine. She had a passion for secrecy, but she herself was merely a Sphinx without a secret.'

'Do you really think so?'

'I am sure of it,' I replied.

He took out the morocco case, opened it, and looked at the photograph. 'I wonder?' he said at last.

E. Œ. SOMERVILLE · 1858–1949
MARTIN ROSS · 1862–1915

Philippa's Fox-Hunt

No one can accuse Philippa and me of having married in haste. As a matter of fact, it was but little under five years from that autumn evening on the river when I had said what is called in Ireland 'the hard word', to the day in August when I was led to the altar by my best man, and was subsequently led away from it by Mrs Sinclair Yeates. About two years out of the five had been spent by me at Shreelane in ceaseless warfare with drains, eaveshoots, chimneys, pumps; all those fundamentals, in short, that the ingenuous and improving tenant expects to find established as a basis from which to rise to higher things. As far as rising to higher things went, frequent ascents to the roof to search for leaks summed up my achievements; in fact, I suffered so general a shrinkage of my ideals that the triumph of making the hall-door bell ring blinded me to the fact that the rat-holes in the hall floor were nailed up with pieces of tin biscuit boxes, and that the casual visitor could, instead of leaving a card, have easily written his name in the damp on the walls.

Philippa, however, proved adorably callous to these and similar shortcomings. She regarded Shreelane and its floundering, foundering ménage of incapables in the light of a gigantic picnic in a foreign land; she held long conversations daily with Mrs Cadogan, in order, as she informed me, to acquire the language; without any ulterior domestic intention she engaged kitchen-maids because of the beauty of their eyes, and housemaids because they had such delightfully picturesque old mothers, and she declined to correct the phraseology of the parlour-maid, whose painful habit it was to whisper 'Do ye choose cherry or clarry?' when proffering the wine. Fast-days, perhaps, afforded my wife her first insight into the sterner realities of Irish housekeeping. Philippa had what are known as High Church proclivities, and took the matter seriously.

'I don't know how we are going to manage for the servants' dinner tomorrow, Sinclair,' she said, coming in to my office one

Thursday morning; 'Julia says she "promised God this long time that she wouldn't eat an egg on a fast-day", and the kitchen-maid says she won't eat herrings "without they're fried with onions", and Mrs Cadogan says she will "not go to them extremes for servants".'

'I should let Mrs Cadogan settle the menu herself,' I suggested.

'I asked her to do that,' replied Philippa, 'and she only said she 'thanked God *she* had no appetite!'

The lady of the house here fell away into unseasonable laughter.

I made the demoralising suggestion that, as we were going away for a couple of nights, we might safely leave them to fight it out, and the problem was abandoned.

Philippa had been much called on by the neighbourhood in all its shades and grades, and daily she and her trousseau frocks presented themselves at hall-doors of varying dimensions in due acknowledgement of civilities. In Ireland, it may be noted, the process known in England as 'summering and wintering' a newcomer does not obtain; sociability and curiosity alike forbid delay. The visit to which we owed our escape from the intricacies of the fast-day was to the Knoxes of Castle Knox, relations in some remote and tribal way of my landlord, Mr Flurry of that ilk. It involved a short journey by train, and my wife's longest basket-trunk; it also, which was more serious, involved my being lent a horse to go out cubbing the following morning.

At Castle Knox we sank into an almost forgotten environment of draught-proof windows and doors, of deep carpets, of silent servants instead of clattering belligerents. Philippa told me afterwards that it had only been by an effort that she had restrained herself from snatching up the train of her wedding-gown as she paced across the wide hall on little Sir Valentine's arm. After three weeks at Shreelane she found it difficult to remember that the floor was neither damp nor dusty.

I had the good fortune to be of the limited number of those who got on with Lady Knox, chiefly, I imagine, because I was as a worm before her, and thankfully permitted her to do all the talking.

'Your wife is extremely pretty,' she pronounced autocratically, surveying Philippa between the candle-shades; 'does she ride?'

Lady Knox was a short square lady, with a weather-beaten face, and an eye decisive from long habit of taking her own line across country and elsewhere. She would have made a very imposing little coachman, and would have caused her stable helpers to rue the day they had the presumption to be born; it struck me that Sir Valentine sometimes did so.

'I'm glad you like her looks,' I replied, 'as I fear you will find her thoroughly despicable otherwise; for one thing, she not only can't ride, but she believes that I can!'

'Oh come, you're not as bad as all that!' my hostess was good enough to say; 'I'm going to put you up on Sorcerer tomorrow, and we'll see you at the top of the hunt—if there is one. That young Knox hasn't a notion how to draw these woods.'

'Well, the best run we had last year out of this place was with Flurry's hounds,' struck in Miss Sally, sole daughter of Sir Valentine's house and home, from her place half-way down the table. It was not difficult to see that she and her mother held different views on the subject of Mr Flurry Knox.

'I call it a criminal thing in any one's great-great-grandfather to rear up a preposterous troop of sons and plant them all out in his own country,' Lady Knox said to me with apparent irrelevance. 'I detest collaterals. Blood may be thicker than water, but it is also a great deal nastier. In this country I find that fifteenth cousins consider themselves near relations if they live within twenty miles of one!'

Having before now taken in the position with regard to Flurry Knox, I took care to accept these remarks as generalities, and turned the conversation to other themes.

'I see Mrs Yeates is doing wonders with Mr Hamilton,' said Lady Knox presently, following the direction of my eyes, which had strayed away to where Philippa was beaming upon her left-hand neighbour, a mildewed-looking old clergyman, who was delivering a long dissertation, the purport of which we were happily unable to catch.

'She has always had a gift for the Church,' I said.

'Not curates?' said Lady Knox, in her deep voice.

I made haste to reply that it was the elders of the Church who were venerated by my wife.

'Well, she has her fancy in old Eustace Hamilton; he's elderly enough!' said Lady Knox. 'I wonder if she'd venerate him as much if she knew that he had fought with his sister-in-law, and they haven't spoken for thirty years! though for the matter of that,' she added, 'I think it shows his good sense!'

'Mrs Knox is rather a friend of mine,' I ventured.

'Is she? H'm! Well, she's not one of mine!' replied my hostess, with her usual definiteness. 'I'll say one thing for her, I believe she's always been a sportswoman. She's very rich, you know, and they say she only married old Badger Knox to save his hounds from being sold to pay his debts, and then she took the horn from him and hunted them herself. Has she been rude to your wife yet? No? Oh, well, she will. It's a mere question of time. She hates all English people. You know the story they tell of her? She was coming home from London, and when she was getting her ticket the man asked if she had said a ticket for York. "No, thank God, Cork!" says Mrs Knox.'

'Well, I rather agree with her!' said I; 'but why did she fight with Mr Hamilton?'

'Oh, nobody knows. I don't believe they know themselves! Whatever it was, the old lady drives five miles to Fortwilliam every Sunday, rather than go to his church, just outside her own back gates,' Lady Knox said with a laugh like a terrier's bark. 'I wish I'd fought with him myself,' she said; 'he gives us forty minutes every Sunday.'

As I struggled into my boots the following morning, I felt that Sir Valentine's acid confidences on cub-hunting, bestowed on me at midnight, did credit to his judgement. 'A very moderate amusement my dear Major,' he had said, in his dry little voice; 'you should stick to shooting. No one expects you to shoot before daybreak.'

It was six o'clock as I crept downstairs, and found Lady Knox and Miss Sally at breakfast, with two lamps on the table, and a foggy daylight oozing in from under the half-raised blinds. Philippa was already in the hall, pumping up her bicycle, in a state of excitement at the prospect of her first experience of hunting that would have been more comprehensible to me had she been going to ride a strange horse, as I was. As I bolted my food I saw the horses being led past the windows, and a faint twang of a horn told that Flurry Knox and his hounds were not far off.

Miss Sally jumped up.

'If I'm not on the Cockatoo before the hounds come up, I shall never get there!' she said, hobbling out of the room in the toils of her safety habit. Her small, alert face looked very childish under her riding-hat; the lamplight struck sparks out of her thick coil of golden-red hair: I wondered how I had ever thought her like her prim little father.

She was already on her white cob when I got to the hall-door, and Flurry Knox was riding over the glistening wet grass with his hounds, while his whip, Dr Jerome Hickey, was having a stirring time with the young entry and the rabbit-holes. They moved on without stopping, up a black avenue, under tall and dripping trees, to a thick laurel covert, at some little distance from the house. Into this the hounds were thrown, and the usual period of fidgety inaction set in for the riders, of whom, all told, there were about half a dozen. Lady Knox, square and solid, on her big, confidential iron-grey, was near me, and her eyes were on me and my mount; with her rubicund face and white collar she was more than ever like a coachman.

'Sorcerer looks as if he suited you well,' she said after a few minutes of silence, during which the hounds rustled and crackled steadily through the laurels; 'he's a little high on the leg, and so are you, you know, so you show each other off.'

Sorcerer was standing like a rock, with his good-looking head in the air and his eyes fastened on the covert. His manners, so far, had been those of a perfect gentleman, and were in marked contrast to those of Miss Sally's cob, who was sidling, hopping, and snatching unappeasably at his bit. Philippa had disappeared from view down the avenue ahead. The fog was melting, and the sun threw long blades of light through the trees; everything was quiet, and in the distance the curtained windows of the house marked the warm repose of Sir Valentine, and those of the party who shared his opinion of cubbing.

'Hark! hark to cry there!'

It was Flurry's voice, away at the other side of the covert. The rustling and brushing through the laurels became more vehement, then passed out of hearing.

'He never will leave his hounds alone,' said Lady Knox disapprovingly.

Miss Sally and the Cockatoo moved away in a series of heraldic capers towards the end of the laurel plantation, and at the same moment I saw Philippa on her bicycle shoot into view on the drive ahead of us.

'I've seen a fox!' she screamed, white with what I believe to have been personal terror, though she says it was excitement; 'it passed quite close to me!'

'What way did he go?' bellowed a voice which I recognised as Dr Hickey's, somewhere in the deep of the laurels.

'Down the drive!' returned Philippa, with a pea-hen quality in her tones with which I was quite unacquainted.

An electrifying screech of 'Gone away!' was projected from the laurels by Dr Hickey.

'Gone away!' chanted Flurry's horn at the top of the covert.

'This is what he calls cubbing!' said Lady Knox, 'a mere farce!' but none the less she loosed her sedate monster into a canter.

Sorcerer got his hind-legs under him, and hardened his crest against the bit, as we all hustled along the drive after the flying figure of my wife. I knew very little about horses, but I realised that even with the hounds tumbling hysterically out of the covert, and the Cockatoo kicking the gravel into his face, Sorcerer comported himself with the manners of the best society. Up a side road I saw Flurry Knox opening half a gate and cramming through it; in a moment we also had crammed through, and the turf of a pasture field was under our feet. Dr Hickey leaned forward and took hold of his horse; I did likewise, with the trifling difference that my horse took hold of me, and I steered for Flurry Knox with single-hearted purpose, the hounds, already a field ahead, being merely an exciting and noisy accompaniment of this endeavour. A heavy stone wall was the first occurrence of note. Flurry chose a place where the top was loose, and his clumsy-looking brown mare changed feet on the rattling stones like a fairy. Sorcerer came at it, tense and collected as a bow at full stretch, and sailed steeply into the air; I saw the wall far beneath me, with an unsuspected ditch on the far side, and I felt my hat following me at the full stretch of its guard as we swept over it, then, with a long slant, we descended to earth some sixteen feet from where we had left it, and I was possessor of the gratifying fact that I had achieved a good-sized 'fly', and had not perceptibly moved in my saddle. Subsequent disillusioning experience has taught me that but few horses jump like Sorcerer, so gallantly, so sympathetically, and with such supreme mastery of the subject; but none the less the enthusiasm that he imparted to me has never been extinguished, and that October morning ride revealed to me the unsuspected intoxication of fox-hunting.

Behind me I heard the scrabbling of the Cockatoo's little hoofs among the loose stones, and Lady Knox, galloping on my left, jerked a maternal chin over her shoulder to mark her daughter's progress. For my part, had there been an entire circus behind me, I was far too much occupied with ramming on my hat and trying to hold Sorcerer, to have looked round, and all my spare faculties were devoted to steering for Flurry, who had taken a right-handed turn, and was at that moment surmounting a bank of uncertain and briary aspect. I surmounted it also, with the swiftness and simplicity for which the Quaker's methods of bank jumping had not prepared me, and two or three fields, traversed at the same steeplechase pace, brought us to a road and to an abrupt check. There, suddenly, were the hounds, scrambling in baffled silence down into the road from the opposite bank, to look for the line they had overrun, and there, amazingly, was Philippa, engaged in excited converse with several men with spades over their shoulders.

'Did ye see the fox, boys?' shouted Flurry, addressing the group.

'We did! we did!' cried my wife and her friends in chorus; 'he ran up the road!'

'We'd be badly off without Mrs Yeates!' said Flurry, as he whirled his mare round and clattered up the road with a hustle of hounds after him.

It occurred to me as forcibly as any mere earthly thing can occur to those who are wrapped in the sublimities of a run, that, for a young woman who had never before seen a fox out of a cage at the Zoo, Philippa was taking to hunting very kindly. Her cheeks were a most brilliant pink, her blue eyes shone.

'Oh, Sinclair!' she exclaimed, 'they say he's going for Aussolas, and there's a road I can ride all the way!'

'Ye can, Miss! Sure we'll show you!' chorused her *cortège*.

Her foot was on the pedal ready to mount. Decidedly my wife was in no need of assistance from me.

Up the road a hound gave a yelp of discovery, and flung himself over a stile into the fields; the rest of the pack went squealing and jostling after him, and I followed Flurry over one of those infinitely varied erections, pleasantly termed 'gaps' in Ireland. On this occasion the gap was made of three razor-edged slabs of slate leaning against an iron bar, and Sorcerer conveyed to me his thorough knowledge of the matter by a lift of his hindquarters that made me feel as if I were being skilfully kicked downstairs. To what extent I looked it, I cannot say, nor providentially can Philippa, as she had already started. I only know that undeserved good luck restored to me my stirrup before Sorcerer got away with me in the next field.

What followed was, I am told, a very fast fifteen minutes; for me time was not; the empty fields rushed past uncounted, fences came and went in a flash, while the wind sang in my ears, and the dazzle of the early sun was in my eyes. I saw the hounds occasionally, sometimes pouring over a green bank, as the charging breaker lifts and flings itself, sometimes driving across a field, as the white tongues of foam slide racing over the sand; and always ahead of me was Flurry Knox, going as a man goes who knows his country, who knows his horse, and whose heart is wholly and absolutely in the right place.

Do what I would, Sorcerer's implacable stride carried me closer and closer to the brown mare, till, as I thundered down the slope of a long field, I was not twenty yards behind Flurry. Sorcerer had stiffened his neck to iron, and to slow him down was beyond me; but I fought his head away to the right, and found myself coming hard and steady at a stonefaced bank with broken ground in front of it. Flurry bore away to the left, shouting something that I did not understand. That Sorcerer shortened his stride at the right moment was entirely due to his own judgement; standing well away from the jump, he rose like a stag out of the tussocky ground, and as he swung my twelve stone six into the air the obstacle revealed itself to him and me as consisting not of one bank but of two, and between the two lay a deep grassy lane, half choked with furze. I have often been asked to state the width of the bohereen, and can only reply that in my opinion it was at least eighteen feet; Flurry Knox and Dr Hickey, who did not jump it, say that it is not more than five. What Sorcerer did with it I cannot say; the sensation was of a towering flight with a kick back in it, a biggish drop, and a landing on cee-springs, still on the downhill grade. That was how one of the best horses in Ireland took one of Ireland's most ignorant riders over a very nasty place.

A sombre line of fir-wood lay ahead, rimmed with a grey wall, and in another couple of minutes we had pulled up on the Aussolas road, and were watching the hounds struggling over the wall into Aussolas demesne.

'No hurry now,' said Flurry, turning in his saddle to watch the Cockatoo jump into the road, 'he's to ground in the big earth inside. Well, Major, it's well for you that's a big-jumped horse. I thought you were a dead man a while ago when you faced him at the bohereen!'

I was disclaiming intention in the matter when Lady Knox and the others joined us.

'I thought you told me your wife was no sportswoman,' she said to me, critically scanning Sorcerer's legs for cuts the while, 'but when I saw her a minute ago she had abandoned her bicycle and was running across country like—'

'Look at her now!' interrupted Miss Sally. 'Oh!—oh!' In the interval between these exclamations my incredulous eyes beheld my wife in mid-air, hand in hand with a couple of stalwart country boys, with whom she was leaping in unison from the top of a bank on to the road.

Everyone, even the saturnine Dr Hickey, began to laugh; I rode back to Philippa, who was exchanging compliments and congratulations with her escort.

'Oh, Sinclair!' she cried, 'wasn't it splendid? I saw you jumping, and everything! Where are they going now?'

'My dear girl,' I said, with marital disapproval, 'you're killing yourself. Where's your bicycle?'

'Oh, it's punctured in a sort of lane, back there. It's all right; and then they'—she breathlessly waved her hand at her attendants—'they showed me the way.'

'Begor! you proved very good, Miss!' said a grinning cavalier.

'Faith she did!' said another, polishing his shining brow with his white flannel coat-sleeve, 'she lepped like a haarse!'

'And may I ask how you propose to go home?' said I.

'I don't know and I don't care! I'm not going home!' She cast an entirely disobedient eye at me. 'And your eye-glass is hanging down your back and your tie is bulging out over your waistcoat!'

The little group of riders had begun to move away.

'We're going on into Aussolas,' called out Flurry; 'come on, and make my grandmother give you some breakfast, Mrs Yeates; she always has it at eight o'clock.'

The front gates were close at hand, and we turned in under the tall beech-trees, with the unswept leaves rustling round the horses' feet, and the lovely blue of the October morning sky filling the spaces between smooth grey branches and golden leaves. The woods rang with the voices of the hounds, enjoying an untrammelled rabbit hunt, while the Master and the Whip, both on foot, strolled along unconcernedly with their bridles over their arms, making themselves agreeable to my wife, an occasional touch of Flurry's horn, or a crack of Dr Hickey's whip, just indicating to the pack that the authorities still took a friendly interest in their doings.

Down a grassy glade in the wood a party of old Mrs Knox's young horses suddenly swept into view, headed by an old mare, who, with her tail over her back, stampeded ponderously past our cavalcade, shaking and swinging her handsome old head, while her youthful friends bucked and kicked and snapped at each other round her with the ferocious humour of their kind.

'Here, Jerome, take the horn,' said Flurry to Dr Hickey; 'I'm going to see Mrs Yeates up to the house, the way these tomfools won't gallop on top of her.'

From this point it seems to me that Philippa's adventures are more worthy of record than mine, and as she has favoured me with a full account of them, I venture to think my version may be relied on.

Mrs Knox was already at breakfast when Philippa was led, quaking, into her formidable presence. My wife's acquaintance with Mrs Knox was, so far, limited to a state visit on either side, and she found but little comfort in Flurry's assurances that his grandmother wouldn't mind if he brought all the hounds in to breakfast, coupled with the statement that she would put her eyes on sticks for the Major.

Whatever the truth of this may have been, Mrs Knox received her guest with an equanimity quite unshaken by the fact that her boots were in the fender instead of on her feet, and that a couple of shawls of varying dimensions and degrees of age did not conceal the inner presence of a magenta flannel dressing-jacket. She installed Philippa at the table and plied her with food, oblivious as to whether the needful implements with which to eat it were forthcoming or no. She told Flurry where a vixen had reared her family, and she watched him ride away, with some biting comments on his mare's hocks screamed after him from the window.

The dining-room at Aussolas Castle is one of the many rooms in Ireland in which Cromwell is said to have stabled his horse (and probably no one would have objected less than Mrs Knox had she been consulted in the matter). Philippa questions if the room had ever been tidied up since, and she endorses Flurry's observation that 'there wasn't a day in the year you wouldn't get feeding for a hen and chickens on the floor'. Opposite to Philippa, on a Louis Quinze chair, sat Mrs Knox's woolly dog, its suspicious little eyes peering at her out of their setting of pink lids and dirty white wool. A couple of young horses outside the windows tore at the matted creepers on the walls, or thrust faces that were half-shy, half-impudent, into the room. Portly pigeons waddled to and fro on the broad window-sill, sometimes flying in to perch on the picture-frames, while they kept up incessantly a hoarse and pompous cooing.

Animals and children are, as a rule, alike destructive to conversation; but Mrs Knox, when she chose, *bien entendu*, could have made herself agreeable in a Noah's ark, and Philippa has a gift of sympathetic attention that personal experience has taught me to regard with distrust as well as respect, while it has often made me realise the worldly wisdom of Kingsley's injunction:

'Be good, sweet maid, and let who will be clever.'

Family prayers, declaimed by Mrs Knox with alarming austerity, followed close on breakfast, Philippa and a vinegar-faced henchwoman forming the family. The prayers were long, and through the open window as they progressed came distinctly a whoop or two; the declamatory tones staggered a little, and then continued at a distinctly higher rate of speed.

'Ma'am! Ma'am!' whispered a small voice at the window.

Mrs Knox made a repressive gesture and held on her way. A sudden outcry of hounds followed, and the owner of the whisper, a small boy with a face freckled like a turkey's egg, darted from the window and dragged a donkey and bath-chair into view. Philippa admits to having lost the thread of the discourse, but she thinks that the 'Amen' that immediately ensued can hardly have come in its usual place. Mrs Knox shut the book abruptly, scrambled up from her knees, and said, 'They've found!'

In a surprisingly short space of time she had added to her attire her boots, a fur cape, and a garden hat, and was in the bath-chair, the small boy stimulating the donkey with the success peculiar to his class, while Philippa hung on behind.

The woods of Aussolas are hilly and extensive, and on that particular morning it seemed that they held as many foxes as hounds. In vain was the horn blown and the whips cracked, small rejoicing parties of hounds, each with a fox of its own, scoured to and fro: every labourer in the vicinity had left his work, and was sedulously heading every fox with yells that would have befitted a tiger hunt, and sticks and stones when occasion served.

'Will I pull out as far as the big rosydandhrum, ma'am?' inquired the small boy; 'I seen three of the dogs go in it, and they yowling.'

'You will,' said Mrs Knox, thumping the donkey on the back with her umbrella; 'here! Jeremiah Regan! Come down out of that with that pitchfork! Do you want to kill the fox, you fool?'

'I do not, your honour, ma'am,' responded Jeremiah Regan, a tall young countryman, emerging from a bramble brake.

'Did you see him?' said Mrs Knox eagerly.

'I seen himself and his ten pups drinking below at the lake 'ere yesterday, your honour, ma'am, and he as big as a chestnut horse!' said Jeremiah.

'Faugh! Yesterday!' snorted Mrs Knox; 'go on to the rhododendrons, Johnny!'

The party, reinforced by Jeremiah and the pitchfork, progressed at a high rate of speed along the shrubbery path, encountering *en route* Lady Knox, stooping on to her horse's neck under the sweeping branches of the laurels.

'Your horse is too high for my coverts, Lady Knox,' said the Lady of the Manor, with a malicious eye at Lady Knox's flushed face and dinged hat; 'I'm afraid you will be left behind like Absalom when the hounds go away!'

'As they never do anything here but hunt rabbits,' retorted her ladyship, 'I don't think that's likely.'

Mrs Knox gave her donkey another whack, and passed on.

'Rabbits, my dear!' she said scornfully to Philippa. 'That's all she knows about it. I declare it disgusts me to see a woman of that age making such a Judy of herself! Rabbits, indeed!'

Down in the thicket of rhododendron everything was very quiet for a time. Philippa strained her eyes in vain to see any of the riders; the horn blowing and the whip cracking passed on almost out of hearing. Once or twice a hound worked through the rhododendrons, glanced at the party, and hurried on, immersed in business. All at once Johnny, the donkey-boy, whispered excitedly:

'Look at he! Look at he!' and pointed to a boulder of grey rock that stood out among the dark evergreens. A big yellow cub was crouching on it; he instantly slid into the shelter of the bushes, and the irrepressible Jeremiah, uttering a rendering shriek, plunged into the thicket after him. Two or three hounds came rushing at the sound, and after this Philippa says she finds some difficulty in recalling the proper order of events; chiefly, she confesses, because of the wholly ridiculous tears of excitement that blurred her eyes.

'We ran,' she said, 'we simply tore, and the donkey galloped, and as for that old Mrs Knox, she was giving cracked screams to the hounds all the time, and they were screaming too; and then somehow we were all out on the road!'

What seems to have occurred was that three couple of hounds, Jeremiah Regan, and Mrs Knox's equipage, amongst them somehow hustled the cub out of Aussolas demesne and up on to a hill on the farther side of the road. Jeremiah was sent back by his mistress to fetch Flurry, and the rest of the party pursued a thrilling course along the road, parallel with that of the hounds, who were hunting slowly through the gorse on the hillside.

'Upon my honour and word, Mrs Yeates, my dear, we have the hunt to ourselves!' said Mrs Knox to the panting Philippa, as they pounded along the road. 'Johnny, d'ye see the fox?'

'I do, ma'am!' shrieked Johnny, who possessed the usual field-glass vision bestowed upon his kind. 'Look at him over-right us on the hill above! Hi! The spotty dog have him! No, he's gone from him! *Gwan out o' that*!' This to the donkey, with blows that sounded like the beating of carpets, and produced rather more dust.

They had left Aussolas some half a mile behind, when, from a strip of wood on their right, the fox suddenly slipped over the bank on to the road just ahead of them, ran up it for a few yards and whisked in at a small entrance gate, with the three couple of hounds yelling on a red-hot scent, not thirty yards behind. The bath-chair party whirled in at their heels, Philippa and the donkey considerably blown, Johnny scarlet through his freckles, but as fresh as paint, the old lady blind and deaf to all things save the chase. The hounds went raging through the shrubs beside the drive, and away down a grassy slope towards a shallow glen, in the bottom of which ran a little stream, and after them over the grass bumped the bath-chair. At the stream they turned sharply and ran up the glen towards the avenue, which crossed it by means of a rough stone viaduct.

' 'Pon me conscience, he's into the old culvert!' exclaimed Mrs Knox; 'there was one of my hounds choked there once, long ago! Beat on the donkey, Johnny!'

At this juncture Philippa's narrative again becomes incoherent, not to say breathless. She is, however, positive that it was somewhere about here that the upset of the bath-chair occurred, but she cannot be clear as to whether she picked up the donkey or Mrs Knox, or whether she herself was picked up by Johnny while Mrs Knox picked up the donkey. From my knowledge of Mrs Knox, I should say she picked up herself and no one else. At all events, the next salient point is the palpitating moment when Mrs Knox, Johnny, and Philippa successively applying an eye to the opening of the culvert by which the stream trickled under the viaduct, while five dripping hounds bayed and leaped around them, discovered by more senses than that of sight that the fox was in it, and furthermore that one of the hounds was in it too.

'There's a sthrong grating before him at the far end,' said Johnny, his head in at the mouth of the hole, his voice sounding as if he were talking into a jug, 'the two of them's fighting in it; they'll be choked surely!'

'Then don't stand gabbling there, you little fool, but get in and pull the hound out!' exclaimed Mrs Knox, who was balancing herself on a stone in the stream.

'I'd be in dread, ma'am,' whined Johnny.

'Balderdash!' said the implacable Mrs Knox. 'In with you!'

I understand that Philippa assisted Johnny into the culvert, and presume that it was in so doing that she acquired the two Robinson Crusoe bare footprints which decorated her jacket when I next met her.

'Have you got hold of him yet, Johnny?' cried Mrs Knox up the culvert.

'I have, ma'am, by the tail,' responded Johnny's voice, sepulchral in the depths.

'Can you stir him, Johnny?'

'I cannot, ma'am, and the wather is rising in it.'

'Well, please God, they'll not open the mill dam!' remarked Mrs Knox philosophically to Philippa, as she caught hold of Johnny's dirty ankles. 'Hold on to the tail, Johnny!'

She hauled, with, as might be expected, no appreciable result. 'Run, my dear, and look for somebody, and we'll have that fox yet!'

Philippa ran, whither she knew not, pursued by fearful visions of bursting mill-dams, and maddened foxes at bay. As she sped up the avenue she heard voices, robust male voices, in a shrubbery, and made for them. Advancing along an embowered walk towards her was what she took for one wild instant to be a funeral; a second glance showed her that it was a party of clergymen of all ages, walking by twos and threes in the dappled shade of the overarching trees. Obviously she had intruded her sacrilegious presence into a Clerical Meeting. She acknowledges that at this awe-inspiring spectacle she faltered, but the thought of Johnny, the hound, and the fox, suffocating, possibly drowning together in the culvert, nerved her. She does not remember what she said or how she said it, but I fancy she must have conveyed to them the impression that old Mrs Knox was being drowned, as she immediately found herself heading a charge of the Irish Church towards the scene of disaster.

Fate has not always used me well, but on this occasion it was mercifully decreed that I and the other members of the hunt should be privileged to arrive in time to see my wife and her rescue party precipitating themselves down the glen.

'Holy Biddy!' ejaculated Flurry, 'is she running a paper-chase with all the parsons? But look! For pity's sake will you look at my grandmother and my Uncle Eustace?'

Mrs Knox and her sworn enemy the old clergyman, whom I had met at dinner the night before, were standing, apparently in the stream, tugging at two bare legs that projected from a hole in the viaduct, and arguing at the top of their voices. The bath-chair lay on its side with the donkey grazing beside it, on the bank a stout Archdeacon was tendering advice, and the hounds danced and howled around the entire group.

'I tell you, Eliza, you had better let the Archdeacon try,' thundered Mr Hamilton.

'Then I tell you I will not!' vociferated Mrs Knox, with a tug at the end of the sentence that elicited a subterranean lament from Johnny. 'Now who was right about the second grating? I told you so twenty years ago!'

Exactly as Philippa and her rescue party arrived, the efforts of Mrs Knox and her brother-in-law triumphed. The struggling, sopping form of Johnny was slowly drawn from the hole, drenched, speechless, but clinging to the stern of a hound, who, in its turn, had its jaws fast in the hind-quarters of a limp, yellow cub.

'Oh, it's dead!' wailed Philippa. 'I *did* think I should have been in time to save it!'

'Well, if that doesn't beat all!' said Dr Hickey.

The Priest

I

Because Father Reen had been reading all day the rain had meant but little for him. Since breakfast time he had not been disturbed, his housekeeper even had not entered, and he had reached an age— he was sixty-two—when a day of unbroken quiet was the best of holidays. Yet any more of the quietness might have taken the edge off his pleasure. In the afternoon, just in good time it seemed, an uncertain sunbeam floated tremulously across the pages of his book; quite unexpectedly, it had stolen in through the still streaming window panes. Father Reen, his mouth suddenly opening, raised his head and stared with his blue eyes, large and clear, across the river valley towards the mountains. He noticed that, even as he looked, hedgerow, branch, and rocky height were emerging through the saturated air, were taking form, unsubstantial still, yet no longer broken in outline. His house was in a good place for the afternoon sunshine; it stood on a rise of ground above the river and looked to the south-west. The soil was sandy, the paths in the garden well kept and kind to the feet; before long, in the mild November sunshine, he was pacing to and fro the full length of his little place. Between this pleasant place in the sun, and the study he had just come from, he had grown into the custom of passing nearly all his free time—too much of it, as he often told himself, for it meant further and further withdrawal from the life of the village, the life of his parish; but then where in the parish was such life to be come upon as he could profitably make use of? He was conscious that in this parish of his, as in many another round about it, there was, speaking from either social or cultural point of view, neither an upper class nor even a middle class—there was only a peasant class that had only comparatively recently emerged from penury, a class that needed spurring, that needed leadership, and that was not finding it. He had long since reasoned out that the time had come for the building up of a middle class, an upper class too, on native lines, to take the place of those that had failed; but as often however as this thought came to him he smiled, for he certainly was not one of those who get things put to right. Now, however, breathing the fresh air, which was chilly enough to make quick walking necessary, he fortunately was free from the thought of all this. Beyond the feel of the fresh air in his nostrils he was free almost from sensation. Film after film of moisture he saw lifting, dissipating themselves in the effulgence of the sun, leaving the wide river valley, the hundred thousand rocky scars and ridges that encumbered it, sharply drawn, one against another, if as yet without colour, a succession of grey tones. But the swollen river made no response to the light above it, for its waters had become stained, were heavy after the scourings from the fords and inches. He could see it tumbling along.

Whenever in his pacing he faced the west his eye traversed not only the river but the village beyond it. He saw the evening smoke of its homely fires ascending, each spire of it alive with the sunshine streaming through it. He had been so long in the place, first as curate and then as parish priest, that he had got into the way of whispering to himself such pet phrases as: My valley, my river, my river, my hills. This afternoon, the ascending smoke spires taking his eye, My people! was the phrase that possessed his lips. It seemed touched with the memory of emotion rather than with any living warmth. He had scarcely uttered the words when he stopped up in his pacing, for in that single patch of open village street that was visible to him, he saw a horseman swinging steadily along, making, he was certain, towards the bridge, towards this hillside, towards this house of his.

II

In less than a half-hour Father Reen was riding alone across the bridge and through the village, faced towards the west, towards Kilmony, a ploughland ten miles away on the farthest edge of his far-flung parish, where, the messenger had informed him, an old man was nearing his end.

Anyhow there would be no more rain. The sky was clearing, the wind was swung round towards the north. Now the sun was hidden behind a barricade of cloud, cold grey in colour, and thick, that rested all along the horizon, shafts of rich light ascending from behind it to the height of heaven. The sun would not show itself again; and the moment it was gone one would feel how hard the night was turning to frost. Father Reen was conscious of this as he made on at a good pace. Yes, the air would become colder and colder, the landscape barer and barer, harder and harder in its features. The village, which he had come through, was wind-swept enough, was hard enough and niggard enough in all its ways, yet it did not lack for trees in various groupings, nor for clipped bushes, shapely hedges, flower plots. And he remembered how, as he passed through, he had heard an outburst of reckless laughter from the stragglers in the forge—their meeting place as long as he could remember. He knew he would come on no other group of gossips as loud voiced or as merry as they: nor on hedgerow trees or clipped hedges or any flowers. Already he was aware of the denuded character of the landscape about him, every feature of it sharp and bare; he foresaw all the long roads and byways, little cared for, stone-strewn, with their surfaces swept away, deep-channelled by the rain torrents from the hills; and, very insidiously, uneasiness intruded on his peace of mind, not induced so much by the discomfort of the roads ahead of him as by the thought of Kilmony itself, to which they led—a place where the people were still living in wretched cabins, on the poorest fare, without a notion of giving attention to, or spending a penny on, anything except the direst necessaries of life—a place where he hardly ever remembered an old person to die without the lust of property troubling the spirit almost to the beginning of the agony. Against the fear that this foreknowledge aroused in him he struggled; he shook his head at it, he set his teeth, he grasped the reins more firmly, consciously giving himself to the onward rhythm of the gallop.

Already, he felt, there was thin frost forming on the pools beneath the horse's hoofs. And what a bite in the north-west as it blew across the marches and the reedy lakes! Soon the stars would begin to come forth sparkling with frost. Everywhere now slabs of rock, pinnacles of rock, hillsides of rock; and not a tree anywhere, not a bush even; scarcely a sign of humanity; hardly a human being. On an upland farm he had seen a boy driving a few scraggy beasts diagonally up a sloping field to the stall. Now, across the inch, he saw an old man bent under a huge mass of bogland cow-fodder, making for a gap—and between man and boy there were miles, it seemed, of rock and heather, of such desolation as hindered the growth of any community spirit, which, of itself, would little by little induce a finer way of living. My people! My people! he thought, so good, so sinless, even so religious, yet so hard, so niggardly, so worldly, even so cruel; and again he blamed himself for not starting, for not forwarding some plan or other—sports or story-telling, or dancing or singing or reading or play-acting—anything that would cut across and baffle that lust of acquisitiveness which everywhere is the peasant's bane. My people! My people! My people! and then: If only I were young again! But this, he chided himself, was but self-deception. What was really wrong with him, he told himself, was that he had unconsciously withdrawn himself from them, with those hard ways of theirs. They were leaderless, at least in the social sense. They had no initiative—yet he had left them to themselves lest—yes, that was it—lest—he was like a doctor falling into age, afraid to use any except the safest remedies—lest complications might ensue—yes, that was the phrase. But it was true he was ageing. And the best day he ever was he had not been one of those blessed people who get things done. Anyway, his duty as a priest—that, O thanks be to God, he had never neglected, so far as he knew.

It was dark night when he turned up the hillside on the ridge of which lay Kilmony—a place where every household was intermarried with every other household. Pluckily his horse stepped up the broken ground, his forehoofs smiting the rocky shelvings, impatient for footing. When the ascent became a little easier Father Reen raised his head and saw the crest of the hill swarthy and sharp against the grey cloudless sky, darker than it, full of roughnesses, of breaks and points, a restless line running east and west with here and there a bright star fallen upon it. He knew he was at the right place. Beyond that ridge, he remembered, were immense slowly rising uplands abandoned to nature, miles on miles, where sheep were driven to pasture at the end of springtime, and left to themselves the length of summer, where turf was dug out, but where no attempt at tillage had ever been made. On his right he now noticed a haphazard group of gables; some of them had once been whitened, and these helped still to separate the whole group from the beetling background. He heard a gate opened, and dimly he made out a tall figure in the middle of the road—it was indeed little more than a rough pathway—standing against the sky awaiting him.

III

'Am I at Miah Neehan's?' he asked.

'Yes, Father. You're better get off here, the yard isn't too clean in itself.'

He dismounted, and already he felt the wind cold on his sweaty limbs.

'I'm in time?' he questioned.

'Good time. In good time,' he was answered, and then he heard the voice raised:

'Isn't it a wonder one of ye wouldn't hold a lamp for Father Reen?'

There was but a dull glimmer of light in the interior of the dwelling: he saw it reflected in the dung pit which, in the old-fashioned way, occupied most of the yard. By peering he made out the causeway of large boulders running through the mire to the doorway. All was just as he had expected. It was one of those places, now happily rare, over which the spirit of the bad old times, as the people say, still seemed to brood, a place where necessity was served, and that only. Among the dark figures on the doorway he saw movement—the effect of a harshly spoken word of his guide—and he was glad, for the sweat was chilly on his limbs. He saw now a flannel-coated middle-aged man emerge, shielding the lamp from the wind with a corner of his wrapper. He made towards him, and by the time he reached the threshold the figures were all withdrawn again into the interior. There were both men and women, but the faces of the women were so deeply hidden within the hoods of their cloaks that all he could see of them was a pale gleam. They were seated by the walls, but the men were standing haphazardly about or leaning their shoulders wherever they could find support. Tall and spare, a mountainy breed, their heads were lost in the darkness that hung beneath the ancient thatch. The fire on the hearth was uncared for; and not a word was passing among those present. He saluted them, his hat in his hand, and waited until the lamp had been again hung on its accustomed nail.

'Where is he?' he said.

There was a slight pause before the reply came: 'Inside, Father.'

Before he entered the lower room, the only other room in the house, he turned towards where the voice had spoken, saying: 'Are his affairs settled, are they in order?'

No answer coming, he turned towards the man who had held the lamp for him, looking at him questioningly, but he, throwing down his eyes, slunk away into the midst of the others. He raised his voice then:

'Are his affairs in order?'

Just then, the man who had welcomed him on the roadway—he had since been seeing after the horse, entered hurriedly—looking like one who had been anxious whether those within might not have been scanting the courtesies. A voice in the semi-darkness, a woman's voice, met him:

'Father Reen wants to know are his affairs settled?'

'Oh yes; that's all right. In good order. In good order. You needn't give yourself any uneasiness about that, Father.'

He spoke loudly, challengingly, the priest felt, to those about them in the room. Indeed he had scarcely finished when one of the tallest of the men flung himself from his place and strode across the room to the doorway where he took his station, his back to those within, his eyes staring out into the black night. 'Sit down, sit down, Jack. Be easy.' He who had answered the priest's question it was who spoke, with the carelessness of contempt, it seemed, rather than in any spirit of good fellowship. But the man in the doorway answered him, flinging round his head suddenly and angrily:

'I'm all right here—just here where I am.'

It appeared to Father Reen the two were fairly matched. 'Very well, very well. Please yourself. Come on in, Father.'

A woman's voice said:

'Tim, you'd want a second candle within.'

'You're right. One is a poor light on these occasions.' He soon had a lighted candle in his hand, showing the way.

'Come on in, Father. Everything is ready for you. Quite ready.'

IV

Father Reen was alone with the dying man. In the squalid room, the rickety contrivance of a bed, the ancient coverings, the stained walls, the tainted air, he again found all he had expected to find. Above all he found his thought realised in the head thrown weakly back upon the pillow, the eyes of which had fastened on him at the moment of entrance. He could feel how grimly the old man's will— he was ninety-one years of age—had been exerted, had been struggling against the craving of the worn-out body for rest, for the lapse of unconsciousness. He drew near to the bedside, seated himself at its edge, and noticed how the old eyes were searching the spaces of the room; he then heard the dry and wearied voice speaking with a distinctness that of itself alone would acquaint one with the triumph of the will over every other faculty in the old man's soul:

'Whisper, Father, is that door shut?'

The priest rose, made certain that the door between them and the crowd of descendants and relatives outside was fastened, then seating himself again said:

' 'Tis all right.'

'Whisper,' the old head was reaching up to his face, 'I'm destroyed, destroyed with them, with them in and out to me all day, all night too, in and out, in and out, watching me, and watching each other too.'

It was a long time before he was satisfied he had done all he could, and could do no more, for that struggling soul, which, he was sure, would enter the next world before the night was out. But the moment he had caught sight of the old face, the tight wisdom of it, the undefeated will in it, the clasp on the lips, the firm old chin, and then the hard-shut fist like a knob on the scraggy forearm that would lift and threaten and emphasise—he knew what was before him—that he would have to call up all the resources of his own brain and will, having asked help from on high, and wrestle, and wrestle, and wrestle, to dislodge that poor old peasant's handful of thoughts from that which had been their centre and stay for seventy or eighty years—the land, the farm, as he called it—a waste of rock and shale, bog and moor, that should never at all have been brought under the spade. He had more than his farm to stay his thoughts upon: as earnest of his long and well-spent life he had his dirty bank-book under his pillow with eighty pounds marked in it to his credit. No sooner was Father Reen aware of this than he knew that it would be easier almost to wrench one of the rocks in the fields abroad from its bed than to wrench that long-accustomed support from the old man's little world of consciousness without shattering it to insanity. Yet this at last Father Reen felt he had succeeded in doing; he thought he found a new look coming into the old man's eyes, overspreading his brow, some expression of hard-won relief, some return of openness, of simplicity, that may not have been there since early manhood; in the voice he thought he found some new timbre, some sudden access of tenderness, of sweetness; and, more surely telling of the new scale of values suddenly come upon by that old battler in a rough world, a flood of aspirations broke impetuously from the trembling lips: 'Jesus Christ, O welcome, O welcome; keep near me, I'm not worthy, I'm not worthy, but welcome. O Blessed Mother, pray for me, now, now'—a flood onward and never-ending once it had started at all; and Father Reen noticed how the two fists, twin knobs, equally hard and small, were pressed fiercely down upon the brows, side by side, covering the eye sockets, hiding almost the whole of the rapt countenance, except the moving chin. Limbs and all, the old peasant had become one knot of concentration, and the thought of what he was leaving behind him was not any longer its secret.

v

When Father Reen re-entered the larger room, the living room, he found the crowd in the self-same positions as when he had gone from them; and he felt that not a syllable had passed among them. Tim, the master mind of the group, the man who had led him to the old man's bedside—he was one of the old man's grandsons—had the middle of the earthen floor to himself. He blurted out, almost with a touch of levity in his voice: 'You had a job with him.'

A murmur of sudden and indignant surprise broke from those against the walls. Father Reen shot one glance at the speaker, he could not help it, the fall from the plane he had been moving in was so terrible—and the man, suddenly realising his fault, made some hopeless, mollifying gesture with a limp hand, speaking no word, however. His wife, as Father Reen perceived, came forward, saying: 'Would Father Reen take some little refreshment? We could make a cup of tea? 'Tis a long journey is before you.'

He motioned her from him, making for the door: he wanted with all his heart to be in the saddle and away under the stars.

vi

It took some little time to get the horse ready. He then had to lead it down that steep decline beneath the crest of the hill. As he did so he noticed a glimmer of light above him on the right hand side. He had noticed no house there when ascending; he would not have noticed it now only that he caught a high-pitched babble of talk above him, and, looking round, spied the dim gleam of a window. As he looked he saw a flash of light—the door had opened—and he heard an angry passionate outburst: 'I'll have the law of him! I'll have the law of him!'

The door was suddenly shut to. There remained the angry onward confusion of talk and the dull glimmer in the tiny window. It was a son's house or a grandson's house, surely; and there was many another house in the neighbourhood thinking the same thought this night. Law, yes, and years and years of it over those stony fields and that dirty bank-book. But this much, he told himself, he had known from the moment of entering that crowded living room.

The remembrance quickened his blood. With almost a touch of savagery he urged his beast forward the moment he found his legs gripping its belly. The hard roads invited it. They, with the frozen pools all along them, were bright enough to see by; there was also the tangle of starshine hanging somehow in the middle air above the landscape. For one no longer young he rode wildly, but then the Reens from time immemorial had been eager horsemen. When he came down on to the level ground he broke into a hard gallop; and when, after an hour's going, he had won to the better-kept road beside the lakes he rode as if for a high wager. He was flying not from Kilmony so much as from that fund of reflections all he had witnessed there had aroused in him. That terrible promiscuity of rock, the little stony fields that only centuries of labour had salvaged from them, the unremitting toil they demanded, the poor return, the niggard scheme of living; and then the ancient face on the pillow, the gathering of greedy descendants—he had known it all before; for years the knowledge of how much of a piece it all was had kept his mind uneasy. He knew he would presently be asking himself: Where do my duties end? And this hard riding of his was but an effort to baffle that inveterate questioning. He rode like a man possessed. If the rhythm of the riding, the need for alertness, the silence of the black, stark landscape, the far-stretching lakes, the mass of starshine in the air, weakened at moments the urgency of the question, it overwhelmingly leaped upon him, that question did, whenever he passed a lonely farm-house clung against its slab of protecting rock at the base of a cliff, or espied one aloft on some *leaca* or other, betrayed to the night by the lamp still dimly burning. Each and every one of them seemed to grab at his very heart, pleading for some human succour that their inmates could not name. And all the time the hoofs of his animal were beating out from the frozen road in perfectly regular rhythm: My people! My people! My people!

The Weaver's Grave

I

Mortimer Hehir, the weaver, had died and they had come in search of his grave to Cloon na Morav, the Meadow of the Dead. Meehaul Lynskey, the nail-maker, was first across the stile. There was excitement in his face. His long warped body moved in a shuffle over the ground. Following him came Cahir Bowes, the stone-breaker, who was so beaten down from the hips forward, that his back was horizontal as the back of an animal. His right hand held a stick which propped him up in front, his left hand clutched his coat behind, just above the small of the back. By these devices he kept himself from toppling head over heels as he walked. Mother earth was the brow of Cahir Bowes by magnetic force, and Cahir Bowes was resisting her fatal kiss to the last. And just now there was animation in the face he raised from its customary contemplation of the ground. Both old men had the air of those who had been unexpectedly let loose. For a long time they had lurked somewhere in the shadows of life, the world having no business for them, and now, suddenly, they had been remembered and called forth to perform an office which nobody else on earth could perform. The excitement in their faces as they crossed over the stile into Cloon na Morav expressed a vehemence in their belated usefulness. Hot on their heels came two dark, handsome, stoutly built men, alike even to the cord that tied their corduroy trousers under their knees, and, being grave-diggers, they carried flashing spades. Last of all, and after a little delay, a firm white hand was laid on the stile, a dark figure followed, the figure of a woman whose palely sad face was picturesquely, almost dramatically, framed in a black shawl which hung from the crown of the head. She was the widow of Mortimer Hehir, the weaver, and she followed the others into Cloon na Morav, the Meadow of the Dead.

To glance at Cloon na Morav as you went by on the hilly road, was to get an impression of a very old burial-ground; to pause on the road and look at Cloon na Morav was to become conscious of its quiet situation, of winds singing down from the hills in a chant for the dead; to walk over to the wall and look at the mounds inside was to provoke quotations from Gray's 'Elegy'; to make the sign of the cross, lean over the wall, observe the gloomy lichened background of the wall opposite, and mark the things that seemed to stray about, like yellow snakes in the grass, was to think of Hamlet moralizing at the graveside of Ophelia, and hear them establish the identity of Yorick. To get over the stile and stumble about inside, was to forget all these things and to know Cloon na Morav for itself. Who could tell the age of Cloon na Morav? The mind could only swoon away into mythology, paddle about in the dotage of paganism, the toothless infancy of Christianity. How many generations, how many septs, how many clans, how many families, how many people, had gone into Cloon na Morav? The mind could only take wing on the romances of mathematics. The ground was billowy, grotesque. Several partially suppressed insurrections—a great thirsting, worming, pushing and shouldering under the sod—had given it character. A long tough growth of grass wired it from end to end. Nature, by this effort, endeavouring to control the strivings of the more daring of the insurgents of Cloon na Morav. No path here; no plan or map or register existed; if there ever had been one or the other it had been lost. Invasions and wars and famines and feuds had swept the ground and left it. All claims to interment had been based on powerful traditional rights. These rights had years ago come to an end—all save in a few outstanding cases, the rounding up of a spent generation. The overflow from Cloon na Morav had already set a new cemetery on its legs a mile away, a cemetery in which limestone headstones and Celtic crosses were springing up like mushrooms, advertising the triviality of a civilization of men and women, who, according to their own epitaphs, had done exactly the two things they could not very well avoid doing: they had all, their obituary notices said, been born and they had all died. Obscure quotations from Scripture were sometimes added by way of apology. There was an almost unanimous expression of forgiveness to the Lord for what had happened to the deceased. None of this lack of humour in Cloon na Morav. Its monuments were comparatively few, and such of them as it had not swallowed were well within the general atmosphere.

No obituary notice in the place was complete; all were either wholly or partially eaten up by the teeth of time. The monuments that had made a stout battle for existence were pathetic in their futility. The vanity of the fashionable of dim ages made one weep. Who on earth could have brought in the white marble slab to Cloon na Morav? It had grown green with shame. Perhaps the lettering, once readable upon it, had been conscientiously picked out in gold. The shrieking winds and the fierce rains of the hills alone could tell. Plain heavy stones, their shoulders rounded with a chisel, presumably to give them some off-handed resemblance to humanity, now swooned at fantastic angles from their settings, as if the people to whose memory they had been dedicated had shouldered them away as an impertinence. Other slabs lay in fragments on the ground, filling the mind with thoughts of Moses descending from Mount Sinai and, waxing angry at sight of his followers dancing about false gods, casting the stone tables containing the Commandments to the ground, breaking them in pieces—the most tragic destruction of a first edition that the world has known. Still other heavy square dark slabs, surely creatures of a pagan imagination, were laid flat down on numerous short legs, looking sometimes like representations of monstrous black cockroaches, and again like tables at which the guests of Cloon na Morav might sit down, goblin-like, in the moonlight, when nobody was looking. Most of the legs had given way and the tables lay overturned, as if there had been a quarrel at cards the night before. Those that had kept their legs exhibited great cracks or fissures across their backs, like slabs of dark ice breaking up. Over by the wall, draped in its pattern of dark green lichen, certain families of dim ages had made an effort to keep up the traditions of the Eastern sepulchres. They had showed an aristocratic reluctance to take to the common clay in Cloon na Morav. They had built low casket-shaped houses against the gloomy wall, putting an enormously heavy iron door with ponderous iron rings—like the rings on a pier by the sea—at one end, a tremendous lock—one wondered what Goliath kept the key—finally cementing the whole thing up and surrounding it with spiked iron railings. In these contraptions very aristocratic families locked up their dead as if they were dangerous wild animals. But these ancient vanities only heightened the general democracy of the ground. To prove a traditional right to a place in its community was to have the bond of your pedigree sealed. The act of burial in

Cloon na Morav was in itself an epitaph. And it was amazing to think that there were two people still over the sod who had such a right—one Mortimer Hehir, the weaver, just passed away, the other Malachi Roohan, a cooper, still breathing. When these two survivors of a great generation got tucked under the sward of Cloon na Morav its terrific history would, for all practical purposes, have ended.

II

Meehaul Lynskey, the nailer, hitched forward his bony shoulders and cast his eyes over the ground—eyes that were small and sharp, but unaccustomed to range over wide spaces. The width and the wealth of Cloon na Morav were baffling to him. He had spent his long life on the look-out for one small object so that he might hit it. The colour that he loved was the golden glowing end of a stick of burning iron; wherever he saw that he seized it in a small sconce at the end of a long handle, wrenched it off by a twitch of the wrist, hit it with a flat hammer several deft taps, dropped it into a vessel of water, out of which it came a cool and perfect nail. To do this thing several hundred times six days in the week, and pull the chain of a bellows at short intervals, Meehaul Lynskey had developed an extraordinary dexterity of sight and touch, a swiftness of business that no mortal man could exceed, and so long as he had been pitted against nail-makers of flesh and blood he had more than held his own; he had, indeed, even put up a tremendous but an unequal struggle against the competition of nail-making machinery. Accustomed as he was to concentrate on a single, glowing, definite object, the complexity and disorder of Cloon na Morav unnerved him. But he was not going to betray any of these professional defects to Cahir Bowes, the stonebreaker. He had been sent there as an ambassador by the caretaker of Cloon na Morav, picked out for his great age, his local knowledge, and his good character, and it was his business to point out to the twin grave-diggers, sons of the caretaker, the weaver's grave, so that it might be opened to receive him. Meehaul Lynskey had a knowledge of the place, and was quite certain as to a great number of grave sites, while the caretaker, being an official without records, had a profound ignorance of the whole place.

Cahir Bowes followed the drifting figure of the nail-maker over the ground, his face hitched up between his shoulders, his eyes keen and grey, glint-like as the mountains of stones he had in his day broken up as road material. Cahir, no less than Meehaul, had his knowledge of Cloon na Morav and some of his own people were buried here. His sharp, clear eyes took in the various mounds with the eye of a prospector. He, too, had been sent there as an ambassador, and as between himself and Meehaul Lynskey he did not think there could be any two opinions; his knowledge was superior to the knowledge of the nailer. Whenever Cahir Bowes met a loose stone on the grass quite instinctively he turned it over with his stick, his sharp old eyes judging its grain with a professional swiftness, then cracking at it with his stick. If the stick were a hammer the stone, attacked on its most vulnerable spot, would fall to pieces like glass. In stones Cahir Bowes saw not sermons but seams. Even the headstones he tapped significantly with the ferrule of his stick, for Cahir Bowes had an artist's passion for his art, though his art was far from creative. He was one of the great destroyers, the reducers, the makers of chaos, a powerful and remorseless critic of the Stone Age.

The two old men wandered about Cloon na Morav, in no hurry whatever to get through with their business. After all they had been a long time pensioned off, forgotten, neglected, by the world. The renewed sensation of usefulness was precious to them. They knew that when this business was over they were not likely to be in request for anything in this world again. They were ready to oblige the world, but the world would have to allow them their own time. The world, made up of the two grave-diggers and the widow of the weaver, gathered all this without any vocal proclamation. Slowly, mechanically as it were, they followed the two ancients about Cloon na Morav. And the two ancients wandered about with the labour of age and the hearts of children. They separated, wandered about silently as if they were picking up old acquaintances, stumbling upon forgotten things, gathering up the threads of days that were over, reviving their memories, and then drew together, beginning to talk slowly, almost casually, and all their talk was of the dead, of the people who lay in the ground about them. They warmed to it, airing their knowledge, calling up names and complications of family relationships, telling stories, reviving all virtues, whispering at past vices, past vices that did not sound like vices at all, for the long years are great mitigators and run in splendid harness with the coyest of all the virtues, Charity. The whispered scandals of Cloon na Morav were seen by the twin grave-diggers and the widow of the weaver through such a haze of antiquity that they were no longer scandals but romances. The rake and the drab, seen a good way down the avenue, merely look picturesque. The grave-diggers rested their spades in the ground, leaning on the handles in exactly the same graveyard pose, and the pale widow stood in the background, silent, apart, patient, and, like all dark, tragic looking women, a little mysterious.

The stonebreaker pointed with his quivering stick at the graves of the people whom he spoke about. Every time he raised that forward support one instinctively looked, anxious and fearful, to see if the clutch were secure on the small of the back. Cahir Bowes had the sort of shape that made one eternally fearful for his equilibrium. The nailer, who, like his friend the stonebreaker, wheezed a good deal, made short, sharp gestures, and always with the right hand; the fingers were hooked in such a way, and he shot out the arm in such a manner, that they gave the illusion that he held a hammer and that it was struck out over a very hot fire. Every time Meehaul Lynskey made this gesture one expected to see sparks flying.

'Where are we to bury the weaver?' one of the grave-diggers asked at last.

Both old men laboured around to see where the interruption, the impertinence, had come from. They looked from one twin to the other, with gravity, indeed anxiety, for they were not sure which was which, or if there was not some illusion in the resemblance, some trick of youth to baffle age.

'Where are we to bury the weaver?' the other twin repeated, and the strained look on the old men's faces deepened. They were trying to fix in their minds which of the twins had interrupted first and which last. The eyes of Meehaul Lynskey fixed on one twin with the instinct of his trade, while Cahir Bowes ranged both and eventually wandered to the figure of the widow in the background, silently accusing her of impatience in a matter in which it would be indelicate for her to show haste.

'We can't stay here for ever,' said the first twin.

It was the twin upon whom Meehaul Lynskey had fastened his small eyes, and, sure of his man this time, Meehaul Lynskey hit him.

'There's many a better man than you,' said Meehaul Lynskey,

'that will stay here for ever.' He swept Cloon na Morav with the hooked fingers.

'Them that stays in Cloon na Morav for ever,' said Cahir Bowes with a wheezing energy, 'have nothing to be ashamed of—nothing to be ashamed of. Remember that, young fellow.'

Meehaul Lynskey did not seem to like the intervention, the help, of Cahir Bowes. It was a sort of implication that he had not—*he*, mind you—had not hit the nail properly on the head.

'Well, where are we to bury him, anyway?' said the twin, hoping to profit by the chagrin of the nailer—the nailer who, by implication, had failed to nail.

'You'll bury him,' said Meehaul Lynskey, 'where all belonging to him is buried.'

'We come,' said the other twin, 'with some sort of intention of that kind.' He drawled out the words, in imitation of the old men. The skin relaxed on his handsome dark face and then bunched in puckers of humour about the eyes; Meehaul Lynskey's gaze, wandering for once, went to the handsome dark face of the other twin and the skin relaxed and then bunched in puckers of humour about *his* eyes, so that Meehaul Lynskey had an unnerving sensation that these young grave-diggers were purposely confusing him.

'You'll bury him,' he began with some vehemence, and was amazed to again find Cahir Bowes taking the words out of his mouth, snatching the hammer out of his hand, so to speak.

'—where you're told to bury him,' Cahir Bowes finished for him.

Meehaul Lynskey was so hurt that his long slanting figure moved away down the graveyard, then stopped suddenly. He had determined to do a dreadful thing. He had determined to do a thing that was worse than kicking a crutch from under a cripple's shoulder; that was like stealing the holy water out of a room where a man lay dying. He had determined to ruin the last day's amusement on this earth for Cahir Bowes and himself by prematurely and basely disclosing the weaver's grave!

'Here,' called back Meehaul Lynskey, 'is the weaver's grave, and here you will bury him.'

All moved down to the spot, Cahir Bowes going with extra-ordinary spirit, the ferrule of his terrible stick cracking on the stones he met on the way.

'Between these two mounds,' said Meehaul Lynskey, and already the twins raised their twin spades in a sinister movement, like swords of lancers flashing at a drill.

'Between these two mounds,' said Meehaul Lynskey 'is the grave of Mortimer Hehir.'

'Hold on!' cried Cahir Bowes. He was so eager, so excited, that he struck one of the grave-diggers a whack of his stick on the back. Both grave-diggers swung about to him as if both had been hurt by the one blow.

'Easy there,' said the first twin.

'Easy there,' said the second twin.

'Easy yourselves,' cried Cahir Bowes. He wheeled about his now quivering face on Meehaul Lynskey.

'What is it you're saying about the spot between the mounds?' he demanded.

'I'm saying,' said Meehaul Lynskey vehemently, 'that it's the weaver's grave.'

'What weaver?' asked Cahir Bowes.

'Mortimer Hehir,' replied Meehaul Lynskey. 'There's no other weaver in it.'

'Was Julia Rafferty a weaver?'

'What Julia Rafferty?'

'The midwife, God rest her.'

'How could she be a weaver if she was a midwife?'

'Not a one of me knows. But I'll tell you what I do know and know rightly: that it's Julia Rafferty is in that place and no weaver at all.'

'Amn't I telling you it's the weaver's grave?'

'And amn't I telling you that it's not?'

'That I may be as dead as my father but the weaver was buried there.'

'A bone of a weaver was never sunk in it as long as weavers was weavers. Full of Raffertys it is.'

'Alive with weavers it is.'

'Heavenly Father, was the like ever heard: to say that a grave was alive with dead weavers.'

'It's full of them—full as a tick.'

'And the clean grave that Mortimer Hehir was never done boasting about—dry and sweet and deep and no way bulging at all. Did you see the burial of his father ever?'

'I did, in troth, see the burial of his father—forty years ago if it's a day.'

'Forty year ago—it's fifty-one year come the sixteenth of May. It's well I remember and it's well I have occasion to remember it, for it was the day after that again that myself ran away to join the soldiers, my aunt hot foot after me, she to be buying me out the week after, I a high-spirited fellow morebetoken.'

'Leave the soldiers out of it and leave your aunt out of it and stick to the weaver's grave. Here in this place was the last weaver buried, and I'll tell you what's more. In a straight line with it is the grave of—'

'A straight line, indeed! Who but yourself, Meehaul Lynskey, ever heard of a straight line in Cloon na Morav? No such thing was ever wanted or ever allowed in it.'

'In a straight direct line, measured with a rule—'

'Measured with crooked, stumbling feet, maybe feet half reeling in drink.'

'Can't you listen to me now?'

'I was always a bad warrant to listen to anything except sense. Yourself ought to be the last man in the world to talk about straight lines, you with the sight scattered in your head, with the divil of sparks flying under your eyes.'

'Don't mind me sparks now, nor me sight neither, for in a straight measured line with the weaver's grave was the grave of the Cassidys.'

'What Cassidys?'

'The Cassidys that herded for the O'Sheas.'

'Which O'Sheas?'

'O'Shea Ruadh of Cappakelly. Don't you know any one at all, or is it gone entirely your memory is?'

'Cappakelly *inagh*! And who cares a whistle about O'Shea Ruadh, he or his seed, breed and generations? It's a rotten lot of landgrabbers they were.'

'Me hand to you on that. Striving ever they were to put their red paws on this bit of grass and that perch of meadow.'

'Hungry in themselves even for the cutaway bog.'

'And Mortimer Hehir a decent weaver, respecting every man's wool.'

'His forehead pallid with honesty over the yarn and the loom.'

'If a bit broad-spoken when he came to the door for a smoke of the pipe.'

'Well, there won't be a mouthful of clay between himself and O'Shea Ruadh now.'

'In the end what did O'Shea Ruadh get after all his striving?'

'I'll tell you that. He got what land suits a blind fiddler.'

'Enough to pad the crown of the head and tap the sole of the foot! Now you're talking.'

'And the devil a word out of him now no more than any one else in Cloon na Morav.'

'It's easy talking to us all about land when we're packed up in our timber boxes.'

'As the weaver was when he got sprinkled with the holy water in that place.'

'As Julia Rafferty was when they read the prayers over her in that place, she a fine, buxom, cheerful woman in her day, with great skill in her business.'

'Skill or no skill, I'm telling you she's not there, wherever she is.'

'I suppose you want me to take her up in my arms and show her to you?'

'Well then, indeed, Cahir, I do not. 'Tisn't a very handsome pair you would make at all, you not able to stand much more hardship than Julia herself.'

From this there developed a slow, laboured, aged dispute between the two authorities. They moved from grave to grave, pitting memory against memory, story against story, knocking down reminiscence with reminiscence, arguing in a powerful intimate obscurity that no outsider could hope to follow, blasting knowledge with knowledge, until the whole place seemed strewn with the corpses of their arguments. The two grave-diggers followed them about in a grim silence; impatience in their movements, their glances; the widow keeping track of the grand tour with a miserable feeling, a feeling, as site after site was rejected, that the tremendous exclusiveness of Cloon na Morav would altogether push her dead man, the weaver, out of his privilege. The dispute ended, like all epics, where it began. Nothing was established, nothing settled. But the two old men were quite exhausted, Meehaul Lynskey sitting down on the back of one of the monstrous cockroaches, Cahir Bowes leaning against a tombstone that was half-submerged, its end up like the stern of a derelict at sea. Here they sat glaring at each other like a pair of grim vultures. The two grave-diggers grew restive. Their business had to be done. The weaver would have to be buried. Time pressed. They held a consultation apart. It broke up after a brief exchange of views, a little laughter.

'Meehaul Lynskey is right,' said one of the twins.

Meehaul Lynskey's face lit up. Cahir Bowes looked as if he had been slapped on the cheeks. He moved out from his tombstone.

'Meehaul Lynskey is right,' repeated the other twin. They had decided to break up the dispute by taking sides. They raised their spades and moved to the site which Meehaul Lynskey had urged upon them.

'Don't touch that place,' Cahir Bowes cried, raising his stick. He was measuring the back of the grave-digger again when the man spun round upon him, menace in his handsome dark face.

'Touch me with that stick,' he cried, 'and I'll—'

Some movement in the background, some agitation in the widow's shawl, caused the grave-digger's menace to dissolve, the words to die in his mouth, a swift flush mounting the man's face. A faint smile of gratitude swept the widow's face like a flash. It was as if she had cried out, 'Ah, don't touch the poor old cranky fellow! you might hurt him.' And it was as if the grave-digger had cried back: 'He has annoyed me greatly, but I don't intend to hurt him. And since you say so with your eyes I won't even threaten him.'

Under pressure of the half threat, Cahir Bowes shuffled back a little way, striking an attitude of feeble dignity, leaning out on his stick while the grave-diggers got to work.

'It's the weaver's grave, surely,' said Meehaul Lynskey.

'If it is,' said Cahir Bowes, 'remember his father was buried down seven feet. You gave into that this morning.'

'There was no giving in about it,' said Meehaul Lynskey. 'We all know that one of the wonders of Cloon na Morav was the burial of the last weaver seven feet, he having left it as an injunction on his family. The world knows he went down the seven feet.'

'And remember this,' said Cahir Bowes, 'that Julia Rafferty was buried no seven feet. If she is down three feet it's as much as she went.'

Sure enough, the grave-diggers had not dug down more than three feet of ground when one of the spades struck hollowly on unhealthy timber. The sound was unmistakable and ominous. There was silence for a moment. Then Cahir Bowes made a sudden short spurt up a mound beside him, as if he were some sort of mechanical animal wound up, his horizontal back quivering. On the mound he made a superhuman effort to straighten himself. He got his ears and his blunt nose into a considerable elevation. He had not been so upright for twenty years. And raising his weird countenance, he broke into a cackle that was certainly meant to be a crow. He glared at Meehaul Lynskey, his emotion so great that his eyes swam in a watery triumph.

Meehaul Lynskey had his eyes, as was his custom, upon one thing, and that thing was the grave, and especially the spot on the grave where the spade had struck the coffin. He looked stunned and fearful. His eyes slowly withdrew their gimlet-like scrutiny from the spot, and sought the triumphant crowing figure of Cahir Bowes on the mound.

Meehaul Lynskey looked as if he would like to say something, but no words came. Instead he ambled away, retired from the battle, and standing apart, rubbed one leg against the other, above the back of the ankles, like some great insect. His hooked fingers at the same time stroked the bridge of his nose. He was beaten.

'I suppose it's not the weaver's grave,' said one of the grave-diggers. Both of them looked at Cahir Bowes.

'Well, you know it's not,' said the stonebreaker. 'It's Julia Rafferty you struck. She helped many a one into the world in her day, and it's poor recompense to her to say she can't be at rest when she left it.' He turned to the remote figure of Meehaul Lynskey and cried: 'Ah-ha, well you may rub your ignorant legs. And I'm hoping Julia will forgive you this day's ugly work.'

In silence, quickly, with reverence, the twins scooped back the clay over the spot. The widow looked on with the same quiet, patient, mysterious silence. One of the grave-diggers turned on Cahir Bowes.

'I suppose you know where the weaver's grave is?' he asked.

Cahir Bowes looked at him with an ancient tartness, then said: 'You suppose!'

'Of course, you know where it is.'

Cahir Bowes looked as if he knew where the gates of heaven were, and that he might—or might not—enlighten an ignorant world. It all depended! His eyes wandered knowingly out over the meadows beyond the graveyard. He said:

'I do know where the weaver's grave is.'

'We'll be very much obliged to you if you show it to us.'

'Very much obliged,' endorsed the other twin.

The stonebreaker, thus flattered, led the way to a new site, one nearer to the wall, where were the plagiarisms of the Eastern sepulchres. Cahir Bowes made little journeys about, measuring so many steps from one place to another, mumbling strange and unintelligible information to himself, going through an extraordinary geometrical emotion, striking the ground hard taps with his stick.

'Glory be to the Lord,' cried Meehaul Lynskey, 'he's like the man they had driving the water for the well in the quarry field, he whacking the ground with his magic hazel wand.'

Cahir Bowes made no reply. He was too absorbed in his own emotion. A little steam was beginning to ascend from his brow. He was moving about the ground like some grotesque spider weaving an invisible web.

'I suppose now,' said Meehaul Lynskey, addressing the marble monument, 'that as soon as Cahir hits the right spot one of the weavers will turn out below. Or maybe he expects one of them to whistle up at him out of the ground. That's it; devil a other! When we hear the whistle we'll all know for certain where to bury the weaver.'

Cahir Bowes was contracting his movements, so that he was now circling about the one spot, like a dog going to lie down.

Meehaul Lynskey drew a little closer, watching eagerly, his grim yellow face, seared with yellow marks from the fires of his workshop, tightened up in a sceptical pucker. His half-muttered words were bitter with an aged sarcasm. He cried:

'Say nothing; he'll get it yet, will the man of knowledge, the know-all, Cahir Bowes! Give him time. Give him until this day twelve month. Look at that for a right-about-turn on the left heel. Isn't the nimbleness of that young fellow a treat to see? Are they whistling to you from below, Cahir? Is it dancing to the weaver's music you are? That's it, devil a other.'

Cahir Bowes was mapping out a space on the grass with his stick. Gradually it took, more or less, the outline of a grave site. He took off his hat and mopped his steaming brow with a red handkerchief, saying:

'There is the weaver's grave.'

'God in Heaven,' cried Meehaul Lynskey, 'will you look at what he calls the weaver's grave? I'll say nothing at all. I'll hold my tongue. I'll shut up. Not one word will I say about Alick Finlay, the mildest man that ever lived, a man full of religion, never at the end of his prayers! But, sure, it's the saints of God that get the worst of it in this world, and if Alick escaped during life, faith he's in for it now, with the pirates and the body-snatchers of Cloon na Morav on top of him.'

A corncrake began to sing in the nearby meadow, and his rasping notes sounded like a queer accompaniment to the words of Meehaul Lynskey. The grave-diggers, who had gone to work on the Cahir Bowes site, laughed a little, one of them looking for a moment at Meehaul Lynskey, saying:

'Listen to that damned old corncrake in the meadow! I'd like to put a sod in his mouth.'

The man's eye went to the widow. She showed no emotion one way or the other, and the grave-digger got back to his work. Meehaul Lynskey, however, wore the cap. He said:

'To be sure! I'm to sing dumb. I'm not to have a word out of me at all. Others can rattle away as they like in this place, as if they owned it. The ancient good old stock is to be nowhere and the scruff of the hills let rampage as they will. That's it, devil a other. Castles falling and dunghills rising! Well, God be with the good old times and the good old mannerly people that used to be in it, and God be with Alick Finlay, the holiest—'

A sod of earth came through the air from the direction of the grave, and, skimming Meehaul Lynskey's head, dropped somewhere behind. The corncrake stopped his notes in the meadow, and Meehaul Lynskey stood statuesque in a mute protest, and silence reigned in the place while the clay sang up in a swinging rhythm from the grave.

Cahir Bowes, watching the operations with intensity, said:

'It was nearly going astray on me.'

Meehaul Lynskey gave a little snort. He asked:

'What was?'

'The weaver's grave.'

'Remember this: the last weaver is down seven feet. And remember this: Alick Finlay is down less than Julia Rafferty.'

He had no sooner spoken when a fearful thing happened. Suddenly out of the soft cutting of the earth a spade sounded harsh on tinware, there was a crash, less harsh, but painfully distinct, as if rotten boards were falling together, then a distinct subsidence of the earth. The work stopped at once. A moment's fearful silence followed. It was broken by a short, dry laugh from Meehaul Lynskey. He said:

'God be merciful to us all! That's the latter end of Alick Finlay.'

The two grave-diggers looked at each other. The shawl of the widow in the background was agitated. One twin said to the other:

'This can't be the weaver's grave.'

The other agreed. They all turned their eyes upon Cahir Bowes. He was hanging forward in a pained strain, his head quaking, his fingers twitching on his stick. Meehaul Lynskey turned to the marble monument and said with venom:

'If I was guilty I'd go down on my knees and beg God's pardon. If I didn't know the ghost of Alick Finlay, saint as he was, would leap upon me and guzzle me—for what right would I have to set anybody at him with driving spades when he was long years in his grave?'

Cahir Bowes took no notice. He was looking at the ground, searching about, and slowly, painfully, began his web-spinning again. The grave-diggers covered in the ground without a word. Cahir Bowes appeared to get lost in some fearful maze of his own making. A little whimper broke from him now and again. The steam from his brow thickened in the air, and eventually he settled down on the end of a headstone, having got the worst of it. Meehaul Lynskey sat on another stone facing him, and they glared, sinister and grotesque, at each other.

'Cahir Bowes,' said Meehaul Lynskey, 'I'll tell you what you are, and then you can tell me what I am.'

'Have it whatever way you like,' said Cahir Bowes. 'What is it that I am?'

'You're a gentleman, a grand oul' stonebreaking gentleman. That's what you are, devil a other!'

The wrinkles on the withered face of Cahir Bowes contracted, his eyes stared across at Meehaul Lynskey, and two yellow teeth showed between his lips. He wheezed:

'And do you know what you are?'

'I don't.'

'You're a nailer, that's what you are, a damned nailer.'

They glared at each other in a quaking, grim silence.

And it was at this moment of collapse, of deadlock, that the widow spoke for the first time. At the first sound of her voice one of the twins perked his head, his eyes going to her face. She said in a tone as quiet as her whole behaviour:

'Maybe I ought to go up to the Tunnel Road and ask Malachi Roohan where the grave is.'

They had all forgotten the oldest man of them all, Malachi Roohan. He would be the last mortal man to enter Cloon na Morav. He had been the great friend of Mortimer Hehir, the weaver, in the days that were over, and the whole world knew that Mortimer Hehir's knowledge of Cloon na Morav was perfect. Maybe Malachi Roohan would have learned a great deal from him. And Malachi Roohan, the cooper, was so long bed-ridden that those who remembered him at all thought of him as a man who had died a long time ago.

'There's nothing else for it,' said one of the twins, leaving down his spade, and immediately the other twin laid his spade beside it.

The two ancients on the headstones said nothing. Not even *they* could raise a voice against the possibilities of Malachi Roohan, the cooper. By their terrible aged silence they gave consent, and the widow turned to walk out of Cloon na Morav. One of the grave-diggers took out his pipe. The eyes of the other followed the widow, he hesitated, then walked after her. She became conscious of the man's step behind her as she got upon the stile, and turned her palely sad face upon him. He stood awkwardly, his eyes wandering, then said:

'Ask Malachi Roohan where the grave is, the exact place.'

It was to do this the widow was leaving Cloon na Morav; she had just announced that she was going to ask Malachi Roohan where the grave was. Yet the man's tone was that of one who was giving her extraordinarily acute advice. There was a little half-embarrassed note of confidence in his tone. In a dim way the widow thought that, maybe, he had accompanied her to the stile in a little awkward impulse of sympathy. Men were very curious in their ways sometimes. The widow was a very well-mannered woman, and she tried to look as if she had received a very valuable direction. She said:

'I will. I'll put that question to Malachi Roohan.'

And then she passed out over the stile.

III

The widow went up the road, and beyond it struck the first of the houses of the near-by town. She passed through faded streets in her quiet gait, moderately grief-stricken at the death of her weaver. She had been his fourth wife, and the widowhoods of fourth wives have not the rich abandon, the great emotional cataclysm, of first, or even second, widowhoods. It is a little chastened in its poignancy. The widow had a nice feeling that it would be out of place to give way to any of the characteristic manifestations of normal widowhood. She shrank from drawing attention to the fact that she had been a fourth wife. People's memories become so extraordinarily acute to family history in times of death! The widow did not care to come in as a sort of dramatic surprise in the gossip of the people about the weaver's life. She had heard snatches of such gossip at the wake the night before. She was beginning to understand why people love wakes and the intimate personalities of wakehouses. People listen to, remember, and believe what they hear at wakes. It is more precious to them than anything they ever hear in school, church, or playhouse. It is hardly because they get certain entertainment at the wake. It is more because the wake is a grand review of family ghosts. There one hears all the stories, the little flattering touches, the little unflattering bitternesses, the traditions, the astonishing records, of the clans. The woman with a memory speaking to the company from a chair beside a laid-out corpse carries more authority than the bishop allocuting from his chair. The wake is realism. The widow had heard a great deal at the wake about the clan of the weavers, and noted, without expressing any emotion, that she had come into the story not like other women, for anything personal to her own womanhood—for beauty, or high spirit, or temper, or faithfulness, or unfaithfulness—but simply because she was a fourth wife, a kind of curiosity, the back-wash of Mortimer Hehir's romances. The widow felt a remote sense of injustice in all this. She had said to herself that widows who had been fourth wives deserved more sympathy than widows who had been first wives, for the simple reason that fourth widows had never been, and could never be, first wives! The thought confused her a little, and she did not pursue it, instinctively feeling that if she did accept the conventional view of her condition she would only crystallize her widowhood into a grievance that nobody would try to understand, and which would, accordingly, be merely useless. And what was the good of it, anyhow? The widow smoothed her dark hair on each side of her head under her shawl.

She had no bitter and no sweet memories of the weaver. There was nothing that was even vivid in their marriage. She had no complaints to make of Mortimer Hehir. He had not come to her in any fiery love impulse. It was the marriage of an old man with a woman years younger. She had recognized him as an old man from first to last, a man who had already been thrice through a wedded experience, and her temperament, naturally calm, had met his half-stormy, half-petulant character, without suffering any sort of shock. The weaver had tried to keep up to the illusion of a perennial youth by dyeing his hair, and marrying one wife as soon as possible after another. The fourth wife had come to him late in life. She had a placid understanding that she was a mere flattery to the weaver's truculent egoism.

These thoughts, in some shape or other, occupied, without agitating, the mind of the widow as she passed, a dark shadowy figure through streets that were clamorous in their quietudes, painful in their lack of all the purposes for which streets have ever been created. Her only emotion was one which she knew to be quite creditable to her situation: a sincere desire to see the weaver buried in the grave which the respectability of his family and the claims of his ancient house fully and fairly entitled him to. The proceedings in Cloon na Morav had been painful, even tragical, to the widow. The weavers had always been great authorities and zealous guardians of the ancient burial place. This function had been traditional and voluntary with them. This was especially true of the last of them, Mortimer Hehir. He had been the greatest of all authorities on the burial places of the local clans. His knowledge was scientific. He had been the grand savant of Cloon na Morav. He had policed the place. Nay, he had been its tyrant. He had over and over again prevented terrible mistakes, complications that would have appalled those concerned if they were not beyond all such concerns. The widow of the weaver had often thought that in his day Mortimer Hehir had made his solicitation for the place a passion, unreasonable, almost violent. They said that all this had sprung from a fear that had come to him in his early youth that through some blunder an alien, an inferior, even an enemy, might come to find his way into the family burial place of the weavers. This fear had made him what he was. And in his later years his pride in the family burial place became a worship. His trade had gone down, and his pride had gone up. The burial ground in Cloon na Morav was the grand proof of his aristocracy. That was the coat-of-arms, the estate, the mark of high breeding, in the weavers. And now the man who had minded everybody's grave had not been able to mind his own. The widow thought that it was one of those injustices which blacken the reputation of the whole earth. She had felt, indeed, that she had been herself slack not to have learned long ago the lie of this precious grave from the weaver himself; and that he himself had been slack in not properly instructing her. But that was the way in this miserable world! In his passion for classifying the rights of others, the weaver had obscured his own. In his long and entirely successful battle in keeping alien corpses out of his own aristocratic pit he had made his own corpse alien to every pit in the place. The living high priest was the dead pariah of Cloon na Morav. Nobody could now tell except, perhaps, Malachi Roohan, the precise spot which he had defended against the blunders and confusions of the entire community, a dead-forgetting, indifferent, slack lot!

The widow tried to recall all she had ever heard the weaver say about his grave, in the hope of getting some clue, something that might be better than the scandalous scatter-brained efforts of Meehaul Lynskey and Cahir Bowes. She remembered various detached things that the weaver, a talkative man, had said about his grave. Fifty years ago since that grave had been last opened, and it had then been opened to receive the remains of his father. It had been thirty years previous to that since it had taken in his father, that is, the newly dead weaver's father's father. The weavers were a long-lived lot, and there were not many males of them; one son was as much as any one of them begot to pass to the succession of the loom; if there were daughters they scattered, and their graves were continents apart. The three wives of the late weaver were buried in the new cemetery. The widow remembered that the weaver seldom spoke of them, and took no interest in their resting place. His heart was in Cloon na Morav and the sweet, dry, deep, aristocratic bed he had there in reserve for himself. But all his talk had been generalization. He had never, that the widow could recall, said anything about the site, about the signs and measurements by which it could be identified. No doubt, it had been well known to many people, but they had all died. The weaver had never realized what their slipping away might mean to himself. The position of the grave was so intimate to his own mind that it never occurred to him that it could be obscure to the minds of others. Mortimer Hehir had passed away like some learned and solitary astronomer who had discovered a new star, hugging its beauty, its exclusiveness, its possession to his heart, secretly rejoicing how its name would travel with his own through heavenly space for all time—and forgetting to mark its place among the known stars grouped upon his charts. Meehaul Lynskey and Cahir Bowes might now be two seasoned astronomers of venal knowledge looking for the star which the weaver, in his love for it, had let slip upon the mighty complexity of the skies.

The thing that is clearest to the mind of a man is often the thing that is most opaque to the intelligence of his bosom companion. A saint may walk the earth in the simple belief that all the world beholds his glowing halo; but all the world does not; if it did the saint would be stoned. And Mortimer Hehir had been as innocently proud of his grave as a saint might be ecstatic of his halo. He believed that when the time came he would get a royal funeral—a funeral fitting to the last of the line of great Cloon na Morav weavers. Instead of that they had no more idea of where to bury him than if he had been a wild tinker of the roads.

The widow, thinking of these things in her own mind, was about to sigh when, behind a window pane, she heard the sudden bubble of a roller canary's song. She had reached, half absent-mindedly, the home of Malachi Roohan, the cooper.

IV

The widow of the weaver approached the door of Malachi Roohan's house with an apologetic step, pawing the threshold a little in the manner of peasant women—a mannerism picked up from shy animals—before she stooped her head and made her entrance.

Malachi Roohan's daughter withdrew from the fire a face which reflected the passionate soul of a cook. The face cooled as the widow disclosed her business.

'I wouldn't put it a-past my father to have knowledge of the grave,' said the daughter of the house, adding, 'The Lord a mercy on the weaver.'

She led the widow into the presence of the cooper.

The room was small and low and stuffy, indifferently served with light by an unopenable window. There was the smell of old age, of decay, in the room. It brought almost a sense of faintness to the widow. She had the feeling that God had made her to move in the ways of old men—passionate, cantankerous, egoistic old men, old men for whom she was always doing something, always remembering things, from missing buttons to lost graves.

Her eyes sought the bed of Malachi Roohan with an unemotional, quietly sceptical gaze. But she did not see anything of the cooper. The daughter leaned over the bed, listened attentively, and then very deftly turned down the clothes, revealing the bust of Malachi Roohan. The widow saw a weird face, not in the least pale or lined, but ruddy, with a mahogany bald head, a head upon which the leathery skin—for there did not seem any flesh—hardly concealed the stark outlines of the skull. From the chin there strayed a grey beard, the most shaken and whipped-looking beard that the widow had ever seen; it was, in truth, a very miracle of a beard, for one wondered how it had come there, and having come there, how it continued to hang on, for there did not seem anything to which it could claim natural allegiance. The widow was as much astonished at this beard as if she saw a plant growing in a pot without soil. Through its gaps she could see the leather of the skin, the bones of a neck, which was indeed a neck. Over this head and shoulders the cooper's daughter bent and shouted into a crumpled ear. A little spasm of life stirred in the mummy. A low, mumbling sound came from the bed. The widow was already beginning to feel that, perhaps, she had done wrong in remembering that the cooper was still extant. But what else could she have done? If the weaver was buried in a wrong grave she did not believe that his soul would ever rest in peace. And what could be more dreadful than a soul wandering on the howling winds of the earth? The weaver would grieve, even in heaven, for his grave, grieve, maybe, as bitterly as a saint might grieve who had lost his halo. He was a passionate old man, such an old man as would have a turbulent spirit. He would surely—. The widow stifled the thoughts that flashed into her mind. She was no more superstitious than the rest of us, but—. These vague and terrible fears, and her moderately decent sorrow, were alike banished from her mind by what followed. The mummy on the bed came to life. And, what was more, he did it himself. His daughter looked on with the air of one whose sensibilities had become blunted by a long familiarity with the various stages of his resurrections. The widow gathered that the daughter had been well drilled; she had been taught how to keep her place. She did not tender the slightest help to her father as he drew himself together on the bed. He turned over on his side, then on his back, and stealthily began to insinuate his shoulder blades on the pillow, pushing up his weird head to the streak of light from the little window. The widow had been so long accustomed to assist the aged that she made some involuntary movement of succour. Some half-seen gesture by the daughter, a sudden lifting of the eyelids on the face of the patient, disclosing a pair of blue eyes, gave the widow instinctive pause. She remained where she was, aloof like the daughter of the house. And as she caught the blue of Malachi Roohan's eyes it broke upon the widow that here in the essence of the cooper there lived a spirit of extraordinary independence. Here, surely, was a man who had been accustomed to look out for himself, who resented the attentions, even in these days of his flickering consciousness. Up he worked his shoulder blades, his mahogany skull, his leathery skin, his sensational eyes, his miraculous beard, to the light and to the full view of the visitor. At a certain stage of the resurrection—when the cooper had drawn two long, stringy arms from under the clothes—his daughter made a drilled movement forward, seeking something in the bed. The widow saw her discover the end of a rope, and this she placed in the hands of her indomitable father. The other end of the rope was fastened to the iron rail of the foot of the bed. The sinews of the patient's hands clutched the rope, and slowly, wonderfully, magically, as it seemed to the widow, the cooper raised himself to a sitting posture in the bed. There was dead silence in the room except for the laboured breathing of the performer. The eyes of the widow blinked. Yes, there was that ghost of a man hoisting himself up from the dead on a length of rope reversing the usual procedure. By that length of rope did the cooper hang on to life, and the effort of life. It represented his connection with the world, the world which had forgotten him, which marched past his window outside without knowing the stupendous thing that went on his room. There he was, sitting up in the bed, restored to view by his own unaided efforts, holding his grip on life to the last. It cost him something to do it, but he did it. It would take him longer and longer every day to grip along that length of rope; he would fail ell by ell, sinking back to the last helplessness on his rope, descending into eternity as a vessel is lowered on a rope into a dark, deep well. But there he was now, still able for his work, unbeholding to all, self-dependent and alive, looking a little vaguely with his blue eyes at the widow of the weaver. His daughter swiftly and quietly propped pillows at his back, and she did it with the air of one who was allowed a special privilege.

'Nan!' called the old man to his daughter.

The widow, cool-tempered as she was, almost jumped on her feet. The voice was amazingly powerful. It was like a shout, filling the little room with vibrations. For four things did the widow ever after remember Malachi Roohan—for his rope, his blue eyes, his powerful voice, and his magic beard. They were thrown on the background of his skeleton in powerful relief.

'Yes, Father,' his daughter replied, shouting into his ear. He was apparently very deaf. This infirmity came upon the widow with a shock. The cooper was full of physical surprises.

'Who's this one?' the cooper shouted, looking at the widow. He had the belief that he was delivering an aside.

'Mrs Hehir.'

'Mrs Hehir—what Hehir would she be?'

'The weaver's wife.'

'The weaver? Is it Mortimer Hehir?'

'Yes, Father.'

'In troth I know her. She's Delia Morrissey, that married the weaver; Delia Morrissey that he followed to Munster, a raving lunatic with the dint of love.'

A hot wave of embarrassment swept the widow. For a moment she thought the mind of the cooper was wandering. Then she remembered that the maiden name of the weaver's first wife was, indeed, Delia Morrissey. She had heard it, by chance, once or twice.

'Isn't it Delia Morrissey herself we have in it?' the old man asked.

The widow whispered to the daughter.

'Leave it so.'

She shrank from a difficult discussion with the spectre on the bed on the family history of the weaver. A sense of shame came to her that she could be the wife to a contemporary of this astonishing old man holding on to the life rope.

'I'm out!' shouted Malachi Roohan, his blue eyes lighting

suddenly. 'Delia Morrissey died. She was one day eating her dinner and a bone stuck in her throat. The weaver clapped her on the back, but it was all to no good. She choked to death before his eyes on the floor. I remember that. And the weaver himself near died of grief after. But he married secondly. Who's this he married secondly, Nan?'

Nan did not know. She turned to the widow for enlightenment. The widow moistened her lips. She had to concentrate her thoughts on a subject which, for her own peace of mind, she had habitually avoided. She hated genealogy. She said a little nervously:

'Sara MacCabe.'

The cooper's daughter shouted the name into his ear.

'So you're Sally MacCabe, from Looscaun, the one Mortimer took off the blacksmith? Well, well, that was a great business surely, the pair of them hot-tempered men, and your own beauty going to their heads like strong drink.'

He looked at the widow, a half-sceptical, half-admiring expression flickering across the leathery face. It was such a look as he might have given to Devorgilla of Leinster, Deirdre of Uladh, or Helen of Troy.

The widow was not the notorious Sara MacCabe from Looscaun; that lady had been the second wife of the weaver. It was said they had led a stormy life, made up of passionate quarrels and partings, and still more passionate reconciliations, Sara MacCabe from Looscaun not having quite forgotten or wholly neglected the blacksmith after her marriage to the weaver. But the widow again only whispered to the cooper's daughter:

'Leave it so.'

'What way is Mortimer keeping?' asked the old man.

'He's dead,' replied the daughter.

The fingers of the old man quivered on the rope.

'Dead? Mortimer Hehir dead?' he cried. 'What in the name of God happened him?'

Nan did not know what happened him. She knew that the widow would not mind, so, without waiting for a prompt, she replied:

'A weakness came over him, a sudden weakness.'

'To think of a man being whipped off all of a sudden like that!' cried the cooper. 'When that's the way it was with Mortimer Hehir what one of us can be sure at all? Nan, none of us is sure! To think of the weaver, with his heart as strong as a bull, going off in a little weakness! It's the treacherous world we live in, the treacherous world, surely. Never another yard of tweed will he put up on his old loom! Morty, Morty, you were a good companion, a great warrant to walk the hills, whistling the tunes, pleasant in your conversation and as broad-spoken as the Bible.'

'Did you know the weaver well, Father?' the daughter asked.

'Who better?' he replied. 'Who drank more pints with him than what myself did? And indeed it's to his wake I'd be setting out, and it's under his coffin my shoulder would be going, if I wasn't confined to my rope.'

He bowed his head for a few moments. The two women exchanged a quick, sympathetic glance.

The breathing of the old man was the breathing of one who slept. The head sank lower.

The widow said:

'You ought to make him lie down. He's tired.'

The daughter made some movement of dissent; she was afraid to interfere. Maybe the cooper could be very violent if roused. After a time he raised his head again. He looked in a new mood. He was fresher, more wide-awake. His beard hung in wisps to the bedclothes.

'Ask him about the grave,' the widow said.

The daughter hesitated a moment, and in that moment the cooper looked up as if he had heard, or partially heard. He said:

'If you wait a minute now I'll tell you what the weaver was.' He stared for some seconds at the little window.

'Oh, we'll wait,' said the daughter, and turning to the widow, added, 'won't we, Mrs Hehir?'

'Indeed we will wait,' said the widow.

'The weaver,' said the old man suddenly, 'was a dream.'

He turned his head to the women to see how they had taken it.

'Maybe,' said the daughter, with a little touch of laughter, 'maybe Mrs Hehir would not give in to that.'

The widow moved her hands uneasily under her shawl. She stared a little fearfully at the cooper. His blue eyes were clear as lake water over white sand.

'Whether she gives in to it, or whether she doesn't give in to it,' said Malachi Roohan, 'it's a dream Mortimer Hehir was. And his loom, and his shuttles, and his warping bars, and his bonnin, and the threads that he put upon the shifting racks, were all a dream. And the only thing he ever wove upon his loom was a dream.'

The old man smacked his lips, his hard gums whacking. His daughter looked at him with her head a little to one side.

'And what's more,' said the cooper, 'every woman that ever came into his head, and every wife he married, was a dream. I'm telling you that, Nan, and I'm telling it to you of the weaver. His life was a dream, and his death is a dream. And his widow there is a dream. And all the world is a dream. Do you hear me, Nan, this world is all a dream?'

'I hear you very well, Father,' the daughter sang in a piercing voice.

The cooper raised his head with a jerk, and his beard swept forward, giving him an appearance of vivid energy. He spoke in a voice like a trumpet blast:

'And I'm a dream!'

He turned his blue eyes on the widow. An unnerving sensation came to her. The cooper was the most dreadful old man she had ever seen, and what he was saying sounded the most terrible thing she had ever listened to. He cried:

'The idiot laughing in the street, the king looking at his crown, the woman turning her head to the sound of a man's step, the bells ringing in the belfry, the man walking his land, the weaver at his loom, the cooper handling his barrel, the Pope stooping for his red slippers—they're all a dream. And I'll tell you why they're a dream: because this world was meant to be a dream.'

'Father,' said the daughter, 'you're talking too much. You'll over-reach yourself.'

The old man gave himself a little pull on the rope. It was his gesture of energy, a demonstration of the fine fettle he was in. He said:

'You're saying that because you don't understand me.'

'I understand you very well.'

'You only think you do. Listen to me now, Nan. I want you to do something for me. You won't refuse me?'

'I will not refuse you, Father; you know very well I won't.'

'You're a good daughter to me, surely, Nan. And do what I tell you now. Shut close your eyes. Shut them fast and tight. No fluttering of the lids now.'

'Very well, Father.'

The daughter closed her eyes, throwing up her face in the attitude of one blind. The widow was conscious of the woman's strong, rough features, something good-natured in the line of the large mouth. The old man watched the face of his daughter with excitement. He asked:

'What is it that you see now, Nan?'

'Nothing at all, Father.'

'In troth you do. Keep them closed tight and you'll see it.'

'I see nothing only—'

'Only what? Why don't you say it?'

'Only darkness, Father.'

'And isn't that something to see? Isn't it easier to see darkness than to see light? Now, Nan, look into the darkness.'

'I'm looking, Father.'

'And think of something—anything at all—the stool before the kitchen fire outside.'

'I'm thinking of it.'

'And do you remember it?'

'I do well.'

'And when you remember it what do you want to do—sit on it, maybe?'

'No, Father.'

'And why wouldn't you want to sit on it?'

'Because—because I'd like to see it first, to make sure.'

The old man gave a little crow of delight. He cried:

'There it is! You want to make sure that it is there, although you remember it well. And that is the way with everything in this world. People close their eyes and they are not sure of anything. They want to see it again before they believe. There is Nan, now, and she does not believe in the stool before the fire, the little stool she's looking at all her life, that her mother used to seat her on before the fire when she was a small child. She closes her eyes, and it is gone! And listen to me now, Nan—if you had a man of your own and you closed your eyes you wouldn't be too sure he was the man you remembered, and you'd want to open your eyes and look at him to make sure he was the man you knew before the lids dropped on your eyes. And if you had children about you and you turned your back and closed your eyes and tried to remember them you'd want to look at them to make sure. You'd be no more sure of them than you are now of the stool in the kitchen. One flash of the eyelids and everything in this world is gone.'

'I'm telling you, Father, you're talking too much.'

'I'm not talking half enough. Aren't we all uneasy about the world, the things in the world that we can only believe in while we're looking at them? From one season of our life to another haven't we a kind of belief that some time we'll waken up and find everything different? Didn't you ever feel that, Nan? Didn't you think things would change, that the world would be a new place altogether, and that all that was going on around us was only a business that was doing us out of something else? We put up with it while the little hankering is nibbling at the butt of our hearts for the something else! All the men there be who believe that some day The Thing will happen, that they'll turn round the corner and waken up in the new great Street!'

'And sure,' said the daughter, 'maybe they are right, and maybe they will waken up.'

The old man's body was shaken with a queer spasm of laughter. It began under the clothes on the bed, worked up his trunk, ran along his stringy arms, out into the rope, and the iron foot of the bed rattled. A look of extraordinarily malicious humour lit up the vivid face of the cooper. The widow beheld him with fascination, a growing sense of alarm. He might say something. He might do anything. He might begin to sing some fearful song. He might leap out of bed.

'Nan,' he said, 'do you believe you'll swing round the corner and waken up?'

'Well,' said Nan, hesitating a little, 'I do.'

The cooper gave a sort of peacock crow again. He cried:

'Och! Nan Roohan believes she'll waken up! Waken up from what? From a sleep and from a dream, from this world! Well, if you believe that, Nan Roohan, it shows you know what's what. You know what the thing around you, called the world, is. And it's only dreamers who can hope to waken up—do you hear me, Nan; it's only dreamers who can hope to waken up.'

'I hear you,' said Nan.

'The world is only a dream, and a dream is nothing at all! We all want to waken up out of the great nothingness of this world.'

'And, please God, we will,' said Nan.

'You can tell all the world from me,' said the cooper, 'that it won't.'

'And why won't we, Father?'

'Because,' said the old man, 'we ourselves are the dream. When we're over the dream is over with us. That's why.'

'Father,' said the daughter, her head again a little to one side, 'you know a great deal.'

'I know enough,' said the cooper shortly.

'And maybe you could tell us something about the weaver's grave. Mrs Hehir wants to know.'

'And amn't I after telling you all about the weaver's grave? Amn't I telling you it is all a dream?'

'You never said that, Father. Indeed you never did.'

'I said everything in this world is a dream, and the weaver's grave is in this world, below in Cloon na Morav.'

'Where in Cloon na Morav? What part of it, Father? That is what Mrs Hehir wants to know. Can you tell her?'

'I can tell her,' said Malachi Roohan. 'I was at his father's burial. I remember it above all burials, because that was the day the handsome girl, Honor Costello, fell over a grave and fainted. The sweat broke out on young Donohoe when he saw Honor Costello tumbling over the grave. Not a marry would he marry her after that, and he sworn to it by the kiss of her lips. "I'll marry no woman that fell on a grave," says Donohoe. "She'd maybe have a child by me with turned-in eyes or a twisted limb." So he married a farmer's daughter, and the same morning Honor Costello married a cattle drover. Very well, then. Donohoe's wife had no child at all. She was a barren woman. Do you hear me, Nan? A barren woman she was. And such childer as Honor Costello had by the drover! Yellow hair they had, heavy as seaweed, the skin of them clear as the wind, and limbs as clean as a whistle! It was said the drover was of the blood of the Danes, and it broke out in Honor Costello's family!'

'Maybe,' said the daughter, 'they were Vikings.'

'What are you saying?' cried the old man testily. 'Amn't I telling you it's Danes they were. Did any one ever hear a greater miracle?'

'No one ever did,' said the daughter, and both women clicked their tongues to express sympathetic wonder at the tale.

'And I'll tell you what saved Honor Costello,' said the cooper. 'When she fell in Cloon na Morav she turned her cloak inside out.'

'What about the weaver's grave, Father? Mrs Hehir wants to know.'

The old man looked at the widow; his blue eyes searched her face and her figure; the expression of satirical admiration flashed over his features. The nostrils of the nose twitched. He said:

'So that's the end of the story! Sally MacCabe, the blacksmith's favourite, wants to know where she'll sink the weaver out of sight! Great battles were fought in Looscaun over Sally MacCabe! The weaver thought his heart would burst, and the blacksmith damned his soul for the sake of Sally MacCabe's idle hours.'

'Father,' said the daughter of the house, 'let the dead rest.'

'Ay,' said Malachi Roohan, 'let the foolish dead rest. The dream of Looscaun is over. And now the pale woman is looking for the black weaver's grave. Well, good luck to her!'

The cooper was taken with another spasm of grotesque laughter. The only difference was that this time it began by the rattling of the rail of the bed, travelled along the rope, down his stringy arms dying out somewhere in his legs in the bed. He smacked his lips, a peculiar harsh sound, as if there was not much meat to it.

'Do I know where Mortimer Hehir's grave is?' he said ruminatingly. 'Do I know where me rope is?'

'Where is it, then?' his daughter asked. Her patience was great.

'I'll tell you that,' said the cooper. 'It's under the elm tree of Cloon na Morav. That's where it is surely. There was never a weaver yet that did not find rest under the elm tree of Cloon na Morav. There they all went as surely as the buds came on the branches. Let Sally MacCabe put poor Morty there; let her give him a tear or two in memory of the days that his heart was ready to burst for her, and believe you me no ghost will ever haunt her. No dead man ever yet came back to look upon a woman!'

A furtive sigh escaped the widow. With her handkerchief she wiped a little perspiration from both sides of her nose. The old man wagged his head sympathetically. He thought she was the long dead Sally MacCabe lamenting the weaver! The widow's emotion arose from relief that the mystery of the grave had at last been cleared up. Yet her dealings with old men had taught her caution. Quite suddenly the memory of the handsome dark face of the gravedigger who had followed her to the stile came back to her. She remembered that he said something about 'the exact position of the grave'. The widow prompted yet another question:

'What position under the elm tree?'

The old man listened to the question; a strained look came into his face.

'Position of what?' he asked.

'Of the grave.'

'Of what grave?'

'The weaver's grave.'

Another spasm seized the old frame, but this time it came from no aged merriment. It gripped his skeleton and shook it. It was as if some invisible powerful hand had suddenly taken him by the back of the neck and shaken him. His knuckles rattled on the rope. They had an appalling sound. A horrible feeling came to the widow that the cooper would fall to pieces like a bag of bones. He turned his face to his daughter. Great tears had welled into the blue eyes, giving them an appearance of childish petulance, then of acute suffering.

'What are you talking to me of graves for?' he asked, and the powerful voice broke. 'Why will you be tormenting me like this? It's not going to die I am, is it? Is it going to die I am, Nan?'

The daughter bent over him as she might bend over a child. She said:

'Indeed, there's great fear of you. Lie down and rest yourself. Fatigued out and out you are.'

The grip slowly slacked on the rope. He sank back, quite helpless, a little whimper breaking from him. The daughter stooped lower, reaching for a pillow that had fallen in by the wall. A sudden sharp snarl sounded from the bed, and it dropped from her hand.

'Don't touch me!' the cooper cried. The voice was again restored, powerful in its command. And to the amazement of the widow she saw him again grip along the rope and rise in the bed.

'Amn't I tired telling you not to touch me?' he cried. 'Have I any business talking to you at all? Is it gone my authority is in this house?'

He glared at his daughter, his eyes red with anger, like a dog crouching in his kennel, and the daughter stepped back, a wry smile on her large mouth. The widow stepped back with her, and for a moment he held the women with their backs to the wall by his angry red eyes. Another growl and the cooper sank back inch by inch on the rope. In all her experience of old men the widow had never seen anything like this old man; his resurrections and his collapse. When he was quite down the daughter gingerly put the clothes over his shoulders and then beckoned the widow out of the room.

The widow left the house of Malachi Roohan, the cooper, with the feeling that she had discovered the grave of an old man by almost killing another.

v

The widow walked along the streets, outwardly calm, inwardly confused. Her first thought was 'the day is going on me!' There were many things still to be done at home; she remembered the weaver lying there, quiet at last, the candles lighting about him, the brown habit over him, a crucifix in his hands—everything as it should be. It seemed ages to the widow since he had really fallen ill. He was very exacting and peevish all that time. His death agony had been protracted, almost melodramatically violent. A few times the widow had nearly run out of the house, leaving the weaver to fight the death battle alone. But her common sense, her good nerves, and her religious convictions had stood to her, and when she put the pennies on the weaver's eyes she was glad she had done her duty to the last. She was glad now that she had taken the search for the grave out of the hands of Meehaul Lynskey and Cahir Bowes; Malachi Roohan had been a sight, and she would never forget him, but he had known what nobody else knew. The widow, as she ascended a little upward sweep of the road to Cloon na Morav, noted that the sky beyond it was more vivid, a red band of light having struck across the grey-blue, just on the horizon. Up against this red background was the dark outline of landscape, and especially Cloon na Morav. She kept her eyes upon it as she drew nearer. Objects that were vague on the landscape began to bulk up with more distinction.

She noted the back wall of Cloon na Morav, its green lichen more vivid under the red patch of the skyline. And presently, above the green wall, black against the vivid sky, she saw elevated the bulk of one of the black cockroaches. On it were perched two drab figures, so grotesque, so still, that they seemed part of the thing itself. One figure was sloping out from the end of the tombstone so curiously that for a moment the widow thought it was a man who had reached down from the table to see what was under it. At the other end of the table was a slender warped figure, and as the widow gazed upon it she saw a sign of animation. The head and face, bleak in their outlines, were raised up in a gesture of despair.

The face was turned flush against the sky, so much so that the widow's eyes instinctively sought the sky too. Above the slash of red, in the west, was a single star, flashing so briskly and so freshly that it might have never shone before. For all the widow knew, it might have been a young star frolicking in the heavens with all the joy of youth. Was that, she wondered, at what the old man, Meehaul Lynskey, was gazing. He was very, very old, and the star was very, very young! Was there some protest in the gesture of the head he raised to that thing in the sky; was there some mockery in the sparkle of the thing of the sky for the face of the man? Why should a star be always young, a man aged so soon? Should not a man be greater than a star? Was it this Meehaul Lynskey was thinking? The widow could not say, but something in the thing awed her. She had the sensation of one who surprises a man in some act that lifts him above the commonplaces of existence. It was as if Meehaul Lynskey were discovered prostrate before some altar, in the throes of a religious agony. Old men were, the widow felt, very, very strange, and she did not know that she would ever understand them. As she looked at the bleak head of Meehaul Lynskey up against the vivid patch of the sky, she wondered if there could really be something in that head which would make him as great as a star, immortal as a star? Suddenly Meehaul Lynskey made a movement. The widow saw it quite distinctly. She saw the arm raised, the hand go out, with its crooked fingers, in one, two, three quick, short taps in the direction of the star. The widow stood to watch, and the gesture was so familiar, so homely, so personal, that it was quite understandable to her. She knew then that Meehaul Lynskey was not thinking of any great things at all. He was only a nailer! And seeing the Evening Star sparkle in the sky he had only thought of his workshop, of the bellows, the irons, the fire, the sparks, and the glowing iron which might be made into a nail while it was hot! He had in imagination seized a hammer and made a blow across interstellar space at Venus! All the beauty and youth of the star frolicking on the pale sky above the slash of vivid redness had only suggested to him the making of yet another nail! If Meehaul Lynskey could push up his scarred yellow face among the stars of the sky he would only see in them the sparks of his little smithy.

Cahir Bowes was, the widow thought, looking down at the earth, from the other end of the tombstone, to see if there were any hard things there which he could smash up. The old men had their backs turned upon each other. Very likely they had had another discussion since, which ended in this attitude of mutual contempt. The widow was conscious again of the unreasonableness of old men, but not much resentful of it. She was too long accustomed to them to have any great sense of revolt. Her emotion, if it could be called an emotion, was a settled, dull toleration of all their little bigotries.

She put her hand on the stile for the second time that day, and again raised her palely sad face over the graveyard of Cloon na Morav. As she did so she had the most extraordinary experience of the whole day's sensations. It was such a sensation as gave her at once a wonderful sense of the reality and the unreality of life. She paused on the stile, and had a clear insight into something that had up to this moment been obscure. And no sooner had the thing become definite and clear than a sense of the wonder of life came to her. It was all very like the dream Malachi Roohan had talked about.

In the pale grass, under the vivid colours of the sky, the two grave-diggers were lying on their backs, staring silently up at the heavens. The widow looked at them as she paused on the stile. Her thoughts of these men had been indifferent, subconscious, up to this instant. They were handsome young men. Perhaps if there had been only one of them the widow would have been more attentive. The dark handsomeness did not seem the same thing when repeated. Their beauty, if one could call it beauty, had been collective, the beauty of flowers, of dark, velvety pansies, the distinctive marks of one faithfully duplicated on the other. The good looks of one had, to the mind of the widow, somehow nullified the good looks of the other. There was too much borrowing of Peter to pay Paul in their well-favoured features. The first grave-digger spoiled the illusion of individuality in the second grave-digger. The widow had not thought so, but she would have agreed if anybody whispered to her that a good-looking man who wanted to win favour with a woman should never have so complete a twin brother. It would be possible for a woman to part tenderly with a man, and, if she met his image and likeness around the corner, knock him down. There is nothing more powerful, but nothing more delicate in life than the valves of individuality. To create the impression that humanity was a thing which could be turned out like a coinage would be to ruin the whole illusion of life. The twin grave-diggers had created some sort of such impression, vague, and not very insistent, in the mind of the widow, and it had made her lose any special interest in them. Now, however, as she hesitated on the stile, all this was swept from her mind at a stroke. The most subtle and powerful of all things, personality, sprang silently from the twins and made them, to the mind of the widow, things as far apart as the poles. The two men lay at length, and exactly the same length and bulk, in the long, grey grass. But, as the widow looked upon them, one twin seemed conscious of her presence, while the other continued his absorption in the heavens above. The supreme twin turned his head, and his soft, velvety brown eyes met the eyes of the widow. There was welcome in the man's eyes. The widow read that welcome as plainly as if he had spoken his thoughts. The next moment he had sprung to his feet, smiling. He took a few steps forward, then, self-conscious, pulled up. If he had only jumped up and smiled the widow would have understood. But those few eager steps forward and then that stock stillness! The other twin rose reluctantly, and as he did so the widow was conscious of even physical differences in the brothers. The eyes were not the same. No such velvety soft lights were in the eyes of the second one. He was more sheepish. He was more phlegmatic. He was only a plagiarism of the original man! The widow wondered how she had not seen all this before. The resemblance between the twins was only skin deep. The two old men, at the moment the second twin rose, detached themselves slowly, almost painfully, from their tombstone, and all moved forward to meet the widow. The widow, collecting her thoughts, piloted her skirts modestly about her legs as she got down from the narrow stonework of the stile and stumbled into the contrariness of Cloon na Morav. A wild sense of satisfaction swept her that she had come back the bearer of useful information.

'Well,' said Meehaul Lynskey, 'did you see Malachi Roohan?' The widow looked at his scorched, sceptical, yellow face, and said: 'I did.'

'Had he any word for us?'

'He had. He remembers the place of the weaver's grave.' The widow looked a little vaguely about Cloon na Morav.

'What does he say?'

'He says it's under the elm tree.'

There was silence. The stonebreaker swung about on his legs, his head making a semi-circular movement over the ground, and his sharp eyes were turned upward, as if he were searching the heavens for an elm tree. The nailer dropped his underjaw and stared tensely across the ground, blankly, patiently, like a fisherman on the edge of the shore gazing over an empty sea. The grave-digger turned his head away shyly, like a boy, as if he did not want to see the confusion of the widow; the man was full of the most delicate mannerisms. The other grave-digger settled into a stolid attitude, then the skin bunched up about his brown eyes in puckers of humour. A miserable feeling swept the widow. She had the feeling that she stood on the verge of some collapse.

'Under the elm tree,' mumbled the stonebreaker.

'That's what he said,' added the widow. 'Under the elm tree of Cloon na Morav.'

'Well,' said Cahir Bowes, 'when you find the elm tree you'll find the grave.'

The widow did not know what an elm tree was. Nothing had ever happened in life as she knew it to render any special knowledge of trees profitable, and therefore desirable. Trees were good; they made nice firing when chopped up; timber, and all that was fashioned out of timber, came from trees. This knowledge the widow had accepted as she had accepted all the other remote phenomena of the world into which she had been born. But that trees should have distinctive names, that they should have family relationships, seemed to the mind of the widow only an unnecessary complication of the affairs of the universe. What good was it? She could understand calling fruit trees fruit trees and all other kinds simply trees. But that one should be an elm and another an ash, that there should be name after name, species after species, giving them peculiarities and personalities, was one of the things that the widow did not like. And at this moment, when the elm tree of Malachi Roohan had raised a fresh problem in Cloon na Morav, the likeness of old men to old trees—their crankiness, their complexity, their angles, their very barks, bulges, gnarled twistiness, and kinks—was very close, and brought a sense of oppression to the sorely-tried brain of the widow.

'Under the elm tree,' repeated Meehaul Lynskey. 'The elm tree of Cloon na Morav.' He broke into an aged cackle of a laugh. 'If I was any good at all at making a rhyme I'd make one about that elm tree, devil a other but I would.'

The widow looked around Cloon na Morav, and her eyes, for the first time in her life, were consciously searching for trees. If there were numerous trees there she could understand how easy it might be for Malachi Roohan to make a mistake. He might have mistaken some other sort of tree for an elm—the widow felt that there must be plenty of other trees very like an elm. In fact, she reasoned that other trees, do their best, could not help looking like an elm. There must be thousands and millions of people like herself in the world who pass through life in the belief that a certain kind of tree was an elm when, in reality, it may be an ash or an oak or a chestnut or a beech, or even a poplar, a birch, or a yew. Malachi Roohan was never likely to allow anybody to amend his knowledge of an elm tree. He would let go his rope in the belief that there was an elm tree in Cloon na Morav, and that under it was the weaver's grave—that is, if Malachi Roohan had not, in some ghastly aged kink, invented the thing. The widow, not sharply, but still with an appreciation of the thing, grasped that a dispute about trees would be the very sort of dispute in which Meehaul Lynskey and Cahir Bowes would, like the very old men that they were, have revelled. Under the impulse of the message she had brought from the cooper they would have launched out into another powerful struggle from tree to tree in Cloon na Morav; they would again have strewn the place with the corpses of slain arguments, and in the net result they would not have been able to establish anything either about elm trees or about the weaver's grave. The slow, sad gaze of the widow for trees in Cloon na Morav brought to her, in these circumstances, both pain and relief. It was a relief that Meehaul Lynskey and Cahir Bowes could not challenge each other to a battle of trees; it was a pain that the tree of Malachi Roohan was nowhere in sight. The widow could see for herself that there was not any sort of a tree in Cloon na Morav. The ground was enclosed upon three sides by walls, on the fourth by a hedge of quicks. Not even old men could transform a hedge into an elm tree. Neither could they make the few struggling briars clinging about the railings of the sepulchres into anything except briars. The elm tree of Malachi Roohan was now non-existent. Nobody would ever know whether it had or had not ever existed. The widow would as soon give the soul of the weaver to the howling winds of the world as go back and interview the cooper again on the subject.

'Old Malachi Roohan,' said Cahir Bowes with tolerant decision, 'is doting.'

'The nearest elm tree I know,' said Meehaul Lynskey, 'is half a mile away.'

'The one above at Carragh?' questioned Cahir Bowes.

'Ay, beside the mill.'

No more was to be said. The riddle of the weaver's grave was still the riddle of the weaver's grave. Cloon na Morav kept its secret. But, nevertheless, the weaver would have to be buried. He could not be housed indefinitely. Taking courage from all the harrowing aspects of the deadlock, Meehaul Lynskey went back, plump and courageously to his original allegiance.

'The grave of the weaver is there,' he said, and he struck out his hooked fingers in the direction of the disturbance of the sod which the grave-diggers had made under pressure of his earlier enthusiasm.

Cahir Bowes turned on him with a withering, quavering glance.

'Aren't you afraid that God would strike you where you stand?' he demanded.

'I'm not—not a bit afraid,' said Meehaul Lynskey. 'It's the weaver's grave.'

'You say that,' cried Cahir Bowes, 'after what we all saw and what we all heard?'

'I do,' said Meehaul Lynskey, stoutly. He wiped his lips with the palm of his hand, and launched out into one of his arguments, arguments, as usual, packed with particulars.

'I saw the weaver's father lowered in that place. And I'll tell you, what's more, it was Father Owen MacCarthy that read over him, he a young red-haired curate in this place at the time, long before ever he became parish priest of Benelog. There was I, standing in this exact spot, a young man, too, with a light moustache, holding me hat in me hand, and there one side of me—maybe five yards from the marble stone of the Keernahans—was Patsy Curtin that drank himself to death after, and on the other side of me was Honor Costello, that fell on the grave and married the cattle drover, a big, loose-shouldered Dane.'

Patiently, half absent-mindedly, listening to the renewal of the dispute, the widow remembered the words of Malachi Roohan, and his story of Honor Costello, who fell on the grave over fifty years ago. What memories these old men had! How unreliable they were, and yet flashing out astounding corroborations of each other. Maybe there was something in what Meehaul Lynskey was saying. Maybe—but the widow checked her thoughts. What was the use of it all? This grave could not be the weaver's grave; it had been grimly demonstrated to them all that it was full of stout coffins. The widow, with a gesture of agitation, smoothed her hair down the gentle slope of her head under the shawl. As she did so her eyes caught the eyes of the grave-digger; he was looking at her! He withdrew his eyes at once, and began to twitch the ends of his dark moustache with his fingers.

'If,' said Cahir Bowes, 'this be the grave of the weaver, what's Julia Rafferty doing in it? Answer me that, Meehaul Lynskey.'

'I don't know what she's doing in it, and what's more, I don't care. And believe you my word, many a queer thing happened in Cloon na Morav that had no right to happen in it. Julia Rafferty, maybe, isn't the only one that is where she had no right to be.'

'Maybe she isn't,' said Cahir Bowes, 'but it's there she is, anyhow, and I'm thinking it's there she's likely to stay.'

'If she's in the weaver's grave,' cried Meehaul Lynskey, 'what I say is, out with her!'

'Very well, then, Meehaul Lynskey. Let you yourself be the powerful man to deal with Julia Rafferty. But remember this, and remember it's my word, that touch one bone in this place and you touch all.'

'No fear at all have I to right a wrong. I'm no backslider when it comes to justice, and justice I'll see done among the living and the dead.'

'Go ahead, then, me hearty fellow. If Julia herself is in the wrong place somebody else must be in her own place, and you'll be following one rightment with another wrongment until in the end you'll go mad with the tangle of dead men's wrongs. That's the end that's in store for you, Meehaul Lynskey.'

Meehaul Lynskey spat on his fist and struck out with the hooked fingers. His blood was up.

'That I may be as dead as my father!' he began in a traditional oath, and at that Cahir Bowes gave a little cry and raised his stick with a battle flourish. They went up and down the dips of the ground, rising and falling on the waves of their anger, and the widow stood where she was, miserable and downhearted, her feet growing stone cold from the chilly dampness of the ground. The twin who did not now count took out his pipe and lit it, looking at the old men with a stolid gaze. The twin who now counted walked uneasily away, bit an end off a chunk of tobacco, and came to stand in the ground in a line with the widow, looking on with her several feet away; but again the widow was conscious of the man's growing sympathy.

'They're a nice pair of boyos, them two old lads,' he remarked to the widow. He turned his head to her. He was very handsome.

'Do you think they will find it?' she asked. Her voice was a little nervous, and the man shifted on his feet, nervously responsive.

'It's hard to say,' he said. 'You'd never know what to think. Two old lads, the like of them, do be very tricky.'

'God grant they'll get it,' said the widow.

'God grant,' said the grave-digger.

But they didn't. They only got exhausted as before, wheezing and coughing, and glaring at each other as they sat down on two mounds.

The grave-digger turned to the widow. She was aware of the nice warmth of his brown eyes.

'Are you waking the weaver again tonight?' he asked.

'I am,' said the widow.

'Well, maybe some person—some old man or woman from the country—may turn up and be able to tell where the grave is. You could make enquiries.'

'Yes,' said the widow, but without any enthusiasm, 'I could make enquiries.'

The grave-digger hesitated for a moment, and said more sympathetically, 'We could all, maybe, make enquiries.' There was a softer personal note, a note of adventure, in the voice.

The widow turned her head to the man and smiled at him quite frankly.

'I'm beholding to you,' she said and then added with a little wounded sigh, 'Everyone is very good to me.'

The grave-digger twirled the ends of his moustache.

Cahir Bowes, who had heard, rose from his mound and said briskly, 'I'll agree to leave it at that.' His air was that of one who had made an extraordinary personal sacrifice. What was he really thinking was that he would have another great day of it with Meehaul Lynskey in Cloon na Morav tomorrow. He'd show that oul' fellow, Lynskey, what stuff Boweses were made of.

'And I'm not against it,' said Meehaul Lynskey. He took the tone of one who was never to be outdone in magnanimity. He was also thinking of another day of effort tomorrow, a day that would, please God, show the Boweses what the Lynskeys were like.

With that the party came straggling out of Cloon na Morav, the two old men first, the widow next, the grave-diggers waiting to put on their coats and light their pipes.

There was a little upward slope on the road to the town, and as the two old men took it the widow thought they looked very spent after their day. She wondered if Cahir Bowes would ever be able for that hill. She would give him a glass of whiskey at home, if there was any left in the bottle. Of the two, and as limp and slack as his body looked, Meehaul Lynskey appeared the better able for the hill. They walked together, that is to say, abreast, but they kept almost the width of the road between each other, as if this gulf expressed the breach of friendship between them on the head of the dispute about the weaver's grave. They had been making liars of each other all day, and they would, please God, make liars of each other all day tomorrow. The widow, understanding the meaning of this hostility, had a faint sense of amusement at the contrariness of old men. How could she tell what was passing in the head which Cahir Bowes hung, like a fuschia drop, over the road? How could she know of the strange rise and fall of the thoughts, the little frets, the tempers, the faint humours, which chased each other there? Nobody—not even Cahir Bowes himself—could account for them. All the widow knew was that Cahir Bowes stood suddenly on the road. Something had happened in his brain, some old memory cell long dormant had become nascent, had a stir, a pulse, a flicker of warmth, of activity, and swiftly as a flash of lightning in the sky, a glow of lucidity lit up his memory. It was as if a searchlight had suddenly flooded the dark corners of his brain.

The immediate physical effect on Cahir Bowes was to cause him to stand stark still on the road, Meehaul Lynskey going ahead without him. The widow saw Cahir Bowes pivot on his heels, his head, at the end of the horizontal body, swinging round like the movement of a hand on a runaway clock. Instead of pointing up the hill homeward the head pointed down the hill and back to Cloon na Morav. There followed the most extraordinary movements—shufflings, gyrations—that the widow had ever seen. Cahir Bowes wanted to run like mad away down the road. That was plain. And Cahir Bowes believed that he was running like mad away down the road. That was also evident. But what he actually did was to make little jumps on his feet, his stick rattling the ground in front, and each jump did not bring him an inch of ground. He would have gone more rapidly in his normal shuffle. His efforts were like a terrible parody on the springs of a kangaroo. And Cahir Bowes, in a voice that was now more a scream than a cackle, was calling out unintelligible things. The widow, looking at him, paused in wonder, then over her face there came a relaxation, a colour, her eyes warmed, her expression lost its settled pensiveness, and all her body was shaken with uncontrollable laughter. Cahir Bowes passed her on the road in his fantastic leaps, his abortive buck-jumps, screaming and cracking his stick on the ground, his left hand still gripped tightly on the small of his back behind, a powerful brake on the small of his back.

Meehaul Lynskey turned back and his face was shaken with an aged emotion as he looked after the stonebreaker. Then he removed his hat and blessed himself.

'The cross of Christ between us and harm,' he exclaimed. 'Old Cahir Bowes has gone off his head at last. I thought there was something up with him all day. It was easily known there was something ugly working in his mind.'

The widow controlled her laughter and checked herself, making the signs of the cross on her forehead, too. She said:

'God forgive me for laughing and the weaver with the habit but fresh upon him.'

The grave-digger who counted was coming out somewhat eagerly over the stile, but Cahir Bowes, flourishing his stick, beat him back again and then himself re-entered Cloon na Morav. He stumbled over the grass, now rising on a mound, now disappearing altogether in a dip of the ground, travelling in a giddy course like a hooker in a storm; again, for a long time, he remained submerged, showing, however, the external stick, his periscope, his indication to the world that he was about his business. In a level piece of ground, marked by stones with large mottled white marks upon them, he settled and cried out to all, and calling God to witness, that this surely was the weaver's grave. There was scepticism, hesitation, on the part of the grave-diggers, but after some parley, and because Cahir Bowes was so passionate, vehement, crying and shouting, dribbling water from the mouth, showing his yellow teeth, pouring sweat on his forehead, quivering on his legs, they began to dig carefully in the spot. The widow, at this rearranged the shawl on her head and entered Cloona na Morav, conscious, as she shuffled over the stile, that a pair of warm brown eyes were, for a moment, upon her movements and then withdrawn. She stood a little way back from the digging and waited the result with a slightly more accelerated beating of the heart. The twins looked as if they were ready to strike something unexpected at any moment, digging carefully, and Cahir Bowes hung over the place, cackling and crowing, urging the men to swifter work. The earth sang up out of the ground, dark and rich in colour, gleaming like gold, in the deepening twilight in the place. Two feet, three feet, four feet of earth came up, the spades pushing through the earth in regular and powerful pushes, and still the coast was clear. Cahir Bowes trembled with excitement on his big stick. Five feet of a pit yawned in the ancient ground. The spade work ceased. One of the grave-diggers looked up at Cahir Bowes and said:

'You hit the weaver's grave this time right enough. Not another grave in the place could be as free as this.'

The widow sighed a quick little sigh and looked at the face of the other grave-digger, hesitated, then allowed a remote smile of thankfulness to flit across her palely sad face. The eyes of the man wandered away over the darkening spaces of Cloon na Morav.

'I got the weaver's grave surely,' cried Cahir Bowes, his old face full of a weird animation. If he had found the Philosopher's Stone he would only have broken it. But to find the weaver's grave was an accomplishment that would help him into a wisdom before which all his world would bow. He looked around triumphantly and said:

'Where is Meehaul Lynskey now; what will the people be saying at all about his attack on Julia Rafferty's grave? Julia will haunt him, and I'd sooner have any one at all haunting me than the ghost of Julia Rafferty. Where is Meehaul Lynskey now? Is it ashamed to show his liary face he is? And what talk had Malachi Roohan about an elm tree? Elm tree, indeed! If it's trees that is troubling him now let him climb up on one of them and hang himself from it with his rope! Where is that old fellow, Meehaul Lynskey, and his rotten head? Where is he, I say? Let him come in here now to Cloon na Morav until I be showing him the weaver's grave, five feet down and not a rib or a knuckle in it, as clean and beautiful as the weaver ever wished it. Come in here, Meehaul Lynskey, until I hear the lies panting again in your yellow throat.'

He went in his extraordinary movement over the ground, making for the stile all the while talking.

Meehaul Lynskey had crouched behind the wall outside when

Cahir Bowes led the diggers to the new site, his old face twisted in
an attentive, almost agonizing emotion. He stood peeping over the
wall, saying to himself:

'Whisht, will you! Don't mind that old madman. He hasn't it at
all. I'm telling you he hasn't it. Whisht, will you! Let him dig away.
They'll hit something in a minute. They'll level him when they find
out. His brain has turned. Whisht, now, will you, and I'll have that
rambling old lunatic, Cahir Bowes, in a minute. I'll leap in on him.
I'll charge him before the world. I'll show him up. I'll take the gab
out of him. I'll lacerate him. I'll lambaste him. Whisht, will you!'

But as the digging went on and the terrible cries of triumph arose
inside Meehaul Lynskey's knees knocked together. His head bent
level to the wall, yellow and grimacing, nerves twitching across it,
a little yellow froth gathering at the corners of the mouth. When
Cahir Bowes came beating for the stile Meehaul Lynskey rubbed
one leg with the other, a little below the calf, and cried brokenly to
himself:

'God in Heaven, he has it! He has the weaver's grave.'

He turned about and slunk along in the shadow of the wall up
the hill, panting and broken. By the time Cahir Bowes had reached
the stile Meehaul Lynskey's figure was shadowily dipping down
over the crest of the road. A sharp cry from Cahir Bowes caused
him to shrink out of sight like a dog at whom a weapon had been
thrown.

The eyes of the grave-digger who did not now count followed the
figure of Cahir Bowes as he moved to the stile. He laughed a little in
amusement, then wiped his brow. He came up out of the grave. He
turned to the widow and said:

'We're down five feet. Isn't that enough in which to sink the
weaver in? Are you satisfied?'

The man spoke to her without any pretence at fine feeling. He
addressed her as a fourth wife should be addressed. The widow was
conscious but unresentful of the man's manner. She regarded him
calmly and without any resentment. On her part there was no
resentment either, no hypocrisy, no make-believe. Her unemotional
eyes followed his action as he stuck his spade into the loose mould
on the ground. A cry from Cahir Bowes distracted the man, he
laughed again, and before the widow could make a reply he said:

'Old Cahir is great value. Come down until we hear him handling
the nailer.'

He walked away down over the ground.

The widow was left alone with the other grave-digger. He drew himself up out of the pit with a sinuous movement of the body which the widow noted. He stood without a word beside the pile of heaving clay and looked across at the widow. She looked back at him and suddenly the silence became full of unspoken words, of flying, ringing emotions. The widow could see the dark green wall, above it the band of still deepening red, above that the still more pallid grey sky, and directly over the man's head the gay frolicking of the fresh star in the sky. Cloon na Morav was flooded with a deep, vague light. The widow scented the fresh wind about her, the cool fragrance of the earth, and yet a warmth that was strangely beautiful. The light of the man's dark eyes were visible in the shadow which hid his face. The pile of earth beside him was like a vague shape of miniature bronze mountains. He stood with a stillness which was tense and dramatic. The widow thought that the world was strange, the sky extraordinary, the man's head against the red sky a wonder, a poem, above it the sparkle of the great young star. The widow knew that they would be left together like this for one minute, a minute which would be as a flash and as eternity. And she knew now that sooner or later this man would come to her and that she would welcome him. Below at the stile the voice of Cahir Bowes was cackling in its aged notes. Beyond this the stillness was the stillness of heaven and earth. Suddenly a sense of faintness came to the widow. The whole place swooned before her eyes. Never was this world so strange, so like the dream that Malachi Roohan had talked about. A movement in the figure of the man beside the heap of bronze had come to her as a warning, a fear, and a delight. She moved herself a little in response, made a step backward. The next instant she saw the figure of the man spring across the open black mouth of the weaver's grave to her.

A faint sound escaped her and then his breath was hot on her face, his mouth on her lips.

Half a minute later Cahir Bowes came shuffling back, followed by the twin.

'I'll bone him yet,' said Cahir Bowes. 'Never you fear I'll make that old nailer face me. I'll show him up at the weaver's wake tonight!'

The twin laughed behind him. He shook his head at his brother, who was standing a pace away from the widow. He said:

'Five feet.'

He looked into the grave and then looked at the widow, saying: 'Are you satisfied?'

There was silence for a second or two, and when she spoke the widow's voice was low but fresh, like the voice of a young girl. She said:

'I'm satisfied.'

The Dead

Lily, the caretaker's daughter, was literally run off her feet. Hardly had she brought one gentleman into the little pantry behind the office on the ground floor and helped him off with his overcoat, than the wheezy hall-door bell clanged again and she had to scamper along the bare hallway to let in another guest. It was well for her she had not to attend to the ladies also. But Miss Kate and Miss Julia had thought of that and had converted the bathroom upstairs into a ladies' dressing-room. Miss Kate and Miss Julia were there, gossiping and laughing and fussing, walking after each other to the head of the stairs, peering down over the banisters and calling down to Lily to ask her who had come.

It was always a great affair, the Misses Morkan's annual dance. Everybody who knew them came to it, members of the family, old friends of the family, the members of Julia's choir, any of Kate's pupils that were grown up enough, and even some of Mary Jane's pupils too. Never once had it fallen flat. For years and years it had gone off in splendid style, as long as anyone could remember; ever since Kate and Julia, after the death of their brother Pat, had left the house in Stoney Batter and taken Mary Jane, their only niece, to live with them in the dark, gaunt house on Usher's Island, the upper part of which they had rented from Mr Fulham, the corn-factor on the ground floor. That was a good thirty years ago if it was a day. Mary Jane, who was then a little girl in short clothes, was now the main prop of the household, for she had the organ in Haddington Road. She had been through the Academy and gave a pupils' concert every year in the upper room of the Antient Concert Rooms. Many of her pupils belonged to the better-class families on the Kingstown and Dalkey line. Old as they were, her aunts also did their share. Julia, though she was quite grey, was still the leading soprano in Adam and Eve's, and Kate, being too feeble to go about much, gave music lessons to beginners on the old square piano in the back room. Lily, the caretaker's daughter, did housemaid's work for them. Though their life was modest, they believed in eating well; the best of everything: diamond-bone sirloins, three-shilling tea and the best bottled stout. But Lily seldom made a mistake in the orders, so that she got on well with her three mistresses. They were fussy, that was all. But the only thing they would not stand was back answers.

Of course, they had good reason to be fussy on such a night. And then it was long after ten o'clock and yet there was no sign of Gabriel and his wife. Besides they were dreadfully afraid that Freddy Malins might turn up screwed. They would not wish for worlds that any of Mary Jane's pupils should see him under the influence; and when he was like that it was sometimes very hard to manage him. Freddy Malins always came late, but they wondered what could be keeping Gabriel: and that was what brought them every two minutes to the banisters to ask Lily had Gabriel or Freddy come.

'O, Mr Conroy,' said Lily to Gabriel when she opened the door for him, 'Miss Kate and Miss Julia thought you were never coming. Good night, Mrs Conroy.'

'I'll engage they did,' said Gabriel, 'but they forget that my wife here takes three mortal hours to dress herself.'

He stood on the mat, scraping the snow from his goloshes, while Lily led his wife to the foot of the stairs and called out:

'Miss Kate, here's Mrs Conroy.'

Kate and Julia came toddling down the dark stairs at once. Both of them kissed Gabriel's wife, said she must be perished alive, and asked was Gabriel with her.

'Here I am as right as the mail, Aunt Kate! Go on up. I'll follow,' called out Gabriel from the dark.

He continued scraping his feet vigorously while the three women went upstairs, laughing, to the ladies' dressing-room. A light fringe of snow lay like a cape on the shoulders of his overcoat and like toecaps on the toes of his goloshes; and, as the buttons of his overcoat slipped with a squeaking noise through the snow-stiffened frieze, a cold, fragrant air from out-of-doors escaped from crevices and folds.

'Is it snowing again, Mr Conroy?' asked Lily.

She had preceded him into the pantry to help him off with his overcoat. Gabriel smiled at the three syllables she had given his surname and glanced at her. She was a slim, growing girl, pale in complexion and with hay-coloured hair. The gas in the pantry made her look still paler. Gabriel had known her when she was a child and used to sit on the lowest step nursing a rag doll.

'Yes, Lily,' he answered, 'and I think we're in for a night of it.'

He looked up at the pantry ceiling, which was shaking with the stamping and shuffling of feet on the floor above, listened for a moment to the piano and then glanced at the girl, who was folding his overcoat carefully at the end of a shelf.

'Tell me, Lily,' he said in a friendly tone, 'do you still go to school?'

'O no, sir,' she answered. 'I'm done schooling this year and more.'

'O, then,' said Gabriel gaily, 'I suppose we'll be going to your wedding one of these fine days with your young man, eh?'

The girl glanced back at him over her shoulder and said with great bitterness:

'The men that is now is only all palaver and what they can get out of you.'

Gabriel coloured, as if he felt he had made a mistake and, without looking at her, kicked off his goloshes and flicked actively with his muffler at his patent-leather shoes.

He was a stout, tallish young man. The high colour of his cheeks pushed upwards even to his forehead, where it scattered itself in a few formless patches of pale red; and on his hairless face there scintillated restlessly the polished lenses and the bright gilt rims of the glasses which screened his delicate and restless eyes. His glossy black hair was parted in the middle and brushed in a long curve behind his ears where it curled slightly beneath the groove left by his hat.

When he had flicked lustre into his shoes he stood up and pulled his waistcoat down more tightly on his plump body. Then he took a coin rapidly from his pocket.

'O Lily,' he said, thrusting it into her hands, 'it's Christmas-time, isn't it? Just . . . here's a little . . .'

He walked rapidly towards the door.

'O no, sir!' cried the girl, following him. 'Really, sir, I wouldn't take it.'

'Christmas-time! Christmas-time!' said Gabriel, almost trotting to the stairs and waving his hand to her in deprecation.

The girl, seeing that he had gained the stairs, called out after him: 'Well, thank you, sir.'

He waited outside the drawing-room door until the waltz should finish, listening to the skirts that swept against it and to the shuffling of feet. He was still discomposed by the girl's bitter and sudden retort. It had cast a gloom over him which he tried to dispel by arranging his cuffs and the bows of his tie. He then took from his waistcoat pocket a little paper and glanced at the headings he had made for his speech. He was undecided about the lines from Robert Browning, for he feared they would be above the heads of his hearers. Some quotation that they would recognise from Shakespeare or from the Melodies would be better. The indelicate clacking of the men's heels and the shuffling of their soles reminded him that their grade of culture differed from his. He would only make himself ridiculous by quoting poetry to them which they could not understand. They would think that he was airing his superior education. He would fail with them just as he had failed with the girl in the pantry. He had taken up a wrong tone. His whole speech was a mistake from first to last, an utter failure.

Just then his aunts and his wife came out of the ladies' dressing-room. His aunts were two small, plainly dressed old women. Aunt Julia was an inch or so the taller. Her hair, drawn low over the tops of her ears, was grey; and grey also, with darker shadows, was her large flaccid face. Though she was stout in build and stood erect, her slow eyes and parted lips gave her the appearance of a woman who did not know where she was or where she was going. Aunt Kate was more vivacious. Her face, healthier than her sister's, was all puckers and creases, like a shrivelled red apple, and her hair, braided in the same old-fashioned way, had not lost its ripe nut colour.

They both kissed Gabriel frankly. He was their favourite nephew, the son of their dead elder sister, Ellen, who had married T. J. Conroy of the Port and Docks.

'Gretta tells me you're not going to take a cab back to Monkstown tonight, Gabriel,' said Aunt Kate.

'No,' said Gabriel, turning to his wife, 'we had quite enough of that last year, hadn't we? Don't you remember, Aunt Kate, what a cold Gretta got out of it? Cab windows rattling all the way, and the east wind blowing in after we passed Merrion. Very jolly it was. Gretta caught a dreadful cold.'

Aunt Kate frowned severely and nodded her head at every word.

'Quite right, Gabriel, quite right,' she said. 'You can't be too careful.'

'But as for Gretta there,' said Gabriel, 'she'd walk home in the snow if she were let.'

Mrs Conroy laughed.

'Don't mind him, Aunt Kate,' she said. 'He's really an awful bother, what with green shades for Tom's eyes at night and making him do the dumb-bells, and forcing Eva to eat the stirabout. The poor child! And she simply hates the sight of it! . . . O, but you'll never guess what he makes me wear now!'

She broke out into a peal of laughter and glanced at her husband, whose admiring and happy eyes had been wandering from her dress to her face and hair. The two aunts laughed heartily, too, for Gabriel's solicitude was a standing joke with them.

'Goloshes!' said Mrs Conroy. 'That's the latest. Whenever it's wet underfoot I must put on my goloshes. Tonight even, he wanted me to put them on, but I wouldn't. The next thing he'll buy me will be a diving-suit.'

Gabriel laughed nervously and patted his tie reassuringly, while Aunt Kate nearly doubled herself, so heartily did she enjoy the joke. The smile soon faded from Aunt Julia's face and her mirthless eyes were directed towards her nephew's face. After a pause she asked:

'And what are goloshes, Gabriel?'

'Goloshes, Julia!' exclaimed her sister. 'Goodness me, don't you know what goloshes are? You wear them over your . . . over your boots, Gretta, isn't it?'

'Yes, said Mrs Conroy. 'Gutta-percha things. We both have a pair now. Gabriel says everyone wears them on the Continent.'

'O, on the Continent,' murmured Aunt Julia, nodding her head slowly.

Gabriel knitted his brows and said, as if he were slightly angered:

'It's nothing very wonderful, but Gretta thinks it very funny because she says the word reminds her of Christy Minstrels.'

'But tell me, Gabriel,' said Aunt Kate, with brisk tact. 'Of course, you've seen about the room. Gretta was saying . . .'

'O, the room is all right,' replied Gabriel. 'I've taken one in the Gresham.'

'To be sure,' said Aunt Kate, 'by far the best thing to do. And the children, Gretta, you're not anxious about them?'

'O, for one night,' said Mrs Conroy. 'Besides, Bessie will look after them.'

'To be sure,' said Aunt Kate again. 'What a comfort it is to have a girl like that, one you can depend on! There's that Lily, I'm sure I don't know what has come over her lately. She's not the girl she was at all.'

Gabriel was about to ask his aunt some questions on this point, but she broke off suddenly to gaze after her sister, who had wandered down the stairs and was craning her neck over the banisters.

'Now, I ask you,' she said almost testily, 'where is Julia going? Julia! Julia! Where are you going?'

Julia, who had gone half-way down one flight, came back and announced blandly: 'Here's Freddy.'

At the same moment a clapping of hands and a final flourish of the pianist told that the waltz had ended. The drawing-room door was opened from within and some couples came out. Aunt Kate drew Gabriel aside hurriedly and whispered into his ear:

'Slip down, Gabriel, like a good fellow and see if he's all right, and don't let him up if he's screwed. I'm sure he's screwed. I'm sure he is.'

Gabriel went to the stairs and listened over the banisters. He could hear two persons talking in the pantry. Then he recognised Freddy Malins's laugh. He went down the stairs noisily.

'It's such a relief,' said Aunt Kate to Mrs Conroy, 'that Gabriel is here. I always feel easier in my mind when he's here ... Julia, there's Miss Daly and Miss Power will take some refreshment. Thanks for your beautiful waltz, Miss Daly. It made lovely time.'

A tall wizen-faced man, with a stiff grizzled moustache and swarthy skin, who was passing out with his partner, said:

'And may we have some refreshment, too, Miss Morkan?'

'Julia,' said Aunt Kate summarily, 'and here's Mr Browne and Miss Furlong. Take them in, Julia, with Miss Daly and Miss Power.'

'I'm the man for the ladies,' said Mr Browne, pursing his lips until his moustache bristled and smiling in all his wrinkles. 'You know, Miss Morkan, the reason they are so fond of me is ...'

He did not finish his sentence, but, seeing that Aunt Kate was out of earshot, at once led the three young ladies into the back room. The middle of the room was occupied by two square tables placed end to end, and on these Aunt Julia and the caretaker were straightening and smoothing a large cloth. On the sideboard were arrayed dishes and plates, and glasses and bundles of knives and forks and spoons. The top of the closed square piano served also as a sideboard for viands and sweets. At a smaller sideboard in one corner two young men were standing, drinking hop-bitters.

Mr Browne led his charges thither and invited them all, in jest, to some ladies' punch, hot, strong and sweet. As they said they never took anything strong, he opened three bottles of lemonade for them. Then he asked one of the young men to move aside, and, taking hold of the decanter, filled out for himself a goodly measure of whisky. The young men eyed him respectfully while he took a trial sip.

'God help me,' he said, smiling. 'It's the doctor's orders.'

His wizened face broke into a broader smile, and the three young ladies laughed in musical echo to his pleasantry, swaying their bodies to and fro, with nervous jerks of their shoulders. The boldest said:

'O, now, Mr Browne, I'm sure the doctor never ordered anything of the kind.'

Mr Browne took another sip of his whisky and said, with sidling mimicry:

'Well, you see, I'm like the famous Mrs Cassidy, who is reported to have said: "Now, Mary Grimes, if I don't take it, make me take it, for I feel I want it." '

His hot face had leaned forward a little too confidentially and he had assumed a very low Dublin accent so that the young ladies, with one instinct, received his speech in silence. Miss Furlong, who was one of Mary Jane's pupils, asked Miss Daly what was the name of the pretty waltz she had played; and Mr Browne, seeing that he was ignored, turned promptly to the two young men who were more appreciative.

A red-faced young woman, dressed in pansy, came into the room, excitedly clapping her hands and crying:

'Quadrilles! Quadrilles!'

Close on her heels came Aunt Kate, crying:

'Two gentlemen and three ladies, Mary Jane!'

'O, here's Mr Bergin and Mr Kerrigan,' said Mary Jane. 'Mr

Kerrigan, will you take Miss Power? Miss Furlong, may I get you a partner, Mr Bergin. O, that'll just do now.'

'Three ladies, Mary Jane,' said Aunt Kate.

The two young gentlemen asked the ladies if they might have the pleasure, and Mary Jane turned to Miss Daly.

'O, Miss Daly, you're really awfully good, after playing for the last two dances, but really we're so short of ladies tonight.'

'I don't mind in the least, Miss Morkan.'

'But I've a nice partner for you, Mr Bartell D'Arcy, the tenor. I'll get him to sing later on. All Dublin is raving about him.'

'Lovely voice, lovely voice!' said Aunt Kate.

As the piano had twice begun the prelude to the first figure Mary Jane led her recruits quickly from the room. They had hardly gone when Aunt Julia wandered slowly into the room, looking behind her at something.

'What is the matter, Julia?' asked Aunt Kate anxiously. 'Who is it?'

Julia, who was carrying in a column of table-napkins, turned to her sister and said, simply, as if the question had surprised her:

'It's only Freddy, Kate, and Gabriel with him.'

In fact right behind her Gabriel could be seen piloting Freddy Malins across the landing. The latter, a young man of about forty, was of Gabriel's size and build, with very round shoulders. His face was fleshy and pallid, touched with colour only at the thick hanging lobes of his ears and at the wide wings of his nose. He had coarse features, a blunt nose, a convex and receding brow, tumid and protruded lips. His heavy-lidded eyes and the disorder of his scanty hair made him look sleepy. He was laughing heartily in a high key at a story which he had been telling Gabriel on the stairs and at the same time rubbing the knuckles of his left fist backwards and forwards into his left eye.

'Good evening, Freddy,' said Aunt Julia.

Freddy Malins bade the Misses Morkan good evening in what seemed an offhand fashion by reason of the habitual catch in his voice and then, seeing that Mr Browne was grinning at him from the sideboard, crossed the room on rather shaky legs and began to repeat in an undertone the story he had just told to Gabriel.

'He's not so bad, is he?' said Aunt Kate to Gabriel.

Gabriel's brows were dark, but he raised them quickly and answered:

'O, no, hardly noticeable.'

'Now, isn't he a terrible fellow!' she said. 'And his poor mother made him take the pledge on New Year's Eve. But come on, Gabriel, into the drawing-room.'

Before leaving the room with Gabriel she signalled to Mr Browne by frowning and shaking her forefinger in warning to and fro. Mr Browne nodded in answer and, when she had gone, said to Freddy Malins:

'Now, then, Teddy, I'm going to fill you out a good glass of lemonade just to buck you up.'

Freddy Malins, who was nearing the climax of his story, waved the offer aside impatiently, but Mr Browne, having first called Freddy Malins's attention to a disarray in his dress, filled out and handed him a full glass of lemonade. Freddy Malins's left hand accepted the glass mechanically, his right hand being engaged in the mechanical readjustment of his dress. Mr Browne, whose face was once more wrinkling with mirth, poured out for himself a glass of whisky while Freddy Malins exploded, before he had well reached the climax of his story, in a kink of high-pitched bronchitic laughter and, setting down his untasted and overflowing glass, began to rub the knuckles of his left fist backwards and forwards into his left eye, repeating words of his last phrase as well as his fit of laughter would allow him.

Gabriel could not listen while Mary Jane was playing her Academy piece, full of runs and difficult passages, to the hushed drawing-room. He liked music, but the piece she was playing had no melody for him and he doubted whether it had any melody for the other listeners, though they had begged Mary Jane to play something. Four young men, who had come from the refreshment-room to stand in the doorway at the sound of the piano, had gone away quietly in couples after a few minutes. The only persons who seemed to follow the music were Mary Jane herself, her hands racing along the keyboard or lifted from it at the pauses like those of a priestess in momentary imprecation, and Aunt Kate standing at her elbow to turn the page.

Gabriel's eyes, irritated by the floor, which glittered with beeswax under the heavy chandelier, wandered to the wall above the piano. A picture of the balcony scene in *Romeo and Juliet* hung there and beside it was a picture of the two murdered princes in the

Tower which Aunt Julia had worked in red, blue, and brown wools when she was a girl. Probably in the school they had gone to as girls that kind of work had been taught for one year. His mother had worked for him as a birthday present a waistcoat of purple tabinet, with little foxes' heads upon it, lined with brown satin and having round mulberry buttons. It was strange that his mother had had no musical talent, though Aunt Kate used to call her the brains carrier of the Morkan family. Both she and Julia had always seemed a little proud of their serious and matronly sister. Her photograph stood before the pier-glass. She held an open book on her knees and was pointing out something in it to Constantine who, dressed in a man-o'-war suit, lay at her feet. It was she who had chosen the names of her sons, for she was very sensible of the dignity of family life. Thanks to her, Constantine was now senior curate in Balbriggan and, thanks to her, Gabriel himself had taken his degree in the Royal University. A shadow passed over his face as he remembered her sullen opposition to his marriage. Some slighting phrases she had used still rankled in his memory; she had once spoken of Gretta as being country cute and that was not true of Gretta at all. It was Gretta who had nursed her during all her last long illness in their house at Monkstown.

He knew that Mary Jane must be near the end of her piece, for she was playing again the opening melody with runs of scales after every bar, and while he waited for the end the resentment died down in his heart. The piece ended with a trill of octaves in the treble and a final deep octave in the bass. Great applause greeted Mary Jane as, blushing and rolling up her music nervously, she escaped from the room. The most vigorous clapping came from the four young men in the doorway who had gone away to the refreshment-room at the beginning of the piece but had come back when the piano had stopped.

Lancers were arranged. Gabriel found himself partnered with Miss Ivors. She was a frank-mannered talkative young lady, with a freckled face and prominent brown eyes. She did not wear a low-cut bodice, and the large brooch which was fixed in the front of her collar bore on it an Irish device and motto.

When they had taken their places she said abruptly:

'I have a crow to pluck with you.'

'With me?' said Gabriel.

She nodded her head gravely.

'What is it?' asked Gabriel, smiling at her solemn manner.

'Who is G. C.?' answered Miss Ivors, turning her eyes upon him.

Gabriel coloured and was about to knit his brows, as if he did not understand, when she said bluntly:

'O, innocent Amy! I have found out that you write for the *Daily Express*. Now, aren't you ashamed of yourself?'

'Why should I be ashamed of myself?' asked Gabriel, blinking his eyes and trying to smile.

'Well, I'm ashamed of you,' said Miss Ivors frankly. 'To say you'd write for a paper like that. I didn't think you were a West Briton.'

A look of perplexity appeared on Gabriel's face. It was true that he wrote a literary column every Wednesday in the *Daily Express*, for which he was paid fifteen shillings. But that did not make him a West Briton surely. The books he received for review were almost more welcome than the paltry cheque. He loved to feel the covers and turn over the pages of newly printed books. Nearly every day when his teaching in the college was ended he used to wander down the quays to the second-hand booksellers, to Hickey's on Bachelor's Walk, to Webb's or Massey's on Aston's Quay, or to O'Clohissey's in the by-street. He did not know how to meet her charge. He wanted to say that literature was above politics. But they were friends of many years' standing and their careers had been parallel, first at the University and then as teachers: he could not risk a grandiose phrase with her. He continued blinking his eyes and trying to smile and murmured lamely that he saw nothing political in writing reviews of books.

When their turn to cross had come he was still perplexed and inattentive. Miss Ivors promptly took his hand in a warm grasp and said in a soft friendly tone:

'Of course, I was only joking. Come, we cross now.'

When they were together again she spoke of the University question and Gabriel felt more at ease. A friend of hers had shown her his review of Browning's poems. That was how she had found out the secret: but she liked the review immensely. Then she said suddenly:

'O, Mr Conroy, will you come for an excursion to the Aran Isles this summer? We're going to stay there a whole month. It will be splendid out in the Atlantic. You ought to come. Mr Clancy is coming, and Mr Kilkelly and Kathleen Kearney. It would be splendid for Gretta too if she'd come. She's from Connacht, isn't she?'

'Her people are,' said Gabriel shortly.

'But you will come, won't you?' said Miss Ivors, laying her warm hand eagerly on his arm.

'The fact is,' said Gabriel, 'I have just arranged to go . . .'

'Go where?' asked Miss Ivors.

'Well, you know, every year I go for a cycling tour with some fellows and so . . .'

'But where?' asked Miss Ivors.

'Well, we usually go to France or Belgium or perhaps Germany,' said Gabriel awkwardly.

'And why do you go to France and Belgium,' said Miss Ivors, 'instead of visiting your own land?'

'Well,' said Gabriel, 'it's partly to keep in touch with the languages and partly for a change.'

'And haven't you your own language to keep in touch with— Irish?' asked Miss Ivors.

'Well,' said Gabriel, 'if it comes to that, you know, Irish is not my language.'

Their neighbours had turned to listen to the cross-examination. Gabriel glanced right and left nervously and tried to keep his good humour under the ordeal, which was making a blush invade his forehead.

'And haven't you your own land to visit,' continued Miss Ivors, 'that you know nothing of, your own people, and your own country?'

'O, to tell you the truth,' retorted Gabriel suddenly, 'I'm sick of my own country, sick of it!'

'Why?' asked Miss Ivors.

Gabriel did not answer for his retort had heated him.

'Why?' repeated Miss Ivors.

They had to go visiting together and, as he had not answered her, Miss Ivor said warmly:

'Of course, you've no answer.'

Gabriel tried to cover his agitation by taking part in the dance with great energy. He avoided her eyes for he had seen a sour expression on her face. But when they met in the long chain he was surprised to feel his hand firmly pressed. She looked at him from under her brows for a moment quizzically until he smiled. Then, just as the chain was about to start again, she stood on tiptoe and whispered into his ear:

'West Briton!'

When the lancers were over Gabriel went away to a remote corner of the room where Freddy Malins's mother was sitting. She was a stout, feeble old woman with white hair. Her voice had a catch in it like her son's and she stuttered slightly. She had been told that Freddy had come and that he was nearly all right. Gabriel asked her whether she had had a good crossing. She lived with her married daughter in Glasgow and came to Dublin on a visit once a year. She answered placidly that she had had a beautiful crossing and that the captain had been most attentive to her. She spoke also of the beautiful house her daughter kept in Glasgow, and of all the friends they had there. While her tongue rambled on Gabriel tried to banish from his mind all memory of the unpleasant incident with Miss Ivors. Of course the girl, or woman, or whatever she was, was an enthusiast, but there was a time for all things. Perhaps he ought not to have answered her like that. But she had no right to call him a West Briton before people, even in joke. She had tried to make him ridiculous before people, heckling him and staring at him with her rabbit's eyes.

He saw his wife making her way towards him through the waltzing couples. When she reached him she said into his ear:

'Gabriel, Aunt Kate wants to know won't you carve the goose as usual. Miss Daly will carve the ham and I'll do the pudding.'

'All right,' said Gabriel.

'She's sending in the younger ones first as soon as this waltz is over so that we'll have the table to ourselves.'

'Were you dancing?' asked Gabriel.

'Of course I was. Didn't you see me? What row had you with Molly Ivors?'

'No row. Why? Did she say so?'

'Something like that. I'm trying to get that Mr D'Arcy to sing. He's full of conceit, I think.'

'There was no row,' said Gabriel moodily, 'only she wanted me to go for a trip to the west of Ireland and I said I wouldn't.'

His wife clasped her hands excitedly and gave a little jump.

'O, do go, Gabriel,' she cried. 'I'd love to see Galway again.'

'You can go if you like,' said Gabriel coldly.

She looked at him for a moment, then turned to Mrs Malins and said:

'There's a nice husband for you, Mrs Malins.'

While she was threading her way back across the room Mrs Malins, without adverting to the interruption, went on to tell Gabriel what beautiful places there were in Scotland and beautiful scenery. Her son-in-law brought them every year to the lakes and they used to go fishing. Her son-in-law was a splendid fisher. One day he caught a beautiful big fish and the man in the hotel cooked it for dinner.

Gabriel hardly heard what she said. Now that supper was coming near he began to think again about his speech and about the quotation. When he saw Freddy Malins coming across the room to visit his mother Gabriel left the chair free for him and retired into the embrasure of the window. The room had already cleared and from the back room came the clatter of plates and knives. Those who still remained in the drawing-room seemed tired of dancing and were conversing quietly in little groups. Gabriel's warm trembling fingers tapped the cold pane of the window. How cool it must be outside! How pleasant it would be to walk out alone, first along by the river and then through the park! The snow would be lying on the branches of the trees and forming a bright cap on the top of the Wellington Monument. How much more pleasant it would be there than at the supper-table!

He ran over the headings of his speech: Irish hospitality, sad memories, the Three Graces, Paris, the quotation from Browning. He repeated to himself a phrase he had written in his review: 'One feels that one is listening to a thought-tormented music.' Miss Ivors had praised the review. Was she sincere? Had she really any life of her own behind all her propagandism? There had never been any ill-feeling between them until that night. It unnerved him to think that she would be at the supper-table, looking up at him while he spoke with her critical quizzing eyes. Perhaps she would not be sorry to see him fail in his speech. An idea came into his mind and gave him courage. He would say, alluding to Aunt Kate and Aunt Julia: 'Ladies and Gentlemen, the generation which is now on the wane among us may have had its faults, but for my part I think it had certain qualities of hospitality, of humour, of humanity, which the new and very serious and hypereducated generation that is growing up around us seems to me to lack.' Very good: that was one for Miss Ivors. What did he care that his aunts were only two ignorant old women?

A murmur in the room attracted his attention. Mr Browne was advancing from the door, gallantly escorting Aunt Julia, who leaned upon his arm, smiling and hanging her head. An irregular musketry of applause escorted her also as far as the piano and then, as Mary Jane seated herself on the stool, and Aunt Julia, no longer smiling, half turned so as to pitch her voice fairly into the room, gradually ceased. Gabriel recognised the prelude. It was that of an old song of Aunt Julia's—*Arrayed for the Bridal*. Her voice, strong and clear in tone, attacked with great spirit the runs which embellish the air and though she sang very rapidly she did not miss even the smallest of the grace notes. To follow the voice, without looking at the singer's face, was to feel and share the excitement of swift and secure flight. Gabriel applauded loudly with all the others at the close of the song and loud applause was borne in from the invisible supper-table. It sounded so genuine that a little colour struggled into Aunt Julia's face as she bent to replace in the music-stand the old leather-bound songbook that had her initials on the cover. Freddy Malins, who had listened with his head perched sideways to hear her better, was still applauding when everyone else had ceased and talking animatedly to his mother, who nodded her head gravely and slowly in acquiescence. At last, when he could clap no more, he stood up suddenly and hurried across the room to Aunt Julia whose hand he seized and held in both his hands, shaking it when words failed him or the catch in his voice proved too much for him.

'I was just telling my mother,' he said, 'I never heard you sing so well, never. No, I never heard your voice so good as it is tonight. Now! Would you believe that now? That's the truth. Upon my word and honour that's the truth. I never heard your voice sound so fresh and so . . . so clear and fresh, never.'

Aunt Julia smiled broadly and murmured something about compliments as she released her hand from his grasp. Mr Browne extended his open hand towards her and said to those who were near him in the manner of a showman introducing a prodigy to an audience:

'Miss Julia Morkan, my latest discovery!'

He was laughing very heartily at this himself when Freddy Malins turned to him and said:

'Well, Browne, if you're serious you might make a worse discovery. All I can say is I never heard her sing half so well as long as I am coming here. And that's the honest truth.'

'Neither did I,' said Mr Browne. 'I think her voice has greatly improved.'

Aunt Julia shrugged her shoulders and said with meek pride:

'Thirty years ago I hadn't a bad voice as voices go.'

'I often told Julia,' said Aunt Kate emphatically, 'that she was simply thrown away in that choir. But she never would be said by me.'

She turned as if to appeal to the good sense of the others against a refractory child while Aunt Julia gazed in front of her, a vague smile of reminiscence playing on her face.

'No,' continued Aunt Kate, 'she wouldn't be said or led by anyone, slaving there in that choir night and day, night and day. Six o'clock on Christmas morning! And all for what?'

'Well, isn't it for the honour of God, Aunt Kate?' asked Mary Jane, twisting round on the piano-stool and smiling.

Aunt Kate turned fiercely on her niece and said:

'I know all about the honour of God, Mary Jane, but I think it's not at all honourable for the Pope to turn the women out of the choirs that have slaved there all their lives and put little whipper-snappers of boys over their heads. I suppose it is for the good of the Church if the Pope does it. But it's not just, Mary Jane, and it's not right.'

She had worked herself into a passion and would have continued in defence of her sister, for it was a sore subject with her, but Mary Jane, seeing that all the dancers had come back, intervened pacifically:

'Now, Aunt Kate, you're giving scandal to Mr Browne who is of the other persuasion.'

Aunt Kate turned to Mr Browne, who was grinning at this allusion to his religion, and said hastily:

'O, I don't question the Pope's being right. I'm only a stupid old woman and I wouldn't presume to do such a thing. But there's such a thing as common everyday politeness and gratitude. And if I were in Julia's place I'd tell that Father Healey straight up to his face . . .'

'And besides, Aunt Kate,' said Mary Jane, 'we really are all hungry and when we are hungry we are all very quarrelsome.'

'And when we are thirsty we are also quarrelsome,' added Mr Browne.

'So that we had better go to supper,' said Mary Jane, 'and finish the discussion afterwards.'

On the landing outside the drawing-room Gabriel found his wife and Mary Jane trying to persuade Miss Ivors to stay for supper. But Miss Ivors, who had put on her hat and was buttoning her cloak, would not stay. She did not feel in the least hungry and she had already overstayed her time.

'But only for ten minutes, Molly,' said Mrs Conroy. 'That won't delay you.'

'To take a pick itself,' said Mary Jane, 'after all your dancing.'

'I really couldn't,' said Miss Ivors.

'I am afraid you didn't enjoy yourself at all,' said Mary Jane hopelessly.

'Ever so much, I assure you,' said Miss Ivors, 'but you really must let me run off now.'

'But how can you get home?' asked Mrs Conroy.

'O, it's only two steps up the quay.'

Gabriel hesitated a moment and said:

'If you will allow me, Miss Ivors, I'll see you home if you are really obliged to go.'

But Miss Ivors broke away from them.

'I won't hear of it,' she cried. 'For goodness' sake go in to your suppers and don't mind me. I'm quite well able to take care of myself.'

'Well, you're the comical girl, Molly,' said Mrs Conroy frankly.

'*Beannacht libh*,' cried Miss Ivors, with a laugh, as she ran down the staircase.

Mary Jane gazed after her, a moody puzzled expression on her face, while Mrs Conroy leaned over the banisters to listen for the hall door. Gabriel asked himself was he the cause of her abrupt departure. But she did not seem to be in ill humour: she had gone away laughing. He stared blankly down the staircase.

At the moment Aunt Kate came toddling out of the supper-room, almost wringing her hands in despair.

'Where is Gabriel?' she cried. 'Where on earth is Gabriel? There's everyone waiting in there, stage to let, and nobody to carve the goose!'

'Here I am, Aunt Kate!' cried Gabriel, with sudden animation, 'ready to carve a flock of geese, if necessary.'

A fat brown goose lay at one end of the table and at the other end, on a bed of creased paper strewn with sprigs of parsley, lay a great ham, stripped of its outer skin and peppered over with crust crumbs, a neat paper frill round its shin, and beside this was a round of spiced beef. Between these rival ends ran parallel lines of side-dishes: two little minsters of jelly, red and yellow; a shallow dish full of blocks of blancmange and red jam, a large green leaf-shaped dish with a stalk-shaped handle, on which lay bunches of purple raisins and peeled almonds, a companion dish on which lay a solid rectangle of Smyrna figs, a dish of custard topped with grated nutmeg, a small bowl full of chocolates and sweets wrapped in gold and silver papers and a glass vase in which stood some tall celery stalks. In the centre of the table there stood, as sentries to a fruit-stand which upheld a pyramid of oranges and American apples, two squat old-fashioned decanters of cut glass, one containing port and the other dark sherry. On the closed square piano a pudding in a huge yellow dish lay in waiting and behind it were three squads of bottles of stout and ale and minerals, drawn up according to the colours of their uniforms, the first two black, with brown and red labels, the third and smallest squad white, with transverse green sashes.

Gabriel took his seat boldly at the head of the table and, having looked to the edge of the carver, plunged his fork firmly into the goose. He felt quite at ease now for he was an expert carver and liked nothing better than to find himself at the head of a well-laden table.

'Miss Furlong, what shall I send you?' he asked. 'A wing or a slice of the breast?'

'Just a small slice of the breast.'

'Miss Higgins, what for you?'

'O, anything at all, Mr Conroy.'

While Gabriel and Miss Daly exchanged plates of goose and plates of ham and spiced beef, Lily went from guest to guest with a dish of hot floury potatoes wrapped in a white napkin. This was Mary Jane's idea and she had also suggested apple sauce for the goose, but Aunt Kate had said that plain roast goose without any apple sauce had always been good enough for her and she hoped she might never eat worse. Mary Jane waited on her pupils and saw that they got the best slices, and Aunt Kate and Aunt Julia opened and carried across from the piano bottles of stout and ale for the gentlemen and bottles of minerals for the ladies. There was a great deal of confusion and laughter and noise, the noise of orders and counter-orders, of knives and forks, of corks and glass-stoppers. Gabriel began to carve second helpings as soon as he had finished the first round without serving himself. Everyone protested loudly so that he compromised by taking a long draught of stout, for he had found the carving hot work. Mary Jane settled down quietly to her supper, but Aunt Kate and Aunt Julia were still toddling round the table, walking on each other's heels, getting in each other's way and giving each other unheeded orders. Mr Browne begged of them to sit down and eat their suppers and so did Gabriel, but they said there was time enough, so that, at last, Freddy Malins stood up and, capturing Aunt Kate, plumped her down on her chair amid general laughter.

When everyone had been well served Gabriel said, smiling:

'Now, if anyone wants a little more of what vulgar people call stuffing let him or her speak.'

A chorus of voices invited him to begin his own supper, and Lily came forward with three potatoes which she had reserved for him.

'Very well,' said Gabriel amiably, as he took another preparatory draught, 'kindly forget my existence, ladies and gentlemen, for a few minutes.'

He set to his supper and took no part in the conversation with which the table covered Lily's removal of the plates. The subject of talk was the opera company which was then at the Theatre Royal. Mr Bartell D'Arcy, the tenor, a dark-complexioned young man with a smart moustache, praised very highly the leading contralto of the company, but Miss Furlong thought she had a rather vulgar style of production. Freddy Malins said there was a Negro chieftain singing in the second part of the Gaiety pantomime who had one of the finest tenor voices he had ever heard.

'Have you heard him?' he asked Mr Bartell D'Arcy across the table.

'No,' answered Mr Bartell D'Arcy carelessly.

'Because,' Freddy Malins explained, 'now I'd be curious to hear your opinion of him. I think he has a grand voice.'

'It takes Teddy to find out the really good things,' said Mr Browne familiarly to the table.

'And why couldn't he have a voice too?' asked Freddy Malins sharply. 'Is it because he's only a black?'

Nobody answered this question and Mary Jane led the table back to the legitimate opera. One of her pupils had given her a pass for *Mignon*. Of course it was very fine, she said, but it made her think of poor Georgina Burns. Mr Browne could go back further still, to the old Italian companies that used to come to Dublin—Tietjens, Ilma de Murzka, Campanini, the great Trebelli, Giuglini, Ravelli, Aramburo. Those were the days, he said, when there was something like singing to be heard in Dublin. He told too of how the top gallery of the old Royal used to be packed night after night, of how one night an Italian tenor had sung five encores to *Let me like a Soldier fall*, introducing a high C every time, and of how the gallery boys would sometimes in their enthusiasm unyoke the horses from the carriage of some great *prima donna* and pull her themselves through the streets to her hotel. Why did they never play the grand old operas now, he asked, *Dinorah*, *Lucrezia Borgia*? Because they could not get the voices to sing them: that was why.

'O, well,' said Mr Bartell D'Arcy, 'I presume there are as good singers today as there were then.'

'Where are they?' asked Mr Browne defiantly.

'In London, Paris, Milan,' said Mr Bartell D'Arcy warmly. 'I suppose Caruso, for example, is quite as good, if not better than any of the men you have mentioned.'

'Maybe so,' said Mr Browne. 'But I may tell you I doubt it strongly.'

'O, I'd give anything to hear Caruso sing,' said Mary Jane.

'For me,' said Aunt Kate, who had been picking a bone, 'there was only one tenor. To please me, I mean. But I suppose none of you ever heard of him.'

'Who is he, Miss Morkan?' askd Mr Bartell D'Arcy politely.

'His name,' said Aunt Kate, 'was Parkinson. I heard him when he was in his prime and I think he had then the purest tenor voice that was ever put into a man's throat.'

'Strange,' said Mr Bartell D'Arcy. 'I never even heard of him.'

'Yes, yes, Miss Morkan is right,' said Mr Browne. 'I remember hearing of old Parkinson, but he's too far back for me.'

'A beautiful, pure, sweet mellow English tenor,' said Aunt Kate with enthusiasm.

Gabriel having finished, the huge pudding was transferred to the table. The clatter of forks and spoons began again. Gabriel's wife served out spoonfuls of the pudding and passed the plates down the table. Midway down they were held up by Mary Jane, who replenished them with raspberry or orange jelly or with blancmange and jam. The pudding was of Aunt Julia's making, and she received praises for it from all quarters. She herself said that it was not quite brown enough.

'Well, I hope, Miss Morkan,' said Mr Browne, 'that I'm brown enough for you because, you know, I'm all brown.'

All the gentlemen, except Gabriel, ate some of the pudding out of compliment to Aunt Julia. As Gabriel never ate sweets the celery had been left for him. Freddy Malins also took a stalk of celery and ate it with his pudding. He had been told that celery was a capital thing for the blood and he was just then under doctor's care. Mrs Malins, who had been silent all through the supper, said that her son was going down to Mount Melleray in a week or so. The table then spoke of Mount Melleray, how bracing the air was down there, how hospitable the monks were and how they never asked for a penny-piece from their guests.

'And do you mean to say,' asked Mr Browne incredulously, 'that a chap can go down there and put up there as if it were a hotel and live on the fat of the land and then come away without paying anything?'

'O, most people give some donation to the monastery when they leave,' said Mary Jane.

'I wish we had an institution like that in our Church,' said Mr Browne candidly.

He was astonished to hear that the monks never spoke, got up at two in the morning and slept in their coffins. He asked what they did it for.

'That's the rule of the order,' said Aunt Kate firmly.

'Yes, but why?' asked Mr Browne.

Aunt Kate repeated that it was the rule that was all. Mr Browne still seemed not to understand. Freddy Malins explained to him, as best he could, that the monks were trying to make up for the sins committed by all the sinners in the outside world. The explanation was not very clear for Mr Browne grinned and said:

'I like that idea very much, but wouldn't a comfortable spring bed do them as well as a coffin?'

'The coffin,' said Mary Jane, 'is to remind them of their last end.'

As the subject had grown lugubrious it was buried in a silence of the table, during which Mrs Malins could be heard saying to her neighbour in an indistinct undertone:

'They are very good men, the monks, very pious men.'

The raisins and almonds and figs and apples and oranges and chocolates and sweets were now passed about the table and Aunt Julia invited all the guests to have either port or sherry. At first Mr Bartell D'Arcy refused to take either, but one of his neighbours nudged him and whispered something to him, upon which he allowed his glass to be filled. Gradually as the last glasses were being filled the conversation ceased. A pause followed, broken only by the noise of the wine and by unsettlings of chairs. The Misses Morkan, all three, looked down at the tablecloth. Someone coughed once or twice and then a few gentlemen patted the table gently as a signal for silence. The silence came and Gabriel pushed back his chair and stood up.

The patting at once grew louder in encouragement and then ceased altogether. Gabriel leaned his ten trembling fingers on the tablecloth and smiled nervously at the company. Meeting a row of upturned faces he raised his eyes to the chandelier. The piano was playing a waltz tune and he could hear the skirts sweeping against the drawing-room door. People, perhaps, were standing in the snow on the quay outside, gazing up at the lighted windows and listening to the waltz music. The air was pure there. In the distance lay the park where the trees were weighted with snow. The Wellington Monument wore a gleaming cap of snow that flashed westwards over the white field of Fifteen Acres.

He began:

'Ladies and Gentlemen,

'It has fallen to my lot this evening, as in years past, to perform a very pleasing task, but a task for which I am afraid my poor powers as a speaker are all too inadequate.'

'No, no!' said Mr Browne.

'But, however that may be, I can only ask you tonight to take the will for the deed, and to lend me your attention for a few moments while I endeavour to express to you in words what my feelings are on this occasion.

'Ladies and Gentlemen, it is not the first time that we have gathered together under this hospitable roof, around this hospitable board. It is not the first time that we have been the recipients—or perhaps, I had better say, the victims—of the hospitality of certain good ladies.'

He made a circle in the air with his arm and paused. Everyone laughed or smiled at Aunt Kate and Aunt Julia and Mary Jane who all turned crimson with pleasure. Gabriel went on more boldly:

'I feel more strongly with every recurring year that our country has no tradition which does it so much honour and which it should guard so jealously as that of its hospitality. It is a tradition that is unique as far as my experience goes (and I have visited not a few places abroad) among the modern nations. Some would say, perhaps, that with us it is rather a failing than anything to be boasted of. But granted even that, it is, to my mind, a princely failing, and one that I trust will long be cultivated among us. Of one thing, at least, I am sure. As long as this one roof shelters the good ladies aforesaid—and I wish from my heart it may do so for many and many a long year to come—the tradition of genuine warm-hearted courteous Irish hospitality, which our forefathers have handed down to us and which we in turn must hand down to our descendants, is still alive among us.'

A hearty murmur of assent ran round the table. It shot through Gabriel's mind that Miss Ivors was not there and that she had gone away discourteously: and he said with confidence in himself:

'Ladies and Gentlemen,

'A new generation is growing up in our midst, a generation actuated by new ideas and new principles. It is serious and enthusiastic for these new ideas and its enthusiasm, even when it is misdirected, is, I believe, in the main sincere. But we are living in a sceptical and, if I may use the phrase, a thought-tormented age: and sometimes I fear that this new generation, educated or hyper-educated as it is, will lack those qualities of humanity, of hospitality, of kindly humour which belonged to an older day. Listening tonight to the names of all those great singers of the past it seemed to me, I must confess, that we were living in a less spacious age. Those days might, without exaggeration, be called spacious days: and if they are gone beyond recall let us hope, at least, that in gatherings such as this we shall still speak of them with pride and affection, still cherish in our hearts the memory of those dead and gone great ones whose fame the world will not willingly let die.'

'Hear, hear!' said Mr Browne loudly.

'But yet,' continued Gabriel, his voice falling into a softer inflection, 'there are always in gatherings such as this sadder thoughts that will recur to our minds: thoughts of the past, of youth, of changes, of absent faces that we miss here tonight. Our path through life is strewn with many such sad memories: and were we to brood upon them always we could not find the heart to go on bravely with our work among the living. We have all of us living duties and living affections which claim, and rightly claim, our strenuous endeavours.

'Therefore, I will not linger on the past. I will not let any gloomy moralising intrude upon us here tonight. Here we are gathered together for a brief moment from the bustle and rush of our everyday routine. We are met here as friends, in the spirit of good-fellowship, as colleagues, also to a certain extent, in the true spirit of *camaraderie*, and as the guests of—what shall I call them?—the Three Graces of the Dublin musical world.'

The table burst into applause and laughter at this allusion. Aunt Julia vainly asked each of her neighbours in turn to tell her what Gabriel had said.

'He says we are the Three Graces, Aunt Julia,' said Mary Jane.

Aunt Julia did not understand, but she looked up, smiling, at Gabriel, who continued in the same vein:

'Ladies and Gentlemen,

'I will not attempt to play tonight the part that Paris played on another occasion. I will not attempt to choose between them. The task would be an invidious one and one beyond my poor powers. For when I view them in turn, whether it be our chief hostess herself, whose good heart, whose too good heart, has become a byword with all who know her; or her sister, who seems to be gifted with perennial youth and whose singing must have been a surprise and a revelation to us all tonight; or, last but not least, when I consider our youngest hostess, talented, cheerful, hard-working and the best of nieces, I confess, Ladies and Gentlemen, that I do not know to which of them I should award the prize.'

Gabriel glanced down at his aunts and, seeing the large smile on Aunt Julia's face and the tears which had risen to Aunt Kate's eyes, hastened to his close. He raised his glass of port gallantly, while every member of the company fingered a glass expectantly, and said loudly:

'Let us toast them all three together. Let us drink to their health, wealth, long life, happiness, and prosperity, and may they long continue to hold the proud and self-won position which they hold in their profession and the position of honour and affection which they hold in our hearts.'

All the guests stood up, glass in hand, and turning towards the three seated ladies, sung in unison, with Mr Browne as leader:

> 'For they are jolly gay fellows,
> For they are jolly gay fellows,
> For they are jolly gay fellows,
> Which nobody can deny.'

Aunt Kate was making frank use of her handkerchief and even Aunt Julia seemed moved. Freddy Malins beat time with his pudding-fork and the singers turned towards one another, as if in melodious conference, while they sang with emphasis:

> 'Unless he tells a lie,
> Unless he tells a lie,'

Then, turning once more towards their hostess, they sang:

> 'For they are jolly gay fellows,
> For they are jolly gay fellows,
> For they are jolly gay fellows,
> Which nobody can deny.'

The acclamation which followed was taken up beyond the door of the supper-room by many of the other guests and renewed time after time, Freddy Malins acting as officer with his fork on high.

The piercing morning air came into the hall where they were standing so that Aunt Kate said:

'Close the door, somebody. Mrs Malins will get her death of cold.'

'Browne is out there, Aunt Kate,' said Mary Jane.

'Browne is everywhere,' said Aunt Kate, lowering her voice.

Mary Jane laughed at her tone.

'Really,' she said archly, 'he is very attentive.'

'He has been laid on here like the gas,' said Aunt Kate in the same tone, 'all during the Christmas.'

She laughed herself this time good-humouredly and then added quickly:

'But tell him to come in, Mary Jane, and close the door. I hope to goodness he didn't hear me.'

At that moment the hall door was opened and Mr Browne came in from the doorstep, laughing as if his heart would break. He was dressed in a long green overcoat with mock astrakhan cuffs and collar and wore on his head an oval fur cap. He pointed down the snow-covered quay from where the sound of shrill prolonged whistling was borne in.

'Teddy will have all the cabs in Dublin out,' he said.

Gabriel advanced from the little pantry behind the office, struggling into his overcoat, and, looking round the hall, said:

'Gretta not down yet?'

'She's getting on her things, Gabriel,' said Aunt Kate.

'Who's playing up there?' asked Gabriel.

'Nobody. They're all gone.'

'O no, Aunt Kate,' said Mary Jane. 'Bartell D'Arcy and Miss O'Callaghan aren't gone yet.'

'Someone is fooling at the piano anyhow,' said Gabriel.

Mary Jane glanced at Gabriel and Mr Browne and said with a shiver:

'It makes me feel cold to look at you two gentlemen muffled up like that. I wouldn't like to face your journey home at this hour.'

'I'd like nothing better this minute,' said Mr Browne stoutly, 'than a rattling fine walk in the country or a fast drive with a good spanking goer between the shafts.'

'We used to have a very good horse and trap at home,' said Aunt Julia sadly.

'The never-to-be-forgotten Johnny,' said Mary Jane, laughing.

Aunt Kate and Gabriel laughed too.

'Why, what was wonderful about Johnny?' asked Mr Browne.

'The late lamented Patrick Morkan, our grandfather, that is,' explained Gabriel, 'commonly known in his later years as the old gentleman, was a glue-boiler.'

'O, now, Gabriel,' said Aunt Kate, laughing, 'he had a starch mill.'

'Well, glue or starch,' said Gabriel, 'the old gentleman had a horse by the name of Johnny. And Johnny used to work in the old gentleman's mill, walking round and round in order to drive the mill. That was all very well; but now comes the tragic part about

Johnny. One fine day the old gentleman thought he'd like to drive out with the quality to a military review in the park.'

'The Lord have mercy on his soul,' said Aunt Kate compassionately.

'Amen,' said Gabriel. 'So the old gentleman, as I said, harnessed Johnny and put on his very best tall hat and his very best stock collar and drove out in grand style from his ancestral mansion somewhere near Back Lane, I think.'

Everyone laughed, even Mrs Malins, at Gabriel's manner and Aunt Kate said:

'O, now, Gabriel, he didn't live in Back Lane really. Only the mill was there.'

'Out from the mansion of his forefathers,' continued Gabriel, 'he drove with Johnny. And everything went on beautifully until Johnny came in sight of King Billy's statue: and whether he fell in love with the horse King Billy sits on or whether he thought he was back again in the mill, anyhow he began to walk round the statue.'

Gabriel paced in a circle round the hall in his goloshes amid the laughter of the others.

'Round and round he went,' said Gabriel, 'and the old gentleman, who was a very pompous old gentleman, was highly indignant. "Go on, sir! What do you mean, sir? Johnny! Johnny! Most extraordinary conduct! Can't understand the horse!" '

The peals of laughter which followed Gabriel's imitation of the incident was interrupted by a resounding knock at the hall door. Mary Jane ran to open it and let in Freddy Malins. Freddy Malins, with his hat well back on his head and his shoulders humped with cold, was puffing and steaming after his exertions.

'I could only get one cab,' he said.

'O, we'll find another along the quay,' said Gabriel.

'Yes,' said Aunt Kate. 'Better not keep Mrs Malins standing in the draught.'

Mrs Malins was helped down the front steps by her son and Mr Browne, and, after many manœuvres, hoisted into the cab. Freddy Malins clambered in after her and spent a long time settling her on the seat, Mr Browne helping him with advice. At last she was settled comfortably and Freddy Malins invited Mr Browne into the cab. There was a good deal of confused talk, and then Mr Browne got into the cab. The cabman settled his rug over his knees, and bent down for the address. The confusion grew greater and the cabmen was directed differently by Freddy Malins and Mr Browne, each of whom had his head out through a window of the cab. The difficulty was to know where to drop Mr Browne along the route, and Aunt Kate, Aunt Julia, and Mary Jane helped the discussion from the doorstep with cross-directions and contradictions and abundance of laughter. As for Freddy Malins he was speechless with laughter. He popped his head in and out of the window every moment to the great danger of his hat, and told his mother how the discussion was progressing, till at last Mr Browne shouted to the bewildered cabman above the din of everybody's laughter:

'Do you know Trinity College?'

'Yes, sir,' said the cabman.

'Well, drive bang up against Trinity College gates,' said Mr Browne, 'and then we'll tell you where to go. You understand now?'

'Yes, sir,' said the cabman.

'Make like a bird for Trinity College.'

'Right, sir,' said the cabman.

The horse was whipped up and the cab rattled off along the quay amid a chorus of laughter and adieus.

Gabriel had not gone to the door with the others. He was in a dark part of the hall gazing up the staircase. A woman was standing near the top of the first flight, in the shadow also. He could not see her face but he could see the terra-cotta and salmon-pink panels of her skirt which the shadow made appear black and white. It was his wife. She was leaning on the banisters, listening to something. Gabriel was surprised at her stillness and strained his ear to listen also. But he could hear little save the noise of laughter and dispute on the front steps, a few chords struck on the piano and a few notes of a man's voice singing.

He stood still in the gloom of the hall, trying to catch the air that the voice was singing and gazing up at his wife. There was grace and mystery in her attitude as if she were a symbol of something. He asked himself what is a woman standing on the stairs in the shadow, listening to distant music, a symbol of. If he were a painter he would paint her in that attitude. Her blue felt hat would show off the bronze of her hair against the darkness and the dark panels of her skirt would show off the light ones. *Distant Music* he would call the picture if he were a painter.

The hall door was closed; and Aunt Kate, Aunt Julia, and Mary Jane came down the hall, still laughing.

'Well, isn't Freddy terrible?' said Mary Jane. 'He's really terrible.'

Gabriel said nothing, but pointed up the stairs towards where his wife was standing. Now that the hall door was closed the voice and the piano could be heard more clearly. Gabriel held up his hand for them to be silent. The song seemed to be in the old Irish tonality and the singer seemed uncertain both of his words and of his voice. The voice, made plaintive by distance and by the singer's hoarseness, faintly illuminated the cadence of the air with words expressing grief:

> 'O, the rain falls on my heavy locks
> And the dew wets my skin,
> My babe lies cold . . .'

'O,' exclaimed Mary Jane. 'It's Bartell D'Arcy singing and he wouldn't sing all the night. O, I'll get him to sing a song before he goes.'

'O, do, Mary Jane,' said Aunt Kate.

Mary Jane brushed past the others and ran to the staircase, but before she reached it the singing stopped and the piano was closed abruptly.

'O, what a pity!' she cried. 'Is he coming down, Gretta?'

Gabriel heard his wife answer yes and saw her come down towards them. A few steps behind her were Mr Bartell D'Arcy and Miss O'Callaghan.

'O, Mr D'Arcy,' cried Mary Jane, 'it's downright mean of you to break off like that when we were all in raptures listening to you.'

'I have been at him all the evening,' said Miss O'Callaghan, 'and Mrs Conroy, too, and he told us he had a dreadful cold and couldn't sing.'

'O, Mr D'Arcy,' said Aunt Kate, 'now that was a great fib to tell.'

'Can't you see that I'm as hoarse as a crow?' said Mr D'Arcy roughly.

He went into the pantry hastily and put on his overcoat. The others, taken aback by his rude speech, could find nothing to say. Aunt Kate wrinkled her brows and made signs to the others to drop the subject. Mr D'Arcy stood swathing his neck carefully and frowning.

'It's the weather,' said Aunt Julia, after a pause.

'Yes, everybody has colds,' said Aunt Kate readily, 'everybody.'

'They say,' said Mary Jane, 'we haven't had snow like it for thirty years; and I read this morning in the newspapers that the snow is general all over Ireland.'

'I love the look of snow,' said Aunt Julia sadly.

'So do I,' said Miss O'Callaghan. 'I think Christmas is never really Christmas unless we have the snow on the ground.'

'But poor Mr D'Arcy doesn't like the snow,' said Aunt Kate, smiling.

Mr D'Arcy came from the pantry, fully swathed and buttoned, and in a repentant tone told them the history of his cold. Every one gave him advice and said it was a great pity and urged him to be very careful of his throat in the night air. Gabriel watched his wife, who did not join in the conversation. She was standing right under the dusty fanlight and the flame of the gas lit up the rich bronze of her hair, which he had seen her drying at the fire a few days before. She was in the same attitude and seemed unaware of the talk about her. At last she turned towards them and Gabriel saw that there was colour on her cheeks and that her eyes were shining. A sudden tide of joy went leaping out of his heart.

'Mr D'Arcy,' she said, 'what is the name of that song you were singing?'

'It's called *The Lass of Aughrim*,' said Mr D'Arcy, 'but I couldn't remember it properly. Why? Do you know it?'

'*The Lass of Aughrim*,' she repeated. 'I couldn't think of the name.'

'It's a very nice air,' said Mary Jane. 'I'm sorry you were not in voice tonight.'

'Now, Mary Jane,' said Aunt Kate, 'don't annoy Mr D'Arcy. I won't have him annoyed.'

Seeing that all were ready to start she shepherded them to the door, where good night was said:

'Well, good night, Aunt Kate, and thanks for the pleasant evening.'

'Good night, Gabriel. Good night, Gretta!'

'Good night, Aunt Kate, and thanks ever so much. Good night, Aunt Julia.'

'O, good night, Gretta, I didn't see you.'

'Good night, Mr D'Arcy. Good night, Miss O'Callaghan.'

'Good night, Miss Morkan.'

'Good night, again.'

'Good night, all. Safe home.'

'Good night. Good night.'

The morning was still dark. A dull, yellow light brooded over the houses and the river; and the sky seemed to be descending. It was slushy underfoot; and only streaks and patches of snow lay on the roofs, on the parapets of the quay and on the area railings. The lamps were still burning redly in the murky air and, across the river, the palace of the Four Courts stood out menacingly against the heavy sky.

She was walking on before him with Mr Bartell D'Arcy, her shoes in a brown parcel tucked under one arm and her hands holding her skirt up from the slush. She had no longer any grace of attitude, but Gabriel's eyes were still bright with happiness. The blood went bounding along his veins; and the thoughts went rioting through his brain, proud, joyful, tender, valorous.

She was walking on before him so lightly and so erect that he longed to run after her noiselessly, catch her by the shoulders and say something foolish and affectionate into her ear. She seemed to him so frail that he longed to defend her against something and then to be alone with her. Moments of their secret life together burst like stars upon his memory. A heliotrope envelope was lying beside his breakfast-cup and he was caressing it with his hand. Birds were twittering in the ivy and the sunny web of the curtain was shimmering along the floor: he could not eat for happiness. They were standing on the crowded platform and he was placing a ticket inside the warm palm of her glove. He was standing with her in the cold, looking in through a grated window at a man making bottles in a roaring furnace. It was very cold. Her face, fragrant in the cold air, was quite close to his; and suddenly he called out to the man at the furnace:

'Is the fire hot, sir?'

But the man could not hear with the noise of the furnace. It was just as well. He might have answered rudely.

A wave of yet more tender joy escaped from his heart and went coursing in warm flood along his arteries. Like the tender fire of stars moments of their life together, that no one knew of or would ever know of, broke up and illumined his memory. He longed to recall to her those moments, to make her forget the years of their dull existence together and remember only their moments of ecstasy. For the years, he felt, had not quenched his soul or hers. Their children, his writing, her household cares had not quenched all their souls' tender fire. In one letter that he had written to her then he had said: 'Why is it that words like these seem to me so dull and cold? Is it because there is no word tender enough to be your name?'

Like distant music these words that he had written years before were borne towards him from the past. He longed to be alone with her. When the others had gone away, when he and she were in the room in the hotel, then they would be alone together. He would call her softly:

'Gretta!'

Perhaps she would not hear at once: she would be undressing. Then something in his voice would strike her. She would turn and look at him . . .

At the corner of Winetavern Steet they met a cab. He was glad of its rattling noise as it saved him from conversation. She was looking out of the window and seemed tired. The others spoke only a few words, pointing out some building or street. The horse galloped along wearily under the murky morning sky, dragging his old rattling box after his heels, and Gabriel was again in a cab with her, galloping to catch the boat, galloping to their honeymoon.

As the cab drove across O'Connell Bridge Miss O'Callaghan said:

'They say you never cross O'Connell Bridge without seeing a white horse.'

'I see a white man this time,' said Gabriel.

'Where?' asked Mr Bartell D'Arcy.

Gabriel pointed to the statue, on which lay patches of snow. Then he nodded familiarly to it and waved his hand.

'Good night, Dan,' he said gaily.

When the cab drew up before the hotel, Gabriel jumped out and, in spite of Mr Bartell D'Arcy's protest, paid the driver. He gave the man a shilling over his fare. The man saluted and said:

'A prosperous New Year to you sir, sir.'

'The same to you,' said Gabriel cordially.

She leaned for a moment on his arm in getting out of the cab and while standing at the kerbstone, bidding the others good night. She leaned lightly on his arm, as lightly as when she had danced with him a few hours before. He had felt proud and happy then, happy that she was his, proud of her grace and wifely carriage. But now, after the kindling again of so many memories, the first touch of her body, musical and strange and perfumed, sent through him a keen pang of lust. Under cover of her silence he pressed her arm closely to his side; and, as they stood at the hotel door, he felt that they had escaped from their lives and duties, escaped from home and friends and run away together with wild and radiant hearts to a new adventure.

An old man was dozing in a great hooded chair in the hall. He lit a candle in the office and went before them to the stairs. They followed him in silence, their feet falling in soft thuds on the thickly carpeted stairs. She mounted the stairs behind the porter, her head bowed in the ascent, her frail shoulders curved as with a burden, her skirt girt tightly about her. He could have flung his arms about her hips and held her still, for his arms were trembling with desire to seize her and only the stress of his nails against the palms of his hands held the wild impulse of his body in check. The porter halted on the stairs to settle his guttering candle. They halted, too, on the steps below him. In the silence Gabriel could hear the falling of the molten wax into the tray and the thumping of his own heart against his ribs.

The porter led them along a corridor and opened a door. Then he set his unstable candle down on a toilet-table and asked at what hour they were to be called in the morning.

'Eight,' said Gabriel.

The porter pointed to the tap of the electric-light and began a muttered apology, but Gabriel cut him short.

'We don't want any light. We have light enough from the street. And I say,' he added, pointing to the candle, 'you might remove that handsome article, like a good man.'

The porter took up his candle again, but slowly, for he was surprised by such a novel idea. Then he mumbled good night and went out. Gabriel shot the lock to.

A ghastly light from the street lamp lay in a long shaft from one window to the door. Gabriel threw his overcoat and hat on a couch and crossed the room towards the window. He looked down into the street in order that his emotion might calm a little. Then he turned and leaned against a chest of drawers with his back to the light. She had taken off her hat and cloak and was standing before a large swinging mirror, unhooking her waist. Gabriel paused for a few moments, watching her, and then said:

'Gretta!'

She turned away from the mirror slowly and walked along the shaft of light towards him. Her face looked so serious and weary that the words would not pass Gabriel's lips. No, it was not the moment yet.

'You look tired,' he said.

'I am a little,' she answered.

'You don't feel ill or weak?'

'No, tired: that's all.'

She went on to the window and stood there, looking out. Gabriel waited again and then, fearing that diffidence was about to conquer him, he said abruptly:

'By the way, Gretta!'

'What is it?'

'You know that poor fellow Malins?' he said quickly.

'Yes. What about him?'

'Well, poor fellow, he's a decent sort of chap, after all,' continued Gabriel in a false voice. 'He gave me back that sovereign I lent him, and I didn't expect it, really. It's a pity he wouldn't keep away from that Browne, because he's not a bad fellow, really.'

He was trembling now with annoyance. Why did she seem so abstracted? He did not know how he could begin. Was she annoyed, too, about something? If she would only turn to him or come to him of her own accord! To take her as she was would be brutal. No, he must see some ardour in her eyes first. He longed to be master of her strange mood.

'When did you lend him the pound?' she asked, after a pause.

Gabriel strove to restrain himself from breaking out into brutal language about the sottish Malins and his pound. He longed to cry to her from his soul, to crush her body against his, to overmaster her. But he said:

'O, at Christmas, when he opened that little Christmas-card shop in Henry Street.'

He was in such a fever of rage and desire that he did not hear her come from the window. She stood before him for an instant, looking at him strangely. Then, suddenly raising herself on tiptoe and resting her hands lightly on his shoulders, she kissed him.

'You are a very generous person, Gabriel,' she said.

Gabriel, trembling with delight at her sudden kiss and at the quaintness of her phrase, put his hands on her hair and began smoothing it back, scarcely touching it with his fingers. The washing had made it fine and brilliant. His heart was brimming over with happiness. Just when he was wishing for it she had come to him of her own accord. Perhaps her thoughts had been running with his. Perhaps she had felt the impetuous desire that was in him, and then the yielding mood had come upon her. Now that she had fallen to him so easily, he wondered why he had been so diffident.

He stood, holding her head between his hands. Then, slipping one arm swiftly about her body and drawing her towards him, he said softly:

'Gretta, dear, what are you thinking about?'

She did not answer nor yield wholly to his arm. He said again, softly:

'Tell me what it is, Gretta. I think I know what is the matter. Do I know?'

She did not answer at once. Then she said in an outburst of tears:

'O, I am thinking about that song, *The Lass of Aughrim*.'

She broke loose from him and ran to the bed and, throwing her arms across the bed-rail, hid her face. Gabriel stood stock-still for a moment in astonishment and then followed her. As he passed in the way of the cheval-glass he caught sight of himself in full length, his broad, well-filled shirt-front, the face whose expression always puzzled him when he saw it in a mirror, and his glimmering gilt-rimmed eyeglasses. He halted a few paces from her and said:

'What about the song? Why does that make you cry?'

She raised her head from her arms and dried her eyes with the back of her hand like a child. A kinder note than he had intended went into his voice.

'Why, Gretta?' he asked.

'I am thinking about a person long ago who used to sing that song.'

'And who was the person long ago?' asked Gabriel, smiling.

'It was a person I used to know in Galway when I was living with my grandmother,' she said.

The smile passed away from Gabriel's face. A dull anger began to gather again at the back of his mind and the dull fires of his lust began to grow angrily in his veins.

'Someone you were in love with?' he asked ironically.

'It was a young boy I used to know,' she answered, 'named Michael Furey. He used to sing that song, *The Lass of Aughrim*. He was very delicate.'

Gabriel was silent. He did not wish her to think that he was interested in this delicate boy.

'I can see him so plainly,' she said, after a moment. 'Such eyes as he had: big, dark eyes! And such an expression in them—an expression!'

'O, then, you are in love with him?' said Gabriel.

'I used to go out walking with him,' she said, 'when I was in Galway.'

A thought flew across Gabriel's mind.

'Perhaps that was why you wanted to go to Galway with that Ivors girl?' he said coldly.

She looked at him and asked in surprise:

'What for?'

Her eyes made Gabriel feel awkward. He shrugged his shoulders and said:

'How do I know? To see him, perhaps.'

She looked away from him along the shaft of light towards the window in silence.

'He is dead,' she said at length. 'He died when he was only seventeen. Isn't it a terrible thing to die so young as that?'

'What was he?' asked Gabriel, still ironically.

'He was in the gasworks,' she said.

Gabriel felt humiliated by the failure of his irony and by the evocation of this figure from the dead, a boy in the gasworks. While he had been full of memories of their secret life together, full of tenderness and joy and desire, she had been comparing him in her mind with another. A shameful consciousness of his own person assailed him. He saw himself as a ludicrous figure, acting as a pennyboy for his aunts, a nervous, well-meaning sentimentalist, orating to vulgarians and idealising his own clownish lusts, the pitiable fatuous fellow he had caught a glimpse of in the mirror. Instinctively he turned his back more to the light lest she might see the shame that burned upon his forehead.

He tried to keep up his tone of cold interrogation, but his voice when he spoke was humble and indifferent.

'I suppose you were in love with this Michael Furey, Gretta,' he said.

'I was great with him at that time,' she said.

Her voice was veiled and sad. Gabriel, feeling now how vain it would be to try to lead her whither he had purposed, caressed one of her hands and said, also sadly:

'And what did he die of so young, Gretta? Consumption, was it?'

'I think he died for me,' she answered.

A vague terror seized Gabriel at this answer, as if, at that hour when he had hoped to triumph, some impalpable and vindictive being was coming against him, gathering forces against him in its vague world. But he shook himself free of it with an effort of reason and continued to caress her hand. He did not question her again, for he felt that she would tell him of herself. Her hand was warm and moist: it did not respond to his touch, but he continued to caress it just as he had caressed her first letter to him that spring morning.

'It was in the winter,' she said, 'about the beginning of the winter when I was going to leave my grandmother's and come up here to the convent. And he was ill at the time in his lodgings in Galway and wouldn't be let out, and his people in Oughterard were written to. He was in decline, they said, or something like that. I never knew rightly.'

She paused for a moment and sighed.

'Poor fellow,' she said. 'He was very fond of me and he was such a gentle boy. We used to go out together, walking, you know, Gabriel, like the way they do in the country. He was going to study singing only for his health. He had a very good voice, poor Michael Furey.'

'Well; and then?' asked Gabriel.

'And then when it came to the time for me to leave Galway and come up to the convent he was much worse and I wouldn't be let see him so I wrote him a letter saying I was going up to Dublin and would be back in the summer, and hoping he would be better then.'

She paused for a moment to get her voice under control, and then went on:

'Then the night before I left, I was in my grandmother's house in Nuns' Island, packing up, and I heard gravel thrown up against the window. The window was so wet I couldn't see, so I ran downstairs as I was and slipped out the back into the garden and there was the poor fellow at the end of the garden, shivering.'

'And did you not tell him to go back?' asked Gabriel.

'I implored of him to go home at once and told him he would get his death in the rain. But he said he did not want to live. I can see his eyes as well as well! He was standing at the end of the wall where there was a tree.'

'And did he go home?' asked Gabriel.

'Yes, he went home. And when I was only a week in the convent he died and he was buried in Oughterard, where his people came from. O, the day I heard that, that he was dead!'

She stopped, choking with sobs, and, overcome by emotion, flung herself face downwards on the bed, sobbing in the quilt. Gabriel held her hand for a moment longer, irresolutely, and then, shy of intruding on her grief, let it fall gently and walked quietly to the window.

She was fast asleep.

Gabriel, leaning on his elbow, looked for a few moments unresentfully on her tangled hair and half-open mouth, listening to her deep-drawn breath. So she had had that romance in her life: a man had died for her sake. It hardly pained him now to think how poor a part he, her husband had played in her life. He watched her while she slept, as though he and she had never lived together as man and wife. His curious eyes rested long upon her face and on her hair: and, as he thought of what she must have been then, in that time of her first girlish beauty, a strange, friendly pity for her entered his soul. He did not like to say even to himself that her face was no longer beautiful, but he knew that it was no longer the face for which Michael Furey had braved death.

Perhaps she had not told him all the story. His eyes moved to the chair over which she had thrown some of her clothes. A petticoat string dangled to the floor. One boot stood upright, its limp upper fallen down: the fellow of it lay upon its side. He wondered at his riot of emotions of an hour before. From what had it proceeded? From his aunt's supper, from his own foolish speech, from the wine and dancing, the merry-making when saying good night in the hall, the pleasure of the walk along the river in the snow. Poor Aunt Julia! She, too, would soon be a shade with the shade of Patrick Morkan and his horse. He had caught that haggard look upon her face for a moment when she was singing *Arrayed for the Bridal*. Soon, perhaps, he would be sitting in that same drawing-room, dressed in black, his silk hat on his knees. The blinds would be drawn down and Aunt Kate would be sitting beside him, crying and blowing her nose and telling him how Julia had died. He would cast about in his mind for some words that might console her, and would find only lame and useless ones. Yes, yes: that would happen very soon.

The air of the room chilled his shoulders. He stretched himself cautiously along under the sheets and lay down beside his wife. One by one, they were all becoming shades. Better pass boldly into that other world, in the full glory of some passion, than fade and wither dismally with age. He thought of how she who lay beside him had locked in her heart for so many years that image of her lover's eyes when he had told her that he did not wish to live.

Generous tears filled Gabriel's eyes. He had never felt that himself towards any woman, but he knew that such a feeling must be love. The tears gathered more thickly in his eyes and in the partial darkness he imagined he saw the form of a young man standing under a dripping tree. Other forms were near. His soul had approached that region where dwell the vast hosts of the dead. He was conscious of, but could not apprehend, their wayward and flickering existence. His own identity was fading out into a grey impalpable world: the solid world itself, which these dead had one time reared and lived in, was dissolving and dwindling.

A few light taps upon the pane made him turn to the window. It had begun to snow again. He watched sleepily the flakes, silver and dark, falling obliquely against the lamplight. The time had come for him to set out on his journey westwards. Yes, the newspapers were right: snow was general all over Ireland. It was falling on every part of the dark central plain, on the treeless hills, falling softly upon the Bog of Allen and, further westwards, softly falling into the dark mutinous Shannon waves. It was falling, too, upon every part of the lonely churchyard on the hill where Michael Furey lay buried. It lay thickly drifted on the crooked crosses and headstones, on the spears of the little gate, on the barren thorns. His soul swooned slowly as he heard the snow falling faintly through the universe and faintly falling, like the descent of their last end, upon all the living and the dead.

My Little Black Ass

translated from the Irish by Eoghan O Tuairisc

It was in Kinvara I first got to know my little black ass. It was a fair-day and there he stood by the ditch with his backside to the wind, heedless of the world and the world of him.

But he caught my interest at once. I needed an ass. I was tired of travelling on foot. Wouldn't he carry me and my bag and overcoat and all that? And who knows, I might get him cheap enough.

I enquired for the owner, but I had to search the town before I found him. He was outside a public house singing for pennies.

Of course he would sell the ass! Why wouldn't he sell, if he got his price? Yes, his price, not a single penny would he take from me bar his price.

And of course only for the hard times he'd never part with him— no, never! A fine young ass fit to go twenty miles a day at his ease. Give him a handful of oats once a month and there wasn't a racehorse in the country fit to keep up with him—no, not even a racehorse.

We both went to have a look at the ass.

Oh how the tinkerman sang his praises! There was never an ass since the first ass came to Ireland as mettlesome, as intelligent, as farsighted—

'D'you know a habit he has,' he said admiringly, 'if you gave him a scrap of oats in the morning he'd put some of it aside for fear it might be scarce the morning after. There's not a word of a lie in that—not one word.'

Somebody laughed. The tinkerman turned on him.

'What are you laughing at, you halfwit? He's that intelligent that he sets some of his oats aside. Isn't it often enough I was so short myself that I had to steal a little of his? Only for that ass we'd often go hungry—myself and my twelve daughters . . .'

I asked whether he could distinguish between what belonged to his master and what belonged to the neighbours.

'He's as innocent as the priest,' the fellow said. 'If every beast was like him there'd be no need for ditch, fence, wall, or dyke—no need at all.'

By this time a big crowd had gathered. His own children were there—I don't know if the whole twelve of them were present, but as for those that were, it would be hard to find such a dirty ragged unkempt flock of children in any other spot in Ireland, and each one of them more impudent than another. His wife was there. Barefoot, bareheaded, wild . . .

She broke into the discussion.

'Peter,' she said to her husband, 'd'you remember the day he went swimming into the river and brought poor Mickileen to land when he was getting carried off by the current?'

'Why wouldn't I remember it, Sive?' said he. 'Yes, and the day I was offered five pounds for him—'

'Five pounds,' she told me, 'he got five pounds for him, five golden sovereigns into the heel of his fist—'

'On my oath I did,' he said interrupting. 'I had the money there in my fist and the bargain made—'

'But when he saw the poor ass,' said she, 'in tears because we were parting with him, all he could do was renege the bargain.'

'Ssh!' he said. 'Speak easy I tell you. He understands every word we say. Look how he cocks his lug.'

I offered a pound for this remarkable animal.

'A pound!' cried the tinkerman.

'A pound!' said the wife.

'A pound!' said the twelve daughters all together.

How astounded they all were. They gathered about to gaze at me. One child took hold of my coat, one took hold of my trousers, the youngest took hold of my knee.

Another one of them put a hand in my trousers pocket. Of course the creature was merely looking to see if I had even the pound—but instead of the pound she got a box in the ear, and not from the gentleman of the roads either . . .

I was quite taken with the little black ass. He'd do. He'd carry me part of the road. And I could sell him whenever I might be tired of him.

'A pound,' I repeated.

'Two pound,' said the tinker.

'Oh woe, woe!' said the wife, 'my fine ass sold for two pound!' And she began to wail and weep.

'For a pound,' I said.

'For a pound—and sixpence each to the children.'

The bargain was settled at that. I gave him the pound. I gave a sixpence to each one of his children round me. Then the wife began to call for Johneen and Eameen and Tomeen and the Lord knows how many more. There wasn't a beggar at the fair who didn't bring me his children all demanding and clamouring. The uproar they made! The tangle, the tussle, the hullaballo all round me! One saying he got ne'er a penny while hiding the silver sixpence under his tongue. Another saying—but who could tell what anyone was saying or trying to say, there was such a bedlam about me.

What a pity I didn't give him the two pounds straight off and not bother with the gratuities!

I left town in fine style. Myself on the ass's back, the tinker gripping the halter on the right, his wife gripping it on the left, the flock of children surrounding us yelling their heads off.

Some of the town boys followed us, each of them giving me his own particular advice. The ass was compared to the most celebrated racehorses of the day; I was told to watch out or he'd take to his heels and never be seen again; I was advised to give him this food and that food—apparently the sight of myself on my little black ass escorted by the tinkers was the biggest lark of their lives.

But what did I care? Hadn't I got the ass, having long wanted such a four-footed beast?

Is it possible to describe how the ass and I parted with the tinkers? Nine times one after the other they all shook my hand; they all spoke to the ass softly, gently, coaxingly, endearingly . . . Seven times over they recounted his qualifications. I was made promise to be kind and good to him, to give him a little fistful of oats when I could afford it, and if I valued my soul not to use a stick on him . . .

Then as we parted they raised the lament. The father began it. The mother joined in. The children took it up, filling all the surrounding wood with the thin sharp wailing they made.

At last I was alone, myself and my little black ass.

He went at a gallop until we had left the wood behind. I had made an excellent bargain I thought: where would you find an ass with the speed of my little black ass?

But when we had left the wood behind it was a different story. He wouldn't stir a foot. I tried coaxing and enticing him with endearing words. He paid no heed. I thought to shift him by using the stick. Not an inch would he budge, he just stood there in the dead centre of the road.

People passed, some of those who had been at the fair and were now more than a little merry. I was advised to do this with him, do that with him, but when one of them advised me to carry him a bit of the way I lost my patience and threw a shower of stones after the fellow.

In the end I had to get down from his back and, yes, pull him along behind me against the drag of his legs and head . . .

How handsomely I prayed for the tinkerman who had sold me such a beast!

But ere long I noticed a peculiar thing. He was skittish and nothing frightened him as much as the musical sound made by the wind through the branches of a tree.

As soon as he came under the branches of trees lining the roadside he always lost his stubbornness and could hardly be held. First he would cock a listening ear, then he'd shake himself like a dog coming out of water, then before you knew where you were he was off at a gallop. Right, said I.

I tied him to a gate, went into the wood and, getting an armful of fresh foliage, made it into a wreath which I fastened round his neck and up above his ears as we emerged from the wood.

Poor animal! He went at an incredible rate. He imagined from the music in his ears that he was still in the wood.

When we reached Ballyvaughan all the townspeople came out to see the wonder—myself and my little black ass wearing his crown of leafy branches . . .

I still have the little black ass and will till he dies. We have gone many a long mile together in rain and drizzle, frost and snow. He has lost some of his bad habits in the course of time—something I failed to do myself. And I think my little black ass knows that as well as anyone.

But he is as proud as punch since I bought him the little bright-green cart. Getting younger he is, poor beast!

The Triangle

Nothing is true for ever. A man and a fact will become equally decrepit and will tumble in the same ditch, for truth is as mortal as man, and both are outlived by the tortoise and the crow.

To say that two is company and three is a crowd is to make a very temporary statement. After a short time satiety or use and wont has crept sunderingly between the two, and, if they are any company at all, they are bad company, who pray discreetly but passionately for the crowd which is censured by the proverb.

If there had not been a serpent in the Garden of Eden it is likely that the bored inhabitants of Paradise would have been forced to import one from the outside wilds merely to relax the tedium of a too-sustained duet. There ought to be a law that when a man and a woman have been married for a year they should be forcibly separated for another year. In the meantime, as our lawgivers have no sense, we will continue to invoke the serpent.

Mrs Mary Morrissy had been married for quite a time to a gentleman of respectable mentality, a sufficiency of money, and a surplus of leisure—Good things? We would say so if we dared, for we are growing old and suspicious of all appearances, and we do not easily recognise what is bad or good. Beyond the social circumference we are confronted with a debatable ground where good and bad are so merged that we cannot distinguish the one from the other. To her husband's mental attainments (from no precipitate, dizzy peaks did he stare; it was only a tiny plain with the tiniest of hills in the centre) Mrs Morrissy extended a courtesy entirely unmixed with awe. For his money she extended a hand which could still thrill to an unaccustomed prodigality, but for his leisure (and it was illimitable) she could find no possible use.

The quality of permanency in a transient world is terrifying. A permanent husband is a bore, and we do not know what to do with him. He cannot be put on a shelf. He cannot be hung on a nail. He will not go out of the house. There is no escape from him, and he is always the same. A smile of a certain dimension, moustaches of this inevitable measurement, hands that waggle and flop like those of automata—these are his. He eats this way and he drinks that way, and he will continue to do so until he stiffens into the ultimate quietude. He snores on this note, he laughs on that, dissonant, unescapable, unchanging. This is the way he walks, and he does not know how to run. A predictable beast indeed! He is known inside and out, catalogued, ticketed, and he cannot be packed away.

Mrs Morrissy did not yet commune with herself about it, but if her grievance was anonymous it was not unknown. There is a back-door to every mind as to every house, and although she refused it house-room, the knowledge sat on her very hearthstone whistling for recognition.

Indeed, she could not look anywhere without seeing her husband. He was included in every landscape. His moustaches and the sun rose together. His pyjamas dawned with the moon. When the sea roared so did he, and he whispered with the river and the wind. He was in the picture but was out of drawing. He was in the song but was out of tune. He agitated her dully, surreptitiously, unceasingly. She questioned of space in a whisper—'Are we glued together?' said she. There was a bee in a flower, a burly rascal who did not care a rap for any one; he sat enjoying himself in a scented and gorgeous palace, and in him she confided:

'If,' said she to the bee, 'If that man doesn't stop talking to me I'll kick him. I'll stick a pin in him if he does not go out for a walk.'

She grew desperately nervous. She was afraid that if she looked at him any longer she would see him. Tomorrow, she thought, I may notice that he is a short, fat man in spectacles, and that will be the end of everything. But the end of everything is also the beginning of everything, and so she was one half in fear and the other half in hope. A little more and she would hate him, and would begin the world again with the same little hope and the same little despair for her meagre capital.

She had already elaborated a theory that man was intended to work, and that male sloth was offensive to Providence and should be forbidden by the law. At times her tongue thrilled, silently as yet, to certain dicta of the experienced Aunt who had superintended her youth, to the intent that a lazy man is a nuisance to himself and to everybody else; and, at last, she disguised this saying as an anecdote and repeated it pleasantly to her husband.

He received it coldly, pondered it with disfavour, and dismissed it by arguing that her Aunt had whiskers, that a whiskered female is a freak, and that the intellectual exercises of a freak are—He lifted his eyebrows and his shoulders. He brushed her Aunt from the tips of his fingers and blew her delicately beyond good manners and the mode.

But time began to hang heavily on both. The intellectual antics of a leisured man become at last wearisome; his methods of thought, by mere familiarity, grow distasteful; the time comes when all the arguments are finished, there is nothing more to be said on any subject, and boredom, without even the covering, apologetic hand, yawns and yawns and cannot be appeased. Thereupon two cease to be company, and even a serpent would be greeted as a cheery and timely visitor. Dismal indeed, and not infrequent, is that time, and the vista therefrom is a long, dull yawn stretching to the horizon and the grave. If at any time we do revalue the values, let us write it down that the person who makes us yawn is a criminal knave, and then we will abolish matrimony and read Plato again.

The serpent arrived one morning hard on Mrs Morrissy's pathetic pressure. It had three large trunks, a toy terrier, and a volume of verse. The trunks contained dresses, the dog insects, and the book emotion—a sufficiently enlivening trilogy! Miss Sarah O'Malley wore the dresses in exuberant rotation, Mr Morrissy read the emotional poetry with great admiration, Mrs Morrissy made friends with the dog, and life at once became complex and joyful.

Mr Morrissy, exhilarated by the emotional poetry, drew, with an instinct too human to be censured, more and more in the direction of his wife's cousin, and that lady, having a liking for comedy, observed the agile posturings of the gentleman on a verbal summit up and down and around which he flung himself with equal dexterity and satisfaction—crudely, he made puns—and the two were further thrown together by the enforced absences of Mrs Morrissy, into a privacy more than sealed, by reason of the attentions of a dog who would climb to her lap, and there, with an angry nose, put to no more than temporary rout the nimble guests of his jacket. Shortly Mrs Morrissy began to look upon the toy terrier with a meditative eye.

It was from one of these, now periodical, retreats that Mrs Morrissey first observed the rapt attitude of her husband, and instantly life for her became bounding, plentiful, and engrossing.

There is no satisfaction in owning that which nobody else covets. Our silver is no more than second-hand, tarnished metal until some one else speaks of it in terms of envy. Our husbands are barely intolerable until a lady friend has endeavoured to abstract their cloying attentions. Then only do we comprehend that our possessions are unique, beautiful, well worth guarding.

Nobody has yet pointed out that there is an eighth sense; and yet the sense of property is more valuable and more detestable than all the others in combination. The person who owns something is civilised. It is man's escape from wolf and monkeydom. It is individuality at last, or the promise of it, while those other ownerless people must remain either beasts of prey or beasts of burden, grinning with ineffective teeth, or bowing stupid heads for their master's loads, and all begging humbly for last straws and getting them.

Under a sufficiently equable exterior Mrs Morrissy's blood was pulsing with greater activity than had ever moved it before. It raced! It flew! At times the tide of it thudded to her head, boomed in her ears, surged in fierce waves against her eyes. Her brain moved with a complexity which would have surprised her had she been capable of remarking upon it. Plot and counterplot! She wove webs horrid as a spider's. She became, without knowing it, a mistress of psychology. She dissected motions and motives. She builded theories precariously upon an eyelash. She pondered and weighed the turning of a head, the handing of a sugar-bowl. She read treason in a laugh, assignations in a song, villainy in a new dress. Deeper and darker things! Profound and vicious depths plunging stark to where the devil lodged in darknesses too dusky for registration! She looked so steadily on these gulfs and murks that at last she could see anything she wished to see; and always, when times were critical, when this and that, abominations indescribable, were separate by no more than a pin's point, she must retire from her watch (alas for a too-sensitive nature!) to chase the enemies of a dog upon which, more than ever, she fixed a meditative eye.

To get that woman out of the house became a pressing necessity. Her cousin carried with her a baleful atmosphere. She moved cloudy with doubt. There was a diabolic aura about her face, and her hair was red! These things were patent. Was one blind or a fool? A straw will reveal the wind, so will an eyelash, a smile, the carriage of a dress. Ankles also! One saw too much of them. Let it be said then. Teeth and neck were bared too often and too broadly. If modesty was indeed more than a name, then here it was outraged. Shame too! was it only a word? Does one do this and that without even a blush? Even vice should have its good manners, its own decent retirements. If there is nothing else let there be breeding! But at this thing the world might look and understand and censure if it were not brass-browed and stupid. Sneak! Traitress! Serpent! Oh, Serpent! do you slip into our very Eden, looping your sly coils across our flowers, trailing over our beds of narcissus and our budding rose, crawling into our secret arbours and whispering-places and nests of happiness? Do you flaunt and sway your crested head with a new hat on it every day? Oh that my Aunt were here, with the dragon's teeth, and the red breath, and whiskers to match! Here Mrs Morrissy jumped as if she had been bitten (as indeed she had been) and retired precipitately, eyeing the small dog that frisked about her with an eye almost petrified with meditation.

To get that woman out of the house quickly and without scandal. Not to let her know for a moment, for the blink and twitter of an eyelid, of her triumph. To eject her with ignominy, retaining one's own dignity in the meantime. Never to let her dream of an uneasiness that might have screamed, an anger that could have bitten and scratched and been happy in the primitive exercise. Was such a task beyond her adequacy?

Below in the garden the late sun slanted upon her husband, as with declamatory hands and intense brows he chanted emotional poetry, ready himself on the slope of opportunity to roll into verses from his own resources. He criticised, with agile misconception, the inner meaning, the involved, hard-hidden heart of the poet; and the serpent sat before him and nodded. She smiled enchantments at him, and allurements, and subtle, subtle disagreements. On the grass at their feet the toy terrier bounded from his slumbers and curved an imperative and furious hind-leg in the direction of his ear.

Mrs Morrissy called the dog, and it followed her into the house, frisking joyously. From the kitchen she procured a small basket, and into this she packed some old cloths and pieces of biscuit. Then she picked up the terrier, cuffed it on both sides of the head, popped it into the basket, tucked its humbly-agitated tail under its abject ribs, closed the basket, and fastened it with a skewer. She next addressed a label to her cousin's home, tied it to the basket, and despatched a servant with it to the railway-station, instructing her that it should be paid for on delivery.

At breakfast the following morning her cousin wondered audibly why her little, weeny, tiny pet was not coming for its brecky.

Mrs Morrissy, with a smile of infinite sweetness, suggested that Miss O'Malley's father would surely feed the brute when it arrived. 'It was a filthy little beast,' said she brightly; and she pushed the toast-rack closer to her husband.

There followed a silence which drowsed and buzzed to eternity, and during which Mr Morrissy's curled moustaches straightened and grew limp and drooped. An edge of ice stiffened around Miss O'Malley. Incredulity, frozen and wan, thawed into swift comprehension and dismay, lit a flame in her cheeks, throbbed burningly at the lobes of her ears, spread magnetic and prickling over her whole stung body, and ebbed and froze again to immobility. She opposed her cousin's kind eyes with a stony brow.

'I think,' said she, rising, 'that I had better see to my packing.'

'Must you go?' said Mrs Morrissy, with courteous unconcern, and she helped herself to cream. Her husband glared insanely at a pat of butter, and tried to look like someone who was somewhere else.

Miss O'Malley closed the door behind her with extreme gentleness.

So the matter lay. But the position was unchanged. For a little time peace would reign in that household, but the same driving necessity remained, and before long another, and perhaps more virulent, serpent would have to be requisitioned for the assuagement of those urgent woes. A man's moustaches will arise with the sun; not Joshua could constrain them to the pillow after the lark had sung reveille. A woman will sit pitilessly at the breakfast table however the male eye may shift and quail. It is the business and the art of life to degrade permanencies. Fluidity is existence, there is no other, and for ever the chief attraction of Paradise must be that there is a serpent in it to keep it lively and wholesome. Lacking the serpent we are no longer in Paradise, we are at home, and our sole entertainment is to yawn when we wish to.

Bush River

A black pony, tied by one leg to the stump of a tree, was eating corn from a wooden bowl. A little brown soldier groomed it furiously, prancing round it in poses of dramatic violence, and twisting his face, like his body, every moment into some unexpected form. Sweat poured down his cheeks and bare chest, on which an identity disc and a leather amulet, on separate cords, performed a kind of African minuet. After every few strokes, he fell back a yard, passing his quivering hand, as small and nervous as a child's, upwards over his whole face and cried loudly in Hausa, 'Oh—beautiful—oh, the lovely one. Oh, God bless him. See how he shines.'

A young officer with an eyeglass in his right eye walked slowly round pony and groom. Now and then he glanced severely upon both. Everything about him, his clipped hair which left him almost bald, his clipped moustache, even his eyeglass increased this air of severity, of an austere and critical aloofness.

'Now then, Mamadu,' he said impatiently, 'get on with it. What about the tail?'

'Oh, what a tail. Did you ever see such a tail?'

'I never saw such a dirty one.'

The little soldier pulled his face into a long, dolorous oval and sent his eyebrows to the top of his skull. But the officer did not notice this performance. He had walked down to the river bank.

The river was an African river never yet banked up, tamed, dredged, canalised; a river still wild. It poured along in tan-coloured flood, carrying with it whole trees, and every part of its surface showed a different agitation. Here it was all in foaming breakers, suddenly cut off by a spear-shaped eddy like pulled brown silk; beyond the eddy was a dark sea, with crisp waves jumping, like a wind flaw; and over on the far side, long manila ropes of water which seemed to turn upon themselves as they were dragged under the banks. This savage river not only moved with agile power; it worked. One saw it at work, digging out its own bed, eating at its banks. Every moment some bluff crumbled; stones, bushes fell and vanished.

The young officer, like most people, found a certain attraction in all rivers and moving waters. But African rivers fascinated him. Looking at them he understood that old phrase 'the devouring element'. He asked himself how Africa survived against such destruction. At the same time, he thought, how magnificent was the gesture with which Africa abandoned herself to be torn, like a lioness who stretches herself in the sun while her cubs bite at her.

A thin old sergeant, with extremely bandy legs, marched up, gave a sketchy war-time salute, and said in a grumbling voice, 'Captain Corner, sir.'

'Yes, sergeant?'

'Germans, sir. They come.'

Young Corner withdrew his eyes slowly from the fascinating river and looked once more at the pony, which had taken its nose from the bowl to nibble at the orderly's legs. He said severely, 'Don't forget the tail, Mamadu.'

And once more he walked slowly round, frowning through his eyeglass at the pony.

It was a Barbary stallion, jet black except beneath the belly, which showed a tinge of bronze. It had legs which looked too fine for its body, a crest like the Parthenon chargers and a forelock swinging to its nose. The little head, with full round eyes and tilted nostrils, was like a stag's. The ears were small and pointed, curled like the husks of an almond.

Corner had never before owned a pony of such quality and he was obsessed with the creature. Indeed he had already committed a great folly for its sake. A week before he had received a command regarded by himself and most of his brother officers as a special distinction, a step to promotion. He was to take charge of a sticky and dangerous operation, the planning of a route through the heart of enemy country, by which a heavy gun could be dragged, in secret, to Mora mountain, a German stronghold that had held out against two assaults. It was thought that the fire of this gun, taking the Germans by surprise, would not only smash their defences on the mountain-top but break the morale of their local troops, who could have no experience of high explosive.

This was the year 1915, before the days of bombing by planes.

The Cameroons campaign of 1914–16, against the German army of occupation, was a war of raids, ambushes, sieges, enormous marches, and especially surprises. There was no reconnaissance by air, no radio, and intelligence could only be got by scouts and spies. Whole columns would disappear for weeks together, to burst out, a thousand miles away, upon a panic-stricken capital. Two patrols would stumble upon each other by accident in high jungle and stare with amazement for a few seconds before grabbing their rifles.

The strategy of such a war was that of the old bush fighters who knew the jungle, who did not expect a field of fire in order to secure a position, who understood how to place a listening sentry in a tree, who could distinguish between the cough of a leopard and a husky, bored Negro *hauptmann* wandering from his post to look for a chicken, who could take a thousand men in line through thick scrub without losing touch and change front without their shooting each other.

Corner's instructions were to avoid anything like a road or even a used track. They were likely to be watched. He was not even to cross a road by daylight. He was to plot his line as far as possible through untouched bush, to avoid any indication that might put the enemy patrols on the alert, and to hide by night.

Officers in that campaign were allowed their horses, but only in the main column—never on scout, point, or patrol duty. For one thing, Nigerian horses in use are all stallions; they will scream at the most distant scent of a mare. For another, a man on a horse can be seen above the top of all but the tallest grass. Corner's assignment was actually that of a man on scout duty all the way. But he had not been able to persuade himself to leave his darling pony behind in some horse lines to be neglected by strangers, starved by thieving camp orderlies, or borrowed by some subaltern for a forced march, or be left dying in a swamp. Few men who parted from their horses in that war ever saw them again. Corner knew his duty, but he said to himself that most of his course lay through high bush where a horse would be as easily hidden as a man. 'And as for mares, there won't be any about—the villages are empty.' But already twice Satan had imagined mares and sent out a trumpet as good as a bugle call for every German within a mile.

Each of these tremendous neighs had scattered the men, diving for cover, and startled the young man out of himself. Each time, in the awful silence which followed, he had sat waiting for a shot, and thinking with amazement, 'My God, what a goddam bloody fool I was to bring this bloody pony. What a hell-fired ass I am.' And the amazement was even stronger than the anger. It was as though he discovered for the first time his own folly, his own mysterious power to forget, simply to abolish common sense and walk gravely, with the most reasonable, dignified air, into impossible situations.

The men creeping back from the scrub would look sulkily at the barb still walking on his toes with ears cocked and nostrils flared. They hated Satan for these alarums. And that was why the young man now said to the sergeant, 'After all the row you've been making down there.' He was defending his darling. He was saying, 'You complain of my pony, but what about your chatter?' And even while he said it, he was ashamed of himself, he was amazed at his own small-mindedness. 'Not like that, Mamadu—don't tear at it.' He took the comb out of the man's hands.

'Captain, sir. Captain Corner, sir.' The sergeant made another war-time salute, and cried in a voice unexpectedly shrill, 'We see 'em, sir.'

Corner, understanding these words at last, looked with surprise at the sergeant and said, 'Who see who, Sargy?'

'Germans, sir. We see 'em, over the river. And the river too big. He too big.'

'That's the style,' Corner murmured to the orderly. He took the excuse of stroking the pony's croup, as if to test the grooming. He did not like to show too openly his passion before Mamadu in case of provoking the latter's admiring outcries, which, for some reason, got on his nerves. His severe air was in fact a defence against this noise and exaggerated praise. 'Gently does it,' he said, and Mamadu cried, 'Oh, what hair—what a tail. God save us, it touches the ground.'

Corner carefully unravelled the tail; Satan, having ground up every bit of corn in the bowl, turned his delicate nose and began to eat the tree stump. His tail switched in the young man's hand, and he glanced sideways at his master. The large black eyes, more brilliant under the thick short lashes than any woman's, expressed something which always gave Corner acute pleasure, though he could scarcely have described it, except by the words, 'The little bastard don't give a damn for me or anybody else.'

He frowned and said, 'Eating still—this horse would eat anything.'

The sergeant turned and walked off, humping his right shoulder in a peculiar manner.

'Oh, a lovely eater—it's a marvel how he eats. Why, he'll eat a desert round himself wherever he is.'

The orderly quite understood that Corner's critical look was simply the outward manner of his obsession; a lover's constraint. Like a lady's maid, he easily penetrated his master's mind. And Corner, like a lady, slightly resented it. He said illogically, 'Then why don't you groom him properly? Look at that mane—look at the dust in the roots.'

'But, sir, it's too thick—just see how thick. Holy God, a wonder for thickness.'

The sergeant reappeared under the huge trees which surrounded the little mud flat. His shoulder was now almost at his ear and he had also begun to limp. He said flatly, 'We no cross here, sir—he too bad place.'

'But we have to cross here; it's the only good place for the gun.'

The duty of the party was to discover if it were practicable to drag a French 75 a hundred miles through the unmapped bush to a certain rendezvous. The idea was to surprise the Germans with this gun, which ranked, in Africa, as heavy artillery.

'The men, they say they no fit to cross.'

'Why?' Corner was startled. He looked thoughtfully at the sergeant. 'There's nobody there, you're not afraid of demons, are you?' he asked.

Sergeant Umaru had, in fact, a great terror of demons, especially in strange bush, and his fear sometimes infected his men. But the men were already frightened of the river, the Germans or demons. Corner found them huddled in a group on the bank, staring through the scrub across the roaring stream. Their faces had the look of panic, a loosened appearance of the flesh had turned soft and sagged a little from the bone. Mouths were hanging slack; one young soldier was showing his lower teeth.

'What's the trouble?' Corner was saying. 'There's no Germans within miles. And this river is too fast for crocodiles or water spirits.'

He was fond of his men and knew them well—brave and cool in action, but subject to unexpected and mysterious panics.

'It's a bad place,' a lance corporal muttered, rolling his eyes about like a child in a cellar.

'Nonsense, it's a very good place. Mamadu, saddle up. Where are the swimmers for the loads?'

On the evening before, there had been eight volunteers eager to take charge of the loads—rifles, ammunition, and rations floated on gourds—but now there were none. Corner looked round him with an air of surprise, which was purely formal. His mind was scarcely interested in this crisis. He was preoccupied with the river. 'A very good place,' he murmured. 'Where's the guide for the ford?'

'No guide, sir—he no come.'

'No guide.' He was startled. And then at once he felt a peculiar sense of anticipation. Not of pleasure, scarcely of excitement. It was as if an opportunity had opened itself before the young man, a gate in the wall of his routine, through which his mind already began to flow. Or rather the force which poured eagerly through this gap was not his at all but that peculiar energy which had possessed him for days; the energy of his passion for Satan, for the wild bush, especially for the wild river. The different streams rushed together at the same gap, and their joined forces where overwhelming. They swept away the whole bank, the whole wall. Young Corner looked severely upon his men and said in a voice of resignation, 'I suppose you want me to give you a lead. Bring Satan, Mamadu.'

Satan was brought. He stretched out his shining neck and nibbled the tassel on the sergeant's fez. But no one laughed. The men were quite dissolved in panic. While Corner mounted, they gazed at him with round eyes which seemed to be liquefying with fear.

The little sergeant alone had his surly veteran's composure. He hitched up his whole right arm and muttered, 'Very bad river, sir. Them crocodiles live, sir. Them Germans live other side, I see 'em.'

But Corner did not even listen to him. He had been carried far away from any notion of Germans, of crocodiles. He had no mind for anything but the river and Satan beneath him, who, by means of the magnificent river, was going to achieve a triumph. He held out each leg in turn to Mamadu to pull off his boots. Bare-legged, he hooked his big toe through the sides of the stirrup irons, gave his eyeglass an additional screw, and jammed on his hat, a disreputable terai. Then, for the first time, he examined the river, not as a fascinating object, but as an obstacle. He measured the weight of the current and the direction of the eddies.

He had swum horses before, but only for a few yards; once on a road after a storm, once in a river pool; never in flood water.

It was not a thing one set out to do. On an ordinary journey, the groom took horses across unbridged rivers from a boat, holding them short by head ropes to keep their noses up. A man who chose to swim his own horse when a boat or a ford was available would have seemed quite mad; and if he managed to drown himself or his horse, he would also seem irresponsible.

Corner, at twenty-six, was an extremely conventional young officer, a little bit of a dandy, a good deal of a coxcomb. He had a strong prejudice against the unusual. It seemed to him affected and he hated affectation. And what gave him a calm personal delight in this opportunity seized upon so eagerly by the forces which possessed him was the knowledge that he *had* to swim this river. He had a first-class excuse for doing what he had often wanted to do. He told himself that he was not his own master, not in any sense of the word.

Satan steppd into the water, moving as usual with the precise muscular liveliness of a dancer, and obeying signals that his rider had not consciously given, the shade of a leg pressure, the very beginning of a wrist turn.

A corporal called out suddenly, 'Don't go there, sir—we find them ford, sir.'

Satan's breast was already under water. He lifted his head; he was swimming within five yards of the bank.

Corner, up to the neck at Satan's hindquarters sank beneath him, took his feet out of the stirrups, hooked his right hand into the pommel of the saddle and floated over it. He found at once that he had no control over the pony. He could only talk to him in Hausa, 'Keep at it, friend—straight ahead.'

And when he spoke, he felt an affection for the little horse, an exultant pride in his courage, so different in quality from anything he had known before that it could not be described. It was more than sympathy, more than the bantering love of a friend; it was a feeling so strong that it seemed to have its own life, full of delight and worship; laughing at Satan and rejoicing in all devotion and courage; the mysterious greatness of the spirit. He wanted to laugh, to call out, like Mamadu. But again, as if constrained by decorum or a sense of what was proper to his responsibilities, he merely looked severe and repeated, this time in English, 'Keep it up, old boy—that's the stuff.'

They were now in mid-current. At this level, the river seemed a mile wide and the waves a little ocean storm. The far bank was a mere line on the horizon. A tree trunk, turning its branches like an enormous screw, went swinging past, three yards from Satan's nose. Satan turned an ear back as if expecting some remark, but his nose never deviated an inch from the course. It pointed like a compass at the opposite bank, now passing at a speed which seemed like a train's.

Once only he showed some emotion, when a wave splashed into his nose. He then gave a snort, not the short loud snort of indignation or surprise, but the longer exhalation which means enquiry and suspended judgement. The bank was now close and it proved to be extremely high and steep—what's more, the eddy under the bank was like a millstream. Satan seemed to be deeper in the water. Another wave struck him in the nose and he snorted loud and sharp. Corner thought, 'If he turns back, we're done.'

But Satan obviously had no notion of turning back. Possibly he was too stupid to think of it; or perhaps wise enough to know its danger. Perhaps it was not in the habit of his mind and breeding to turn back. He struck with his forefeet at the clay, now flying past at the rate of four miles an hour. But it was as hard as brick above water level, and his unshod hoofs brought down only small shoots of dust. Corner murmured, 'That's it, old boy, go at it.' But he did not see exactly what was to be gone at. They whirled along the bank and Satan continued to stab at it furiously; he sank suddenly over his nose and, coming up again with a terrific snort, again stabbed and again sank.

They were carried round a point and struck a snag, itself caught against a stump. The cliff behind was breached by some recent avalanche which was heaped among the roots of the stump. Corner threw himself on the snag and backed up the slope, hauling on the reins. Satan made a powerful effort and heaved himself out of the river. In a moment both were on the level ground ten feet above, among short bushes.

Corner felt as if he too had swum a river. He was tired as only a swimmer can be. He chose a patch of young grass and lay flat on his back, holding Satan by the loose rein.

Suddenly he heard a click and turned his head towards it. Over a bush, not ten yards away, he saw the outline of a head in a German soldier's cap and a rifle barrel.

'The Germans,' he thought, or rather the realisation exploded inside his brain like a bomb on a time fuse, illuminating a whole landscape of the mind. He was stupefied again by the spectacle of his own enormous folly, but also by something incomprehensible behind it and about it. And it was with a kind of despair that he said to himself, 'You've done it at last, you fool. You asked for it. But why, why—'

He hadn't even a revolver, so he lay quite still, fatalistic, but not resigned. For he was resentful. He detested this monster of his own stupidity.

At the same time, he was in great terror, the calm helpless terror of the condemned. He was holding his breath for the shot. He had a queer sensation so vivid that he still remembered it twenty years after, of floating lightly off the ground.

Nothing happened. There was a deep silence. And then suddenly a cold touch on his bare calf made him shiver. But he perceived at once that it was Satan's nose. The pony wanted a tuft of grass that was just under his leg.

The young man jumped up and looked angrily at the bushes. But no German fired.

'Captain.' The sergeant's voice behind was full of exultation. Dripping, he saluted almost well enough for a recruit on parade.

'Oh, you've got over at last.' Corner turned upon the man.

'All present, sir.' And he saluted again. 'We find them ford—dem guide come.'

'I suppose he was there all the time. We stop here. We'll have to ramp this bank. Put out two pickets at once. And tell the men to keep on the alert.'

The men, shouting and laughing in triumph as they climbed the bank, were annoyed to be put on picket. They were quite sure that there were no Germans within miles. As the sergeant said in Hausa, 'If the Germans were here, they would have fired before this.'

Corner, with a brisk efficient air, marched up and down, inspected the pickets, pegged out a section of bank to be cut away. He could hear the orderly's voice raised in a song of praise loud enough to reach his ear, and intended to do so.

'Oh, the marvellous swimmer. Oh, the brave horse. Oh, princely horse—the worthy son of kings among horses. Look at him, my brothers. How nobly he moves his lovely ears. Oh, wise horse, he's as wise as a clerk. God bless him in his bravery—in his beauty. Oh, God bless him in his eating.'

Corner frowned and walked further away, as if from contagion. Why had that German not fired—orders to give no alarms?—panic at the sudden appearance of his own men coming up the bank in force? But what was the good of wondering at chance, at luck, here in Africa? Next time it would be different.

He turned his thought from the event, from Satan—he would not even look at the river. But all the more, they were present to his feeling, the feeling of one appointed to a special fate, to gratitude.

LIAM O'FLAHERTY · 1896–1984

The Pedlar's Revenge

Old Paddy Moynihan was dead when the police appeared on the scene of the accident. He lay stretched out on his back at the bottom of the deep ravine below the blacksmith's house. His head rested on a smooth granite stone and his hands were crossed over his enormous stomach. His battered old black hat was tied on to his skull with a piece of twine that passed beneath his chin. Men and boys from the village stood around him in a circle, discussing the manner of his death in subdued tones. Directly overhead, women and girls leaned in a compact group over the low stone wall of the blacksmith's yard. They were all peering down into the shadowy depths of the ravine at the dim shape of the dead man, with their mouths wide open and a fixed look of horror in their eyes.

Sergeant Toomey made a brief inspection of the corpse and then turned to Joe Finnerty, the rate collector.

'Tommy Murtagh told me,' he said, 'that it was you . . .'

'Yes,' said Finnerty. 'It was I sent Tommy along to fetch you. I told him to get a priest as well, but no priest came.'

'Both the parish priest and the curate are away on sick calls at the moment,' said the sergeant.

'In any case,' said Finnerty, 'there was little that a priest could do for him. The poor old fellow remained unconscious from the moment he fell until he died.'

'Did you see him fall?' said the sergeant.

'I did,' said Finnerty. 'I was coming down the road when I caught sight of him on the blacksmith's wall there above. He was very excited. He kept shouting and brandishing his stick. "The Pedlar poisoned me," he said. He kept repeating that statement in a sing-song shout, over and over again, like a whinging child. Then he got to his feet and moved forward, heading for the road. He had taken only half a step, though, when he seemed to get struck by some sort of colic. He dropped his stick, clutched his stomach with both hands and staggering backwards, bent almost double, to sit down again on the wall. The next thing I knew, he was going head over heels into the ravine, backwards, yelling like a stuck pig. Upon my soul! His roaring must have been heard miles away.'

'It was a terrific yell, all right,' said Peter Lavin, the doctor's servant. 'I was mowing down there below in the meadow when I heard it. I raised my head like a shot and saw old Paddy go through the air. Great God! He looked as big as a house. He turned somersault twice before he passed out of my sight, going on away down into the hole. I heard the splash, though, when he struck the ground, like a heavy sack dropped into the sea from a boat's deck.'

He pointed towards a deep wide dent in the wet ground to the right and said:

'That was where he landed, sergeant.'

The sergeant walked over and looked at the hollow. The whole ground was heavily laden with water that flowed from the mossy face of the cliff. Three little boys had stuck a rolled dock-leaf into a crevice and they were drinking in turn at the thin jet of water that came from the bright green funnel.

'Why did he think he was poisoned?" said the sergeant.

'I've no idea,' said Finnerty. 'It's certain, in any case, that he had swallowed something that didn't agree with him. The poor fellow was in convulsions with pain just before he fell.'

The sergeant looked up along the sheer face of the cliff at a thick cluster of ivy that grew just beneath the overarching brow. A clutch of young sparrows were chirping plaintively for food from their nest within the ivy.

'According to him,' the sergeant said, as he walked back to the corpse, 'The Pedlar was responsible for whatever ailed him.'

'That's right,' said Finnerty. 'He kept repeating that The Pedlar had poisoned him, over and over again. I wouldn't pay much attention to that, though, The Pedlar and himself were deadly enemies. They have accused one another of every crime in the calendar scores of times.'

' 'Faith, I saw him coming out of The Pedlar's house a few hours ago,' said Anthony Gill. 'He didn't look like a poisoned man at that time. He had a broad smile on his face and he was talking to himself, as he came shuffling down along the road towards me. I asked him where he was going in such a great hurry and he told me to mind my own business. I looked back after he had passed and saw him go into Pete Maloney's shop.'

'I was there when he came in,' said Bartly Timoney. 'He was looking for candles.'

'Candles?' said the sergeant.

'He bought four candles,' Timoney said. 'He practically ran out of the shop with them, mumbling to himself and laughing. Begob, like Anthony there said, he seemed to be in great form at the time.'

'Candles?' said the sergeant again. 'Why should he be in such a great hurry to buy candles?'

'Poor man!' said Finnerty. 'He was very old and not quite right in the head. Lord have mercy on him, he's been half-mad these last two years, ever since he lost his wife. Ah! The poor old fellow is better off dead than the way he was, living all alone in his little cottage, without anybody to feed him and keep him clean.'

The sergeant turned to Peter Lavin and said:

'Did the doctor come back from town yet?'

'He won't be back until this evening,' Lavin said. 'He's waiting over for the result of the operation on Tom Kelly's wife.'

'All right, lads,' the sergeant said. 'We might as well see about removing poor old Moynihan.'

'That's easier said than done,' said Anthony Gill. 'We weighed him a few weeks ago in Quinn's scales against three sacks of flour to settle a bet. Charley Ridge, the lighthouse keeper, bet a pound note that he was heavier than three sacks of flour and Tommy Perkins covered the pound, maintaining that he would fall short of that weight. The lighthouse keeper lost, but it was only by a whisker. I never saw anything go so close. There were only a few ounces in the difference. Well! Three sacks of flour weigh three hundred and thirty-six pounds. How are we going to carry that much dead weight out of this hole?'

'The simplest way, sergeant,' said Guard Hynes, 'would be to get a rope and haul him straight up to the blacksmith's yard.'

Everybody agreed with Hynes.

'I've got a lot of gear belonging to my boat up at the house,' said Bartly Timoney. 'I'll go and get a strong rope.'

He began to clamber up the side of the ravine.

'Bring a couple of slings as well,' the sergeant called after him. 'They'll keep him steady.'

All the younger men followed Timoney, in order to give a hand with the hauling.

'There may be heavier men than old Moynihan,' said Finnerty to those that remained below with the corpse, 'but he was the tallest and the strongest man seen in his part of the country within living memory. He was six feet inches in his bare feet and there was no known limit to his strength. I've seen him toss a full-grown bullock without hardly any effort at all, in the field behind Tom Daly's pub at Gortmor. Then he drank the three gallons of porter that he won for doing it, as quickly as you or I would drink three pints.'

'He was a strong man, all right,' said Gill. 'You could heap a horse's load on to his back and he'd walk away with it, as straight as a rod, calmly smoking his pipe.'

'Yet he was as gentle as a child,' said Lavin, 'in spite of his strength. They say that he never struck anybody in his whole life.'

'Many is the day he worked on my land,' said Sam Clancy, 'and I'll agree that he was as good as ten men. He could keep going from morning to night without slacking pace. However, it was the devil's own job giving him enough to eat. The side of a pig, or even a whole sheep, would make no more than a good snack for him. The poor fellow told me that he suffered agonies from hunger. He could never get enough to eat. It must have been absolute torture for him, when he got too old to work and had to live on the pension.'

Timoney came back and threw down two slings, over the low wall where the women and girls were gathered. Then he let down the end of a stout rope. Sergeant Toomey made one sling fast about Moynihan's upper chest and the other about his knees. Then he passed the end of the rope through the slings and knotted it securely.

'Haul away now,' he said to Timoney.

The two old sparrows fluttered back and forth across the ravine, uttering shrill cries, when they saw the corpse drawn up slowly along the face of the cliff. The fledglings remained silent in obedience to these constantly repeated warnings, until old Moynihan's dangling right hand brushed gently against the ivy outside their nest. The light sound being like that made by the bodies of their parents, when entering with food, they broke into a frenzied chatter. Thereupon, the old birds became hysterical with anxiety. The mother dropped a piece of worm from her beak. Then she and her cock hurled themselves at old Moynihan's head, with all their feathers raised. They kept attacking him fiercely, with beak and claw, until he was drawn up over the wall into the yard.

When the corpse was stretched out on the blacksmith's cart, Sergeant Toomey turned to the women that were there and said:

'It would be an act of charity for ye to come and get him ready for burial. He has nobody of his own to wash and shave him.'

'In God's name,' they said, 'we'll do whatever is needed.'

They all followed the men that were pushing the cart up the road towards the dead man's cottage.

'Listen,' the sergeant said to Finnerty, as they walked along side by side. 'Didn't The Pedlar bring old Moynihan to court at one time over the destruction of a shed.'

'He did, 'faith,' said Finnerty, 'and he was awarded damages, too, by District Justice Roche.'

'How long ago was that?' the sergeant said.

'It must be over twenty years,' said Finnerty.

'A long time before I came here,' said the sergeant. 'I never heard the proper details of the story.'

'It was only a ramshackle old shed,' said Finnerty, 'where The Pedlar used to keep all the stuff that he collected around the countryside, rags and old iron and bits of ancient furniture and all sorts of curiosities that had been washed ashore from wrecked ships. Moynihan came along one day and saw The Pedlar's ass tied to the iron staple in the door-jamb of the shed. Lord have mercy on the dead, he was very fond of playing childish pranks, like all simple-minded big fellows. So he got a turnip and stuck it on to the end of his stick. Then he leaned over the wall of The Pedlar's backyard and began to torment the ass, drawing the unfortunate animal on and on after the turnip. The ass kept straining at its rope until the door-jamb was dragged out of the wall. Then the wall collapsed and finally the whole shed came down in a heap. The Pedlar was away at the time and nobody saw the damage being done except old Moynihan himself. The poor fellow would have got into no trouble if he had kept his mouth shut. Instead of doing so, it was how he ran down into the village and told everybody what had happened. He nearly split his sides laughing at his own story. As a result of his confessions, he very naturally didn't have a foot to stand on when the case came up before the court.'

The dead man's cottage looked very desolate. The little garden in front was overgrown with weeds. There were several large holes in the roof. The door was broken. The windows were covered with sacking. The interior was in a shocking state of filth and disorder.

'He'll have to stay on the cart,' said Sergeant Toomey, after he had inspected the two rooms, 'until there is a proper place to lay him out like a christian.'

He left Guard Hynes in charge of the body and then set off with Joe Finnerty to The Pedlar's cottage.

'I couldn't find the candles,' he said on the way. 'Neither could I find out exactly what he had for his last meal. His little pot and his frying pan were on the hearth, having evidently been used to prepare whatever he ate. There was a small piece of potato skin at the bottom of the pot, but the frying pan was licked as clean as a new pin. God only knows what he fried on it.'

'Poor old Paddy!' said Finnerty. 'He had been half-starved for a long time. He was going around like a dog, scavenging for miserable scraps in shameful places. Yet people gave him sufficient food to satisfy the appetite of any ordinary person, in addition to what he was able to buy with his pension money.'

The Pedlar's cottage was only a few yards away from Moynihan's sordid hovel, to which its neatness offered a very striking contrast. It was really very pretty, with its windows painted dark blue and its walls spotlessly white and the bright May sunlight sparkling on its slate roof. The garden was well stocked with fruit trees and vegetables and flowers, all dressed in a manner that bore evidence to the owner's constant diligence and skill. It also contained three hives of honey-bees which made a pleasant clamour as they worked among the flowers. The air was charged with a delicious perfume, which was carried up by the gentle breeze from the different plants and flowers.

The Pedlar hailed the two men as they were approaching the house along a narrow flagged path that ran through the centre of the garden.

'Good day,' he said to them. 'What's goin' on over at Paddy Moynihan's house? I heard a cart and a lot of people arrive there.'

He was sitting on a three-legged stool to the right of the open door-way. His palsied hands moved up and down, constantly, along the blackthorn stick that he held erect between his knees. His legs were also palsied. The metalled heels of his boots kept beating a minute and almost inaudible tattoo on the broad smooth flagstone beneath his stool. He was very small and so stooped that he was bent almost double. His boots, his threadbare black suit, his white shirt and his black felt hat were all very neat; like his house and his garden. Indeed, he was immaculately clean from head to foot, except for his wrinkled little face. It was in great part covered with stubbly grey hair, that looked more like an animal's fur than a proper human beard.

'It was old Paddy Moynihan himself,' said the sergeant in a solemn tone, 'that they brought home on the cart.'

The Pedlar laughed drily in his throat, making a sound that was somewhat like the bleating of a goat, plaintive and without any merriment.

'Ho! Ho! Did the shameless scoundrel get drunk again?' he said in a thin high-pitched voice. 'Two months ago, he got speechless in Richie Tallon's pub with two sheep-jobbers from Castlegorm. He had to be taken home on Phil Manion's ass-cart. There wasn't room for the whole of him on the cart. Two lads had to follow along behind, holding up the lower parts of his legs.'

'Old Paddy is dead,' the sergeant said in a stern tone.

The Pedlar became motionless for a few moments on hearing this news, with his shrewd blue eyes looking upwards at the sergeant's face from beneath his bushy grey eyebrows. Then his heels began once more to beat their minute tattoo and his fingers moved tremulously along the surface of the blackthorn stick, up and down, as if it were a pipe from which they were drawing music.

'I'll ask God to have mercy on his soul,' he said coldly, 'but I won't say that I'm sorry to hear he's dead. Why should I? To tell you the honest truth, the news that you bring lifts a great weight off my mind. How did he die?'

He again laughed drily in his throat, after the sergeant had told him the manner of old Moynihan's death. His laughter now sounded gay.

'It must have been his weight that killed him,' he said, 'for John Delaney, a carpenter that used to live in Srulane long ago, fell down at that very same place without hurting himself in the least. It was a terrible night, about forty years ago. Delaney was coming home alone from a funeral at Tirnee, where he had gone to make the coffin. As usual, he was dead drunk, and never let a word out of him as he fell. He stayed down there in the hole for the rest of that night and all next day. He crawled out of it at nightfall, as right as rain. That same Delaney was the king of all drunkards. I remember one time he fell into a coffin he was making for an old woman at . . .'

'I must warn you,' Sergeant Toomey interrupted, 'that Paddy Moynihan made certain allegations against you, in the presence of Joe Finnerty here, shortly before he died. They were to the effect that you had . . .'

'Ho! Ho! Bad cess to the scoundrel!' The Pedlar interrupted in turn. 'He's been making allegations against me all his life. He's been tormenting me, too. God forgive me! I've hated that man since I was a child.'

'You've hated him all that time?' said the sergeant.

'We were the same age,' said The Pedlar. 'I'll be seventy-nine next month. I'm only a few weeks older than Paddy. We started going to school on the very same day. He took a violent dislike to me from the first moment he laid eyes on me. I was born stooped, just the same as I am now. I was delicate into the bargain and they didn't think I'd live. When I was seven or eight years old, I was no bigger than a dwarf. On the other hand, Paddy Moynihan was already a big hefty block of a lad. He was twice the size of other boys his own age. He tortured me in every way that he could. His favourite trick was to sneak up behind me and yell into my ear. You know what a powerful voice he had as a grown man. Well! It was very nearly as powerful when he was a lad. His yell was deep and rumbling, like the roar of an angry bull. I always fell down in a fit whenever he sneaked up behind me and yelled into my ear.'

'That was no way to treat a delicate lad,' said the sergeant in a sympathetic tone. 'It was no wonder that you got to hate him.'

'Don't believe a word of what he's telling you,' said Finnerty to the sergeant. 'Paddy Moynihan never did anything of the sort.'

The Pedlar again became motionless for a few seconds, as he looked at Finnerty's legs. Then he resumed his dance and turned his glance back to the sergeant's face.

'He did worse things to me,' he said. 'He made the other scholars stand around me in a ring and beat my bare feet with little pebbles. He used to laugh at the top of his voice while he watched them do it. If I tried to break out of the ring, or sat down on the ground and put my feet under me, he'd threaten me with worse torture. "Stand there," he'd say, "or I'll keep shouting into your ear until you die." Of course, I'd rather let them go on beating me than have him do the other thing. Oh! God! The shouting in my ear was a terrible torture. I used to froth at the mouth so much, when I fell down, that they thought for a long time I had epilepsy.'

'You old devil!' cried Finnerty angrily. 'You should be ashamed of yourself for telling lies about the dead.'

'Let him have his say,' the sergeant said to Finnerty. 'Every man has a right to say what he pleases on his own threshold.'

'He had no right to speak ill of the dead, all the same,' said Finnerty, 'especially when there isn't a word of truth in what he says. Sure, it's well known that poor old Paddy Moynihan, Lord have mercy on him, wouldn't hurt a fly. There was no more harm in him than in a babe unborn.'

'Take it easy, Joe,' said the sergeant. 'There are two sides to every story.'

Then he turned to The Pedlar and added:

' 'Faith, you had cause to hate Moynihan, all right. No wonder you planned to get revenge on him.'

'I was too much afraid of him at that time,' said The Pedlar, 'to think of revenge. Oh! God! He had the life nearly frightened out of me. He and his gang used to hunt me all the way home from school, throwing little stones at me and clods of dirt. "Pedlar, Pedlar, Pedlar," they'd shout and they coming after me.'

'Musha, bad luck to you,' said Finnerty, 'for a cunning old rascal, trying to make us believe it was Paddy Moynihan put the scholars up to shouting "Pedlar" after you. Sure, everybody in the parish has shouted "Pedlar" after a Counihan at one time or other and thought nothing of it. Neither did the Counihans. Why should they? They've all been known as "The Pedlars" from one generation to another, every mother's son of them.'

The sergeant walked over to the open doorway and thrust his head into the kitchen.

'Leave the man alone,' he said to Finnerty.

The fireplace, the dressers that were laden with beautiful old brown delft-ware and the flagged floor were all spotlessly clean and brightly polished.

'Ah! Woe!' The Pedlar cried out in a loud voice, as he began to rock himself like a lamenting woman. 'The Counihans are all gone except myself and I'll soon be gone, too, leaving no kith or kin behind me. The day of the wandering merchant is now done. He and his ass will climb no more up from the sea along the stony mountain roads, bringing lovely bright things from faraway cities to the wild people of the glens. Ah! Woe! Woe!'

'If you were that much afraid of Moynihan,' said the sergeant, as he walked back from the doorway to The Pedlar's stool, 'it must have been the devil's own job for you to get revenge on him.'

The Pedlar stopped rocking himself and looked up sideways at the sergeant, with a very cunning smile on his little bearded face.

'It was easy,' he whispered in a tone of intense pleasure, 'once I had learned his secret.'

'What secret did he have?' said the sergeant.

'He was a coward,' said The Pedlar.

'A coward!' cried Finnerty. 'Paddy Moynihan a coward!'

'Keep quiet, Joe,' said the sergeant.

'I was nineteen years of age at the time,' said The Pedlar, 'and in such a poor state of health that I was barely able to walk. Yet I had to keep going. My mother, Lord have mercy on her, had just died after a long sickness, leaving me alone in the world with hardly a penny to my name. I was coming home one evening from Ballymullen, with a load of goods in my ass's creels, when Moynihan came along and began to torment me. "Your load isn't properly balanced," he said. "It's going to overturn." Then he began to pick up loose stones from the road and put them into the creels, first into one and then into the other, pretending that he was trying to balance the load. I knew very well what he had in mind, but I said nothing. I was speechless with fright. Then he suddenly began to laugh and he took bigger stones from the wall and threw them into the creels, one after the other. Laughing at the top of his voice, he kept throwing in more and more stones, until the poor ass fell down under the terrible weight. That was more than I could bear. In spite of my terror, I picked up a stone and threw it at him. It wasn't much of a stone and I didn't throw it hard, but it struck him in the cheek and managed to draw blood. He put up his hand and felt the cut. Then he looked at his fingers. "Lord God!" he said in a weak little voice. "Blood is coming from my cheek. I'm cut." Upon my soul, he let a terrible yell out of him and set off down the road towards the village as fast as he could, with his hand to his cheek and he screaming like a frightened girl. As for me, 'faith, I raised up my ass and went home happy that evening. There was a little bird singing in my heart, for I knew that Moynihan would never again be able to torture me.'

'Right enough,' said the sergeant, 'you had him in your power after that. You had only to decide . . .'

'Best of all, though,' The Pedlar interrupted excitedly, 'was when I found out that he was mortally afraid of bees. Before that, he was able to steal all my fruit and vegetables while I was out on the roads. It was no use keeping a dog. The sight of him struck terror into the fiercest dog there ever was.'

'You wicked old black spider!' said Finnerty. 'Why do you go on telling lies about the dead?'

'Keep quiet, Joe,' said the sergeant. 'Let him finish his story!'

'All animals loved Moynihan,' said Finnerty, 'because he was gentle with them. They knew there was no harm in him. Children loved him, too. Indeed, every living creature was fond of the poor old fellow except this vindictive little cripple, who envied his strength and his good nature and his laughter. It was his rollicking laughter, above all else, that aroused the hatred of this cursed little man.'

'So you got bees,' the sergeant said to The Pedlar.

'I bought three hives,' The Pedlar said, 'and put them here in the garden. That did the trick. Ho! Ho! The ruffian has suffered agonies on account of those bees, especially since the war made food scarce in the shops. Many is the good day's sport I've had, sitting here on my stool, watching him go back and forth like a hungry wolf, with his eyes fixed on the lovely fruit and vegetables that he daren't touch. Even so, I'm glad to hear he's dead.'

'You are?' said Sergeant Toomey.

'It takes a load off my mind,' The Pedlar said.

'It does?' said the sergeant.

'Lately,' said The Pedlar, 'I was beginning to get afraid of him again. He was going mad with hunger. You can't trust a madman. In spite of his cowardice, he might attack me in order to rob my house and garden.'

'Was that why you decided to poison him?' said the sergeant.

The Pedlar started violently and became motionless, with his upward-glancing eyes fixed on the sergeant's chest. He looked worried for a moment. Then his bearded face became suffused with a cunning smile and his palsied limbs resumed their uncouth dance. The metalled heels of his boots now made quite a loud and triumphant sound as they beat upon the flagstone.

'You are a clever man, Sergeant Toomey,' he whispered in a

sneering tone, 'but you'll never be able to prove that I'm guilty of having caused Paddy Moynihan's death.'

'He was in your house today,' said the sergeant.

'He was,' said The Pedlar.

'Did you give him anything?' said the sergeant.

'I gave him nothing,' said The Pedlar.

'You might as well tell the truth,' said the sergeant. 'When the doctor comes back this evening, we'll know exactly what old Moynihan had for his last meal.'

'I can tell you that myself,' said The Pedlar.

'You can?' said the sergeant.

'He burst into my kitchen,' said The Pedlar, 'while I was frying a few potatoes with some of the bacon fat that I collect in a bowl. "Where did you get the bacon?" he said. He loved bacon and he was furious because there was none to be had in the shops. "I have no bacon," I said. "You're a liar," said he. "I can smell it." I was afraid to tell him the truth, for fear he might ransack the house and find my bowl of bacon fat. Then he'd kill me if I tried to prevent him from marching off with it. So I told him it was candles I was frying with the potatoes. God forgive me, I was terribly frightened by the wild look in his eyes. So I told him the first thing that came into my head, in order to get him out of the house. "Candles!" he said. "In that case, I'll soon be eating fried potatoes myself." Then he ran out of the house. I locked the door as soon as he had gone. Not long afterwards, he came back and tried to get in, but I pretended not to hear him knocking. "You old miser!" he shouted, as he gave the door a terrible kick that nearly took it off its hinges. "I have candles myself now. I'll soon be as well fed as you are." He kept laughing to himself as he went away. That was the last I saw or heard of him.'

'You think he ate the candles?' said the sergeant.

'I'm certain of it,' said The Pedlar. 'He'd eat anything.'

The sergeant folded his arms across his chest and stared at The Pedlar in silence for a little while. Then he shook his head.

'May God forgive you!' he said.

'Why do you say that?' The Pedlar whispered softly.

'You are a very clever man,' said the sergeant. 'There is nothing that the law can do to a man as clever as you, but you'll have to answer for your crime to Almighty God on the Day of Judgement all the same.'

Then he turned to Finnerty and said sharply:

'Come on, Joe. Let's get out of here.'

Finnerty spat on the ground at The Pedlar's feet.

'You terrible man!' he said. 'You wicked dwarf! You'll roast in hell for all eternity in payment for your crime.'

Then he followed the sergeant down along the narrow flagged path that divided the garden.

'Ho! Ho!' The Pedlar cried in triumph as he stared after them. 'Ho! Ho! My lovelies! Isn't it great to hear the mighty of this earth asking for God's help to punish the poor? Isn't it great to see the law of the land crying out to God for help against the weak and the persecuted.'

He broke into a peal of mocking laughter, which he suddenly cut short.

'Do ye hear me laugh out loud?' he shouted after them. 'No man heard me laugh like this in all my life before. I'm laughing out loud, because I fear neither God nor man. This is the hour of my delight. It is, 'faith. It's the hour of my satisfaction.'

He continued to laugh at intervals, on a shrill high note, while the two men went down the flagged path to the gate and then turned right along the road that led back to Moynihan's sordid cottage.

'Ho! Ho!' he crowed between the peals of laughter. 'I have a lovely satisfaction now for all my terrible shame and pain and sorrow. I can die in peace.'

The metalled heels of his boots now beat a frantic tattoo upon the flagstones and his palsied hands continued to move back and forth over the surface of his blackthorn stick, as if it were a pipe from which they were drawing music.

The Fanatic

Everything in the gloomy tavern, which also served as a general store, was literally covered with dirt. The old wooden counter was dappled like a leopard's hide with dried daubs of porter froth and a labyrinthine pattern of rings left by the bottoms of pint measures. The floor was pocked with holes, some of which were large enough to let a child fall through into the cellar. Rats made a great tumult down below, as they scurried to and fro. The light of day was barely able to penetrate the foul mass of dust and garbage on the window panes. There were thousands of flies roaming about the place, feeding and making love and gambolling at their leisure. The air was laden with a nauseating stench. The sound of normal healthy life, that came through the open street door from the little country town outside, seemed to be unreal and even plaintive.

Good Lord! It really was like a place invented by Father Mathew, the famous apostle of temperance, while preaching a sermon about the horrors of indulgence in alcohol.

'God save all here,' I said in a loud voice.

Nobody answered and it was hardly reasonable to expect that anybody should; for it seemed that there was nothing alive in the place above ground except flies and the spiders that were trying to catch them in their webs up among the rafters.

'Anybody here?' I called out once more.

'Yes,' said a voice.

I looked to my left and saw a man's face framed between the two posts of the open door that led to the kitchen in the rear. Owing to the poor light, I could see nothing attached to the face. It was like an apparition, that yellow countenance hanging without attachment on the dark air. I got somewhat frightened.

'Good Heavens!' I said to myself, while a tremor of apprehension passed slowly down my spine. 'What place is this? The tavern of the dead? Or has the unaccustomed heat unhinged my reason?'

Then a polite little cough issued from the face and I saw a tall lean man come towards me very slowly behind the counter. He walked with downcast head and he was rubbing the palms of his blue-veined hands together, back and forth continually, in front of his navel. He went past me without glancing in my direction, walking silently on the tips of his toes. After he had passed, he shrugged his narrow drooping shoulders three times in quick succession, a gesture that usually denotes a habitual drunkard.

'Thanks be to God,' he said in a gentle low voice, after he had come to a halt in front of the window, 'it's a lovely fine day.'

'Praised be God,' I replied, 'it would be difficult to find fault with it, right enough.'

'It may keep fine like this now for a good spell,' the man said. 'A good spell of it would come in handy.'

'It would,' I agreed. 'It would come in very handy.'

'Oh! Indeed, it would,' he said. 'There's no doubt at all but that a good long spell of it would suit the country down to the ground, in God's holy name.'

Then he clasped his hands behind the small of his back and let the upper part of his body come slanting gently towards me; exactly like a person on a ship's deck in breezy weather striving to keep his balance against the anarchy of the sea's movement.

'Where was your hurry taking you?' he asked politely.

'It was how I dropped in for a bottle,' I replied.

'Ha! Then,' said he, 'it was a wish for a bottle that brought you.'

'Yes indeed,' said I. 'It was a wish for a bottle of porter.'

He straightened himself suddenly, raised his shoulders and shook his head violently, like a man suffering from cold.

'Upon my soul,' he said, 'you have no reason at all for feeling ashamed of such a wish on a day as boiling hot as this.'

'True enough,' I said, 'it was the heat made me thirsty.'

'Oh! Indeed,' he said with deep feeling, 'it's proud of your thirst you should be on a day like this, instead of feeling the least little bit ashamed.'

Then he looked at me, back over his shoulder.

'Don't be afraid, good man,' he added in a very friendly tone. 'I have a nice fresh bottle for you here, full of porter that is just as sweet and wholesome as the milk of any cow you ever saw in all your natural life. It is, 'faith and no doubt about it.'

He was stiff-necked. He had to turn his whole body right up from his knees before he was able to look me in the face from that position. Good Lord! His eyes were of an extraordinary beauty. They were like a woman's eyes soft and gentle and amorous. It was quite impossible to identify their colour in that dark room. They seemed to be a mixture of brown and grey and green; like the little smooth multi-coloured stones that lie at the bottom of a swiftly-running mountain torrent on whose surface the bright rays of the sun are dancing.

'Come now,' said I. 'Oblige me, in God's name, by handing me that fine bottle. Will you have one yourself, good man?'

He shook his head sadly.

'Thank you, treasure,' he said, 'but I haven't tasted a drop, either good or bad, for the past two years.'

Then he started and began to turn his body ever so slowly, with his head poised in ludicrous immobility on his stiff neck. When he had finally put about, he gave his shoulders a nervous twitch, coughed in his throat, and walked towards me on tip-toe. He kept his face turned from me as he went past and his hands were clasped before his navel like a person at prayer. Judging by the movement of his jaw muscles, his lips were framing words. Yet I heard no sound of uttered speech issue from them.

'Oh! Yes,' I said to myself. 'The poor fellow is deranged.'

He picked up a bottle, pulled the cork and filled a glass, which he placed before me on the counter. I gave him a half-crown.

'You are like a man,' he said, while looking for my change in the till, 'that has travelled a fair share of the world.'

'I've been here and there,' I said.

'That's what I thought,' he said. 'You have the cut of a traveller about your wise face.'

'Thank you,' I said.

'You're welcome,' said he.

He approached me once more behind the counter with downcast head. As he was going past, he handed me the change without glancing in my direction. Then he kept moving along slowly on tip-toe, until he reached a tiny wooden cubicle that lay between the end of the counter and the open door that led out into the street. The business accounts of the shop were kept in the cubicle. He thrust his head into it and then stood stock still, with his hands clasped behind his back and his legs spread out wide away behind him;

exactly like a frightened sheep hiding its head in a hole and exposing its big tremulous rump to the oncoming danger.

'He's deranged without a doubt,' I said to myself once more.

Then I drank some of the porter and lit a cigarette. In spite of the man's boast, the liquor was sour and almost repulsively tepid. It left a frightful taste on my tongue. Neither of us spoke for some time. The only sound in the shop was the scuffling of the rats down in the cellar. Away out along a country road beyond the town, cart wheels were turning and a man was singing a gay song of love.

'Listen to me,' the tavern-keeper said at last.

'Yes?' I said.

'Were you ever in England?' he said.

'I was,' I said to him. 'Why do you ask?'

He shrugged his shoulders like a toper, pulled his head out of the cubicle and looked at me, turning his body slowly up from his knees, with his head sitting motionless on his stiff neck. His head was like a 'hobby horse' going round in a circle at a fun fair. Now I noticed that it was shaped in a very peculiar fashion. At first, I decided that it was very like the head of a seal, since the skull was no wider than any part of the neck on which it was based. Furthermore, the yellow greasy face was as smooth as a pebble exposed at low tide on a strand. On reflection, however, I came to the conclusion that it was much more like the head of an old stallion, with the neck emerging from the shoulders powerful and broad, tapering as it rose and slanting forward slightly, until it ended in a blunt and naked skull. Except for his eye-brows, his whole countenance was utterly devoid of hair. Even his brows would not provide quite enough material to line a wren's nest.

'It's easy to see,' he muttered in a tone that had suddenly become hostile, 'that you have been in England.'

'Really?' I said.

'Yes,' he said with great emphasis. 'England leaves her mark on everybody that sets foot on her soil.'

'What sort of mark?' I said.

He fixed his glance on the lighted cigarette in my hand.

'The people of England,' he said with maniacal intensity, 'are all pagans, every single one of them. They are, 'faith. Every single one of them is sold to the devil, lock stock and barrel. Sold to the devil in Hell. Red roasting and damnation is their lot in the next world and devil mend them for their greed, that made them sell their souls.'

I looked at him in astonishment and said:

'Are you joking?'

'Joking?' said he. 'Devil a fear of me. I'm in dead earnest. The English are all rotten. That's my final word.'

Thereupon, he thrust his head once more into the cubicle and became absolutely motionless; except for his fingers that were trying to catch one another behind the small of his back. By Jove! The poor fellow's clothes were not worth the ten of clubs. As for dirt! they were really filthy. Neither his shirt nor his jacket possessed a button between them. His twisted shoes were yellow, old with age and neglect. Their tongues were hanging out. They were unlaced. Their leather was scarred and they were down at heel. His bare skin could be seen, here and there, through the holes in his flannel trousers.

'Have you travelled in France?' he said after a while.

I admitted that I knew that country quite well.

'May God forgive you!' he said.

'Why on earth do you say that?' I said.

The queer fellow got excited. He pulled his head out of the cubicle and stared at me in an evil fashion. Now there was bitter hatred in his lovely eyes that were so soft and gentle a short time previously: drowsy with yearning like the eyes of a woman that is dreaming of passionate love. Good Lord! I got afraid that his lunacy had taken charge of his will and that he was becoming possessed by an evil intention.

'The French people are worse than the English,' he said.

'Why do you say that?' I said in a non-committal tone.

'They are lecherous people,' he said. 'There's nothing in that terrible country but dirt and sinful filth. Anybody is in danger of losing his immortal soul that sets foot in it.'

After he had hidden his head once more in the cubicle, I decided to slip away from the place quietly. So I swallowed about half of the porter and then began to make for the door on tip-toe for fear of attracting the strange fellow's attention. However, I did not succeed in effecting my escape. I was just level with the cubicle when he thrust his head suddenly around its side and stared at me. I halted abruptly and returned his stare, with my eyes fixed and my mouth wide open. There we were, the two of us, on either side of the counter, with our faces only a few inches apart, the queer fellow's countenance quivering with hysteria and mine rigid with apprehension. Neither of us spoke for almost a minute.

'Wait,' he whispered at length. 'Wait 'till I tell you.'

'Go ahead,' I said.

'The Americans are the worst of all,' he said. 'They have ruined the whole world with their dirty pictures. They are spreading adultery and every other kind of sexual filth over the wide world, in the same way that dung is spread to manure a garden.'

'The Americans?' I said.

'Yes,' said he. 'The people of America and it's a terrible thing to admit that some of our own holy race are over there among them.'

'Devil take that for a story,' I said to myself. 'Whether he's mad or sane, that is going a bit too far.'

I put my elbows on the counter and said to him:

'Listen, my good man. You should be ashamed of yourself for insulting in that fashion the whole human race, with the exception of the few that populate this rather insignificant island. Like the fox, you seem unable to smell your own filth. If the first stone could only be cast by a person without sin, it would never be cast.'

I regretted my outburst before I had finished speaking. The poor fellow had begun to shiver from head to foot. The look of hatred had vanished from his eyes, which were soft and dreamy once more. Now, however, it was for pity and forgiveness that they yearned.

'Ah! My dear brother,' he said, 'don't blame me for being foolish and loud-mouthed. I am half dead with loneliness, since my sister went away two years ago.'

'I understand, brother,' I said. 'In God's name, don't blame me, either, for the unmannerly and unkind things that I said.'

'I won't, darling,' he said. 'I know well that it wasn't through wickedness you let out your hasty words into the light of day.'

'Indeed, it was not,' I said. 'A few untidy words very often slip out through a corner of one's mouth, without the mind knowing a thing about them.'

'That's very true, brother,' he said. 'I find myself doing that same, time and again, during the past two years. It's hard to keep the tongue in order when the heart is mad with sorrow. Oh! Darling, I'm telling you that loneliness is a terrible disease.'

'Your sister went away?' I said.

'She did, my pulse,' said he. 'Kate went away to America. She was two years gone away last Feast of St Brigid. God help us! That was the defenceless blow and don't be talking. It was a death-blow!'

'Yes?' said I. 'There was just the two of you?'

'That was all,' he said, 'since mother died, Lord have mercy on her soul. At that time, Nora had already gone to America and Kate was at a convent school in Dublin. It was to me the place was left and Kate came back home to look after me, since I was in a very delicate state of health. She came back home, right enough, the poor creature and stayed there seventeen years. She did, 'faith. Oh! Indeed, she was as steady a girl as you could meet. As for work! She had no equal as a willing and capable and tidy worker. Ah! Brother, she was a regular saint and no doubt about it. No man ever had a mother kinder that my sister Kate was to me. Look after me? She waited on me hand and foot, as if I were a little naked fledgling in her nest. Oh! Indeed, the two of us were blessed by God and comfortable here in this shop, food and drink and shelter to our name as God ordained for a Christian life, without any need for us to go outside our own door to look for a bit of butter, or a loaf of wheaten bread, or a slice of meat, or a hansel of tea. The good neighbours were going in and out the whole time. The chapel was less than a hundred yards away, down at the end of the street. On a fair day, we'd celebrate a little and drink a sup and sing a couple of songs. Ah! Lord God! That was the lovely life and don't be talking.'

The poor fellow was overcome with emotion and burst into tears.

'Oh! Kate, Kate,' he wailed through his tears, 'you were so gentle and so kind and so holy. Why did you do it? Oh! Why did you?'

Then he turned away from me and went over to the window. His fingers now seemed to be attacking one another savagely behind the small of his back. There was a rattle in his throat. By Jove! I admit that his grief affected me considerably.

'What did she do?' I said gently.

With his back turned towards me, he leaned back from the hips and stared at the roof in the grotesque fashion of a stiff-necked man. His jaws were now bare and his eyes looked savage.

'American pictures!' he said. 'My curse on them!'

'What sort of pictures?' I said. 'Do you mean films?'

'Pictures, I tell you,' he shouted. 'The devil's own pictures, God forgive me.'

He shuddered and continued in a less violent tone.

'They came to our town,' he said, 'about five years ago. A little dark foreigner of a fellow brought them here from Dublin. He used to show them once a week and only young blackguards and corner boys went into the hall, throwing clods of dirt and shouting insults at the foreign lad and breaking the seats. Then the priest spoke from the altar, saying it was only fair to let the foreign fellow earn his living. After that, respectable people began to go to the pictures, especially the women. Soon there were three shows a week and the house full every time. Full of women, young and old. Listen, good man. Women are responsible for all the foreign filth that comes into this holy country. Women! Goats are supposed to be the most inquisitive of all creatures. It is said that if a goat is let as far as the church door, she will end up by eating the altar cloth. Women, though, are even more inquisitive and daring than goats in search of opportunities for committing sin. Women are inclined to sin by nature and a hard discipline is needed to keep them on the right road. Man alive, they are lecherous in the very cradle. Soon after, in any way, they begin to smarten and titivate themselves, getting ready for debauch.'

'Don't blame the poor creatures for their nature,' I said. 'They are just as God created them.'

'Kate began to go to the pictures,' he said, 'and I have it on my conscience that I didn't try to stop her. What could I say after the parish priest gave the foreign fellow his blessing?'

He turned towards me and he raised his two hands in front of his face, with the fingers turned inward like claws. His eyes shone.

'If I had a hold of that foreign fellow now,' he said viciously, 'I tell you that I'd choke him to death first and then tear the flesh off his bones, strip by strip.'

I moved over gently along the side of the counter until I reached my glass. I swallowed the remainder of the porter, which no longer tasted sour. Upon my soul! I am always timid of lunatics. After I had lit another cigarette, I looked back over my shoulder at the tavern-keeper. He had again thrust his head into the cubicle. His wide-spread legs were far back and his fingers were in frenzied movement behind his back. He was sobbing.

'I had better leave here,' I said to myself. 'It is unmannerly to watch a human soul, when it is laid bare and quivering in the grasp of a great sorrow.'

I was sneaking away on tip-toe to the door, when the heartbroken man gave forth once more in a voice that was hoarse with sobbing. So I came to a halt, lest he might think my going away showed a lack of kindness and sympathy.

'Alas,' he wailed. 'The filthy pictures didn't take long to corrupt her. It was a sort of fright they gave her at first. She used to come home after watching them with terror in her eyes. Then she had nightmares when she went to bed, as if the devil were between the sheets with her and he trying to get a strangle-hold on her immortal soul. The damage was done within a month. One day she went to Galway on the bus and when she returned in the evening I hardly knew her. Oh! Lord! She had cropped her hair and all that was left of it on her skull was twisted in the foreign fashion and wet with the sweet oil of lechery. When I began to give her a bit of my mind, it was how she put her fists on her hips and laughed in my face. Making fun of me! Calling me a silly old codger and worse, saving your presence! From that very moment, we took a dislike to each other. There was only argument and complaint between the two of us, that used to be so loving. She kept asking me for money, to buy this and that, from morning to night. She complained about how she had spent the best of her life slaving for me without any reward. True enough, I hadn't given her any money, but it was all between the two of us. All that was earned in the house was put away and neither of us spent any of it. Now, though, she wanted everything changed. She wanted her share and she had to have it. Lord God! May I be forgiven for my sin on the day of judgement! When I should have knocked sparks out of her hide with a stick, it was how I gave way to her in everything. I did, 'faith. I gave her all the money she wanted, for fear she'd go away and leave me alone. I threw it at her without counting it, money that had been hard to earn. Money! She was scattering it like chaff in this direction and in that, just like a mad creature; buying flashy clothes and titivating herself like a whore; painting her finger nails and covering her face with stinking powder; a music-box from England in her bedroom; buying every sort of dainty for the table; sprinkling herself with sweet oil that you could smell from a distance; like the whiff you get in the fall of autumn from a herd of rutting goats. Oh! Lord! The worst of all was when she began to go about in motor cars with the dancing blackguards of the county. Ah! Then, indeed, the sight of her would bring tears from a stone; lovely modest girl that had a saintly mind before America's dirty pictures dragged her down into the ways of sin. At last she took to drink. I'll never forget the night she came home in a motor car and she not able to stand on her feet. When I came down in my shirt to open the door, two men had a hold of her and they barely able to keep her from falling. All three of them, with Kate in the middle, were swaying from side to side in front of the door, singing at the top of their voices. People were sticking their heads out through windows all the way up and down the street. Oh! The terrible shame of it! The three drunkards roared out laughing when they saw me in my shirt. They started to point at my legs and they splitting their sides with laughter. There I was right enough, at three o'clock in the morning, standing in my doorway practically naked and the whole town, you might say, looking at me. Oh! God! That was too much. The whole town seeing me naked! Naked! With only a little shirt that was barely able to . . . Oh! God! It was too much. To have her standing there drunk was bad enough, but to have me naked was worse. Naked! You might as well say I was stark naked. I was worse than naked, trying to cover myself with my poor hands. So I cursed her right then and there. I did and I closed the door on her and I shouted out that I never wanted to see her again. Neither did I ever lay eyes on her since. A few days later, a relative came for her clothes. I handed them over, together with half of what money was left in the bank. She went to England then and stayed there a while, until Nora took her out to America. There's where she is now, over in America, thousands of miles away, while I'm here all alone. She might as well be dead for all the good she is to me. Alone! Rotting with loneliness! My heart broken! Oh! Indeed, the devil can have his fun now and plenty of it. He can boast, too, of the fine trick he played on a lovely virgin that was without sin before God. Now it's I myself that has the nightmares and the devil between sheets with me, making terrible fun in the darkness of the night. There isn't anybody even to hear me screech, or to take notice if they heard. Night and day, the devil is whispering in my ear, jeering at me and boasting, saying wicked things that I don't want to understand and there is a great noise, too, a long way off, with thousands of people threatening me. They have their fists raised and they are shouting a wicked word, over and over again, although what word it is . . .'

I could understand no more, although he continued to talk in this disjointed fashion for some time further. His words no longer made any sense. His voice, too, gradually became weaker, like a dying breeze, until there was only a pitiful moaning sound coming from his throat. Then he suddenly became silent.

'I must leave here,' I said to myself. 'This is the confessional house of the insane.'

Even so, I was loath to go away without offering a few words of comfort to the stricken man.

'Listen, brother,' I said. 'Why don't you send for her? Perhaps she would come back if you asked her to do so gently, from the fullness of your loving heart.'

He withdrew his head from the cubicle and looked at me in silence for a little while. Now there was dark wisdom in his beautiful eyes and resignation that was much more terrifying than his recent rage.

'Is it Kate?' he said at length.

'Yes,' I said. 'You should write and ask her to come home.'

'She got married six months ago,' he said softly.

Good Lord! I have rarely seen a countenance so forlorn.

'Is that so?' I said.

He went past me without making any reply, walking slowly on tip-toe, on the far side of the counter, with his face turned away and his hands joined in front of his navel, like a person at prayer. After he had gone through the open door leading to the kitchen, he turned and stared at me from out the darkness.

I shuddered again when I saw his yellow countenance hanging, without apparent attachment, on the gloomy air.

Now, however, it was through pity that I shuddered and not at all through fear.

Her Table Spread

Alban had few options on the subject of marriage; his attitude to
women was negative, but in particular he was not attracted to Miss
Cuffe. Coming down early for dinner, red satin dress cut low, she
attacked the silence with loud laughter before he had spoken. He
recollected having heard that she was abnormal—at twenty-five, of
statuesque development, still detained in childhood. The two other
ladies, in beaded satins, made entrances of a surprising formality. It
occurred to him, his presence must constitute an occasion: they
certainly sparkled. Old Mr Rossiter, uncle to Mrs Treye, came last,
more sourly. They sat for some time without the addition of
lamplight. Dinner was not announced; the ladies by remaining on
guard, seemed to deprecate any question of its appearance. No
sound came from other parts of the Castle.

Miss Cuffe was an heiress to whom the Castle belonged and
whose guests they all were. But she carefully followed the
movements of her aunt, Mrs Treye; her ox-eyes moved from face
to face in happy submission rather than expectancy. She was
continually preoccupied with attempts at gravity, as though
holding down her skirts in a high wind. Mrs Treye and Miss Carbin
combined to cover her excitement; still, their looks frequently stole
from the company to the windows, of which there were too many.
He received a strong impression someone outside was waiting to
come in. At last, with a sigh they got up: dinner had been
announced.

The Castle was built on high ground, commanding the estuary; a
steep hill, with trees, continued above it. On fine days the view was
remarkable, of almost Italian brilliance, with that constant reflection
up from the water that even now prolonged the too-long day. Now,
in continuous evening rain, the winding wooded line of the further
shore could be seen and, nearer the windows, a smothered island
with the stump of a watch-tower. Where the Castle stood, a higher
tower had answered the island's. Later a keep, then wings, had been

added; now the fine peaceful residence had French windows opening on to the terrace. Invasions from the water would henceforth be social, perhaps amorous. On the slope down from the terrace, trees began again; almost, but not quite concealing the destroyer. Alban, who knew nothing, had not yet looked down.

It was Mr Rossiter who first spoke of the destroyer—Alban meanwhile glancing along the table; the preparations had been stupendous. The destroyer had come today. The ladies all turned to Alban: the beads on their bosoms sparkled. So this was what they had here, under their trees. Engulfed by their pleasure, from now on he disappeared personally. Mr Rossiter, rising a note, continued. The estuary, it appeared, was deep, with a channel buoyed up it. By a term of the Treaty, English ships were permitted to anchor in these waters.

'But they've been afraid of the rain!' chimed in Valeria Cuffe.

'Hush,' said her aunt, 'that's silly. Sailors would be accustomed to getting wet.'

But, Miss Carbin reported, that spring there *had* already been one destroyer. Two of the officers had been seen dancing at the hotel at the head of the estuary.

'So,' said Alban, 'you are quite in the world.' He adjusted his glasses in her direction.

Miss Carbin—blonde, not forty, and an attachment of Mrs Treye's—shook her head despondently. 'We were all away at Easter. Wasn't it curious they should have come then? The sailors walked in the demesne but never touched the daffodils.'

'As though I should have cared!' exclaimed Valeria passionately.

'Morale too good,' stated Mr Rossiter.

'But next evening,' continued Miss Carbin, 'the officers did not go to the hotel. They climbed up here through the trees to the terrace—you see, they had no idea. Friends of ours were staying here at the Castle, and they apologized. Our friends invited them in to supper . . .'

'Did they accept?'

The three ladies said in a breath: 'Yes, they came.'

Valeria added urgently, 'So don't you *think*—?'

'So tonight we have a destroyer to greet you,' Mrs Treye said quickly to Alban. 'It is quite an event; the country people are coming down from the mountains. These waters are very lonely; the steamers have given up since the bad times; there is hardly a pleasure-boat. The weather this year has driven visitors right away.'

'You are beautifully remote.'

'Yes,' agreed Miss Carbin. 'Do you know much about the Navy? Do you think, for instance, that this is likely to be the same destroyer?'

'*Will they remember?*' Valeria's bust was almost on the table. But with a rustle Mrs Treye pressed Valeria's toe. For the dining-room also looked out across the estuary, and the great girl had not once taken her eyes from the window. Perhaps it was unfortunate that Mr Alban should have coincided with the destroyer. Perhaps it was unfortunate for Mr Alban too.

For he saw now he was less than half the feast; unappeased, the party sat looking through him, all grouped at an end of the table—to the other, chairs had been pulled up. Dinner was being served very slowly. Candles—possible to see from the water—were lit now; some wet peonies glistened. Outside, day still lingered hopefully. The bushes over the edge of the terrace were like heads—you could have sworn sometimes you saw them mounting, swaying in manly talk. Once, wound up in the rain, a bird whistled, seeming hardly a bird.

'Perhaps since then they have been to Greece, or Malta?'

'That would be the Mediterranean fleet,' said Mr Rossiter.

They were sorry to think of anything out in the rain tonight.

'The decks must be streaming,' said Miss Carbin.

Then Valeria, exclaiming 'Please excuse me!' pushed her chair in and ran from the room.

'She is impulsive,' explained Mrs Treye. 'Have *you* been to Malta, Mr Alban?'

In the drawing-room, empty of Valeria, the standard lamps had been lit. Through their ballet-skirt shades, rose and lemon, they gave out a deep, welcoming light. Alban, at the ladies' invitation, undraped the piano. He played, but they could see he was not pleased. It was obvious he had always been a civilian, and when he had taken his place on the piano-stool—which he twirled round three times, rather fussily—his dinner-jacket wrinkled across the shoulders. It was sad they should feel so indifferent, for he came from London. Mendelssohn was exasperating to them—they opened all four windows to let the music downhill. They preferred not to draw the curtains; the air, though damp, being pleasant tonight, they said.

The piano was damp, but Alban played almost all his heart out. He played out the indignation of years his mild manner concealed. He had failed to love; nobody did anything about this; partners at dinner gave him less than half their attention. He knew some spring had dried up at the root of the world. He was fixed in the dark rain, by an indifferent shore. He played badly, but they were unmusical. Old Mr Rossiter, who was not what he seemed, went back to the dining-room to talk to the parlour maid.

Valeria, glittering vastly, appeared in a window.

'Come *in*!' her aunt cried in indignation. She would die of a chill, childless, in fact unwedded; the Castle would have to be sold and where would they all be?

But—'Lights down there!' Valeria shouted above the music.

They had to run out for a moment, laughing and holding cushions over their bare shoulders. Alban left the piano; they looked boldly down from the terrace. Indeed, there they were: two lights like arc-lamps, blurred by rain and drawn down deep in reflection into the steady water. There were, too, ever so many portholes, all lit up.

'Perhaps they are playing bridge,' said Miss Carbin.

'Now I wonder if Uncle Robert ought to have called,' said Mrs Treye. 'Perhaps we have seemed remiss—one calls on a regiment.'

'Patrick could row him out tomorrow.'

'He hates the water.' She sighed. 'Perhaps they will be gone.'

'Let's go for a row now—let's go for a row with a lantern,' besought Valeria, jumping and pulling her aunt's elbow. They produced such indignation she disappeared again—wet satin skirts and all—into the bushes. The ladies could do no more: Alban suggested the rain might spot their dresses.

'They must lose a great deal, playing cards throughout an evening for high stakes,' Miss Carbin said with concern as they all sat down again.

'Yet, if you come to think of it, somebody must win.'

But the naval officers who so joyfully supped at Easter had been, Miss Carbin knew, a Mr Graves, and a Mr Garrett: *they* would certainly lose. 'At all events, it is better than dancing at the hotel; there would be nobody of their type.'

'There is nobody there at all.'

'I expect they are best where they are . . . Mr Alban, a Viennese waltz?'

He played while the ladies whispered, waving the waltz time a little distractedly. Mr Rossiter, coming back, momentously stood: they turned in hope: even the waltz halted. But he brought no news. 'You should call Valeria in. You can't tell who may be round the place. She's not fit to be out tonight.'

'Perhaps she's not out.'

'She is,' said Mr Rossiter crossly. 'I just saw her racing past the window with a lantern.'

Valeria's mind was made up: she was a princess. Not for nothing had she had the dining-room silver polished and all set out. She would pace around in red satin that swished behind, while Mr Alban kept on playing a loud waltz. They would be dazed at all she had to offer—also her new statues and the leopard-skin from the auction.

When he and she were married (she inclined a little to Mr Garrett) they would invite all the Navy up the estuary and give them tea. Her estuary would be filled up, like a regatta, with loud excited battleships tooting to one another and flags flying. The terrace would be covered with grateful sailors, leaving room for the band. She would keep the peacocks her aunt did not allow. His friends would be surprised to notice that Mr Garrett had meanwhile become an admiral, all gold. He would lead the other admirals into the Castle and say, while they wiped their feet respectfully: 'These are my wife's statues; she has given them to me. One is Mars, one is Mercury. We have a Venus, but she is not dressed. And wait till I show you our silver and gold plates . . .' The Navy would be unable to tear itself away.

She had been excited for some weeks at the idea of marrying Mr Alban, but now the lovely appearance of the destroyer put him out of her mind. He would not have done; he was not handsome. But she could keep him to play the piano on quiet afternoons.

Her friends had told her Mr Garrett was quite a Viking. She was so very familiar with his appearance that she felt sometimes they had already been married for years—though still, sometimes, he could not realize his good luck. She still had to remind him the island was hers too . . . Tonight, Aunt and darling Miss Carbin had so fallen in with her plans, putting on their satins and decorating the drawing-room, that the dinner became a betrothal feast. There was some little hitch about the arrival of Mr Garrett—she had heard that gentlemen sometimes could not tie their ties. And now he was late and would be discouraged. So she must now go half-way down to the water and wave a lantern.

But she put her two hands over the lantern, then smothered it in her dress. She had a panic. Supposing she should prefer Mr Graves?

She had heard Mr Graves was stocky, but very merry; when he came to supper at Easter he slid in the gallery. He would teach her to dance, and take her to Naples and Paris . . . Oh, dear, oh, dear, then they must fight for her; that was all there was to it . . . She let the lantern out of her skirts and waved. Her fine arm with bangles went up and down, up and down, with the staggering light; the trees one by one jumped up from the dark, like savages.

Inconceivably, the destroyer took no notice.

Undisturbed by oars, the rain stood up from the water; not a light rose to peer, and the gramophone, though it remained very faint, did not cease or alter.

In mackintoshes, Mr Rossiter and Alban meanwhile made their way to the boat-house, Alban did not know why. 'If that goes on,' said Mr Rossiter, nodding towards Valeria's lantern, 'they'll fire one of their guns at us.'

'Oh, no. Why?' said Alban. He buttoned up, however, the collar of his mackintosh.

'Nervous as cats. It's high time that girl was married. She's a nice girl in many ways, too.'

'Couldn't we get the lantern away from her?' They stepped on a paved causeway and heard the water nibble the rocks.

'She'd scream the place down. She's of age now, you see.'

'But if—'

'Oh, she won't do that; I was having a bit of fun with you.' Chuckling equably, Mrs Treye's uncle unlocked and pulled open the boat-house door. A bat whistled out.

'Why are we here?'

'She might come for the boat; she's a fine oar,' said Mr Rossiter wisely. The place was familiar to him; he lit an oil-lamp and, sitting down on a trestle with a staunch air of having done what he could, reached a bottle of whisky out of the boat. He motioned the bottle to Alban. 'It's a wild night,' he said. 'Ah, well, we don't have these destroyers every day.'

'That seems fortunate.'

'Well, it is and it isn't.' Restoring the bottle to the vertical, Mr Rossiter continued: 'It's a pity you don't want a wife. You'd be the better for a wife, d'you see, a young fellow like you. She's got a nice character; she's a girl you could shape. She's got a nice income.' The bat returned from the rain and knocked round the lamp. Lowering the bottle frequently, Mr Rossiter talked to Alban (whose attitude remained negative) of women in general and the parlour-maid in particular . . .

'*Bat!*' Alban squealed irrepressibly, and with his hand to his ear—where he still felt it—fled from the boat-house. Mr Rossiter's conversation continued. Alban's pumps squelched as he ran; he skidded along the causeway and balked at the upward steps. His soul squelched equally: he had been warned, he had been warned. He had heard they were all mad; he had erred out of headiness and curiosity. A degree of terror was agreeable to his vanity: by express wish he had occupied haunted rooms. Now he had no other pumps in this country, no idea where to buy them, and a ducal visit ahead. Also, wandering as it were among the apples and amphoras of an art school, he had blundered into the life room: woman revolved gravely.

'Hell,' he said to the steps, mounting, his mind blank to the outcome.

He was nerved for the jumping lantern, but half-way up to the Castle darkness was once more absolute. Her lantern had gone out; he could orientate himself—in spite of himself—by her sobbing. Absolute desperation. He pulled up so short that, for balance, he had to cling to a creaking tree.

'Hi!' she croaked. Then: 'You *are* there! I hear you!'

'Miss Cuffe—'

'How too bad you are! I never heard you rowing. I thought you were never coming—'

'Quietly, my dear girl.'

'Come up quickly. I haven't even seen you. Come up to the windows—'

'Miss Cuffe—'

'Don't you remember the way?' As sure but not so noiseless as a cat in the dark, Valeria hurried to him.

'Mr Garrett—' she panted. 'I'm Miss Cuffe. Where have you been? I've destroyed my beautiful red dress and they've eaten up your dinner. But we're still waiting. Don't be afraid; you'll soon be there now. I'm Miss Cuffe; this is my Castle—'

'Listen, it's I, Mr Alban—'

'Ssh, ssh, Mr Alban: *Mr Garrett has landed*.'

Her cry, his voice, some breath of the joyful intelligence, brought the others on to the terrace, blind with lamplight.

'Valeria?'

'Mr Garrett has landed!'

Mrs Treye said to Miss Carbin under her breath, 'Mr Garrett has come.'

Miss Carbin, half weeping with agitation, replied, 'We must go in.' But uncertain who was to speak next, or how to speak, they remained leaning over the darkness. Behind, through the windows, lamps spread great skirts of light, and Mars and Mercury, unable to contain themselves, stooped from their pedestals. The dumb keyboard shone like a ballroom floor.

Alban, looking up, saw their arms and shoulders under the bright rain. Close by, Valeria's fingers creaked on her warm wet satin. She laughed like a princess, magnificently justified. Their unseen faces were all three lovely, and, in the silence after the laughter, such a strong tenderness reached him that, standing there in full manhood, he was for a moment not exiled. For the moment, without moving or speaking, he stood, in the dark, in a flame, as though all three said: 'My darling . . .'

Perhaps it was best for them all that early, when next day first lightened the rain, the destroyer steamed out—below the extinguished Castle where Valeria lay with her arms wide, past the boathouse where Mr Rossiter lay insensible and the bat hung masked in its wings—down the estuary into the open sea.

The Faithless Wife

He had now been stalking his beautiful Mlle Morphy, whose real name was Mrs Meehawl O'Sullivan, for some six weeks, and she had appeared to be so amused at every stage of the hunt, so responsive, *entraînante*, even *aguichante*, that he could already foresee the kill over the next horizon. At their first encounter, during the Saint Patrick's Day cocktail party at the Dutch embassy, accompanied by a husband who had not a word to throw to a cat about anything except the scissors and shears that he manufactured somewhere in the West of Ireland, and who was obviously quite ill at ease and drank too much Irish whiskey, what had attracted him to her was not only her splendid Boucher figure (whence his sudden nickname for her, La Morphée), or her copper-coloured hair, her lime-green Irish eyes and her seemingly poreless skin, but her calm, total and subdued elegance: the Balenciaga costume, the peacock-skin gloves, the gleaming crocodile handbag, a glimpse of tiny, lace-edged lawn handkerchief and her dry, delicate scent. He had a grateful eye and nose for such things. It was, after all, part of his job. Their second meeting, two weeks later, at his own embassy, had opened the doors. She came alone.

Now, at last, inside a week, perhaps less, there would be an end to all the probationary encounters that followed—mostly her inventions, at his persistent appeals—those wide-eyed fancy-meeting-you-heres at the zoo, at race-meetings, afternoon cinemas, in art galleries, at more diplomatic parties (once he had said gaily to her, 'The whole diplomacy of Europe seems to circle around our interest in one another'), those long drives over the Dublin mountains in his Renault coupé, those titillating rural lunches, nose to nose, toe to toe (rural because she quickly educated him to see Dublin as a stock exchange for gossip, a casino of scandal), an end, which was rather a pity, to those charming unforeseen-foreseen, that is to say proposed but in the end just snatched, afternoon *promenades champêtres* under the budding leaves and closing skies of the Phoenix Park, with the first lights of the city springing up below them to mark the end of another boring day for him in Ailesbury Road, Dublin's street of embassies, for her another possibly cosier but, he selfishly hoped, not much more exciting day in her swank boutique on Saint Stephen's Green. Little by little those intimate encounters, those murmured confessions had lifted acquaintance to friendships, to self-mocking smiles over some tiny incident during their last meeting, to eager anticipation of the next, an aimless tenderness twanging to appetite like an arrow. Or, at least, that was how he felt about it. Any day now, even any hour, the slow countdown, slower than the slow movement of Mendelssohn's Concerto in E Minor, or the swoony sequence from the *Siegfried Idyll*, or that floating spun-sugar balloon of Mahler's 'Song of the Earth', to the music of which on his gramophone he would imagine her smiling sidelong at him as she softly disrobed, and his ingenious playing with her, his teasing and warming of her moment by moment for the roaring, blazing takeoff. To the moon!

Only one apprehension remained with him, not a real misgiving, something nearer to a recurring anxiety. It was that at the last moments when her mind and her body ought to take leave of one another she might take to her heels. It was a fear that flooded him whenever, with smiles too diffident to reassure him, she would once again mention that she was a Roman Catholic, or a Cat, a Papist or a Pape, a convent girl, and once she laughed that during her schooldays in the convent she had actually been made an *Enfant de Marie*. The words never ceased to startle him, dragging him back miserably to his first sexual frustration with his very pretty but unexpectedly proper cousin Berthe Ohnet during his lycée years in Nancy; a similar icy snub a few years later in Quebec; repeated still later by that smack on the face in Rio that almost became a public scandal; memories so painful that whenever an attractive woman nowadays mentioned religion, even in so simple a context as, 'Thank God I didn't buy that hat, or frock, or stock, or mare', a red flag at once began to flutter in his belly.

Obsessed, every time she uttered one of those ominous words he rushed for the reassurance of what he called The Sherbet Test, which meant observing the effect on her of some tentatively sexy joke, like the remark of the young princess on tasting her first sherbet:—'Oh, how absolutely delicious! But what a pity it isn't a sin!' To his relief she not only always laughed merrily at his stories but always capped them, indeed at times so startling him by her coarseness that it only occurred to him quite late in their day that this might be her way of showing her distaste for his diaphanous indelicacies. He had once or twice observed that priests, peasants and children will roar with laughter at some scavenger joke, and growl at even a veiled reference to a thigh. Was she a child of nature? Still, again and again back would come those disturbing words. He could have understood them from a prude, but what on earth did *she* mean by them? Were they so many herbs to season her desire with pleasure in her naughtiness? Flicks of nasty puritan sensuality to whip her body over some last ditch of indecision? It was only when the final crisis came that he wondered if this might not all along have been her way of warning him that she was neither a light nor a lecherous woman, neither a flirt nor a flibbertigibbet, that in matters of the heart she was *une femme très sérieuse*.

He might have guessed at something like it much earlier. He knew almost from the first day that she was *bien élevée*, her father a judge of the Supreme Court, her uncle a monsignor at the Vatican, a worldly, sport-loving, learned, contriving priest who had per-suaded her papa to send her for a finishing year to Rome with the Sisters of the Sacred Heart at the top of the Spanish Steps; chiefly, it later transpired, because the convent was near the *centre hippique* in the Borghese Gardens and it was his right reverend's opinion that no rich girl could possibly be said to have completed her education until she had learned enough about horses to ride to hounds. She had told him a lot, and most amusingly, about this uncle. She had duly returned from Rome to Dublin, and whenever he came over for the hunting, he always rode beside her. This attention had mightily flattered her until she discovered that she was being used as a cover for his uncontrollable passion for Lady Kinvara and Loughrea, then the master, some said the mistress, of the Clare-Galway hounds.

'How old were you then?' Ferdy asked, fascinated.

'I was at the university. Four blissful, idling years. But I got my degree. I was quick. And,' she smiled, 'good-looking. It helps, even with professors.'

'But riding to hounds as a student?'

'Why not? In Ireland everybody does. Children do. You could

ride to hounds on a plough horse if you had nothing else. So long as you keep out of the way of real hunters. I only stopped after my marriage, when I had a miscarriage. And I swear that was only because I was thrown.'

A monsignor who was sport-loving, worldly and contriving. He understood, and approved, and it explained many things about her.

The only other ways in which her dash, beauty and gaiety puzzled and beguiled him were trivial. Timid she was not, she was game for any risk. But the coolness of her weather eye often surprised him.

'The Leopardstown Races? Oh, what a good idea, Ferdy! Let's meet there . . . The Phoenix Park Races? No, not there. Too many doctors showing off their wives and their cars, trying to be noticed. And taking notice. Remember, a lot of my college friends married doctors . . . No, not *that* cinema. It has become vogueish . . . In fact, no cinema on the south side of the river. What we want is a good old fleabitten picture house on the north side where they show nothing but westerns and horrors, and where the kids get in on Saturday mornings for thruppence . . . Oh, and do please only ring the boutique in an emergency. Girls gossip.'

Could she be calculating? For a second of jealous heat he wondered if she could possibly have another lover. Cooling, he saw that if he had to keep a wary eye in his master's direction she had to think of her bourgeois clientele. Besides, he was a bachelor, and would remain one. She had to manage her inexpressibly dull, if highly successful old scissors and shears manufacturer, well past fifty and probably as suspicious as he was boring; so intensely, so exhaustingly boring that the only subject about which she could herself nearly become boring was in her frequent complaints about his boringness. Once she *was* frightening—when she spat out that she had hated her husband ever since the first night of their marriage when he brought her for their honeymoon—it was odd how long, and how intensely this memory had rankled—not, as he had promised, to Paris, but to his bloody scissors and shears factory in the wet wilds of northern Donegal. ('Just, me dear, haha, to let 'em see, haha, t'other half of me scissors.')

Ferdy had of course never asked her why she had married such a cretin; not after sizing up her house, her furniture, her pictures, her clothes, her boutique. Anyway, only another cretin would discourage any pretty woman from grumbling about her husband:

(a) because such grumblings give a man a chance to show what a deeply sympathetic nature he has, and (b) because the information incidentally supplied helps one to arrange one's assignations in places and at times suitable to all concerned.

Adding it all up (he was a persistent adder-upper) only one problem had so far defeated him: that he was a foreigner and did not know what sort of women Irish women are. It was not as if he had not done his systematic best to find out, beginning with a course of reading through the novels of her country. A vain exercise. With the exception of the Molly Bloom of James Joyce the Irish Novel had not only failed to present him with any fascinating woman but it had presented him with, in his sense of the word, no woman at all. Irish fiction was a lot of nineteenth-century *connerie* about half-savage Brueghelesque peasants, or urban *petits fonctionnaires* who invariably solved their frustrations by getting drunk on religion, patriotism or undiluted whiskey, or by taking flight to England. Pastoral melodrama. (Giono at his worst.) Or pastoral humbuggery. (Bazin at his most sentimental.) Or, at its best, pastoral lyricism. (Daudet and rosewater.) As for Molly Bloom! He enjoyed the smell of every kissable pore of her voluptuous body without for one moment believing that she had ever existed. James Joyce in drag.

'But,' he had finally implored his best friend in Ailesbury Road, Hamid Bey, the third secretary of the Turkish embassy, whose amorous secrets he willingly purchased with his own, 'if it is too much to expect Ireland to produce a bevy of Manons, Mitsous, Gigis, Claudines, Kareninas, Oteros, Leahs, San Severinas, what about those great-thighed, vast-bottomed creatures dashing around the country on horseback like Diana followed by all her minions? Are they not interested in love? And if so why aren't there novels about them?'

His friend laughed as toughly as Turkish Delight and replied in English in his laziest Noel Coward drawl, all the vowels frontal as if he were talking through bubble gum, all his r's either left out where they should be, as in *deah* or *cleah*, or inserted where they should not be, as in *India-r* or *Iowa-r*.

'My dear Ferdy, did not your deah fatheh or your deah mamma-r eveh tell you that all Irish hohsewomen are in love with their hohses? And anyway it is well known that the favourite pin-up gihl of Ahland is a gelding.'

'Naked?' Ferdinand asked coldly, and refused to believe him, remembering that his beloved had been a hohsewoman, and satisfied that he was not a gelding. Instead, he approached the Italian ambassador at a cocktail party given by the Indonesian embassy to whisper to him about *l'amore irlandese* in his best stage French, and stage French manner, eyebrows lifted above fluttering eyelids, voices as hoarse as, he guessed, His Excellency's mind would be on its creaking way back to memories of Gabin, Jouvet, Brasseur, Fernandel. Yves Montand. It proved to be another futile exercise. His Ex groaned as operatically as every Italian groans over such vital, and lethal, matters as the Mafia, food, taxation and women, threw up his hands, made a face like a more than usually desiccated De Sica and sighed, '*Les femmes d'Irlande? Mon pauvre gars! Elles sont d'une chasteté . . .*' He paused and roared the adjective, '. . . FORMIDABLE!'

Ferdinand had heard this yarn about feminine chastity in other countries and (with those two or three exceptions already mentioned) found it true only until one had established the precise local variation of the meaning of 'chastity'. But how was he to discover the Irish variation? In the end it was Celia herself who, unwittingly, revealed it to him and in doing so dispelled his last doubts about her susceptibility, inflammability and volatility—despite the very proper Sisters of the Spanish Steps.

The revelation occurred one night in early May—her Meehawl being away in the West, presumably checking what she contemptuously called his Gaelic-squeaking scissors. Ferdy had driven her back to his flat for a nightcap after witnessing the prolonged death of Mimi in *La Bohème*. She happened to quote to him Oscar Wilde's remark about the death of Little Nell that only a man with a heart of stone could fail to laugh at it, and in this clever vein they had continued for a while over the rolling brandy, seated side by side on his settee, his hand on her bare shoulder leading him to hope more and more fondly that this might be his Horizon Night, until suddenly, she asked him a coldly probing question.

'Ferdy! Tell me exactly why we did not believe in the reality of Mimi's death.'

His palm oscillated gently between her clavicle and her scapula.

'Because, my little cabbage, we were not expected to. Singing away like a lark? With her last breath? And no lungs? I am a

Frenchman. I understand the nature of reality and can instruct you about it. Art, my dear Celia, is art because it is not reality. It does not copy or represent nature. It improves upon it. It embellishes it. This is the kernel of the classical French attitude to life. And,' he beamed at her, 'to love. We make of our wildest feelings of passion the gentle art of love.'

He suddenly stopped fondling her shoulder and surveyed her with feelings of chagrin and admiration. The sight of her belied his words. Apart from dressing with taste, and, he felt certain, undressing with even greater taste, she used no art at all. She was as innocent of makeup as a peasant girl of the Vosges. Had he completely misread her? Was she that miracle, a fully ripe peach brought into the centre of the city some twenty years ago from a walled garden in the heart of the country, still warm from the sun, still glowing, downy, pristine, innocent as the dew? He felt her juice dribbling down the corner of his mouth. Was this the missing piece of her jigsaw? An ensealed innocence. If so he had wasted six whole weeks. This siege could last six years.

'No, Ferdy!' she said crossly. 'You have it all wrong. I'm talking about life, not about art. The first and last thought of any real Italian girl on her deathbed would be to ask for a priest. She was facing her God.'

God at once pointed a finger at him through the chandelier, and within seconds they were discussing love among the English, Irish, French, Indians, Moslems, Italians, naturally the Papacy, Alexander the Sixth and incest, Savonarola and dirty pictures, Joan of Arc and martyrdom, death, sin, hellfire, Cesare Borgia who, she insisted, screamed for a priest to pray for him at the end.

'A lie,' he snarled, 'that some beastly priest told you in a sermon when you were a schoolgirl. Pray! I suppose,' he challenged furiously, 'you pray even against me.'

Abashed, she shook her autumn-brown head at him, threw a kipper-eyed glance up to the chandelier, gave him a ravishingly penitential smile, and sighed like an unmasked sinner.

'Ah, Ferdy! Ferdy! If you only knew the real truth about me! Me pray against you? I don't pray at all. You remember Mimi's song at the end of the first act? "I do not always go to Mass, but I pray quite a bit to the good Lord." Now, I hedge my bets in a very different way. I will not pray because I refuse to go on my knees to anybody. Yet, there I go meekly trotting off to Mass every Sunday and holy day. And why? Because I am afraid not to, because it would be a mortal sin not to.' She gripped his tensed hand, trilling her r's over the threshold of her lower lip and tenderly umlauting her vowels. Dürling. Cöward. Li-er. 'Amn't I the weak cöward, dürling? Amn't I the awful li-er? A crook entirrely?'

Only a thin glint of streetlight peeping between his curtains witnessed the wild embrace of a man illuminated by an avowal so patently bogus as to be the transparent truth.

'You a liar?' he gasped, choking with laughter. 'You a shivering coward? A double-faced hedger of bets? A deceiving crook? A wicked sinner? For the last five minutes you have been every single one of them by pretending to be them. What you really are is a woman full of cool, hard-headed discretion, which you would like to sell to me as a charming weakness. Full of dreams that you would like to disguise as wicked lies. Of common sense that it suits you to pass off as crookedness. Of worldly wisdom still moist from your mother's nipple that, if you thought you would get away with the deception, you would stoop to call a sin. My dearest Celia, your yashmak reveals by pretending to conceal. Your trick is to be innocence masquerading as villainy. I think it is enchanting.'

For the first time he saw her in a rage.

'But it is *all* true. I *am* a liar. I *do* go to Mass every Sunday. I do *not* pray. I *am* afraid of damnation. I . . .'

He silenced her with three fingers laid momentarily on her lips.

'Of course you go to Mass every Sunday. My father, a master tailor of Nancy, used to go to Mass every Sunday not once but three times, and always as conspicuously as possible. Why? Because he was a tailor, just as you run a boutique. You don't pray? Sensible woman. Why should you bother your *bon Dieu*, if there is a *bon Dieu*, with your pretty prattle about things that He knew all about one billion years before you were a wink in your mother's eye? My dearest and perfect love, you have told me everything about Irishwomen that I need to know. None of you says what you think. Every one of you means what you don't say. None of you thinks about what she is going to do. But every one of you knows it to the last dot. You dream like opium eaters and your eyes are as calm as resting snow. You are all of you realists to your bare backsides. Yes, yes, yes, yes, yes, you will say this is true of all women, but it is not. It is not even true of Frenchwomen. They may be realists in lots of things. In love, they are just as stupid as all the rest of us. But not

Irishwomen! Or not, I swear it, if they are all like you. I'll prove it to you with a single question. Would you, like Mimi, live for the sake of love in a Paris garret?'

She gravely considered a proposition that sounded delightfully like a proposal.

'How warm would the garret be? Would I have to die of tuberculosis? You remember how the poor Bohemian dramatist had to burn his play to keep them all from being famished with the cold.'

'Yes!' Ferdy laughed. 'And as the fire died away he said, "I always knew that last act was too damned short." But you are dodging my question.'

'I suppose, dürling, any woman's answer to your question would depend on how much she was in love with whoever he was. Or wouldn't it?'

Between delight and fury he dragged her into his arms.

'You know perfectly well, you sweet slut, that what I am asking you is, "Do you love me a lot or a little? A garretful or a palaceful?" Which is it?'

Chuckling she slid down low in the settee and smiled up at him between sleepycat eyelashes.

'And you, Ferdy, must know perfectly well that it is pointless to ask any woman silly questions like that. If some man I loved very much were to ask me, "Do you love me, Celia?" I would naturally answer, "No!" in order to make him love me more. And if it was some man I did not like at all I would naturally say, "Yes, I love you so much I think we ought to get married," in order to cool him off. Which, Ferdy, do you want me to say to you?'

'Say,' he whispered adoringly, 'that you hate me beyond the tenth circle of Dante's hell.'

She made a grave face.

'I'm afraid, Ferdy, the fact is I don't like you at all. Not at all! Not one least little bit at all, at all.'

At which lying, laughing, enlacing and unlacing moment they kissed pneumatically and he knew that if all Irishwomen were Celias then the rest of mankind were mad ever to have admired women of any other race.

Their lovemaking was not as he had foredreamed it. She hurled her clothes to the four corners of the room, crying out, 'And about time too! Ferdy, what the hell have you been fooling around for during the last six weeks?' Within five minutes she smashed him into bits. In her passion she was more like a lion than a lioness. There was nothing about her either titillating or erotic, indolent or indulgent, as wild, as animal, as unrestrained, as simple as a forest fire. When, panting beside her, he recovered enough breath to speak he expressed his surprise that one so cool, so ladylike in public could be so different in private. She grunted peacefully and said in her muted brogue, 'Ah, shure, dürling, everything changes in the beddaroom.'

He woke at three twenty-five in the morning with that clear bang so familiar to everybody who drinks too much after the chimes of midnight, rose to drink a pint of cold water, lightly opened his curtains to survey the pre-dawn May sky and, turning toward the bed, saw the pallid streetlamp's light fall across her sleeping face, as calm, as soothed, as innocently sated as a baby filled with its mother's milk. He sat on the side of the bed looking down at her for a long time, overcome by the terrifying knowledge that, for the first time in his life, he had fallen in love.

The eastern clouds were growing as pink as petals while they drank the coffee he had quietly prepared. Over it he arranged in unnecessarily gasping whispers for their next meeting the following afternoon—'*This* afternoon!' he said joyously—at three twenty-five, henceforth his Mystic Hour for Love, but only on the strict proviso that he would not count on her unless she had set three red geraniums in a row on the windowsill of her boutique before three o'clock and that she, for her part, must divine a tragedy if the curtains of his flat were not looped high when she approached at three twenty o'clock. He could, she knew, have more easily checked with her by telephone, but also knowing how romantically, voluptuously, erotically minded he was she accepted with an indulgent amusement what he obviously considered ingenious devices for increasing the voltage of passion by the trappings of conspiracy. To herself she thought, 'Poor boy! He's been reading too many dirty books.'

Between two o'clock and three o'clock that afternoon she was entertained to see him pass her boutique three times in dark glasses. She cruelly made him pass a fourth time before, precisely at three o'clock, she gave him the pleasure of seeing two white hands with pink fingernails—not, wickedly, her own: her assistant's—emerge from under the net curtains of her window to arrange three small scarlet geraniums on the sill. He must have hastened perfervidly to the nearest florist to purchase the pink rose whose petals—when found (to her tolerant amusement at his boyish folly) tessellating the silk sheets of his bed. His gramophone, muted by a bath towel, was murmuring Wagner. A joss stick in a brass bowl stank cloyingly. He had cast a pink silk headscarf over the beside lamp. His dressing-table mirror had been tilted so that from where they lay they could see themselves. Within five minutes he neither saw, heard nor smelled anything, tumbling, falling, hurling headlong to consciousness of her mocking laughter at the image of her bottom mottled all over by his clinging rose petals. It cost him a brutal effort to laugh at himself.

All that afternoon he talked only of flight, divorce and remarriage. To cool him she encouraged him. He talked of it again and again every time they met. Loving him she humoured him. On the Wednesday of their third week as lovers they met briefly and chastely because her Meehawl was throwing a dinner at his house that evening for a few of his business colleagues previous to flying out to Manchester for a two-day convention of cutlers. Ferdy at once promised her to lay in a store of champagne, caviar, *pâté de foie* and brioches so that they need not stir from their bed for the whole of those two days.

'Not even once?' she asked coarsely, and he made a moue of disapproval.

'You do not need to be all that realistic, Celia!'

Already by three fifteen that Thursday afternoon he was shuffling nervously from window to window. By three twenty-five he was muttering, 'I hope she's not going to be late.' He kept feeling the champagne to be sure it was not getting too cold. At three thirty-five he moaned, 'She *is* late!' At three forty he cried out in a jealous fury, glaring up and down the street, 'The slut is betraying me!' At a quarter to four his bell rang, he leaped to the door. She faced him as coldly as a newly carved statue of Carrara marble. She repulsed his arms. She would not stir beyond his doormat. Her eyes were dilated by fear.

'It is Meehawl!' she whispered.

'He has found us out?'

'It's the judgement of God on us both!'

The word smacked his face.

'He is dead?' he cried hopefully, brushing aside fear and despair.

'A stroke.'

She made a violent, downward swish with the side of her open palm.

'*Une attaque? De paralysie?*'

'He called at the boutique on his way to the plane. He said goodbye to me. He walked out to the taxi. I went into my office to prepare my vanity case and do peepee before I met you. The taxi driver ran in shouting that he had fallen in a fit on the pavement. We drove him to 96. That's Saint Vincent's. The hospital near the corner of the Green. He is conscious. But he cannot speak. One side of him is paralysed. He may not live. He has had a massive coronary.'

She turned and went galloping down the stairs.

His immediate rebound was to roar curses on all the gods that never were. Why couldn't the old fool have his attack next week? His second thought was glorious. 'He will die, we will get married.' His third made him weep, 'Poor little cabbage!' His fourth thought was, 'The brioches I throw out, the rest into the fridge.' His fifth sixth and seventh were three Scotches while he rationally considered all her possible reactions to the brush of the dark angel's wing. Only Time, he decided, would tell.

But when liars become the slaves of Time what can Time do but lie like them? A vat solid-looking enough for old wine, it leaks at every stave. A ship rigged for the wildest seas, it is rust-bound to its bollards on the quay. She said firmly that nothing between them could change. He refuted her. Everything had changed, and for the better. He rejoiced when the doctors said their patient was doomed. After two more weeks she reported that the doctors were impressed by her husband's remarkable tenacity. He spoke of Flight. She now spoke of Time. One night as she lay hot in his arms in his bed he shouted triumphantly to the chandelier that when husbands are imprisoned lovers are free. She demurred. She could never spend a night with him in her own bed; not with a resident housekeeper upstairs. He tossed it aside. What matter where they slept! He would be happy sleeping with her in the Phoenix Park. She pointed out snappishly that it was raining. 'Am I a seal?' He proffered her champagne. She confessed the awful truth. This night was the last night they could be together anywhere.

'While he was dying, a few of his business pals used to call on him at the Nursing Home—the place all Dublin knows as 96. Now that the old devil is refusing to die they refuse to call on him anymore. I am his only faithful visitor. He so bores everybody. And with his paralysed mouth they don't know what the hell he is saying. Do you realise, Ferdy, what this means? He is riding me like a nightmare. Soaking me up like blotting paper. He rang me four times the day before yesterday at the boutique. He rang again while I was here with you having a drink. He said whenever I go out I must leave a number where he can call me. The night before last he rang me at three o'clock in the morning. Thank God I was back in my own bed and not here with you. He said he was lonely. Has terrible dreams. That the nights are long. That he is frightened. That if he gets another stroke he will die. Dürling! I can never spend a whole night with you again!'

Ferdy became Napoleon. He took command of the campaign. He accompanied her on her next visit to 96. This, he discovered, was a luxury (i.e. Victorian) nursing home in Lower Leeson Street, where cardinals died, coal fires were in order, and everybody was presented with a menu from which to choose his lunch and dinner. The carpets were an inch thick. The noisiest internal sound heard was the Mass bell tinkling along the corridors early every morning as the priest went from room to room with the Eucharist for the dying faithful. The Irish, he decided, know how to die. Knowing no better, he bore with him copies of *Le Canard Enchaîné*, *La Vie Parisienne*, and *Playboy*. Celia deftly impounded them. 'Do you want him to die of blood pressure? Do you want the nuns to think he's an Irish queer? A fellow who prefers women to drink?' Seated at one side of the bed, facing her seated at the other, he watched her, with her delicate lace-edged handkerchief (so disturbingly reminiscent of her lace-edged panties) wiping the unshaven chin of the dribbling half-idiot on the pillow. In an unconsumed rage he lifted his eyebrows into his hair, surveyed the moving mass of clouds above Georgian Dublin, smoothened his already blackboard-smooth hair, gently touched the white carnation in his lapel, forced himself to listen calmly to the all-but-unintelligible sounds creeping from the dribbling corner of the twisted mouth in the unshaven face of the revolting cretin on the pillow beneath his eyes, and agonisingly asked himself by what unimaginably devious machinery, and for what indivinable purpose the universe had been so arranged since the beginning of Time that this bronze-capped, pastel-eyed, rosy-breasted, round-buttocked, exquisite flower of paradise sitting opposite to him should, in the first place, have matched and mated with this slob between them, and then, or rather *and then*, or rather AND THEN make it so happen that he, Ferdinand Louis Jean-Honoré Clichy, of 9 *bis* rue des Dominicains, Nancy, in the Department of Moselle et Meurthe, population 133,532, altitude 212 metres, should happen to discover her in remote Dublin, and fall so utterly into her power that if he were required at that particular second to choose between becoming Ambassador to the Court of Saint James's for life and one night alone in bed with her he would have at once replied, 'Even for one hour!'

He gathered that the object on the pillow was addressing him.

'Oh, Mosheer! Thacks be to the ever cliving and cloving Gog I khav mosht devote clittle wife in all Khlistendom ... I'd be chlost without her ... Ah, Mosheer! If you ever dehide to marry, marry an Irikhwoman ... Mosht fafeful cleatures in all exhishtench ... Would any Frenchwoman attend shoopid ole man chlike me the way Chelia doesh?'

Ferdy closed his eyes. She was tenderly dabbing the spittled corners of the distorted mouth. What happened next was that a Sister took Celia out to the corridor for a few private words and that Ferdy at once leaned forward and whispered savagely to the apparently immortal O'Sullivan, 'Monsieur O'Sullivan, your wife does not look at all well. I fear she is wilting under the strain of your illness.'

'Chlstrain!' the idiot said in astonishment. 'What chlstrain? I khlsee no khlsignch of kkchlstrain!'

Ferdy whispered with fierceness that when one is gravely ill one may sometimes fail to observe the grave illness of others.

'We have to remember, Monsieur, that if your clittle wife were to collapse under the chlstr ... under the *strain* of your illness it would be very serious, for *you*!'

After that day the only reason he submitted to accompany his love on these painful and piteous visits to 96 was that they always ended with O'Sullivan begging him to take his poor clittle, loving clittle, devoted clittle pet of a wife to a movie for a relaxation and a rest, or for a drink in the Russell, or to the evening races in the park; whereupon they would both hasten, panting, to Ferdy's flat to make love swiftly, wildly and vindictively—swiftly because their time was limited, wildly because her Irish storms had by now become typhoons of rage, and he no longer needed rose petals, Wagner, Mendelssohn, dim lights or pink champagne, and vindictively to declare and to crush their humiliation at being slaves to that idiot a quarter of a mile away in another bed saying endless rosaries to the Virgin.

Inevitably the afternoon came—it was now July—when Ferdy's pride and nerves cracked. He decided that enough was enough. They must escape to freedom. At once.

'Celia! If we have to fly to the end of the world! It won't really ruin my career. My master is most sympathetic. In fact since I hinted to him that I am in love with a *belle mariée* he does nothing but complain about his wife to me. And he can't leave her, his career depends on her, she is the daughter of a Secretary of State for Foreign Affairs—and rich. He tells me that at worst I would be moved off to someplace like Los Angeles or Reykjavik. Celia! My beloved flower! We could be as happy as two puppies in a basket in Iceland.'

She permitted a meed of Northern silence to create itself and then wondered reflectively if it is ever warm in Iceland, at which he pounced with a loud 'What do you mean? What are you actually asking? What is really in your mind?' She said, 'Nothing, dürling,' for how could she dare to say that whereas he could carry his silly job with him wherever he went she, to be with him, would have to give up her lovely old, friendly old boutique on the Green where her friends came to chat over morning coffee, where she met every rich tourist who visited Dublin, where she made nice money of her own, where she felt independent and free; just as she could never hope to make him understand why she simply could not just up and out and desert a dying husband.

'But there's nothing to hold you here. In his condition you'd be sure to get custody of the children. Apart from the holidays they could remain in school here the year round.'

So he had been thinking it all out. She stroked his hairy chest.

'I know.'

'The man, even at his best, you've acknowledged it yourself, over and over, is a fool. He is a moujik. He is a bore.'

'I know!' she groaned. 'Who should better know what a crasher he is? He is a child. He hasn't had a new idea in his head for thirty years. There have been times when I've hated the smell of him. He reminds me of an unemptied ashtray. Times when I've wished to God that a thief would break into the house some night and kill him. And,' at which point she began to weep on his tummy, 'I know

now that there is only one thief who will come for him and he is so busy elsewhere that it will be years before he catches up with him. And then I think of the poor old bastard wetting his hospital bed, unable to stir, let alone talk, looking up at his ceiling, incontinent, with no scissors, no golf, no friends, no nothing, except me. How *can* I desert him?'

Ferdy clasped his hands behind his head, stared up at heaven's pure ceiling and heard her weeping like the summer rain licking his windowpane. He created a long Irish silence. He heard the city whispering. Far away. Further away. And then not at all.

'And to think,' he said at last, 'that I once called you a realist!'

She considered this. She too no longer heard the muttering of the city's traffic.

'This is how the world is made,' she decided flatly.

'I presume,' he said briskly, 'that you do realise that all Dublin knows that you are meanwhile betraying your beloved Meehawl with me?'

'I know that there's not one of those bitches who wouldn't give her left breast to be where I am at this moment.'

They got out of bed and began to dress.

'And, also meanwhile, I presume you do *not* know that they have a snotty name for you?'

'What name?'—and she turned her bare back for the knife.

'They call you The Diplomatic Hack.'

For five minutes neither of them spoke.

While he was stuffing his shirt into his trousers and she, dressed fully except for her frock, was patting her penny-brown hair into place before his mirror he said to her, 'Furthermore I suppose you do realise that whether I like it or not I shall one day be shifted to some other city in some other country. What would you do then? For once, just for once in your life tell me the plain truth! Just to bring you to the crunch. What would you really do then?'

She turned, comb in hand, leaned her behind against his dressing table and looked him straight in the fly which he was still buttoning.

'Die,' she said flatly.

'That,' he said coldly, 'is a manner of speech. Even so, would you consider it an adequate conclusion to a love that we have so often said is forever?'

They were now side by side in the mirror, she tending her copper hair, he his black, like any long-married couple. She smiled a little sadly.

'Forever? Dürling, does love know that lovely word? You love me. I know it. I love you. You know it. We will always know it. People die but if you have ever loved them they are never gone. Apples fall from the tree but the tree never forgets its blossoms. Marriage is different. You remember the way he advised you that if you ever marry you should marry an Irishwoman. Don't, Ferdy! If you do that she will stick to you forever. And you wouldn't really want that?' She lifted her frock from the back of a chair and stepped into it. 'Zip me up, dürling, will you? Even my awful husband. There must have been a time when I thought him attractive. We used to sail together. Play tennis together. He was very good at it. After all, I gave him two children. What's the date? They'll be home for the holidays soon. All I have left for him now is contempt and compassion. It is our bond.'

Bewildered he went to the window, buttoned his flowered waistcoat. He remembered from his café days as a student a ruffle of aphorisms about love and marriage. Marriage begins only when love ends. Love opens the door to Marriage and quietly steals away. *Il faut toujours s'appuyer sur les principes de l'amour—ils finissent par en céder.* What would she say to that? Lean heavily on the principles of love—they will always conveniently crumple in the end. Marriage bestows on Love the tenderness due to a parting guest. Every *affaire de coeur* ends as a *mariage de convenance*. He turned to her, arranging his jacket, looking for his keys and his hat. She was peeking into her handbag, checking her purse for her keys and her lace handkerchief, gathering her gloves, giving a last glance at her hat. One of the things he liked about her was that she always wore a hat.

'You are not telling me the truth, Celia,' he said quietly. 'Oh, I don't mean about loving me. I have no doubt about you on that score. But when you persuade yourself that you can't leave him because you feel compassion for him that is just your self-excuse for continuing a marriage that has its evident advantages.'

She smiled lovingly at him.

'Will you ring me tomorrow, dürling?'

'Of course.'

'I love you very much, dürling.'

'And I love you too.'
'Until tomorrow then.'
'Until tomorrow, dürling.'
As usual he let her go first.

That afternoon was some two years ago. Nine months after it he was transferred to Brussels. As often as he could wangle special leave of absence, and she could get a relative to stay for a week with her bedridden husband, now back in his own house, they would fly to Paris or London to be together again. He would always ask solicitously after her husband's health, and she would always sigh and say his doctors had assured her that 'he will live forever'. Once, in Paris, passing a church he, for some reason, asked her if she ever went nowadays to confession. She waved the question away with a laugh, but later that afternoon he returned to it pertinaciously.

'Yes. Once a year.'
'Do you tell your priest about us?'
'I tell him that my husband is bedridden. That I am in love with another man. That we make love. And that I cannot give you up. As I can't, dürling.'
'And what does he say to that?'
'They all say the same. That it is an impasse. Only one dear old Jesuit gave me a grain of hope. He said that if I liked I could pray to God that my husband might die.'
'And have you so prayed?'
'Dürling, why should I?' she asked gaily, as she stroked the curly hair between his two pink buttons. 'As you once pointed out to me yourself all this was foreknown millions of years ago.'

He gazed at the ceiling. In her place, unbeliever though he was, he would, for love's sake, have prayed with passion. Not that she had said directly that she had not. Maybe she had? Two evasions in one sentence! It was all more than flesh and blood could bear. It was the Irish variation all over again: never let your left ass know what your right ass is doing. He decided to give her one more twirl. When she got home he wrote tenderly to her, 'You are the love of my life!' He could foresee her passionate avowal, 'And me too, dürling!' What she actually replied was, 'Don't I know it?' Six months later he had manœuvred himself into the consular service and out of Europe to Los Angeles. He there consoled his broken heart with a handsome creature named Rosie O'Connor. Quizzed about his partiality for the Irish, he could only flap his hands and say, 'I don't know what they have got. They are awful liars. There isn't a grain of romance in them. And whether as wives or mistresses they are absolutely faithless!'

The Sugawn Chair

Every autumn I am reminded of an abandoned sugawn chair that languished for years, without a seat, in the attic of my old home. It is associated in my mind with an enormous sack which the carter used to dump with a thud on the kitchen floor around every October. I was a small kid then, and it was as high as myself. This sack had come 'up from the country', a sort of diplomatic messenger from the fields to the city. It smelled of dust and hay and apples, for the top half of it always bulged with potatoes, and, under a layer of hay, the bottom half bulged with apples. Its arrival always gave my mother great joy and a little sorrow, because it came from the farm where she had been born. Immediately she saw it she glowed with pride in having a 'back', as she called it— meaning something behind her more solid and permanent than city streets, though she was also saddened by the memories that choked her with this smell of hay and potatoes from the home farm, and apples from the little orchard near the farmhouse. My father, who had also been born on a farm, also took great pleasure in these country fruits, and as the two of them stood over the sack, in the kitchen, in the middle of the humming city, everything that their youth had meant to them used to make them smile and laugh and use words that they had never used during the rest of the year, and which I thought magical: words like *late sowing, clover crop, inch field, marl bottom, headlands, tubers*, and the names of potatoes, British Queens or Arran Banners, that sounded to me like the names of regiments. For those moments my father and mother became a young, courting couple again. As they stood over that sack, as you might say warming their hands to it, they were intensely happy, close to each other, in love again. To me they were two very old people. Counting back now, I reckon that they were about forty-two or forty-three.

One autumn evening after the sack arrived, my father went up to the attic and brought down the old sugawn chair. I suppose he had

had it sent up from his home farm. It was the only thing of its kind in our house, which they had filled—in the usual peasants' idea of what constitutes elegance—with plush chairs, gold-framed pictures of Stags at Bay, and exotic tropical birds, pelmets on the mantelpieces, Delft shepherdesses, Chinese mandarins with nodding heads, brass bedsteads with mighty knobs and mother-of-pearl escutcheons set with bits of mirror, vast mahogany chiffoniers, and so on. But the plush-bottomed chairs, with their turned legs and their stiff backs, were for show, not for comfort, whereas in the old country sugawn chair my da could tilt and squeak and rock to his behind's content.

It had been in the place for years, rockety, bockety, chipped and well-polished, and known simply as 'your father's chair', until the night when, as he was reading the *Evening Echo* with his legs up on the kitchen range, there was a sudden rending noise, and down he went through the seat of it. There he was then, bending over, with the chair stuck on to him, and my mother and myself in the splits of laughter, pulling it from him while he cursed like a trooper. This was the wreck that he now suddenly brought down from the dusty attic.

The next day, he brought in a great sack of straw from the Cornmarket, a half-gallon of porter and two old buddies from the street—an ex-soldier known to the kids around as 'Tear-'em-and-ate-'em' and a little dwarf of a man who guarded the stage door at the Opera House when he was not behind the sacristan at the chapel. I was enchanted when I heard what they were going to do. They were going to make ropes of straw—a miracle I had never heard of—and reseat the chair. Bursting with pride in my da, I ran out and brought in my best pal, and the two of us sat quiet as cats on the kitchen table, watching the three men filling the place with dust, straw, and loud arguments as they began to twist the ropes for the bottom of the chair.

More strange words began to float in the air with the dust: *scallops, flat tops, bulrushes, cipeens, fields in great heart* . . . And when the three sat down for a swig of porter, and looked at the old polished skeletons in the middle of the floor, they began to rub the inside of their thighs and say how there was no life at all like the country life, and my mother poured out more porter for them, and laughed happily when my da began to talk about horses, and harrows, and a day after the plough, and how, for *that* much, he'd throw up this blooming city life altogether and settle down on a bit of a farm for the heel of his days.

This was a game of which he, she, and I never got tired, a fairy tale that was so alluring it did not matter a damn that they had not enough money to buy a window box, let alone a farm of land.

'Do you remember that little place,' she would say, 'that was going last year down at Nantenan?'

When she said that, I could see the little reedy fields of Limerick that I knew from holidays with my uncle, and the crumbling stone walls of old demesnes with the moss and saffron lichen on them, and the willow sighing softly by the Deel, and I could smell the wet turf rising in the damp air, and, above all, the tall wildflowers of the mallow, at first cabbage-leaved, then pink and coarse, then gosamery, then breaking into cakes that I used to eat—a rank weed that is the mark of ruin in so many Irish villages, and whose profusion and colour is for me the sublime emblem of Limerick's loneliness, loveliness, and decay.

'Ah!' my da would roar, 'You and your blooming ould Limerick! That bog of a place! Oh, but, God blast it why didn't I grab that little farm I was looking at two years ago there below Emo!'

'Oho, ho, ho!' she would scoff. 'The Queen's! The Lousy Queen's! God, I'd live like a tiger and die like a Turk for Limerick. For one patch of good old Limerick. Oh, Limerick, my love, and it isn't alike! Where would you get spuds and apples the like of them in the length and breadth of the Queen's County?'

And she grabbed a fist of hay from the bag and buried her face in it, and the tears began to stream down her face, and me and my pal screaming with laughter at her, and the sacristan lauding Tipperary, and the voices rose as Tear-'em-and-ate-'em brought up the River Barrow and the fields of Carlow, until my da jumped up with:

'Come on, lads, the day is dyin' and acres wide before us!'

For all that, the straw rope was slow in emerging. Their arguments about it got louder and their voices sharper. At first all their worry had been whether the kitchen was long enough for the rope; but so far, only a few, brief worms of straw lay on the red tiles. The sacristan said: 'That bloody straw is too moist.' When he was a boy in Tipp he never seen straw the like o' that. Tear-'em-and-ate-'em said that straw was old straw. When he was a lad in Carlow they never used old straw. Never! Under no possible circumstances! My da said: 'What's wrong with that straw is it's too bloomin' short!' And they began to kick the bits with their toes, and grimace at the heap on the floor, and pick up bits and fray them apart and throw them aside until the whole floor was like a stable. At last they put on their coats, and gave the straw a final few kicks, and my pal jumped down and said he was going back to his handball and, in my heart, I knew that they were three impostors.

The kitchen was tidy that evening when I came back with the *Evening Echo*. My da was standing by the sack of potatoes. He had a spud in his fist, rubbing off the dust of its clay with his thumb. When he saw me he tossed it back in the sack, took the paper, took one of the plush-bottom chairs and sat on it with a little grimace. I did not say anything, but young as I was, I could see that he was not reading what he was looking at. God knows what he was seeing at that moment.

For years the anatomy of the chair stood in one of the empty attics. It was there for many years after my father died. When my mother died and I had to sell out the few bits of junk that still remained from their lives, the dealer would not bother to take the useless frame, so that when, for the last time, I walked about the echoing house, I found it standing alone in the middle of the bare attic. As I looked at it I smelled apples, and the musk of Limerick's dust, and the turf-tang from its cottages, and the mallows among the limestone ruins, and I saw my mother and my father again as they were that morning—standing over the autumn sack, their arms about one another, laughing foolishly, and madly in love again.

Guests of the Nation

I

At dusk the big Englishman, Belcher, would shift his long legs out of the ashes and say 'Well, chums, what about it?' and Noble and myself would say 'All right, chum' (for we had picked up some of their curious expressions), and the little Englishman, Hawkins, would light the lamp and bring out the cards. Sometimes Jeremiah Donovan would come up and supervise the game, and get excited over Hawkins' cards, which he always played badly, and shout at him, as if he was one of our own, 'Ah, you divil, why didn't you play the tray?'

But ordinarily Jeremiah was a sober and contented poor devil like the big Englishman, Belcher, and was looked up to only because he was a fair hand at documents, though he was slow even with them. He wore a small cloth hat and big gaiters over his long pants, and you seldom saw him with his hands out of his pockets. He reddened when you talked to him, tilting from toe to heel and back, and looking down all the time at his big farmer's feet. Noble and myself used to make fun of his broad accent, because we were both from the town.

I could not at the time see the point of myself and Noble guarding Belcher and Hawkins at all, for it was my belief that you could have planted that pair down anywhere from this to Claregalway and they'd have taken root there like a native weed. I never in my short experience saw two men take to the country as they did.

They were passed on to us by the Second Battalion when the search for them became too hot, and Noble and myself, being young, took them over with a natural feeling of responsibility, but Hawkins made us look like fools when he showed that he knew the country better than we did.

'You're the bloke they call Bonaparte,' he says to me. 'Mary Brigid O'Connell told me to ask what you'd done with the pair of her brother's socks you borrowed.'

For it seemed, as they explained it, that the Second had little evenings, and some of the girls of the neighbourhood turned up, and, seeing they were such decent chaps, our fellows could not leave the two Englishmen out. Hawkins learned to dance 'The Walls of Limerick', 'The Siege of Ennis' and 'The Waves of Tory' as well as any of them, though he could not return the compliment, because our lads at that time did not dance foreign dances on principle.

So whatever privileges Belcher and Hawkins had with the Second they just took naturally with us, and after the first couple of days we gave up all pretence of keeping an eye on them. Not that they could have got far, because they had accents you could cut with a knife, and wore khaki tunics and overcoats with civilian pants and boots, but I believe myself they never had any idea of escaping and were quite content to be where they were.

It was a treat to see how Belcher got off with the old woman in the house where we were staying. She was a great warrant to scold, and cranky even with us, but before ever she had a chance of giving our guests, as I may call them, a lick of her tongue, Belcher had made her his friend for life. She was breaking sticks, and Belcher who had not been more than ten minutes in the house, jumped up and went over to her.

'Allow me, madam,' he said, smiling his queer little smile. 'Please allow me,' and he took the hatchet from her. She was too surprised to speak, and after that, Belcher would be at her heels, carrying a bucket, a basket, or a load of turf. As Noble said, he got into looking before she leapt, and hot water, or any little thing she wanted, Belcher would have ready for her. For such a huge man (and though I am five foot ten myself I had to look up at him) he had an uncommon lack of speech. It took us a little while to get used to him, walking in and out like a ghost, without speaking. Especially because Hawkins talked enough for a platoon, it was strange to hear Belcher with his toes in the ashes come out with a solitary 'Excuse me, chum,' or 'That's right, chum.' His one and only passion was cards, and he was a remarkably good card player. He could have skinned myself and Noble, but whatever we lost to him, Hawkins lost to us, and Hawkins only played with the money Belcher gave him.

Hawkins lost to us because he had too much old gab, and we probably lost to Belcher for the same reason. Hawkins and Noble argued about religion into the early hours of the morning, and Hawkins worried the life out of Noble, who had a brother a priest, with a string of questions that would puzzle a cardinal. Even in treating of holy subjects, Hawkins had a deplorable tongue. I never met a man who could mix such a variety of cursing and bad language into any argument. He was a terrible man, and a fright to argue. He never did a stroke of work, and when he had no one else to argue with, he got stuck in the old woman.

He met his match in her, for when he tried to get her to complain profanely of the drought she gave him a great comedown by blaming it entirely on Jupiter Pluvius (a deity neither Hawkins nor I had ever heard of, though Noble said that among the pagans it was believed that he had something to do with the rain). Another day he was swearing at the capitalists for starting the German war when the old lady laid down her iron, puckered up her little crab's mouth and said: 'Mr Hawkins, you can say what you like about the war, and think you'll deceive me because I'm only a simple poor country-woman, but I know what started the war. It was the Italian Count that stole the heathen divinity out of the temple of Japan. Believe me, Mr Hawkins, nothing but sorrow and want can follow people who disturb the hidden powers.'

A queer old girl, all right.

II

One evening we had our tea and Hawkins lit the lamp and we all sat into cards. Jeremiah Donovan came in too, and sat and watched us for a while, and it suddenly struck me that he had no great love for the two Englishmen. It came as a surprise to me because I had noticed nothing of it before.

Late in the evening a really terrible argument blew up between Hawkins and Noble about capitalists and priests and love of country.

'The capitalists pay the priests to tell you about the next world so that you won't notice what the bastards are up to in this,' said Hawkins.

'Nonsense, man!' said Noble, losing his temper. 'Before ever a capitalist was thought of people believed in the next world.'

Hawkins stood up as though he was preaching.

'Oh, they did, did they?' he said with a sneer. 'They believed all the things you believe—isn't that what you mean? And you believe God created Adam, and Adam created Shem, and Shem created Jehoshophat. You believe all that silly old fairytale about Eve and Eden and the apple. Well listen to me, chum! If you're entitled to a silly belief like that, I'm entitled to my own silly belief—which is that the first thing your God created was a bleeding capitalist, with morality and Rolls-Royce complete. Am I right, chum?' he says to Belcher.

'You're right, chum,' says Belcher with a smile, and he got up from the table to stretch his long legs into the fire and stroke his moustache. So, seeing that Jeremiah Donovan was going, and that there was no knowing when the argument about religion would be over, I went out with him. We strolled down to the village together, and then he stopped, blushing and mumbling, and said I should be behind, keeping guard. I didn't like the tone he took with me, and anyway I was bored with life in the cottage, so I replied by asking what the hell we wanted to guard them for at all.

He looked at me in surprise and said: 'I thought you knew we were keeping them as hostages.'

'Hostages?' I said.

'The enemy have prisoners belonging to us, and now they're talking of shooting them,' he said. 'If they shoot our prisoners, we'll shoot theirs.'

'Shoot Belcher and Hawkins?' I said.

'What else did you think we were keeping them for?' he asked.

'Wasn't it very unforeseen of you not to warn Noble and myself of that in the beginning?' I said.

'How was it?' he said. 'You might have known that much.'

'We could not know it, Jeremiah Donovan,' I said. 'How could we when they were on our hands so long?'

'The enemy have our prisoners as long and longer,' he said.

'That's not the same thing at all,' said I.

'What difference is there?' said he.

I couldn't tell him, because I knew he wouldn't understand. If it was only an old dog that you had to take to the vet's, you'd try and not get too fond of him, but Jeremiah Donovan was not a man who would ever be in danger of that.

'And when is this to be decided?' I said.

'We might hear tonight,' he said. 'Or tomorrow or the next day at latest. So if it's only hanging round that's a trouble to you, you'll be free soon enough.'

It was not the hanging round that was a trouble to me at all by this time. I had worse things to worry about. When I got back to the cottage the argument was still on. Hawkins was holding forth in his best style, maintaining that there was no next world, and Noble saying that there was; but I could see that Hawkins had had the best of it.

'Do you know what, chum?' he was saying with a saucy smile. 'I think you're just as big a bleeding unbeliever as I am. You say you believe in the next world, and you know just as much about the next world as I do, which is sweet damn-all. What's heaven? You don't know. Where's heaven? You don't know. You know sweet damn-all! I ask you again, do they wear wings?'

'Very well, then,' said Noble. 'They do. Is that enough for you? They do wear wings.'

'Where do they get them then? Who makes them? Have they a factory for wings? Have they a sort of store where you hand in your chit and take your bleeding wings?'

'You're an impossible man to argue with,' said Noble. 'Now, listen to me—' And they were off again.

It was long after midnight when we locked up and went to bed. As I blew out the candle I told Noble. He took it very quietly. When we'd been in bed about an hour he asked if I thought we should tell the Englishmen. I didn't, because I doubted if the English would shoot our men. Even if they did, the Brigade officers, who were always up and down to the Second Battalion and knew the Englishmen well, would hardly want to see them plugged. 'I think so too,' said Noble. 'It would be great cruelty to put the wind up them now.'

'It was very unforeseen of Jeremiah Donovan, anyhow,' said I.

It was next morning that we found it so hard to face Belcher and Hawkins. We went about the house all day, scarcely saying a word. Belcher didn't seem to notice; he was stretched into the ashes as usual, with his usual look of waiting in quietness for something unforeseen to happen, but Hawkins noticed it and put it down to Noble being beaten in the argument of the night before.

'Why can't you take the discussion in the proper spirit?' he said severely. 'You and your Adam and Eve! I'm a Communist, that's what I am. Communist or Anarchist, it all comes to much the same thing.' And he went round the house, muttering when the fit took him: 'Adam and Eve! Adam and Eve! Nothing better to do with their time than pick bleeding apples!'

III

I don't know how we got through that day, but I was very glad when it was over, the tea things were cleared away, and Belcher said in his peaceable way: 'Well, chums, what about it?' We sat round the table and Hawkins took out the cards, and just then I heard Jeremiah Donovan's footsteps on the path and a dark presentiment crossed my mind. I rose from the table and caught him before he reached the door.

'What do you want?' I asked.

'I want those two soldier friends of yours,' he said, getting red.

'Is that the way, Jeremiah Donovan?' I asked.

'That's the way. There were four of our lads shot this morning, one of them a boy of sixteen.'

'That's bad,' I said.

At that moment Noble followed me out, and the three of us walked down the path together, talking in whispers. Feeney, the local intelligence officer, was standing by the gate.

'What are you going to do about it?' I asked Jeremiah Donovan.

'I want you and Noble to get them out; tell them they're being shifted again; that'll be the quietest way.'

'Leave me out of that,' said Noble, under his breath.

Jeremiah Donovan looked at him hard.

'All right,' he says. 'You and Feeney get a few tools from the shed and dig a hole by the far end of the bog. Bonaparte and myself will be after you. Don't let anyone see you with the tools. I wouldn't like it to go beyond ourselves.'

We saw Feeney and Noble go round to the shed and went in ourselves. I left Jeremiah Donovan to do the explanations. He told them that he had orders to send them back to the Second Battalion. Hawkins let out a mouthful of curses, and you could see that though Belcher didn't say anything, he was a bit upset too. The old woman was for having them stay in spite of us, and she didn't stop advising them until Jeremiah Donovan lost his temper and turned on her. He had a nasty temper, I noticed. It was pitch dark in the cottage by this time, but no one thought of lighting the lamp, and in the darkness the two Englishmen fetched their topcoats and said goodbye to the old woman.

'Just as a man makes a home of a bleeding place, some bastard at headquarters thinks you're too cushy and shunts you off,' said Hawkins, shaking her hand.

'A thousand thanks, madam,' said Belcher. 'A thousand thanks for everything'—as though he'd made it up.

We went round to the back of the house and down towards the bog. It was only then that Jeremiah Donovan told them. He was shaking with excitement.

'There were four of our fellows shot in Cork this morning and now you are to be shot as a reprisal.'

'What are you talking about?' snaps Hawkins. 'It's bad enough being mucked about as we are without having to put up with your funny jokes.'

'It isn't a joke,' said Donovan. 'I'm sorry, Hawkins, but it's true,' and begins on the usual rigmarole about duty and how unpleasant it is. I never noticed that people who talk a lot about duty find it much of a trouble to them.

'Oh, cut it out!' said Hawkins.

'Ask Bonaparte,' said Donovan, seeing that Hawkins wasn't taking him seriously. 'Isn't it true, Bonaparte?'

'It is,' I said, and Hawkins stopped.

'Ah, for Christ's sake, chum!'

'I mean it, chum,' I said.

'You don't sound as if you meant it.'

'If he doesn't mean it, I do,' said Donovan, working himself up.

'What have you against me, Jeremiah Donovan?'

'I never said I had anything against you. But why did your people take out four of your prisoners and shoot them in cold blood?'

He took Hawkins by the arm and dragged him on, but it was impossible to make him understand that we were in earnest. I had the Smith and Wesson in my pocket and I kept fingering it and wondering what I'd do if they put up a fight for it or ran, and wishing to God they'd do one or the other. I knew if they did run for it, that I'd never fire on them. Hawkins wanted to know was Noble in it, and when we said yes, he asked us why Noble wanted to plug him. Why did any of us want to plug him? What had he done to us? Weren't we all chums? Didn't we understand him and didn't he understand us? Did we imagine for an instant that he'd shoot us for all the so-and-so officers in the so-and-so British Army?

By this time we'd reached the bog, and I was so sick I couldn't even answer him. We walked along the edge of it in the darkness, and every now and then Hawkins would call a halt and begin all over again, as if he was wound up, about our being chums, and I knew that nothing but the sight of the grave would convince him that we had to do it. And all the time I was hoping that something would happen; that they'd run for it or that Noble would take over the responsibility from me. I had the feeling that it was worse on Noble than on me.

IV

At last we saw the lantern in the distance and made towards it. Noble was carrying it, and Feeney was standing somewhere in the darkness behind him, and the picture of them so still and silent in the bogland brought it home to me that we were in earnest, and banished the last bit of hope I had.

Belcher, on recognising Noble, said: 'Hallo, chum,' in his quiet way, but Hawkins flew at him at once, and the argument began all over again, only this time Noble had nothing to say for himself and stood with his head down, holding the lantern between his legs.

It was Jeremiah Donovan who did the answering. For the twentieth time, as though it was haunting his mind, Hawkins asked if anybody thought he'd shoot Noble.

'Yes, you would,' said Jeremiah Donovan.

'No, I wouldn't, damn you!'

'You would, because you'd know you'd be shot for not doing it.'

'I wouldn't, not if I was to be shot twenty times over. I wouldn't shoot a pal. And Belcher wouldn't—isn't that right, Belcher?'

'That's right, chum,' Belcher said, but more by way of answering the question than of joining in the argument. Belcher sounded as though whatever unforeseen thing he'd always been waiting for had come at last.

'Anyway, who says Noble would be shot if I wasn't? What do you think I'd do if I was in his place, out in the middle of a blasted bog?'

'What would you do?' asked Donovan.

'I'd go with him wherever he was going, of course. Share my last bob with him and stick by him through thick and thin. No one can ever say of me that I let down a pal.'

'We've had enough of this,' said Jeremiah Donovan, cocking his revolver. 'Is there any message you want to send?'

'No, there isn't.'

'Do you want to say your prayers?'

Hawkins came out with a cold-blooded remark that even shocked me and turned on Noble again.

'Listen to me, Noble,' he said. 'You and me are chums. You can't come over to my side, so I'll come over to your side. That show you I mean what I say? Give me a rifle and I'll go along with you and the other lads.'

Noble answered him. We knew that was no way out.

'Hear what I'm saying?' he said. 'I'm through with it. I'm a deserter or anything else you like. I don't believe in your stuff, but it's no worse than mine. That satisfy you?'

Noble raised his head, but Donovan began to speak and he lowered it again without replying.

'For the last time, have you any messages to send?' said Donovan in a cold, excited sort of voice.

'Shut up, Donovan! You don't understand me, but these lads do. They're not the sort to make a pal and kill a pal. They're not the tools of any capitalist.'

I alone of the crowd saw Donovan raise his Webley to the back of Hawkins's neck, and as he did so I shut my eyes and tried to pray. Hawkins had begun to say something else when Donovan fired, and as I opened my eyes at the bang, I saw Hawkins stagger at the knees and lie out flat at Noble's feet, slowly and as quiet as a kid falling asleep, with the lantern-light on his lean legs and bright farmer's boots. We all stood very still, watching him settle out in the last agony.

Then Belcher took out a handkerchief and began to tie it about his own eyes (in our excitement we'd forgotten to do the same for Hawkins), and, seeing it wasn't big enough, turned and asked for the loan of mine. I gave it to him, and he knotted the two together and pointed with his foot at Hawkins.

'He's not quite dead,' he said. 'Better give him another.'

Sure enough, Hawkins's left knee was beginning to rise. I bent down and put my gun to his head; then recollecting myself, I got up again. Belcher understood what was in my mind.

'Give him his first,' he said. 'I don't mind. Poor bastard, we don't know what's happening to him now.'

I knelt and fired. By this time I didn't seem to know what I was doing. Belcher, who was fumbling a bit awkwardly with the handkerchiefs, came out with a laugh as he heard the shot. It was the first time I had heard him laugh and it sent a shudder down my back; it sounded so unnatural.

'Poor bugger!' he said quietly. 'And last night he was so curious about it all. It's very queer, chums, I always think. Now he knows as much about it as they'll ever let him know, and last night he was all in the dark.'

Donovan helped him to tie the handkerchiefs about his eyes. 'Thanks, chum,' he said. Donovan asked if there were any messages he wanted sent.

'No, chum,' he said. 'Not for me. If any of you would like to write to Hawkins's mother, you'll find a letter from her in his pocket. He and his mother were great chums. But my missus left me eight years ago. Went away with another fellow and took the kid with her. I like the feeling of a home, as you may have noticed, but I couldn't start another again after that.'

It was an extraordinary thing, but in those few minutes Belcher said more than in all the weeks before. It was just as if the sound of the shot had started a flood of talk in him and he could go on the whole night like that, quite happily, talking about himself. We stood around like fools now that he couldn't see us any longer. Donovan looked at Noble, and Noble shook his head. Then Donovan raised his Webley, and at that moment Belcher gave his queer laugh again. He may have thought we were talking about him, or perhaps he noticed the same thing I'd noticed and couldn't understand it.

'Excuse me, chums,' he said. 'I feel I'm talking the hell of a lot, and so silly, about my being so handy about a house and things like that. But this thing came on me suddenly. You'll forgive me, I'm sure.'

'You don't want to say a prayer?' asked Donovan.

'No, chum,' he said. 'I don't think it would help. I'm ready, and you boys want to get it over.'

'You understand that we're only doing our duty?' said Donovan.

Belcher's head was raised like a blind man's, so that you could only see his chin and the top of his nose in the lantern-light.

'I never could make out what duty was myself,' he said. 'I think you're all good lads, if that's what you mean. I'm not complaining.'

Noble, just as if he couldn't bear any more of it, raised his fist at Donovan, and in a flash Donovan raised his gun and fired. The big man went over like a sack of meal, and this time there was no need for a second shot.

I don't remember much about the burying, but that it was worse than all the rest because we had to carry them to the grave. It was all mad lonely with nothing but a patch of lantern-light between ourselves and the dark, and birds hooting and screeching all round, disturbed by the guns. Noble went through Hawkins's belongings to find the letter from his mother, and then joined his hands together. He did the same with Belcher. Then, when we'd filled in the grave, we separated from Jeremiah Donovan and Feeney and took our tools back to the shed. All the way we didn't speak a word. The kitchen was dark and cold as we'd left it, and the old woman was sitting over the hearth, saying her beads. We walked past her into the room, and Noble struck a match to light the lamp. She rose quietly and came to the doorway with all her cantankerousness gone.

'What did ye do with them?' she asked in a whisper, and Noble started so that the match went out in his hand.

'What's that?' he asked without turning round.

'I heard ye,' she said.

'What did you hear?' asked Noble.

'I heard ye. Do you think I didn't hear ye, putting the spade back in the houseen?'

Noble struck another match and this time the lamp lit for him.

'Was that what ye did to them?' she asked.

Then, by God, in the very doorway, she fell on her knees and began praying, and after looking at her for a minute or two Noble did the same by the fireplace. I pushed my way out past her and left them at it. I stood at the door, watching the stars and listening to the shrieking of the birds dying out over the bogs. It is so strange what you feel at times like that you can't describe it. Noble says he saw everything ten times the size, as thought there were nothing in the whole world but that little patch of bog with the two Englishmen stiffening into it, but with me it was as if the patch of bog where the Englishmen were was a million miles away, and even Noble and the old woman, mumbling behind me, and the birds and the bloody stars were all far away, and I was somehow very small and very lost and lonely like a child astray in the snow. And anything that happened to me afterwards, I never felt the same about again.

The Majesty of the Law

Old Dan Bride was breaking brosna for the fire when he heard a step on the path. He paused, a bundle of saplings on his knee.

Dan had looked after his mother while the life was in her, and after her death no other woman had crossed his threshold. Signs on it, his house had that look. Almost everything in it he had made with his own hands in his own way. The seats of the chairs were only slices of log, rough and round and thick as the saw had left them, and with the rings still plainly visible through the grime and polish that coarse trouser-bottoms had in the course of long years imparted. Into these Dan had rammed stout knotted ash-boughs that served alike for legs and back. The deal table, bought in a shop, was an inheritance from his mother and a great pride and joy to him though it rocked whenever he touched it. On the wall, unglazed and fly-spotted, hung in mysterious isolation a Marcus Stone print, and beside the door was a calendar with a picture of a racehorse. Over the door hung a gun, old but good, and in excellent condition, and before the fire was stretched an old setter who raised his head expectantly whenever Dan rose or even stirred.

He raised it now as the steps came nearer and when Dan, laying down the bundle of saplings, cleaned his hands thoughtfully on the seat of his trousers, he gave a loud bark, but this expressed no more than a desire to show off his own watchfulness. He was half human and knew people thought he was old and past his prime.

A man's shadow fell across the oblong of dusty light thrown over the half-door before Dan looked round.

'Are you alone, Dan?' asked an apologetic voice.

'Oh, come in, come in, sergeant, come in and welcome,' exclaimed the old man, hurrying on rather uncertain feet to the door which the tall policeman opened and pushed in. He stood there, half in sunlight, half in shadow, and seeing him so, you would have realized how dark the interior of the house really was.

One side of his red face was turned so as to catch the light, and behind it an ash tree raised its boughs of airy green against the sky. Green fields, broken here and there by clumps of red-brown rock, flowed downhill, and beyond them, stretched all across the horizon, was the sea, flooded and almost transparent with light. The sergeant's face was fat and fresh, the old man's face, emerging from the twilight of the kitchen, had the colour of wind and sun, while the features had been so shaped by the struggle with time and the elements that they might as easily have been found impressed upon the surface of a rock.

'Begor, Dan,' said the sergeant, ' 'tis younger you're getting.'

'Middling I am, sergeant, middling,' agreed the old man in a voice which seemed to accept the remark as a compliment of which politeness would not allow him to take too much advantage. 'No complaints.'

'Begor, 'tis as well because no one would believe them. And the old dog doesn't look a day older.'

The dog gave a low growl as though to show the sergeant that he could remember this unmannerly reference to his age, but indeed he growled every time he was mentioned, under the impression that people had nothing but ill to say of him.

'And how's yourself, sergeant?'

'Well, now, like the most of us, Dan, neither too good nor too bad. We have our own little worries, but, thanks be to God, we have our compensations.'

'And the wife and family?'

'Good, praise be to God, good. They were away from me for a month, the lot of them, at the mother-in-law's place in Clare.'

'In Clare, do you tell me?'

'In Clare. I had a fine quiet time.'

The old man looked about him and then retired to the bedroom, from which he returned a moment later with an old shirt. With this he solemnly wiped the seat and back of the log-chair nearest the fire.

'Sit down now, sergeant. You must be tired after the journey. 'Tis a long old road. How did you come?'

'Teigue Leary gave me the lift. Wisha now, Dan, don't be putting yourself out. I won't be stopping. I promised them I'd be back inside an hour.'

'What hurry is on you?' asked Dan. 'Look, your foot was only on the path when I made up the fire.'

'Arrah, Dan, you're not making tea for me?'

'I am not making it for you, indeed; I'm making it for myself, and I'll take it very bad of you if you won't have a cup.'

'Dan, Dan, that I mightn't stir, but 'tisn't an hour since I had it at the barracks!'

'Ah, whisht, now, whisht! Whisht, will you! I have something here to give you an appetite.'

The old man swung the heavy kettle on to the chain over the open fire, and the dog sat up, shaking his ears with an expression of deepest interest. The policeman unbuttoned his tunic, opened his belt, took a pipe and a plug of tobacco from his breast pocket, and, crossing his legs in an easy posture, began to cut the tobacco slowly and carefully with his pocket knife. The old man went to the dresser and took down two handsomely decorated cups, the only cups he had, which, though chipped and handleless, were used at all only on very rare occasions, for himself he preferred his tea from a basin. Happening to glance into them, he noticed that they bore signs of disuse and had collected a lot of the fine white dust-turf that always circulated in the little smoky cottage. Again he thought of the shirt, and, rolling up his sleeves with a stately gesture, he wiped them inside and out till they shone. Then he bent and opened the cupboard. Inside was a quart bottle of pale liquid, obviously untouched. He removed the cork and smelt the contents, pausing for a moment in the act as though to recollect where exactly he had noticed that particular smoky smell before. Then, reassured, he stood up and poured out with a liberal hand.

'Try that now, sergeant,' he said with quiet pride.

The sergeant, concealing whatever qualms he might have felt at the idea of drinking illegal whiskey, looked carefully into the cup, sniffed, and glanced up at old Dan.

'It looks good,' he commented.

'It should be good,' replied Dan with no mock modesty.

'It tastes good too,' said the sergeant.

'Ah, sha,' said Dan, not wishing to praise his own hospitality in his own house, ' 'tis of no great excellence.'

'You'd be a good judge, I'd say,' said the sergeant without irony.

'Ever since things became what they are,' said Dan, carefully guarding himself against a too-direct reference to the peculiarities of the law administered by his guest, 'liquor isn't what it used to be.'

'I've heard that remark made before now, Dan,' said the sergeant thoughtfully. 'I've heard it said by men of wide experience that it used to be better in the old days.'

'Liquor,' said the old man, 'is a thing that takes time. There was never a good job done in a hurry.'

' 'Tis an art in itself.'

'Just so.'

'And an art takes time.'

'And knowledge,' added Dan with emphasis. 'Every art has its secrets, and the secrets of distilling are being lost the way the old songs were lost. When I was a boy there wasn't a man in the barony but had a hundred songs in his head, but with people running here, there, and everywhere, the songs were lost ... Ever since things became what they are,' he repeated on the same guarded note, 'there's so much running about the secrets are lost.'

'There must have been a power of them.'

'There was. Ask any man today that makes whiskey do he know how to make it out of heather.'

'And was it made of heather?' asked the policeman.

'It was.'

'You never drank it yourself?'

'I didn't, but I knew old men that did, and they told me that no whiskey that's made nowadays could compare with it.'

'Musha, Dan, I think sometimes 'twas a great mistake of the law to set its hand against it.'

Dan shook his head. His eyes answered for him, but it was not in nature for a man to criticize the occupation of a guest in his own home.

'Maybe so, maybe not,' he said non-committally.

'But sure, what else have the poor people?'

'Them that makes the laws have their own good reasons.'

'All the same, Dan, all the same, 'tis a hard law.'

The sergeant would not be outdone in generosity. Politeness required him not to yield to the old man's defence of his superiors and their mysterious ways.

'It is the secrets I'd be sorry for,' said Dan, summing up. 'Men die and men are born, and where one man drained another will plough, but a secret lost is lost forever.'

'True,' said the sergeant mournfully. 'Lost forever.'

Dan took his cup, rinsed it in a bucket of clear water by the door and cleaned it again with the shirt. Then he placed it carefully at the sergeant's elbow. From the dresser he took a jug of milk and a blue bag containing sugar; this he followed up with a slab of country butter and—a sure sign that he had been expecting a visitor—a round cake of home-made bread, fresh and uncut. The kettle sang and spat and the dog, shaking his ears, barked at it angrily.

'Go away, you brute!' growled Dan, kicking him out of his way.

He made the tea and filled the two cups. The sergeant cut himself a large slice of bread and buttered it thickly.

'It is just like medicines,' said the old man, resuming his theme with the imperturbability of age. 'Every secret there was is lost. And leave no one tell me that a doctor is as good a man as one that had the secrets of old times.'

'How could he be?' asked the sergeant with his mouth full.

'The proof of that was seen when there were doctors and wise people there together.'

'It wasn't to the doctors the people went, I'll engage?'

'It was not. And why?' With a sweeping gesture the old man took in the whole world outside his cabin. 'Out there on the hillsides is the sure cure for every disease. Because it is written'—he tapped the table with his thumb—'it is written by the poets "wherever you find the disease you will find the cure". But people walk up the hills and down the hills and all they see is flowers. Flowers! As if God Almighty—honour and praise to Him!—had nothing better to do with His time than be to making old flowers!'

'Things no doctor could cure the wise people cured,' agreed the sergeant.

'Ah, musha, 'tis I know it,' said Dan bitterly. 'I know it, not in my mind but in my own four bones.'

'Have you the rheumatics at you still?' the sergeant asked in a shocked tone.

'I have. Ah, if you were alive, Kitty O'Hara, or you, Nora Malley of the Glen, 'tisn't I'd be dreading the mountain wind or the sea wind; 'tisn't I'd be creeping down with my misfortunate red ticket for the blue and pink and yellow dribble-drabble of their ignorant dispensary.'

'Why then indeed,' said the sergeant, 'I'll get you a bottle for that.'

'Ah, there's no bottle ever made will cure it.'

'That's where you're wrong, Dan. Don't talk now till you try it. It cured my own uncle when he was that bad he was shouting for the carpenter to cut the two legs off him with a handsaw.'

'I'd give fifty pounds to get rid of it,' said Dan magniloquently. 'I would and five hundred.'

The sergeant finished his tea in a gulp, blessed himself, and struck a match which he then allowed to go out as he answered some question of the old man. He did the same with a second and third, as though titillating his appetite with delay. Finally he succeeded in getting his pipe alight and the two men pulled round their chairs, placed their toes side by side in the ashes, and in deep puffs, lively bursts of conversation, and long, long silences enjoyed their smoke.

'I hope I'm not keeping you?' said the sergeant, as though struck by the length of his visit.

'Ah, what would you keep me from?'

'Tell me if I am. The last thing I'd like to do is waste another man's time.'

'Begor, you wouldn't waste my time if you stopped all night.'

'I like a little chat myself,' confessed the policeman.

And again they became lost in conversation. The light grew thick and coloured and, wheeling about the kitchen before it disappeared, became tinged with gold; the kitchen itself sank into cool greyness with cold light on the cups and basins and plates of the dresser. From the ash tree a thrush began to sing. The open hearth gathered brightness till its light was a warm, even splash of crimson in the twilight.

Twilight was also descending outside when the sergeant rose to go. He fastened his belt and tunic and carefully brushed his clothes. Then he put on his cap, tilted a little to side and back.

'Well, that was a great talk,' he said.

' 'Tis a pleasure,' said Dan, 'a real pleasure.'

'And I won't forget the bottle for you.'

'Heavy handling from God to you!'

'Good-bye now, Dan.'

'Good-bye, sergeant, and good luck.'

Dan didn't offer to accompany the sergeant beyond the door. He sat in his old place by the fire, took out his pipe once more, blew through it thoughtfully, and just as he leaned forward for a twig to kindle it, heard the steps returning. It was the sergeant. He put his head a little way over the half-door.

'Oh, Dan!' he called softly.

'Ay, sergeant?' replied Dan, looking round, but with one hand still reaching for the twig. He couldn't see the sergeant's face, only hear his voice.

'I suppose you're not thinking of paying that little fine, Dan?'

There was a brief silence. Dan pulled out the lighted twig, rose slowly, and shambled towards the door, stuffing it down in the almost empty bowl of the pipe. He leaned over the half-door while the sergeant with hands in the pockets of his trousers gazed rather in the direction of the laneway, yet taking in a considerable portion of the sea line.

'The way it is with me, sergeant,' replied Dan unemotionally, 'I am not.'

'I was thinking that, Dan; I was thinking you wouldn't.'

There was a long silence during which the voice of the thrush grew shriller and merrier. The sunken sun lit up rafts of purple cloud moored high above the wind.

'In a way,' said the sergeant, 'that was what brought me.'

'I was just thinking so, sergeant, it only struck me and you going out the door.'

'If 'twas only the money, Dan, I'm sure there's many would be glad to oblige you.'

'I know that, sergeant. No, 'tisn't the money so much as giving that fellow the satisfaction of paying. Because he angered me, sergeant.'

The sergeant made no comment on this and another long silence ensued.

'They gave me the warrant,' the sergeant said at last, in a tone which dissociated him from all connection with such an un-neighbourly document.

'Did they so?' exclaimed Dan, as if he was shocked by the thoughtlessness of the authorities.

'So whenever 'twould be convenient for you—'

'Well, now you mention it,' said Dan, by way of throwing out a suggestion for debate, 'I could go with you now.'

'Ah, sha, what do you want going at this hour for?' protested the sergeant with a wave of his hand, dismissing the notion as the tone required.

'Or I could go tomorrow,' added Dan, warming to the issue.

'Would it be suitable for you now?' asked the sergeant, scaling up his voice accordingly.

'But, as a matter of fact,' said the old man emphatically, 'the day that would be most convenient to me would be Friday after dinner, because I have some messages to do in town, and I wouldn't have the journey for nothing.'

'Friday will do grand,' said the sergeant with relief that this delicate matter was now practically disposed of. 'If it doesn't they can damn well wait. You could walk in there yourself when it suits you and tell them I sent you.'

'I'd rather have yourself there, sergeant, if it would be no inconvenience. As it is, I'd feel a bit shy.'

'Why then, you needn't feel shy at all. There's a man from my own parish there, a warder; one Whelan. Ask for him; I'll tell him you're coming, and I'll guarantee when he knows you're a friend of mine he'll make you as comfortable as if you were at home.'

'I'd like that fine,' Dan said with profound satisfaction. 'I'd like to be with friends, sergeant.'

'You will be, never fear. Good-bye again now, Dan. I'll have to hurry.'

'Wait now, wait till I see you to the road.'

Together the two men strolled down the laneway while Dan explained how it was that he, a respectable old man, had had the grave misfortune to open the head of another old man in such a way as to require his removal to hospital, and why it was that he couldn't give the old man in question the satisfaction of paying in cash for an injury brought about through the victim's own unmannerly method of argument.

'You see, sergeant,' Dan said, looking at another little cottage up the hill, 'the way it is, he's there now, and he's looking at us as sure as there's a glimmer of sight in his weak, wandering, watery eyes, and nothing would give him more gratification than for me to pay. But I'll punish him. I'll lie on bare boards for him. I'll suffer for him, sergeant, so that neither he nor any of his children after him will be able to raise their heads for the shame of it.'

On the following Friday he made ready his donkey and butt and set out. On his way he collected a number of neighbours who wished to bid him farewell. At the top of the hill he stopped to send them back. An old man, sitting in the sunlight, hastily made his way indoors, and a moment later the door of his cottage was quietly closed.

Having shaken all his friends by the hand, Dan lashed the old donkey, shouted: 'Hup there!' and set out alone along the road to prison.

Pastorale

God knows, no one would want to belittle a neighbouring farmer
and his family. The more so when there's been a chair for you at
their kitchen fire every night for a score or more years. But not to
put a tooth in it and to make due allowance for bitter tongues, the
Bennetts are known throughout the length and breadth of the
parish as notorious bloody land-grabbers. They've gobbled up
every small holding in the townland that went on the market for
years past. Even where it was a forced sale. A halt was put to their
gallop a while back when James—the old man—took to the bed.
Still by that time they had gathered together a few hundred acres of
the best land hereabouts. With a world of cattle and sheep to keep it
stocked up.

But if they are big farmers itself, they are bloody wee in their
ways. They may grant you the heat of the fire, but you'll not be left
long enough sitting idle to scorch the knees of your pants. From the
time you cross the threshold till you say goodnight, it's a constant
litany.

'There's turf wanted. Take the big creel. It'll save the double
journey.'

'Put another few sods on the fire, will you.'

'The heifer's roaring. Better go out to the byre and make sure
she's all right.'

'Bring in a couple of buckets of water.'

'The morrow's Sunday. The shoes could do with a lick of
polish.'

The rest of the time you're hunched up beside the bellows wheel
keeping the fire going, or shifting the kettle up and down on the
arm of the crane, or poking around with the tongs gathering up the
scattered embers.

So it's easy to tell there's something wrong when for once you're
let take your seat by the fire without being called to order. Susie,
the mother, is not around herself. Only the two young fellows.

'A brave class of a night, lads.'

A civil enough remark, you'd think. But for all the heed paid to it, you might have been talking to two dummies.

'Good growthy weather, wouldn't you say?'

Not a mute out of either of them.

'That sup of rain this morning'll do no harm.'

No reply.

The thick, ignorant whelps. Sitting there crouched over the fire. Without a word to throw to a dog.

'Is your father improving any?'

John, the elder buck, turns his head, a stupid look on his face.

'Hey?' says he.

'What form is the old fellow in the day?'

'The Boss-man is it?' says he. 'He got a bad turn around tea-time. Didn't he, Martin?'

'Aye.'

Not very forthcoming, you'd be at liberty to say.

'He's had the priest and the doctor. He's in a poor way. Isn't he, Martin?'

'Aye.'

'His breathing's a class of choked. It's a fret to listen to it.'

No word of a lie in that statement. You could hear the wheezing through the closed door of the bedroom upstairs.

'He'll not last the night. Isn't that what the doctor said, Martin?'

The young chap gives him a look that would sour your stomach.

'Damned well you know what the doctor said. Weren't you there at the time?'

'I was only asking a civil question.'

'Weren't you right beside me when I was talking to the doctor?'

'I was only asking—'

'You ask too many bucking questions, if you ask me. And you know the answers to them all before you start.'

And Martin into him with the castigating and the casting up. Allowing for John being a class of an idiot and Martin himself maybe having enough on his plate, it's still a bit bloody thick. There's a time and a place for everything. It's a disgrace to be chawing the fat with your poor father dying above in the room.

'You blabber too much,' says Martin.

'Only for you're a big-mouthed slob,' says he, 'there'd have been no need for either priest or doctor.'

'How do you mean?'

'What need was there to tell the Boss about the malicious antics of the neighbours.'

'Malicious antics?'

'Aye. Leaking out to him that Gormley is running up an extension to the haggard. You must have known that would put him frothing at the mouth.'

In the name of God, what's this? The river field again. For years past, the source of contention and doggery. It is a scraggy strip of land that wouldn't graze a goat, but it meres on the Bennett property, blocking them off from watering their stock in the river. Old James has been trying these many years to buy it from the owner, Peter Gormley, a half-baked sheep-farmer who has as much regard for the Bennett family as he has for sheep-dip. The river field lies on the far side of the road from the Gormley farmstead, so he describes it as the 'Out Farm'. It is littered with rusting, second-hand farm machinery that Gormley trucks in as a side line. There is an old timber shed on it, used for storing what is described in the local paper as 'SPECIAL OFFERS, FOR ONE WEEK ONLY'. A man in his right mind wouldn't take a gift of the whole rickmatick—shed, machinery and land. But Gormley won't sell. At any price. Claims the shed has become a class of a bloody emporium. With farmers coming from all arts and parts to buy top-grade farm equipment. And Bennett grinding his teeth with rage every time he sees a harrow or a binder or a potato-digger towed into the river field. To say nothing but the truth, for the last while back the poor man can think of nothing else but 'Gormley's haggard'. No wonder, in his present state of health, he gets a bad turn when he hears your man is running up an addition to it.

'There's no use in you trying to make excuses,' Martin is still giving out the pay. 'You put your two big ignorant feet in it, as usual.'

'Aw jay, Martin, have a heart. You're always larding into me.'

'Haven't I every right to? The Lord knows what manner of misfortune you're after bringing about with your tattling tongue. There could be a poor enough way on us if the Boss doesn't pull out of this turn.'

Now what's all this about? You'd think to listen to him that they haven't a shilling to their name. Instead of being the wealthiest ranchers in the whole barony. Begod, some people don't know when they're well off.

John is digging the wax out of one ear, his forefinger working like the plunger of a churn.

'Och, things can't be as bad as that,' says he.

'We could well be walking the road,' says Martin, 'without a roof over our heads if the ould fellow hasn't put his affairs in order.'

'Hey?'

Finger still jammed in his ear, John gapes at the brother. Properly flummoxed. And no wonder. A statement the like of yon would put the hair standing on your head. Walking the roads, no less. The arse out of their breeches. And sleeping at the back of a ditch with the winds of the world for company. Fat chance of that happening to greedy corbies the like of the Bennetts. Unless—? Hold on now!

'Have you no savvy, man?' says Martin. 'Don't you know that if the Boss hasn't made a will, that bloody brother of ours will fall in for his share of the property? We'll be ruined paying him out his portion.'

'Francis, is it?' John is frowning at the wax on his fingernail. 'Sure he's abroad in Tasmania, the last we heard of him.'

'Wherever he is, it won't be long till he finds out that he can get something for nothing.'

Ho-ho! So that's it! Old James hasn't settled his affairs. Loth, like many another, to quit the jockey-seat. Well, it looks as if it's too late now. If the old fellow snuffs it, Francie can claim his share of the kitty—house, lands, stock and the nest egg that's surely in the Bank. You can hardly fault Martin for being worried. After all, when Francie was hunted out of the country twenty years ago, the Bennetts were small farmers like the rest of us. And now that they're wealthy ranchers, the black sheep of the family can levy a toll on all those years of sweat and skullduggery.

Martin is on his feet, prowling about the kitchen, every so often stopping at the foot of the stairs to cock an ear towards the room above.

'Bad enough,' says he, 'if we have to cripple ourselves for life paying him out his share, as long as he stays away from us. In Australia or Tasmania or wherever the hell he's supposed to be. But,' says he, with a look of horror on his face, the like of what you'd see on a Redemptorist when he's describing the fate of the damned, 'what will we do if he takes it into his hands to come home and squat here, drinking the piece out till he has us ruined and disgraced with his blackguardly behaviour?'

It's a queer thing about young bucks the like of Martin. They're all the time beefing off to other people. Laying down the law as though they are the only ones who know the answers. But if you listen closely, you find they are really talking to themselves. Especially if they are worried or excited. It would seem as if they build up such a head of steam that they must let it off. No matter who is listening. So here is Martin giving out the pay like a whore at a christening.

'That Francie fellow,' says he, 'was a proper affliction. No wonder the Boss gave him the run. If he had been let fly his kite for much longer, the whole bloody farm would have come under the hammer. He was nothing but a drunken bum.'

You could say a lot more than that about Francie without repeating yourself. He would drink the cross off an ass. For the price of a pint, he'd perform any manner of villainy, let it be grand larceny itself. And when he was drunk—which was every night of the week—he was a notorious ruffian. Singing and shouting, arguing the point, spilling drinks, breaking glasses, puking up his guts, before he wrecked the jakes. He would latch on to you at the bar counter. Never let up till he had you milked dry. Then you'd be lucky if he didn't mill you with a bottle for refusing to buy him a drink. A barbarous bloody savage, that's what he was. And yet he could get any woman he wanted. Whatever they saw in him.

'Sure you're maybe worrying your head about nothing,' says John. 'The Boss-man would never overlook a thing like making a will.'

'Well, you're wrong there. He has no will made. I'm positive of that.'

'Isn't it a wonder now you never tackled him about it long since?'

'Tackled him about it?' Martin, neck outstretched, hisses like an angry goose. 'Haven't I been harping at him since he took to the bed six months ago? But it's no use. He keeps on saying that he can't put his affairs in order till he has the river field got. He can think of nothing else but that bloody field. And the wretched haggard. He has himself convinced that Gormley put up yon ould shed just to annoy him. Between the pair of them, I'm bloody near demented.'

And God knows, the sight of him striding up and down, waving his arms and spitting out maledictions against the poor, dying father, would put you wondering. After all, the Bennetts were a queer bloody class of a connection. You would never know where you were with them. There was Uncle Dan, a godless heathen if ever there was one, always giving off about relics and statues and religion in general, who had a framed picture of the Sacred Heart, almost as big as himself, tied round his bare chest with a hay rope. And Rosie, the aunt, a withered up old maid, who used to go out to the dark fields every morning at daybreak and roll herself stark naked in the dew so as to keep her skin young. And the grandfather, who would wear you down with talk of temperance, the while he was lapping up the booze in the security of his bedroom until at the latter end, overcome by the horrors of drink, he would parade the village in the small hours of the morning clad in nothing but his shirt and pledgepin, a lighted candle in each hand and him roaring: 'Sprinkle me for fear of God!' Not to speak of the present company, for John was never considered to be more than a half-wit. If the truth be told, there was a want in the whole seed, breed, and generation of them.

'So help me, Jaysus, I'd be better off—' Martin is just getting properly into his stride when Susie comes out of the bedroom, the finger to her lips.

'Ssh!' says she. 'He's just dozed off.'

She's at the foot of the stairs before she says:

'Oh, *you're* here!'

There's barely time to mutter: 'Sorry to hear poor James was taken bad', before she starts giving off.

'My God!' says she. 'What's come over you? Sitting there with the fire dying out before your eyes. No! No! Gather up the embers first. Get a few sods of turf. Small dry ones. Put them at the back where they'll light quicker. Not that way! On their ends. Now give a spin to the bellows wheel. Take it easy! Don't you see you're scattering sparks?'

She's a professional cribber, the Susie one. Satisfied with nothing. If the old fellow above in the room were to croak, she would be grumbling about how inconsiderate it was of him to die and him knowing full well how expensive it would be, what with feeding the mourners and stuffing them with drink and cigarettes, and keeping fires going day and night in every room and folk trampling about everywhere, ruining the floors with their dirty boots; and the cost of a funeral with hearse, mourning-cars, and a coffin, more than likely of unseasoned timber that would buckle and warp before it's rightly underground; and what in God's holy name will a High Mass run to, with priests to no end loafing around inside the altar rails making no effort to earn their money; and grave diggers that get better paid than County Council workers for digging a bit of a hole in the ground and then filling it up again.

'How is he, Ma?' says John, who, dim-witted as he is, has still more savvy than to get up off his arse and help with the fire.

'I've seen him worse,' says she. 'He'll maybe pull out of it.' She draws up a chair to the fire and squats down straddle-legged, toasting her thighs.

'The doctor says he won't last till morning,' says Martin. And you would know by the whine in his voice what class of a worry is on him.

'Och, I suppose if it's laid down,' says she, 'it'll come to pass.'

She starts swaying back and forth, massaging her legs with the flat of her hands. Says she:

'Father Bourke was talking to me after he gave your poor father the last rites. "Don't worry, Mrs Bennett," says he. "I never saw a man better prepared for death. Completely resigned," says he. "It was a most edifying sight. There is no doubt in my mind," says he, "that God will forgive him his trespasses as James himself," says he, "has forgiven those of his neighbours." And what's more—'

Before she can say any more, Martin reins her back on her haunches.

'What about Gormley?' says he.

'Gormley?' says she.

'Aye. If there's trespasses to be forgiven, wouldn't it be as well, before it's too late, for himself and the Boss to make the peace?'

Could you beat that for sheer effrontery? Proposing a death-bed reconciliation so that he can lay hands on the loot. He has the neck of a giraffe, that young fellow.

Susie gapes at him, goggle-eyed.

'Are you gone out of your mind?' says she. 'Allow that ruffian into the house to rant and rave at your poor father's bedside? Dragging up old scandals that are best forgotten? Sure there's no sense to the man. Nothing will convince him but that our Francie was responsible for—'

'Ma!' says Martin. You'd think he's checking a dog that's after lifting a leg against the dresser.

And no wonder. Susie's chapfallen expression tells its own story. She has let the cat out of the bag. A disreputable tomcat by the name of Francie. Very liable to commit scandal when on the prowl. And in this parish, scandal means only the one thing—poling a woman. So very likely that's why Francie decamped. And wait now! A short while after the flitting didn't Gormley's daughter, Helen, get herself, what her father described as 'a grand job' in England? A notorious kittling-ground for colleens in disgrace. Bejeezus, that's it! She sneaked off to that immoral country to have her ba. And . . . Hold on! Hold on! Hold on! Wasn't that the same year that Robert, Helen's brother, left the Seminary in his last term. Just before he was due for ordination. They were bloody strict in those days. One rattle from the closet where your family skeleton was stored and you were out the window. Nothing for it but creep home in the guise of a spoiled priest, giving out at all and sundry that you had the misfortune to lose your vocation. After all, if it became known that you were turfed out of the College because your sister was a manifest trollop, your family could never hold their heads up in the village again.

So Robert is shipped off to the States where if he opens his mouth too wide over a few pints, it'll not give rise to local gossip. And everybody sympathises with his poor father in his sad bereavement, for spoiled priests are a rare enough commodity in this part of the country.

Can you beat it? Over all these years Mister Slippy-tit has been codding the natives with his bragging and boasting that no one can point the finger of scorn at one of the Gormleys. But the cost of keeping his halo intact has been high. There he is, clocking in a big barn of a house, with nothing but the walls for company. Small blame to him if he hates the guts of the Bennett family and holds them to ransom for a patch of ground and a rickety shed.

Susie has recovered herself and is holding forth once more as though nothing has happened.

'He was a good man, your father,' says she. 'None better. In the front seat at Mass every Sunday. Year in, year out. Always attended to his Easter duty. Headed the list in every church collection. Father Burke claims there wasn't a pick of malice in his bones. It's a great comfort to hear the like of that from a priest.'

Over by the fireplace, John wags his poll in agreement.

'Aye, indeed,' say she. 'A great comfort.'

Martin is gritting his teeth like he's chewing granite. But before he can get a word in edgeways, the uproar breaks out in the room above. It is a cross between a howl and a moan. The sort of a bellow a person lets out of him when he is struggling out of a nightmare.

Susie throws up her hands in holy horror.

'Mother of God!' she says. 'He's done for!'

There's a rush for the stairs with everyone stumbling and tripping over each other and muttering pious ejaculations and getting wedged in the bedroom door.

Now you'll always discover in upstarts the like of the Bennetts that no matter how much land or coin they muster together, never can they shake off the mean streak that was their driving force from the beginning. Stingy they were reared and they'll give up the ghost in the same condition. Still you'd think they'd throw a strip of lino on the bare boards of a sick room or have something better than an army blanket on the bed, or stretch a curtain itself across the window.

The old fellow is propped up on the pillow, hands clawing at the blanket, eyes squeezed shut. His jaw is hanging and there's a shocking wheeze to his breathing. You can see by the look of him he's a done duck. So it's down on your knees and into the prayers for the dying, with Susie reading out the litany at the rate of no man's business from a battered old prayer-book. It's maybe as well the poor bugger perishing in the bed is panting too loud to hear the words, for it would be cold comfort to him to hear his wife rattling off the blood and thunder invocations, with their talk of damnation and eternal night, punishment with darkness, chastisement with flames, and condemnation to torments. She is going full blast when his breathing eases a little and he opens his eyes. As he glowers at her, she keeps babbling on, one eye on the book, the other on the bed.

'Deliver, O Lord,' she says, 'the soul of Thy servant from all danger of hell, from all pain and tribulation.'

'What's all this commotion about?' says he, in a hoarse whisper.

They scramble to their feet. Not a cheep out of one of them. Their hands hanging the one length with embarrassment.

'You'll not get shut of me before my time,' says he.

He's badly out in that statement, but a cranky little weasel he always was and you can hardly expect him to change at the latter end of his days.

Martin clears his throat and starts rummaging in the inner pocket of his jacket.

'What else could we do?' says he. 'And you getting another attack just after you were anointed.'

The old fellow is puffing through his pursed lips like a goods train labouring on a hill.

'There's men,' says he, 'got the last rites . . . years ago . . . and they're still . . . walking the roads.'

'What did the doctor tell you?' says he.

Martin pays no heed. He is studying the rumpled paper he has pulled from his pocket.

'What did the doctor say?' says the old fellow.

Martin looks up. Casual like.

'He said you're dying,' says he.

Christ, that's sinking the boot in to the uppers with a vengeance. Jeffreys, the hanging judge, could hardly have made a better job of passing sentence at the Bloody Assizes.

'My Jesus, mercy!' says Susie. And you wouldn't know whether it was pity or piety was moving her.

'Amen,' says John.

'Dying?' says the old fellow.

'Aye.' Martin spreads the paper out on the blanket and takes a pen from his pocket. 'Wouldn't this be a good time to settle your affairs?'

Well, you'd have to hand it to that young thick. He never takes his eye off the ball. Not till it's in the back of the net. He must have been carrying that paper around with him for months. Only waiting for the chance to get it signed. And what better time than when the party concerned is stretched on the bed with nothing between himself and the Day of Judgement but the last few gasps? What harm if it is your own old fellow? He's a Bennett like yourself and there'll be no hard feelings.

Old James is staring down at the paper spread out on the blanket. The breathing is coming hard on him again and there's a class of a whistle to it that you'd find in a horse with the heaves.

'The doctor,' says he, wheezing out the words. 'Was he . . . positive?'

'He was,' says Martin. 'He said 'tis beyond dispute.' He is crouched over the bed, tapping the paper with his pen.

'You sign your name down here,' says he.

The old fellow goes into a fit of coughing and spluttering. 'Beyond . . . dispute,' says he. 'That's . . . a good one.'

The next thing his head is back on the pillow, and he's quaking and quivering and jerking till the bed is clattering under him like a rattley-box. The eyes are squinting out of his head. He's slobbering at the mouth. His jaws are gaping open with the teeth showing to the roots. And there are queer clucking noises coming out of the back of his throat that you'd hear nowhere barring a fowl-house. To say nothing but the truth, the sight and sound of him would scare the living daylights out of you.

Susie is wringing her hands.

'He's done for this time,' says she. 'It's the last agony.'

'He's gone into convulsions,' says she.

'Convulsions, begor,' says John, the eyebrows up in his hair.

'Convulsions, me arse!' says Martin. 'He's making a mock of us all.'

And sure enough, the old fellow is cackling away to himself. Laughing his head off as though he hadn't a care in the world.

Martin is fit to be tied. There's a scowl on his face that would scare rats and he's muttering away under his breath. You can be full sure it's not the praying he's at, but laying maledictions on his silly old fool of a father for making a buck idiot of himself on his deathbed, when he'd be better employed regulating his testamentary obligations.

The old man has cackled himself to a standstill. He is stretched out on the bed, groaning and gasping, his chest going like a bellows. If the sweat pouring out of him is any indication, he is well and truly invoiced.

'Martin,' says he, and you'd hardly hear him, the voice is so weak. 'Come here, son.'

Martin is like a man that's after getting a glimpse of the Promised Land. You can see the glory of this vision shining out of his greedy little eyes. Land and cattle and coin to be had for the scribbling of a couple of words. He wastes no time moving in for the kill.

'Now,' says he, prodding the old man's fingers with the pen. 'Down here you sign.'

Not so much as a 'by your leave' or 'after you, MacNaughton'.

It's a case of disgorge the loot and away you go to Kingdom Come.

But James has no notion of signing wills or the like. He pushes the pen aside.

'Martin,' says he. 'What do you think yourself?

'Will I last till morning?' says he.

Martin is still stooped over the bed, trying to get the unwilling fingers to grasp the pen.

'Not a hope,' says he, without looking up.

The old fellow gathers himself together, lips working, eyebrows drawn down in concentration. You can see by the queer gleam in his eye that he has something important to say. Something that'll not let him die easy till he's got it off his chest. Perhaps he's worried about what'll happen to Susie after he's gone. Or it could be the question about where he wants to be buried. Or maybe 'tis some old debt that's still outstanding.

He levers himself up in the bed, knocking pen and paper flying.

'Listen, son,' says he. 'This would be the blessed night to burn down Gormley's haggard.'

MAIRTIN O CADHAIN · 1906–1970

The Hare-Lip

Translated from the Irish by Eoghan O Tuairisc

Nora Liam Bhid spent the night as she had spent the previous one making tea for the wedding party. But now the light of an early February morning, fogged and white, was seeping into the half-deserted parlour, and since she had cleared up after yesterday and was now free, again the strangeness of it came nagging at her. The strangeness of being married, the change, the outlandish Plain: that same flicker of unease astir in her ever since the night her father came home from the Galway Fair and began telling her mother in private that he had 'fixed up a strong farmer on the Plain for Nora'. And it had been no cure for that cut-off feeling to see the man himself and his sisters for the first time last week at the matchmaking. Like a female salmon locked in a choked up side-channel and destined never to reach the breeding beds in the clear shallows upriver, Nora had undertaken the marriage bond in the chapel of Ard late last evening. And now, finding no comfort in her mother's mild words, her father's boozy cajolery, her husband's bland imperturbability, or in the chatter of her female in-laws friendly and sly, she went down into the kitchen to the group of her old neighbours who had come from Ard with the wedding party.

The dancing-barn outside had been for some time deserted and the kitchen was now thronged with people who fell silent when she appeared. Wheezing beerladen breaths, trails of tobacco smoke, specks of sand from the concrete floor floating in a frostfog—all this made the silence a palpable thing confronting her, a phantom, to try and drag from her the words that would express the anguish of her being. It was that time of a wedding morning when a man might go about starting a row and find none to hinder him. The fire had gone out of the drunken voices, the laughter was lifeless. The young folk, it seemed to her, got up without much heart to dance the jig, afraid that the married couples and oldtimers might take advantage of the quiet that was beginning to close in about the house and say it was time to go. Even the young folk from Ard, hardened to revelling and constant labour, every one of them by now was bleary of voice, weary of foot. The only one in the house left with some flinty fire in his footwork and the flush of life in his cheek was Beairtlin, her father's servant-boy.

Nora dropped her head and let that flintspark penetrate her mind, that flush invade her being, till the silence and the unhomely thing receded. She remembered the many spells of innocent courting with him, snatching dulse from him in summer, or in the autumn the two of them on the flags of the dooryard cracking the nuts he had brought her from the hazelgrove of Liss, and nights of fireside chat together when the old couple were gone to bed and she was waiting up for Padraig her brother to come home from a visit. The girls of Ard, who were at the wedding tonight, had often given her a sly dig, suggesting Beairtlin for her. Tonight was the one night none of them would think of him for her, but it was the one night she wouldn't have minded. Beairtlin's witty remarks, that's what used take the bitter edge off her laughter whenever her father and mother were settling a match for her. A pain of regret, dulled not healed. That she had been so slow to speak her mind to him that day, so unwilling to find fault with Providence, when Beairtlin told her that 'the old fellow was making a match for her again, and no one would be given a wisp of consideration except a shopkeeper or a boss-man of the Plain'.

It wasn't because she had been vexed with Beairtlin for what he said that she passed remarks that day about his hare-lip. Instead, she had intended to say that she'd go off warm and willing with him there and then. For when all is said and done, it wasn't his slim and shapely person, his skygrey eye, his cheek red as foxglove, no, it was the hare-lip, that disfigurement he was marked with from the womb—he didn't even try to hide it with a moustache—that attracted her eyes and her passionate lips. It attracted and repelled her, often her disgust got the upper hand, too often, that's what left the web of her young life a heap of grey dust today. Even now it was the hare-lip she saw coming at her like a bloodsucking lamprey through a grey sea-lough. Beairtlin grumbled that 'the Plainers had taken over the house all night with their reel sets', but she couldn't attend to him till the pair of them were out on the middle of the floor dancing the plain set of home.

'So you're spancelled at last?' he said humorously, appearing to hide his vexation.

'God willing,' she answered. She realised fully for the first time what neither match, marriage, nor the wedding itself had given her clearly to understand.

'Have no regrets. You've made a good swap, lashings and leavings and being your own mistress here on the level Plain, in place of the rocks and the slave-labour—and not to mention the vigilant eye of your old fellow—out at Ardbeg. We'll send you an odd cargo of dulse, an odd bottle of poteen, and a bundle of nuts in the autumn.'

Nora's heart missed a beat. She had forgotten until now that there was no dulse, no nuts, no poteen here.

'I spent last night looking for you, Beairtlin, to sing *The Deer's Wood by Casla* for me, but there wasn't a sight of you in the crowd. You'll sing it after this dance. Do. I'm longing to hear it again . . .'

But Beairtlin had hardly cleared his throat for the song when her mother and her husband's sister came and carried her off again to the parlour.

'Time for us to be home,' said the mother. 'Look, it's broad daylight, and your husband Martin here without sleep since the night before last. You two are at home, God bless you, but look at the journey we have before us.'

'Eleven miles to Gaalwaay,' said Martin Ryan, the new husband. He had a slow congealed kind of a voice and the unhomely accent of the Plain. 'And fifteen miles farther west again, isn't that it? That's what he used to tell me, a labouring man I had here one year from Ard.'

Despite their talk of the long miles and the scurry there was for coats and shawls, Nora wouldn't admit that her family and friends were leaving her. She was made to realise it when the Ardbeg girls came kissing her and saying 'not to be homesick, they'd slip over an odd time on a visit'. She recognised every individual shout of the Ardbeg boys going wildly on their bikes back down the Galway road, and that left the Plainsfolk more alien than ever as they took leave of her in the misty morning light. And all with their 'Missus Ryan' so pat on the tongue causing her cold shivers of fears. The cars that had brought the Ardbeg people were humming out on the road, the drivers hooting the horns. As she had done so many times before at the end of a wedding Nora put on her overcoat and walked out to the road. Beairtlin was the last one to crush into the car that held her family.

'It's God's will, Beairtlin,' she said. 'Keep me a handful of dulse.'

Beairtlin had fixed the cape-ends of his raincoat across his mouth. Though her senses swam she caught the meaning in his words which came squeezed out through the hare-lip opening. 'Don't worry. And I'll bring you a bag of nuts too. In the autumn.'

'There's plenty of noots in the cregs hereabouts,' said her husband standing alongside her.

She stood unmoving at the gate, looking after the car until it had passed Crossroads rise, pretending not to have heard her mother's parting words, 'not to be homesick, she'd see them soon again'.

Homesick? That anchor, keeping the spirit though in exile fixed in its native harbour? No, she wasn't homesick. Tossed on a wave's crest at the caprice of God, having cut her life's cable, not a single link left with her natural element since Beairtlin went, she drove on straight ahead like a boat that has lost its bearings to the Crossways rise. She had never been nearer than Galway to this district and it had been dark during the wedding-drive last night, still it wasn't to view the country that she walked to the crest of this hill. Her only idea was to climb the first rise that came her way and get out of this smothering trough between the two waves of past and present. At that moment she couldn't tell whether Martin Ryan was to the left or right of her, she took no interest in the stem of his pipe circling the prominent points while he himself stabbed the queer uncouth names in the face of her illwill and detestation. She didn't notice Ryan leaving her and going back to the house.

The fog was being rolled and thinned out and dragged by a freshening wind in grey diminishing strips to the edge of the Plain. As far as her eye could see, nothing but immense flat fields, no stones, no rock-heaps, and every foot of fencing as straight as a fishing-line except where they were submerged in winter flooding. Here and there a stand of trees, a thicket, down below her a few outcrops of bedrock like knots in a deal table that had been bleached and scoured. The spot where she stood was the most airy hill of all the dull rich expanse. The houses were not strung together here, the nearest wavering thread of smoke seemed to her a mile away. All the houses alike. And the same set of trees sheltering the walls of the haggards. It appeared to her fancy that one immense house had split in the night and all its parts had separated as far as they might out of sheer unneighbourliness. She looked back at her husband's house. Not too unlike her father's house in make and appearance, two-storey, slated. But her father's house had looked newer, with a view of the sea, bare hills at the back of it, the house itself seeming a section of granite sliced out of the rock country to be set up as some tall symbolic stone in the middle of the group of thatched houses called Ardbeg. But there was a greater difference still. The two houses were as different as chalk from cheese. Like all the surrounding countryside her new house had a certain stupid arrogance, it reminded her of the smug smile of a shopkeeper examining his bankbook. Boasting to her face that it was no mushroom growth but a part of the everlasting. She knew it was a 'warm' house. She knew her father wouldn't have set her there if it wasn't, in view of her dowry and all the well-heeled upstarts he had refused on her behalf. She shivered to think that from now on she would be simply one of the conveniences among the conveniences of this house.

Here there was no barrier of mountain and sea to restrain a rambling foot or limit a wandering imagination. Nothing but the smooth monotonous Plain to absorb one's yearnings and privacies and weave them into the one drab undifferentiated fabric, as each individual drop, whatever its shade, whatever its nature before being engulfed in the womb of it, the ocean transmutes into its own grey phantom face. From now on whatever contact she'd have with home would be only a thin thread in this closeknit stuff.

There was a chilliness in the morning, not a genuine cold—rather like the friendliness of her sisters-in-law. She went in. She noticed there was nothing out of place within. After all the merrymaking the kitchen wasn't disordered enough to be called homely, not to say Irish. Their own kitchen at home had often been more of a shambles after a couple of hours dancing during a neighbourly visit. Apart from the two tables set end to end in the parlour, the attendants had set everything to rights before they went, and there wasn't the slightest thing crooked to mark that an event had taken place, that two lives had been spiritually and bodily woven together in the tie of intercourse under the one roof to ensure the spring of life in that house. The prime events of a man's destiny skimmed across the wide placid surface of this countryside as lightly as a finger-stone is flicked across water.

Sitting she looked about the kitchen, it was the first chance she had got of examining it since she came to the house. There were signs of careful housekeeping, nursing things to last long, on every single item from the saucepans cleaned and scoured to the two tall presses blond and mellow. A burial chamber, the image might have occurred, vessels and furniture set in it never to be moved until time should undo them; but, ignorant of the antiquities, what she did ask herself was how Ryan all on his own had kept the place so spick and span. This house needed no woman's hand. Strangest of all, neither hearth nor fire to be seen. Instead there was a metal range, dull and unwelcoming. The last spark had died somewhere within its womb.

'I wonder where's the turf?' she said to herself, getting up. In order to change this alien cold into a warm intimacy she must heap up a fire that would make the iron range red hot and prove to herself that a warm fire was more than a match for the rigid iron.

'I use nothing but coal,' he said. 'Wouldn't it be better not bother with a fire and take a lie-down on the bed?'

She took fright. Till now she hadn't thought of the bed. That drowsy voice, assured, self-assertive, set up waves of repulsion in her, yet she recognised it as the voice of authority, not to be denied if he felt like bringing the thing to a head.

'I'm not sleepy,' she said at last. But her husband had gone out for the coal. He soon returned and shot a shovelful of it into the maw of the range. His jabs with the poker at the embers got on Nora's nerves. Like a soul gripped by the demon on the edge of desire, the embers were quickly breaking apart and trying to flame. She'd give anything if her husband's father, mother, any of his prating sisters or even a silent one, were here at the hearth.

The smoke of Ryan's pipe was rising up to the loft in measured puffs, unruffled, unconcerned. The smoke of her father's pipe, or Beairtlin's, always made twists and angles as if they were wrestling with something in the air. There was none of the unfenced regions of her homeland in her husband's conversation, none of the wild oats of speech. Prosy and precise, he could hardly be otherwise, for his mind was a smooth plain without the slightest up or down from end to end . . . With his rare attempts at a joke, a smile crinkling the stiff crease of his nose, he reminded her of the god of wisdom trying to be merry a minute. The more she grew accustomed to the local accent the more alien she felt it. She longed for a new twist in the tune—a change of person, change of day, change of time, that it might be night again, or that his voice might be angry, anything but that gentle deadly drone that did nothing now but linger in her ears.

She got up and stood in the doorway in the fresh air. Plump hens just let out were already scrabbling in the flowerbeds on each side of the concrete path that led from the steps at the front gate. What scant flowers had already poked up through the earth had been trampled last night. There was Beairtlin's footprint—how could she mistake it, the many times it had caught her eye, on the bog, in the earth, on the seasand. She was examining the shape of the boot when a heavyfooted man with the soft hat of the region and a cord breeches passed on the road. Nora remembered he was some neighbour of her husband's, he had been given special treatment in the parlour last night. Without slowing his step and with only the slightest turn of his head her way he greeted her briefly. Sparing his words as if every syllable was worth another penny towards the rent. The fog had come down again in a drab shawl over the Plain with only odd slits of visibility. Still she wouldn't have gone back in so quickly if a filthy hen hadn't angered her by scratching away the footprint with a mindless claw from the soft impressionable earth . . .

She sat again in the same chair by the range. With the heat of the fire and the weariness her husband was asleep and snoring—a dull measured snore, peaceful and passionless. The gentle ripple of a languid sea on the shingle in a summer calm. She studied him for the first time as she might some insignificant item of her new life. Long limbs, angular shoulders. Centuries of sun and shower, soil and drudgery, had shaped and marked that robust body, the sinewy neck, the sallow features. A black head of hair edged with grey, sign of strength. Lids shut on those slow dull eyes in which she could imagine neither smile of pleasure nor flash of anger nor the soft haze of desire. Flaring nostrils that wouldn't be too squeamish of smells. A sootblack moustache—she had caught it out of the corner of her eye a few times previously and felt it needed badly to be cut. And now particularly, realising that those thick seal's bristles weren't hiding a hare-lip.

MICHAEL McLAVERTY · 1907–1992

The Poteen Maker

When he taught me some years ago he was an old man near his retirement, and when he would pass through the streets of the little town on his way from school you would hear the women talking about him as they stood at their doors knitting or nursing their babies: 'Poor man, he's done ... Killing himself ... Digging his own grave!' With my bag of books under my arm I could hear them, but I could never understand why they said he was digging his own grave, and when I would ask my mother she would scold me: 'Take your dinner, like a good boy, and don't be listening to the hard backbiters of this town. Your father has always a good word for Master Craig—so that should be enough for you!'

'But why do they say he's killing himself?'

'Why do who say? Didn't I tell you to take your dinner and not be repeating what the idle gossips of this town are saying? Listen to me, son! Master Craig is a decent, good-living man—a kindly man that would go out of his way to do you a good turn. If Master Craig was in any other town he'd have got a place in the new school at the Square instead of being stuck for ever in that wee poky bit of a school at the edge of the town!'

It was true that the school was small—a two-roomed ramshackle of a place that lay at the edge of the town beyond the last street lamp. We all loved it. Around it grew a few trees, their trunks hacked with boy's names and pierced with nibs and rusty drawing-pins. In summer when the windows were open we could hear the leaves rubbing together and in winter see the raindrops hanging on the bare twigs.

It was a draughty place and the master was always complaining of the cold, and even in the early autumn he would wear his overcoat in the classroom and rub his hands together: 'Boys, it's very cold today. Do you feel it cold?' And to please him we would answer: 'Yes, sir, 'tis very cold.' He would continue to rub his hands and he would look out at the old trees casting their leaves or at the broken spout that flung its tail of rain against the window. He always kept his hands clean and three times a day he would wash them in a basin and wipe them on a roller towel affixed to the inside of his press. He had a hanger for his coat and a brush to brush away the chalk that accumulated on the collar in the course of the day.

In the wet windy month of November three buckets were placed on the top of the desks to catch the drips that plopped here and there from the ceiling, and those drops made different music according to the direction of the wind. When the buckets were filled the master always called me to empty them, and I would take them one at a time and swirl them into the drain at the street and stand for a minute gazing down at the wet roofs of the town or listen to the rain pecking at the lunch-papers scattered about on the cinders.

'What's it like outside?' he always asked when I came in with the empty buckets.

'Sir, 'tis very bad.'

He would write sums on the board and tell me to keep an eye on the class and out to the porch he would go and stand in grim silence watching the rain nibbling at the puddles. Sometimes he would come in and I would see him sneak his hat from the press and disappear for five or ten minutes. We would fight then with rulers or paper-darts till our noise would disturb the mistress next door and in she would come and stand with her lips compressed, her fingers in her book. There was silence as she upbraided us: 'Mean, low, good-for-nothing corner boys. Wait'll Mister Craig comes back and I'll let him know the angels he has. And I'll give him special news about *you!*'—and she shakes her book at me: 'An altar boy on Sunday and a corner boy for the rest of the week!' We would let her barge away, the buckets plink-plonking as they filled up with rain and her own class beginning to hum, now that she was away from them.

When Mr Craig came back he would look at us and ask if we had disturbed Miss Lagan. Our silence or our tossed hair always gave him the answer. He would correct the sums on the board, flivell the pages of a book with his thumb, and listen to us reading; and occasionally he would glance out of the side window at the river that flowed through the town and, above it, the bedraggled row of houses whose tumbling yard-walls sheered to the water's edge. 'The loveliest county in Ireland is County Down!' he used to say, with a sweep of his arm to the river and the tin cans and the chalked walls of the houses.

During that December he was ill for two weeks and when he came back amongst us he was greatly failed. To keep out the draughts he nailed perforated plywood over the ventilators and stuffed blotting paper between the wide crevices at the jambs of the door. There were muddy marks of a ball on one of the windows and on one pane a long crack with fangs at the end of it: 'So someone has drawn the River Ganges while I was away,' he said; and whenever he came to the geography of India he would refer to the Ganges delta by pointing to the cracks on the pane.

When our ration of coal for the fire was used up he would send me into the town with a bucket, a coat over my head to keep off the rain, and the money in my fist to buy a stone of coal. He always gave me a penny to buy sweets for myself, and I can always remember that he kept his money in a waistcoat pocket. Back again I would come with the coal and he would give me disused exercise books to light the fire. 'Chief stoker!' he called me, and the name has stuck to me to this day.

It was at this time that the first snow had fallen, and someone by using empty potato bags had climbed over the glass-topped wall and stolen the school coal, and for some reason Mr Craig did not send me with the bucket to buy more. The floor was continually wet from our boots, and our breath frosted the windows. Whenever the door opened a cold draught would rush in and gulp down the breath-warmed air in the room. We would jig our feet and sit on our hands to warm them. Every half-hour Mr Craig would make us stand and while he lilted *O'Donnell Abu* we did a series of physical exercises which he had taught us, and in the excitement and the exaltation we forgot about our sponging boots and the snow that pelted against the windows. It was then that he did his lessons in Science; and we were delighted to see the bunsen burner attached to the gas bracket which hung like an inverted T from the middle of the ceiling. The snoring bunsen seemed to heat up the room and we all gathered round it, pressing in on top of it till he scattered us back to our places with the cane: 'Sit down!' he would shout. 'There's no call to stand. Everybody will be able to see!'

The cold spell remained, and over and over again he repeated one lesson in Science, which he called: *Evaporation and Condensation*.

'I'll show you how to purify the dirtiest of water,' he had told us. 'Even the filthiest water from the old river could be made fit for drinking purposes.' In a glass trough he had a dark brown liquid and when I got his back turned I dipped my finger in it and it tasted like treacle or burnt candy, and then I remembered about packets of brown sugar and tins of treacle I had seen in his press.

He placed some of the brown liquid in a glass retort and held it aloft to the class: 'In the retort I have water which I have discoloured and made impure. In a few minutes I'll produce from it the clearest of spring water.' And his weary eyes twinkled and although we could see nothing funny in that, we smiled because he smiled.

The glass retort was set up with the flaming bunsen underneath, and as the liquid was boiling, the steam was trapped in a long-necked flask on which I sponged cold water. With our eyes we followed the bubbling mixture and the steam turning into drops and dripping rapidly into the flask. The air was filled with a biscuity smell, and the only sound was the snore of the bunsen. Outside was the cold air and the falling snow. Presently the master turned out the gas and held up the flask containing the clear water.

'As pure as crystal!' he said, and we watched him pour some of it into a tumbler, hold it in his delicate fingers, and put it to his lips. With wonder we watched him drink it and then our eyes travelled to the dirty, cakey scum that had congealed on the glass sides of the retort. He pointed at this with his ruler: 'The impurities are sifted out and the purest of pure water remains.' And for some reason he gave his roguish smile. He filled up the retort again with the dirty brown liquid and repeated the experiment until he had a large bottle filled with the purest of pure water.

The following day it was still snowing and very cold. The master filled up the retort with the clear liquid which he had stored in the bottle: 'I'll boil this again to show you that there are no impurities left.' So once again we watched the water bubbling, turning to steam, and then to shining drops. Mr Craig filled up his tumbler: 'As pure as crystal,' he said, and then the door opened and in walked the Inspector. He was muffled to the ears and snow covered his hat and his attaché case. We all stared at him—he was the old, kind man we had seen before. He glanced at the bare firegrate and at the closed windows with their sashes edged with snow. The water continued to bubble in the retort, giving out its pleasant smell.

The Inspector shook hands with Mr Craig and they talked and smiled together, the Inspector now and again looking towards the empty grate and shaking his head. He unrolled his scarf and flicked the snow from off his shoulders and from his attaché case. He sniffed the air, rubbed his frozen hands together, and took a black notebook from his case. The snow ploofed against the windows, the wind hummed under the door.

'Now, boys,' Mr Craig continued, holding up the tumbler of water from which a thread of steam wriggled in the air. He talked to us in a strange voice and told us about the experiment as if we were seeing it for the first time. Then the Inspector took the warm tumbler and questioned us on our lesson. 'It should be perfectly sure water,' he said, and he sipped at it. He tasted its flavour. He sipped at it again. He turned to Mr Craig. They whispered together, the Inspector looking towards the retort which was still bubbling and sending out its twirls of steam to be condensed to water of purest crystal. He laughed loudly, and we smiled when he again put the tumbler to his lips and this time drank it all. Then he asked us more questions and told us how, if we were shipwrecked, we could make pure water from the salt sea water.

Mr Craig turned off the bunsen and the Inspector spoke to him. The master filled up the Inspector's tumbler and poured out some for himself in a cup. Then the Inspector made jokes with us, listened to us singing, and told us we were the best class in Ireland. Then he gave us a few sums to do in our books. He put his hands in his pockets and jingled his money, rubbed a little peep-hole in the breath-covered window, and peered out at the loveliest sight in Ireland. He spoke to Mr Craig again and Mr Craig shook hands with him and they both laughed. The Inspector looked at his watch. Our class was let out early, and while I remained behind to tidy up the Science apparatus the master gave me an empty treacle tin to throw in the bin and told me to carry the Inspector's case up to the station. I remember that day well as I walked behind them through the snow, carrying the attaché case, and how loudly they talked and laughed as the snow whirled cold from the river. I remember how they crouched together to light their cigarettes, how match after match was thrown on the road, and how they walked off with the unlighted cigarettes still in their mouths. At the station Mr Craig took a penny from his waistcoat pocket and as he handed it to me it dropped on the snow. I lifted it and he told me I was the best boy in Ireland . . .

When I was coming from his funeral last week—God have mercy on him—I recalled that wintry day and the feel of the cold penny and how much more I know now about Mr Craig than I did then. On my way out of the town—I don't live there now—I passed the school and saw a patch of new slates on the roof and an ugly iron barrier near the door to keep the home-going children from rushing headlong on to the road. I knew if I had looked at the trees I'd have seen rusty drawing-pins stuck into their rough flesh. But I passed by. I heard there was a young teacher in the school now, with an array of coloured pencils in his breast pocket.

The Ring

I should like you to have known my grandmother. She was my mother's mother, and as I remember her she was a widow with a warm farm in the Kickham country in Tipperary. Her land was on the southern slope of a hill, and there it drank in the sun which, to me, seemed always to be balanced on the teeth of the Galtees. Each year I spent the greater part of my summer holidays at my grandmother's place. It was a great change for me to leave our home in a bitter sea-coast village in Kerry and visit my grandmother's. Why, man, the grass gone to waste on a hundred yards of the roadside in Tipperary was as much as you'd find in a dozen of our sea-poisoned fields. I always thought it a pity to see all that fine grass go to waste by the verge of the road. I think so still.

Although my Uncle Con was married, my grandmother held the whip hand in the farm. At the particular time I am trying to recall, the first child was in the cradle. (Ah, how time has galloped away! That child is now a nun in a convent on the Seychelles Islands.) My Uncle Con's wife, my Aunt Annie, was a gentle, delicate girl who was only charmed in herself to have somebody to assume the responsibility of the place. Which was just as well indeed, considering the nature of woman my grandmother was. Since that time when her husband's horse had walked into the farmyard unguided, with my grandfather, Martin Dermody, dead in the body of the car, her heart had turned to stone in her breast. Small wonder to that turning, since she was left with six young children—five girls and one boy, my Uncle Con. But she faced the world bravely and did well by them all. Ah! but she was hard, main hard.

Once at a race-meeting I picked up a jockey's crop. When I balanced it on my palm it reminded me of my grandmother. Once I had a twenty-two pound salmon laced to sixteen feet of Castleconnell greenheart; the rod reminded me of my grandmother. True, like crop and rod, she had an element of flexibility, but like them there was no trace of fragility. Now after all these years I cannot recall her person clearly; to me she is but something tall and dark and austere. But lately I see her character with a greater clarity. Now I understand things that puzzled me when I was a boy. Towards me she displayed a certain black affection. Oh, but I made her laugh warmly once. That was when I told her of the man who had stopped me on the road beyond the limekiln and asked me if I were a grandson of Martin Dermody. Inflating with a shy pride, I had told him that I was. He then gave me a shilling and said, 'Maybe you're called Martin after your grandfather?' 'No,' I said, 'I'm called Con after my Uncle Con.' It was then my grandmother had laughed a little warmly. But my Uncle Con caught me under the armpits, tousled my hair and said I was a clever Kerry rascal.

The solitary occasion on which I remember her to have shown emotion was remarkable. Maybe remarkable isn't the proper word; obscene would be closer to the mark. Obscene I would have thought of it then, had I known the meaning of the word. Today I think it merely pathetic.

How was it that it all started? Yes, there was I with my bare legs trailing from the heel of a loaded hay-float. I was watching the broad silver parallels we were leaving in the clean after-grass. My Uncle Con was standing in the front of the float guiding the mare. Drawing in the hay to the hayshed we were. Already we had a pillar and a half of the hayshed filled. My grandmother was up on the hay, forking the lighter trusses. The servant-boy was handling the heavier forkfuls. A neighbour was throwing it up to them.

When the float stopped at the hayshed I noticed that something was amiss. For one thing the man on the hay was idle, as indeed was the man on the ground. My grandmother was on the ground, looking at the hay with cold calculating eyes. She turned to my Uncle Con.

'Draw in no more hay, Con,' she said. 'I've lost my wedding ring.'

'Where? In the hay?' he queried.

'Yes, in the hay.'

'But I thought you had a keeper?'

'I've lost the keeper, too. My hands are getting thin.'

'The story could be worse,' he commented.

My grandmother did not reply for a little while. She was eyeing the stack with enmity.

' 'Tis in that half-pillar,' she said at last. 'I must look for it.'

'You've a job before you, mother,' said Uncle Con.

She spoke to the servant-boy and the neighbour. 'Go down and shake out those couple of pikes at the end of the Bog Meadow,' she ordered. 'They're heating in the centre.'

'Can't we be drawing in to the idle pillar, mother?' my Uncle Con asked gently.

'No, Con,' she answered. 'I'll be putting the hay from the middle pillar there.'

The drawing-in was over for the day. That was about four o'clock in the afternoon. Before she tackled the half-pillar my grandmother went down on her hands and knees and started to search the loose hay in the idle pillar. She searched wisp by wisp, even sop by sop. My Uncle Con beckoned to me to come away. Anyway, we knew she'd stop at six o'clock. 'Six to six' was her motto for working hours. She never broke that rule.

That was a Monday evening. On Tuesday we offered to help— my Uncle Con and I. She was down on her knees when we asked her. 'No, no,' she said abruptly. Then, by way of explanation, when she saw that we were crestfallen: 'You see, if we didn't find it I'd be worried that ye didn't search as carefully as ye should, and I'd have no peace of mind until I had searched it all over again.' So she worked hard all day, breaking off only for her meals and stopping sharp at six o'clock.

By Wednesday evening she had made a fair gap in the hay but had found no ring. Now and again during the day we used to go down to see if she had had any success. She was very wan in the face when she stopped in the evening.

On Thursday morning her face was still more strained and drawn. She seemed reluctant to leave the rick even to take her meals. What little she ate seemed like so much dust in her mouth. We took down tea to her several times during the day.

By Friday the house was on edge. My Uncle Con spoke guardedly to her at dinner-time. 'This will set us back a graydle, mother,' he said. 'I know, son; I know, son; I know,' was all she said in reply.

Saturday came and the strain was unendurable. About three o'clock in the afternoon she found the keeper. We had been watching her in turns from the kitchen window. I remember my uncle's face lighting up and his saying, 'Glory, she's found it!' But he drew a long breath when again she started burrowing feverishly in the hay. Then we knew it was only the keeper. We didn't run out at all. We waited till she came in at six o'clock. There were times between three and six when our three heads were together at the small window watching her. I was thinking she was like a mouse nibbling at a giant's loaf.

At six she came in and said, 'I found the keeper.' After her tea she couldn't stay still. She fidgeted around the kitchen for an hour or so. Then, 'Laws were made to be broken,' said my grandmother with a brittle bravery, and she stalked out to the hayshed. Again we watched her.

Coming on for dusk she returned and lighted a stable lantern and went back to resume her search. Nobody crossed her. We didn't say yes, aye or no to her. After a time my Uncle Con took her heavy coat off the rack and went down and threw it across her shoulders. I was with him. 'There's a touch of frost there tonight, mother,' said my Uncle Con.

We loitered for a while in the darkness outside the ring of her lantern's light. But she resented our pitying eyes so we went in. We sat around the big fire waiting—Uncle Con, Aunt Annie and I. That was the lonely waiting—without speaking—just as if we were waiting for an old person to die or for a child to come into the world. Near twelve we heard her step on the cobbles. 'Twas typical of my grandmother that she placed the lantern on the ledge of the dresser and quenched the candle in it before she spoke to us.

'I found it,' she said. The words dropped out of her drawn face.

'Get hot milk for my mother, Annie,' said Uncle Con briskly.

My grandmother sat by the fire, a little to one side. Her face was as cold as death. I kept watching her like a hawk but her eyes didn't even flicker. The wedding ring was inside its keeper, and my grandmother kept twirling it round and round with the fingers of her right hand.

Suddenly, as if ashamed of her fingers' betrayal, she hid her hands under her check apron. Then, unpredictably, the fists under the apron came up to meet her face, and her face bent down to meet the fists in the apron. 'Oh, Martin, Martin,' she sobbed, and then she cried like the rain.

Sarah

Sarah had a bit of a bad name. That was the worst her neighbours would say of her, although there was a certain fortuity about her choice of fathers for the three strapping sons she'd born—all three outside wedlock.

Sarah was a great worker, strong and tireless, and a lot of women in the village got her in to scrub for them. Nobody was ever known to be unkind to her. And not one of her children was born in the County Home. It was always the most upright matron in the village who slapped life into every one of them.

'She's unfortunate, that's all,' this matron used to say. 'How could she know any better—living with two rough brothers? And don't forget she had no father herself!'

If Sarah had been one to lie in bed on a Sunday and miss Mass, her neighbours might have felt differently about her, there being greater understanding in their hearts for sins against God than for sins against his Holy Church. But Sarah found it easy to keep the Commandments of the church. She never missed Mass. She observed abstinence on all days abstinence was required. She frequently did the Stations of the Cross as well. And on Lady Day when an annual pilgrimage took place to a holy well in the neighbouring village Sarah was an example to all—with her shoes off walking over the sharp flinty stones, doing penance like a nun. If on that occasion some outsider showed disapproval of her, Sarah's neighbours were quicker than Sarah herself to take offence. All the same charity was tempered with prudence, and women with grown sons, and women not long married, took care not to hire her.

So when Oliver Kedrigan's wife, a newcomer to the locality, spoke of getting Sarah in to keep house for her while she was going up to Dublin for a few days, two of the older women in the district felt it their duty to step across to Kedrigan's and offer a word of advice.

'I know she has a bit of a bad name,' Kathleen conceded, 'but she's a great worker. I hear it's said she can bake bread that's nearly as good as my own.'

'That may be!' said one of the women, 'but if I was you, I'd think twice before I'd leave her to mind your house while you're away!'

'Who else is there I can get?' Kathleen said stubbornly.

'Why do you want anyone? You'll only be gone for three days, isn't that all?'

'Three days is a long time to leave a house in the care of a man.'

'I'd rather let the roof fall in on him than draw Sarah Murray about my place!' said the women. 'She has a queer way of looking at a man. I wouldn't like to have her give my man one of those looks.' Kathleen got their meaning at last.

'I can trust Oliver,' she said coldly.

'It's not right to trust any man too far,' the women said, shaking their heads.

'Oliver isn't that sort,' Kathleen said, and her pale papery face smiled back contempt for the other women.

Stung by that smile, the women stood up and prepared to take their leave.

'I suppose you know your own business,' said the first one who had raised the subject, 'but I wouldn't trust the greatest saint ever walked with Sarah Murray.'

'I'd trust Oliver with any woman in the world,' Kathleen said.

'Well he's your man, not ours,' said the two women, speaking together as they went out the door. Kathleen looked after them resentfully. She may not have been too happy herself about hiring Sarah but as she closed the door on the women she made up her mind for once and for all to do so, goaded on by pride in her legitimate power over her man. She'd let everyone see she could trust him.

As the two women went down the road they talked for a while about the Kedrigans but gradually they began to talk about other things, until they came to the lane leading up to the cottage where Sarah Murray lived with her brothers and the houseful of children. Looking up at the cottage their thoughts went back to the Kedrigans again and they came to a stand. 'What ever took possession of Oliver Kedrigan to marry that bleached out bloodless thing?' one of them said.

'I don't know,' said the other one. 'I wonder why she's going up to Dublin?'

'Why do you think!' said the first woman, contemptuous of her companion's ignorance. 'Not that she looks to me like a woman would ever have a child, no matter how many doctors she might go to—in Dublin or elsewhere.'

Sarah went over to Mrs Kedrigan's the morning Mrs Kedrigan was going away and she made her a nice cup of tea. Then she carried the suitcase down to the road and helped her on the bus because it was a busy time for Oliver. He had forty lambing ewes and there was a predatory vixen in a nearby wood that was causing him alarm. He had had to go out at the break of day to put up a new fence.

But the bus was barely out of sight when Oliver's cart rattled back into the yard. He'd forgotten to take the wire-cutters with him. He drew up outside the kitchen door and called to Sarah to hand him out the clippers, so he wouldn't have to get down off the cart. But when he looked down at her, he gave a laugh. 'Did you rub sheep-raddle into your cheeks?' he asked, and he laughed again—a loud happy laugh that could give no offence. And Sarah took none. But her cheeks went redder, and she angrily swiped a bare arm across her face as if to stem the flux of the healthy blood in her face. Oliver laughed for the third time. 'Stand back or you'll frighten the horse and he'll bolt,' he said, as he jerked the reins and the cart rattled off out of the yard again.

Sarah stared after him, keeping her eyes on him until the cart was like a toy cart in the distance, with a toy horse under it, and Oliver himself a toy farmer made out of painted wood.

When Kathleen came home the following Friday her house was cleaner than it had ever been. The boards were scrubbed white as rope, the windows glinted and there was bread cooling on the sill. Kathleen paid Sarah and Sarah went home. Her brothers were glad to have her back to clean the house and make the beds and bake. She gave them her money. The children were glad to see her too because while she was away their uncles made them work all day footing turf and running after sheep like collie dogs.

Sarah worked hard as she had always done, for a few months. Then one night as she was handing round potato-cakes to her brothers and the children who were sitting around the kitchen table with their knives and forks at the ready in their hands, the elder brother Pat gave a sharp look at her. He poked Joseph, the younger brother, in the ribs with the handle of his knife. 'For God's sake,' he said, 'will you look at her!'

Sarah ignored Pat's remark, except for a toss of her head. She sat down and ate her supper greedily, swilling it down with several cups of boiling tea. When she'd finished she got up and went out into the wagon-blue night. Her brothers stared after her. 'Holy God,' Pat said, 'something will have to be done about her this time.'

'Ah what's the use of talking like that?' Joseph said, twitching his shoulders uneasily. 'If the country is full of blackguards, what can we do about it?'

Pat put down his knife and fork and thumped the table with his closed fist.

'I thought the talking-to she got from the priest the last time would knock sense into her. The priest said a Home was the only place for the like of her. I told him we'd have no part in putting her away—God Almighty what would we do without her? There must a woman in the house!—we can't stand for much more of this.'

'Her brats need her too,' Joseph said, pondering over the plight they'd be in without her, 'leastways until they can be sent out to service themselves.' He looked up. 'That won't be long now though; they're shaping into fine strong boys.'

But Pat stood up. 'All the same something will have to be done. When the priest hears about this he'll be at me again. And this time I'll have to give him a better answer than the other times.'

Joseph shrugged his shoulders. 'Ah tell him you can get no rights of her. And isn't it the truth?' He gave an easy-going chuckle. 'Tell him to tackle the job himself!'

Pat gave a sort of a laugh too but it was less easy. 'Do you remember what he said the last time? He said if she didn't tell the name of the father, he'd make the new born infant speak and name him!'

'How well he didn't do it! Talk is easy!' Joseph said.

'He didn't do it,' said Pat, 'because Sarah took care not to let him catch sight of the child till the whole thing was put to the back of his mind by something else—the Confirmation—or the rewiring of the chapel.'

'Well, can't she do the same with this one?' Joseph said. He stood up. 'There's one good thing about the whole business, and that is that Mrs Kedrigan didn't notice anything wrong with her, or she'd never have given her an hour's work!'

Pat twitched with annoyance. 'How could Mrs Kedrigan notice anything? Isn't it six months at least since she was working in Kedrigan's?'

'It is I suppose,' Joseph said.

The two brothers moved about the kitchen for a few minutes in silence. The day with its solidarity of work and eating was over and they were about to go their separate ways when Joseph spoke.

'Pat?'

'What?'

'Oh nothing,' said Joseph. 'Nothing at all.'

'Ah quit your hinting! What are you trying to say? Speak out man.'

'I was only wondering,' said Joseph. 'Have you any idea at all who could be the father of this one?'

'Holy God,' Pat cried in fury. 'Why would you think I'd know the father of this one any more than the others? But if you think I'm going to stay here all evening gossiping like a woman, you're making a big mistake. I'm going out. I'm going over to the quarry field to see that heifer is all right that was sick this morning.'

'Ah the heifer'll be all right,' Joseph said. But feeling his older brother's eyes were on him he shrugged his shoulders. 'You can give me a shout if she's in a bad way and you want me.' Then when he'd let Pat get as far as the door he spoke again. 'I won't say anything to her, I suppose, when she comes in?' he asked.

Pat swung around. 'And what would you say, I'd like to know? Won't it be all beyond saying anyway in a few weeks when everyone in the countryside will see for themselves what's going on?'

'That's right,' said Joseph.

Sarah went out at the end of the day's work, as she had always done. And her brothers kept silent tongues in their heads about the child she was carrying. She worked even better than before and she sang at her work. She carried the child deep in her body and she boldly faced an abashed congregation at Mass on Sundays, walking down the centre aisle and taking her usual place under the fourth station of the cross.

Meantime Mrs Kedrigan too was expecting her long-delayed child, but she didn't go to Mass: the priest came to her. She was looking bad. By day she crept from chair to chair around the kitchen, and only went out at night for a bit of a walk up and down their own lane. She was self-conscious about her condition and her nerves were frayed. Oliver used to have to sit up half the night with her and hold her moist hands in his until she fell asleep, but all the same she woke often and was frightened and peevish and, in bursts of hysteria, she called him a cruel brute. One evening she was taking a drop of tea by the fire. Oliver had gone down to the Post Office to see if there was a letter from the Maternity Hospital in Dublin, where she had engaged a bed for the following month. When he came back Oliver had a letter in his hand. Before he gave it to her, he told her what was in it. It was an anonymous letter and it named him as the father of the child Sarah Murray was going to bring into the world in a few weeks. He told Kathleen it was an unjust accusation.

'For God's sake, say something, Katty,' he said. 'You don't believe the bloody letter, do you?' Kathleen didn't answer. 'You don't believe it, sure you don't?' He went over to the window and laid his burning face against the cold pane of glass. 'What will I do, Katty?'

'You'll do nothing,' Kathleen said, speaking for the first time. 'Nothing. Aren't you innocent? Take no notice of that letter.'

She stooped and with a wide and grotesque swoop she plucked up the letter. She put it under a plate on the dresser and began to get the tea ready with slow, tedious journeyings back and forth across the silent kitchen. Oliver stood looking out over the fields until the tea was ready and only once or twice looked at his wife. At last he turned away from the window and went over to the dresser. 'I'll tear up the letter,' he said.

'You'll do nothing of the kind,' Kathleen said, and with a lurch she reached the dresser before him. 'Here's where that letter belongs.'

There was a sound of crackling and a paper-ball went into the heart of the flames. Oliver watched it burn, and although he thought it odd that he didn't see the writing on it, he still believed that it was Sarah's letter that coiled into a black spiral in the grate.

The next evening Sarah was sitting by the fire as Kathleen Kedrigan had been sitting by hers. She too was drinking a cup of tea, and she didn't look up when her brothers came into the kitchen. No one spoke, but after a minute or two Sarah went to get up to prepare the supper. Her brother Pat pushed her down again on the chair. The cup shattered against the range and the tea slopped over the floor.

'Is this letter yours? Did you write it?' he shouted at her, holding out a letter addressed to Oliver Kedrigan—a letter that had gone through the post, and been delivered and opened. 'Do you hear me talking to you? Did you write this letter?'

'What business is it of yours?' Sarah said sullenly, and again she tried to get to her feet.

'Sit down, I tell you,' Pat shouted, and he pressed her back. 'Answer my question. Did you write this letter?'

Sarah stared dully at the letter in her brother's hand. The firelight flickered in her yellow eyes. 'Give it to me,' she snarled, and she snatched it from him. 'What business is it of yours, you thief?'

'Did you hear that, Pat? She called you a thief!' the younger brother shouted.

'Shut up, you,' Pat said. He turned back to his sister. 'Answer me. Is it true what it says in this letter?'

'How do I know what it says! And what if it's true? It's no business of yours.'

'I'll show you whose business it is!' Pat said. For a minute he stood as if not knowing what to do. Then he ran into the room off the kitchen where Sarah slept with the three children. He came out with an armful of clothes, a red dress, a coat, and a few bits of underwear. Sarah watched him. There was no one holding her down now but she didn't attempt to rise. Again her brother stood for a moment in the middle of the floor irresolute. Then he heard the outer door rattle in a gust of wind, and he ran towards it and dragging it open he threw out the armful of clothing and ran back into the room. This time he came out with a jumper and a red cap, an alarm clock, and a few other odds and ends. He threw them out the door, too.

'Do you know it's raining, Pat?' the younger brother asked cautiously.

'What do I care if it's raining?' Pat said. He went into the other room a third time. He was a while in there rummaging and when he came out he had a picture-frame, a prayer book, a pair of high-heeled shoes, a box of powder and a little green velvet box stuck all over with pearly shells.

Sarah sprang to her feet. 'My green box. Oh! Give me my box!' She tried to snatch it from him.

But Joseph suddenly put out a foot and tripped her.

When Sarah got to her feet Pat was standing at the door throwing her things out one by one, but he kept the green box till last and when he threw it out he fired it with all his strength as far as it would go as if trying to reach the dunghill at the other end of the yard. At first Sarah made as if to run out to get the things back. Then she stopped and started to pull on her coat, but her brother caught her by the hair, at the same time pulling the coat off her. Then, by the hair he dragged her across the kitchen and pushed her out into the rain, where she slipped and fell again on the wet slab stone of the doorway. Quickly then he shut out the sight of her from his eyes by banging the door closed.

'That ought to teach her,' he said. 'Carrying on with a married man! No one is going to say I put up with that kind of thing. I didn't mind the other times when it was probably old Molloy or his like that would have been prepared to pay for his mistakes if the need arose, but I wasn't going to stand for a thing like this.'

'You're sure it was Kedrigan?'

'Ah! didn't you see the letter yourself! Wasn't it Sarah's writing? And didn't Mrs Kedrigan herself give it to me this morning?'

'Sarah denied it, Pat,' Joseph said. His spurt of courage had given out and his hands were shaking as he went to the window and pulled back a corner of the bleached and neatly sewn square of a flour bag that served as a curtain.

'She did! And so did he, I suppose? Well, she can deny it somewhere else now.'

'Where do you suppose she'll go?'

'She can go where she bloody well likes. And shut your mouth, you. Keep away from that window! Can't you sit down? Sit down, I tell you.'

All this took place at nine o'clock on a Tuesday night. The next morning at seven o'clock, Oliver Kedrigan went to a fair in a neighbouring town where he bought a new ram. He had had his breakfast in the town and he wanted to get on with his work, but he went to the door of the kitchen to see his wife was all right and called it to her from the yard. 'Katty! Hand me the tin of raddle. It's on top of the dresser.'

Kathleen Kedrigan came to the door and she had the tin of raddle in her hand.

'You won't be troubled with any more letters,' she said.

Oliver laughed self-consciously. 'That's a good thing, anyhow,' he said. 'Hurry, give me the raddle.'

His wife held the tin in her hand, but she didn't move. She leaned against the jamb of the door. 'I see you didn't hear the news?'

'What news?'

'Sarah Murray got what was coming to her last night. Her brothers turned her out of the house, and threw out all her things after her.'

Oliver's face darkened.

'That was a cruel class of thing for brothers to do. Where did she go?'

'She went where she and her likes belong; into a ditch on the side of the road!'

Oliver said nothing. His wife watched him closely and she clenched her hands. 'You can spare your sympathy. She won't need it.'

Oliver looked up.

'Where did she go?'

'Nowhere,' Kathleen said slowly.

Oliver tried to think clearly. It had been a bad night, wet and windy. 'She wasn't out all night in the rain?' he asked, a fierce light coming into his eyes.

'She was,' Kathleen said, and she stared at him. 'At least that's where they found her in the morning, dead as a rat. And the child dead beside her!'

Her pale eyes held his, and he stared uncomprehendingly into them. Then he looked down at her hand that held the tin of red sheep-raddle.

'Give me the raddle!' he said, but before she had time to hand it to him he yelled at her again. 'Give me the raddle. Give it to me. What are you waiting for? Give me the God-damn' stuff.'

Desert Island

The Barclays bought Grangemore to house their famous collection. It was the largest mansion in that part of the country, and on this particular afternoon in June the guests were so numerous that it was impossible to get through the hall. I was standing on the lawn, wondering how our host would bear up under the strain. He must have been suffering agonies of apprehension about his precious things at the mercy of this throng.

'Funny thing about Barclay,' my companion said, as another car drew up at the door. 'He hasn't a friend in the world.'

As a caption under a drawing of the milling crowd it would have been worthy of *The New Yorker*; but it was not said for fun, nor was it malicious. The Barclays always struck me, for all the entertaining that they did, as essentially a lonely pair. They filled the house at week-ends with English friends, who regarded them, I often thought, as if they were Robinson Crusoes; and when they came back and found me on the guest list again I was given the sort of attention appropriate to Man Friday.

And that exactly was the sort of role I played at Grangemore. Mrs Barclay, whom, after a time, I was invited to call 'Helen', never went to any trouble to disguise the fact that in England I could hardly have expected to find myself at their board. 'You are the only Irish person we know,' she used to say; and always added 'except Michael, of course'. Michael trained their three racehorses, and he was made a very special fuss of. I had no cause of complaint. In course of time I became quite the Mayor of the Palace. There were occasions when the guests were particularly uninteresting, when Helen would say 'You show them around.'

Faces fell at this. To begin with not everyone wants to behave as if he were in a museum when visiting a private house, especially after dinner. And being given no choice in the matter and left to the care of another guest—and one of no importance—did nothing to sweeten the circumstances. It was usually a grim-faced group that I conducted round the reception rooms. Occasionally a guest would rebel and refuse to move. So far from annoying the hosts, this was always well received and produced an approximation to hilarity on several occasions. The Barclays, you see, were merely doing their duty. It gave them no pleasure to send parties of inspection round their premises; but they felt obliged to. It relieved their sense of guilt for being so rich. And they could think of nothing else for their guests to do. When the tours of inspection were over—having sat down to dinner at eight and with the prospect of a longish drive for anyone who had to return to Dublin—there was very little time for more than a nightcap before the party broke up. By then a fearful solemnity had set in, and parting was on all sides a blessed relief.

I could never think of the Barclays apart from their possessions; not only because I met them always in their own house, but because the subject of conversation seldom travelled far away from objects of art. And all through dinner one knew that it was only the prelude to that inevitable inspection and the enlightened comments worn out by over-use.

Among his books, in the library he had built on as an extension to the mansion, Humphrey was livelier than in the house proper. This was natural enough; he had collected them himself, and he knew a great deal about bindings. Every sale catalogue came to him. He had someone to buy for him in the principal capitals. I hesitate to guess what he must have spent on his hobby, but as he got the best advice it was really a gilt-edged investment. Not that he looked on it in that way. He had the pure passion of a collector. His pale eyes lit up when he told us about a rare bible on papyrus that he had run to earth with the directors of all the great libraries in the world on his heels. The inside of books did not interest him. It was the covers he cared for. I always picture the Barclays surrounded by copies of *Vogue* and the expensive art magazines, with the latest novel beside them. When they were alone they played patience, if he wasn't looking through book catalogues or studying *Apollo* and *The Connoisseur*.

The origin of our friendship was a lucky guess on my part. I arrived at the house with a group of earnest people whom the Barclays had permitted to visit the collection. They had greeted us wanly in the hall, then he took one group to the library and Mrs Barclay led another round the treasures in the house. My companions were not acquitting themselves very well; our guide, no doubt, described them to herself as 'very Irish'. One in particular was making a show of herself, regarding it as a point of national pride to dispute every attribution. I could have kicked her. It was bad manners, even if she had the knowledge, which she hadn't. Hers was the impregnable front of complacent ignorance; but she was not going to allow an English woman to get away with the idea that she had anything that could not be bettered in the national collections.

'That's a nice little Teniers you have,' this importunate woman said when we entered a closet off the drawing-rooms. For once she felt sure of an attribution; and pride mellowed her for the moment. I knew a little about Dutch painting, and I was sufficiently irritated by her manners throughout the afternoon to contradict. 'A Brouwer, I should have thought.'

'You are quite right,' Mrs Barclay turned to me gratefully. 'My husband's uncle bought it from Duveen. He said at the time it was the best Brouwer outside Holland.'

My companion made a face, expressing her unconcern for a mere slip of the tongue of no more significance than Duveen (whoever he was). The incident served a useful purpose. It shut her up; she went round doggedly and silently after that, as if she were making an inventory of national grievances.

But when we gathered in the hall to make our farewells—no refreshment was provided—Mr Barclay took me aside. 'I hear you recognised the Brouwer,' he said. 'Everyone calls it a Teniers. It's such a relief to meet anyone who appreciates our few things.'

I met them again somewhere and she came up to me at once, recalling the incident. I began to think of it as my signature tune. Soon after that I received an invitation to dine. Some of the guests were from England and were staying in the house. They had the air of knowing their hosts only slightly better than the local visitors, who did not know them at all. We had all been collected in a haphazard way; but everyone had 'a reason' for being present— being the head of this or of that; a representative figure—I was unique in being of no significance whatever. I was surprised to find myself beside my hostess at dinner. She talked away in a flutteringly confidential manner of the troubles of transplantation, the difficulty of getting servants, the worry of leaving the precious things. In London they had a flat, and a villa in Provence. It was the devil to get servants in France, she told me. I listened sympathetically. In comparison to hers, my life seemed to be singularly free of care. One of their horses had gone lame on the eve of a race. Another had failed to justify the enormous sum they paid for it. The National Gallery in London wanted to borrow their Fra Angelico; it was difficult to refuse; but the wall would look sad without it. A restorer was coming from Italy to deal with the flaking paint in the Tintoretto. This meant that they would have to retrench this year in some of their expenses. And Humphrey had his eye on a Chaucer.

I made appropriately sympathetic noises. It was the only demand the conversation made on me. 'You work in Dublin?' was the extent of her curiosity about my—admittedly—not very eventful life. I assumed they were childless. There seemed in all their apartments no room for one. What would a child do in such a house? But I was wrong.

'It's such a bore that Julia doesn't hunt—she lost her nerve—and there is literally nothing else to do here in the winter,' she said, adding 'Julia is our daughter.'

'Could you not stay here in the summer and spend the winter in London?'

'We don't like leaving the collection for so long. We always spend Easter in France and Christmas in London, but except to fly over when we have dentists to see and that sort of thing, we have decided that we are better off here. I love Ireland,' she added rather surprisingly. 'The people are so friendly. I mean the working-class people. But we don't seem to be able to get to know anyone else— as friends, I mean. There seems to be an unbridgeable gap. I can't quite describe it exactly. As if we spoke a different language. That is why we were so delighted to meet you.'

All I had done was to recognise the Brouwer, and it astonished me to find that it had made such an impression, and could possibly be the basis of a friendship. But it was. I found myself so frequently at the Barclays' parties that I lost count. Each was exactly like the other, and the conversation on every occasion was almost identical. At some stage or other during the evening Mrs Barclay would say to me of some acquaintance 'He is Irish, but not what *you* would call Irish.' It was an unintended snub. I came to look forward to it, and had bets about it with myself. Sometimes there were among the guests from England people who answered to this description. One was called 'Pat', and another was a major in the Irish Guards, but certainly nobody would suspect either of any Irish connection, without being told.

The Barclays never said anything amusing: and that might explain why they built up a character as a humorist for me. If I had gained admission to their friendship by an appearance of expertise, I held my place as a court jester. It was no strain. There was no competition. Anything more recondite than a reference to the weather was greeted with a smirk from him and a peal of laughter from her. 'It's the way you put things,' she said. 'You must meet'—referring to some celebrity—'he'd adore you.'

I acquired another function. I became a social register for the local scene. Helen (we had come to that) rang me up at least once a week to enquire about some new acquaintance. The Barclays seemed to have no faculty themselves to determine what people were like. It was as though they had come to live in the jungle or the further reaches of Mongolia. 'They seemed nice. Tell me about them.'

At first I was flattered, and then I began to despise myself and disliked my role. I was being a social quisling. It came to an end without my having shown the courage to resign. I failed to get briefs at the bar, and took a job in a lawyer's office in Canada. I sent a card to the Barclays at Christmas but got none in return, and felt a little hurt. I didn't look them up when I came back to Ireland on annual leave; but one day I walked into Julia in Dublin. She was in black, and I hesitated to enquire for her parents. She was, as always, direct.

'Mummy died on Wednesday. I was away. It was very sudden.'

I said what one says. Julia made it easy. I only once saw her express any emotion, and so far as appearances went now, she was perfectly calm. I enquired after her father. He must be distraught, I said.

'He's all right.'

'I don't suppose he wants to see anyone at the moment.'

'I'm sure he would like to see you. He's on his own. But I'd ring up if I were you. He hates droppers-in.'

It was as encouraging as Julia could be. I decided to telephone. They had been kind to me in their way; and I had been a little sad as well as piqued to find that out of sight I was also out of mind.

Perhaps I was to blame. I should have written. They got millions of Christmas cards. Mine had probably gone unnoticed.

Humphrey greeted me on the telephone as if I had never been away. 'I knew you would be upset,' he said. 'I'm all alone. Come down tonight and have a chop with me.'

Of all the evenings I had spent there I enjoyed that one most. We sat at a small table in the library. He talked away about his books. He was on the track of the Chaucer again. It was touch and go. He never mentioned Helen. I asked about Julia. Would she live with him? I was curious to know if there were any prospects of her marrying, but if there were I suppose he would not have told me.

'She won't leave London,' he said.

I hoped she was well. In spite of her grief, I thought she looked as pretty as ever when I met her, I said. I remembered that Humphrey always talked about Julia as if she were a beauty. It was somehow endearing. She was, for her mother's daughter, surprisingly plain.

'Even now,' he smiled wanly, 'I can't make out why she isn't married,' he said.

I was a very young man when the Barclays took me up, and averagely susceptible. There was only one likeness of Julia in their house, a painting done by somebody who did everybody's child that year. It hung in a little room they called their 'den', Julia at the age of six—a mass of yellow hair in a primrose dress, nursing a cat. One could just make out the suggestion of features under the hair. A clever formula; I wondered if the artist employed it when the children were pretty. But I only thought of that after I met Julia. Her absence, casual references to her doings—she moved from one exotic spot to another—and her father's way of referring to her built up an image in my mind that gave the evening she was going to appear an excitement that her parents' parties never aroused in me.

She ought to have been outstandingly pretty. Helen was like a Gainsborough, and Humphrey was so elegant that he conveyed an impression of being much better looking than in fact he was. My disappointment when I saw Julia was of the kind I experienced when I saw the Mona Lisa for the first time. In that case I had been brought up on reproductions and should have known what to expect; but Pater's prose had bitten deep, and I expected to be overcome when I saw the original. I wasn't.

I hope I didn't show my disappointment on this occasion. What made it more poignant was her marked resemblance to both her parents. She was too tall. Then, her father was tall. Her eyes were large and blue—as her mother's were—but the mother's sparkled like frost; the daughter's were frozen over. Her hair was pepper colour now and worn long. She had a trick of moving it from one side of her face to the other when she was talking as if it had some function that had gone out of order. Her clothes were very expensive, but somehow wrong. They might have been selected by her father, not for her, but for his idea of her.

I thought that he doted on his daughter; but when she was present neither of the parents took any notice of her. She had her silent place among the guests, the usual visitors from England, and the Irish contingent—the Director of this, the President of that— gallantly pretending to be friends. There was never anybody of her own age, which I guessed to be about twenty.

I was right. She had a coming-out party the next year; it was in London, and I was not invited. The Barclays kept their worlds apart. That summer they had a house-party for the Horse Show; for once it included young people. I met them on the Sunday after the week's diversions. They seemed—perhaps I was prejudiced—rather a colourless lot. They had paired off, but nobody seemed to belong to Julia. The week of dances had done nothing for her, except to make her sleepy. She yawned quite a lot.

I always found her very difficult to talk to, and although we were much more of an age, I was not enlisted for her entertainment, but remained exclusively a friend of the parents. It would have caused me chagrin had I had any romantic feelings; but I had none and preferred the status I was accorded.

In any event, the Horse Show apart, no effort seemed to be made to entertain for Julia. One assumed that her social life took place in London, where, if she met the Irish, they were, in Helen's phrase, 'not what you would call Irish'.

One morning Helen rang me up. Julia, she explained, had been invited to a hunt ball and told to bring a partner. A suitable one had been found in London and was to have been flown in; but, at the last moment, he had failed. Would I help out? It was very short notice. She asked me to do it for her. She couldn't have been nicer about it. I had to accept, but I did not look forward to the evening. And in proof it was worse than I feared. I called for Julia and we drove thirty miles to one house where we had dinner and then twenty miles to another where the dance took place.

It might have been pleasant to assume the role of cavalier for a change, and I was prepared to play up if Julia, for her part, made the smallest effort. But she threw cold water on any charade of that description from the start. It was a bore for me, she said. It must be. She had been looking forward to Charley's coming. They had been seeing quite a lot of one another, but he had started to take someone else out—a Chinese girl—and his sudden attack of flu was a diplomatic excuse. She knew it. Most of her friends bored her, but Charley had been different. He could do things like playing the guitar. He was also a good mimic. She was sorry she couldn't attempt to imitate him. She had protested when she heard that her mother had invited me to fill the gap. It would have been much better to have called the evening off. She disliked the people we were going to dine with particularly and she hated dances at any time. After that she lapsed into silence, interrupted once when she asked if I had a cigarette about me. She had forgotten to bring her own. She was forbidden to smoke, I remembered.

We arrived at a crowded house where nobody seemed to know anyone, and dinner arrived on the table as if by a miracle. I said as much, and thought how Helen would have laughed and drawn attention to another pearl of wit. Julia made an expression of mild disgust.

'Something hot at last,' I said when the champagne arrived. A joke of Disraeli's that had proved useful on similar occasions in the past. It fell flat; so, it happened, did the wine.

After dinner a move was made towards the cars, and I found myself driving Julia and another couple, who flirted in the back and ignored us.

I never danced very well, and Julia asked me why I had never learnt to at our first attempt. 'I think we had better sit down,' she said, after the second circuit. The evening dragged on. Once or twice she was claimed from me, usually by older men whom I had met at her parents. It was quite a surprise when a youth with a very red face and an obviously borrowed evening suit came up and asked awkwardly if she would dance with him. He looked like a farm-hand, and I half expected Julia to refuse; but, on the contrary, she jumped up at once. I caught a glimpse of them whirling round. Her face was flushed, her eyes were approximately gay. I lost sight of her after that until five o'clock, when I was aroused from sleep in a chair in the bar by a touch on my shoulder.

'We're going home,' Julia said.

In the car, she stared straight before her and never turned her head towards me, so that I could only catch a vague impression of her face in the windscreen. But even from that reflection I saw that she had become transformed. There was a hard brightness about her as if she was drugged.

She never stopped talking, in a low excited voice. I wondered if she had been drinking; it was hard to believe that dancing, or even flirting, with that gauche youth could have worked such a metamorphosis.

She never referred to him or to the dance or seemed to be warmed by any aftermath of pleasure. Her talk was bitter—and incessant.

She described the boredom of her life, the dullness of her parents, their selfishness. She hated antiques and paintings, ancient or modern, and silver and ivories and rare books. She hated art and she hated artists. She enjoyed the cinema; she worshipped Elvis Presley. He might be getting on, but he was still divine. She found her parents' friends intolerable. Pansies, for the most part. If she could have her way she would burn the house down and see its contents go up in smoke with a cheer.

I let her go on, except when she attacked her parents. I said they had been very good to me.

'They hate the Irish,' she said. 'They despise them. They left England because they thought it was breaking up. They don't really care for anyone very much. Humphrey prefers his bindings to anyone on earth. And Helen thinks about nothing except her appearance. She spends hours on it every day. Hours. How old do you think she is?'

I preferred not to guess.

'I'll tell you. She will be sixty next birthday. I know. They were married ten years before I arrived. I was an accident. The worst accident they ever had except the day the butler put his foot through a Ming vase. Humphrey hit him and had to pay through the nose when he sued for assault. I got hysteria, I laughed so much. The parents sent me away for three months. Humphrey began to go grey after that. He's seventy. Did you know?'

She said 'seventy' with a venom that made me start; she must have remarked it, because she stopped abruptly, and never opened her mouth until we arrived at her house. She opened the door, yawning; the light was on in the hall.

'Do you know the way to your room?'

I said I did and found when I got upstairs that I had spoken the truth. There was a bust of Socrates on the landing and I remembered that my door was on the far side of it.

I was curious to see whether Julia's outburst and unwelcome confidences would change our relations in any way. These things, as a rule, create a secret understanding, or she might regret her loss of self-control and hate me in consequence. But I was unaware of any alteration in her manner towards me; when I came to dinner again I got the usual welcomes, the synthetically effusive ones from the parents, from Julia a nod and a stare.

Helen died as I said; and I went back to Canada. For various reasons I did not come to Ireland again for my holidays, and I never heard a word about the Barclays until one day I saw in a newspaper that Humphrey was dead. His age was given as seventy-three—so Julia was right!—and the paragraph said that his collection had been left to the Irish government. That was as it should be if Julia hated it. There would be more than enough money to keep her in comfort. And I hoped that now at last she would feel free to live as she wanted to. A vivid recollection of the strange night at the ball came back to me. The only time I had ever seen Julia look animated, when she was dancing with a farm-hand. Perhaps she had married him already, or would now, and grow fat and comfortable, surrounded by pigs, and little fat philistines of children. Free from parents and possessions at last. I wrote her a letter of sympathy, but remembering that nocturnal confidence I was not fulsome. But I said, and I wanted to say, that her father had always treated me hospitably and kindly. She sent no reply.

Ten years later in a Dublin hotel I saw a notice advertising the Barclay Museum—open to the public every afternoon except Monday. As I had nothing to do and a car was at my disposal I decided to indulge a nostalgic urge. I always regret these impulses. As Dr Johnson said, it is a melancholy form of pleasure.

Nothing had changed very much at Grangemore; but now there was a turnstile in the doorway. The house was obviously a tourist attraction; there were several buses in waiting outside; and there was a handful of people in the hall. Suddenly I regretted my visit. We should bury certain parts of the past, and this, for me, was one of them. But, having come so far—thirty miles—it was easier to go on. I paid six shillings, but refused to buy a catalogue; after all, I was practically qualified to act as a guide to the establishment.

There was a group of Americans in the hall, talking very loudly. They wanted a guide, it seemed, and I very nearly offered my services. Fortunately I held my tongue, for at that moment a party which had been touring the house debouched into the hall again.

The next conducted tour would be at four, I heard the porter say. The Americans obediently formed a queue. The guide turned away, to rest I suppose until the time came to lead the next party round. I caught a glimpse of her. 'Julia,' I cried. She stopped to see who had called her name. But as I crossed the hall she gave no sign of recognition. She had changed very little, and I would have known her anywhere. I knew I had put on weight and shed some hair, but had I become totally unrecognisable?

'Have you forgotten me?'

She remembered then. I asked her how she was. She said she was quite well. I asked her where she was living. 'Here,' she said. 'What are you doing now?' she enquired, after a pause. I was still in Canada, I explained. 'I was in Dublin for a few days and wanted to recall the pleasant times I had in this wonderful house.'

She let the remark pass, and nothing came to mind to add to it.

'If you will forgive me,' she said, 'I must bring the next lot round.'

She didn't wait for my reply, but stepped into the hall and shouted 'This way, please.'

It didn't sound like Julia's voice, as I remembered it; but, then, I had not heard it very often. Nor was it like her mother's, which had the tinkle of small glass. And this had a different kind of hardness. Then I remembered Humphrey hailing a taxi. She had her father's voice. It was something else he had left her.

The Pilgrims

Blue was the colour of the rosary, the colour of the Mother of God, of the hot steam screaming up from the black engine, of the sky arched over the morning town and the tiny station. Long before the train started the pilgrims were saying the rosary, a separate rosary in each carriage, blue voices swelling out, falling and rising, to the blue morning. Then with five decades finished the pilgrims rested from praying and talked about the world they lived in, about the town they were leaving and the town they were going to, about the journey before them to the holy place where the brown skull of the martyr dead for centuries was kept as a sign and a memorial in a glass box.

Listening to the talk, he looked out of the window at the coloured advertisements nailed to the railings on the opposite platform. He put his hands on his bare knees, his own flesh touching his own flesh, and shuddered with self-pity at the ignominy of short pants. He thought of the greater ignominy of dry shaves to sandpaper from his cheeks and chin the white cat-hairs that were less like a man's beard than they were like the fluff that gathered around what the cat left in the coal-hole. George had long trousers, good grey flannels with a fine crease in them. But then George was a man with seven years' experience of shaving and the brown wisdom of twenty-one in his eyes. George sat facing him and taking part in the conversation.

The advertisements slowly moved away from him. Wheels clanked, gathering speed, over the metal of a bridge. He looked down at narrow backyards and small windows with blinds still drawn. That was a Protestant part of the town and Protestants didn't make pilgrimages and stayed in bed on Sunday mornings reading the English newspapers. When his ma and da reached for their rosaries a second time he made a sudden excuse-me noise that could mean only one of two things. He slipped out of the compartment into the empty swaying corridor. He watched the humpy ridges of the roofs going away from him to be swallowed up in the fields. George joined him.

'Your mother sent me out to see were you sick or something.'

He said, 'I'm not sick or anything.'

'They've got praying on the brain in there,' George said. 'They'll say the fifteen decades of the rosary if the Lord himself doesn't halt them. I can tell by the look in their eyes.'

A slow river curved through the green fields.

He said, 'Isn't that what a pilgrimage is for? All praying. An excursion is all drinking and fighting.'

'And a wee bit of coorting,' George said. 'But you wouldn't know about that.'

'I heard tell of it.'

'I was a year in a seminary,' George said. 'You can't tell me anything about pilgrimages.'

'You know everything.'

'I know that the people who go on excursions go on pilgrimages too. The only difference is they don't fight and there isn't much drink.'

Green was the colour of the fields on both sides of the railway, the colour of childhood and fun and the first kiss.

'Come on up the train,' said George. 'There might be card-playing somewhere.'

From end to end the train was blue with the rosary. They waited in a corner of the corridor outside a lavatory and gave the people time to tire of praying. Then they slipped into another compartment and sat down side by side. The old lady sitting opposite them manœuvred her newspaper with the awkwardness of one unaccustomed to reading a newspaper in a moving vehicle. It was a local newspaper with wide clumsy pages and black blotchy print. She was a small, stout stump of a woman, her long black skirt billowing outwards and downwards to meet the shiny blackness of buttoned boots of patent leather, her solemn black bonnet almost sitting beside her, its ribbons dangling over the edge of the seat like two thin legs. She sighed loudly behind the newspaper. She folded the newspaper into very small folds. It crackled like a fire catching in weeds and dry sticks. Her face was fat with a hard square fatness and two black moles on her forehead were like the tops of screwnails holding the tough yellow skin in place and preserving it from wrinkles.

She sighed again and said loudly: 'It's a terrible thing to read a third cousin's name in the newspaper in connection with something as terrible as a wilful murder.'

She was as black as the soot up the chimney, he thought, and her face was as yellow as goose grease. But inside in her mind she was meditating on murder, and red was the colour of blood and murder, and of martyrdom, and the colour of the vestments the priest wore reading the mass in memory of a man or woman who died for the love of Christ.

The other people in the carriage sighed sympathetically. George was curious. George was always curious. Curiosity was stamped all over his thin, freckled face and sharp question-mark of a nose. It set his round protruding eyes shining like headlights. He leaned across the compartment and tapped the old lady on the knee. She was long gone past the time of life when a stranger's tap on the knee could be interpreted as anything other than courtesy. George said, 'Was it that your third cousin murdered somebody, ma'am?'

'He was murdered,' she sighed. 'Had his poor head battered clean off. On the threshold of his own barn. The motive was robbery.'

Her face wrinkled suddenly, the yellow skin defying for a moment the tightening pressure of the moles. It might have been the grimace of great grief or mental agony. It might just as readily have been the satisfied smile of a princess among her courtiers or an actress surrounded by her admirers, of any man or woman becoming for a moment the centre of interest and attention. For everybody in the compartment had suddenly sat up to listen. The case was in all the papers. When she spoke again it was not only to George but to her alert audience, to the whole world of prosaic people who had never a murdered relative.

'God rest the poor man,' she said. 'He was civil and innocent all the days of his life. Too trusting, by far. Very unlike his half-brother who two years ago had his name in the papers for something similar.'

'Was he murdered as well?' said George.

She blessed herself. She said, 'God between us and all harm it was worse. Farandaway worse. He murdered a poor girl and, by all accounts, marrying instead of murdering would have been better for both of them.'

The compartment shuddered.

'They were an unfortunate family,' she said. 'Those of you that are old enough might remember the time the servant man murdered the three unmarried sisters.'

Nobody seemed to remember it. She was queen and mistress of a horrified silence that absorbed everybody except George.

'Colm here heard his grandfather talking about it,' lied George.

He indicated Colm by putting his left hand upon Colm's right knee so that Colm for a moment forgot about murder and remembered the mortifying lack of long trousers.

'Well, the granduncle of this poor fellow that cut the girl's throat . . .'

'Was he the servant man that killed the three unmarried sisters?'

'No. But he found the bodies. And wasn't the murderer his best friend. They say the shock of the discovery affected the creature's mind. He never did a day's good afterwards. He ended his life by jumping into a canal in England.'

George leaned back in his seat and breathed out slowly and audibly. Brown was the colour of freckles and of curiosity and even the brownest curiosity had to come sometime to the point of satiety. Green was the colour of the first kiss given and taken in the quiet corner of a field, and red was the colour of a man murdering a girl that he should have married, and black was the colour of the devil and of the clothes of a woman who knew too much about murder.

'May God have mercy on all their souls,' said George—with a panache of piety.

He raised his round eyes to the white ceiling of the compartment and beyond the ceiling was the blue heaven.

'That they may share in all the graces of the pilgrimage,' said the woman.

She whipped out a rosary as long as a measuring tape and with each individual bead the size of a schoolboy's marble, and before George or Colm could escape, the gentleness of prayer was around them as blue as the air, and red murder was forgotten and martyrdom and green kisses, and the prayers they said were set like jewels around the mysteries of the resurrection, the ascension, the descent of the Holy Ghost, the assumption, and the crowning of the Mother of God in the blue courts of heaven.

*   *   *

Grey was the colour of age, the colour of the hair of old men and women, of old streets and high tottering houses and ancient towers, the colour of history.

His mother said, 'Where were you all the time, boy?'

'Got stuck in the crowd far up the train, ma.'

'Did you say your rosary?'

'We said several,' George replied. 'Isn't there a great crowd on the pilgrimage?'

Colm's mother smiled and said there was surely. She always smiled when George spoke politely to her and George always spoke politely to elderly ladies who, for some reason surpassing Colm's comprehension, always liked George.

And there most certainly was a great crowd on the pilgrimage. The pilgrims jammed the exits from the platform. The sun was shining. Outside on the roadway a brass band was slowly, solemnly, playing the music of a hymn. Some of the pilgrims began to sing with the band. George and Colm waited cautiously on the edge of the crowd. A thin monkish man coming from behind caught George by the arm. He said, 'George. The right man in the right place, the very man I want.'

'Hello, Mr Richards,' George said. 'Hello, Rosaleen.'

Rosaleen stood at a little distance and smiled sweetly. Her father was baldheaded and blackavised, as solemn, in his dark suit, as the high grey houses of the antique town, but Rosaleen was plump, pretty, yellow-haired, and her little body curved attractively. George had one eye on the father and one on Rosaleen. Colm had one eye on Rosaleen and one on George. Green was the colour of the first kiss but the colour of the second kiss and afterwards, or the colour of warm curves, could easily be the yellow colour of ripening corn.

'You're an educated young man, George,' said Mr Richards.

He handed George a short length of red ribbon.

'Tie this ribbon around your left arm and that'll make you a steward.'

George tied the ribbon around his left arm.

'I'm a steward,' he said. 'What happens now?'

'You stand outside the station and help to direct the people to the church.'

'I was never in this town in my life.'

'We'll soon mend that,' said Mr Richards.

He sketched with a pencil on the back of an envelope. He handed the sketch to George.

'That's the town,' he said.

George glanced at the sketch, then put it into his breast pocket with what seemed to Colm a pantomime of carefulness. In the background Rosaleen was laughing silently at the antics of George. The solemn man was looking solemnly at the struggling crowd. He said, 'Tell them to go straight down the hill, turn right over the bridge, turn left in the centre of the town and stop at the first church on the right.'

George, beating time with the index finger of his right hand, repeated the words as if he was memorising them. George was a card. When he had repeated his instructions twice he gave a military salute and said, 'Aye, aye, sir.' The solemn man didn't even know he was being fooled. Rosaleen was laughing quietly behind her father's back. Yellow and gold were the colours of her laughter and the colours of the strengthening sunshine. Colm wished to God that he could be a card like George.

Headed by the band the pilgrims were going in a shapeless mass down the slope towards the centre of the town. Colm hesitated. He said, 'What about directing the people?'

George laughed.

'Would you pay any attention to that holymary of a man? I wouldn't mind directing his wee daughter.'

'She's a nice girl.'

'She's all that and something else too,' George said.

He looked sideways at Colm. He patted Colm's shoulder. He said, 'Take the advice of an older man. Don't worry your head about her or the likes of her. She's bad medicine for the young.'

'She's only three years older than I am myself.'

George halted to lean on the wall at the side of the road, to look down on the town, streets and houses and factories, on the wide river with two steamers moored at the quayside, and to look across the river at grey steeples that could chime and grey towers that were always silent.

'A girl of sixteen is a lot older than a boy of thirteen,' he said. 'Especially when the girl is Rosaleen and the boy has short-pants.'

Colm said nothing. His soul was weak with the bitter shame of those bare knees. The old suit he wore going to school had long pants but his mother wouldn't allow him to wear his old suit on a Sunday and his father wouldn't buy him a new suit until the one he had was worn out. For a moment, walking in the blinding sun, he understood the colours of anger and murder.

'What I want now,' George said, 'is something to eat.'

They turned to the right over the bridge. The pavements were crowded with pilgrims gulping down the salt air that came blowing in cool from the sea. In the middle of the bridge a girl called to George. She was tall and sunburned and darkheaded and she wore a blue coat. Her voice had all the round, rough, friendly vowels of country places. The blue coat had about it the musky odour of turf smoke and faintly from her clean skin Colm smelled the smell of plain, unscented soap. She said, 'George, it's generations since I've seen you.'

George eyed her calmly. He said mechanically, 'Go straight down the hill, turn right over the bridge, turn left in the centre of the town and stop at the first church on the right.'

She wasn't easy to snub. She laughed. She said, 'You're as daft as ever, George. You never come to the crossroads now.'

'I'm a steward now,' he said. 'I haven't a minute. I'm run off my feet directing people.'

A passing crowd of pilgrims swept between them. Colm saw George moving away speedily across the bridge and he followed as fast as he could, looking back once or twice for a sight of the tall girl. But the crowd had swallowed her and her coat that was the colour of the rosary and the colour of the sea and of the wide river flowing down to the sea. The smell of her washed skin troubled his senses and he marvelled at the greatness of George who could afford to despise such riches.

The big event of the day was the procession and the procession was all the colours of the rainbow: no less than seven bands blaring golden music; the Children of Mary dressed in blue-and-white; the silken banners of all the confraternities; the Sunday clothes of all the marching men and women; the white surplices of the priests and altar-boys; the brown Franciscans and the white Dominicans, and always the yellow sunlight pouring out of a blue sky and brightening the walls that were grey with age.

Colm liked the procession, the slow solemn movement, the music of the bands, the wind flapping the banners, the watching crowds lining the street that led up to the church where the shrine was. He liked it because, in spite of the indecency of short pants, he walked with the men who walked strongly and steadily and four deep. He was a man moving in a world of men and for a while he forgot the girl with the blue coat and the girl with the yellow hair.

The bands stopped playing as they approached the church. The bandsmen stood in silence at the sides of the street while the procession turned to the right through wide iron gates and went up steps and through a high-arched doorway. Candles burned on a distant altar. Organ music accompanied shuffling steps as the pilgrims filed into the pews. A priest stood waiting in the pulpit, motionless as a statue, until the shuffling ceased and the pews were filled. Then he crossed himself with the crucifix of his rosary beads and commenced the rosary. The voices of the pilgrims rose in the responses, swelling upwards and outwards, filling the church up to the carved wooden angels on the high rafters.

Colm and George knelt side by side at the outer end of a pew in the aisle to the right of the pulpit. It was a pleasant enough place to be. The breeze blew cool in through an open doorway. You could look out through the doorway at green trees and sunshine. Colm would have looked out through the doorway all the time but his mother was sitting two seats behind him and he could feel her eyes boring into the small of his back.

The rosary ended. The pilgrims rose from their knees and sat down on the hard seats. The priest said in a loud voice, 'The souls of the just are in the hand of God and the torment of death shall not touch them. In the sight of the unwise they seemed to die and their departure was taken for misery; and their going away from us for utter destruction: but they are in peace.'

George leaned towards Colm and whispered something unintelligible, then rose from his seat, genuflected, and was gone into the sunshine.

The priest was saying, 'As gold in the furnace he hath proved them, and as a victim of a holocaust he hath received them, and in time there shall be respect had to them.'

George might be back in a minute. He might have been feeling ill. He might merely have wanted to go out for a mouthful of air. But for some reason that he could not yet quite understand Colm was nervous and fidgetty. He listened uneasily to the priest, 'The just shall shine, and shall run to and fro like sparks among the reeds. They shall judge nations, and rule over people, and their Lord shall reign for ever.'

The space on the seat left by George was cold and empty. He felt it with his left hand. But he didn't risk a sideways look that his mother might consider a yielding to distraction. He kept his eyes on the priest in the pulpit. The priest said, 'Words taken, my dearly beloved brethren, from the Book of Wisdom, the third chapter.'

Then he led the pilgrims in making the sign of the cross. He cleared his throat, steadied himself by resting the palms of his hands on the edge of the pulpit, and was off into the sermon. He was good for an hour at least, thought Colm, looking at the size of him and listening to the sound of him, and George was gone like a spark among the reeds, but not in the least like one of the just. For the just who had in the sight of the unwise seemed to die had hardly bothered much about maidens with yellow hair, and Colm's instinct, shivering on the threshold of knowledge, told him that Rosaleen was gone also, like a yellow flame between grey, ancient walls. He rested his hands on his bare knees and gritted his teeth. George had known that he couldn't follow because his mother's eyes were nailing him to his place on the hard wooden seat. That thought set a red mist before his eyes and the priest and the pulpit and the pilgrims faded away and the words of the sermon thundered in his ears as if God were speaking to him alone.

Afterwards, searching the town for George, the words came back to him and fragments of the ceremony that followed the sermon.

He leaned on the parapet of the bridge, losing his own identity in the movement of the blue water going in one mass and glittering with the sun to the neighbouring sea.

After the text the preacher had said, 'These words apply most appropriately, dear brethren, to the martyr whose memory we celebrate today.'

So many centuries had turned the town grey, all the time the river flowing down to the sea, since the martyr had lived the life of a wandering hunted man. The preacher had preached about those wanderings, about the journey to Europe and the quiet years spent there in studious and cloistered preparation, about the return to Ireland in a small ship sailing precariously over stormy seas. The preacher had gone into great detail about the perils of stormy seas.

Studying the smooth movement of the river, Colm tried to imagine what a stormy sea looked like: dark water rising and falling under dark skies.

The preacher had gone into greater detail about the wandering years that followed the martyr's return to Ireland: the minister of a proscribed religion going from house to house with a price on his head, celebrating mass in open places when the hills were white with snow. White was the colour of silence and of eternity. The preacher had grown red in the face and loud with anger when he came to the capture, the betrayal of false friends, the lying charges, the torture and brutal execution.

With his left hand Colm felt the cold empty seat where George had sat: the false friend gone with a girl whose hair was yellow like gold, the yellow gold of the lifted monstrance, the gold of the flames of the candles burning on the altar, the golden voices of the choristers singing Latin words in praise of God, chanting Latin words as the pilgrims filed one by one past the shrine of the martyr and out again into golden sunshine.

Once in the course of his search for George he saw his father and mother at a distance along a crowded street. He was hungry and he guessed they were on their way to have tea before the train left. But he stifled his hunger and avoided them, running along a side street that narrowed to a lane and along the lane until it changed into a path that went by the side of the river and away from the town. He followed the path, the gossiping water to his right and a whispering meadow to his left, until the town was far behind him, and the sunlight weakening, and shadows gathering in corners of distant fields.

He found George and Rosaleen sitting on the grass by the edge of the path. George had his legs crossed like a tailor squatting. He was chewing a piece of grass and saying something to Rosaleen out of the corner of his mouth. Rosaleen was combing her yellow hair, her arms raised, her soft mouth fenced with hairpins, her breasts and shoulders disturbed with laughter at the humour of what George was saying.

'Fancy meeting you here,' George said.

'It's a free country, isn't it?'

'It's all that and heaven too,' George said.

He stood up and stretched himself lazily.

'Is the praying all over?'

'It is.'

'My apologies for deserting you,' George said. 'But I couldn't wait to hear about the martyr's sufferings. It would have broken my heart.'

Rosaleen, standing straight while George dusted fragments of grass from the back of her skirt, tinkled with merriment. George grinned. Colm smiled weakly. Slowly and silently they walked back towards the town, Rosaleen walking between George and Colm, Rosaleen and George holding hands and now and again pressing against each other. The river went gossiping beside them and the whispering of the meadow-grass died away into shadows.

In the crowded street near the big bridge they came so suddenly on his father and mother that he had no time to run or dodge. His mother said, 'Where were you all the time, boy? We searched the town for you.'

'We went walking after the devotions,' George said. 'Wasn't it a fine sermon?'

A lie, no matter how shameless, was never the least trouble to lucky George.

'It was indeed,' his mother said. 'But you'd want to hurry to get something to eat before the train goes.'

'I'm waiting for the late train,' George said.

'Can't I wait too?' he asked.

'Indeed you can't,' his mother said. 'It's all very well for George. George is a grown man.'

She looked at George and George looked at her and they laughed with understanding.

Walking away between his father and mother he didn't speak a word, didn't look back once over his shoulder. He knew that George and Rosaleen were going somewhere hand-in-hand and that they had already forgotten about him.

There was no room for him in the compartment so his mother sent him up the train to find a seat for himself. From end to end the train was blue-black with the rosary. He stumbled along the swaying corridor looking into compartment after compartment, seeing quiet hands holding rosary beads and quiet faces with eyes staring into infinity. Nobody noticed him, a pale face passing the glass, a small boy staggering along the corridor, weak and shivering, and ready to cry with the overpowering force of his anger. The train was crowded. There was no room for him in any compartment.

He went on until a doorknob refused to turn in his hand and he knew that there was nothing but the engine, steel and coal as black as night and the devil. Holding the doorknob in his two hands he sobbed painful dry sobs. What had the martyr suffered that was worse than this: the shame and ignominy and humiliation, the bullying and the betrayal. He turned back down the corridor, looking mechanically into compartment after compartment, looking suddenly into one pair of eyes that did not stare into infinity. It was the girl with the blue coat and the sight of her renewing his agony he fled, hiding for a while in a dimly lighted water-closet, watching his pale reflection in a dirty, spotted mirror. When he opened the door and came out into the corridor she was standing patiently waiting.

'Hello,' she said. 'You left George behind you.'

'George left me.'

The light in the corridor was blue, a lighter shade than the blue of her coat. The rocking of the train bumped them suddenly against each other, he steadied himself, his right hand on her shoulder.

'That's a way George has,' she said bitterly. 'Leaving people behind him.'

Looking over her shoulder into the darkness he knew how she had been hurt when George snubbed her, hurt painfully somewhere behind her loud talk and careless laughter.

'A person like George always meets his match,' she said. 'He won't leave the girl with the yellow hair.'

They stood side by side in the corridor looking out into the black world that was spotted now and again with the light in the window of some farmhouse. Their shoulders touched. He pressed closer. His nose was once again troubled with the odour of skin scrubbed clean with plain, unperfumed soap. Her left arm was around his shoulders, the way two friendly boys might walk home from school.

'Do you ride a bike?' she asked.

'I do.'

'Then you should cycle out to the crossroads.'

'What for?'

'We have great fun there in the evenings. Dancing to the bagpipes and everything.'

He didn't like dancing. He didn't like the bagpipes, but he knew that dancing and the bagpipes could be the beginning of something. Sitting in loneliness and anger could only be the end of everything: sitting in loneliness and anger remembering George and yellow-haired Rosaleen walking hand-in-hand beside the smooth river and the lovely shadowy evening going behind them and gathering in the old streets and around the towers and spires. Remembering was death. Cycling and dancing to bagpipes and smelling the smell of plain soap was life.

'I'll go out surely,' he said.

Her arm tightened about his shoulders. He turned towards her and kissed her. He had to raise himself a little on tiptoes in order to reach her lips. She had to steer her own mouth carefully down to his. He had never kissed a girl before, and anyway the train was jolting wildly from side to side. He smelled and tasted the cigarettes she had been smoking.

From end to end the train was blue-black with the rosary. Blue was the colour of the rosary, the colour of the Mother of God, of the light in the corridor and the coat that covered the body of the laughing, sunburned girl. Black was the colour of the night all around them, of mouth finding mouth in the darkness and making a beginning and an end.

JAMES PLUNKETT · 1920–2003

Weep for our Pride

The door of the classroom was opened by Mr O'Rourke just as Brother Quinlan was about to open it to leave. They were both surprised and said 'Good morning' to one another as they met in the doorway. Mr O'Rourke, although he met Brother Quinlan every morning of his life, gave an expansive but oddly unreal smile and shouted his good morning with blood-curdling cordiality. They then withdrew to the passage outside to hold a conversation.

In the interval English Poetry books were opened and the class began to repeat lines. They had been given the whole of a poem called *Lament for the Death of Eoghan Roe* to learn. It was very patriotic and dealt with the poisoning of Eoghan Roe by the accursed English, and the lines were very long, which made it difficult. The class hated the English for poisoning Eoghan Roe because the lines about it were so long. What made it worse was that it was the sort of poem Mr O'Rourke loved. If it was *Hail to thee blithe spirit* he wouldn't be so fond of it. But he could declaim this one for them in a rich, fruity, provincial baritone and would knock hell out of anybody who had not learned it.

Peter had not learned it. Realising how few were the minutes left to him he ran his eyes over stanza after stanza and began to murmur fragments from each in hopeless desperation. Swaine, who sat beside him, said, 'Do you know this?'

'No,' Peter said, 'I haven't even looked at it.'

'My God!' Swaine breathed in horror. 'You'll be mangled!'

'You could give us a prompt.'

'And be torn limb from limb,' said Swaine with conviction; 'not likely.'

Peter closed his eyes. It was all his mother's fault. He had meant to come to school early to learn it but the row delayed him. It had been about his father's boots. After breakfast she had found that there were holes in both his shoes. She held them up to the light which was on because the November morning was wet and dark.

'Merciful God, child,' she exclaimed, 'there's not a sole in your shoes. You can't go out in those.'

He was anxious to put them on and get out quickly, but everybody was in bad humour. He didn't dare to say anything. His sister was clearing part of the table and his brother Joseph, who worked, was rooting in drawers and corners and growling to everybody:

'Where the hell is the bicycle pump? You can't leave a thing out of your hand in this house.'

'I can wear my sandals,' Peter suggested.

'And it spilling out of the heavens—don't be daft, child.' Then she said, 'What am I to do at all?'

For a moment he hoped he might be kept at home. But his mother told his sister to root among the old boots in the press. Millie went out into the passage. On her way she trod on the cat, which meowed in intense agony.

'Blazes,' said his sister, 'that bloody cat.'

She came in with an old pair of his father's boots, and he was made try them on. They were too big.

'I'm not going out in those,' he said, 'I couldn't walk in them.'

But his mother and sister said they looked lovely. They went into unconvincing ecstasies. They looked perfect they said, each backing up the other. No one would notice.

'They look foolish,' he insisted, 'I won't wear them.'

'You'll do what you're told,' his sister said. They were all older than he and each in turn bullied him. But the idea of being made look ridiculous nerved him.

'I won't wear them,' he persisted. At that moment his brother Tom came in and Millie said quickly:

'Tom, speak to Peter—he's giving cheek to Mammy.'

Tom was very fond of animals. 'I heard the cat,' he began, looking threateningly at Peter who sometimes teased it. 'What were you doing to it?'

'Nothing,' Peter answered, 'Millie walked on it.' He tried to say something about the boots but the three of them told him to shut up and get to school. He could stand up to the others but he was afraid of Tom. So he had flopped along in the rain feeling miserable and hating it because people would be sure to know they were not his own boots.

The door opened and Mr O'Rourke came in. He was a huge man in tweeds. He was a fluent speaker of Irish and wore the gold fáinne in the lapel of his jacket. Both his wrists were covered with matted black hair.

'*Filíocht*,' he roared and drew a leather from his hip pocket.

Then he shouted, '*Dún do leabhar*,' and hit the front desk a ferocious crack with the leather. Mr O'Rourke was an ardent Gael who gave his orders in Irish—even during English class. Someone had passed him up a poetry book and the rest closed theirs or turned them face downwards on their desks.

Mr O'Rourke, his eyes glaring terribly at the ceiling, from which plaster would fall in fine dust when the third year students overhead tramped in or out, began to declaim:

> 'Did they dare, did they dare, to slay Eoghan Roe
> O'Neill?
> Yes they slew with poison him they feared to meet with
> steel.'

He clenched his powerful fists and held them up rigidly before his chest.

> 'May God wither up their hearts, may their blood cease
> to flow!
> May they walk in living death who poisoned Eoghan
> Roe!'

Then quite suddenly, in a business-like tone, he said, 'You—Daly.'

'Me, sir?' said Daly, playing for time.

'Yes, you fool,' thundered Mr O'Rourke. 'You.'

Daly rose and repeated the first four lines. When he was half-way through the second stanza Mr O'Rourke bawled, 'Clancy.' Clancy rose and began to recite. They stood up and sat down as Mr O'Rourke commanded while he paced up and down the aisles between the seats. Twice he passed close to Peter. He stood for some time by Peter's desk bawling out names. The end of his tweed jacket lay hypnotically along the edge of Peter's desk. Cummins stumbled over the fourth verse and dried up completely.

'Line,' Mr O'Rourke bawled. Cummins, calmly pale, left his desk and stepped out to the side of the class. Two more were sent out. Mr O'Rourke walked up and down once more and stood with his back to Peter. Looking at the desk at the very back he suddenly bawled, 'Farrell.'

Peter's heart jerked. He rose to his feet. The back was still towards him. He looked at it, a great mountain of tweed, with a frayed collar over which the thick neck bulged in folds. He could see the antennae of hair which sprouted from Mr O'Rourke's ears and could smell the chalk-and-ink schoolmaster's smell of him. It was a trick of Mr O'Rourke's to stand with his back to you and then call your name. It made the shock more unnerving. Peter gulped and was silent.

'Wail . . .' prompted Mr O'Rourke.

Peter said, 'Wail . . .'

Mr O'Rourke paced up to the head of the class once more.

'Wail—wail him through the island,' he said as he walked. Then he turned around suddenly and said, 'Well, go on.'

'Wail, wail him through the island,' Peter said once more and stopped.

'Weep,' hinted Mr O'Rourke.

He regarded Peter closely, his eyes narrowing.

'Weep,' said Peter, ransacking the darkness of his mind but finding only emptiness.

'Weep, weep, weep,' Mr O'Rourke said, his voice rising.

Peter chanced his arm. He said, 'Wail, wail him through the island weep, weep, weep.'

Mr O'Rourke stood up straight. His face conveyed at once shock, surprise, pain.

'Get out to the line,' he roared, 'you thick lazy good-for-nothing bloody imbecile. Tell him what it is, Clancy.' Clancy dithered for a moment, closed his eyes and said:

> 'Sir—Wail, wail him through the island, weep, weep
>   for our pride
> Would that on the battle field our gallant chief had
>   died.'

Mr O'Rourke nodded with dangerous benevolence. As Peter shuffled to the line the boots caught the iron upright of the desk and made a great clamour. Mr O'Rourke gave him a cut with the leather across the behind. 'Did you look at this, Farrell?' he asked.

Peter hesitated and said uncertainly, 'No, sir.'

'It wasn't worth your while, I suppose?'

'No, sir. I hadn't time, sir.'

Just then the clock struck the hour. The class rose. Mr O'Rourke put the leather under his left armpit and crossed himself. '*In ainm an Athar*,' he began. While they recited the *Hail Mary* Peter, unable to pray, stared at the leafless rain-soaked trees in the square and the serried rows of pale, prayerful faces. They sat down.

Mr O'Rourke turned to the class.

'Farrell hadn't time,' he announced pleasantly. Then he looked thunderously again at Peter. 'If it was an English penny dreadful about Public Schools or London crime you'd find time to read it quick enough, but when it's about the poor hunted martyrs and felons of your own unfortunate country by a patriot like Davis you've no time for it. You've the makings of a fine little Britisher.' With genuine pathos Mr O'Rourke then recited:

'The weapon of the Sassenach met him on his way
And he died at Cloch Uachter upon St Leonard's day.'

'That was the dear dying in any case, but if he died for the likes of you, Farrell, it was the dear bitter dying, no mistake about it.'

Peter said, 'I meant to learn it.'

'Hold out your hand. If I can't preach respect for the patriot dead into you, then honest to my stockings I'll beat respect into you. Hand.'

Peter held it out. He pulled his coat sleeve down over his wrist. The leather came down six times with a resounding impact. He tried to keep his thumb out of the way because if it hit you on the thumb it stung unbearably. But after four heavy slaps the hand began to curl of its own accord, curl and cripple like a little piece of tinfoil in a fire, until the thumb lay powerless across the palm, and the pain burned in his chest and constricted every muscle. But worse than the pain was the fear that he would cry. He was turning away when Mr O'Rourke said:

'Just a moment, Farrell. I haven't finished.'

Mr O'Rourke gently took the fingers of Peter's hand, smoothing them out as he drew them once more into position. 'To teach you I'll take no defiance,' he said in a friendly tone and raised the leather. Peter tried to hold his crippled hand steady.

He could not see properly going back to his desk and again the boots deceived him and he tripped and fell. As he picked himself up Mr O'Rourke, about to help him with another, though gentler, tap of the leather, stopped and exclaimed:

'Merciful God, child, where did you pick up the boots?'

The rest looked with curiosity. Clancy, who had twice excelled himself, tittered. Mr O'Rourke said, 'And what's the funny joke, Clancy?'

'Nothing, sir.'

'Soft as a woman's was your voice, O'Neill, bright was your eye,' recited Mr O'Rourke, in a voice as soft as a woman's, brightness in his eyes. 'Continue, Clancy.' But Clancy, the wind taken out of his sails, missed and went out to join the other three. Peter put his head on the desk, his raw hands tightly under his armpits, and nursed his wounds while the leather thudded patriotism and literature into the other, unmurmuring, four.

Swaine said nothing for a time. Now and then he glanced at Peter's face. He was staring straight at the book. His hands were tender, but the pain had ebbed away. Each still hid its rawness under a comfortably warm armpit.

'You got a heck of a hiding,' Swaine whispered at last. Peter said nothing.

'Ten is too much. He's not allowed to give you ten. If he gave me ten I'd bring my father up to him.'

Swaine was small, but his face was large and bony and when he took off his glasses sometimes to wipe them there was a small red weal on the bridge of his nose. Peter grunted and Swaine changed the subject.

'Tell us who owns the boots. They're not your own.'

'Yes they are,' Peter lied.

'Go on,' Swaine said, 'who owns them? Are they your brother's?'

'Shut up,' Peter menaced.

'Tell us,' Swaine persisted. 'I won't tell a soul. Honest.' He regarded Peter with sly curiosity. He whispered: 'I know they're not your own, but I wouldn't tell it. We sit beside one another. We're pals. You can tell me.'

'Curiosity killed the cat . . .' Peter said.

Swain had the answer to that. With a sly grin he rejoined, 'Information made him fat.'

'If you must know,' Peter said, growing tired, 'they're my father's. And if you tell anyone I'll break you up in little pieces. You just try breathing a word.'

Swaine sat back, satisfied.

Mr O'Rourke was saying that the English used treachery when they poisoned Eoghan Roe. But what could be expected of the English except treachery?

'Hoof of the horse,' he quoted, 'horn of a bull, smile of a Saxon.' Three perils. Oliver Cromwell read his Bible while he quartered infants at their mother's breasts. People said let's forget all that. But we couldn't begin to forget it until we had our full freedom. Our own tongue, the sweet Gaelic *teanga*, must be restored once more as the spoken language of our race. It was the duty of all to study and work towards that end.

'And those of us who haven't time must be shown how to find the time. Isn't that a fact, Farrell?' he said. The class laughed. But the clock struck and Mr O'Rourke put the lament regretfully aside.

'Mathematics,' he announced, '*Céimseachta*.'

He had hoped it would continue to rain during lunchtime so that they could stay in the classroom. But when the automatic bell clanged loudly and Mr O'Rourke opened the frosted window to look out, it had stopped. They trooped down the stairs. They pushed and jostled one another. Peter kept his hand for safety on the banisters. Going down the stairs made the boots seem larger. He made straight for the urinal and stayed there until the old brother whose duty it was for obscure moral reasons to patrol the place had passed through twice. The second time he said to him: 'My goodness, boy, go out into the fresh air with your playmates. Shoo—boy—shoo,' and stared at Peter's retreating back with perplexity and suspicion.

Dillon came over as he was unwrapping his lunch and said, 'Did they dare, did they dare to slay Eoghan Roe O'Neill.'

'Oh, shut up,' Peter said.

Dillon linked his arm and said, 'You got an awful packet.' Then with genuine admiration he added: 'You took it super. He aimed for your wrist, too. Not a peek. You were wizard. Cripes. When I saw him getting ready for the last four I was praying you wouldn't cry.'

'I never cried yet,' Peter asserted.

'I know, but he lammed his hardest. You shouldn't have said you hadn't time.'

'He wouldn't make me cry,' Peter said grimly, 'not if he got up at four o'clock in the morning to try it.'

O'Rourke had lammed him all right, but there was no use trying to do anything about it. If he told his father and mother they would say he richly deserved it. It was his mother should have been lammed and not he.

'You were super, anyway,' Dillon said warmly. They walked arm in arm. 'The Irish,' he added sagaciously, 'are an unfortunate bloody race. The father often says so.'

'Don't tell me,' Peter said with feeling.

'I mean, look at us. First Cromwell knocks hell out of us for being too Irish and then Rorky slaughters us for not being Irish enough.'

It was true. It was a pity they couldn't make up their minds.

Peter felt the comfort of Dillon's friendly arm. 'The boots are my father's,' he confided suddenly. 'My own had holes.' That made him feel better.

'What are you worrying about?' Dillon said, reassuringly. 'They look all right to me.'

When they were passing the row of water taps with the chained drinking vessels a voice cried. 'There's Farrell now.' A piece of crust hit Peter on the nose.

'Caesar sends his legate,' Dillon murmured. They gathered round. Clancy said, 'Hey, boys, Farrell is wearing someone else's boots.'

'Who lifted you into them?'

'Wait now,' said Clancy, 'let's see him walk. Go on—walk, Farrell.'

Peter backed slowly towards the wall. He backed slowly until he felt the ridge of a downpipe hard against his back. Dillon came with him. 'Lay off, Clancy,' Dillon said. Swaine was there too. He was smiling, a small cat fat with information.

'Where did you get them, Farrell?'

'Pinched them.'

'Found them in an ashbin.'

'Make him walk,' Clancy insisted; 'let's see you walk, Farrell.'

'They're my own,' Peter said; 'they're a bit big—that's all.'

'Come on, Farrell—tell us whose they are.'

The grins grew wider.

Clancy said, 'They're his father's.'

'No, they're not,' Peter denied quickly.

'Yes, they are. He told Swaine. Didn't he, Swaine? He told you they were his father's.'

Swaine's grin froze. Peter fixed him with terrible eyes.

'Well, didn't he, Swaine? Go on, tell the chaps what he told you. Didn't he say they were his father's?'

Swaine edged backwards. 'That's right,' he said, 'he did.'

'Hey, you chaps,' Clancy said, impatiently, 'let's make him walk. I vote . . .'

At that moment Peter, with a cry, sprang on Swaine. His fist smashed the glasses on Swaine's face. As they rolled over on the muddy ground, Swaine's nails tore his cheek. Peter saw the white terrified face under him. He beat at it in frenzy until it became covered with mud and blood.

'Cripes,' Clancy said in terror, 'look at Swaine's glasses. Haul him off, lads.' They pulled him away and he lashed out at them with feet and hands. He lashed out awkwardly with the big boots which had caused the trouble. Swaine's nose and lips were bleeding so they took him over to the water tap and washed him. Dillon, who stood alone with Peter, brushed his clothes as best he could and fixed his collar and tie.

'You broke his glasses,' he said. 'There'll be a proper rucky if old Quinny sees him after lunch.'

'I don't care about Quinny.'

'I do then,' Dillon said fervently. 'He'll quarter us all in our mother's arms.'

They sat with their arms folded while Brother Quinlan, in the high chair at the head of the class, gave religious instruction. Swaine kept his bruised face lowered. Without the glasses it had a bald, maimed look, as though his eyebrows, or a nose, or an eye, were missing. They had exchanged no words since the fight. Peter was aware of the boots. They were a defeat, something to be ashamed of. His mother only thought they would keep out the rain. She didn't understand that it would be better to have wet feet. People did not laugh at you because your feet were wet.

Brother Quinlan was speaking of our relationship to one another, of the boy to his neighbour and of the boy to his God. We communicated with one another, he said, by looks, gestures, speech. But these were surface contacts. They conveyed little of what went on in the mind, and nothing at all of the individual soul. Inside us, the greatest and the humblest of us, a whole world was locked. Even if we tried we could convey nothing of that interior world, that life which was nourished, as the poet had said, within the brain. In our interior life we stood without friend or ally—alone. In the darkness and silence of that interior and eternal world the immortal soul and its God were at all times face to face. No one else could peer into another's soul, neither our teacher, nor our father or mother, nor even our best friend. But God saw all. Every stray little thought which moved in that inaccessible world was as plain to Him as if it were thrown across the bright screen of a cinema. That was why we must be as careful to discipline our thoughts as our actions. Custody of the eyes, custody of the ears, but above all else custody . . .

Brother Quinlan let the sentence trail away and fixed his eyes on Swaine.

'You—boy,' he said in a voice which struggled to be patient, 'what are you doing with that handkerchief?'

Swaine's nose had started to bleed again. He said nothing. 'Stand up, boy,' Brother Quinlan commanded. He had glasses himself, which he wore during class on the tip of his nose. He was a big man too, and his head was bald in front, which made his large forehead appear even more massive. He stared over the glasses at Swaine.

'Come up here,' he said, screwing up his eyes, the fact that something was amiss with Swaine's face dawning gradually on him. Swaine came up to him, looking woebegone, still dabbing his nose with the handkerchief. Brother Quinlan contemplated the battered face for some time. He turned to the class.

'Whose handiwork is this?' he asked quietly. 'Stand up, the boy responsible for this.'

For a while nobody stirred. There was an uneasy stillness. Poker faces looked at the desks in front of them and waited. Peter looked around and saw Dillon gazing at him hopefully. After an unbearable moment feet shuffled and Peter stood up.

'I am, sir,' he said.

Brother Quinlan told Clancy to take Swaine out to the yard to bathe his nose. Then he spoke to the class about violence and what was worse, violence to a boy weaker than oneself. That was the resort of the bully and the scoundrel—physical violence—The Fist. At this Brother Quinlan held up his large bunched fist so that all might see it. Then with the other hand he indicated the picture of the Sacred Heart. Charity and Forebearance, he said, not vengeance and intolerance, those were qualities most dear to Our Blessed Lord.

'Are you not ashamed of yourself, Farrell? Do you think what you have done is a heroic or a creditable thing?'

'No, sir.'

'Then why did you do it, boy?'

Peter made no answer. It was no use making an answer. It was no use saying Swaine had squealed about the boots being his father's. Swaine's face was badly battered. But deep inside him Peter felt battered too. Brother Quinlan couldn't see your soul. He could see Swaine's face, though, when he fixed his glasses on him properly. Brother Quinlan took his silence for defiance.

'A blackguardly affair,' he pronounced. 'A low, cowardly assault. Hold out your hand.'

Peter hesitated. There was a limit. He hadn't meant not to learn the poetry and it wasn't his fault about the boots.

'He's been licked already, sir,' Dillon said. 'Mr O'Rourke gave him ten.'

'Mr O'Rourke is a discerning man,' said Brother Quinlan, 'but he doesn't seem to have given him half enough. Think of the state of that poor boy who has just gone out.'

Peter could think of nothing to say. He tried hard but there were no words there. Reluctantly he presented his hand. It was mudstained. Brother Quinlan looked at it with distaste. Then he proceeded to beat hell out of him, and charity and forebearance into him, in the same way as Mr O'Rourke earlier had hammered in patriotism and respect for Irish History.

It was raining again when he was going home. Usually there were three or four to go home with him, but this afternoon he went alone. He did not want them with him. He passed some shops and walked by the first small suburban gardens, with their sodden gravel paths and dripping gates. On the canal bridge a boy passed him pushing fuel in a pram. His feet were bare. The mud had splashed upwards in thick streaks to his knees. Peter kept his left hand under his coat. There was a blister on the ball of the thumb which ached now like a burn. Brother Quinlan did that. He probably didn't aim to hit the thumb as Mr O'Rourke always did, but his sight was so bad he had a rotten shot. The boots had got looser than they were earlier. He realised this when he saw Clancy with three or four others passing on the other side of the road. When Clancy waved and called to him, he backed automatically until he felt the parapet against his back.

'Hey, Farrell,' they called. Then one of them, his head forward, his behind stuck out, began to waddle with grotesque movements up the road. The rest yelled to call Peter's attention. They indicated the mime. Come back if you like, they shouted. Peter waited until they had gone. Then he turned moodily down the bank of the canal. He walked with a stiff ungainly dignity, his mind not yet quite made up. Under the bridge the water was deep and narrow, and a raw wind which moaned in the high arch whipped coldly at his face. It might rain tomorrow and his shoes wouldn't be mended. If his mother thought the boots were all right God knows when his shoes would be mended. After a moment of indecision he took off the boots and dropped them, first one—and then the other—into the water.

There would be hell to pay when he came home without them. But there would be hell to pay anyway when Swaine's father sent around the note to say he had broken young Swaine's glasses. Like the time he broke the Cassidys' window. Half regretfully he stared at the silty water. He could see his father rising from the table to reach for the belt which hung behind the door. The outlook was frightening; but it was better to walk in your bare feet. It was better to walk without shoes and barefooted than to walk without dignity. He took off his stockings and stuffed them into his pocket. His heart sank as he felt the cold wet mud of the path on his bare feet.

VAL MULKERNS · 1925–

Loser

On the last day of his life Dan decided that women who haunted
you were not those whom you had enjoyed or even known remotely
well, but strangers who had at one time or another troubled you
with the most transient flicker of desire. He hadn't a face for most
of them. One was represented by a pair of crossed ankles on the
Dalkey tram, another by a smile which had temporarily blotted out
the entrance of Mitchell's where he was going to meet a friend,
another was remembered only by a laugh or a gasp of greeting or a
pair of chubby breasts bare below him in the parterre when fashion
had newly decreed flattening and covering. He was troubled by all
the women in turn, all over again, as he rocked along by tram after
Fairyhouse to visit his sister in Ballsbridge. It was no use anyhow
planning how he would approach her for money. That was
something you had to play by ear every time. Now that poor
Mother is dead you are my only refuge. No. That failed last time.
Play the thing by ear. As he knew.

She was tinkering as usual in the garden and didn't look pleased
to see him. He kissed her playfully, then lifted up the hand which
was not carrying a flowerpot and searched for green fingers.

'No use. You may as well leave the cuttings alone, sister Harriet.
Your fingers are shelly pink and much too pretty. Come in and
brew your famished relative the pot of tea he's been dreaming of.
Look, I brought you meringues from Mitchell's.' Smiling he held up
the blue and white box and then she had to smile too.

'Oh very well. At all events I was nearly finished.'

Sparrows chattered among the ivy that lined her front walls, and
the spring breeze had a touch of the sea in it. She would have
preferred to remain out of doors. But there, even now as a wife she
was at the beck and call of her brothers and sisters just like long ago
at home. He saw the complaint in her face and set about amusing
her in the spotless tiled kitchen that yet seemed dark after the
spring light outside. A canary in a domed wicker cage sang shrilly

at the open window. There were geranium pots on the deeply recessed ledge, a few of them overflowing already with new growth.

'So Medway was too bally lazy to see to it himself and left the booking once again to yours truly. It's true I approached the Carl Rosa for the same week but I didn't finalise the arrangements. Medway did that and then forgot to put it in the book. He says he discussed it fully with me to the last detail but I've no recollection of it. It can't be denied that I could have been a wee bit the worse for wear after Leopardstown but the fact remains it should have gone down in the book. Failing to write it up was the root of that particular little problem.'

'What little problem?'

He laughed merrily like a beloved younger brother and complimented her on the tea. 'Oh, but wait until you hear! Dear Noel himself couldn't have done better.' He jumped up and put on the soft black hat again, this time at a rakish angle over the untrustworthy china blue eyes. He settled one shoulder against the fireplace and struck an attitude.

'Here am I, sister mine, in the absence of Medway entertaining the manager of the Carl Rosa to coffee in the top office with a choice selection of his stars. It's only eleven o'clock in the morning and rehearsals start in half an hour and will go on all day. Their men are helping ours to clear the dress circle bar for the Tosca rehearsals—they'll open with Tosca next week. Everything in the garden is rosy.' He swept off the hat and bowed, kissing imaginary hands. 'Compliments have been exchanged all round. The stars are delighted with their suites in the Shelbourne. Ireland is a charming country, devoted to grand opera. Best audiences in the British Isles. All that sort of thing. Your little brother is feeling sanguine at the prospect of a good season and Medway's praise (with a practical expression of it perhaps in next month's cheque) when Stan comes in with that agitated expression on his beery old face. "Mr Montgomery, sir, I'm sorry to butt in. Gentleman downstairs says he must see you. Shocking urgent, sir. Gentleman from Moody Manners, sir."

'Stan has only finished this rigmarole and light is suddenly and horribly beginning to dawn on yours truly when a very large gentleman in a bowler hat explodes into the office. Language most unfit for the ears of ladies—horrible. Consternation at happy coffee ceremony. Somebody spills a scalding cup on somebody else's foot and dear Dolly starts to scream from sheer nerves. It's the contralto's foot not Dolly's which is scalded but *she* is stunned into silence. Shocking scene.'

'But what was it all about?' Harriet felt she ought to be able to interpret her brother by now but this scene defeated her.

'Dear old girl—patience. You shall hear. Picture the annoyance of the manager of a well-known opera company when he arrived with his little band at the North Wall and there's nobody to meet them. Irish courtesy and hospitality and all that. Not a sign of it. He takes a taxi to the theatre and what does he find?'

'Dear goodness!' Harriet understood at last. 'Oh, Baby, how could you?'

That was a good sign. Calling him Baby was a good sign. Dear little chap that she had dandled on her knee and cared for like a mother.

'Not my fault, ducky. Reflect. There's nothing in the book—no record of the booking. No way I could have understood that I was booking in the Carl Rosa for a fortnight already agreed on with Moody Manners. Medway's Method was at fault—nothing whatsoever to do with yours truly. But who must take the knock? Whose career is in ruins at this moment? Not Medway's, I assure you.'

'Come and sit down, Baby, and drink your tea. These meringues are delicious. Have another. I'll warm up that cup for you. There must be something you can do.'

This was the cue he had been waiting for, and he sat down heavily again in front of the geraniums, head in his hands. 'Have you any remote conception of what this means to me?' he said brokenly. 'They were at first claiming all their costs and also damages. Now Medway has softened up the manager to the extent that he will accept return travel costs with a firm booking for May on much better terms.'

'Isn't that splendid? Cheer up now, Dan, like a good boy, and stop breaking your heart over it.'

'Travel costs to be recovered from *me*, Harriet. From *me* who haven't a penny in the wide world except my salary—totally inadequate for some time now.'

'I'm sure you're being too gloomy about it, dear. Mr Medway would never be so unreasonable.'

'Wouldn't he though? It's pay up or get out. As simple as that. Theatre finances are tricky enough at the moment.'

'Wouldn't your bank accommodate you?'

'Not a chance!'

'Father then?'

'The old man has paid up a few small personal debts too recently for me to ask so soon again. You are my only hope.'

'I? You must be dreaming, Dan—several hundred pounds might be involved?'

'Say an even thousand and everybody would be happy. You'll be paid back of course, with interest.'

'I think you must be joking, Daniel. Richard and I simply do not have on hand a huge sum like that.'

'Never mind Richard—you had more than that salted away yourself before you married him.' It was a fact well known in the family that she had the first halfpenny she ever earned.

'That's quite enough of that sort of talk. You're forgetting yourself as usual, Daniel—I never heard such a proposition in all my born days. If poor Mother could only hear you . . .'

'If Mother was alive I wouldn't even have to ask. She'd do the offering—you know that!'

'Poor Mother was in a stronger position financially than I am. I'll have to ask you to excuse me—I must get back to the garden and finish before it's time to see to Richard's meal. In fact I'm late as it is. I'm truly sorry, Daniel.'

True to form he wasn't even Dan now, not to speak of Baby. He was Daniel, the same troublemaker he always was, a nuisance to the family even at school. Fancying himself a hero and joining Fianna Eireann and drilling out in Santry when he ought to have been at his books. A brave young soldier laddie until he was needed and then causing endless trouble to them all trying to escape his involvement. She remembered the white feather some Eccles Street girl had sent him and how lightly he had taken it. 'Take a trophy for your chapeau, sister mine. Somebody has kindly sent me a premature decoration.'

He was only a schoolboy but it was true they were all ashamed of him just the same. It was the time for heroic gestures. He had two brothers out in Flanders fighting for little Belgium. He had burned his Fianna uniform in the back garden and applied himself so well to his studies over the next six years that he was barely twenty-three when he was called to the bar. Amateur dramatics became his craze, however, and eventually took over from the law. Some small parts, a lot of luck, occasional professional chances with touring companies, brought him in due course to the position of house manager in the Gaiety Theatre with a safe progression to manager and a seat on the board on Mr Medway's forthcoming retirement. If only he would keep his nose clean. If only he would develop a belated sense of responsibility even now. But no. This sounded like his most serious piece of trouble to date.

'Dear Harriet, listen to me before you go back to your tulips. I need your help now as I've never needed it before. I implore you not to throw me to the lions.' He turned the full battery of his desperate charm on her and smiled the smile whose various stages she could remember from child to man.

'I'm truly sorry, Dan. You'll have to accept that I can't go on helping you for ever. It wouldn't be in your own ultimate interest even if I could.'

'Then goodbye, Harriet, and thanks for the tea. But remember I warned you that you wouldn't like the pieces the lions leave behind.' On their way along the side door, he put two fingers into his breast pocket and pulled out an envelope. 'I almost forgot. I brought you a couple of briefs for the show next week.'

'You never do hold grudges, do you? Bless you, Dan.'

'It's called style, darling, and it's much rarer than talent. Goodbye.'

Quite suddenly he was gone, banging the door behind him. She sat down on the bottom step of the stairs to cry, her garden forgotten at last.

Outside the cherry trees in all the front gardens gave off their acrid smell in the sunshine and Richard was coming with his shiny briefcase and rolled umbrella from the direction of Lansdowne Road. You poor vanquished bastard, Dicky. She'll suck you dry and polish up the remains and send you out a prosperous citizen with your briefcase every morning in good time for the eight-thirty and nobody will ever know that you're dead, that you died a dozen years ago.

'How's the form, Dan? You don't look your usual perky self I must say.'

'Come on over with me for a snifter before supper and I'll tell you all, Dicky.'

'Thanks for the offer but Harriet has something planned for this evening. I promised her faithfully I'd be on time.' The pale blue eyes were apprehensive, yet looking longingly in the direction of Mooney's pub.

'It won't take us ten minutes. Come on, Dick. Be a devil for once. She's not ready for you anyway—I've just been there.'

It was cool and quiet in the pub. There was only a scattering of men drinking, but the snug door was half open showing a neat pair of ankles and high-heeled green shoes. Dan called for two small Jamesons. Then Richard ordered two large ones and listened with widened eyes to the highly coloured tale of the bungled bookings. Finally he laughed enviously.

'Never a dull moment, Dan. You'll never grow old like the rest of us. Would you believe I had a nice voice myself when I was a boy. Sang in the choir in Berkeley Road, did you know that? Might have made a name for myself if I'd got the chance. But my old man was always pushing me at the books—like your own father, I suppose— wanted me in the legal partnership, don't you know? Now that I have responsibilities I suppose it's just as well but sometimes, just sometimes, I wish . . .'

He stared so distantly into his glass that Dan could have strangled him. Listen, you old fool. Understand.

'My responsibility at the moment, Dicky, is to cough up enough money to cover the company's losses. If I can do that, I'm away again. Old Medway is prepared to let bygones be bygones. But if I don't . . .'

'Poor fellow,' Richard said, 'it's a difficult situation.' Suddenly Dan felt he had to tell somebody the truth. Even Dick Reidy.

'Listen, Dick, old skin, I very nearly made it today on a borrowed fifty quid. Two-thirty at Fairyhouse—my tip was a certainty at a hundred to one. Outsider called Fox Trot couldn't lose, the chappie said. So I'd made up my mind. Fifty for a win. Made up my *mind*, Dicky, you understand? But going in the gate I met the Nag Montague—remember him? Haunted the stables since he was a nipper. Said I was mad, misinformed. Fox Trot hadn't an earthly. The horse that was a certainty for the two-thirty was Bitter Sweet— the tip came from the trainer who knew the form of the whole field.'

Now it seemed at last Richard understood. Drink suspended, he gave Dan all his appalled attention.

'You changed your mind?'

'Changed my mind. Fox Trot won, Dicky. Fucking Fox Trot won the fucking race by three lengths.'

Richard looked uneasily around at the few other drinkers to make sure nobody could see his brother-in-law actually breaking down, actually blubbing like a woman. Now Richard knew all he wanted to do was to make his escape home to Harriet as quickly as possible. He should never have come to the pub with Dan in the first place.

'There, there, old man. Don't take it so much to heart. Nothing is ever as bad as it seems at first.' He would apologise first to Harriet before she attacked him for being late, maybe take her a bunch of daffodils from the corner shop. There were daffodils in the garden but she hated plucking them.

'This is worse, and can only get entirely hopeless if I can't lay hands on a thousand quid inside twenty-four hours.' But Dan was not blubbing any more. He had raised his voice and Richard looked uneasily in the direction of the snug door which was open now. A young woman with avid eyes was watching them. A young woman of a certain class drinking gin alone.

'Maybe you should go over to the northside and see Fanny—how about that?' Richard offered shakily. The prominent blue eyes of his brother-in-law took on an ugly glitter. Richard knew himself that even mentioning Fanny in relation to borrowing money was treacherous, and worse, silly.

'My sister Fanny would give me her last farthing and so would her husband. It's to be regretted that that's not where the money is to be found in this family.'

'You'll have to excuse me, Dan. Would you not have another drink before I rush off? As I told you before, Harriet has something arranged for this evening.'

'I will have another Jameson since you offer it.'

Rapidly draining his own glass, Richard ordered another for his brother-in-law, who had relapsed into gloom again. 'Good luck, old man. The situation might change entirely after you've slept on it. Mr Medway might even see his way . . .'

The farewell monosyllable from his brother-in-law was not one Richard cared to remember. Dan always had been ugly in drink. He hurried into the sunshine in the direction of the flower shop just as the young woman in the snug emerged and moved quite close to Dan, shamelessly giving him the glad eye.

She was not, Dan decided, a gift from the gods, their parting gift. She was neither as young nor as pretty as her ankles but she looked clean enough and cheerful enough and suddenly she seemed to Dan to embody all the women who had ever momentarily stirred him. She could be put in even more agreeable form by the single pound he had left in his pockets. When she told him she lived in a top room in Holles Street, a cosy attic under the slates with a window looking at the stars, he knew they would take a cab there and that his final exit had been reasonably stage-managed by the gods. It wouldn't provoke spontaneous applause, but it would be an exit that could scarcely go unnoticed, even by his family.

The Bird I Fancied

Charing Cross Station, apparently, exists no longer. At Embankment a recorded male voice hollowly intoned 'Mind the Gap!' over and over. And then I was away. An hour too early, missing you again, seeing love-bowers below, rolling cornfields of Sussex, stands of beech buffeted by the breeze, ferny gripes. Then Hither Green, Petts Wood, immense strato-cumulus over the weald. Wadhurst and a fat smiling girl on a fat piebald pony following a pretty blackhaired friend on a sorrel, off for a day's trekking. Stonegate ('England, Home & Beauty'), Etchingham, a heron flying over the stubble-fields, and what I took to be the ghost of Douglas Bader, the air-ace, stumping heavily up and down Tunbridge Station, waiting for the London train.

Cut wheatfields around Frant. Then Tunbridge Wells Central, the inevitable pottery, Sevenoaks. I counted only seven cabbage whites along the woody railway embankments between Petts Wood (lacking a possessive) and Battle. Pesticides destroy the butterflies, our world.

Then High Brooms, Grove Junction, Robertsbridge without the possessive and Brownies embarking on Battle Station for a day's outing to Hastings. A damp mess of used clothes thrown out under a tree near a caravan site at the end of the road leading to the station; the balmy air of High Street. I walked over the famous battlefield with Professor Burns, felt nothing much; history's pomps are toylike.

A Mexican couple were studying the battle array mounted in a glass case; toy lead soldiers on a field of green, an arrow in King Harold's eye.

'Look up in the sky, Hal, and tell me what you see.'

'I see the moon.'

'Well, how much further do you want to see?'

The attack had been made uphill, great foolishness, over undulating terrain. The hidden bowmen, releasing their flights from a distance, killed at will. Modern warfare as such had begun—odd that the phlegmatic and peace-loving English should have invented it. The armoured knights attacked splendidly uphill with battle-axes raised, leaving behind them only a pool of blood. The battle-area was smaller than expected; as Lord Byron, riding over it, had remarked upon the smallness of the field of Waterloo. Great deeds, as murder, require little space. To kill a man there is required a bright, shining and clear light. No sooner had a bloodred sun set behind the hazy border hills of Sussex than a paper-thin, bone-white sickle moon appeared in the sky, shrouded in cloud, to shine obliquely down on disordered and ghostly battle-dead at Hastings.

Overheard, orbiting in space, fixed upon an undeviating course, a trajectory of aligned accuracy that had not changed since observed in 87 BC by the seventeen-year-old stripling Caius Julius—in a time that went backwards—Halley's Comet had come around again, dragging a tail of luminous gas said to be a hundred million kilometers long; a monster of antiquity breeding in the upper air.

Ahead, unknown to Caesar, were the years on horseback, sanguinary campaigns, promotion, war in Gaul. Not to mention the Rubicon, the Ides of March, and a text to trouble future generations of inkstained schoolboys baffled by *De Bello Gallico*.

Orbiting overhead, letting off steam, the *rara avis* went rocketing onward, dropping off gross tonnage of itself in its haste to get beyond the sun. Nothing would be clear from the crib, except gleams of half-extinguished light, diffuse illusions; increasing and decreasing, no sooner seen than gone. This manifestation not to be seen again by human eye for seventy-six years, our lifespan, passing by without leaving a trace—heaven's gas, *numinous rejectamenta*, a will-o'-the-wisp in the night sky.

Jupiter's red spot indicates where it has been raining, not bleeding, nonstop for seven hundred years. There is always a sign, if you look for it. But William Duke of Normandy was ignorant of all this as he dined with his army chiefs.

Celibate as an Abelite or the albatross that mates every three years—chastity springing from lack of choice and a fastidious mood (abstinence, as absence, makes the heart grow less fond, *au fond*, makes it weary, also distorts the reality of the absent one); and I'd been eighteen months in that sorry condition when I first set eyes on you. The range of the squonk is limited.

*　　*　　*

How come you in these parts? Where were you bred? To escape into nothingness, struggle upwards out of the Nothing, struggle on. Expect few favours; we live in modern times, after all. Sometimes you got tight by evening. One day we had thirty-two 'jars' in The Nightingale, beginning with Bloody Mary and ending with bitter.

All your projects were to come to nothing. Working, as you put it, for '*Your* bunch' (the Irish Tourist Board), for the deaf, designing sandals, sculpting, making paper funeral-flowers for an undertaker; nothing came of all this. Another life was pacing alongside your own.

Then you were in Somerset where your mother was dying of cancer. You feared to stay in the house with your father. You said: 'I can't stand it.'

'We must have a child.' We'd call it Jarleth. You'd drag me from a pub, drive away in a large limousine stocked with a private bar, come to a rural retreat all whitewashed; and we'd live forever and forever there, eating rabbits. You had such sweet fancies.

At first I couldn't even remember your name. Not even that most primitive courtesy. It was an odd name of two syllables with a bucolic ring to it: Fairfax, Fielding, Rutland, Greenwood, Moormist, Thorncroft, Atwood, Woodfall, Honeycombe, Summerbee, Oldfield, Loveridge. *Liebe*, lord, how does that come in! Love, an accomplice between two ailing beings. Why, one must fear even to be liked.

You, as Harbinger of Woe, with your dose of bad news every morning, to wake up the estranged husband, Moose. Your name, when I did recall it, seemed to suit you, it fitted: Sally Underwood.

You took jobs that were beneath you, worked for a mini-cab firm, the deaf, kept the family going, knew petty criminals. To the yobbos and geezers you were the witchy-looking bird with the tits. The burglar with revolver in bag had offered you fifty quid to show your breasts. You said you needed the money but not that badly. Moose threw up his job, went bankrupt, buried his bills in the garden. The VAT man was after him. The Somerset rooks were building high in the trees that spring; but other creatures were on the wing about the rape-fields.

Howling like attacking Dervishes, savages at tribal rites deep in the jungle, the damned in deepest Hell, some wildly excited coloured youths were engaging in burying an unconscious drunken comrade in an open drain outside The Green Man on Muswell Hill.

'Darkies,' your mother called them. Head-butters were in action between Oscar's and Chicago 20, and Flynn the drug-pusher slinking home.

You had not many years to live, you said sadly, showing me your palms. Yet in Glastonbury they lived to a ripe old age—Uncle Gilbert was 102. Your moods went on and off like traffic lights. You belonged in spirit to the fast set of a previous time: Emily Coleman and Mary Pyne, the daring lost ones—Thelma Wood accelerating about the Etoile in a red Bugatti with the muffler removed. Stingos at the Dome. Sipping tea laced with absinthe with McAlmon at the Berlin Adlon.

We drank White Shields at Harry's Bar in Hampstead near the ponds. The river flooded the valley and the sea came in, while Wells' Choir sang Vivaldi's 'Gloria' as if Cromwell's hangman had never strung up the Abbot. Our maternal grandmothers had the same Christian name: Lily. The double of John Arlott drank Guinness in The Shepherds on Archway Road, and you told me how as a young girl you had offered to sleep with the English wicket-keeper. He said you are too nice for that, and sent you home in a taxi. Mike the barman at The Alexandra, a Mack Sennett heavy, was polishing a glass, one bloodshot eye fixed on me.

'Where's the lovely lady?'

And in you came, blown in by the morning, breathless.

'My trouble is—I can't say no and I can't say yes.'

The 'Deafies' were foaming at the mouth with excitement on the stairs. When you left the Royal Institute of the Deaf at Gower Street, the deaf and staff wept to see you go. Moose's fury was just contained. You sold the old house, which you had cleaned yourself from cellar to attic, found a buyer, got the right price, spent two days in bed. Then bought another house not ten miles from the old one, in a rougher area, for exactly the same price. In the first four months it was broken into twice, the back door smashed in with a sledgehammer. Moose began burying his bills in the garden again. He drank vodka, came back footless from the Railway Tavern and The Finishing Post.

You told me stories of Glastonbury; a schoolfriend, one of the 'fast' girls serving in a tea-shop at the age of sixteen, had been raped in a lane. She couldn't tell her own father, who had already molested her at an even more tender age. She had marked the face of the attacker, a customer known to her. That's how it was in Glastonbury.

Sometimes you said your mother was dying down there, at other times you yourself were dying in Finsbury Park. The confusion was total. I didn't know whom to believe, or who was dying.

You said to Moose: 'You want to kill me.' Moose said no, not you; it was evident whom he meant. Sometimes you had to sleep with him; it was no good. You made up your own room upstairs; he followed you up. You crept down, slept alone in his own room; he followed you down. He was a hundred per cent physical, a Harringay second-row forward, the heavy in the boiler-house. He began to break things up. You and he could neither part nor live amicably together. It was a classical situation—the Marital Impasse. All concerned were having a bad time. The three children suffered; Saxon, Titus and Liza. The eldest son was twenty-two; Liza had been molested at the age of eight by an artist with a studio in Kentish Town. You knew him. He told me what would happen when you caught him.

You left Moose and went to stay with a redheaded business-woman who had three redheaded daughters, having left her Jewish husband, a dentist in Golders Green. It is quite rare to meet interesting people in the Golders Green area. Beth Brockelhurst, breathing fire, followed you into her bathroom, sat smoking on the edge of the tub, praised your figure, enquired of your love-life, begged a goodnight kiss. She was attracted to lesbians and ladies with leanings. Her livingroom was decorated with posters of sinewy masculine-looking females who had legs long as Fanny Blankers Koen.

Her gardener was a Professor whose son had jumped to his death from a tower-block. He was a cowed man, his spirit broken, which suited his Boss, who treated him like a dog when she didn't treat him like dirt. I encountered this depressed Professor in the kitchen, smelling of garden-loam and fear, uneasy on the other side of the long table, being patronisingly offered instant coffee by the mistress of Haus Herzenstod. And from the attic window of the former servant's room rented out to Sally, I watched him moodily raking up pears in the dewy garden below. The house next door was owned by the brother or son of the man who wrote 'Gormanghast' and 'Titus Groan'.

We were 'married' by the middle daughter Trixie, aged six, in the kitchen. Sixteen rings from a broken white necklace ringed our fingers, our names were repeated. Sally-and-Brian joined and sworn sixteen times; well and truly joined in wedlock by this innocent. Mahaud the Saudi with tribal markings who drank in The Prince had taken us for brother and sister. He was gunman or gardener in a great mansion overlooking Hampstead Heath. Freddy Baker, the Liverpudlian drunk, embraced you by the serving-hatch. He said that the Irish were only good for digging holes in the road.

We lived high up in the dim attic as man and wife, in a bedroom permeated with old sorrows. Sally went out to work in Gower Street, got up in fatigues and battle dress, never a skirt, having some notion about her legs. In fact she had a very nice pair, and had danced on a table in The Prince of Wales with Dr Graham Chapman, later to become famous as one of the Monty Python jokers.

Sally's rigout might be a mixture of English Lesbos and Italian *partisani*, a style later developed by Kirsten Teisner. In-Wear 'Savage Spirit' nana socks and camel jeans, kan bag and savanna boots, shore kit, jungle casual wear. She garbed herself in the colours of autumn and winter, though I always associated her with summer and the things of summer.

The bull in a field of heifers at Brickendon Green. The great Beast had exposed a pizzle long as a red-hot poker and attempted to mount a five-barred gate, as Sally backed off. You found this as startling as the antics of the belly-dancer downstairs at The Four Lanterns. If summers would ever be like summer again, in England, they would be linked with you under the beech tree in Hadley Wood, dressed in savanna boots and earrings. Or with nothing on at all in the reedy riverbed at Brickendon Green, with drinks in The Ploughboy after.

We drank pints at Ye Olde Monken Holt and took a Barnet bus with foul-mouthed Mohawks out for an evening of booze and Wogbashing in dirty Leicester Square. We frequented The Prince of Wales, the Angel, Gate House, Rose and Crown, Duke of Norfolk in Highgate village; sometimes The Flask or The Wrestlers, Red Lion and Sun, The Victoria, The Bull, The Clissold Arms, that morgue, or two Irish pubs on the Archway Road, The Shepherds, Whittington and Cat, patronised by labouring Irish, like bad spuds, all ears.

At Oscar's, The Green Man, The John Baird we were known. A morning of Bloody Marys down at The Royal Oak, an evening of White Shields at The Alexandra; mixing 'em in Dick's Bar on Tottenham Lane or at Odd Bob's in East Finchley. We passed by The Bull and Gate, The Drum and Monkey, The Tally Ho, avoided the meat-heads in The Mother Red Cap at Camden Town.

In The Prince one morning I spoke to Mick Minogue, late of Scariff in the County Clare. He was doing a job in Cromwell's old townhouse off Pond Square, praised the ornate woodwork. His mother had called him from the Beyond; Mick heard her distinctly, his hair stood on end. He sat down and drank a bottle of Scotch as if it were water. He gave me a hot tip for White City, the crabbed finger went down the list of runners, Mystical Hound, Peaceful Rouge. Drummond and McAllister were drinking with the Cockney Henry who had done time for manslaughter.

The poor beast Sweeney had his testicles surgically treated by the local vet. The gingery Rory Beamish was dragged about the Broadway by the frantic labrador, but pulled between The Baird and Oscar's, or between The Green Man and The Royal Oak. No flies on Mr B.

You said I was a badger, my youngest son a fox. You liked Elkie Brooks, Brian Ferry ('These Foolish Things'), the Aloha Boys ('Only You'). Katie Deering's white portable throbbed, we danced across the sanded floor, the three small Deerings poking at our private parts. Buzz was your best friend; she came from the Windward Islands. 'Katie doesn't know if she's brown or black.'

You were generous; when your dying mother gave you her own mother's jewellery, you handed it on to Liza. You looked after your mother, slept with her despite the terrible smell, washed her, put her on the pot. She was 'going down like a balloon', shrunken. 'My death comes in a direct line through her.' The old man had moved into the spare room, protesting that he was shy. Your mother had grown sharp; the old man didn't want to watch her dying. She had always been pretty, and now was pretty again; 'making sense at last'. She whispered to you: 'Your children are grown up now . . . Save yourself while you can.'

Recently you had begun to live. We were staying at Wandsworth in a friend's place near the prison. Well-fed wardens drank pints in The Country Arms, handcuffs hung from their hip-pockets. You told me of your past: At sixteen you had a pet jackdaw, at twenty were besotted with David Attenborough, rode Jupiter the stallion without a saddle through Glastonbury. You praised the peace of Somerset; the dawn chorus, the look of the winter sea, the village of Wells under the Mendips. 'Come down,' you said. 'I don't play games.'

You were drinking at the Prince of Wales, The Nightingale, the back bar of The Alexandra; you were waiting for me there, talking to Big Mike. The estranged husband of Katie Deering was on speed, jogging in the dark. He asked you to show your breasts; you obliged. You flew into The John Baird, sat on my lap like a bird.

'I have the spondoolicks.'

The unhappy jogger passed. You spent a wet winter's night in the ruins of Alexandra Palace, a foolish thing to do; arrived home with chattering teeth for Moose to throw open the door. He asked no questions, had murder on his mind. We had nowhere to go.

'I could sleep for a week.'

For Moose the footer season opened with fractured ribs, ended with broken teeth. At a rowdy party for rugger friends, all drinking their heads off, he forced you to sit on a hot and hairy lap, the only woman there. A part-time barman 'chatted you up' at The Baird, became aggressive, asked where was the Brain-of-Britain, demanded attention.

'I don't take no from a bird I fancy.'

You told him to go home, that he was pushing his luck. He slunk away, cursing. You took chances, thinking yourself safe in mini-cabs, asked the coloured driver to kiss you, you were kissing me. He said he was gay; you said it didn't matter, he kissed you. A kerb-crawler drove you home, you changed, were driven to Highgate Golf Club. You asked the fare, but it wasn't even a mini-cab. You might have been raped. You were moving fast in several directions at once, lost, 'shattered'. Your skin-aroma: Geranium. Your hair: Meadowsweet.

It was around that time that your electricity supply had been cut off, and the Falklands débâcle ended. 'The Antipodes really grate on me,' a morose drinker admitted at The Gate House. You chased a Peeping Tom out of Highgate Wood as if chasing a goose, not a flasher, a flustered biker carrying a white crash-helmet into which he may have been masturbating.

'*Christ is Coming*' went the graffiti on a wall, below it a wit had finely amended: '*When?*' and below that another hand had written: '*So is Tom (Perrier)*.'

One night Katie Deering phoned late, saying a friend wished to speak to me. The name? 'Patricia.' It was Sally unsober at The Four Lanterns. Buzz prayed to the Lord, referring to Him as The Man. The Hereafter would be as bad as this world, run by heavenly Mafia; prayer was a kind of bribe, payola. Katie sat mesmerised before the large colour TeeVee; Torvill and Dean skated 'Bolero'; the three kids clung to her, transfixed, thumbs in mouths, Lizzy, Dizzy and Whizzy, watched the skaters twirling.

You yourself had a tendency to bolt. One night after closing-time outside Chicago 20 you abandoned me for the *third* time, fled weeping into the dark. You were feeling edgy, shattered, had gone mad again. If I was a badger, you were a hare, both Pisceans. You wrote me a postcard from Somerset: 'My dear Brian—Going down on the train now. Hawthorn blossom all over the hedges all the way. Snow-in-June. Sally.'

Moose's sister had arrived from Copenhagen. Liza, aged thirteen, worried about her thin ankles and big bust. Titus, aged eighteen, kept piranha fish, was attacked in the school yard. Large coloured youths drove in at recess, to do him properly, because of a quarrel over a coloured girl; he was taken to hospital with fractured ribs and a broken nose.

One Saturday night the standoff half of Moose's team, having just left The Green Man in an unsober condition, was struck by a white Cortina driven by a Cypriot, and carried as far as The Odeon. He was kept alive in a life support machine until his parents arrived from Sheffield. He was breathing, but 'had no face to talk with. They asked that the machine be turned off.'

You liked the big city for the edge it gave you, but were 'shattered' once more by events in the country. The deaths of Uncle Gilbert and your Grandfather, both in their nineties. You'd remembered the pleasant peaty aroma of old men, when as a child you had sat on their laps, the warmth and protection (more imaginary than real) it afforded.

'P'sst, Missy! Y'uve gotta nice fice, Missy!' the tough coloured youths whispered spookily outside The Court House. A knife was shown, you had to walk the gauntlet of their threats. The attacker was known for previous violent behaviour. You had to give evidence. Then all that trouble ended; the case went to a higher court, the attacker was arrested. He had a record. Titus slept with his bedroom door locked, a shiv under his pillow. Big Mike had done a bunk to Hatfield.

You wept on the cobb at Lyme Regis at seven o'clock one morning in August, were photographed on Axminster Station, looking very brown and Mediterranean. In Buzz's garden you fell over the handlebars of a child's bike and cut open your chin, got sick in the flowerbeds, had to have five stitches at The Whittington. You were like that.

The small red Bugatti buzzed into Juan-les-Pins with muffler removed, into a broad street with tramlines leading to the harbour, the glittering sea. In the Bar Basque a band was tuning up, before launching into 'I'm Looking for Sally'. The large smiling gent in beige suiting sprawled with legs apart, pulling on a thick cigar, watching us dance over the sanded dance-floor under the turning fairie lights. A sea-breeze, smell of resin, cigar smoke. Sanded dance-floor, glittering lights.

You, only you; a chestful of breasts, a bird's ever-suspicious eye with permanently enlarged pupils, on the lookout for predators. Slightly knock-kneed, with the inturned toes of a wide-hipped breeder. A warmly sexual nature, the barest hint of a rural burr. Say Lardy Cake. Say Beacon Hill. Say Wells. Say Mendips. The dark gods of Somerset are listening.

Bugger my old boots, but of all the birds in the air that ever floated on dark water, twittered, hid in reeds, flew in the night, skidded on ice, sang from treetop, perched in impossible places, lamented, rose early, retired late, had young, choked on chicken reappeared next morning, drank to excess, went on the wagon, regretted nothing, died on the wing, struck against lighthouses, were incapable of restraint, I surely fancied you.

A shadow passing, a female presence gone. As sure as God is in bleeding Gloucestershire, it's true, dear heart.

WILLIAM TREVOR · 1928–

Death in Jerusalem

'Till then,' Father Paul said, leaning out of the train window. 'Till Jerusalem, Francis.'

'Please God, Paul.' As he spoke the Dublin train began to move and his brother waved from the window and he waved back, a modest figure on the platform. Everyone said Francis might have been a priest as well, meaning that Francis's quietness and meditative disposition had an air of the cloister about them. But Francis contented himself with the running of Daly's hardware business which his mother had run until she was too old for it. 'Are we game for the Holy Land next year?' Father Paul had asked that July. 'Will we go together, Francis?' He had brushed aside all Francis's protestations, all attempts to explain that the shop could not be left, that their mother would be confused by the absence of Francis from the house. Rumbustiously he'd pointed out that there was their sister Kitty, who was in charge of the household of which Francis and their mother were part and whose husband Myles could surely be trusted to look after the shop for a single fortnight. For thirty years, ever since he was seven, Francis had wanted to go to the Holy Land. He had savings which he'd never spent a penny of: you couldn't take them with you, Father Paul had more than once stated that July.

On the platform Francis watched until the train could no longer be seen, his thoughts still with his brother. The priest's ruddy countenance smiled again behind cigarette smoke; his bulk remained impressive in his clerical clothes, the collar pinching the flesh of his neck, his black shoes scrupulously polished. There were freckles on the backs of his large, strong hands; he had a fine head of hair, grey and crinkly. In an hour and a half's time the train would creep into Dublin, and he'd take a taxi. He'd spend a night in the Gresham Hotel, probably falling in with another priest, having a drink or two, maybe playing a game of bridge after his meal. That was his brother's way and always had been—an extravagant, easy kind of way, full of smiles and good humour. It was what had taken him to America and made him successful there. In order to raise money for the church that he and Father Steigmuller intended to build before 1980 he took parties of the well-to-do from San Francisco to Rome and Florence, to Chartres and Seville and the Holy Land. He was good at raising money, not just for the church but for the boys' home of which he was president, and for the Hospital of Our Saviour, and for St Mary's Old People's Home on the west side of the city. But every July he flew back to Ireland, to the town in Co. Tipperary where his mother and brother and sister still lived. He stayed in the house above the shop which he might have inherited himself on the death of his father, which he'd rejected in favour of the religious life. Mrs Daly was eighty now. In the shop she sat silently behind the counter, in a corner by the chicken-wire, wearing only clothes that were black. In the evenings she sat with Francis in the lace-curtained sitting-room, while the rest of the family occupied the kitchen. It was for her sake most of all that Father Paul made the journey every summer, considering it his duty.

Walking back to the town from the station, Francis was aware that he was missing his brother. Father Paul was fourteen years older and in childhood had often taken the place of their father, who had died when Francis was five. His brother had possessed an envied strength and knowledge; he'd been a hero, quite often worshipped, an example of success. In later life he had become an example of generosity as well: ten years ago he'd taken their mother to Rome, and their sister Kitty and her husband two years later; he'd paid the expenses when their sister Edna had gone to Canada; he'd assisted two nephews to make a start in America. In childhood Francis hadn't possessed his brother's healthy freckled face, just as in middle age he didn't have his ruddy complexion and his stoutness and his easiness with people. Francis was slight, his sandy hair receding, his face rather pale. His breathing was sometimes laboured because of wheeziness in the chest. In the ironmonger's shop he wore a brown cotton coat.

'Hullo, Mr Daly,' a woman said to him in the main street of the town. 'Father Paul's gone off, has he?'

'Yes, he's gone again.'

'I'll pray for his journey so,' the woman promised, and Francis thanked her.

*   *   *

A year went by. In San Francisco another wing of the boys' home was completed, another target was reached in Father Paul's and Father Steigmuller's fund for the church they planned to have built by 1980. In the town in Co. Tipperary there were baptisms and burial services and First Communions. Old Loughlin, a farmer from Bansha, died in Flynn's grocery and bar, having gone there to celebrate a good price he'd got for a heifer. Clancy, from behind the counter in Doran's drapery, married Maureen Talbot; Mr Nolan's plasterer married Miss Driscoll; Johneen Lynch married Seamus in the chip shop, under pressure from her family to do so. A local horse, from the stables on the Limerick road, was said to be an entry for the Fairyhouse Grand National, but it turned out not to be true. Every evening of that year Francis sat with his mother in the lace-curtained sitting-room above the shop. Every weekday she sat in her corner by the chicken-wire, watching while he counted out screws and weighed staples, or advised about yard brushes or tap-washers. Occasionally, on a Saturday, he visited the three Christian Brothers who lodged with Mrs Shea and afterwards he'd tell his mother about how the authority was slipping these days from the nuns and the Christian Brothers, and how Mrs Shea's elderly maid, Agnes, couldn't see to cook the food any more. His mother would nod and hardly ever speak. When he told a joke—what young Hogan had said when he'd found a nail in his egg or how Agnes had put mint sauce into a jug with milk in it—she never laughed and looked at him in surprise when he laughed himself. But Dr Grady said it was best to keep her cheered up.

All during that year Francis talked to her about his forthcoming visit to the Holy Land, endeavouring to make her understand that for a fortnight next spring he would be away from the house and the shop. He'd been away before for odd days, but that was when she'd been younger. He used to visit an aunt in Tralee, but three years ago the aunt had died and he hadn't left the town since.

Francis and his mother had always been close. Before his birth two daughters had died in infancy, and his very survival had often struck Mrs Daly as a gift. He had always been her favourite, the one among her children whom she often considered least able to stand on his own two feet. It was just like Paul to have gone blustering off to San Francisco instead of remaining in Co. Tipperary. It was just like Kitty to have married a useless man. 'There's not a girl in the town who'd touch him,' she'd said to her daughter at the time, but

Kitty had been headstrong and adamant, and there was Myles now, doing nothing whatsoever except cleaning other people's windows for a pittance and placing bets in Donovan's the turf accountant's. It was the shop and the arrangement Kitty had with Francis and her mother that kept her and the children going, three of whom had already left the town, which in Mrs Daly's opinion they mightn't have done if they'd had a better type of father. Mrs Daly often wondered what her own two babies who'd died might have grown up into, and imagined they might have been like Francis, about whom she'd never had a moment's worry. Not in a million years would he give you the feeling that he was too big for his boots, like Paul sometimes did with his lavishness and his big talk of America. He wasn't silly like Kitty, or so sinful you couldn't forgive him, like you couldn't forgive Edna, even though she was dead and buried in Toronto.

Francis understood how his mother felt about the family. She'd had a hard life, left a widow early on, trying to do the best she could for everyone. In turn he did his best to compensate for the struggles and disappointments she'd suffered, cheering her in the evenings while Kitty and Myles and the youngest of their children watched the television in the kitchen. His mother had ignored the existence of Myles for ten years, ever since the day he'd taken money out of the till to pick up the odds on Gutsy Spirit at Phoenix Park. And although Francis got on well enough with Myles he quite understood that there should be a long aftermath to that day. There'd been a terrible row in the kitchen, Kitty screaming at Myles and Myles telling lies and Francis trying to keep them calm, saying they'd give the old woman a heart attack.

She didn't like upsets of any kind, so all during the year before he was to visit the Holy Land Francis read the New Testament to her in order to prepare her. He talked to her about Bethlehem and Nazareth and the miracle of the loaves and fishes and all the other miracles. She kept nodding, but he often wondered if she didn't assume he was just casually referring to episodes in the Bible. As a child he had listened to such talk himself, with awe and fascination, imagining the walking on the water and the temptation in the wilderness. He had imagined the cross carried to Calvary, and the rock rolled back from the tomb, and the rising from the dead on the third day. That he was now to walk in such places seemed extraordinary to him, and he wished his mother was younger so that she could appreciate his good fortune and share it with him when she received the postcards he intended, every day, to send her. But her eyes seemed always to tell him that he was making a mistake, that somehow he was making a fool of himself by doing such a showy thing as going to the Holy Land. *I have the entire itinerary mapped out*, his brother wrote from San Francisco. *There's nothing we'll miss.*

It was the first time Francis had been in an aeroplane. He flew by Aer Lingus from Dublin to London and then changed to an El Al flight to Tel Aviv. He was nervous and he found it exhausting. All the time he seemed to be eating, and it was strange being among so many people he didn't know. 'You will taste honey such as never before,' an Israeli businessman in the seat next to his assured him. 'And Galilean figs. Make certain to taste Galilean figs.' Make certain too, the businessman went on, to experience Jerusalem by night and in the early dawn. He urged Francis to see places he had never heard of, the Yad Va-Shem, the treasures of the Shrine of the Book. He urged him to honour the martyrs of Masada and to learn a few words of Hebrew as a token of respect. He told him of a shop where he could buy mementoes and warned him against Arab street traders.

'The hard man, how are you?' Father Paul said at Tel Aviv airport, having flown in from San Francisco the day before. Father Paul had had a drink or two and he suggested another when they arrived at the Plaza Hotel in Jerusalem. It was half-past nine in the evening. 'A quick little nightcap,' Father Paul insisted, 'and then hop into bed with you, Francis.' They sat in an enormous open lounge with low round tables and square modern armchairs. Father Paul said it was the bar.

They had said what had to be said in the car from Tel Aviv to Jerusalem. Father Paul had asked about their mother, and Kitty and Myles. He'd asked about other people in the town, old Canon Mahon and Sergeant Malone. He and Father Steigmuller had had a great year of it, he reported: as well as everything else, the boys' home had turned out two tip-top footballers. 'We'll start on a tour at half-nine in the morning,' he said. 'I'll be sitting having breakfast at eight.'

Francis went to bed and Father Paul ordered another whisky, with ice. To his great disappointment there was no Irish whiskey in the hotel so he'd had to content himself with Haig. He fell into conversation with an American couple, making them promise that if they were ever in Ireland they wouldn't miss out Co. Tipperary. At eleven o'clock the barman said he was wanted at the reception desk and when Father Paul went there and announced himself he was given a message in an envelope. It was a telegram that had come, the girl said in poor English. Then she shook her head, saying it was a telex. He opened the envelope and learnt that Mrs Daly had died.

Francis fell asleep immediately and dreamed that he was a boy again, out fishing with a friend whom he couldn't now identify.

On the telephone Father Paul ordered whisky and ice to be brought to his room. Before drinking it he took his jacket off and knelt by his bed to pray for his mother's salvation. When he'd completed the prayers he walked slowly up and down the length of the room, occasionally sipping at his whisky. He argued with himself and finally arrived at a decision.

For breakfast they had scrambled eggs that looked like yellow ice-cream, and orange juice that was delicious. Francis wondered about bacon, but Father Paul explained that bacon was not readily available in Israel.

'Did you sleep all right?' Father Paul enquired. 'Did you have the jet-lag?'

'Jet-lag?'

'A tiredness you get after jet flights. It'd knock you out for days.'

'Ah, I slept great, Paul.'

'Good man.'

They lingered over breakfast. Father Paul reported a little more of what had happened in his parish during the year, in particular about the two young footballers from the boys' home. Francis told about the decline in the cooking at Mrs Shea's boarding-house, as related to him by the three Christian Brothers. 'I have a car laid on,' Father Paul said, and twenty minutes later they walked out into the Jerusalem sunshine.

The hired car stopped on the way to the walls of the old city. It drew into a lay-by at Father Paul's request and the two men got out and looked across a wide valley dotted with houses and olive trees.

A road curled along the distant slope opposite. 'The Mount of Olives,' Father Paul said. 'And that's the road to Jericho.' He pointed more particularly. 'You see that group of eight big olives? Just off the road, where the church is?'

Francis thought he did, but was not sure. There were so many olive trees, and more than one church. He glanced at his brother's pointing finger and followed its direction with his glance.

'The Garden of Gethsemane,' Father Paul said.

Francis did not say anything. He continued to gaze at the distant church, with the clump of olive trees beside it. Wild flowers were profuse on the slopes of the valley, smears of orange and blue on land that looked poor. Two Arab women herded goats.

'Could we see it closer?' he asked, and his brother said that definitely they would. They returned to the waiting car and Father Paul ordered it to the Gate of St Stephen.

Tourists heavy with cameras thronged the Via Dolorosa. Brown, bare-foot children asked for alms. Stall-keepers pressed their different wares—cotton dresses, metal-ware, mementoes, sacred goods. 'Get out of the way,' Father Paul kept saying to them, genially laughing to show he wasn't being abrupt. Francis wanted to stand still and close his eyes, to visualise for a moment the carrying of the Cross. But the ceremony of the Stations, familiar to him for as long as he could remember, was unreal. Try as he would, Christ's journey refused to enter his imagination, and his own plain church seemed closer to the heart of the matter than the noisy lane he was now being jostled on. 'God damn it, of course it's genuine,' an angry American voice proclaimed, in reply to a shriller voice which insisted that cheating had taken place. The voices argued about a piece of wood, neat beneath plastic in a little box, a sample or not of the cross that had been carried.

They arrived at the Church of the Holy Sepulchre, and at the Chapel of the Nailing to the Cross, where they prayed. They passed through the Chapel of the Angel, to the tomb of Christ. Nobody spoke in the marble cell, but when they left the church Francis overheard a quiet man with spectacles saying it was unlikely that a body would have been buried within the walls of the city. They walked to Hezekiah's Pool and out of the old city at the Jaffa Gate, where their hired car was waiting for them. 'Are you peckish?' Father Paul asked, and although Francis said he wasn't they returned to the hotel.

Delay funeral till Monday was the telegram Father Paul had sent. There was an early flight on Sunday, in time for an afternoon one from London to Dublin. With luck there'd be a late train on Sunday evening and if there wasn't they'd have to fix a car. Today was Tuesday. It would give them four and a half days. *Funeral eleven Monday* the telegram at the reception desk now confirmed. 'Ah, isn't that great?' he said to himself, bundling the telegram up.

'Will we have a small one?' he suggested in the open area that was the bar. 'Or better still a big one.' He laughed. He was in good spirits in spite of the death that had taken place. He gestured at the barman, wagging his head and smiling jovially.

His face had reddened in the morning sun; there were specks of sweat on his forehead and his nose. 'Bethlehem this afternoon,' he laid down. 'Unless the jet-lag . . .?'

'I haven't got the jet-lag.'

In the Nativity Boutique Francis had bought for his mother a small metal plate with a fish on it. He had stood for a moment, scarcely able to believe it, on the spot where the manger had been, in the Church of the Nativity. As in the Via Dolorosa it had been difficult to rid the imagination of the surroundings that now were present, of the exotic Greek Orthodox trappings, the foreign-looking priests, the oriental smell. Gold, frankincense, and myrrh, he'd kept thinking, for somehow the church seemed more the church of the kings than of Joseph and Mary and their child. Afterwards they returned to Jerusalem, to the Tomb of the Virgin and the Garden of Gethsemane. 'It could have been anywhere,' he heard the quiet, bespectacled sceptic remarking in Gethsemane. 'They're only guessing.'

Father Paul rested in the late afternoon, lying down on his bed with his jacket off. He slept from half-past five until a quarter-past seven and awoke refreshed. He picked up the telephone and asked for whisky and ice to be brought up and when it arrived he undressed and had a bath, relaxing in the warm water with the drink on a ledge in the tiled wall beside him. There would be time to take in Nazareth and Galilee. He was particularly keen that his brother should see Galilee because Galilee had atmosphere and was beautiful. There wasn't, in his own opinion, very much to Nazareth but it would be a pity to miss it all the same. It was at the Sea of Galilee that he intended to tell his brother of their mother's death.

We've had a great day, Francis wrote on a postcard that showed an aerial view of Jerusalem. *The Church of the Holy Sepulchre, where Our Lord's tomb is, and Gethsemane and Bethlehem. Paul's in great form.* He addressed it to his mother, and then wrote other cards, to Kitty and Myles and to the three Christian Brothers in Mrs Shea's, and to Canon Mahon. He gave thanks that he was privileged to be in Jerusalem. He read St Mark and some of St Matthew. He said his rosary.

'Will we chance the wine?' Father Paul said at dinner, not that wine was something he went in for, but a waiter had come up and put a large padded wine-list into his hand.

'Ah, no, no,' Francis protested, but already Father Paul was running his eye down the listed bottles.

'Have you local wine?' he enquired of the waiter. 'A nice red one?'

The waiter nodded and hurried away, and Francis hoped he wouldn't get drunk, the red wine on top of the whisky he'd had in the bar before the meal. He'd only had the one whisky, not being much used to it, making it last through his brother's three.

'I heard some gurriers in the bar,' Father Paul said, 'making a great song and dance about the local red wine.'

Wine made Francis think of the Holy Communion, but he didn't say so. He said the soup was delicious and he drew his brother's attention to the custom there was in the hotel of a porter ringing a bell and walking about with a person's name chalked on a little blackboard on the end of a rod.

'It's a way of paging you,' Father Paul explained. 'Isn't it nicer than bellowing out some fellow's name?' He smiled his easy smile, his eyes beginning to water as a result of the few drinks he'd had. He was beginning to feel the strain: he kept thinking of their mother lying there, of what she'd say if she knew what he'd done, how she'd savagely upbraid him for keeping the fact from Francis. Out of duty and humanity he had returned each year to see her because, after all, you only had the one mother. But he had never cared for her.

Francis went for a walk after dinner. There were young soldiers with what seemed to be toy guns on the streets, but he knew the guns were real. In the shop windows there were television sets for sale, and furniture and clothes, just like anywhere else. There were advertisements for some film or other, two writhing women without a stitch on them, the kind of thing you wouldn't see in Co. Tipperary. 'You want something, sir?' a girl said, smiling at him with broken front teeth. The siren of a police car or an ambulance shrilled urgently near by. He shook his head at the girl. 'No, I don't want anything,' he said, and then realised what she had meant. She was small and very dark, no more than a child. He hurried on, praying for her.

When he returned to the hotel he found his brother in the lounge with other people, two men and two women. Father Paul was ordering a round of drinks and called out to the barman to bring another whisky. 'Ah, no, no,' Francis protested, anxious to go to his room and to think about the day, to read the New Testament and perhaps to write a few more postcards. Music was playing, coming from speakers that could not be seen.

'My brother Francis,' Father Paul said to the people he was with, and the people all gave their names, adding that they came from New York. 'I was telling them about Tipp,' Father Paul said to his brother, offering his packet of cigarettes around.

'You like Jerusalem, Francis?' one of the American women asked him, and he replied that he hadn't been able to take it in yet. Then, feeling that that didn't sound enthusiastic enough, he added that being there was the experience of a lifetime.

Father Paul went on talking about Co. Tipperary and then spoke of his parish in San Francisco, the boys' home and the two promising footballers, the plans for the new church. The Americans listened and in a moment the conversation drifted on to the subject of their travels in England, their visits to Istanbul and Athens, an argument they'd had with the Customs at Tel Aviv. 'Well, I'm for the hay-pile,' one of the men announced eventually, standing up.

The others stood up too and so did Francis. Father Paul remained where he was, gesturing again in the direction of the barman. 'Sit down for a nightcap,' he urged his brother.

'Ah, no, no—' Francis began.

'Bring us two more of those,' the priest ordered with a sudden abruptness, and the barman hurried away. 'Listen,' said Father Paul. 'I've something to tell you.'

After dinner, while Francis had been out on his walk, before he'd dropped into conversation with the Americans, Father Paul had said to himself that he couldn't stand the strain. It was the old woman stretched out above the hardware shop, as stiff as a board already, with the little lights burning in her room: he kept seeing all that, as if she wanted him to, as if she was trying to haunt him. Nice as the idea was, he didn't think he could continue with what he'd planned, with waiting until they got up to Galilee.

Francis didn't want to drink any more. He hadn't wanted the whisky his brother had ordered him earlier, nor the one the Americans had ordered for him. He didn't want the one that the barman now brought. He thought he'd just leave it there, hoping his brother wouldn't see it. He lifted the glass to his lips, but he managed not to drink any.

'A bad thing has happened,' Father Paul said.

'Bad? How d'you mean, Paul?'

'Are you ready for it?' He paused. Then he said, 'She died.'

Francis didn't know what he was talking about. He didn't know who was meant to be dead, or why his brother was behaving in an odd manner. He didn't like to think it but he had to: his brother wasn't fully sober.

'Our mother died,' Father Paul said. 'I'm after getting a telegram.'

The huge area that was the lounge of the Plaza Hotel, the endless tables and people sitting at them, the swiftly moving waiters and barmen, seemed suddenly a dream. Francis had a feeling that he was not where he appeared to be, that he wasn't sitting with his brother, who was wiping his lips with a handkerchief. For a moment he appeared in his confusion to be struggling his way up the Via Dolorosa again and then in the Nativity Boutique.

'Take it easy, boy,' his brother was saying. 'Take a mouthful of whisky.'

Francis didn't obey that injunction. He asked his brother to repeat what he had said, and Father Paul repeated that their mother had died.

Francis closed his eyes and tried as well to shut away the sounds around them. He prayed for the salvation of his mother's soul. 'Blessed Virgin, intercede,' his own voice said in his mind. 'Dear Mary, let her few small sins be forgiven.'

Having rid himself of his secret, Father Paul felt instant relief. With the best of intentions in the world it had been a foolish idea to think he could maintain the secret until they arrived in a place that was perhaps the most suitable in the world to hear about the death of a person who'd been close to you. He took a gulp of his whisky and wiped his mouth with his handkerchief again. He watched his brother, waiting for his eyes to open.

'When did it happen?' Francis asked eventually.

'Yesterday.'

'And the telegram only came—'

'It came last night, Francis. I wanted to save you the pain.'

'Save me? How could you save me? I sent her a postcard, Paul.'

'Listen to me, Francis—'

'How could you save me the pain?'

'I wanted to tell you when we got up to Galilee.'

Again Francis felt he was caught in the middle of a dream. He couldn't understand his brother: he couldn't understand what he meant by saying a telegram had come last night, why at a moment like this he was talking about Galilee. He didn't know why he was sitting in this noisy place when he should be back in Ireland.

'I fixed the funeral for Monday,' Father Paul said.

Francis nodded, not grasping the significance of this arrangement. 'We'll be back there this time tomorrow,' he said.

'No need for that, Francis. Sunday morning's time enough.'

'But she's dead—'

'We'll be there in time for the funeral.'

'We can't stay here if she's dead.'

It was this, Father Paul realised, he'd been afraid of when he'd argued with himself and made his plan. If he'd have knocked on Francis's door the night before Francis would have wanted to return immediately without seeing a single stone of the land he had come so far to be moved by.

'We could go straight up to Galilee in the morning,' Father Paul said quietly. 'You'll find comfort in Galilee, Francis.'

But Francis shook his head. 'I want to be with her,' he said.

Father Paul lit another cigarette. He nodded at a hovering waiter, indicating the need of another drink. He said to himself that he must keep his cool, an expression he was fond of.

'Take it easy, Francis,' he said.

'Is there a plane out in the morning? Can we make arrangements now?' He looked about him as if for a member of the hotel staff who might be helpful.

'No good'll be done by tearing off home, Francis. What's wrong with Sunday?'

'I want to be with her.'

Anger swelled within Father Paul. If he began to argue his words would become slurred: he knew that from experience. He must keep his cool and speak slowly and clearly, making a few simple points. It was typical of her, he thought, tò die inconveniently.

'You've come all this way,' he said as slowly as he could without sounding peculiar. 'Why cut it any shorter than we need? We'll be losing a week anyway. She wouldn't want us to go back.'

'I think she would.'

He was right in that. Her possessiveness in her lifetime would have reached out across a dozen continents for Francis. She'd known what she was doing by dying when she had.

'I shouldn't have come,' Francis said. 'She didn't want me to come.'

'You're thirty-seven years of age, Francis.'

'I did wrong to come.'

'You did no such thing.'

The time he'd taken her to Rome she'd been difficult for the whole week, complaining about the food, saying everywhere was dirty. Whenever he'd spent anything she'd disapproved. All his life, Father Paul felt, he'd done his best for her. He had told her before anyone else when he'd decided to enter the priesthood, certain that she'd be pleased. 'I thought you'd take over the shop,' she'd said instead.

'What difference could it make to wait, Francis?'

'There's nothing to wait for.'

As long as he lived Francis knew he would never forgive himself. As long as he lived he would say to himself that he hadn't been able to wait a few years, until she'd passed quietly on. He might even have been in the room with her when it happened.

'It was a terrible thing not to tell me,' he said. 'I sat down and wrote her a postcard, Paul. I bought her a plate.'

'So you said.'

'You're drinking too much of that whisky.'

'Now, Francis, don't be silly.'

'You're half drunk and she's lying there.'

'She can't be brought back no matter what we do.'

'She never hurt anyone,' Francis said.

Father Paul didn't deny that, although it wasn't true. She had hurt their sister Kitty, constantly reproaching her for marrying the man she had, long after Kitty was aware she'd made a mistake She'd driven Edna to Canada after Edna, still unmarried, had had a miscarriage that only the family knew about. She had made a shadow out of Francis although Francis didn't know it. Failing to hold on to her other children, she had grasped her last-born to her, as if she had borne him to destroy him.

'It'll be you'll say a mass for her?' Francis said.

'Yes, of course it will.'

'You should have told me.'

Francis realised why, all day, he'd been disappointed. From the moment when the hired car had pulled into the lay-by and his brother had pointed across the valley at the Garden of Gethsemane he'd been disappointed and had not admitted it. He'd been disappointed in the Via Dolorosa and in the Church of the Holy Sepulchre and in Bethlehem. He remembered the bespectacled man who'd kept saying that you couldn't be sure about anything. All the people with cameras made it impossible to think, all the jostling and pushing was distracting. When he'd said there'd been too much to take in he'd meant something different.

'Her death got in the way,' he said.

'What d'you mean, Francis?'

'It didn't feel like Jerusalem, it didn't feel like Bethlehem.'

'But it is, Francis, it is.'

'There are soldiers with guns all over the place. And a girl came up to me on the street. There was that man with a bit of the Cross. There's you, drinking and smoking in this place—'

'Now, listen to me, Francis—'

'Nazareth would be a disappointment. And the Sea of Galilee. And the Church of the Loaves and Fishes.' His voice had risen. He lowered it again. 'I couldn't believe in the Stations this morning. I couldn't see it happening the way I do at home.'

'That's nothing to do with her death, Francis. You've got a bit of jet-lag, you'll settle yourself up in Galilee. There's an atmosphere in Galilee that nobody misses.'

'I'm not going near Galilee.' He struck the surface of the table, and Father Paul told him to contain himself. People turned their heads, aware that anger had erupted in the pale-faced man with the priest.

'Quieten up,' Father Paul commanded sharply, but Francis didn't.

'She knew I'd be better at home,' he shouted, his voice shrill and reedy. 'She knew I was making a fool of myself, a man out of a shop trying to be big—'

'Will you keep your voice down? Of course you're not making a fool of yourself.'

'Will you find out about planes tomorrow morning?'

Father Paul sat for a moment longer, not saying anything, hoping his brother would say he was sorry. Naturally it was a shock, naturally he'd be emotional and feel guilty, in a moment it would be better. But it wasn't and Francis didn't say he was sorry. Instead he began to weep.

'Let's go up to your room,' Father Paul said, 'and I'll fix about the plane.'

Francis nodded but did not move. His sobbing ceased, and then he said, 'I'll always hate the Holy Land now.'

'No need for that, Francis.'

But Francis felt there was and he felt he would hate, as well, the brother he had admired for as long as he could remember. In the lounge of the Plaza Hotel he felt mockery surfacing everywhere. His brother's deceit, and the endless whisky in his brother's glass, and his casualness after a death, seemed like the scorning of a Church which honoured so steadfastly the mother of its founder. Vivid in his mind, his own mother's eyes reminded him that they'd told him he was making a mistake, and upbraided him for not heeding her. Of course there was mockery everywhere, in the splinter of wood beneath plastic, and in the soldiers with guns that were not toys, and the writhing nakedness in the Holy City. He'd become part of it himself, sending postcards to the dead. Not speaking again to his brother, he went to his room to pray.

'Eight a.m., sir,' the girl at the reception desk said, and Father Paul asked that arrangements should be made to book two seats on the plane, explaining that it was an emergency, that a death had occurred. 'It will be all right, sir,' the girl promised.

He went slowly downstairs to the bar. He sat in a corner and lit a cigarette and ordered two whiskies and ice, as if expecting a companion. He drank them both himself and ordered more. Francis would return to Co. Tipperary and after the funeral he would take up again the life she had ordained for him. In his brown cotton coat he would serve customers with nails and hinges and wire. He would regularly go to Mass and to Confession and to Men's Confraternity. He would sit alone in the lace-curtained sitting-room, lonely for the woman who had made him what he was, married forever to her memory.

Father Paul lit a fresh cigarette from the butt of the last one. He continued to order whisky in two glasses. Already he could sense the hatred that Francis had earlier felt taking root in himself. He wondered if he would ever again return in July to Co. Tipperary, and imagined he would not.

At midnight he rose to make the journey to bed and found himself unsteady on his feet. People looked at him, thinking it disgraceful for a priest to be drunk in Jerusalem, with cigarette ash all over his clerical clothes.

BRIAN FRIEL · 1929–

The Diviner

During twenty-five years of married life, Nelly Devenny was
ashamed to lift her head because of Tom's antics. He was seldom
sober, never in a job for more than a few weeks at a time, and
always fighting. When he fell off his bicycle one Saturday night and
was killed by a passing motor-cycle, no one in the village of
Drumeen was surprised that Nelly was not heartbroken. She took
the death calmly and with quiet dignity and even shed a few tears
when the coffin was lowered into the grave. After a suitable period
of mourning, she went out to work as a charwoman, and the five
better-class families she asked for employment were blessed for
their prompt charity, because Nelly was the perfect servant—silent,
industrious, punctual, spotlessly clean. Later, when others, hearing
of her value, tried to engage her, they discovered that her schedule
was full; all her time was divided among the bank manager, the
solicitor, the dentist, the doctor, and the prosperous McLaughlins
of the Arcade.

Father Curran, the parish priest, was the only person she told
she was getting married again, and he knew she told him only
because she had to have a baptismal certificate and letters of
freedom.

'He's not from around these parts, Nelly, is he?' the priest
asked.

'He's not, Father.'

'Is he from County Donegal at all?'

'He's from the West, Father,' said Nelly, smoothing down the
hem of her skirt. 'Of course, Mr Doherty's retired now. He's not a
young man, but he's very fresh-looking.'

'Retired?' the priest said promptingly.

'Yes, Father,' said Nelly. 'Mr Doherty's retired.'

'And you'll live here in Drumeen with—with Mr Doherty?'

'That is our intention, Father.'

'Well, I wish you every blessing, Nelly,' said Father Curran in dismissal, because he was an inquisitive man and Nelly was giving nothing away. 'I'll see you when you get back.' Then quickly—an old trick of his—'The wedding is in the West, did you say?'

'That has to be settled yet, Father,' said Nelly calmly. 'It will just be a quiet affair. At our time of day, Father, we would prefer no fuss and no talk.'

He took the hint and let her go.

Nelly Devenny became Nelly Doherty, and she and her husband moved into her cottage at the outskirts of the village. Drumeen's speculation on Mr Doherty was wild and futile. What age was he? Was he younger than Nelly? What part of the West did he come from? What had he been—a train driver, a skipper of a fishing boat, a manager of a grocery shop, a plumber, a carpenter? Had he any relatives? Had he even a Christian name? Where had they met? Was it true that she had put an advertisement in the paper and that his was the only answer? But Nelly parried all their probings and carefully sheltered Mr Doherty from their clever tongues. The grinding humiliation of having her private life made public every turnabout in bars and courthouses for twenty-five years had made her skilled in reticence and fanatically jealous of her dignity. He stayed in the house during the day while she worked, and in the evening, if the weather was good, they could be seen going out along the Mill Road for a walk, Nelly dressed entirely in black and Mr Doherty in his gabardine raincoat, checked cap, and well-polished shoes, the essence of respectability. And in time the curiosity died and the only person to bring up the subject now and again was McElwee, the postman, who had been a drinking pal of Tom Devenny, her first husband. 'I'm damned if I can make head or tail of Doherty!' he would say to the others in McHugh's pub. 'A big, grown man with rough hands and dressed up in good clothes and taking walks like that—it's not natural!' And McElwee was also puzzled because, he said, Mr Doherty had never received a letter, not even a postcard, since the day he arrived in Drumeen.

On the first Sunday in March, three months after their marriage, Mr Doherty was drowned in the bog-black water of Lough Keeragh. Several of the mountainy Meenalargan people who passed the lake on their way to last Mass in the village saw him fishing from Dr Boyle's new punt, and on their way home from the chapel they found the boat, waterlogged, swaying on its keel in the shallow water along the south shore. In it were Mr Doherty's fishing bag, his checked cap, and one trout.

Father Curran went to Nelly's house and broke the news to her. When he told her, she hesitated, her face a deep red, and then said, 'As true as God, Father, he was out at first Mass with me,' as if he had accused her of having a husband who skipped Mass for a morning's fishing. (When he thought about her strange reaction later that day, he concluded that Mr Doherty most likely had not been out at first Mass.) He took her in his car out to the lake and parked it at right angles to the shore, and there she sat in the front seat right through that afternoon and evening and night, never once moving, as she watched the search for her husband. When Father Curran had to go back to Drumeen for the seven o'clock devotions—in an empty chapel, as it turned out, because by then the whole of the village was at Lough Keeragh—he had not the heart to ask her to get out. So he borrowed the curate's car, and the curate took the parish priest's place beside Nelly. Every hour or so, they said a rosary together, and between prayers Nelly watched quietly and patiently and responded respectfully to the curate's ponderous consolings.

Everyone toiled unsparingly, not only the people to whose houses she went charring every day—her clients, as she called them: Dr Boyle; Mr Mannion, of the bank; Mr Groome, the solicitor; Dr Timmons, the dentist; the McLaughlins—but the ordinary villagers, people of her own sort, although many of them were only names to her. Logan, the fish merchant, sent his lorry to the far end of Donegal to bring back boats for the job of dragging the lake; O'Hara, the taximan, sent his two cars to Derry to fetch the frogmen from the British Admiralty base there; and Joe Morris, the bus conductor, drove to Killybegs for herring nets.

The women worked as generously as the men. They condoled with Nelly first, each going to where she sat in the parish priest's car and saying how deeply sorry she was about the great and tragic loss. To each of them Nelly gave her red, washer-woman's hand, said a few suitable words of thanks, and even had the presence of mind to enquire about a sick child or a son in America or a cow that was due to calve. Then the women set up a canteen in Dr Boyle's boathouse and made tea and snacks for the workers on the lake. Among themselves they marvelled at Nelly's calm, at her dignified resignation.

'The poor soul! As if one tragedy wasn't enough.'

'Just when she was beginning to enjoy life, too.'

'And they were so attached to each other, so complete in themselves.'

'Have his people been notified?'

'Someone mentioned that to Nelly, but she said his people are all dead or in England.'

'He must have got a heart attack, the poor man.'

'Maybe that . . .'

'Why? What did you hear?'

'Nothing, nothing . . . Nobody knows for certain but himself and his Maker.'

'Is it true that he took the Doctor's boat without permission? That he broke the chain with a stone?'

'Sure, if he had gone to the Doctor straight and asked him, he would have got the boat and welcome.'

'Poor Nelly!'

'Poor Nelly indeed. But isn't it people like her that always get the sorest knocks?'

It was late afternoon before the search was properly organized. The mile-long lake was divided into three strips, which were separated by marker buoys. Each strip was dragged by a seine net stretched between two yawls. The work was slow and frustrating, the men unskilled in the job. Ropes were stretched too taut and snapped. The outboard motors got fouled in the weeds. Then dusk fell and imperceptibly thickened into darkness, and every available vehicle from Drumeen was lined up along the shore and its headlights beamed across the water. Submerged tar barrels were brought to the surface, the hulk of an old boat, the carcass of a sheep, a plough, and a cart wheel, but there was no trace of Mr Doherty. At intervals of half an hour a man in shirt and trousers went to the parish priest's car to report progress to Nelly.

'Thank you,' she said each time. 'Thank you all. You are all so kind.'

And immediately the priest beside her would resume prayers, because he imagined that sooner or later she would break down.

Father Curran had just returned from devotions and released the curate when the two frogmen arrived. They were English, dispassionate, businesslike, and brought with them all the complicated apparatus of their trade. Their efficiency gave the searchers new hope. They began at the north end, one taking the east side, the other the west. Carrying big searchlights, they went down six times in all and then told Dr Boyle and Mr Mannion that it was futile making any further attempts. The bottom of the lake, they explained, had once been a turf bog; the floor was even for perhaps ten yards and then dropped suddenly to an incalculable depth. If the body were lying on one of these shelves, they might have found it, but the chances were that it had dropped into one of the chasms, where it could never be found. In the circumstances, they saw no point in diving again. They warmed themselves at the canteen fire, loaded their gear into O'Hara's taxis, and departed.

The searchers gathered behind the parish priest's car and discussed the situation. Nelly's clients, the executives, who had directed operations up to this point, now listened to the suggestions of the workers. Some proposed calling the search off until daylight; some proposed pouring petrol on portions of the lake and igniting it to give them light; some proposed calling on all the fire brigades in the country and having the lake drained. And while the Drumeen people were conferring, the mountainy Meenalaragan men, who had raised the alarm in the first place and had stood, silent, watching, beside the drowned man's waterlogged boat throughout the whole day as if somehow it would divulge its secret, now baled out the water and, armed with long poles, searched the whole southern end of the lake. When they had no success, they returned the boat and slipped off home in the darkness.

The diviner was McElwee's idea. The postman admitted that he knew little about him except that he lived somewhere in the north of County Mayo, that he was infallible with water, and that his supporters claimed that he could find anything provided he got the 'smell of the truth in it'.

'We're concerned with a man, not a spring,' said Dr Boyle testily, 'A Mr Doherty, who lies somewhere in that lake there. And the question is, should we carry on with the nets or should we wait until the morning and decide what to do then?'

'He'll come if we go for him,' McElwee persisted. 'They say he's like a priest—he can never refuse a call. But whether he takes the job on when he gets here—well, that depends on whether he gets the smell of the—'

'I suggest we drag the south end again,' said Groome, the solicitor. 'The boat was waterlogged when it was found; therefore, it can't have drifted far after the accident. If he's anywhere, that's where he'll be.'

'We'll wait until the morning,' said McLaughlin of the Arcade. 'There's no great urgency, is there? Wait until we have proper light.'

'I vote for getting the diviner,' said McElwee. 'He likes to work while the scent is hot.'

'It's worth trying,' said one of Logan's men. 'Anyhow, what are you going to do tomorrow—try the nets again? After what the frogmen told you?'

Most of the men agreed.

'All right! All right!' said Dr Boyle. 'We'll get this fellow, whoever he is. But we'll tell Father Curran first.' They went round to the front of the car, and the Doctor spoke in to the priest.

'It has been suggested, Father,' he said, choosing his words as carefully as if he were giving evidence at an inquest, 'that we send for a diviner in County Mayo, a man who claims to be able—to locate—'

'A what?' the priest demanded.

'A diviner, Father. A water diviner.'

'What about him?'

'It appears, Father, according to McElwee and some of the men here—it appears that this diviner has been successful on occasion in the past. We are thinking of sending for him.'

Father Curran turned to Nelly.

'They're going to send for a water diviner now,' he said, putting a little extra emphasis on the word 'now'.

'Whatever you say, Father,' said Nelly. 'I'll never be able to repay you for all your kindness this night.'

'Well, Father?' said the Doctor.

'It's up to yourselves,' said the priest. Then, in dismissal, 'Let us begin another rosary. "I believe in God the Father Almighty, creator of Heaven and earth . . ." '

McElwee and one of McLaughlin's apprentices set off after midnight for County Mayo. None of Nelly's clients offered a car, so they travelled in a fifteen-year-old van belonging to McElwee's brother-in-law. After they left, the searchers broke up into small groups, sat in the cars and lorries and tractors lined along the shore, turned off the headlights, and waited. The night was thick and breathless. The men talked of the accident and of Mr Doherty. Each group knew something more about the man than had been known previously. In one car, it was known that his name was Arthur. Two lorries away, it was decided that Mr Doherty was not as retiring as one might have thought; one night a boisterous bass voice was heard coming through Nelly's kitchen window. In the Arcade delivery van, someone said that Dr Boyle was seen going into the cottage at least once a fortnight, and Nelly was never known to be sick. In one of the tractors, Nelly's frequent visits to the chemist were commented on. But these scraps of knowledge meant nothing; they were the kind of vague tales that might attach themselves to any stranger with a taste for privacy. The man at the bottom of the lake was still that respectable stranger in the good raincoat and the well-polished shoes.

The night was at its blackest when the pale lights of the returning van came bobbing over the patchy road. Immediately, fifty headlamps shot across the water and picked out tapering paths on the gleaming surface. Car doors slammed and the lake-side hummed with subdued excitement. Father Curran had been dozing. He opened his eyes and smacked his lips a dozen times. 'What? What is it?' he asked.

'They're back,' said Nelly, sitting forward in her seat. 'And they have him with them.'

The diviner was a tall man, inclined to flesh, and dressed in the same deep black as Nelly and the priest. He wore a black, greasy homburg, tilted the least fraction to the side, and carried a flat package, wrapped in newspaper, under his arm. The first impression was, What a fine man! But when he stepped directly in front of the headlights of one car there were signs of wear—faded, too active eyes, fingernails stained with nicotine, the trousers not a match for the jacket, the shoes cracking across the toecap, cheeks lined by the ready smiles. He spoke with the attractive, lilting accent of the west coast.

McElwee and McLaughlin's apprentice, fluttering about the diviner like nervous acolytes, led him to Father Curran's car. He opened the door, removed his hat, and bowed to Nelly and the priest. His hair was carefully stretched across a bald patch. 'I am the diviner,' he said with coy simplicity.

Father Curran leaned across Nelly to get a closer look at him. 'What's your name? Who's your parish priest?'

He ignored the questions and addressed himself to Nelly. 'I will need something belonging to your husband, something that was close to his person—a tie, a handkerchief, a—'

'Will this do?' asked McElwee, thrusting the checked cap over the man's shoulder into the car.

'Yes, that will do,' the diviner said. 'Thank you.' Then, to Nelly, 'His name was Arthur Doherty.'

'Arthur Doherty,' Nelly repeated, almost in a whisper.

'And he was born and reared in the townland of Drung, thirteen miles north of Athenry.'

'Drung,' said Nelly. She licked her lips. 'Did you know him?'

'I travel the country and I meet many people. I will search for the stonemason, but I will promise nothing.'

'How did you know he was a stonemason? You must have known him.'

'In a manner of speaking. Just as I recognize you,' he said.

She leaned away from him. 'You don't know me! I never saw you before!'

'You are Nelly Devenny, a highly respectable and respected woman. You work for the best people in Drumeen.'

'That dirty toper McElwee,' McLaughlin of the Arcade broke in.

'I will do my best,' the diviner said, withdrawing from the car and smiling at her—a sly, knowing smile, a sort of wink without an eye being closed.

'Father—!' Nelly began. She clutched the priest's elbow, her face working with agitation.

Father Curran did not heed her; he was sniffing the air. 'Whiskey!' he announced. 'That man reeks of whiskey!'

'Father, what will he do? D'you think he's going to do anything, Father?'

'A fake! A quack! A charlatan! Get a grip on yourself, woman! We'll say another rosary and then I'll leave you home. They're wasting their time with that—that pretender!' And he blessed himself extravagantly.

Neither Dr Boyle nor Mr Groome nor Dr Timmons nor Mr Mannion nor MacLaughlin of the Arcade volunteered to take the diviner out. McElwee and he went alone, the postman at the oars, the diviner sitting on the bench across the stern. The checked cap lay on his knees. He had removed the newspaper wrapping from his package, revealing a Y-shaped twig, and now he held it carelessly in his hands by the forked portion, the tail of the Y pointing away from him. The others gathered along the shore in the gloomy corridors between the headlights and watched them pull out. Before the boat was ten yards away from the edge of the water, Nelly left the priest's car for the first time that day and ran to join the watchers. The women gathered protectively around her.

The boat moved evenly up the lake. One minute it was part of the blackness, the next it was caught, exposed, frozen in a line of light projected by a headlight, then lost, then caught. Calmly, imperturbably, exasperatingly it went on revealing itself and losing itself, until the minutes of blackness seemed endless and the seconds of exposure mere flashes. But the pattern was regular—the vehicles were evenly spaced—and soon the eyes of the watchers knew to relax when the boat and blackness were one, but when it crossed a ribbon of light they devoured it, noted the new position of the oars, the slant of McElwee's back, the hunched, tensed shoulders of the diviner. No one spoke; no one dared speak. A word to a neighbour, a glance at once's watch, a look at Nelly's face and one might never find the punt again.

Then it disappeared. The watchers fastened on the next beam, waited, blinked, wondered had they missed it, stared again, murmured. Had it stopped? Where was it? Why the delay? Had it found something? Then it appeared again, moving slowly into the spotlight, first the bow, then McElwee, then the oars poised above the water, then the diviner, now standing rigid, his elbows bent, his hands at his chest, his head stiffly forward. There it sat, a yellow picture projected against the night. Seconds passed. A minute. Two minutes. Three minutes. To watch was pain. The picture dissolved, men and boat merging in a blur, then took shape again.

'Come out! Come out! Bring out the boat hooks!'

McElwee was on his feet, his face screaming into the light, his arms gesticulating wildly to an audience he could not see. 'He's here! Bring out the boats! He's here!'

No one stirred. Then, after a minute, a youth broke away from the crowd and leaped into a yawl, and another followed him, and then everyone was moving and calling for oars and lighting cigarettes and wading heedlessly out into the water. The women held Nelly's arms, because she was trembling violently.

The body lay in twenty feet of water directly below the diviner's quivering twig. They brought it in to the shore and carried it up the gravel immediately in front of Father Curran's car. There they laid it on top of a brown sail.

McElwee got down on his knees beside the body. He closed the eyes and the sagging mouth and knitted together the fingers of the rough hands. Then he adjusted the good gabardine raincoat and the trousers and placed the two feet together.

'He was a good man,' said the priest. He was standing beside the car door, close to the group of women that surrounded Nelly. He lifted his chin and allowed his eyelids to droop. 'He was a man who lived a quiet life and loved his God and his neighbours,' he said in his pulpit voice. 'At this moment, he is enjoying his just reward. At the hour of his demise, he was carrying his rosary beads—am I correct, McElwee?'

'I'll see, Father,' said McElwee.

He knelt again. While he worked, the men and women in the circle around the body looked away, gravely studying each other or staring off into the darkness beyond the cars. Then McElwee rose to his feet and moved quickly out of the circle, holding the dead man's belongings against his chest, his shoulders rounded as if to protect them. 'I—I—we'll have to look again, Father,' he said, facing away from the car. He took off his jacket and placed it on the ground and laid several objects on it. Then he folded the jacket around them.

'Did you find the beads?' the priest said.

'The clothes are soaking wet, Father. It's hard to get your hand into the pockets.'

'What do you have there?'

The postman straightened up and turned towards the light. 'There are these,' he said, holding something in his wet hands.

'Is that his wallet?'

'Yes. And the watch.'

'Give them to me.'

Someone handed the wallet and the watch to the priest, who gave them at once to Nelly.

'What else is there?' the priest asked.

'Nothing, Father.'

'There is something else in your jacket there, McElwee.'

'Show him, McElwee,' said the Doctor quietly.

McElwee looked at his jacket on the ground. Then he opened it. There were two dark-green pint whiskey bottles lying on it, side by side. One of them had no cork; the other had been opened, but the cork was still in it.

'Ho-ho, so that's it!' said Father Curran. 'And what are you doing with two bottles?'

'I found them,' said McElwee quietly.

'He found them!' the priest cried. 'And what—' He saw the faces in the circle, and then realization hit him. He opened his mouth to speak again, but closed it without a word.

Imperceptibly, it was dawn, a new day vying with the priest's headlamps. No one spoke; no one moved. Then McElwee bent and folded his jacket over the bottles once more. He turned and glanced at the priest, and then, in a voice that was no more than a whisper but which carried clearly about the lapping of the water and the first uncertain callings of the birds, he said, 'We'll say a rosary for the repose of the soul of Arthur Doherty, stonemason, of Drung, in the County Galway.' He began the Creed, and they all joined him.

While they prayed, Nelly cried, helplessly, convulsively, her wailing rising above the drone of the prayers. Hers, they knew, were not only the tears for twenty-five years of humility and mortification but, more bitter still, tears for the past three months, when appearances had almost won, when a foothold on respectability had almost been established.

Beyond the circle around the drowned man, the diviner mopped the perspiration on his forehead and on the back of his neck with a soiled handkerchief. Then he sat on the fender of a car and waited for someone to remember to drive him back to County Mayo.

An Occasion of Sin

About ten miles south of Dublin, not far from Blackrock, there is a small bathing place. You turn down a side road, cross a railway bridge, and there, below the wall, is a little bay with a pier running out into the sea on the left. The water is not deep, but much calmer and warmer than at many points further along the coast. When the tide comes in, it covers the expanse of green rocks on the right, lifting the seaweed like long hair. At its highest, one can dive from the ledge of the Martello Tower, which stands partly concealed between the pier and the sea wall.

Françoise O'Meara began coming there shortly after Easter of '56. A chubby, open-faced girl, at ease with herself and the world, she had arrived from France only six months before, after her marriage. At first she hated it: the damp mists of November seemed to eat into her spirit; but she kept quiet, for her husband's sake. And when winter began to wear into spring, and the days grew softer, she felt her heart expand; it was as simple as that.

Early in the new year, her husband bought her a car, to help her pass the time when he was at the office. It was nothing much, an old Austin, with wide running boards and rust-streaked roof, but she cleaned and polished it till it shone. With it, she explored all the little villages around Dublin: Delgany, where a pack of beagles came streaming across the road; Howth, where she wandered for hours along the cliffs; the roads above Rathfarnham. And Seacove, where she came to bathe as soon as her husband would allow her.

'But nobody bathes at this time of the year,' he said in astonishment, 'except the madmen at the Forty Foot!'

'But I *want* to!' she cried. 'What does it matter what people do. I won't melt!'

She stretched her arms wide as she spoke, and he had to admit that she didn't look as if she would; her breasts pushing her blouse, her stocky, firm hips, her wide grey eyes—he had never seen anyone look so positive in his life.

At first it was marvellous being on her own, feeling the icy shock of the water as she plunged in. It brought back a period of her childhood, spent at Etretat, on the Normandy coast: she had bathed through November, running along the deserted beach afterwards, the water drying on her body in the sharp wind. She doubted if she could do that at Seacove, but she found a corner of the wall which trapped whatever sun there was, and when the rain spat she went into the Martello Tower Café and had a bar of chocolate and a cup of tea. Sometimes it was so cold that her skin was goose-pimpled, but she loved it all; she felt she had never been so completely alive.

It was mid-May before anyone joined her along the sea wall. The earliest comer was a small fat man, who unpeeled to show a paunch carpeted with white hair. He waved to her before diving off the pierhead and trundling straight out to sea. When he came back, his face was lobster-red with exertion, and he pummelled himself savagely with a towel. He had surprisingly small, almost dainty feet, she noticed, as he danced up and down on the stones, blowing a white column of breath into the air. As he left, he always gave her a friendly wink or called (his words swallowed by the wind): 'That beats Banagher!'

She liked him a lot. She didn't feel as much at ease with the others. An English couple came down from the Stella Maris boarding house to eat a picnic lunch and read the *Daily Express*. Though sitting side by side, they rarely spoke, casting mournful glances at the sky which, even at its brightest, always had a faintly threatening aspect, like a chemical solution on the point of precipitation. And more and more local men came, mainly on bicycles. They swung to a halt along the sea wall, removing the clips from their trousers, removing their togs from the carrier, and tramping purposefully down towards the sea. One of them, who looked like a clerk (lean, bespectacled, his mouth cut into his face), carried equipment for underwater fishing, goggles, flippers, and spear.

What troubled her was their method of undressing: she had never seen anything like it. First they spread a paper on the ground. Upon this they squatted, slowly unpeeling their outer garments. When they were down to shirt and trousers, they took a swift look round, and then gave a kind of convulsive wriggle, so that the lower half of the trousers hung limply. There was a brief glimpse of white before a towel was wrapped across the loins; gradually the full length of the trousers unwound, in a series of convulsive shudders. A further lunge and the togs went sliding up the thighs, until they struck the outcrop of the hipbone. A second look round, a swift pull of the towel with the left hand, a jerk of the togs with the right, and the job was done. Or nearly: creaking to their feet, they pulled their thigh-length shirts over their heads to reveal pallid torsos.

At the beginning, this procedure amused her: it looked like a comedy sequence, especially as it had to be performed in reverse, when they came out of the water. But then it began to worry her: why were they doing it? Was it because there were women present? But there were none apart from the Englishman's wife, who sat gazing out to sea, munching her sandwiches: and herself. But she had seen men undressing on beaches ever since she was a child and hardly even noticed it. In any case, the division of the human race into male and female was an interesting fact with which she had come to terms long ago: she did not need to have her attention called to it in such an extraordinary way.

What troubled her even more was the way they watched her when she was undressing. She usually had her togs on under her dress; when she hadn't, she sat on the edge of the sea wall, sliding the bathing suit swiftly up her body, before jumping down to pull the dress over her head: the speed and cleanness of the motion pleased her. But as she fastened the straps over her back she could feel eyes on her every move: she felt like an animal in a cage. And it was not either curiosity or admiration, because when she raised her eyes, they all looked swiftly away. The man with the goggles was the worst: she caught him gazing at her avidly, the black band pushed up around his ears, like a racing motorist. She smiled to cover her embarrassment but to her surprise he turned his head, with an angry snap. What was wrong with her?

Because there was something: it just wasn't right, and she wanted to leave. She mentioned her doubts to her husband who laughed and then grew thoughtful.

'You're not very sympathetic,' he pointed out. 'After all, this is a cold country. People are not used to the sun.'

'Rubbish,' she replied. 'It's as warm as Normandy. It's something more than that.'

'Maybe it's just modesty.'

'Then why do they look at me like that? They're as lecherous as troopers but they won't admit it.'

'You don't understand,' he retreated.

It was mid-June when the clerical students appeared at Seacove. They came along the coast road from Dun Laoghaire on bicycles, black as a flock of crows. Their coats flapped in the sea-wind as they tried to pass each other out, rising on the pedals. Then they curved down the side-road towards the Martello Tower, where they piled their machines into the wooden racks, solemn-looking Raleighs and low-handled racers.

When they appeared, some of them had started undressing, taking off their coats and hard clerical collars as they came. Most already had their togs on, stepping out of their trousers on the beach, to create a huddle of identical black clothes. The others undressed in a group under the shadow of the sea wall, and then came racing down; together they trooped towards the pierhead.

For the next quarter of an hour the sea was teeming with them, dense as a shoal of mackerel. They plunged, they splashed, they turned upside down. One who was timid kept retreating to the shallow water, but two others stole up and ducked him vigorously, only to be buffeted, from behind, in their turn. The surface of the water was cut into clouds of spray. Far out the arms of the three strongest swimmers flashed, in a race to the lighthouse point.

When they came out of the sea to dry and lie down, they generally found a space cleared around their clothes, the people having withdrawn to give them more room. But the clerical students did not seem to observe, or mind, plumping themselves down in whatever space offered. One or two had brought books, but the majority lay on their backs, talking and laughing. At first their chatter disturbed Françoise from the novel she was reading, but it soon sank into her consciousness, like a litany.

'But Pius always had a great cult of the Virgin. They say he saw her in the Vatican gardens.'

'If Carlow had banged in that penalty, they'd be in the final Sunday.'

'Father Conroy says that after the second year in the bush you nearly forget home exists.'

While she was amused by their energy, Françoise would probably not have spoken to them, but for the accident of falling asleep one day, a yellow edition of Mauriac lying across her stomach. When she awoke, the students were settling around her. It was a warm day, and their usual place near the water had been taken by a group of English families with children, so they looked for the nearest free area. Although they pretended indifference, she could feel a current of curiosity running through them at finding her so close; now and again she caught a shy glance, or a chuckle, as one glanced at another meaningfully. Among their white skins and long shorts, she became suddenly conscious of her gay blue- and red-striped suit, blazing like a flag in the sunshine. And of her already browning legs and arms.

'Is that French you're reading?' said one finally. Just back from a second plunge in the sea, he was towelling himself slowly, shaking drops of water over everyone. He had a coarse, friendly face, covered with blotches, and a shock of carroty hair, which stuck up in wet tufts.

She held up the volume in answer. '*Le Fleuve de Feu*,' she spelled; 'the river of fire, one of Mauriac's novels.'

'He's a Catholic writer, isn't he?' said another, with sudden interest. The other turned to look at him, and he flushed brick-red, sitting his ground.

'Well,' she grimaced, remembering certain episodes in the novel, 'he is and he isn't. He's very bleak, in an old-fashioned sort of way. The river of fire is meant to be,' she searched for the words, 'the flood of human passion.'

There was silence for a minute or two. 'Are you French?' said a wondering voice.

'Yes, I am,' she confessed, apologetically, 'but I'm married to an Irishman.'

'We thought you couldn't be from here,' said another voice, triumphantly. Everyone seemed more at ease, now that her national identity had been established. They talked idly for a few minutes before the red-haired boy, who seemed to be in charge, looked at his watch and said it was time to go. They all dressed quickly, and as they sailed along the sea wall on their bicycles (she could only see their heads, like moving targets in a funfair) they waved to her.

'See you tomorrow,' they called gaily.

By early July the meetings between Françoise and the students had become a daily affair. As they rode up on their bicycles they would call out to her, 'Hello, Françoise.' And after they bathed, they came clambering up the rocks, to sit around her in a semi-circle. Usually the big red-haired boy (called 'Ginger' by his companions) would start the conversation with a staccato demand, 'What part of France are you from?' or, 'Do ye like it here?' but the others soon took over, while he sank back into a satisfied silence, like a dog that has performed an expected trick.

At first the conversation was general: Françoise felt like a teacher as they questioned her about life in Paris. And whatever she told them seemed to take on such an air of unreality, more like a lesson than real life. They liked to hear about the Louvre, or Notre Dame, but when she tried to tell them of what she knew best, the student life around the Latin Quarter, their attention slid away. But it was not her fault, because when she questioned them about their own future (they were going on to the Missions), they were equally vague. It was as though only what related to the present was real, and anything else exotic; unless one was plunged into it, when, of course, it became normal. Such torpidity angered her.

'But wouldn't you like to see Paris?' she exclaimed.

They looked at each other. Yes, they would like to see Paris, and might, some day, on the way back from Africa. But what they really wanted to do was to learn French: all they got was a few lessons a week from Father Dundee.

Another day they spoke of the worker priests. Fresh from the convent, a *jeune fille bien pensante*, Françoise had plunged into social work, around the rue Belhomme and the fringes of Montmartre. And she had come to know several of the worker priests. One she knew had fallen in love with a prostitute and had to struggle to save his vocation: she thought him a wonderful man. But her story was received in silence; a world where people did not go to mass, where passion was organised and dangerous, did not exist for them, except as a textbook vision of evil.

'Things must be very lax in France,' said Ginger, rising up.

She could have brained him.

Still, she enjoyed their company, and felt quite disappointed whenever (because of examinations or some religious ceremony) they did not show up. And it was not just because they fulfilled a woman's dream to find herself surrounded by admiring men. Totally at ease with her, they offered no calculation of seduction or flattery, except a kind of friendly teasing. It reminded her of when she had played with her brothers (she was the only girl) through the long summer holidays; that their relationship might not seem as innocent to others never crossed her mind.

She was lying on the sea wall after her swim, one afternoon, when she felt a shadow move across her vision. At first she thought it was one of the students, though they had told her the day before that they might not be coming. But no; it was the small fat man who had been one of the first to join her at Seacove. She smiled up at him in welcome, shielding her eyes against the sun. But he did not smile back, sitting down beside her heavily, his usual cheery face set in an attempt at solemnity.

'Missing your little friends today?'

She laughed. 'Yes, a bit,' she confessed. 'I rather like them, they're very pleasant company.'

He remained silent for a moment. 'I'm not sure it's right for you to be talking to them,' he plunged.

'Lots of people on the beach'—he was obviously uncomfortable—'are talking.'

'But they're only children!' Her shock was so deep that she was trembling: if such an inoffensive man believed this, what must the others be thinking?

'They're clerical students,' he said stubbornly. 'They're going to be priests.'

'But all the more reason: one can't,' she searched for the word, '*isolate* them.'

'That's not how we see it. You're giving bad example.'

'I'm giving what?'

'Bad example.'

Against her will, she felt tears prick the corners of her eyes. 'Do you believe that?' she asked, attempting to smile.

'I don't know,' he said seriously. 'It's a matter for your conscience. But it's not right for a single girl to be making free with clerical students.'

'But I'm not single!'

It was his turn to be shocked. 'You're a married woman! And you come—'

He did not end the sentence but she knew what he meant.

'Yes, I'm a married woman, and my husband lets me go to the beach on my own, and talk to whoever I like. You see, he trusts me.'

He rose slowly. 'Well, daughter,' he said, with a baffled return to kindliness, 'it's up to yourself. I only wanted to warn you.'

As he padded heavily away, she saw that the whole beach was watching her. This time she did not smile, but stared straight in front of her. There was a procession of yachts making towards Dun Laoghaire harbour, their white sails like butterflies. Turning over, she hid her face against the concrete, and began to cry.

But what was she going to do? As she drove back towards Dublin, Françoise was so absorbed that she nearly got into an accident, obeying an ancient reflex to turn on the right into the Georgian street where they lived. An oncoming Ford hooted loudly, and she swung her car up onto the pavement, just in time. She saw her husband's surprised face looking through the window: thank God he was home.

She did not mention the matter, however, until several hours later, when she was no longer as upset as she had been at the beach. And when she did come round to it, she tried to tell it as lightly as possible, hoping to distance it for herself, to see it clearly. But though her husband laughed a little at the beginning, his face became more serious, and she felt her nervousness rising again.

'But what right had he to say that to me?' she burst out, finally.

Kieran O'Meara did not answer, but kept turning the pages of the *Evening Press*.

'What right has anyone to accuse people like that?' she repeated.

'Obviously he thought he was doing the right thing.'

She hesitated. 'But surely *you* don't think . . .'

His face became a little red, as he answered, 'No, of course not. But I don't deny that in certain circumstances you might be classed as an occasion of sin.'

She sat down with a bump in the armchair, a dishcloth in her hand. At first she felt like laughing, but after repeating the phrase 'an occasion of sin' to herself a few times, she no longer found it funny and felt like crying. Did everyone in this country measure things like this? At a party, a few nights before, one of her husband's friends had solemnly told her that sex was the worst sin because it was the most pleasant. Another had gripped her arm, once, crossing the street: 'Be careful.' 'But you're in danger too!' she laughed, only to hear his answer: 'It's not myself I'm worried about, it's you. I'm in the state of sanctifying grace.' The face of the small fat man swam up before her, full of painful self-righteousness, as he told her she was 'giving bad example'. What in the name of God was she doing in this benighted place?

'Do you find me an occasion of sin?' she said, at last, in a strangled voice.

'It's different for me,' he said, impatiently. 'After all, we're married.'

It came as a complete surprise to him to see her rise from the chair, throw the dishcloth on the table, and vanish from the room. Soon he heard the front door bang, and her feet running down the steps.

Hands in the pockets of her white raincoat, Françoise O'Meara strode along the bank of the Grand Canal. There was a thin rain falling, but she ignored it, glad if anything for its damp imprint upon her face. Trees swam up to her, out of the haze: a pair of lovers were leaning against one of them, their faces blending. Neither of them had coats, they must be soaked through, but they did not seem to mind.

Well, there was a pair who were enjoying themselves, anyway. But why did they have to choose the dampest place in all Dublin, risking double pneumonia to add to their troubles? What was this instinct to seek darkness and discomfort, rather than the friendly light of day? She remembered the couples lying on the deck of the Holyhead boat when she had come over: she had to stumble over them in order to get down the stairs. It was like night-time in a bombed city, people hiding from the blows of fate; she had never had such a sense of desolation. And then, when she had negotiated the noise and porter stains of the Saloon and got to the Ladies, she found that the paper was strewn across the floor and that someone had scrawled FUCK CAVAN in lipstick on the mirror.

Her husband had nearly split his sides laughing when she asked what that meant. And yet, despite his education and travel, he was as odd as any of them. From the outside, he looked completely normal, especially when he left for the office in the morning in his neat executive suit. But inside he was a nest of superstition and stubbornness; it was like living with a Zulu tribesman. It emerged in all kinds of small things: the way he avoided walking under ladders, the way he always blessed himself during thunderstorms, the way he saluted every church he passed, a hand flying from the wheel to his forehead even in the thick of city traffic. And that wasn't the worst. One night she had woken up to see him sitting bolt upright in bed, his face tense and white.

'Do you hear it?' he managed to say.

Faintly, on the wind, she heard a crying sound, a sort of wail. It sounded weird all right, but it was probably only some animal locked out, or in heat, the kind of thing one hears in any garden, only magnified by the echo-chamber of the night.

'It's a banshee,' he said. 'They follow our family. Aunt Margaret must be going to die.'

And, strangely enough, Aunt Margaret did die, but several weeks later, and from old age more than anything else: she was over eighty and could have toppled into the grave at any time. But all through the funeral, Kieran kept looking at Françoise reproachfully, as if to say *you see*! And now the disease was beginning to get at her, sending her to stalk through the night like a Mauriac heroine, melancholy eating at her heart. As she approached Leeson Street Bridge, she saw two swans, a cob and a pen, moving slowly down the current. Behind them, almost indistinguishable because of their grey feathers, came four young ones. The sight calmed her: it was time to go back. Though he deserved it, she did not want her husband to be worrying about her. In any case, she had more or less decided what she was going to do.

The important thing was not to show, by the least sign, that she was troubled by what they thought of her. Swinging her togs in her left hand, Françoise O'Meara sauntered down towards the beach at Seacove. It was already pretty full, but, as though by design, a little space had been left, directly under the sea wall, where she usually sat. So she was to be ostracised as well! She would show them: with a delicious sense of her audience she hoisted herself up onto the concrete and began to undress. But she was only halfway through changing when the students arrived. In an ordinary way, she would have taken this in her stride, but she saw the people watching them as they tramped over, and the clasp of her bra stuck, and she was left to greet them half in, half out of her dress. And when she did get the bathing suit straightened she saw that, since they had all arrived more or less together, they were expecting her to join them in a swim. Laying his towel out carefully on the ground, like an altar-cloth, Ginger turned towards the sea: 'Coming?'

Scarlet-faced, she marched down with him to the pierhead. The tide was high, and just below the Martello Tower the man with the goggles broke surface, spluttering, as though on purpose to stare at her. A little way out, a group of clerical students were horse-playing: she wasn't going to join in *that*. Without speaking to her companion, she struck out towards the Lighthouse Point, cutting the water with a swift sidestroke. But before she had gone far, she found Ginger at her side: and another boy on the other. Passing (they both knew the crawl), falling back, repassing, they accompanied her out to the point, and back again. Were they never to leave her alone?

And afterwards, when they lay on the beach, they kept pestering her with questions. And not the usual ones, but much bolder, in an innocent sort of way: what had got into them? It was the boy who had asked about Mauriac who began it, wanting to know if she had ended the book, whether she knew any people like that, what she thought of its view of love. And then, out of the blue:

'What's it like, to be married?'

She rolled over on her stomach and looked at him. No, he was not being roguish, he was quite serious, gazing at her with interest, as were most of the others. But how could one answer such a question, before such an audience?

'Well, it's very important for a woman, naturally,' she began, feeling as ripe with clichés as a woman's page columnist. 'And not just because people—society—imply that if a woman is not married she's a failure: that's a terrible trap. And it is not merely living together, though—' she looked at them: they were still intent '—that's pleasant enough, but in order to fulfil herself, in the process of giving. And that's the whole paradox, that if it's a true marriage, she feels freer, just because she has given.'

'Freer?'

'Yes, freer after marriage than before it. It's not like an affair, where though the feeling may be as intense, one knows that one can escape. The freedom in marriage is the freedom of having committed oneself: at least that's true for the woman.' Her remarks were received in silence, but it was not the puzzled silence of their first meetings, but a thoughtful one, as though, while they could not quite understand what she meant, they were prepared to examine it. But she still could not quiet a nagging doubt in her mind, and demanded: 'What made you ask me that?'

It was not her questioner, but Ginger, who had hardly been listening, who gave her her answer. 'Sure, it's well known,' he said pleasantly, gathering up his belongings, 'that French women think about nothing but love.'

He pronounced it 'luve', with a deep curl in the vowel. Before she could think of a reply, they were half-way across the beach.

She was still raging when she got home, all the more so since she knew she could not tell her husband about it. She was still raging when she went to bed, shifting so much that she made her husband grunt irritably. She was still raging when she woke up, from a dream in which the experience lay curdled.

She dreamt that she was at Seacove in the early morning. The sea was a deep running green, with small waves hitting the pierhead. There was no one in sight so she took off her clothes and slipped into the water. She was half-way across to the Lighthouse Point when she sensed something beneath her: it was the man with the goggles, his back flippers beating the water soundlessly as he surged up towards her. His eyes roved over her naked body as he reached out for her leg. She felt herself being pulled under, and kicked out strongly. She heard the glass of his goggles smash as she broke to the surface again; where her husband was drawing the blinds to let in the morning light.

Today, she decided, she must end the whole stupid affair: it had gone on too long, caused her too much worry. After all, the people who had protested were probably right: the fact that the boys were getting fresh with her proved it. She toyed with the idea of just not going back to the beach, but it seemed cowardly. Better to face the students directly, and tell them she could not see them again.

So when they arrived at the beach in the mid-afternoon they found her sitting stiffly against the sea wall, a book resting on her knees. Saluting her with their usual friendliness, they got hardly any reply. At the time, they passed no remarks, but lying on the beach after their swim they found the silence heavy and tried to coax her with questions. But she cut them short each time, ostentatiously returning to her book.

'Is there anything wrong?' one of them asked, at last.

Keeping her eyes fixed on the print, she nodded. 'More or less.'

'It wouldn't have anything to do with us?' This from Ginger, with sudden probing interest.

'As a matter of fact, it has.' Shyness slowly giving way to relief, she told about her conversation with the little fat man. 'But, of course, it's really my fault,' she ended lamely. 'I should have known better.'

Waiting their judgement, she looked up. To her surprise, they were smiling at her, affectionately.

'Is that all?'

'Isn't it enough?'

'But sure we knew all that before.'

'You knew it!' she exclaimed in horror. 'But how . . .'

'Somebody came to the College a few days ago and complained to the Dean.'

'And what did he say?'

'He asked us what you were like.'

'And what did you say?' she breathed.

'We said'—the tone was teasing but sincere—'we said you were a better French teacher than Father Dundee.'

The casual innocence of the remark, restoring the whole heart of their relationship, brought a shout of laughter from her. But as her surprise wore off, she could not resist picking at it, suspiciously, at least once more.

'But what about what the people said? Didn't it upset you?'

Ginger's gaze seemed to rest on her for a moment, and then moved away, bouncing like a rubber ball down the steps towards the sea.

'Ach, sure some people would see bad in anything,' he said easily.

And that was all: no longer interested, they turned to talk about something else. They were going on their holidays soon (no wonder they were so frisky!) and wouldn't be seeing her much again. But they had enjoyed meeting her; maybe she would be there next year? She lay with her back against the sea wall, listening to them, her new book (it was Simone de Beauvoir's *Le Deuxième Sexe*) at her side. A movement caught her eye down the beach: someone was trying to climb on to the ledge of the Martello Tower. First came the spear, then the black goggles, then the flippers, like an emerging sea monster. Remembering her dreams, she began to laugh again, so much so that her companions looked at her inquiringly. Yes, she said quickly, she might be at Seacove next year.

Though in her heart she knew that she wouldn't.

Irish Revel

Mary hoped that the rotted front tyre would not burst. As it was, the tube had a slow puncture, and twice she had to stop and use the pump, maddening, because the pump had no connection and had to be jammed on over the corner of a handkerchief. For as long as she could remember she had been pumping bicycles, carting turf, cleaning outhouses, doing a man's work. Her father and her two brothers worked for the forestry, so that she and her mother had to do all the odd jobs—there were three children to care for, and fowl and pigs and churning. Theirs was a mountainy farm in Ireland, and life was hard.

But this cold evening in early November she was free. She rode along the mountain road, between the bare thorn hedges, thinking pleasantly about the party. Although she was seventeen this was her first party. The invitation had come only that morning from Mrs Rodgers of the Commercial Hotel. The postman brought word that Mrs Rodgers wanted her down that evening, without fail. At first, her mother did not wish Mary to go, there was too much to be done, gruel to be made, and one of the twins had earache, and was likely to cry in the night. Mary slept with the year-old twins, and sometimes she was afraid that she might lie on them or smother them, the bed was so small. She begged to be let go.

'What use would it be?' her mother said. To her mother all outings were unsettling—they gave you a taste of something you couldn't have. But finally she weakened, mainly because Mrs Rodgers, as owner of the Commercial Hotel, was an important woman, and not to be insulted.

'You can go, so long as you're back in time for the milking in the morning; and mind you don't lose your head,' her mother warned. Mary was to stay overnight in the village with Mrs Rodgers. She plaited her hair, and later when she combed it it fell in dark crinkled waves over her shoulders. She was allowed to wear the black lace dress that had come from America years ago and belonged to no one in particular. Her mother had sprinkled her with Holy Water, conveyed her to the top of the lane and warned her not to touch alcohol.

Mary felt happy as she rode along slowly, avoiding the pot-holes that were thinly iced over. The frost had never lifted that day. The ground was hard. If it went on like that, the cattle would have to be brought into the shed and given hay.

The road turned and looped and rose; she turned and looped with it, climbing little hills and descending again towards the next hill. At the descent of the Big Hill she got off the bicycle—the brakes were unreliable—and looked back, out of habit, at her own house. It was the only house back there on the mountain, small, whitewashed, with a few trees around it, and a patch at the back which they called a kitchen-garden. There was a rhubarb bed, and shrubs over which they emptied tea-leaves and a stretch of grass where in the summer they had a chicken run, moving it from one patch to the next, every other day. She looked away. She was now free to think of John Roland. He came to their district two years before, riding a motor-cycle at a ferocious speed; raising dust on the milk-cloths spread on the hedge to dry. He stopped to ask the way. He was staying with Mrs Rodgers in the Commercial Hotel and had come up to see the lake, which was noted for its colours. It changed colour rapidly—it was blue and green and black, all within an hour. At sunset it was often a strange burgundy, not like a lake at all, but like wine.

'Down there,' she said to the stranger, pointing to the lake below, with the small island in the middle of it. He had taken a wrong turning.

Hills and tiny cornfields descended deeply towards the water. The misery of the hills was clear, from all the boulders. The cornfields were turning, it was midsummer; the ditches throbbing with the blood-red of fuchsia; the milk sour five hours after it had been put in the tanker. He said how exotic it was. She had no interest in views herself. She just looked up at the high sky and saw that a hawk had halted in the air above them. It was like a pause in her life, the hawk above them, perfectly still; and just then her mother came out to see who the stranger was. He took off his helmet and said 'Hello', very courteously. He introduced himself as John Roland, an English painter, who lived in Italy.

She did not remember exactly how it happened, but after a while he walked into their kitchen with them and sat down to tea.

Two long years since; but she had never given up hoping—perhaps this evening. The mail-car man said that someone special in the Commercial Hotel expected her. She felt such happiness. She spoke to her bicycle, and it seemed to her that her happiness somehow glowed in the pearliness of the cold sky, in the frosted fields going blue in the dusk, in the cottage windows she passed. Her father and mother were rich and cheerful; the twin had no earache, the kitchen fire did not smoke. Now and then, she smiled at the thought of how she would appear to him—taller and with breasts now, and a dress that could be worn anywhere. She forgot about the rotted tyre, got up and cycled.

The five street lights were on when she pedalled into the village. There had been a cattle fair that day, and the main street was covered with dung. The townspeople had their windows protected with wooden half-shutters and makeshift arrangements of planks and barrels. Some were out scrubbing their own piece of footpath with bucket and brush. There were cattle wandering around, mooing, the way cattle do when they are in a strange street, and drunken farmers with sticks were trying to identify their own cattle in dark corners.

Beyond the shop window of the Commercial Hotel, Mary heard loud conversation, and men singing. It was opaque glass so that she could not identify any of them, she could just see their heads moving about, inside. It was a shabby hotel, the yellow-washed walls needed a coat of paint as they hadn't been done since the time De Valera came to that village during the election campaign five years before. De Valera went upstairs that time, and sat in the parlour and wrote his name with a penny pen in an autograph book, and sympathized with Mrs Rodgers on the recent death of her husband.

Mary thought of resting her bicycle against the porter barrels under the shop window, and then of climbing the three stone steps that led to the hall door, but suddenly the latch of the shop door clicked and she ran in terror up the alley by the side of the shop, afraid it might be someone who knew her father and would say he saw her going in through the public bar. She wheeled her bicycle into a shed and approached the back door. It was open, but she did not enter without knocking.

Two townsgirls rushed to answer it. One was Doris O'Beirne, the daughter of the harness-maker. She was the only Doris in the whole village, and she was famous for that, as well as for the fact that one of her eyes was blue and the other a dark brown. She learnt shorthand and typing at the local technical school, and later she meant to be a secretary to some famous man or other in the Government, in Dublin.

'God, I thought it was someone important,' she said when she saw Mary standing there, blushing, pretty and with a bottle of cream in her hand. Another girl! Girls were two a penny in that neighbourhood. People said that it had something to do with the lime water that so many girls were born. Girls with pink skins, and matching eyes, and girls like Mary with long, wavy hair and good figures.

'Come in, or stay out,' said Eithne Duggan, the second girl, to Mary. It was supposed to be a joke but neither of them liked her. They hated shy mountainy people.

Mary came in carrying cream which her mother had sent to Mrs Rodgers, as a present. She put it on the dresser and took off her coat. The girls nudged each other when they saw her dress. In the kitchen was a smell of cow dung and fried onions.

'Where's Mrs Rodgers?' Mary asked.

'Serving,' Doris said in a saucy voice, as if any fool ought to know. Two old men sat at the table eating.

'I can't chew, I have no teeth,' said one of the men, to Doris. ' 'Tis like leather,' he said, holding the plate of burnt steak towards her. He had watery eyes and he blinked childishly. Was it so, Mary wondered, that eyes got paler with age, like bluebells in a jar?

'You're not going to charge me for that,' the old man was saying to Doris. Tea and steak cost five shillings at the Commercial.

' 'Tis good for you, chewing is,' Eithne Duggan said, teasing him.

'I can't chew with my gums,' he said again, and the two girls began to giggle. The old man looked pleased that he had made them laugh, and he closed his mouth and munched once or twice on a piece of fresh, shop bread. Eithne Duggan laughed so much that she had to put a dish-cloth between her teeth. Mary took off her coat and went through to the shop.

Mrs Rodgers came from the counter for a moment to speak to her.

'Mary, I'm glad you came, that pair in there are no use at all, always giggling. Now first thing we have to do is to get the parlour upstairs straightened out. Everything has to come out of it except the piano. We're going to have dancing and everything.'

Quickly, Mary realized that she was being given work to do, and she blushed with shock and disappointment.

'Pitch everything into the back bedroom, the whole shootin' lot,' Mrs Rodgers was saying as Mary thought of her good lace dress, and of how her mother wouldn't even let her wear it to Mass on Sundays.

'And we have to stuff a goose too and get it on,' Mrs Rodgers said, and went on to explain that the party was in honour of the local Customs and Excise Officer who was retiring because his wife won some money in the Sweep. Two thousand pounds. His wife lived thirty miles away at the far side of Limerick and he lodged in the Commercial Hotel from Monday to Friday, going home for the weekends.

'There's someone here expecting me,' Mary said, trembling with the pleasure of being about to hear his name pronounced by someone else. She wondered which room was his, and if he was likely to be in at that moment. Already in imagination she had climbed the rickety stairs and knocked on the door, and heard him move around inside.

'Expecting you!' Mrs Rodgers said, and looked puzzled for a minute. 'Oh, that lad from the slate quarry was enquiring about you, he said he saw you at a dance once. He's as odd as two left shoes.'

'What lad?' Mary said, as she felt the joy leaking out of her heart.

'Oh, what's his name?' Mrs Rodgers said, and then to the men with empty glasses who were shouting for her, 'Oh all right, I'm coming.'

Upstairs Doris and Eithne helped Mary move the heavy pieces of furniture. They dragged the sideboard across the landing and one of the castors tore the linoleum. She was expiring, because she had the heaviest end, the other two being at the same side. She felt that it was on purpose: they ate sweets without offering her one, and she caught them making faces at her dress. The dress worried her too in case anything should happen to it. If one of the lace threads caught in a splinter of wood, or on a porter barrel, she would have no business going home in the morning. They carried out a varnished bamboo whatnot, a small table, knick-knacks and a chamber-pot with no handle which held some withered hydrangeas. They smelt awful.

'How much is the doggie in the window, the one with the waggledy tail?' Doris O'Beirne sang to a white china dog and swore that there wasn't ten pounds' worth of furniture in the whole shibeen.

'Are you leaving your curlers in, Dot, till it starts?' Eithne Duggan asked her friend.

'Oh def.,' Doris O'Beirne said. She wore an assortment of curlers—white pipe-cleaners, metal clips, and pink, plastic rollers. Eithne had just taken hers out and her hair, dyed blonde, stood out, all frizzed and alarming. She reminded Mary of a moulting hen about to attempt flight. She was, God bless her, an unfortunate girl with a squint, jumbled teeth and almost no lips; like something put together hurriedly. That was the luck of the draw.

'Take these,' Doris O'Beirne said, handing Mary bunches of yellowed bills crammed on skewers.

Do this! Do that! They ordered her around like a maid. She dusted the piano, top and sides, and the yellow and black keys; then the surround, and the wainscoting. The dust, thick on everything, had settled into a hard film because of the damp in that room. A party! She'd have been as well off at home, at least it was clean dirt attending to calves and pigs and the like.

Doris and Eithne amused themselves, hitting notes on the piano at random and wandering from one mirror to the next. There were two mirrors in the parlour and one side of the folding fire-screen was a blotchy mirror too. The other two sides were of water-lilies painted on black cloth, but like everything else in the room it was old.

'What's that?' Doris and Eithne asked each other, as they heard a hullabullo downstairs. They rushed out to see what it was and Mary followed. Over the banisters they saw that a young bullock had got in the hall door and was slithering over the tiled floor, trying to find his way out again.

'Don't excite her, don't excite her I tell ye,' said the old, toothless man to the young boy who tried to drive the black bullock out. Two more boys were having a bet as to whether or not the bullock would do something on the floor when Mrs Rodgers came out and dropped a glass of porter. The beast backed out the way he'd come, shaking his head from side to side.

Eithne and Doris clasped each other in laughter and then Doris drew back so that none of the boys would see her in her curling pins and call her names. Mary had gone back to the room, downcast. Wearily she pushed the chairs back against the wall and swept the linoleumed floor where they were later to dance.

'She's bawling in there,' Eithne Duggan told her friend Doris. They had locked themselves into the bathroom with a bottle of cider.

'God, she's a right-looking eejit in the dress,' Doris said. 'And the length of it!'

'It's her mother's,' Eithne said. She had admired the dress before that, when Doris was out of the room, and had asked Mary where she bought it.

'What's she crying about?' Doris wondered, aloud.

'She thought some lad would be here. Do you remember that lad stayed here the summer before last and had a motor-cycle?'

'He was a Jew,' Doris said. 'You could tell by his nose. God, she'd shake him in that dress, he'd think she was a scarecrow.' She squeezed a blackhead on her chin, tightened a curling pin which had come loose and said, 'Her hair isn't natural either, you can see it's curled.'

'I hate that kind of black hair, it's like a gipsy's,' Eithne said, drinking the last of the cider. They hid the bottle under the scoured bath.

'Have a cachou, take the smell off your breath,' Doris said as she hawed on the bathroom mirror and wondered if she would get off with that fellow O'Toole, from the slate quarry, who was coming to the party.

In the front room Mary polished glasses. Tears ran down her cheeks so she did not put on the light. She foresaw how the party would be; they would all stand around and consume the goose, which was now simmering in the turf range. The men would be drunk, the girls giggling. Having eaten, they would dance, and sing, and tell ghost stories, and in the morning she would have to get up early and be home in time to milk. She moved towards the dark pane of window with a glass in her hand and looked out at the dirtied streets, remembering how once she had danced with John on the upper road to no music at all, just their hearts beating, and the sound of happiness.

He came into their house for tea that summer's day and on her father's suggestion he lodged with them for four days, helping with the hay and oiling all the farm machinery for her father. He understood machinery. He put back doorknobs that had fallen off. Mary made his bed in the daytime and carried up a ewer of water from the rain-barrel every evening, so that he could wash. She washed the check shirt he wore, and that day, his bare back peeled in the sun. She put milk on it. It was his last day with them. After supper he proposed giving each of the grown-up children a ride on the motor-cycle. Her turn came last, she felt that he had planned it that way, but it may have been that her brothers were more persistent about being first. She would never forget that ride. She warmed from head to foot in wonder and joy. He praised her as a good balancer and at odd moments he took one hand off the handlebar and gave her clasped hands a comforting pat. The sun went down, and the gorse flowers blazed yellow. They did not talk for miles; she had his stomach encased in the delicate and frantic grasp of a girl in love and no matter how far they rode they seemed always to be riding into a golden haze. He saw the lake at its most glorious. They got off at the bridge five miles away, and sat on the limestone wall, that was cushioned by moss and lichen. She took a tick out of his neck and touched the spot where the tick had drawn one pin-prick of blood; it was then they danced. A sound of larks and running water. The hay in the fields was lying green and ungathered, and the air was sweet with the smell of it. They danced.

'Sweet Mary,' he said, looking earnestly into her eyes. Her eyes were a greenish-brown. He confessed that he could not love her, because he already loved his wife and children, and anyhow he said, 'You are too young and too innocent.'

Next day, as he was leaving, he asked if he might send her something in the post, and it came eleven days later: a black-and-white drawing of her, very like her, except that the girl in the drawing was uglier.

'A fat lot of good, that is,' said her mother, who had been expecting a gold bracelet or a brooch. 'That wouldn't take you far.'

They hung it on a nail in the kitchen for a while and then one day it fell down and someone (probably her mother) used it to sweep dust on to, ever since it was used for that purpose. Mary had wanted to keep it, to put it away in a trunk, but she was ashamed to. They were hard people, and it was only when someone died that they could give in to sentiment or crying.

'Sweet Mary,' he had said. He never wrote. Two summers passed, devil's pokers flowered for two seasons, and thistle seed blew in the wind, the trees in the forestry were a foot higher. She had a feeling that he would come back, and a gnawing fear that he might not.

'Oh it ain't gonna rain no more, no more, it ain't gonna rain no more; How in the hell can the old folks say it ain't gonna rain no more.'

So sang Brogan, whose party it was, in the upstairs room of the Commercial Hotel. Unbuttoning his brown waistcoat, he sat back and said what a fine spread it was. They had carried the goose up on a platter and it lay in the centre of the mahogany table with potato stuffing spilling out of it. There were sausages also and polished glasses rim downwards, and plates and forks for everyone.

'A fork supper' was how Mrs Rodgers described it. She had read about it in the paper; it was all the rage now in posh houses in Dublin, this fork supper where you stood up for your food and ate with a fork only. Mary had brought knives in case anyone got into difficulties.

' 'Tis America at home,' Hickey said, putting turf on the smoking fire.

The pub door was bolted downstairs, the shutters across, as the eight guests upstairs watched Mrs Rodgers carve the goose and then tear the loose pieces away with her fingers. Every so often she wiped her fingers on a tea-towel.

'Here you are, Mary, give this to Mr Brogan, as he's the guest of honour.' Mr Brogan got a lot of breast and some crispy skin as well.

'Don't forget the sausages, Mary,' Mrs Rodgers said. Mary had to do everything, pass the food around, serve the stuffing, ask people whether they wanted paper plates or china ones. Mrs Rodgers had bought paper plates, thinking they were sophisticated.

'I could eat a young child,' Hickey said.

Mary was surprised that people in towns were so coarse and outspoken. When he squeezed her finger she did not smile at all. She wished that she were at home—she knew what they were doing at home; the boys at their lessons; her mother baking a cake of wholemeal bread, because there was never enough time during the day to bake; her father rolling cigarettes and talking to himself. John had taught him how to roll cigarettes, and every night since he rolled four and smoked four. He was a good man, her father, but dour. In another hour they'd be saying the Rosary in her house and going up to bed: the rhythm of their lives never changed, the fresh bread was always cool by morning.

'Ten o'clock,' Doris said, listening to the chimes of the landing clock.

The party began late; the men were late getting back from the dogs in Limerick. They killed a pig on the way in their anxiety to get back quickly. The pig had been wandering around the road and the car came round the corner; it got run over instantly.

'Never heard such a roarin' in all me born days,' Hickey said, reaching for a wing of goose, the choicest bit.

'We should have brought it with us,' O'Toole said. O'Toole worked in the slate quarry and knew nothing about pigs or farming; he was tall and thin and jagged. He had bright green eyes and a face like a greyhound; his hair was so gold that it looked dyed, but in fact it was bleached by the weather. No one had offered him any food.

'A nice way to treat a man,' he said.

'God bless us, Mary, didn't you give Mr O'Toole anything to eat yet?' Mrs Rodgers said as she thumped Mary on the back to hurry her up. Mary brought him a large helping on a paper plate and he thanked her and said that they would dance later. To him she looked far prettier than those good-for-nothing townsgirls—she was tall and thin like himself; she had long black hair that some people might think streelish, but not him, he liked long hair and simple-minded girls; maybe later on he'd get her to go into one of the other rooms where they could do it. She had funny eyes when you looked into them, brown and deep, like a bloody bog-hole.

'Have a wish,' he said to her as he held the wishbone up. She wished that she were going to America on an aeroplane and on second thoughts she wished that she would win a lot of money and could buy her mother and father a house down near the main road.

'Is that your brother the Bishop?' Eithne Duggan, who knew well that it was, asked Mrs Rodgers, concerning the flaccid-faced cleric over the fireplace. Unknown to herself Mary had traced the letter J on the dust of the picture mirror, earlier on, and now they all seemed to be looking at it, knowing how it came to be there.

'That's him, poor Charlie,' Mrs Rodgers said proudly, and was about to elaborate, but Brogan began to sing, unexpectedly.

'Let the man sing, can't you,' O'Toole said, hushing two of the girls who were having a joke about the armchair they shared; the springs were hanging down underneath and the girls said that any minute the whole thing would collapse.

Mary shivered in her lace dress. The air was cold and damp even though Hickey had got up a good fire. There hadn't been a fire in that room since the day De Valera signed the autograph book. Steam issued from everything.

O'Toole asked if any of the ladies would care to sing. There were five ladies in all—Mrs Rodgers, Mary, Doris, Eithne, and Crystal the local hairdresser, who had a new red rinse in her hair and who insisted that the food was a little heavy for her. The goose was greasy and undercooked, she did not like its raw, pink colour. She liked dainty things, little bits of cold chicken breast with sweet pickles. Her real name was Carmel, but when she started up as a hairdresser she changed to Crystal and dyed her brown hair red.

'I bet you can sing,' O'Toole said to Mary.

'Where she comes from they can hardly talk,' Doris said.

Mary felt the blood rushing to her sallow cheeks. She would not tell them, but her father's name had been in the paper once, because he had seen a pine-marten in the forestry plantation; and they ate with a knife and fork at home and had oil cloth on the kitchen table, and kept a tin of coffee in case strangers called. She would not tell them anything. She just hung her head, making clear that she was not about to sing.

In honour of the Bishop O'Toole put 'Far away in Australia' on the horn gramophone. Mrs Rodgers had asked for it. The sound issued forth with rasps and scratchings and Brogan said he could do better than that himself.

'Christ, lads, we forgot the soup!' Mrs Rodgers said suddenly, as she threw down the fork and went towards the door. There had been soup scheduled to begin with.

'I'll help you,' Doris O'Beirne said, stirring herself for the first time that night, and they both went down to get the pot of dark giblet soup which had been simmering all that day.

'Now we need two pounds from each of the gents,' said O'Toole, taking the opportunity while Mrs Rodgers was away to mention the delicate matter of money. The men had agreed to pay two pounds each, to cover the cost of the drink; the ladies did not have to pay anything, but were invited so as to lend a pleasant and decorative atmosphere to the party, and, of course, to help.

O'Toole went around with his cap held out, and Brogan said that as it was *his* party he ought to give a fiver.

'I ought to give a fiver, but I suppose ye wouldn't hear of that,' Brogan said, and handed up two pound notes. Hickey paid up, too, and O'Toole himself and Long John Salmon—who was silent up to then. O'Toole gave it to Mrs Rodgers when she returned and told her to clock it up against the damages.

'Sure that's too kind altogether,' she said, as she put it behind the stuffed owl on the mantelpiece, under the Bishop's watchful eye.

She served the soup in cups and Mary was asked to pass the cups around. The grease floated like drops of molten gold on the surface of each cup.

'See you later, alligator,' Hickey said, as she gave him his; then he asked her for a piece of bread because he wasn't used to soup without bread.

'Tell us, Brogan,' said Hickey to his rich friend, 'what'll you do, now that you're a rich man?'

'Oh go on, tell us,' said Doris O'Beirne.

'Well,' said Brogan, thinking for a minute, 'we're going to make some changes at home.' None of them had ever visited Brogan's home because it was situated in Adare, thirty miles away, at the far side of Limerick. None of them had ever seen his wife either, who it seems lived there and kept bees.

'What sort of changes?' someone said.

'We're going to do up the drawing-room, and we're going to have flower-beds,' Brogan told them.

'And what else?' Crystal asked, thinking of all the lovely clothes she could buy with that money, clothes and jewellery.

'Well,' said Brogan, thinking again, 'we might even go to Lourdes. I'm not sure yet, it all depends.'

'I'd give my two eyes to go to Lourdes,' Mrs Rodgers said.

'And you'd get 'em back when you arrived there,' Hickey said, but no one paid any attention to him.

O'Toole poured out four half-tumblers of whiskey and then stood back to examine the glasses to see that each one had the same amount. There was always great anxiety among the men, about being fair with drink. Then O'Toole stood bottles of stout in little groups of six and told each man which group was his. The ladies had gin and orange.

'Orange for me,' Mary said, but O'Toole told her not to be such a goody, and when her back was turned he put gin in her orange.

They drank a toast to Brogan.

'To Lourdes,' Mrs Rodgers said.

'To Brogan,' O'Toole said.

'To myself,' Hickey said.

'Mud in your eye,' said Doris O'Beirne, who was already unsteady from tippling cider.

'Well we're not sure about Lourdes,' Brogan said. 'But we'll get the drawing-room done up anyhow, and the flower-beds put in.'

'We've a drawing-room here,' Mrs Rodgers said, 'and no one ever sets foot in it.'

'Come into the drawing-room, Doris,' said O'Toole to Mary, who was serving the jelly from the big enamel basin. They'd had no china bowl to put it in. It was red jelly with whipped egg-white in it, but something went wrong because it hadn't set properly. She served it in saucers, and thought to herself what a rough-and-ready party it was. There wasn't a proper cloth on the table either, just a plastic one, and no napkins, and that big basin with the jelly in it. Maybe people washed in that basin, downstairs.

'Well, someone tell us a bloomin' joke,' said Hickey, who was getting fed up with talk about drawing-rooms and flower-beds.

'I'll tell you a joke,' said Long John Salmon, erupting out of his silence.

'Good,' said Brogan, as he sipped from his whiskey glass and his stout glass alternately. It was the only way to drink enjoyably. That was why, in pubs, he'd be much happier if he could buy his own drink and not rely on anyone else's meanness.

'Is it a funny joke?' Hickey asked of Long John Salmon.

'It's about my brother,' said Long John Salmon, 'my brother Patrick.'

'Oh no, don't tell us that old rambling thing again,' said Hickey and O'Toole, together.

'Oh let him tell it,' said Mrs Rodgers who'd never heard the story anyhow.

Long John Salmon began, 'I had this brother Patrick and he died; the heart wasn't too good.'

'Holy Christ, not this again,' said Brogan, recollecting which story it was.

But Long John Salmon went on, undeterred by the abuse from the three men:

'One day I was standing in the shed, about a month after he was buried, and I saw him coming out of the wall, walking across the yard.'

'Oh what would you do if you saw a thing like that,' Doris said to Eithne.

'Let him tell it,' Mrs Rodgers said. 'Go on, Long John.'

'Well it was walking toward me, and I said to myself, "What do I do now?"; 'twas raining heavy, so I said to my brother Patrick, "Stand in out of the wet or you'll get drenched." '

'And then?' said one of the girls anxiously.

'He vanished,' said Long John Salmon.

'Ah God, let us have a bit of music,' said Hickey, who had heard that story nine or ten times. It had neither a beginning, a middle or an end. They put a record on, and O'Toole asked Mary to dance. He did a lot of fancy steps and capering; and now and then he let out a mad 'Yippee'. Brogan and Mrs Rodgers were dancing too and Crystal said that she'd dance if anyone asked her.

'Come on, knees up Mother Brown,' O'Toole said to Mary, as he jumped around the room, kicking the legs of chairs as he moved. She felt funny: her head was swaying round and round, and in the pit of her stomach there was a nice, ticklish feeling that made her want to lie back and stretch her legs. A new feeling that frightened her.

'Come into the drawing-room, Doris,' he said, dancing her right out of the room and into the cold passage where he kissed her clumsily.

Inside Crystal O'Meara had begun to cry. That was how drink affected her; either she cried or talked in a foreign accent and said, 'Why am I talking in a foreign accent?' This time she cried.

'Hickey, there is no joy in life,' she said as she sat at the table with her head laid in her arms and her blouse slipping up out of her skirtband.

'What joy?' said Hickey, who had all the drink he needed, and a pound note which he slipped from behind the owl when no one was looking.

Doris and Eithne sat on either side of Long John Salmon, asking if they could go out next year when the sugar plums were ripe. Long John Salmon lived by himself, way up the country, and he had a big orchard. He was odd and silent in himself; he took a swim every day, winter and summer, in the river, at the back of his house.

'Two old married people,' Brogan said, as he put his arm round Mrs Rodgers and urged her to sit down because he was out of breath from dancing. He said he'd go away with happy memories of them all, and sitting down he drew her on to his lap. She was a heavy woman, with straggly brown hair that had once been a nut colour.

'There is no joy in life,' Crystal sobbed, as the gramophone made crackling noises and Mary ran in from the landing, away from O'Toole.

'I mean business,' O'Toole said, and winked.

O'Toole was the first to get quarrelsome.

'Now ladies, now gentlemen, a little laughing sketch, are we ready?' he asked.

'Fire ahead,' Hickey told him.

'Well, there was these three lads, Paddy th'Irishman, Paddy th'Englishman, and Paddy the Scotsman, and they were badly in need of a . . .'

'Now, no smut,' Mrs Rodgers snapped, before he had uttered a wrong word at all.

'What smut?' said O'Toole, getting offended. 'Smut!' And he asked her to explain an accusation like that.

'Think of the girls,' Mrs Rodgers said.

'Girls,' O'Toole sneered, as he picked up the bottle of cream— which they'd forgotten to use with the jelly—and poured it into the carcass of the ravaged goose.

'Christ's sake, man,' Hickey said, taking the bottle of cream out of O'Toole's hand.

Mrs Rodgers said that it was high time everyone went to bed, as the party seemed to be over.

The guests would spend the night in the Commercial. It was too late for them to go home anyhow, and also Mrs Rodgers did not want them to be observed staggering out of the house at that hour. The police watched her like hawks and she didn't want any trouble, until Christmas was over at least. The sleeping arrangements had been decided earlier on—there were three bedrooms vacant. One was Brogan's, the room he always slept in. The other three men were to pitch in together in the second big bedroom, and the girls were to share the back room with Mrs Rodgers herself.

'Come on, everyone, blanket street,' Mrs Rodgers said, as she put a guard in front of the dying fire and took the money from behind the owl.

'Sugar you,' O'Toole said, pouring stout now into the carcass of the goose, and Long John Salmon wished that he had never come. He thought of daylight and of the swim in the mountain river at the back of his grey, stone house.

'Ablution,' he said, aloud, taking pleasure in the word and in thought of the cold water touching him. He could do without people, people were waste. He remembered catkins on a tree outside his window, catkins in February as white as snow; who needed people?

'Crystal, stir yourself,' Hickey said, as he put on her shoes and patted the calves of her legs.

Brogan kissed the four girls and saw them across the landing to the bedroom. Mary was glad to escape without O'Toole noticing; he was very obstreperous and Hickey was trying to control him.

In the bedroom she sighed; she had forgotten all about the furniture being pitched in there. Wearily they began to unload the things. The room was so crammed that they could hardly move in it. Mary suddenly felt alert and frightened, because O'Toole could be heard yelling and singing out on the landing. There had been gin in her orangeade, she knew now, because she breathed closely on to the palm of her hand and smelt her own breath. She had broken her Confirmation pledge, broken her promise; it would bring her bad luck.

Mrs Rodgers came in and said that five of them would be too crushed in the bed, so that she herself would sleep on the sofa for one night.

'Two of you at the top and two at the bottom,' she said, as she warned them not to break any of the ornaments, and not to stay talking all night.

'Night and God bless,' she said, as she shut the door behind her.

'Nice thing,' said Doris O'Beirne, 'bunging us all in here; I wonder where she's off to?'

'Will you loan me curlers?' Crystal asked. To Crystal, hair was the most important thing on earth. She would never get married because you couldn't wear curlers in bed then. Eithne Duggan said she wouldn't put curlers in now if she got five million for doing it, she was that jaded. She threw herself down on the quilt and spread her arms out. She was a noisy, sweaty girl but Mary liked her better than the other two.

'Ah me old segotums,' O'Toole said, pushing their door in. The girls exclaimed and asked him to go out at once as they were preparing for bed.

'Come into the drawing-room, Doris,' he said to Mary, and curled his forefinger at her. He was drunk and couldn't focus her properly but he knew that she was standing there somewhere.

'Go to bed, you're drunk,' Doris O'Beirne said, and he stood very upright for an instant and asked her to speak for herself.

'Go to bed, Michael, you're tired,' Mary said to him. She tried to sound calm because he looked so wild.

'Come into the drawing-room, I tell you,' he said, as he caught her wrist and dragged her towards the door. She let out a cry, and Eithne Duggan said she'd brain him if he didn't leave the girl alone.

'Give me that flower-pot, Doris,' Eithne Duggan called, and then Mary began to cry in case there might be a scene. She hated scenes. Once she heard her father and a neighbour having a row about boundary rights and she'd never forgotten it; they had both been a bit drunk, after a fair.

'Are you cracked or are you mad?' O'Toole said, when he perceived that she was crying.

'I'll give you two seconds,' Eithne warned, as she held the flower-pot high, ready to throw it at O'Toole's stupefied face.

'You're a nice bunch of hard-faced aul crows, crows,' he said. 'Wouldn't give a man a squeeze,' and he went out cursing each one of them. They shut the door very quickly and dragged the sideboard in front of the door so that he could not break in when they were asleep.

They got into bed in their underwear; Mary and Eithne at one end with Crystal's feet between their faces.

'You have lovely hair,' Eithne whispered to Mary. It was the nicest thing she could think of to say. They each said their prayers, and shook hands under the covers and settled down to sleep.

'Hey,' Doris O'Beirne said a few seconds later, 'I never went to the lav.'

'You can't go now,' Eithne said, 'the sideboard's in front of the door.'

'I'll die if I don't go,' Doris O'Beirne said.

'And me, too, after all that orange we drank,' Crystal said. Mary was shocked that they could talk like that. At home you never spoke of such a thing, you just went out behind the hedge and that was that. Once a workman saw her squatting down and from that day she never talked to him, or acknowledged that she knew him.

'Maybe we could use that old pot,' Doris O'Beirne said, and Eithne Duggan sat up and said that if anyone used a pot in that room she wasn't going to sleep there.

'We have to use something,' Doris said. By now she had got up and had switched on the light. She held the pot up to the naked bulb and saw what looked to be a hole in it.

'Try it,' Crystal said, giggling.

They heard feet on the landing and then the sound of choking and coughing, and later O'Toole cursing and swearing and hitting the wall with his fist. Mary curled down under the clothes, thankful for the company of the girls. They stopped talking.

'I was at a party. Now I know what parties are like,' Mary said to herself, as she tried to force herself asleep. She heard a sound as of water running, but it did not seem to be raining outside. Later, she dozed, but at daybreak she heard the hall door bang, and she sat up in bed abruptly. She had to be home early to milk, so she got up, took her shoes and her lace dress, and let herself out by dragging the sideboard forward, and opening the door slightly.

There were newspapers spread on the landing floor and in the lavatory, and a heavy smell pervaded. Downstairs, porter had flowed out of the bar into the hall. It was probably O'Toole who had turned on the taps of the five porter barrels, and the stone-floored bar and sunken passage outside was swimming with black porter. Mrs Rodgers would kill somebody. Mary put on her high-heeled shoes and picked her steps carefully across the room to the door. She left without even making a cup of tea.

She wheeled her bicycle down the alley and into the street. The front tyre was dead flat. She pumped for a half-an-hour but it remained flat.

The frost lay like a spell upon the street, upon the sleeping windows, and the slate roofs of the narrow houses. It had magically made the dunged street white and clean. She did not feel tired, but relieved to be out, and stunned by lack of sleep she inhaled the beauty of the morning. She walked briskly, sometimes looking back to see the track which her bicycle and her feet made on the white road.

Mrs Rodgers wakened at eight and stumbled out in her big nightgown from Brogan's warm bed. She smelt disaster instantly and hurried downstairs to find the porter in the bar and the hall; then she ran to call the others.

'Porter all over the place; every drop of drink in the house is on the floor—Mary Mother of God help me in my tribulation! Get up, get up.' She rapped on their door and called the girls by name.

The girls rubbed their sleepy eyes, yawned, and sat up.

'She's gone,' Eithne said, looking at the place on the pillow where Mary's head had been.

'Oh, a sneaky country one,' Doris said, as she got into her taffeta dress and went down to see the flood. 'If I have to clean that, in my good clothes, I'll die,' she said. But Mrs Rodgers had already brought brushes and pails and got to work. They opened the bar door and began to bail the porter into the street. Dogs came to lap it up, and Hickey, who had by then come down, stood and said what a crying shame it was, to waste all that drink. Outside it washed away an area of frost and revealed the dung of yesterday's fair day. O'Toole the culprit had fled since the night; Long John Salmon was gone for his swim, and upstairs in bed Brogan snuggled down for a last-minute warm and deliberated on the joys that he would miss when he left the Commercial for good.

'And where's my lady with the lace dress?' Hickey asked, recalling very little of Mary's face, but distinctly remembering the sleeves of her black dress which dipped into the plates.

'Sneaked off, before we were up,' Doris said. They all agreed that Mary was no bloody use and should never have been asked.

'And 'twas she set O'Toole mad, egging him on and then disappointing him,' Doris said, and Mrs Rodgers swore that O'Toole, or Mary's father, or someone, would pay dear for the wasted drink.

'I suppose she's home by now,' Hickey said, as he rooted in his pocket for a butt. He had a new packet, but if he produced that they'd all be puffing away at his expense.

Mary was half-a-mile from home, sitting on a bank.

If only I had a sweetheart, something to hold on to, she thought, as she cracked some ice with her high heel and watched the crazy splintered pattern it made. The poor birds could get no food as the ground was frozen hard. Frost was general all over Ireland; frost like a weird blossom on the branches, on the river-bank from which Long John Salmon leaped in his great, hairy nakedness, on the ploughs left out all winter; frost on the stony fields, and on all the slime and ugliness of the world.

Walking again she wondered if and what she would tell her mother and her brothers about it, and if all parties were as bad. She was at the top of the hill now, and could see her own house, like a little white box at the end of the world, waiting to receive her.

First Conjugation

She was from Cremona: a patrician creature in her forties, who had
followed her refugee husband to our town and taught Italian in our
local university. Her colleagues here were peasants' grandsons
abandoned by ambition at the top of Ireland's academic tree.
Noncoms in an army with nowhere to go, they treated their meek
students with weary irony. Among them, the signora's presence was
like moonlight in a well. Each glimpse of her was tonic in that tight,
cast-concrete arena where the inner walls were painted a washable
urine-green.

She alone supplied the hyper-vividness I had expected from
college and did so in the first few weeks. In their academic gowns,
other teachers became moulting crows or funeral mutes. She wore
hers like a ball-dress and her green-shadowed Parmigianino neck
rose thrillingly from between its gathered billows. Her hair circled
her head with the austere vigour of black mountain-streams. Her
body moved like channelled water and she had a higher charge of
life than anyone I had ever seen.

Her controlled vibrancy enthralled me as did an aloof pity for
our simplicity, and the prodigality with which, perhaps for her
private amusement, she proposed considerations too fine for our
grasp. Had I been a male student I would have been in love with
her.

As it was, her beauty set standards towards which, despairingly,
I aspired. At night in bed I thought of her, sometimes making up
stories in which I won her esteem, sometimes letting myself become
her and move through marvellous though shadowy adventures. At
sixteen I was pursuing my waking dreams with flagging zest. I
longed for something actual to happen and was beginning to think
of men. To reconcile my yearnings, I, as the signora, fancied I was
courted by a man. 'Oh thou,' he whispered, 'art wondrous as the
evening air / In wanton Arethusa's azure arms . . .' Who was he? It
was hard to give him a face for I did not know any worthy men.

Only students who, if they were not clerics, were pimply, or had necks like plucked quails or faces, as my friend Ita put it, 'like babies' bottoms': a sexual disgrace to any girl they might approach. Not that they approached Ita or me. Or rather only Nick Lucy did, whose sad puffy face appeared with inappropriate suddeness in my dream, staring with his hang-dog look at me-the-signora just as he stared at me-myself every morning in the coffee shop.

Clot! Squirt! How *dare* he disturb my private fancies! I hated him! Maybe he was thinking of me? Telepathically bullying me into thinking of *him*? At the thought that no one but Nick Lucy would do the like I bit the pillow with rage.

'Hold on to Nick,' Ita had recommended that morning when he'd gone to buy us both some doughnuts. 'He'll be useful!'

'He's awful looking!'

'They all are,' said Ita looking round the coffee shop. 'We've no choice.'

'Mike McGillacuddy isn't so bad.' I argued. 'You wouldn't go round with him if he looked like Nick!'

'Mike's ghastly really,' said Ita, 'he's stuck on himself! But he has VV.'

'What's that?'

'Vehicular value. VV! It means he has a car. A fellow with a car can take you places where you meet other fellows. If you stay home you never meet any. No fear of *them* coming looking for us!'

'Well, Nick has no VV—car.'

'One car's enough,' Ita said. 'But we need a man each. Don't you see! Any sort of stooge will do so long as we can go to a dance with him or into a pub. Girls can't go into pubs alone and *that's* where you meet men. When we meet some attractive ones we can drop the stooges. So my sister says. She says Irish fellows don't *like* girls,' Ita explained patiently, 'so it has to be a tough chase with no holds barred.'

Ita's sister was four years older than we and engaged so she, I supposed, must know. I agreed to put up with Nick.

'Though,' I said, 'he gives me the creeps.'

He did. In the last few months my body had become an Aeolian harp, resonant to the slighest breath. If I stirred the down on my arms or the nape of my neck with a pencil tip, pleasure rippled up my spine. When Nick Lucy picked books from my desk, the brush of his sleeve against my cheek had the toad pressure of jellied frogspawn.

'Put down those books, Lucy! I don't want you carrying my books!'

'OK, OK, spitfire!' he said and went off, sauntering and hurt, for he was as moody and torn by yens as myself.

'She's awful to me,' he said to Ita.

'Ah,' Ita said as people do, 'she likes you really.'

I didn't. I was embarrassed by him: a pasty drip whose plight however upset me. For I knew he dreamed of me as I did of Signora Perruzzi and that I had 'led him on'. I knew a gawky face was not the emanation of a gawky soul but that handsome was as handsome did. Or I tried to know. Yes! Yes! But the leaven of my sensuality was stuck deep in the dough of snobbery. I couldn't *make* myself like him, could I? The man who would set my veins foaming was going to have to be spiffing to look at, dream-standard, unlike poor Nick whose plainness seemed somehow contagious.

'Don't follow me to Italian class,' I told him.

I could be kind to him at coffee or, better still, in the leaf-screened alleys of the college grounds where he amused me with stories of his country childhood; but I dreaded being seen with him by the signora. Nick's niceness was not of the sort that met the eye, and I imagined *her* eye as more exacting than my own. Her high-arched brows looked ironic, and I could not imagine her tall neck flexing in pity. Or didn't want to imagine it.

To show he wouldn't be bullied, Nick followed me to Italian class anyhow, and sat in the back row drawing my profile.

I ignored him. It was 'conversation' where the signora gave of her best. She must have been dazzling in the Fascist *salons* of ten years before. Now she exercised her high-powered weapons on three seminarists, four nuns, a few flat-vowelled peasants from the midlands, and myself. I strained towards her. *Why* had she had to leave Italy? Why wound up in this provincial stopping-place from which we all—even the four blue nuns bound eventually to nurse Florentine aristocrats and Prato businessmen—intended to progress? What war crimes were hers that she taught here for a pittance, wasting her coruscations in this pee-green room, under the bare electric light bulb and the painted-over crucifix on the wall? (A

Radical professor had insisted on having all crucifixes in the classrooms painted over and now, it was rumoured, objected on political grounds to the signora's being on the staff. The pale patch hung behind her like a reproof.)

'In our patriotic time in Italy,' the signora sighed, 'we used the *voi* not the *Lei*. It is nearer the ancient Roman *tu*.'

She laughed an opulent laugh. Unnecessarily lavish, its throatiness evoked the pile of deep carpets and the fur of snuggly coats in a Lombard winter. She was a gay, not a pitiful exile. 'The Romans,' she said sweetly, 'were democratic. The *Lei* was a subservient Spanish importation.'

Nick whose father had been in the British army muttered in the back row.

I turned round. 'Shut up!' I whispered.

When I looked back up the signora's eyes were on me. She frowned. Then her lips formed a brief, tight smile.

'I see,' she cried sprightly. 'You are impatient for conversation! Well, *I* shall converse and you may note my phrases, since your Italian is perhaps not up to replying. What,' she murmured dreamily, 'shall we discuss? I have it: love. Love is the great Italian subject. Or so,' she mocked, 'foreigners think. Who care for it perhaps more than Italians themselves. Well, we have the verb *amare*, first conjugation, regular. *Io amo*, I love. *Tu ami*,' she beamed her attention at a point in the back row, and I stirred apprehensively, 'you love. *Tu ami la ragazza*.' Unbelievably, she was addressing herself to Nick. 'You love the girl,' she told him. '*Egli ama*, he loves.' She turned to the others, and nodded so unmistakably, first in Nick's direction and then in mine, that even the blue nuns giggled and stared from him to me. 'He loves the girl,' said the cruel signora. Oh belle dame sans merci! Dry-mouthed, I listened in horror. She was more beautiful than ever. And bad! Just as I had supposed! But why with me? Why? 'He comes to class because he loves the girl. *Elia ama* or *essa* or we may say *lei ama*,' said Signora Perruzzi with maddening sloth, 'may all mean—for Italian is a rich language—she loves.'

I felt as though she were putting worms on me, as though she were stripping and streaking me with filth. 'If she couples me with him again. . . . If she says . . .' I could not think what she might say next. Had she X-ray eyes? Did she know I had worshipped her? Was this her way of refusing my devotion? I felt the paralysing embarrassment, the shame I used to feel as a child when I was dreaming out loud and suddenly suspected that my brother had crept under my bed to surprise and deride me. The agony of those few seconds while I used to grope for the electric light switch returned, now realized and suffocating. 'I'll get up,' I thought weakly, 'I'll walk out.' It was Nick I loathed even while the signora tormented me. 'He's enjoying this,' I thought with ferocious injustice, 'he's happy at being connected with me.' *Odiare*, to hate, supplied my grammar: First Conjugation, regular.

'Does she love him?' pronounced the signora, 'may be rendered in Italian without any inversion: *Leo lo ama?*' She stared at me. '*Lo ama?*' she repeated enquiringly, 'which may also mean "do *you* love him". Do you?' she asked me. 'Do you?'

I picked up my books and left the room.

As I passed the four nuns, their sleek, blue-veiled heads bent low over the verbs of the First Conjugation.

That's all: a child's humiliation. Even as 'my most embarrassing moment' it would hardly rate in competition with men who lost their trunks on the beach or girls surprised in hair-curlers by their suitors. Signora Perruzzi, if she remembered her own teens, may have felt a tiny twinge of compunction. But more likely not. How could she know on what tumid, thin-skinned areas she had trodden or that for me the offence was absolute?

I, absorbed in the symmetries of my own taboos, was just as unaware of her—the real signora. And when I hurt her it was not a planned *quid pro quo*, but the random flailing movement of a creature uncertain of its own location.

In the next few weeks she tried to win me round, inviting me to her flat where she had little Italian evenings with fried polenta and great moments from Italian opera on records. Before the pivotal conversation class (BC), nothing would have given me more joy. Now I refused. Her verve I fancy flagged a little under my disdain. She could *have* her flat-vowelled midlanders, seminarists and nuns. I stayed aloof. I did agree to do a paper on D'Annunzio for the Modern Language Society but only to deride the poet of 'our patriotic time in Italy'. She gave me good marks. She had not noticed my idolizing of herself and did not seem to care when I attacked her idol.

* * *

And then our worlds impinged.

A bachelor friend of my parents begged me to come and make sandwiches for an adult party he was giving and, as a reward, invited me to stay. It was a musical party to celebrate the arrival in our town of a well-known pianist, and among the guests was Signor Perruzzi, my signora's husband. She herself did not come.

He couldn't have been more than half her height.

'Are you sure,' I asked my host, 'that that's he?'

'Yes,' he said, 'that's Signor Perruzzi.'

He was a fat blackbird of a fellow from Rome with all his weight tilted forward so that his evening tails rose a little on his behind, as though he were constantly considering leaning over to kiss someone's hand. He had a lively blackberry eye, a wet mouth, and warm jolly contours to a face which didn't have a single hollow in it. He was altogether astonishingly unlike his wife and kept flinging little candied cherries into his mouth which puffed his cheeks out so that he looked like Tweedledum. And yet it was he, our host told me, who was the cause of their exile. He had been an ardent Fascist, had composed hymns and marching tunes for Mussolini and had even committed imprudences during the days of the Badoglio government.

'Not only political, rather scabrous I gather. Something to do with assaulting a minor,' said the host and then, having looked at me, clearly decided to get off that tack. 'He can't go back,' he told me. 'And he can't get work. He was a well-known conductor, you know, but there's a ban against him. His antisemitism . . .'

'And she?' I asked, thinking of her green-tinged skin, her fine, violent face.

'Oh, she's just a housewife. Nobody has anything against *her*. She adores him and puts up with a lot. He's a bastard to her,' said the host and moved off to welcome someone new.

I was carrying a tray of sandwiches and moved towards Signor Perruzzi. Would he have one, I asked, in careful Italian. He swung round. His hands revolved like a conjuror's. Words flowed with the rush of an open faucet. He was common, a stage Italian, a charm-vendor. He dished out technicolour, cream-topped compliments with the familiar phoney friendliness of his Irish equivalent. I didn't need to know Rome to know *him*.

'*Ma guarda, guarda che bella signorina!*'

He lengthened the i-i-i of signorina as the Irish uncle-type would have done with that of cailín. ('Isn't she a gorgeous little cailín antirely!')

'And you know Italian? You are studying with my wife? Are all her students as pretty as you? No wonder she keeps them hidden!'

The tone was the same but the look in his fruity eyes was not. Unblinking, cat-like, they changed quality, seemed to change substance as they stared into mine. There was a shameless, peeled excitement in them which I had never seen, never imagined and which contrasted disquietingly with the platitudes which emerged soothingly from his soft lips. 'Is she a good teacher?' he asked. The eyes were black basalt. 'She'll give you a Lombard accent! You should come and have lessons with me. I talk the best Italian. *Lingua toscana in bocca romana!* Do you know what that means? The Tuscan tongue in a Roman mouth!' His own tongue travelled the damp surface of his lips. Suddenly he leaned almost toppled towards me. He was smaller than I was—how much smaller than she? *'Conosce l'amore?'* he asked. 'Do you know love?' I stared at him. What could he mean? One *felt* love. How could one *know* it?' And why was he asking *me* such a thing? Remembering how the signora had conjugated the verb to love, I blushed.

He did not smile as an Irishman might. His spearing gaze and my giggle were interrupted by our host who said that my father was leaving and that I should get my coat. I went, but on my way back passed Signor Perruzzi again. 'Going so soon?' he asked. 'Little girls have to get their beauty sleep!' His tone was light and I felt let down as though he had reneged on a promise. But at the door he was there again. 'When,' he whispered swiftly for my father had already gone out to the lift.

'When what?'

'Our conversation lesson?'

'Oh,' I said, 'that was a joke, wasn't it?' and ran out to the landing. 'Goodbye,' I called. 'Give my regards to your wife.' As the lift went down I saw him turn. He was a fat little man.

I thought of him as I sat in Italian class, where the signora now seemed less marvellous to me. Coldly, I noted the wrinkles at the corners of her eyes. The poetry she liked to quote seemed soppy.

'*Ecco settembre*,' she read, '*O amore mio triste, sogneremo.*
In questo ciel l'estramo sogno si dileguera.
D'un pensoso dolore, settembre il ciel riempie,
Gli languon sulle tempoe, le rose dell'esta.'

Was *he* her *amore triste*? What had our host meant by his being a
bastard to her? Perruzzi's eyes came back to me when I closed
my own, imperiously. Black, I thought, like beetles. Round and
black like fresh excrement of goats. But that did not send them
away.

Then one morning I took a book the signora had lent me and
went around to their flat. It was a Saturday and I thought she might
be out shopping as my mother often was on Saturday mornings.
Signor Perruzzi opened the door.

'Ah,' he said. 'The little signorina!'

Even in my flat-heeled shoes I was taller than he but I knew he
had said 'little' to reassure me and exorcise something imminent
and furtive in the air.

'I brought back the signora's book,' I said and stood there.

He took it. 'Will you have a coffee?'

'If you're having some,' I said, 'thank you.' And I followed him
into the signora's kitchen.

It was an Irish kitchen, rented, with only a few foreign touches: a
half-moon shaped meat-chopper, a coffee machine. Signor Perruzzi
reached up to the shelf for this. His hand brushed my neck and I
trembled. '*Piccola*!' He relinquished the gadget on its shelf, took
hold of my shoulders and, pulling them downwards, kissed my
neck which he could just reach. He seized my two weakly struggling
hands. '*Bambina*,' he whispered and, squashing one hand into his
tightly encased stomach, started pushing it determinedly downwards.
I jerked it away, then, as he grabbed me, braced my knee against his
thigh and, freeing myself with a wrench, fell backwards to collide
with someone who had just opened the back door. It was the
signora who was arriving, loaded with parcels.

She gave a little scream: 'Eugenio!' then picked up her fallen
groceries and put them on the table.

I tried to stand up but my ankle was hurt and shot sharp pains up
my leg when I tried to lean on it. I had to sit on a chair, massaging
myself and waiting while Signor and Signora Perruzzi quarrelled in
rapid Italian. He screamed and she spoke with calm, cold clarity so

that anything I did understand came from her. 'Ah no,' she kept saying, 'not again, not any more!' And then: 'I'd rather leave right now!' And later: 'Scandal, I can't stand scandal! This one's only sixteen!' Neither of them paid any attention to me and I had time to make two or three more attempts to stand up and go but each time my leg collapsed under me and I had to sit back on the chair. It was so dreadful to have to sit there listening that the pain was almost a relief. When finally Signor Perruzzi after a particularly shrill crescendo of shouting, paused, bowed to me and walked with slow dignity out the inner door, I began to wonder whether the signora might not assault me physically. Guilt is an isolating feeling and I felt no pity for either of the Perruzzis. Not even wonder at myself. All I wanted was to get home as quickly as possible and forget.

'Are you hurt?' the signora asked quietly. She was probably as eager to get rid of me as I was to go. 'It's probably just a sprain. Lean on my shoulder. See if you can hop as far as the car and I'll give you a lift home.'

We did as she said and she drove me home without saying anything more. I kept looking out the window on my side and only once, when a van braked suddenly on the other side and gave me an excuse, did I glance at her face. It was expressionless but, from close up, the wrinkles were encroaching tendrils of shadows on the apricot lightness.

'This is our gate,' I said. 'Thank you for the lift. I think I can get out myself.' I didn't want her meeting my parents.

She faced me. 'I have to ask you something. It's important to me. You're old enough to understand . . .' Suddenly her lips were puckering. The Signora Perruzzi had begun to cry.

Ashamed for both of us, holding my hands tightly in my lap, I waited. I would not have known how to help her if I had still loved her and I did not love her.

'Did he,' she asked, 'did my husband ask you to come to the flat this morning? Did he tell you *I* would be there?'

I looked at her.

'Did he *ask* you to come?' she repeated a little sharply.

I hesitated and then: 'Yes,' I told her, 'yes, he did. He was most insistent,' I said, 'actually. I'm sorry about everything, Signora Perruzzi. Goodbye.'

I hopped out of the car by myself in spite of the pain and dragged myself inside our gate. When I heard the car drive off I called to the maid to come and help me.

'I fell,' I told her, 'getting off the bus.'

It was April, almost the end of the academic year. With the excuse of my ankle I was able to stay home and avoid going to any more Italian classes. In June we had exams. It was during the luncheon break, one examination day, that I ran into Signor Perruzzi in the college grounds. He was feeding the ducks with a little boy of about five, and I would have sneaked by behind their backs but that he caught sight of me and called: 'Signorina!'

'Hullo,' I said, gave him a great gush of a smile and rushed on.

But he ran after me. 'Signorina, wait! I have been wanting to ask . . .' He was trotting to keep up with me, dragging the child by the hand so I had to stop.

'Please,' I begged, 'can't we forget . . .'

'No, no!' Signor Perruzzi's eyes leaped in all directions. He was no longer bouncy but deflated. Muddy, semi-circular shadows furrowed the flesh at the corners of his eyes and mouth. When he turned round to the child he took the opportunity of checking up on the alley behind us. 'My son,' he explained. 'Say "hullo",' he told the child but turned away from him at once. 'My wife has got the wrong impression,' he told me. 'It is most unfortunate. For reasons you can't know . . .' he spoke rapidly and with a vague urgency. 'Most grave. For me. I must ask you to help me . . .' His eyes shifted. 'You remember the last time . . . we met? It was merely a moment of tenderness,' said Signor Perruzzi while the child pulled out of his arm. 'An impulse. If *you* could tell my wife that. Tell her,' he begged, 'that it was not premeditated . . .'

At that moment I saw the signora herself. 'Mama!' yelled the child, running towards her. The signora opened her arms to sweep it up and the black bat-wings of her BA gown closed vengefully around it. She strode towards us. Pitiful and repellent, the wrinkles in her face moved in the sun like the long-jointed legs of agonizing insects. Both she and her husband looked old to me.

'So,' she said in English, 'you continue to make appointments! My God Eugenio, I cannot sleep, cannot work with worrying about a fresh scandal. If you would even pick on adults . . .'

'Maria, I swear,' said her husband. 'There was no appointment. I just met the signorina by chance, two minutes ago. Ask her, I have never given her an appointment. *Ask her!*'

'I asked her the last time,' the signora retorted sourly, 'and she told me then that you *had* made an appointment to meet behind my back! Eugenio, it is too much . . .'

This time, unhampered by any twisted ankle, I fled. As I went I could hear the ebb and suspiration of their voices incomprehensibly wrangling. Bitter, painful and obscure, the sounds pursued me across the garden.

I felt guilt of course, remorse which I buried as fast and deeply as I could. What, I argued with myself, could I do anyway? Even if I were to retract my lie, tell the signora that her husband had *not* invited me to their flat that morning or arranged to meet me in the college gardens, she would not believe me. Would she? Besides, wasn't he clearly a bad hat? A weak, lecherous, morally soft creature? I flailed in him my own uncertain shames. She would be well rid of him.

It was October and the start of a new academic year when I heard that she had returned with the child to Italy. She was looking for an annulment it was thought, and he was hanging round town living on expedients. Eventually, I caught sight of him in the street, looking no longer like a blackbird but like a mournful thrush in a tweed coat which someone must have given him, for its padded shoulders drooped half-way to his elbow. He did not see me and I cannot remember if I spared him a passing regret.

I had given up Italian and was busy competing with Ita for the attentions of Nick Lucy who had become muscular, tanned and worldly during a summer in the south of France. If we ever did mention Signora Perruzzi after that, it was to laugh—happily—at the way she had made fun of us during conversation class.

The Beginning of an Idea

*The word Oysters was chalked on the wagon that carried
Chekhov's body to Moscow for burial. The coffin was carried in
the oyster wagon because of the fierce heat of early July.*

Those were the first sentences in Eva Lindberg's loose notes,
written in a large childish hand, and she started reading them at the
table again as she waited for Arvo Meri to come to the small flat.
The same pair of sentences was repeated throughout the notes in a
way which suggested that she leaned on them for inspiration. *The
word Oysters was chalked on the wagon that carried Chekhov's
body to Moscow for burial. The coffin was carried in the oyster
wagon because of the fierce heat of early July.* There was also
among the notes a description of Chekhov's story called 'Oysters'.

The father and son were on the streets of Moscow in that rainy
autumn evening. They were both starving. The father had failed to
find work after trudging about Moscow for five months, and he
was trying to muster up enough courage to beg for food. He had
drawn the tops of a pair of old boots round his calves so that people
wouldn't notice that his feet were bare under the galoshes. Above
father and son was a blue signboard with the word *Restaurant* and
on a white placard on the wall was written the word *Oysters*. The
boy had been alive for eight years and three months and had never
come across the word oysters before.

'What does oysters mean, Father?'

The father had touched a passerby on the sleeve, but not being
able to beg he was overcome with confusion and stammered.
'Sorry.' Then he swayed back against the wall. He did not hear the
boy's voice.

'What does oysters mean, Father?' the child repeated.

'It's an animal . . . it lives in the sea,' the father managed.

The boy imagined something between a fish and a crab, delicious
made into a hot fish soup, flavoured with pepper and laurel, or with
crayfish sauce and served cold with horse-radish. Brought from the

market, quickly cleaned, quickly thrown into the pot, quick-quick-quick, everyone was starving. A smell of steaming fish and crayfish soup came from the kitchen. The boy started to work his jaws, oysters, blessed oysters, chewing and slugging them down. Overcome by this feeling of bliss he grabbed at his father's elbow to stop himself from falling, leaned against the wet summer overcoat. His father was shivering with the cold.

'Are oysters a Lenten food, Father?'

'They are eaten alive . . . they come in shells, like tortoises but . . . in two halves.'

'They sound horrible, Father,' the boy shivered.

A frog sat in a shell, staring out with great glittering eyes, its yellow throat moving—that was an oyster. It sat in a shell with claws, eyes that glittered like glass, slimy skin; the children hid under the table, while the cook lifted it by its claw, put it on a plate, and gave it to the grown-ups. It squealed and bit at their lips as they ate it alive—claws, eyes, teeth, skin and all. The boy's jaws still continued to move, up and down; the thing was disgusting but he managed to swallow it, swallowed another one, and then another, hurriedly, fearful of getting their taste. He ate everything in sight, his father's galoshes, the white placard, the table napkin, the plate. The eyes of the oysters glittered but he wanted to eat. Nothing but eating would drive this fever away.

'Oysters. Give me some oysters,' he cried, and stretched out his hands.

'Please help us, sir. I am ashamed to ask but I can't stand it any more,' he heard his father's voice.

'Oysters,' the boy cried.

'Do you mean to say you eat oysters? As small a fellow as you eats oysters?' he heard laughter close. A pair of enormous men in fur coats were standing over him. They were looking into his face and laughing. 'Are you sure it's oysters you want? This is too rich. Are you sure you know how to eat them?' Strong hands drew him into the lighted restaurant. He was sat at a table. A crowd gathered round. He ate something slimy, it tasted of sea water and mould. He kept his eyes shut. If he opened them he'd see the glittering eyes and claws and teeth. And then he ate something hard, for it crunched.

'Good lord. He's eating the bloody shells! Don't you know you can't eat the shells? Here, waiter!'

The next thing he remembered was lying in bed with a terrible thirst, he could not sleep with heartburn, and there was a strange taste in his parched mouth. His father was walking up and down the small room and waving his arms about.

'I must have caught cold. My head is splitting. Maybe it's because I've eaten nothing today. I am quite useless. Those men must have spent ten roubles on the oysters today and I stood there and did nothing. Why hadn't I the sense to go up to them and ask them, ask them to lend me something? They would have given me something.'

Towards evening the child fell asleep and dreamt of a frog sitting in a shell, moving its eyes. At noon he was woken by thirst and looked for his father. His father was still pacing up and down and waving his arms around.

The word Oysters was chalked on the wagon that carried Chekhov's body to Moscow for burial. The coffin was carried in the oyster wagon because of the fierce heat of early July, she found she had written it down once more. Chekhov was that boy outside the restaurant with his father in the autumn rain, was that starving boy crunching the oysters in the restaurant while they laughed, was the child in the bed woken by thirst at noon, watching the father pace up and down the small room and waving his arms around. She wanted to write an imaginary life of Chekhov, from the day outside the restaurant to the day the body of the famous writer reached Moscow in the oyster wagon for burial. It would begin with oysters and end with oysters, some of the oysters, after the coffin had been taken away for burial, delivered to the same restaurant in which the child Chekhov had eaten shells. She wasn't yet sure whether she would write it as a novel or a play. The theatre was what she knew best but she was sure that it would probably never get written at all unless more order and calm entered her life than was in it now. She closed the folder very quietly on the notes and returned them to their drawer. Then she showered and changed into a blue woollen dress and continued to wait for Arvo Meri to come.

That morning Arvo's wife had rung her at the theatre, where she was directing the rehearsals of Ostrovsky's *The Dragon*. At the end of much abuse she shouted, 'You're nothing but a whore,' and then began to sob hysterically. Eva used the old defence of silence and put down the receiver, and told the doorman that no matter how urgent any call claimed to be she was not to be interrupted in rehearsal. She was having particular difficulty with one of the leads, an actress of some genius who needed directing with a hand of iron since her instinct was to filch more importance for her own part than had been allotted to it. She had seen her ruin several fine plays by acting everybody else off the stage and was determined that it wasn't going to happen in this production. Once she began to rehearse again she put the call out of her mind but was able to think of nothing else during the midday break, and rang Arvo at his office. He was a journalist, with political ambitions on the Left, who had almost got into parliament at the last election and was almost certain to get in at the next. When he apologized for the call and blamed it on his wife's drinking she lost her temper.

'That makes a pair of you then,' and went on to say that she wanted a life of her own, preferably with him, but if not—without him. She had enough of to-ing and fro-ing, of what she called his Hamlet act. This time he would have to make up his mind, one way or the other. He countered by saying that it wasn't possible to discuss it over the phone and arranged to call at her flat at eight. As she waited for him in the blue woollen dress after showering, she determined to have that life of her own. The two sentences *The word Oysters was chalked on the wagon that carried Chekhov's body to Moscow for burial. The coffin was carried in the oyster wagon because of the fierce heat of early July* echoed like a revenant in her mind and would not stay still.

There was snow on Arvo Meri's coat and fur hat when he came and he carried a sheaf of yellow roses. Once she saw the flowers she knew nothing would change. She laid them across a sheepskin that covered a large trunk at the foot of the bed without removing their wrapping.

'Well?'

'I'm so sorry about this morning, Eva . . .'

'That doesn't matter,' she stopped him, 'but I do want to know what you propose to do.'

'I don't know what to do,' he said guiltily. 'You know I can't get a divorce.'

'I don't care about a divorce.'

'But what else is there to do?'

'I can take a larger flat than this. We can start to live seriously together,' she said, and he put his head in his hands.

'Even though there's nothing left between us she still depends on the relationship. If I was to move out completely she'd just go to pieces.'

'That's not my problem.'

'Can't we wait a little longer?'

'More than two years seems long enough to me. You go to Moscow by going to Moscow. If you wait until all the conditions are right you can wait your whole life.'

'I've booked a table at the Mannerheim. Why don't we talk it out there?'

'Why not?' she shrugged with bright sarcasm, and lifted the yellow roses from the sheepskin. 'I ask you for a life and you offer me yellow roses and a dinner at the Mannerheim,' but he did not answer as he started to dial a taxi, and she let the roses drop idly down on the sheepskin and pulled on her fur coat and boots and sealskin cap.

Charcoal was blazing in two braziers on tall iron stems on either side of the entrance to the Mannerheim. They hadn't spoken during the taxi drive and she remarked as she got out, 'They must have some important personage tonight.' She felt a sinking as in an aeroplane take-off as the lift went up. A uniformed attendant took their furs and they had a drink in the bar across from the restaurant while they gave their order to the waiter. The restaurant was half empty: three older couples and a very large embassy party. They knew it was an embassy party because of a circle of toy flags that stood in the centre of the table. Through the uncurtained glass they could see out over the lights of the city to the darkness that covered the frozen harbour and sea. He had drunk a number of vodkas by the time the main course came, and she was too tense to eat as she nibbled at the shrimp in the avocado and sipped at the red wine.

'You don't mind me drinking? I have a need of vodka tonight.'

'Of course not . . . but it won't be any use.'

'Why?' he looked at her.

'When I got pregnant you took me to the Mannerheim and said, "I don't know what to do. It's not the right time yet. That is all I know," and drank vodka and were silent for hours, except every now and then you'd say, "All I'm certain of is that it's not the right time for us to have a child." I had some hard thinking to do when I left the Mannerheim that night. And when I arranged for and had the abortion without telling you, and rang you after coming out of the clinic, you said the whole week had been like walking round under a dark cloud, but that I had made you so happy now. I was so understanding. One day we'd have a child when everything was right. And you came that evening with yellow roses and took me to the Mannerheim and later we danced all night at that place on the shore.'

She spoke very slowly. He didn't want to listen, but he didn't know what to say to stop her, and he ordered more vodka.

'And now when we spend three days in a row together your wife rings up and calls me a whore. You bring me yellow roses and take me to the Mannerheim. The vodka won't do any good . . .'

'But what are we to do?'

'I've given my answer. I'll take a larger flat. We'll live together as two people, from now on.'

'But can't we wait till after the elections?'

'No. It's always been "wait". And there will always be something to wait for. They say there's no good time to die either. That it's as difficult to leave at seventy as at twenty. So why not now?'

'But I love you, Eva.'

'If you loved me enough you'd come and live with me,' and he went silent. He had more vodka, and as they were leaving she noticed the attendant's look of disapproval as he swayed into the lift. The tall braziers had been taken in, and as they waited while the doorman hailed a taxi he asked, 'Can I come back with you tonight?' 'Why not. If you want,' she laughed in a voice that made him afraid. He was violently ill when he got to the flat and then fell at once into a drugged sleep sprawled across the bed. She looked at him a moment with what she knew was the dangerous egotism of the maternal instinct before she made up a bed on the carpet and switched off the lights. He woke early with a raging thirst and she got him a glass of water. 'Was I sick last night?' 'Yes, but don't worry, in the bathroom.' 'Why didn't you sleep in the bed?' 'I'd have to wake you, the way you were in bed.' 'I'm sorry.' 'It doesn't matter.' 'Why don't you come in now?' 'All right,' she rose from the blankets on the floor. The night conversation seemed to her like dialogue from a play that had run too long and the acting had gone stale. He drew her towards him on the bed, more, she knew, to try to escape through pleasure from the pain of the hangover than from desire. She grew impatient with his tired fumbling and pulled him on top of her, provoking him with her own body till he came. Afterwards they both slept. She shook her head later when he asked her, 'When will we meet?' 'It's no use.' 'But I love you.' She still shook her head. 'I'm fond of you but you can't offer me what I want.' As he moved to speak she stopped him. 'No, I can't wait. I have work I want to do.' 'Is it that damned Chekhov's body?' 'That's right.' 'It'll never come to anything,' he said in hatred. 'I don't care, but I intend to try.' 'You're nothing but a selfish bitch.' 'I am selfish and I want you to go now.'

That morning there were several calls for her during rehearsals but she had left strict instructions that she wasn't to be disturbed, and when she got home that evening she took the phone off the hook.

She was surprised during the following days how little she yearned for him, it was as if a weight had lifted; she felt an affection for him that she felt for that part of her life that she had passed with him, but she saw clearly that it was for her own life and not for his that she had yearning. She would go on alone, and when he demanded to see her she met him with a calm that was indifference which roused him to fury. She had not built a life with him, she had built nothing: but out of these sentences *The word Oysters was chalked on the wagon that carried Chekhov's body to Moscow for burial. The coffin was carried in the oyster wagon because of the fierce heat of early July* she would build, and for that she had to be alone. She would leave this city that had so much of her past life, the theatre where she had worked so long. She would leave them like a pair of galoshes in the porch, and go indoors. She rang rich friends: Was their offer of the house in Spain still open? It was. They only used it in July. They would be delighted to loan it to her. She could be their cuckoo there till then. She went and offered her resignation to the old manager.

'But you can't leave in the middle of a production.'

'I'm sorry. I didn't explain properly. Of course I'll see the production though, but I won't be renewing my contract when it expires at the end of the year.'

'Is it salary?' he sat down behind his big desk and motioned to her to sit.

'No. I am leaving the theatre. I want to try to write,' she blurted out to save explanation.

'It's even more precarious than the theatre, and now that you've made your way there why throw it over for something worse still?' he was old and kindly and wise, though he too must have had to be ruthless in his day.

'I must find out whether I can or not. I'll only find out by finding out. I'll come back if I fail.'

'You know, contrary to the prodigal son story, few professions welcome back their renegades?'

'I'll take that risk.'

'Well, I see you're determined,' he rose.

As soon as a production begins to take shape it devours everybody around it so that one has no need for company or friends or anything outside it, and in the evening one takes a limp life home with no other idea but to restore it so that it can be devoured anew the next day. As she went home on the tram two days before the dress rehearsal she hadn't enough strength to be angry when she saw her photo in the evening paper and read that she was leaving the theatre to write. She was leaving to *try* to write. She should have been more careful. Kind as he was she should have known that the old manager would use any publicity in any way to fill the theatre. *To write* was better copy than the truthful *try to write*. She wondered tiredly if there was a photo of the coffin being lifted out of the oyster wagon or of the starving man in his summer coat in the rain outside the restaurant while the boy crunched on the oyster shells within: and whether it was due to the kindness usually reserved for the dear departed or just luck, no production of hers had ever opened before to such glowing notices. And she left on New Year's Eve for Spain, by boat and train, passing through Stockholm and Copenhagen, and stopping five days in Paris where she knew some people. She had with her the complete works of Chekhov, and the two sentences were more permanently engraved than ever in her mind: *The word Oysters was chalked on the wagon that carried Chekhov's body to Moscow for burial. The coffin was carried in the oyster wagon because of the fierce heat of early July.*

She stayed five days in the Hotel Celtique on the rue Odessa, and all her waking hours seemed taken up with meeting people she already knew. Most of them scraped a frugal living from translation or journalism or both and all of them wrote or wanted to be artists in one way or another. They lived in small rooms and went out to cheap restaurants and movie houses. She saw that many of them were homesick and longed for some way to go back without injuring their self-esteem, and that they thought her a fool for leaving. In their eyes she read contempt. 'So she too has got the bug. That's all we need. One more,' and she began to protect herself by denying that there was any foundation to the newspaper piece. On the evening before she took the train to Spain she had dinner in a Russian restaurant off the Boulevard St Michel with the cleverest of them all: the poet Severi. He had published three books of poems, and the previous year she had produced a play of his that had been taken off after a week though it was highly praised by the critics. His threadbare dark suit was spotless, and the cuffs and collar of the white shirt shone, the black bow knotted with a studied carelessness. They were waited on by the owner, a little old hen of a Russian woman, who spoke heavily accented French, and whose thinning hair was dyed carrot. A once powerful man played an accordion at the door.

'Well, Eva Lindberg, can you explain to me what you're doing haring off to Spain instead of staying up there to empty that old theatre of yours with my next play?' the clever mordant eyes looked at her through unrimmed spectacles with ironic amusement.

'I was offered a loan of a house there,' she was careful.

'And they informed me you intend to write there. You know there's not room for the lot of us,' he did not let up.

'That's just a rumour that got into a newspaper.'

'What'll you do down there, a single woman among hordes of randy Spaniards?'

'For one thing I have a lot of reading to catch up on,' she was safe now, borrowing aggression from his aggression.

'And why did you leave the theatre?'

'I felt I was getting stale. I wasn't enjoying it any more.'

'And have you money?'

'I have enough money. And what about your work?'

He started to describe what he was working on with an even more ferocious mockery that he usually reserved for the work of others. The accordion player came round the tables with a saucer and bullied those who offered him less than a franc. They had a second carafe of red wine and finished with a peppered vodka. Warmed by the vodka he asked her to sleep with him, his face so contorted into a fury at having to leave himself open to rejection that she felt sorry for him.

'Why not?' he pushed, soon he would begin to mock his own desire.

'I've told you,' she said gently enough. 'I've had enough of sleeping, with the Arvo business. I want to be alone for a time.'

She was left completely alone for the whole of the journey the next evening and night, going early to her sleeper, changing at the frontier the next morning in the wider Spanish train, which got into Barcelona just before noon. A taximan took her to the small Hotel New York in the Gothic quarter and it proved as clean and cheap as he said it would be. She stayed five days in Barcelona and was happy. As an army in peacetime she was doing what she had to do by being idle and felt neither guilt nor need to strive to make the holiday, always the death of any chance of actually enjoying it.

She walked the narrow streets, went to a few museums and churches, bought a newspaper on the Ramblas, vivid with the flower stalls under the leafless trees in the cold dry weather, and ate each evening at the Casa Agut, a Catalan restaurant a few minutes' walk from the hotel. She sat where she could watch the kitchen, and always had Gaspacho, ensalada and a small steak with a half-bottle of red Rioja, enjoying the march of the *jefe* who watched for the slightest carelessness, the red and white towel on his shoulder like an epaulet. After five such days she took the train to Valencia, where she got the express bus to Almeria. She would get off at Vera and get a taxi to the empty house on the shore. It was on this bus that she made her first human contact since leaving Paris, a Swedish homosexual who must have identified her as Scandinavian by her clothes and blonde hair and who asked if he could sit beside her. 'How far are you going?' she asked when she saw she was stuck with him for the journey. 'I don't know. South. I can go as far as I want,' though the hair was dyed blond the lines in the brittle feminine face showed that he was sixty or more. He spoke only his own language and some English, and was impressed by her facility for acquiring languages. She wondered if the homosexual love of foreignness was that having turned away from the mother or being turned away they needed to do likewise with their mother tongue. 'Aren't you a lucky girl to find languages so easy?' She resented the bitchiness that inferred a boast she hadn't made.

'It's no more than being able to run fast or jump. It means you can manage to say more inaccurately in several languages what you can say better in your own. It's useful sometimes but it doesn't seem very much to me if that's all it achieves.'

'That's too deep for me,' he was resentful and impressed and a little scared. 'Are you on a holiday?'

'No. I'm going to live here for a time.'

'Do you have a house?'

'Yes. I've been loaned a house.'

'Will you be with people or alone?' his questioning grew more eager and rapid.

'I'll be alone.'

'Do you think I could take a room in the house?'

She was grateful to be able to rest her eyes on the blue sea in the distance. At least it would not grow old. Its tides would ebb and flow, it would still yield up its oyster shells long after all the living had become the dead.

'I'm sorry. One of the conditions of the loan is that I'm not allowed to have people to stay,' she lied.

'I could market for you and cook.'

'It's impossible. I'm sorry,' he would cling to any raft to shut out of mind the grave ahead.

'You? Are you going far?' she diverted.

'The bus goes to Almería.'

'And then?'

'I don't know. I thought to Morocco.'

She escaped from him in Alicante, where they had a half-hour break and changed buses. She saw the shirtsleeved porters pat the Swede's fur coat in amusement, '*Mucho frio, mucho frio,*' as they transferred it to the boot of the bus returning to Almería, and she waited till she saw him take the same seat in the new bus, and then took her place beside an old Spanish woman dressed in black who smelled of garlic and who, she learned later, had been seeing her daughter in hospital. She felt guilty at avoiding the Swede so pointedly but it would be worse to join him again now as it would be to get up and leave him if she were with him, as once alive it is better to go on than die, the best not to have been born at all, and she did not look back when she got off at Vera.

The house was low and flatroofed and faced the sea. The mountain was behind, a mountain of the moon, sparsely sprinkled with the green of farms that grew lemon trees and had often vine or olive on terraces of stone built on the mountainside. In the dried-up beds of rivers the cacti flourished. The village was a mile away and had a covered market built of stone and roofed with tiles the colour of sand. She was alarmed when the old women hissed at her when she first entered the market but then she saw it was only their way of trying to draw people to their stalls. Though there was a fridge in the house she went every day to the market, and it became her daily outing. The house had four rooms but she arranged it so that she could live entirely in the main room.

She reread all of Chekhov, ate and drank carefully, and in the solitude of her days felt her life for the first time in years in order. And the morning came when she decided to face the solitary white page. She had an end, the coffin of the famous writer coming to Moscow for burial that hot July day; and a beginning, the boy crunching on the oyster shells in the restaurant while the man starved in his summer coat in the rain outside: what she had to do was to imagine the life in between. She wrote in a careful hand *The word Oysters was chalked on the wagon that carried Chekhov's body to Moscow for burial. The coffin was carried in the oyster wagon because of the fierce heat of early July*, and then became curiously agitated. She rose and looked at her face in the small silver-framed mirror. Yes, there were lines, but faint still, and natural. Her nails needed filing. She decided to change into a shirt and jeans and then to rearrange all her clothes and jewellery. A week, two weeks, passed in this way. She got nothing written. The early sense of calm and order left her.

She saw one person fairly constantly during that time, a local *guardia* whose name was Manolo. He had first come to the house with a telegram from her old theatre, asking her if she would do a translation of a play of Mayakovsky's for them. She offered him a drink when he came with the telegram. He asked for water, and later he walked with her back to the village where she cabled her acceptance of the theatre's offer, wheeling his rattling bicycle, the thin glittering barrel of his rifle pointed skyward. The Russian manuscript of the play arrived by express delivery a few days afterwards, and now she spent all her mornings working on the translation; and how easy it was, the good text solidly and reliably under her hand: it was play compared with the pain of trying to pluck the life of Chekhov out of the unimaginable air.

Manolo began to come almost daily, in the hot lazy three or four of the afternoon. She could hear his boots scrape noisily on the gravel to give her warning. He would leave his bicycle against the wall of the house in the shade, his gun where the drinking water dripped slowly from the porous clay jars into catching pails. They would talk for an hour or more across the bare Scandinavian table, and he would smoke and drink wine or water. His talk turned often to the social ills of Spain and the impossibility of the natural division between men and women. She wondered why someone as intelligent as he could have become a *guardia*. There was nothing else to do, he told her: he was one of the lucky ones in the village, he got a salary, it was that or Germany. And then he married, and bang-bang, he said—two babies in less than two years. A third was on its way. All his wife's time was taken up with the infants now. There was nothing left between them but babies, and that was the way it would go on, without any money, seven or eleven or more . . .

'But that's criminal in this age,' she said.

'What is there to do?'

'There's contraception.'

'In Spain there's not.'

'They could be brought in.'

'Could you get some in? If you could I'd pay you,' he said eagerly, and when she sent back the completed translation she asked the theatre's editor if he could send the contraceptives with the next commission. She explained why she wanted them, though she reflected that he would think what he wanted anyhow. The contraceptives did get through with the next commissioned play. They wanted a new translation of *The Seagull*, which delighted her; she felt it would bring her closer to her Chekhov and that when she had finished it she would be able to begin what she had come here to try to do in the first place. The only objection the editor had to sending the contraceptives was that he was uneasy for her safety: it was against the law, and it was Spain, and policemen were as notorious as other people for wanting promotion. She thought Manolo was nervous and he left her quickly after she handed him the package that afternoon, but she put it out of mind as natural embarrassment in taking contraceptives from a woman, and went back to reading *The Seagull*. She was still reading it and making notes towards her translation on the margins when she heard boots and voices coming up the gravel, and a loud knock with what sounded like a gun butt came on the door. She was frightened as she called out, 'Who's there?' and a voice she didn't know called back, 'Open. It's the police.' When she opened the door she saw Manolo and the *jefe* of the local *guardia*, a fat oily man she had often seen lolling about the market, and he at once barged into the house. Manolo closed the door behind them as she instinctively got behind the table.

The *jefe* threw the package she had given Manolo earlier in the day on to the table. 'You know this?' and as she nodded she noticed in growing fear that both of them were very drunk. 'You know it's against the law? You can go to prison for this,' he said, the small oily eyes glittering across the table, and she decided there was no use answering any more.

'Still, Manolo and myself have agreed to forget it if we can try them out here,' his oily eyes fell pointedly on the package on the table but the voice was hesitant. 'That's if you don't prefer it Spanish style,' he laughed back to Manolo for support, and started to edge round the table.

They were drunk and excited. They would probably take her anyhow. How often had she heard this problem argued. Usually it was agreed that it was better to yield than to get hurt. After all, sex wasn't all it was cracked up to be: in Paris the butcher and the baker shook hands with the local whore when they met, as people simply plying different trades.

'All right. As long as you promise to leave as soon as it's done,' her voice stopped him, it had a calm she didn't feel.

'Okay, it's a promise,' they both nodded eagerly, and they reminded her of mastered boys as they asked apprehensively, 'With the . . . or without?'

'With.'

The *jefe* followed her first into the room. 'All the clothes off,' was his one demand, and she complied. She averted her face sideways while it took place. A few times after parties when she was younger hadn't she held almost total strangers in her arms? Then she fixed completely on the two sentences *The word Oysters was chalked on the wagon that carried Chekhov's body to Moscow for burial. The coffin was carried in the oyster wagon because of the fierce heat of early July*, her mind moving over them from beginning to end, and from beginning to end, again and again. Manolo rushed out of the room when he had finished. They kept their word and left, subdued and quiet. It had not been as jolly as they must have imagined it would be.

She showered and washed and changed into new clothes. She

poured herself a large glass of cognac at the table, noticing that they must have taken the condoms with them, and then began to sob, dry and hard at first, rising to a flood of rage against her own foolishness. 'There is only one real sin—stupidity. You always get punished for behaving stupidly,' the poet Severi was fond of repeating.

When she quietened she drank what was left of the cognac and then started to pack. She stayed up at night packing and putting the house in order for her departure. Numbed with tiredness she walked to the village the next morning. All the seats on the express that passed through Vera were booked for that day but she could take the *rápido* to Granada and go straight to Barcelona from there. She arranged for the one taxi in the village to take her to the train. The taximan came and she made listless replies to his ebullient talk on the drive by the sea to meet the train. The *rápido* was full of peasants and as it crawled from station to small station she knew it would be night before it reached Granada. She would find some hotel close to the station. In the morning she would see a doctor and then go to Barcelona. A woman in a black shawl on the wooden seat facing her offered her a sliver of sausage and a gourd of wine. She took the sausage but refused the wine as she wasn't confident that her hands were steady enough to direct the thin stream into her mouth. Then she nodded to sleep, and when she woke she thought the bitter taste of oysters was in her mouth and that an awful lot of people were pacing up and down and waving their arms around, and she had a sudden desire to look out the window to see if the word *Oysters* was chalked on the wagon; but then she saw that the train had just stopped at a large station and that the woman in the black shawl was still there and was smiling on her.

Life Drawing

After darkness fell and he could no longer watch the landscape from the train window, Liam Diamond began reading his book. He had to take his feet off the seat opposite and make do with a less comfortable position to let a woman sit down. She was equine and fifty and he didn't give her a second glance. To take his mind off what was to come he tried to concentrate. The book was a study of the Viennese painter Egon Schiele who, it seemed, had become so involved with his thirteen-year-old girl models that he ended up in jail. Augustus John came to mind—'To paint someone you must first sleep with them'—and he smiled. Schiele's portraits, mostly of himself, exploded off the page beside the text, distracting him. All sinew and gristle and distortion. There was something decadent about them, like Soutine's pictures of hanging sides of beef.

Occasionally he would look up to see if he knew where he was but saw only the darkness and himself reflected from it. The street-lights of small towns showed more and more snow on the roads the further north he got. To stretch he went to the toilet and noticed the faces as he passed between the seats. Like animals being transported. On his way back he saw a completely different set of faces but he knew they looked the same. He hated train journeys, seeing so many people, so many houses. It made him realize he was part of things whether he liked it or not. Seeing so many unknown people through their back windows, standing outside shops, walking the streets, moronically waving from level crossings—they grew amorphous and repulsive. They were going about their static lives while he had a sense of being on the move. And yet he knew he was not. At some stage any one of those people might travel past his flat on a train and see him in the act of pulling his curtains. The thought depressed him so much that he could no longer read. He leaned his head against the window and, although he had his eyes closed, he did not sleep.

*　　*　　*

The snow, thawed to slush and quickly re-frozen, crackled under his feet and made walking difficult. For a moment he was not sure which was the house. In the dark he had to remember it by number and shade his eyes against the yellow glare of the sodium street-lights to make out the figures on the small terrace doors. He saw 56 and walked three houses further along. The heavy wrought-iron knocker echoed in the hallway as it had always done. He waited, looking up at the semicircular fan light. Snow was beginning to fall again, tiny flakes swirling in the corona of light. He was about to knock again or look to see if they had got a bell when he heard shuffling from the other side of the door. It opened a few inches and a white-haired old woman peered out. Her hair was held in place by a hair-net a shade different from her own hair colour. It was one of the Miss Harts but for the life of him he couldn't remember which. She looked at him, not understanding.

'Yes?'

I'm Liam,' he said.

'Oh thanks be to goodness for that. We're glad you could come.' Then she shouted over her shoulder, 'It's Liam.'

She shuffled backwards opening the door and admitting him. Inside she tremulously shook his hand, then took his bag and set it on the ground. Like a servant she took his coat and hung it on the hall-stand. It was still in the same place and the hallway was still a dark electric yellow.

'Bertha's up with him now. You'll forgive us sending the telegram to the College but we thought you would like to know,' said Miss Hart. If Bertha was up the stairs then she must be Maisie.

'Yes, yes, you did the right thing,' said Liam. 'How is he?'

'Poorly. The doctor has just left—he had another call. He says he'll not last the night.'

'That's too bad.'

By now they were standing in the kitchen. The fireplace was black and empty. One bar of the dished electric fire took the chill off the room and no more.

'You must be tired,' said Miss Hart. 'It's such a journey. Would you like a cup of tea? I tell you what, just you go up now and I'll bring you your tea when it's ready. All right?'

'Yes thank you.'

When he reached the head of the stairs she called after him, 'And send Bertha down.'

Bertha met him on the landing. She was small and withered and her head reached to his chest. When she saw him she started to cry and reached out her arms to him saying, 'Liam, poor Liam.' She nuzzled against him weeping. 'The poor old soul,' she kept repeating. Liam was embarrassed, feeling the thin arms of this old woman he hardly knew about his hips.

'Maisie says you have to go down now,' he said, separating himself from her and patting her crooked back. He watched her go down the stairs, one tottering step at a time, gripping the banister, her rheumatic knuckles standing out like limpets.

He paused at the bedroom door and for some reason flexed his hands before he went in. He was shocked to see the state his father was in. He was now almost completely bald except for some fluffy hair above his ears. His cheeks were sunken, his mouth hanging open. His head was back on the pillow so that the strings of his neck stood out.

'Hello, it's me, Liam,' he said when he was at the bed. The old man opened his eyes flickeringly. He tried to speak. Liam had to lean over but failed to decipher what was said. He reached out and lifted his father's hand in a kind of wrong handshake.

'Want anything?'

His father signalled by a slight movement of his thumb that he needed something. A drink? Liam poured some water and put the glass to the old man's lips. Arcs of scum had formed at the corners of his sagging mouth. Some of the water spilled on to the sheet. It remained for a while in droplets before sinking into dark circles.

'Was that what you wanted?' The old man nodded no. Liam looked around the room trying to see what his father could want. It was exactly as he had remembered it. In twenty years he hadn't changed the wallpaper, yellow roses looping on an umber trellis. He lifted a straight-backed chair and drew it up close to the bed. He sat with his elbows on his knees, leaning forward.

'How do you feel?'

The old man made no response and the question echoed around and around the silence in Liam's head.

Maisie brought in tea on a tray, closing the door behind her with her elbow. Liam noticed that two red spots had come up on her cheeks. She spoke quickly in an embarrassed whisper, looking back and forth between the dying man and his son.

'We couldn't find where he kept the teapot so it's just a tea-bag in a cup. Is that all right? Will that be enough for you to eat? We sent out for a tin of ham, just in case. He had nothing in the house at all, God love him.'

'You've done very well,' said Liam. 'You shouldn't have gone to all this trouble.'

'If you couldn't do it for a neighbour like Mr Diamond—well? Forty-two years and there was never a cross word between us. A gentleman we always called him, Bertha and I. He kept himself to himself. Do you think he can hear us?' The old man did not move.

'How long has he been like this?' asked Liam.

'Just three days. He didn't bring in his milk one day and that's not like him, y'know. He'd left a key with Mrs Rankin, in case he'd ever lock himself out again—he did once, the wind blew the door shut—and she came in and found him like this in the chair downstairs. He was frozen, God love him. The doctor said it was a stroke.'

Liam nodded, looking at his father. He stood up and began edging the woman towards the bedroom door.

'I don't know how to thank you, Miss Hart. You've been more than good.'

'We got your address from your brother. Mrs Rankin phoned America on Tuesday.'

'Is he coming home?'

'He said he'd try. She said the line was as clear as a bell. It was like talking to next door. Yes, he said he'd try but he doubted it very much.' She had her hand on the door knob. 'Is that enough sandwiches?'

'Yes thanks, that's fine.' They stood looking at one another awkwardly. Liam fumbled in his pocket. 'Can I pay you for the ham . . . and the telegram?'

'I wouldn't dream of it,' she said. 'Don't insult me now, Liam.'

He withdrew his hand from his pocket and smiled his thanks to her.

'It's late,' he said. 'Perhaps you should go now and I'll sit up with him.'

'Very good. The priest was here earlier and gave him . . .' she groped for the word with her hands.

'Extreme Unction?'

'Yes. That's twice he has been in three days. Very attentive. Sometimes I think if our ministers were half as good . . .'

'Yes but he wasn't what you would call gospel greedy.'

'He was lately,' she said.

'Changed times.'

She half turned to go and said, almost coyly, 'I'd hardly have known you with the beard.' She looked up at him, nodding her head in disbelief. He was trying to make her go, standing close to her but she skirted round him and went over to the bed. She touched the old man's shoulder.

'I'm away now, Mr Diamond. Liam is here. I'll see you in the morning,' she shouted into his ear. Then she was away.

Liam heard the old ladies' voices in the hallway below, then the slam of the front door. He heard the crackling of their feet over the frozen slush beneath the window. He lifted the tray off the chest of drawers and on to his knee. He hadn't realized it but he was hungry. He ate the sandwiches and the piece of fruit-cake, conscious of the chewing noise he was making with his mouth in the silence of the bedroom. There was little his father could do about it now. They used to have the most terrible rows about it. You'd have thought it was a matter of life and death. At table he had sometimes trembled with rage at the boys' eating habits, at their greed as he called it. At the noises they made 'like cows getting out of muck'. After their mother had left them he took over the responsibility for everything. One night as he served sausages from the pan Liam, not realizing the filthy mood he was in, made a grab. His father in a sudden downward thrust jabbed the fork he had been using to cook the sausages into the back of Liam's hand.

'Control yourself.'

Four bright beads of blood appeared as Liam stared at them in disbelief.

'They'll remind you to use your fork in future.'

He was sixteen at the time.

The bedroom was cold and when he finally got round to drinking his tea it was tepid. He was annoyed that he couldn't heat it by pouring more. His feet were numb and felt damp. He went downstairs and put on his overcoat and brought the electric fire up to the bedroom, switching on both bars. He sat huddled over it, his fingers fanned out, trying to get warm. When the second bar was switched on there was a clicking noise and the smell of burning dust. He looked over at the bed but there was no movement.

'How do you feel?' he said again, not expecting an answer. For a long time he sat staring at the old man whose breathing was audible but quiet—a kind of soft whistling in his nose. The alarm clock, its face bisected with a crack, said twelve thirty. Liam checked it against the red figures of his digital watch. He stood up and went to the window. Outside the roofs tilted at white snow-covered angles. A faulty gutter hung spikes of icicles. There was no sound in the street but from the main road came the distant hum of a late car that faded into silence.

He went out on to the landing and into what was his own bedroom. There was no bulb when he switched the light on so he took one from the hall and screwed it into the shadeless socket. The bed was there in the corner with its mattress of blue stripes. The lino was the same with its square pock-marks showing other places the bed had been. The cheap green curtains that never quite met on their cord still did not meet.

He moved to the wall cupboard by the small fireplace and had to tug at the handle to get it open. Inside the surface of everything had gone opaque with dust. Two old radios, one with a fretwork face, the other more modern with a tuning dial showing such places as Hilversum, Luxembourg, Athlone; a Dansette record player with its lid missing and its arm bent back showing wires like severed nerves and blood vessels; the empty frame of the smashed glass picture was still there; several umbrellas, all broken. And there was his box of poster paints. He lifted it out and blew off the dust.

It was a large Quality Street tin; he eased the lid off, bracing it against his stomach muscles. The colours in the jars had shrunk to hard discs. Viridian Green, Vermillion, Jonquil Yellow. At the bottom of the box he found several sticks of charcoal, light in his fingers when he lifted them, warped. He dropped them into his pocket and put the tin back into the cupboard. There was a pile of magazines and papers and beneath that again he saw his large Windsor and Newton sketch-book. He eased it out and began to look through the work in it. Embarrassment was what he felt most turning the pages, looking at the work of this schoolboy. He could see little talent in it, yet he realized he must have been good. There were several drawings of hands in red pastel which had promise.

The rest of the pages were blank. He set the sketch-book aside to take with him and closed the door.

Looking round the room it had the appearance of nakedness. He crouched and looked under the bed but there was nothing there. His fingers coming in contact with the freezing lino made him aware how cold he was. His jaw was tight and he knew that if he relaxed it he would shiver. He went back to his father's bedroom and sat down.

The old man had not changed his position. He had wanted him to be a lawyer or a doctor but Liam had insisted, although he had won a scholarship to the university, on going to art college. All that summer his father tried everything he knew to stop him. He tried to reason with him:

'*Be* something. And you can carry on doing your art. Art is OK as a sideline.'

But mostly he shouted at him, 'I've heard about these art students and what they get up to. Shameless bitches prancing about with nothing on. And what sort of a job are you going to get? Drawing on pavements?' He nagged him every moment they were together about other things. Lying late in bed, the length of his hair, his outrageous appearance. Why hadn't he been like the other lads and got himself a job for the summer? It wasn't too late because he would willingly pay him if he came in and helped out in the shop.

One night, just as he was going to bed, Liam found the old framed print of cattle drinking. He had taken out the glass and had begun to paint on the glass itself with small tins of Humbrol enamel paints left over from aeroplane kits he had never finished. They produced a strange and exciting texture which was even better when the paint was viewed from the other side of the pane of glass. He sat stripped to the waist in his pyjama trousers painting a self-portrait reflected from the mirror on the wardrobe door. The creamy opaque nature of the paint excited him. It slid on to the glass, it built up, in places it ran scalloping like cinema curtains and yet he could control it. He lost all track of time as he sat with his eyes focused on the face staring back at him and the painting he was trying to make of it. It became a face he had not known, the holes, the lines, the spots. He was in a new geography.

His brother and he used to play a game looking at each other's faces upside down. One lay on his back across the bed, his head flopped over the edge reddening as the blood flooded into it. The other sat in a chair and stared at him. After a time the horror of seeing the eyes where the mouth should be, the inverted nose, the forehead gashed with red lips, would drive him to cover his eyes with his hands. 'It's your turn now,' he would say and they would change places. It was like familiar words said over and over again until they became meaningless and once he ceased to have purchase on the meaning of a word it became terrifying, an incantation. In adolescence he had come to hate his brother, could not stand the physical presence of him just as when he was lying upside down on the bed. It was the same with his father. He could not bear to touch him and yet for one whole winter when he had a bad shoulder he had to stay up late to rub him with oil of wintergreen. The old boy would sit with one hip on the bed and Liam would stand behind him massaging the stinking stuff into the white flesh of his back. The smell, the way the blubbery skin moved under his fingers, made him want to be sick. No matter how many times he washed his hands, at school the next day he would still reek of oil of wintergreen.

It might have been the smell of the Humbrol paints or the strip of light under Liam's door—whatever it was his father came in and yelled that it was half past three in the morning and what the hell did he think he was doing sitting half-naked drawing at this hour of the morning. He had smacked him full force with the flat of his hand on his bare back and, stung by the pain of it, Liam had leapt to retaliate. Then his father had started to laugh, a cold snickering laugh. 'Would you? Would you? Would you indeed?' he kept repeating with a smile pulled on his mouth and his fists bunched to knuckles in front of him. Liam retreated to the bed and his father turned on his heel and left. Thinking the incident was over Liam gritted his teeth and fists and cursed his father. He looked over his shoulder into the mirror and saw the primitive daub of his father's hand, splayed fingers outlined across his back. He heard him on the stairs and when he came back into the bedroom with the poker in his hand he felt his insides turn to water. But his father looked away from him with a sneer and smashed the painting to shards with one stroke. As he went out the door he said,

'Watch your feet in the morning.'

He had never really 'left home'. It was more a matter of going to art college in London and not bothering to come back. Almost as soon as he was away from the house his hatred for his father eased. He simply stopped thinking about him. Of late he had wondered if he was alive or dead—if he still had the shop. The only communication they had had over the years was when Liam sent him, not without a touch of vindictiveness, an invitation to some of the openings of his exhibitions.

Liam sat with his fingertips joined, staring at the old man. It was going to be a long night. He looked at his watch and it was only after two. He paced up and down the room listening to the tick of snow on the window pane. When he stopped to look down he saw it flurrying through the haloes of the street-lamps. He went into his own bedroom and brought back the sketch-book. He moved his chair to the other side of the bed so that the light fell on his page. Balancing the book on his knee he began to draw his father's head with the stick of charcoal. It made a light hiss each time a line appeared on the cartridge paper. When drawing he always thought of himself as a wary animal drinking, the way he looked up and down, up and down, at his subject. The old man had failed badly. His head scarcely dented the pillows, his cheeks were hollow and he had not been shaved for some days. Earlier when he had held his hand it had been clean and dry and light like the hand of a girl. The bedside light deepened the shadows of his face and highlighted the rivulets of veins on his temple. It was a long time since he had used charcoal and he became engrossed in the way it had to be handled and the different subtleties of line he could get out of it. He loved to watch a drawing develop before his eyes.

His work had been well received and among the small Dublin art world he was much admired—justly he thought. But some critics had scorned his work as 'cold' and 'formalist'—one had written 'Like Mondrian except that he can't draw a straight line'—and this annoyed him because it was precisely what he was trying to do. He felt it unfair to be criticized for succeeding in his aims.

His father began to cough—a low, wet, bubbling sound. Liam leaned forward and touched the back of his hand gently. Was this man to blame in any way? Or had he only himself to blame for the shambles of his life? He had married once and lived with two other women. At present he was on his own. Each relationship had ended in hate and bitterness, not because of drink or lack of money or any of the usual reasons but because of a mutual nauseating dislike.

He turned the page and began to draw the old man again. The

variations in tone from jet black to pale grey depending on the pressure he used fascinated him. The hooded lids of the old man's eyes, the fuzz of hair sprouting from the ear next the light, the darkness of the partially open mouth. Liam drew several more drawings, absorbed, working slowly, refining the line of each until it was to his satisfaction. He was pleased with what he had done. At art school he had loved the life class better than any other. It never ceased to amaze him how sometimes it could come just right, better than he had hoped for; the feeling that something was working through him to produce a better work than at first envisaged.

Then outside he heard the sound of an engine followed by the clinking of milk bottles. When he looked at his watch he was amazed to see that it was five thirty. He leaned over to speak to his father.

'Are you all right?'

His breathing was not audible and when Liam touched his arm it was cold. His face was cold as well. He felt for his heart, slipping his hand inside his pyjama jacket, but could feel nothing. He was dead. His father. He was dead, and the slackness of his dropped jaw disturbed his son. In the light of the lamp his dead face looked like the open-mouthed moon. Liam wondered if he should tie it up before it set. In a Pasolini film he had seen Herod's jaw being trussed and he wondered if he was capable of doing it for his father.

Then he saw himself in his hesitation, saw the lack of any emotion in his approach to the problem. He was aware of the deadness inside himself and felt helpless to do anything about it. It was why all his women had left him. One of them accused him of making love the way other people rodded drains.

He knelt down beside the bed and tried to think of something good from the time he had spent with his father. Anger and sneers and nagging was all that he could picture. He knew he was grateful for his rearing but he could not *feel* it. If his father had not been there somebody else would have done it. And yet it could not have been easy—a man left with two boys and a business to run. He had worked himself to a sinew in his tobacconist's, opening at seven in the morning to catch the workers and closing at ten at night. Was it for his boys that he worked so hard? The man was in the habit of earning and yet he never spent. He had even opened for three hours on Christmas Day.

Liam stared at the dead drained face and suddenly the mouth

held in that shape reminded him of something pleasant. It was the only joke his father had ever told and to make up for the smallness of his repertoire he had told it many times, of two ships passing in mid-Atlantic. He always megaphoned his hands to tell the story.

'Where are you bound for?' shouts one captain.

'Rio—de—Janeir—o. Where are you bound for?'

And the other captain not to be outdone yells back, 'Cork—a—lork—a—lor—io.'

When he had finished the joke he always repeated the punch-line, laughing and nodding in disbelief that something could be so funny.

'Cork—a—lork—a—lorio.'

Liam found that his eyes had filled with tears. He tried to keep them coming but they would not. In the end he had to close his eyes and a tear spilled from his left eye on to his cheek. It was small and he wiped it away with a crooked index finger.

He stood up from the kneeling position and closed the sketch-book that was lying open on the bed. He might work on them later. Perhaps a charcoal series. He walked to the window. Dawn would not be up for hours yet. In America it would be daylight and his brother would be in shirt-sleeves. He would have to wait until Mrs Rankin was up before he could phone him—and the doctor would be needed for a death certificate. There was nothing he could do at the moment, except perhaps tie up the jaw. The Miss Harts when they arrived would know everything that ought to be done.

The Airedale

The door of their house and the side gate to the archway leading to their yard, their proliferation of sheds and subsequently to their garden were painted fresh bright green. Green was the colour of the door and the side gate of the last house on the street, the house just before the convent. The nuns were always eager to get hold of the house and they did eventually. If you pay a visit to the town now it is merely an eventual part of the convent premises.

The stone of the house was dark grey and if you peeped through the bony windows you'd see shining wooden floors and above them paintings of the maroon and purple mountains of the West. We lived in the Western Midlands. East Galway. Mrs Bannerton was from Poland. She had blonde sleeked hair. She had taken a bus from the war and arrived in Ireland. In Dublin she'd married a surgeon. They lived now in our town. Denny was the son. Their one child. He was my friend. I came from a family of five brothers. There were certain obscenities within my family. I can now see that friendship was one of them. Denny should have been from a suitable class background for closeness with me but my mother detected something she did not approve of there. Looking out the window at Denny trailing along on the other side of the street, beside rugged curtains she spat 'You're not to play with him. He's wild.'

Denny was wild; he had wild chestnut hair, wild confluences of freckles, wild and expansive short trousers. He kept a milling household of pets, lily white, quivering-nosed rabbits, garden trekking tortoises, cats of many colours, at one stage a dying jackdaw, but monarch among the pets was Sir Lesley the airedale. Denny tended his menagerie carefully, kneeling to comb the fur of cats and rabbits with a horn comb he assured me had been part of his grandmother's heirloom in Lublin. Later discovering that Lublin had been the site of a concentration camp struck home memories of a childhood where imaginary storks cascaded over a town which often looked, in its loop of the river, as if it had been constructed as a concentration camp. Denny in white sleeveless jersey and white trousers combed a cat's fur and muttered a prayer he insisted was Polish. It was in fact gibberish. Denny did not know a word of Polish because his mother refused even to speak a consonant of it. Some languages are best forgotten. The town had its language. My family had its language. But the Bannertons spoke a different language and I owe them something; I owe them what I am now, for better or for worse, because without them, without their house, I would have been subject to a lineage which perforated madness and violence. Denny's gibberish addressed to one of his cats is a language I still hear. We move from one country to another; we move from one language to another. But certain remembrances bind us with sanity. Denny's addresses to his cats is one of them for me. Another is the red in Denny's hair. Denny's red. My own hair was dull brown and I always vied for red hair so when I first came to live in this city I had a craze and dumped a bottle of henna into my crewcut, stared into my eyes in a mirror then and saw myself as an inmate in a concentration camp.

Denny and I sat together at school and we heard the words of William Allingham together, 'Adieu to Ballyshannon! where I was bred and born; Go where I may, I'll think of you, as sure as night and morn.' That we were elevated at an early age by the romance of words was also a saving grace of this town. The speaker of these words, a grey-haired headmaster with a worn and lathery black leather strap, is now lying in his grave. After doing his purgatory for the mutilation of poor boys'—boys from the 'Terrace', the slum area of town—hands he will surely be transported to Heaven on a stanza of Thomas Moore. That was the duality we lived with. But Denny's home in the afternoons dominated at school. Toys on the wooden floor were trains winding through central Europe. Snow toppling on the trains litter from Denny's hands. We saw a midget woman alight from a carriage on the floor, look around her and wander through the bustling streets of an anonymous central European city.

Mr Bannerton had a large penis. From Denny I first heard mention of the word penis. He kept me in touch with his father's and mother's attributes. I presumed Mr Bannerton's large penis was to do with his medical profession.

Denny taught me history; the entire history of the world; he knew this from books; Denny read Dickens and Louisa M. Alcott. These authors owed their life in the town to Denny. He frequented their worlds. He borrowed their books from the library. Denny was a parent. At eleven he had a wide and middle-aged freckled face.

Everything was lovely about Denny, his father, his mother, his hair, his clothes, everything except his face. He had an ugly face. When I met him in later life he had kept that face like a chalking up area for pain.

In Denny's home I first heard Mozart; I first spoke to a jackdaw; I first was kissed by a blonde woman; I first acquainted myself with the names of herbs. In Denny's home I first hated my mother and my father. I despised my brothers. There were no cats or dogs in our home. No airedales. I swapped passports in their home and took out citizenship of a country situated between bare wooden walls.

I was ten when Denny left. God threw snow out of a spiteful heaven. He was borne away in the furniture van. On the main street I cried. They were going to a city in the very South. I was wearing a short blue coat. Tears stung in my eyes and if I stay awake long enough at night I can still feel them.

All their property had gone, everything, except the airedale. He'd been too big to carry away and whether they donated him to a neighbour or not he strode majestically around for weeks. In the mornings on my way to school I nodded to him though he did not acknowledge me. Then one day I passed his carcass beside a dustbin. They left his carcass there for weeks, below the dustbin, until fleas got into it. I supposed it was to demonstrate to everyone the folly of being lofty and having once been the pet of a gifted family. The Bannertons went on to be part of a big city. There was an opera house in this city and a river which divided into two. There were many hills in this city and many churches. Now that I had been left my brothers turned upon me, beat me up, locked me into rooms on grey afternoons. It was a grey February afternoon for a long time now. One grey February afternoon I left to be a priest in Maynooth.

What happened in the meantime had been a kind of breakdown. My parents, fearful of consequences, confiscated stamp albums, books. Stamps were slightly suspicious, books were dangerous for me. They knew no better, my parents. They were peasant people, their parents having graduated to businesses in towns. The only book my mother had ever read was the penny catechism and my father, a more jovial sort, had his joviality truncated by my mother. My brothers were all going to be accountants. At fifteen I borrowed my father's razor blade and slashed my wrists. Blood ran from the wound of a white hamster. They did not bring me to the main hospital but to the mental hospital. On the way there like Denny I began muttering gibberish. Gibberish saved my life.

Maynooth was rusted pipes alongside the grey walls of premises which were alleged to be haunted by catonic ghosts; Maynooth was young clerics in black soutanes, hands digging deep into their soutanes, staring collectively at gutters; Maynooth was razor blades the colour of congealed blood, deftly taken from private lockers. There were sonorous prayers and professors of medieval philosophy who went around spraying snippets of Simon and Garfunkel. But eventually a prayer became too nasal for me; a part of my brain leapt into self awareness again; before being ordained, a hitherto placid clerical student boarded a plane from Dublin to London, first having attended a film in his favourite cinema on Eden Quay. The city I arrived in was experiencing its first buffeting of punk hairdos; skies were bleached, dustbins overladen. Hands were generally shrouded in pockets. From a room in Plumstead I looked for work, got a job on a building site and a year later started attending a film school. Boats pushed past on the Thames outside my door. Plumstead marshes nearby conjured skeletal boats on the Thames. There was a ghost running through me as I sat, meditating, in my room in Plumstead. I could make little communication with fellow students. Something in me was impotent and my favourite occupation was sitting on a stool, meditating on my multiple impotences and creating a route out of them. One day I knew I'd walk out of inability. Charitable notes drifted through from Maynooth. There were short films made. There were eventually relationships made. Sex stirred like a ship on the Thames, a rusty and an outworn frigate. But I touched one or two people. I made gestures to one or two people. I was released from the school with accolades. I made my first film outside school. A short film. On that ticket I returned to Ireland.

'Adieu to Ballyshannon! where I was bred and born; Go where I may, I'll think of you, as sure as night and morn.'

A plane veered across lamb-like clouds. Below me was a Southern Irish city. My film was being shown in the annual film festival. I was sitting next to the window. I'd never been to this country before. I was an outsider now. I'd prepared myself and preened myself for that role. But a wind on the airport tarmac ruffled my demeanour and cowed me back again to Good Fridays and Pentecost Sundays on a grey small-town Irish street.

Cocktails were barraged towards the glitter of the light. Young women in scanty dresses and with silken bodies flashed venomous eyes at me. I was invited to bed chambers that always seem by implication to be above the bars of cinemas. I declined these invitations. The night my film was shown, afterwards, I met Denny Bannerton. Doctor Denny Bannerton. We said hello, made polite comments to one another, and arranged to meet the next night. There was no award for my film. Silence. Unmuttered blame. It had been a trip to Ireland though and I was glad of it. In a gents' toilet full of mirrors I congratulated myself on my black, polka-dotted tie, a narrow stripe of a tie purchased on Portobello Road and subsequently endearingly laundered and ironed. It was as if someone was affectionately pulling my tie in the direction of London. But first I had an appointment. A camera went off and took a photograph of me, dark glasses on and a smile winter days living by London cemeteries had given me.

A blank, broad freckled face with black glasses. A grey suit—a collar and tie. Unusual accoutrement for a film reception. Denny's face was still the same in a way. We met in a pub the night after. The night was young, Denny explained when we met; there were many bars in this city to travel through. I sat on a high stool and gazed into a purple spotlight falling on a many ringed male finger. We had ventured into the gay scene of this city. We were about to step further.

Swans, very clean swans; little neon emblazoned retreats; hills; wave-line lanes. A spiralling journey. Conversation. I was the film maker. Denny Bannerton was an auspicious and regular part of the newspapers and behaved as such. I was treated to propaganda. I listened to the water, the breeze and the swans. The tricolour flew for some reason over a Roman pillared church. As Denny's conversation battled with the breeze, as young men in white shirts behind counters, glasses being cleaned in their hands, enthusiastically saluted him among purple light, I made a mental film of his life.

The most important discovery in Denny Bannerton's life had been that of his homosexuality. He discovered at thirteen with a white rabbit. In the back garden of a red suburban house. The tenderness of his impediment connected him with inmates in a concentration camp near Lublin. He was still in short trousers at the time. Broad, blank faced, at fifteen he had an actual beauty. He had a brief affair with a corporeal monk who was directing a Gilbert and Sullivan operetta. Afterwards, having been rejected by the monk, Denny's face resigned itself to ugliness. At university he took girls out. But such relationships quickly collapsed. A young doctor he toured the world. Had posts in Iran, in Venezuela, in Bristol. He returned to Ireland. Returning to his city in the South he announced his homosexuality. Affairs with Moslem, short-socked boys in oil deserts. An affair with a piano-playing prodigy in Caracas. Nights of promiscuity in Bristol. Back home he politicized his loneliness. A doctor he travelled the city with an expansive rose on his lapel. He was in the newspapers. He wrote irate letters to editors. He was a mirage on television discussion programmes. He'd peculiarly found his way home.

The questions asked of me were for the most part very factual; I knew what he was driving at. What were my sexual proclivities. I refused to answer. I just allowed myself to be led and occasionally I indulged in reminiscence. But it seemed reminiscence brought me back further than a garden. It brought me to a concentration camp in the suburbs of a Polish city.

Some of the nights in the desert had been like a concentration camp for Denny; the hot air, the arid flesh. Petrol had burned like pillars of flame. They had returned him to a geography before birth. Shirts were purple and pink in the dimly lit bars we slipped through. I was introduced to many people. A blond, furry-haired boy revolved his hand in mine in the pretence of shaking it. There had been the question of where Mrs Bannerton had really been from but now I knew. She'd been a mutual mother. Denny yapped on in a flaxen brogue, regardless of the images in my mind, furnaces lighting the night on the perimeter of a concentration camp in Poland.

Whether in reality or in dream she had traversed that camp. The skeletons had piled up in the dark. She'd heard the screams from those freshly dying. But in the middle of the skeletons and the screams she'd had an intuition of a limestone street, of an oak tree over a simple and pastoral pea garden, of an airedale.

'So you're the film maker. Heard your film was lousy. What are you doing beyond there in England? Pandering to Britannia. You should be home and drawing the turf of our native art.' An academic's lips seared with effeminacy. A gold chain sheathed the brushing of black hairs on display in the v of his pastel shirt, the chain sinking into a tan picked up in Mexico. 'You're one of the quislings who won't admit they're queer.' He was asking me to concede my ratio of queerness. I said nothing, looked to the photograph of a scarlet-sailed yacht in Kinsale. Denny muttered something about camera work. The one word reserved for special treatment by the academic was Britannia; I saw a spring shower dripping off a stone, slouching lion.

Back in the night Denny ran down the list of his endeavours to bring gay liberation to Ireland; planting flags on the top of low, buttercup-covered mountains, leading straddling tiny marches through the city, chaining himself to the pillars of the town hall. He'd been wearing a brown tee shirt the day he'd chained himself to the town hall. Not a grey suit as now. A breeze from the sea suddenly slapped me with a drop or two of rain on the face.

The edges of her hair had burnt against the lights of the concentration camp; again and again she strode across my vision. She wanted to exorcise it. She'd come a long way. Suddenly she'd been in Ireland and she'd lain down.

'My ma discovered I was gay. She was informed by a neighbour I was gay. She wasn't sure what that meant but contacted the mother of a boy who was known to be gay. That woman declared "Mrs Finuacane don't fret. There were always gay men and gay women in Blarney but they didn't have the word for it then." '

I was speaking to a youth in one of the bars, interviewing him really. His hand was on a pint of Guinness. These rests in pubs interspersed with Denny's intense and self-engrossed mouthings.

In the same pub as I spoke to the boy in I enquired from Denny about his mother. She had stepped from a red brick suburban house into a big red brick hilltop mental hospital. Denny's mother had begun to eat her own fur coats. She was totally mad, Denny said. Totally mad.

In the airedale I had seen it all; a crossroads. Denny had gone his way. I had gone mine. But some creatures lie down and die. Living becomes too much for them. Memory becomes too much for them. What she remembered I did not know. Could only guess. But she and her household of deranged hamsters had given me a residence in my mind. A new home. I had gone from their house, their world, with a life I would not otherwise have had; Denny had departed to his world. There'd been a juncture. An airedale had marked the crossing. But a woman had held its thrall.

What had really caused an eddy in my gait had been the way Denny had referred to his mother. It was as if there was plain reason to be dismissory about her. She had sunk for him. Legend and myth had walked out of his life but I had cherished it. She had grown for me. She had marched across nights for me. In fact the first film I made at film school I had thought of her. The blonde, ice-maiden-faced Polish lady. The lights had centred on her. When Denny had made his farewells I headed on into the night. There was a lot of way to go.

'See you now. Good luck with the films. I might see you tomorrow.' The phrases rang in my ears. I shovelled my hands into my jacket. Denny was an arabesque of remarks. But I had sauntered away from the airedale of long time ago in this predestined black jacket. There were already films in my face and Denny had already changed in slinking away. There were worlds and corrosive thoughts to stride through tonight.

'Goodnight. See you.' There'd been a room in her mind. A chamber of torture. It had not necessarily been a concentration camp, the proximity to a concentration camp, but the experience and anguish of war. The worst anguish of surviving it. Storks and domed palaces had perished in this war. But she had survived.

The scintillating blonde-haired lady in the garden imperiously called to her husband. 'Bring me some lemonade.' A white rabbit stuck its ears up at her. I watched from behind an oak tree, my right hand clinging to the hoary bark.

The lights focused in on a girl's face. She had the features of Mrs Bannerton. Why do I remember this face? What had this face to say for me?

The city at night wound on. I unravelled the streets. There had been a point on which I had coincided with this lady. You go past pain. You come to meaning. I jotted little sentences in my mind. The city by the river, its slim outlying houses, was Italianate.

The first time I made love to a woman I thought of her. Her buttocks had asserted themselves through summer dresses, the disdaining quiver at the side of her buttocks. That quiver had said a lot. 'I'm not happy here. I'm not happy here.'

In the first few years after they went I used jumble words on blue squared paper at school; 'loss' 'severity'. Gulls had looked in on me, perching by an inedible crumb. I wanted to write to them, to all of them, but letters seemed inadequate to contain my feelings and anyway envelopes too frail to contain such corrosive letters as they might be. So I allowed myself to suffer. The airedale had died. John F. Kennedy had died. My mother bought me a white sleeveless jersey one Christmas. At that point the Bannertons' house had been turned into classrooms by the nuns.

I'd wanted to write to her as well as to Denny. A letter to her had composed itself over my adolescence. There was a place of pain we shared with one another. Not having any brothers I got on with I invented brothers in others, in boys who filtered through school— off to England after a short spate of studying at the priest-run boys' secondary school. There was chestnut hair, there were certain chest muscles behind white jerseys I envied in other boys. Boys from the 'Terrace'. Dionne Warwick sang me into a night of suicide. I woke up in Poland.

'Dear Mrs Bannerton . . .' Always there was a beginning of a letter to her. But after my exercise in suicide attempts whatever they did to me in the mental hospital part of my brain slumbered. They had cajoled me into their universe. Maynooth College, its black bricks, was a logical upshoot from that universe.

On a night vaguely ingrained with rain in a hilly city in the very south of Ireland I finally scrambled off that letter to Mrs Bannerton. She was in a mental hospital in the vicinity, a house I thought I detected, shining with a light or two on a hill.

The times I was on the verge of doing something truly disastrous—being ordained a priest—when there was the immediate imminence of some irreparable lunacy she stopped me. She took strides with me when I was in my black soutane. It was that room that carried me from Ireland to England. The room where her blonde hair had looked red. Where toy trains spun around. Where trains stopped in towns you crept out into and had cold eggs showered in paprika in small cafes, the autumn sunshine shining through white wine and a leaf sweeper singing like a minstrel outside.

As a child I'd run up that street and peer in. There had been many ways of approaching a sight of the inside of that home. In the grey convent yard, a proudly decked member of the convent band, in claret dickie bow (which alternated occasionally with a miniature scarlet tie), in white shirt, white long trousers, clashing a triangle, tripping in my clashing of it, one blue eye on the Bannertons' garden. What were Mrs Bannerton's limbs up to? Through the oblong window that stretched itself with narrowness on the street level you saw the brown wooden room and the journeys that the trains encompassed. Your mind gyrated with Europe's railways. Sometimes she stood in the middle of that room returning over these journeys, trembling in a leafy tight summer dress in the room. There was a person or a budgie she spoke to often. If it was a budgie it was to be seen, a cheeky lemon and lime thing. If a human being he was invisible. There were also ways you spied into that house in your dreams, through the chimney, on that roof that sent slates flying down in March. One night I travelled in the sky over their house on a broomstick and in my magician's capacity observed her dreams, trains snuggling into stations packed with marigolds and girls. But even being inside the house was always just an attempt. There were barriers. I was not one of them. The airedale disdained me with one eye.

'How are you?'

A middle-aged man in a Charlie Chaplin-type bowler hat cascaded into me in the night. 'You're the young man who makes the films.' As a celebrity in my own right I sat beside him on a high stool in a late night cafe on a hill, Elvis Presley in maroon and pink on the wall, looking as if he'd been blasted on to it, as we discussed my films and my intentions with new films. As a cappuccino lever was pulled down—the cafe was Italian—a voice in my head in a County Galway accent said 'Now you are their world.'

A woman in a room crossed her own barrier to be again in the boulevards and the parks of childhood. The edges of her hair had been red in remembrance. They had stood out, flames. Mrs Bannerton had had red hair as a child. She'd coveted a wooden sleigh with emerald tattoos on it. I too had a barrier to cross to remember. In the night my relatives webbed in me, no longer the demons I'd always presented to myself, but innocent. My mother, her frail sisters beside her, on station platforms in June during their youths. Many of my mother's sisters had died. Of purple lilac. Of tuberculosis. Purple lilac had flagged on russet, peeling railway bridges. Further back there was a room in history. A concentration camp. A war. A famine. There had been an operation theatre where innocence and joy had been removed. I had to make my way through ancestral minds to the joy in myself. The task in a black jacket seemed easy.

'Dear Mrs Bannerton . . .'

It was not to her I ended up giving most of my thoughts but to the young man I'd spent the evening with, her son. Whether we knew it or not those times we enacted pageants in the thick shrubbery outside the men's club—a black canvas-covered hut—we were seeking to return to a corner of history; Ireland before subjugation. In white bed sheets we had been the kings of an undefiled Munster and undefiled hobgoblin world. The garden had pointed the way to an innocence. The oak had shaded the wounds of history; the memory of war. It had covered a part of a human being quaking because the sores distributed on her body were not apparent.

'There was a bus; there was a journey. I'm not sure any more what I left behind. I just remember a little boy in white trousers holding the white handbag of a woman. He was holding it up for the world to see. As if to ask why he was holding it. Why wasn't it with its owner who was probably dead or mutilated.'

The film scripts were beginning again. I could not stop them. A woman's voice reached me from the twinkle of a mental hospital light.

In a church at dawn under a cinder-blackened Christ I prayed for her and for her son who had disappeared into his grey jacket, into his spectacles and into the manifold expostulations of his cause. I tried to restate a part of myself I'd tried to forget. Pain too, the crossed mangled legs were necessary. They were a connecting point with the dots of our ancestors on the atlas. The world inside me now was created from childhood; from a gruesome logic of art. An attempt at art. But attempts at art could only lead back. To a room. In an ornately lettered mirror in a bar the edges of my hair were ghostly henna.

'We try to build; we try to grow. But we always build backwards. May God help me both to forget and to remember.' There were swans on the river. Graffiti flung itself against a urinal. There were turkey feet of aeroplane tracks through the clear sky. A path led out of here now. I had a ticket to depart. To leave a place where Mrs Bannerton was incarcerated, where Denny Bannerton fought among the profusion of media attention, where a garden had been cemented over and an oak tree slashed down. The blood from the oak tree landed on the pavement of this city. I wanted to say over again, 'Thanks. Thanks for giving me birth.' But a chill had entered the air. It fingered the exposed headlines of newspapers. This was no country. It was no place. It no longer existed for me. All I was aware of were the aeroplane tracks in the sky. But there was a country in me now. There was a demesne. Sometime in the middle of the night I had gone back and picked up a child who'd been waiting on a street in Poland for a long time. There was a country where my child could be born or failing that where I could give birth to the latent little boy in myself. The terms of reference had changed; the language had changed. The chill in the air here no longer tortured me. The fate of the airedale no longer bothered me. Soon Mrs Bannerton and Denny Bannerton would be forgotten. But walking back to the hotel I heard what I had not permitted myself to hear for many years.

The sound of Polish.

ACKNOWLEDGEMENTS

The editor and publishers are grateful for permission to include the following copyright stories in this anthology:

Elizabeth Bowen: 'Her Table Spread', copyright 1941 and renewed 1969 by Elizabeth Bowen, reprinted from *The Collected Short Stories of Elizabeth Bowen* by permission of Jonathan Cape Ltd. on behalf of the Estate of Elizabeth Bowen, and Alfred A. Knopf, Inc.

Patrick Boyle: 'Pastorale' reprinted from *Winter's Tales from Ireland 2* (1972), ed. by Kevin Casey, by permission of Gill and Macmillan, Dublin, and Proscenium Press.

Joyce Cary: 'Bush River' reprinted from *Spring Song and Other Stories* (Michael Joseph, 1960), copyright © 1960 by Joyce Cary, by permission of John Farquharson Ltd., and Curtis Brown Ltd.

Daniel Corkery: 'The Priest' from *The Stormy Hills* (Dublin: Talbot/ London: Jonathan Cape, 1929). Used with permission.

The Cow that ate the Piper reprinted from *Folktales of Ireland*, ed. & trans. by Sean O'Sullivan, copyright 1966, by permission of the University of Chicago Press.

Cromwell and the Friar reprinted from *Folktales of Ireland*, ed. & trans. Sean O'Sullivan, copyright 1966, by permission of the University of Chicago Press.

Terence de Vere White: 'Desert Island' reprinted from *Big Fleas and Little Fleas*, © Terence de Vere White 1977, by permission of Richard Scott Simon Ltd.

Fionn in Search of his Youth reprinted from *Folktales of Ireland*, ed. & trans. Sean O'Sullivan, copyright 1966, by permission of the University of Chicago Press.

The Four-leafed Shamrock and the Cock reprinted from *Folktales of Ireland*, ed. & trans. Sean O'Sullivan, copyright 1966, by permission of the University of Chicago Press.

Brian Friel: 'The Diviner' reprinted from *The Gold in the Sea* (Gollancz, 1966). First appeared in *The New Yorker*. Reprinted by permission of Curtis Brown Ltd.

The Girl and the Sailor reprinted from *Folktales of Ireland*, ed. & trans. by Sean O'Sullivan, copyright 1966, by permission of the University of Chicago Press.

Desmond Hogan: 'The Airedale' reprinted from *A Link with the River*, copyright © 1989, by permission of Farrar, Straus & Giroux, Inc.

566 Acknowledgements

The Hour of Death reprinted from *Folktales of Ireland*, ed. & trans. by Sean O'Sullivan (1966), by permission of the University of Chicago Press.

James Joyce: 'The Dead' reprinted from *Dubliners*. Copyright 1916 by B. W. Huebsch. Definitive text copyright © 1967 by the Estate of James Joyce. All rights reserved. By permission of Jonathan Cape Ltd., the Society of Authors on behalf of the Executors of the James Joyce Estate, and Viking Penguin, Inc.

Benedict Kiely: 'The Pilgrims' reprinted from *A Journey to the Seven Streams*, copyright © 1963, by Benedict Kiely, by permission of A. P. Watt Ltd., and Curtis Brown Ltd., New York.

Mary Lavin: 'Sarah' reprinted from *Tales of Bective Bridge* (1943) by permission of Constable Publishers and the author.

John McGahern: 'The Beginning of an Idea' reprinted from *Getting Through* (1978) by permission of Faber & Faber Ltd.

Bernard Mac Laverty: 'Life Drawing' reprinted from *A Time to Dance* (1982) by permission of Jonathan Cape Ltd. on behalf of the author.

Michael McLaverty: 'The Poteen Maker' reprinted from *Collected Short Stories* (1978) by permission of Poolbeg Press Ltd.

Bryan MacMahon: 'The Ring' reprinted from *The End of the World & Other Stories* (1976), copyright 1976, by Bryan MacMahon, by permission of A. P. Watt Ltd.

John Montague: 'An Occasion of Sin' reprinted from *Death of a Chieftain and Other Stories* (MacGibbon & Kee Ltd., 1964/Poolbeg, 1978), by permission of the author.

Val Mulkerns: 'Loser' reprinted from *Antiquities* by permission of André Deutsch.

Edna O'Brien: 'Irish Revel' reprinted from *The Love Object* copyright 1968 by Edna O'Brien, by permission of A. M. Heath on behalf of the author, and Farrar, Straus & Giroux, Inc.

Mairtin O Cadhain: 'The Hare-Lip' reprinted from *The Road to Brightcity* (1981), trans. by Eoghan O Tuairisc, by permission of Poolbeg Press Ltd.

Padraic O Conaire: 'My Little Black Ass' reprinted from *The Woman at the Window*, trans. by Eoghan O Tuairisc (Poolbeg Press, 1966).

Frank O'Connor: 'The Majesty of the Law' and 'Guests of the Nation' reprinted from *The Stories of Frank O'Connor* (Hamish Hamilton Ltd.) by permission of A. D. Peters & Co. Ltd.

Julia O'Faolain: 'First Conjugation' reprinted from *Melancholy Baby*. Reprinted by permission of Rogers, Coleridge & White Ltd.

Sean O'Faolain: 'The Sugawn Chair', © 1961 by Sean O'Faolain. First appeared in *The Atlantic*. Published in the UK in *Selected Stories of Sean O'Faolain* (Constable, 1978). 'The Faithless Wife', © 1976 by Sean O'Faolain. Published in the UK in *Foreign Affairs and Other Stories* (Constable, 1976). Both published in the US in *The Collected Stories of*

Sean O'Faolain. Reprinted by permission of A. P. Watt Ltd., and Little Brown & Co.

Liam O'Flaherty: 'The Pedlar's Revenge' and 'The Fanatic' reprinted from *The Pedlar's Revenge & Other Stories* by permission of Wolfhound Press.

James Plunkett: 'Weep for Our Pride' reprinted from *The Trusting and the Maimed* (Hutchinson) by permission of A. D. Peters & Co. Ltd.

E. Œ. Somerville and Martin Ross: 'Philippa's Fox-Hunt' from *Some Experiences of an Irish R.M.* (Longman, Green & Co., 1902). Reprinted by permission of John Farquharson Ltd.

James Stephens: 'The Triangle' reprinted from *Here Are The Ladies* by permission of The Society of Authors on behalf of the copyright owner, Mrs Iris Wise.

William Trevor: 'Death in Jerusalem' reprinted from *Lovers of Their Time and Other Stories* (Bodley Head) by permission of Peters Fraser & Dunlop.

INDEX OF AUTHORS